Doing Something

Matt Mason

All characters in this book are fictitious and any resemblance to anyone, living or dead, is purely coincidental.

Copyright© Matthew Mason 2019.

For my son, Alex.

Prologue

That great inevitability, that heaving mass descends at sometime in every life. The rationale must be made, whereby the merits inherent thus in breathing must be measured against the unenviable, lifelong labour of trudging humanity. And so we crawl, clawing the ground in front of us, pulling our mass towards the goal that is this relative wealth and all the baubles this pittance unto us all will bring. And what would you do, or not, to achieve this coin? Who would you drag with you pawing at the paper and the empty space that become the draughts around our souls? Where in this life is the page entitled *Happiness* and *Fulfilment* and where is the tussocked path to guide us there? What lurks glowing behind that door as golden and bright as a sunrise in summer? Selflessness here lives, like a quiet child in a classroom who cannot lift her hand for fear of failure and derision that comes with the choice to engage, join in, compromise the comfort, question the daily radiant blast of the moving wallpaper in the corner of the living-room, that flickering spectre, that shimmering pulp which spews out its *truth* and into lives, insisting we are happy. Yes, we laugh, but on Sundays it stops and the stealthy, cloying smell of want force forward into drudgery those dark mornings of rain, creeping queues of traffic, bus-stops of silent watchers who left the kids to go to school, left the house now empty and alone, cold, waiting for its space to groan again when returning lives bump around like equally polarised atoms at a deity's whim. Among the pillars and porticoes of hallowed chambers, office and hall, sites of sludge, steel-enclosed cathedrals of machinery, cord-carpeted portacabins and shops enladened with *things*, is a species of love, unable to grasp that which is there and as extant as the skin that seals it, but entombed and dead as the Neanderthals that were. Lost are we, urbanised in plastic, whoring for Mammon and looking through the trees as if summer never was. We gaze at shapes and blocks, walls with clocks, things that fill that void we know is there, which has dimension, weight and form but silently assents to the denial, absorbing space and time with the tangible, tactile and true, that which we agree is *nice* and *real* and never nod to another *something* in painted colours seldom seen, kissed by spiralling air, vortexing to that otherness and curling somewhere beyond or between, somewhere untouchable with hand, unspoken in word but as real as you and me. Tarry in time, be slack in courage and life will rip the meaning that it is to be human from within you until beads and tinsel become deeds less sinful and time's deep slow drip from which we hide, frees and unenseas us all, at last.

Chapter 1

Filching Hasek

Thursday, 7th June, 1984

He was thirty-three, liked to be known by his surname, unmarried, had no girlfriend nor no real friends, neither had he a regular job, but he liked books, however, had never finished one and didn't wash too often. His intelligence galvanised his selfishness and ego and he was going to get into a mess that would change his life forever.

Kelly was wandering around an office block in The Cowgate of Edinburgh. It was being refurbished in the unusually warm summer heat of 1984 and he didn't like it. He was wandering around the office block because he was searching for water, and he was searching for water because, just as unusually, he had been working. He had been working as a Painter and Decorator but he wasn't, nor ever would be, a Painter and Decorator but he did have cursory skills with a roller and sported white overalls that declared him a brother of the brush. These were borrowed from an acquaintance of his who *was* a bona fide decorator and needed his help to fulfil his contractual agreement to paint some of the office block. For this he would receive ninety pounds for three days work, naturally tax-free, and this was his second day.

This late afternoon saw him a furtive figure creeping into spaces that had been refurbished and painted and were in the process of being made good to fulfil their function as offices. The water had been turned off by the plumbers who were running new pipe from floor to floor so had ceased the flow of Kelly's most needful of liquids and consequently his desperation led to potential pilfering in the shape of a bottle of water, possibly brought to work by those who now occupied some of the finished offices. His problem, apart from the fact that he was parched, was that he still had the taste of piss in his mouth. And now he had just struck gold.

He still had the taste of piss in his mouth because he had told an entirely felonious story of a non-existent foreman called *Bob* who had told him to ask two plumbers to turn on the water because the mixing of plaster, elsewhere on the site, was required, however, his ruse was discovered by them as they knew of no foreman called *Bob*, but they did offer him a drink from a bottle of what they said was a fruit drink of glistening amber. Suffice to say, it was the temporary toilet arrangements for the plumbers who both agreed that it was a much more convenient arrangement than walking down four floors to a chemical toilet outside and then back up again when their task of running pipe was already so labour intensive. To this end, Kelly had recently swallowed a mouthful of plumber piss, to whit, the plumbers found this extremely amusing, but before him now beheld a wondrous sight, a bottle of fresh water, not his of course, but no compunction to desist from his larceny occurred in him nor probably any contrition for the theft. He drank deeply.

On a desk nearest the door was a book, *The Good Soldier Sveyk,* by Jaroslav Hasek. He'd never heard of it and didn't like that he'd never heard of it. He looked at the door and into the corridor, beyond. No-one about. He opened the front cover without lifting it, again looking towards the staircase through the glass partition. It was a Penguin Classic. He prided himself on knowing many of the classics and had, within a few years ago, subscribed to a magazine which took you through the themes, characters and history of the work and author. The subscriber also got the book, itself. He lasted four: *Great Expectations,* a Wilkie Collins, of which, he couldn't remember nor ever liked. *Silas Marner* and *The Picture of Dorian Gray* which he considered brilliant, moreso, the preface by Oscar Wilde, anatomising concisely the nature of Art and something about Caliban looking at himself in a mirror? He couldn't remember all of that, either, but it did prompt him to discover that Oscar Wilde was gay and Caliban was a deformed creature with murder a goal.

He would often engineer discussions to illuminate his apparent knowledge and gird his standing amongst the regulars in his local, *The Old Duke.* It was an earthy establishment, which barred none by race, class or gender, but they had recently moved a motion; *Is this the Beginning of the End?* then enthusiastically and uninformedly discussed the arrival of AIDS. Kelly took his opportunity, naturally, and dropped Oscar into the debate never forgetting to mention that the year was 1984 and George Orwell had written something concerning that year a while back. He really enjoyed using the word *dystopian,* too. Others threw their sometimes virulent social observations of the unfortunate malady about the debating chamber freely until all agreed it was *a bastard of a virus* but safe to say the pub fraternity were still a little unsure about this one so probably would've frowned on any *bottom grazers* quaffing in *The Old Duke* until UNICEF, or some other body they knew equally as little about, gave them the green light. To this end, beer and *The Old Duke* became a distraction and eventually an obstruction for Kelly to *The Classics.*

He flicked to the contents page with which each chapter was all laid out, Dickensesque with a title. Intriguing. The Introduction sat across the page, and Kelly read about this dude from Prague called Jaroslav Hasek and as he read on it became clearer that Hasek had had an impoverished childhood, lost his dad who drank himself into an early grave, and then around the age of thirteen started to live his life like a tramp but the irony was, he was something of a Bohemian. Kelly had heard of this before and knew it meant people from the arty set that had beards, wore berets and painted shit pictures. And wrote books. Well he'd written this tome, hadn't he so he had to be a Bohemian. Right?

Anyway, turns out this fatherless, beatnik tramp was something of a character and Kelly knew he liked him already. Adequate justification for appropriation. He squeezed it next to the bottle of water inside his overalls and left the office. He certainly wasn't going to buy it and the library had thrown him out recently for falling asleep at one of their tables one spring afternoon. It was shortly after an *al fresco* session nearby after which he had need of their facilities. They publicly and quite insensitively declared his unsuitability for their municipal resource asking him to go and snore elsewhere. *Sveyk* came with him.

He was leaving the office quietly closing the door as the sound of brisk footsteps were coming up the stairwell. He quickly pulled his filling knife from his overalls and started to spit on it and appear to clean it in masturbatory fashion as he passed a very smartly dressed young man with floppy blond hair, the shiniest of shoes and a discernibly fruity aftershave and gait. Probably a junior clerk of works, or something similar? The young man looked at Kelly as he passed and Kelly gave him a noiseless builder's twist of the neck still masturbating his filling knife and the semblance of a wink where the word *alright* would have been. Standard practice for construction workers acknowledgement of others of whom one doesn't know but sweat on the same job. He looked up the stairs to see where the young man was going, afraid he may well be arrested for theft, just as the young man looked back down at Kelly. This look appeared to have had the subtext of something other than casual greeting, potential assignation perhaps? The phallic filling knife confirmed it.

"Shit!" he whispered to himself realising the signals he'd just given out.

He knew this part of the job had been more or less completed and he would have no reason to be there, other than to steal water and paperbacks, and may appear that he was lurking with the intent of a fortuitous liaison. He stopped and craned his neck out to see if the young man had gone into the office from which he had just pilfered. As his head slowly reached a position able to covertly determine this, the young man's head craned out, too, from above and their eyes met. Time stopped. Kelly panicked. Young man smiled. He smiled back. The reason he wanted to see where he went were not the reasons Mr. Immaculate had, obviously, and then he hurried down the stairs. He had heard about this ability of *The Friends of Dorothy* of determining the personal proclivities of one of their own with lightning speed, however, on this occasion, their apparently paid-up member was patently wrong. That said, he was wanking a filling knife and was where he should not have been, a skill shared by many Dorothians, and smiled vapidly back at him. What was the poor boy supposed to think?

He burst quickly into the office where Joe Delaney, his current employer, a well-kept fifty and thoroughly decent fellow, and he were working. The door had hardly opened before the tirade boomed out.

"Where the holy Christ have you been, Kells! We're here 'til this is done...." Joe protested at him. "....need to get it all coated tomorrow."

"We will. Dry as soon as it hits the stud in this heat. I'll be late though. I have to sign on. Should've been there on Tuesday."

"You'll still be doin' eight hours!" Joe reminded him.

"Last day. I don't give a fuck. Who's the young fella in the suit?"

"What?"

"Young fella in a sharp suit. Blonde hair. Can't be more than twenty one."

"Oh him. Just got here. Government team checkin' everythin's in order before Sir Clive Harrow gets here."

"Who's he?"

"Foreign Office. Minister. Some government *Billy Big Time*, anyway. He's opening this on Monday so this has to be second-coated by the end of tomorrow. A'right?"

No answer.

"Kelly!"

"Aye ok!"

"I'm pricin' another job tomorrow night at five, so I'll be gone. Don't let me down. I'll square you up in the pub."

Kelly, covertly, put the bottle and book in his bag and picked up his sanding block and began to wearily rub the walls. The dust was intolerable and went in his eyes and mouth and he coughed and swore. Joe smiled and started to sing to the tune of *Summertime* with a pub singer's finish on each line for emphasis.

Summertime, you wanna get yersel' a mask…ah!
Yer eyes are streamin' and youre gonna die………ah!
Ah've got a spare yin, sittin' in ma tool box……ah!
But you can just choke, because it's mine!

George Gershwin slowly turned in his grave.

"Hilarious, Joe!" Sarcasm wasn't his strong suit and shook his head, however, he quietly admired Joe's improvisational skills.

Then he began to think. He thought of the shit he was going to get at the dole office tomorrow and of how he would have to deliver another tale of illness or woe that softened the heart of whoever had to listen and despised having to dance to their tune. Equally, Kelly decided that the thought of throwing one's life and liberty away to join the daily grind was a crime against humanity. He knew he didn't need much to survive on and accepted that there would be compromises to make with regard to foreign holidays, fabulously delicious malt whiskies or the latest video player, etc. when in receipt of the government's pittance but he also thought that there had to be a better way of accruing coin of the realm than any of the traditional methods. He considered a well-planned raid on a Post-Office and then told himself he didn't fancy fending off wrong-intentioned, libidinous inmates in prison nor had the balls to wield a gun. The sale of knock-off goods at a local market? He'd need a van and he couldn't drive......*Oh well...*he thought.... *better just top myself now, eh?*

Joe sang softly to himself..

Summertime.... and the livin' is easy....

Kelly didn't look at him when he said, "Really? What are you so cheery about?"

"This. This contract has really been a payer, Kells. Dug me out, paid off some long-standin' bills and dribbled lots more down into the company coffers over these few months. So much so that I'm goin' to do something. Somethin' I've wanted to for a long time but never really had the guts."

"Don't start wearin' dresses, Joe. You won't get another contract."

"Scoff away, my friend. Scoff freely but I'm going to do it."

"Do what?"

"Expand. Grow the business. Take on some men. Take on bigger jobs" Joe glowed smiling across to Kelly.

"I've had enough of *this job* so don't look at me."

"You're not a tradesman, Kells. I couldn't take you on."

"Good."

"It is good. Very good and your unenthusiastic grid won't make me feel different." Joe smiled relentlessly at Kelly. Then he started to whistle. A sure but irritating sign of a man happy in his work and Kelly groaned inwardly at the thought of dedicating his life to the daily grind and the words, *there has to be another* way rattled around his head

He sneaked a look at Joe who did seem content with his lot and delighted that he'd made his decision but moreso that he'd told someone. But he had a bad back and knees. Kelly didn't want to be Joe knowing that his joints would only get worse with wear or have the stress of having an expanding company to deal with. He knew remarkably little about him beyond work and the pub. Why should he? He's never asked him where he grew up, what music he liked, where he went to school or the women he might have romanced in his time, or of how life might be in *Joeworld*.

He concluded that being Joe would be boring. But if he was Joe then his thoughts would change and he'd like what he does, would he not? However, from the perspective of workshy loafer, it still appeared.... *difficult*. Then he thought of the coming evening's first pint.

Chapter 2

Brylcreem and Beer

The Old Duke was one of those Edinburgh pubs that was set into the ground floor of a tenement building and would appear to be made of three-foot wide sandstone blocks, however, upon entering one wouldn't be blamed for thinking you'd just entered a hundred year old dilapidated sauna that had been patched up with various degrees of cladding that hid the state of the walls from disparaging eyes.

The bar was a stretch of solid dark oak that probably exceeded the current lifespan of any other wooden artefact in the hostelry with dents and marks that could tell of a thousand evenings and a hundred fights and was reportedly hewn down in Glen Lyon and brought to Edinburgh by the man responsible for creating the premises in 1892. To this end, the strength and sturdy longevity of this length of shaped timber deserved to be called, Hector.

A viciously closing hatch clattered heavily at the end of Hector, as if belting out brusque profanity, likely disgruntled at having been removed from the oaken mainland and roughly hinged to lift and fall with its own angry sound. This Son of Hector fell back to its ledge often, ignored by staff and tolerated by punters, and met the wall that hid the men's toilets.

The toilet door was an anomaly to the general pine setting because it had been replaced many times with a flush-panel concern, now *sans handle* and with occasional depressions due to stout-booted tradesmen and general lack of care. Brusque male-posturing, alcohol and angry regulars that found offence with each other, wreaked revenge on this innocent toilet door and it had been bullied several times as had been his older and now deceased and disposed of forebears. If it ever had the misfortune to pass through the Scottish education system it would probably have gone by the name of Richard, shortened, appropriately, to Dick.

Along two walls was a fixed bench with a high back and a headrest that harkened back to a time when the landlord cared about the comfort of his clientele. These were benches where men had smoked long clay pipes in frock coats and quaffed ale and porter from pewter mugs by the fire. There was an open fire but not one that had had the care of any pyrophile. It sported the remnants of a blaze long extinguished but had been given birth due to an unseasonable blast of winter last March. It was squat and unremarkable for the size of room and had a quite ordinary wooden mantelshelf, frequently the resting place of pint glasses, and if it was ever to be given a name it would most probably be called, John. The current landlord, Norrie, knew that *The Old Duke* had descended to the rank of scruffy local admitting few tourists or strangers and those that had braved The Duke's unique ambience were quick to leave and warn the world of the iniquity within.

Pride of place, dominating and drawing gaze was a square elevated planken platform with a rectangular table fixed to the floor and set in the back left corner of the room with two tall windows behind it that had been covered over with plywood and painted black, originally, but with a gloss paint that sank into the wood with little recourse to a priming coat and were now complaining loudly to the world. Longitudinal cracks coursed up and down the length of the window boards uncaring of the subsequent layers of emulsion and god-knows-what that had been carelessly applied through the decades, and that paint now sat raised, proud like black butterfly wings waiting for an auspicious wind.

Stan, the single syllable, no-nonsense, calvinist platform and table was a place where philosophical imperatives and current cultural issues were discussed such as the outline planning to make Tynecastle Stadium, the home of Heart of Midlothian Football Club, an all-seated affair. This significant social question had lately met with vociferous antipathy from some of the regulars citing the fact that they would have to use the toilets at half-time, whereas, currently the convenience of fixed viewing and urination point was largely and agreeably, preferable. Stan was both debating chamber and entertainment location of *The Old Duke* and had experienced some memorable performances throughout the sixties and seventies of solo artists with three chords ever at the ready and rising acts that had lately garnered column coverage in *The Edinburgh Evening News*, one page before the obituaries. No such bravery had been displayed for the best part of a decade and any sentimental or memorable souvenir had long since passed into common folklore.

A juke box belted out *The Wild Side of Life*. May the Man stood at the bar collecting two bottles of stout and a nip of whisky shepherding them skilfully into both hands while shifting delicately and languidly from one foot to the other as *Status Quo* drove on. She sang louder than was necessary to the lyrics, proud of her ability to maintain the pace despite having started six bottles of stout and three nips, ago, and danced over towards Stan shuffling two steps backwards and looking up at Spider Blackwood in the corner who smiled back, vacantly, and then timed it to arrive on Stan just as the key phrase in the song repeated and dropped her drinks to a full stop just as the coda concluded.

Spider Blackwood sat with May the Man at Stan. May was a most disagreeable version of the fairer sex and she would have been the first to acknowledge this with her quite masculine demeanour, broad shoulders and flat chest. She was forty-something, unmarried it seemed as she had never spoken of a significant other, had a square jaw and a mouth that could spit the worst vitriol when cornered in an argument. She didn't dress femininely but for a perennial headscarf that held her hair pinned in place which seemed quite voluminous but was tucked away beneath the checked triangle. The outfit ran to no more than a brown stained coat that remained on whatever the weather. She chose male company and kept the social hours of many of the men in *The Duke* and kept up with the best of them when on *a session*. Spider radiated the best of toothy beamers.

"What're you grinning at?" she barked at Spider.

His ruddy visage smiled a row of yellowing but straight teeth from the framework of a tidy goatee beard and moustache. His hair was black and swept straight back; some say dyed black but he just smiled inanely and often drunkenly when contentiously confronted on this. He always wore black or dark coloured clothes without much variation and with his dark features often seemed a shadowy figure but for the wide grin starkly contrasting this almost satanic presentation.

"Dancin'" Not one for lengthy conversation starters, was Spider.

"What about it?" May said.

"Dancin'. Good dancin'."

"That was just a few wee shuffles, Spider, son. Don't get excited 'til you see me tango. Cheers"

She took a deep draught of the stout from a half pint glass dropping the level down to half and then sipped her whisky carefully.

"Cheers." Spider returned but didn't touch his pint.

He was divorced. He had two lads that were now young adults who never saw him, which hurt him but he never said so or knew how to. He had an inertia about him that was cited by his ex-wife as a reason for the eventual break-up and adopted by his boys having heard their mother's frequent rants, and watched their father do nothing but accept it, take it and say nothing. His inability, or perhaps refusal, to defend himself when bludgeoned in a tirade of criticism levelled at his fatherhood, manhood and passivity, had lost him the respect of his children long ago and he knew this but at the time couldn't or wouldn't find the impetus or desire to confront his silence or their denigration of him and so gradually he sought out the company of others less challenging. Then they all left. The truth be told, Spider thought he had done well to achieve wedlock at all, but he really didn't want the complications of children and having to communicate meaningfully with a woman. That was difficult. They were difficult. What he wanted was a facsimile of his mother who was there and stolidly functioned. His father was there in the picture but passive, too, sitting in an armchair with a small side-table adjacent which had organised all the necessary and habitual accoutrements of his life; ashtray, cigarettes, matches, newspaper, penknife and intermittent teacup and biscuits. Simple. So Spider went to work in a factory each day, went home then came to the pub. Nothing else.

The bar was interspersed with a smattering of drinkers. Thursday signalled the beginning of the weekend for much of its clientele, however it was still early. Two greasy suits were at the bar with even greasier hair flattened resolutely to their scalps with *Brylcreem*. You knew it was *Brylcreem* by the smell. These were men that spurned the advent of pansified expensive hair gels and wore *Old Spice* at the weekend. These fifty-something men were the smell of the sixties who ignored the seventies and declared themselves unchangeable in the eighties and realised they might never see the nineties, so remained constant in their habits.

A grey-bearded elderly man called Eric sat in a seat next to the door dropping crisps onto the floor for his ageing black Labrador dog, Lenni. Lenni wore a bright red, old leather collar with a silver name tag and was lying under the table next to his master's legs and slowly and skilfully swept up the crisps with its tongue. Eric had an old suit jacket on with a woollen grey jumper underneath and that atop a white shirt with frayed collar. On his head was a knitted woollen hat. Before him on the table was a tightly nursed pint of Younger's Special now marking an hour since he last went to the bar. Soft deep murmurs were sent under the table affectionately to his dog which licked his hand as Eric stroked the ageing mutt.

The pub door opened as Guy Mitchell began singing *A White Sport Coat* on the juke box and in shuffled a massive man. He moved uncertainly with little surety of himself. At least six feet four in his bare feet but was six-six in his ex-army boots. He had a shock of hair that was greying, unkempt and uncut for some time which seemed to grow outwards augmenting his scale and a discernible week's growth on his face. He crossed to the bar and pulled up a tall stool from behind Son of Hector. This was exclusively for the use of the bar staff but he took it without a by-your-leave from the young woman serving who eyed him with a quiet alarm. The two greasy suits then moved further down Hector's dark stretch to an apparently safe distance. This man made no eye-contact with anyone nor spoke but settled himself and shortly a pint of Guinness was softly placed in front of him and then a Bushmills Irish whiskey was slid tentatively towards him. All of this was performed with no apparent communication as he placed a twenty pound note on the bar which was put in an empty glass with a note of what he had just bought. He lifted the glass without looking at the pint, his eyes elsewhere, drank deeply, replaced the glass and gazed at the floor.

Behind the bar a young woman, plainly somewhat pretty but neither entirely pretty nor plain busied herself mopping the top of Hector with a cloth and replacing beer mats, thereabouts.

Kelly pushed the door slowly open and eased in, tiredly. "Eric."

Without acknowledgement or pleasantry returned, Eric hoarsed back, "Shut the door, Son! Lenni feels it!"

Kelly turned without breaking his weary stride muttering something about it being nearly summer and pushed the door. It swung and slammed in its frame as the old brass latch complained.

"Kells!! You'll have the glass out of that again! Be careful."

Megan, the sometime barmaid, rarely called him *Kells* and Kelly noticed this but was too tired to do much more than order. He hadn't washed after the day's labours, merely splashed his face after taking off his borrowed overalls, ate sauceless cold pasta and lay on his couch, drowsily going under into sleep and reawakening only when his mouth decided he needed a drink. He donned his large Crombie overcoat and crossed the short distance from his flat over to *The Duke*.

"Pint."

"Of what?"

"Heavy!"

"Alright! I don't know what you drink!"

"Yes you do."

"My dad does! Not me." She started to pour the pint.

"Where is he?" Kelly said craning to look in the back.

"Night off."

"What for?"

"I need the money."

"You should get a proper job not serve us reprobates. You can have mine."

Megan affected a loud sarcastic laugh as she one-handedly swirled the pint to put a head on it and pushed a fallen tress of her dark hair back to its headquarters. Another minor moment that Kelly read.

"You laughin' at?"

Kelly tried to appear affected or miffed by her sarcasm but knew the truth, and knew that Megan also knew the truth. The pursuit of any apparently credible refutation of her assertions painted in affected indignation, was pointless and so let a small smile curl the ends of his mouth. Too tiring. It fell as quickly as it arrived.

"Are you?" asked Megan.

"Workin'?"

"Keep up, Kells," placing the pint in front of him.

He grabbed hold of it and heaved it to his mouth expertly sucking in the dark liquid and let three large gulps descend before swilling the last one around his mouth then swallowing. He replaced it on the bar wiped his mouth and then made to speak to Megan but he eyed his pint again, picked it up quickly and again greedily gulped down the last of it in one go, finally erasing the smell, taste and psychologically damaging memory of plumber piss. He then lifted a lazy finger toward the pint as he wiped his mouth and Megan took it to the pump then started to pour another. May shouted over,

"Haw, Kelly! Your round, by the way! I seen that! Sneaky quick one"

Kelly smiled, put two pound notes onto Hector, rolled his eyes and nodded in apparent bonhomie over to her and Satan sitting on Stan.

"Somethin' you'll never get, you ugly cow! Fuck off."

The Brylcreem Boys laughed, loudly. Megan suppressed a grin. Spider as was. Eric muttered at the noise. May shook her head and twisted her face into a retort that tried to say *well aren't you the smart bastard*, but uttered nothing as she leaned back in her seat. Kelly, enjoying his riposte basked in the glow of his humorous wit for a few seconds and turned to look at the big man sitting on the barstool who flatly gazed back at him with empty unblinking eyes. Kelly knew not to expect a reaction from him as his smile dropped and turned back to Megan.

"Doin' a three day shift with Joe. What do you need the money for?" returning to Megan.

"Doing a TEFL course. Might need it when it's all done."

"What's that?"

"Teaching English as a Foreign Language."

"Start with Sasquatch. He says nothing." he said nodding over at the big man.

"Yes he does. He points." said Megan.

"That's not communication!"

"I think it is. It's *his* communication. He's just sad."

"How the feckin' feck would you know that, Sigmund? Why isn't he just a very large nutter?"

"Ssshh! He's just there!" she nodded, then said, "Sigmund?"

But before he had the chance to dazzle her with his learning May stood and shouted again.

"I wasn't jokin' about that round, Kelly boy! We know you're diggin' Joe out, so you can dig down in yer pockets and get a round in or I'll get Spider to shag me and make you watch!"

Grimaces from the Brylcreem Boys. More muttering from Eric. A smile from Megan to Kelly.

Kelly adopted a classical Shakespearean actor's tone and accent. "Heaven forfend. My public awaits." and then eased over towards Stan and slid his backside onto the bench.

Megan cleaned and busied herself for the next half hour as Kelly, May the Man and the grinning Spider talked of not much.

She was indeed off on a new direction planning to get herself onto a professional footing coaching exchange students how to differentiate between *there, their and they're* and exactly what the United Kingdom is, as opposed to Great Britain, four apparently separate countries. She was now twenty-eight and panicking slightly about doing something with her life. Truth is, she was never academically able enough to consider university but dearly craved to be one of that set of bright young things who seemed so carefree and sure of their future and themselves. She couldn't articulate this but intuitively did understand that somewhere ahead the clarity of money, detached houses and all the wealth of friends, knowledge, career, social position and probably happiness awaited these damned clever people and now she'd got in the back door attending Edinburgh University on a part-time day course that allowed her to mix and laugh and drink black coffee, eat brown rice at vegetarian café's, wear black denims, outlandish hats and be applauded for it. She couldn't keep up when Descartes or Hume entered the dialogue but she could nod sagely when general approval at either of these two monoliths of The Enlightenment were mooted abroad and she would snort bravely, at the risk of being interrogated as to her stance on said topic if some palpably ill-considered poppycock arraigned the conversation. She liked them. She liked their learning and desire to learn and their brains that were three litre Mercs but knew her engine was an Austin Allegro, albeit a Cartesian one, and would always remain so. Mostly, she liked it when they talked of characters from novels as if they were alive and with free will to think and breathe and love and really enjoyed it when academic arguments ensued loudly in bars and cafes as to the particular motivations of these chimeras. Nothing thrilled her more than two male rugby-playing literature students rutting as to whether Joe Gargery was the personified emblem of an agrarian working-class of integrity that were innocent, ignored, and then eventually lost and of Dickens's obvious denigration of the Victorian ruling class

An hour passed. Kelly was tiredly reclining on Stan and fending off the blunt enquiries of May the Man as to his current financial wealth while Spider enjoyed their jibes and parries.

A white shirted paunchy middle-aged man appeared behind the bar. He wore polyester Farah slacks with a U-bend belt detouring underneath a most definite gut, had a sharply knotted tie beneath a lined forehead, which was above a severely ruddy complexion. This was Norrie, Megan's father who owned *The Old Duke.* He looked around the bar immediately noting and counting the individual sources of his wealth, reckoned quickly their spending habits, the time of the evening and the day of the week and hit the button that opened the till. With very deliberate stillness he gazed intensely into the various sections counting the paper notes quickly with a skilled appraisal of the loose change while deducting the initial float. He turned his head to the massive man sitting alone at the bar. He looked over at the glass containing his twenty and picked out the accompanying note, read it and replaced it. He took his hand across his dark hair swept back from his receding temples taking extra care to flatten behind his ears. He looked almost regimental but for his hair that was growing out of the eighty-pence cut he got, however, only when absolutely necessary. But when he did he always gave the barber a quid. He bought some quasi-superiority for twenty pence even though it still smarted, somewhat, when he nodded to the barber who muttered some noise of deference and gratitude and then he enjoyed the next thirty seconds of sycophancy being brushed across the shoulders, coat offered and door held open. He always liked to stop in the doorway momentarily before he left. He was, seemingly, checking the weather, a pocket, straightening his tie, or his best one which was to pretend to see some renegade hair still on his shoulder and flick it off with a cursory glance to the barber, almost threatening to take the twenty pence back. The door had to be held at his convenience elongating the moment of obsequiousness and annoying the other customers, which he thoroughly enjoyed despite his stony outward expression. The barber knew him, his reputation and the commonly agreed opinion of all that crossed him and wished he was a barber of yore who amputated more than hair but, resignedly, observed the rules of repeated custom.

Megan knew the ritual, saw all of this and Kelly, too. Nobody liked Norrie. Not even Megan.

"I've got it Dad. I'm fine. It's not busy." Megan appealed.

"Yet…!." came back to her. Monosyllabic grunts akin to words was a particular skill of Norrie's.

"I'll manage if it does. It's just Thursday!" She was quietly miffed at his presence.

The sub-text irking Megan was that she knew her father would, with little hesitancy, dock her wage for the evening if he had to step in behind the bar if it got really busy. Family didn't get in the way of profit in *The Old Duke*. Norrie poured himself a pint.

The pub door opened and a beige raincoat and tousled suit which hung complaining of its ill fit, tiredly entered and immediately acknowledged Eric and bent down to stroke Lenni. This greying man of middle-height had the early onset of hang-dog expression and the tired physical gait to match, despite being just south of fifty. He exchanged a few pleasantries with Eric and stopped to deliver affectionate noises and his hand across the mane of Lenni then drew himself into what was his usual place in the corner, just along from Eric. From this vantage he could see the entire populous of the bar and of whomsoever crossed the threshold before they could see him. He took out his copy of *The Evening News* and laid it on the table before him and placed a small black notebook next to it.

Norrie had taken his pint to the far end of Hector. He reached to a shelf beneath and took out a cigar and lit it as he saw him come in and he promptly enacted an apparently well-worn signal to Megan who glanced over to the corner and began to pour a pint. Megan took it over to him and placed it at the top of the table away from his paper and notebook on a fresh beer mat.

"Evening, Mr McQuarrie. Any joy today?" Megan smiled at him.

He wearily smiled and returned,

"Megan, if you mean villains, certainly, but if you mean the nags, *well....*but this will comfort me. Thank you." and then raised his pint across to Norrie which Norrie, largely and visually returned for the benefit of all the regulars. Megan returned back to the bar.

A raised salutation that confirmed Norrie's connection to protection for the price of DI McQuarrie's first pint of every evening. Norrie's demonstration that he was moving in circles that could wield power if required, unearth information to advantage or have someone *spoken to* should they ever overstep the mark. All pretentious bollocks that DI McQuarrie tolerated and chuckled inwardly at, knowing the popular opinion of Norrie, abroad. However he played this facile game because... well there was an aspect of it that he egotistically enjoyed, quite frankly. He knew it was something that defined him, put him in the broad picture of this study of humanity in this small room of distinctive characters and so he happily allowed Norrie his undisplayed but unmistaken delight. So what the hell. Let him have his moment. This aside, he was frequently given free beer and the occasional single malt but also had a fixation with giving his money to various bookies across town and when he had exhausted his salary he set up a credit arrangement with whichever turf accountant agreed to this facility, thinking they were always good for their debt with Plod.

Nobody willingly shared much with DI McQuarrie, except Eric whom he seemed to have almost a parental affection for and often shared a quiet joke or observation that elevated Eric, somewhat in the eyes of all that beheld him. McQuarrie was a single man who'd enjoyed dalliance with the fairer sex in his time but quickly wearied of the chase and the emotional effort required to manage a relationship alongside catching crooks. The truth was he enjoyed hunting miscreants so much more and bringing them to book. He also liked a beer, a decent malt and a frequent flutter that shifted the geography of his testicles when his nag ran a close one. Or won. This and the job could be said to have supplanted any aspirations he once had to successfully love another human being and so, despite ostensible position, he also did befit these unambitious misfits.

Kelly observed all of this from Stan as Spider and May tried to sing along to *Ebony and Ivory* with dreadfully large, however meaningful, hand gestures as Paul McCartney and Stevie wonder cringed three thousand miles away. He despised Norrie's sad attempts to tell the world he was important and mulled over what it was that kept Norrie catering for such an uninspiring sometimes iniquitous and noisome crew? He probably had enough money to give up the trade or get a manager in or sell up and buy a share in a pub of a more salubrious address and comportment. He wondered what the man was like outside the pub. At home? In the street? Did he actually have conversations? Which paper did he read? Kelly didn't know if there was a Mrs Norrie and realised he'd never heard Megan speak of her mother. Kelly then made an imaginative projection into Norrie's sex life, which in his depiction, was cold and functional with a faceless Mrs Norrie being ground into a mattress with flannelette fitted sheets, winceyette nightgown and ninety seconds of publican quality beneath a dodgy headboard. He chuckled to himself and settled for the fact that he didn't like him, despised him actually, or would ever want to be like him and then seized his moment and made his way to the bar.

"Evening, Norman." Affected. Bright and breezy.

Nought but a grunt came back with a sideways look as he gripped his pint. Kelly knew Norrie didn't like this familiarity.

"One more pint of your delectable ale, please, Mine Host. Hang the expense! One for yourself as well! What care we for coin of the realm when we are coined but in the realm of Bacchus. Oh, you have the advantage of me, Norman. I see your ambrosia, golden and glittering, has found its home."

Kelly, of course, knew that Norrie had already poured himself a pint and Norrie knew that Kelly knew this, too. What he didn't know was that he had made up the phrase not really knowing how a realm could be coined as a verb in this context but it didn't matter. The effect was made and Norrie wasn't going to debate it with him. Norrie didn't like Kelly but liked taking his money and his insistence at spending it in his pub but had to deal with Kelly and his guileful stabs at his dourness and inability to joust with him from time to time in order to get it. So he coldly passed him on.

"Megan…."

Megan scowled to herself and started to pour Kelly's pint.

"You're as bad as each other! He knows you just try to wind him up." she said shaking her head.

"Does he? Is he as bad as me? How am I bad, Megan, how bad am I or how bad would you like me to be?"

"And me!"

"Megan, you are the sun in my sky. You are to me what Therese Raquin was to Emile Zola! I wouldn't wilfully wind you up, at all, unless wondrous wooing deemed I was sure of reciprocal passion."

She had no idea who Therese Raquin was but knew what alliteration was and had heard of Emile Zola, not sure if he wrote *Therese Raquin* or if he was her lover in the story so she smiled as if she knew and gave him his pint.

"There'll be no *wondrous wooing* while you're dressed like that, Kells."

Kells again! And a smile! Much fluttering of butterfly wings beneath the Crombie. Signals seemed to be sent across Hector, Kellyward, unasked for, however welcome.

"Do you mean there would be if I cut a dash in my rags from George Street?" he ventured.

Megan smiled again.

"Maybe I'd *run the risk*." was all she could muster alliteratively, but it was unmistakably flirtatious and knew it so decided curtailing such girlish hoo-ha now retained her unblemished reputation, and anyway her dad was there. She glided further down Hector and served Eric another two-hour sipper.

Kelly had heard that Megan had some new university type friends and that some had visited The Old Duke to see her, once or twice, and therefore considered his chances of ever landing her as a catch was now null and void, completely. Actually, to ever have had hope when she was witness to some of his worst excesses some evenings was ridiculous, he thought, but regained ground often when he talked with her, or *apologised,* the next day. He knew she liked to hear about literature and he was armed with enough knowledge, phrases, references and titles to blag around some novels and poetry that placed him above *shiftless waster* in the hierarchy of the pub, plus he was the only one of the regulars that was of an eligible age for Megan and this current smattering of flirtatious badinage was a surprise beyond surprises. He decided to extend the show.

"Eric. Does *The Duke* not remind one of *The Admiral Benbow?*"

"I don't know. *One* has never drank there." Sarcasm apparent.

"All this wood? The thud of pirate heel on timber? The dull

approach of resonating hooves from without, promising the creak of door on rusty hinge? Pewter scraping flecked oak? I sometimes expect Ben Gunn to cross the threshold to regale us with yarns of loneliness and cheese."

All declared loudly enough in earshot of Megan as if it was representative of a genuine conundrum Kelly wrestled with, daily.

"Norman, this room has venerability and mystery tacked to the very walls. What secrets lie, herein, perchance?"

Nothing from Norrie. May had heard, though.

"Is that him wi' verbal diahorrea, again? What the fuck is he sayin' now?" she barked across the room.

"I point only to the treasures that this island hostelry and Benn Gunn's island may conceal!"

"What fuckin' island?" six whiskies returned.

"*Treasure Island* by Robert Louis Stevenson." Eric said, balancing his pint and making his way back to his seat. "If you'd any eddication at a' ye'd ken it. S'on the wa' at Deacon Brodies."

DI McQuarrie looked up from the racing page over to May as Eric reached his table and shakily planted his pint.

May was becoming quite confused. Deacon Brodie's was a pub in the heart of Edinburgh's Old Town.

"What's on the wa' at Deacon Brodie's"

Eric spat back, "Treasure Island!"

"Where?" May threw back.

Eric had started to get frustrated at her lack of knowledge.

"The Wa'! It's on the fuckin' wa'!"

"Where?"

"Deacon Brodie's!"

"There's an island on the wa'?"

"There's a story about Jeckyll an' Hyde an' Robert Louis Stevenson!"

"What about the island?"

"He wrote about it!"

"Who did?"

"Him! Fuckin' him!"

"Fuckin' who?"

"Fuckin' Stevenson! Wrote Jeckyll an' fuckin' Hyde!"

"Why'd he hide on an island?"

"He didn't hide on a fuckin' island, for fuck sake!! The story o' Stevenson writin' Jeckyll an' Hyde is on the wa' but it says somethin' aboot, Treasure fuckin' Island, too, ya fuckin' dense hoor!"

"Well what the fuck is it aboot then if it's on the fuckin' wa' at Deacon Brodies? Why the fuck is there a story aboot somebody called Stevenson who wanted to hide on an island on the wa' of a fuckin pub!"

Eric got louder and much more vehement. "It's a study o' good and evil! It questions the soul of humanity and the darkness of the self. Opposites! Purity and filth. Wealth and want! Not that you'd ever question any o' these conundrums o' life, ye lumpen proletarian heap, o' crud!"

"Hey! Less o' the lumpytarian, shit, auld yin. No idea whit it means but I ken it's no a compliment!"

Eric was starting to spit as he talked. DI McQuarrie twisted an affectionate and quizzical look over to Eric as if to say *don't bother* but May had now lost the thread completely who was standing on Stan with a come-and-have-a-go posture shouting back. Eric reached into his inside pocket and then slid a small pink tablet into the side of his mouth. DI McQuarrie saw this.

May became the man. "Jeckyll an' fuckin' Hyde? Deacon fuckin' Brodie? Robert Louis fuckin' Stevenson? Make yer fuckin' mind up! Who the fuck are you talkin' about?"

Presumably, all of these notable personages had little inkling that within a few measly decades beyond a hundred that their monikers would be augmented profanely to a more modern usage.

"All o' them! I'm talkin' aboot all of them...." Eric forced out bereft of breath.

Lenni, underneath the table, started to howl a low moan as he felt his master's rage, intuitively knowing that he now cut a reasonable hue of vermillion. Then the big man in army boots on the barstool at Hector had started to breathe heavily as this exchange became more heated and personal.

DI McQuarrie darted a look to Norrie who understood.

"Enough!" Norrie obediently barked.

Kelly smirked, delightedly.

"Jeez....." Megan leaned on Hector with her head in her hands

The Brylcreem Boys looked at each other, Eric consoled Lenni.

May was keen to shift the blame. "See the fuckin' bother you cause wi' yer fuckin' smartarse mouth, Kelly, ya fuckin' ….. …..smartarse!"

May maintained her volume but remained defiant realising she repeated herself, not good in any verbal joust, and Spider smiled at it all.

The huge man at the bar was squeezing his whisky glass tightly as his breathing got heavier and a low moan emanated from him. Lenni started to howl louder. Everybody in the pub started to nod to each other and nod to him knowing what was about to occur.

May muttered something about putting him out of his misery and put her whole hands over her ears. Spider leaned his elbows on the table and squeezed a finger onto each ear. His breathing got quicker then wound up to a tighter pattern, stretched his neck and started to moan louder. Megan quite fearfully retreated to the back of the bar away from the massive man wary of this instability and the Brylcreem boys turned away from him huddling up next to the juke box. DI McQuarrie who was writing in his notebook used the pen in one ear and the notebook to cover the other. Eric, anticipating Lenni's dislike of this, began to hush soft sounds to the dog and stroke him.

His eyes began to show white as his head craned to the ceiling with the moan getting louder and louder as he then released a long, deep, guttural howl as everything stopped and time seemed to stand still in the pub. He began to strained for air and then the exhausted lungs gave up and with a quick intake shifted his head level and into a thousand-yard stare as scream after scream bedecked in fear and horror rebounded off the walls and then as gradually as it arrived he subsided to a steady and regular heaving of the chest and then down to a tired, weary resignation as his massive shoulders rounded, curling over Hector into stillness. Megan quickly placed a replenished glass of whisky before him and retreated as sharply. Everyone uncovered their ears. Megan wrote up the whisky onto his note in the glass. The huge man leaned over Hector, now visually smaller, and slid the whisky over to his mouth and drew it in. The he rubbed his hands.

This was Sasquatch. He never spoke but the only time he communicated anything was when he howled and he only howled at the sound and sights of confrontation or pain. Nobody really knew his real name but agreed that if he was to attend *The Old Duke,* a moniker was required and so, appropriately, perhaps affectionately, this is how he became known. He had become something of a local legend, particularly to the children of the south side who would giggle nervously and point with the odd brat daring to speak to him, which was less ignored more psychologically unacknowledged. There was also some throwing of stones or whatever was considered a worthy missile, at him in the hope of a reaction. However, none came. Stories and myths of strength and violence abounded but the only truth that was known was that he arrived in *The Old Duke* in the winter of 1982 wearing a camouflage jacket with insignia, still apparent, but with time was replaced with other apparel.

The door opened and Joe came in with a younger, very thin man who belied his twenty-four years with the complexion of a boy. They arrived at one of those moments in a room when a family is informed that a close relative has been arrested for loitering around public toilets. Eric got up crossed in front of Joe and pushed Dick open. The sound of Eric muttering and complaining about the smell faded as Joe reached Hector. Lenni lay still beneath the table watching his master go.

"Who's died?" Joe asked.

"Sasquatch." Spider almost whispered over the room.

Joe and the young man both looked at Sasquatch together. Then looked askance back to Spider.

Kelly cleared it up.

"No .. not *died*….had one of his *moments*."

Joe and the young man understood and went to the bar. The young man spoke, "I'll get these, Joe. Turn up the telly, Megan!"

Top of the Pops was in full flow above them on a shelved black and white TV, circa 1970, traversing a corner, whose layer of dust was profound and had obvious nicotine streaks on its screen.

"Good man, Bullet. And I'll let you." With that Joe took a seat at Stan with May and Spider. Bullet asked her to turn up the TV.

"Magic word?" Megan replied patronisingly to Bullet.

"Please!"

Megan enjoyed serving Bullet full in the knowledge she was his intellectual superior and often, when serving him alone, tried to convince him of this state of relative intelligence between them, however, on this occasion, Kelly was lurking, close by.

She grabbed a long pole from the corner behind the bar and leant against the side of the volume knob on the TV and moved it downwards to roll the knob clockwise. This method frequently didn't set the TV to the desired volume and in this case was louder than she intended to make it, nevertheless, experience had taught her that she could be there trying to set the volume for ages before everyone was content and in consensus. So left it where it was.

"And how is Ford, this evening?"

Bullet hated his first name and had no idea how Megan had got hold of it. It wasn't that difficult as she had heard the rest of the gang calling him such names as *Mustang* and *Henry* one drunken dreich night near Christmas, last. She was quite proud of herself having worked this one out knowing Mustang was an American Classic car and that Henry Ford kicked off the whole motorised production line some seventy years ago, but she desperately fought the desire at the time to shout it out, let them all know that she understood the historical source of their jibes, so she just resorted to loudly using his first name.. This was somewhat shameful of her because she knew that he was called Bullet, ironically, because of his lugubrious inability to keep up with the ribaldry and aggressive badinage that frequently resonated around The Duke.

Bullet squirmed slightly looking back towards Stan.

"Aye. Okay."

"And have your labours satisfied you, this week?" she asked.

"What?"

Kelly rescued him. "How's work?"

"Great." Bullet returned and meant it. He emptied the bins of Edinburgh for a living and loved it. He needed nothing more in life but the ability to complete an unchallenging daily routine and the company within *The Old Duke*.

"Anything turn up?" Kelly asked, referring to the frequent stories of dead dogs and ballroom gowns that appeared in Edinburgh's refuse, occasionally.

"No." He took his drinks from Megan who was desperately trawling her grey imagination for a jibe to belittle Bullet. None arrived. Kelly pitched in.

"No firearms or lightning conductors?"

Megan immediately smiled to Kelly although she sensed that this wasn't his best material but enjoyed their conjoined, however, condescending, superiority. Bullet knew the word *gun* and the only conductors he'd ever known had worked on the buses. Any references to speed were beyond him.

"No, why?" He knew he was a target.

"Just wondering how fast you can get around in a day?" Megan joined.

Again, not brilliant but she was in and liked that. Kelly liked it more knowing that this unison of denigration may lead to coital unison.

"Fast." said Bullet walking over to Stan knowing he was extricating himself from....*something?*

Megan's smug smile to Kelly was interrupted by one of the Brylcreem Boys sidling up to the bar with a fiver in his hand. She sailed over to him and took his order.

Kelly looked up at the TV and heard the end of Madness singing *One Better Day* which he'd been aware of while Bullet had been getting served. It was quite a tuneful plaintive song seeming to bemoan the plight of the hapless and homeless and Kelly quite liked it. The camera swung around to one of the presenters as the clapping continued and a group he hadn't seen before called *The Smiths* were introduced and a jangling, rolling, guitar quickly preceded the singer, who with his hand in the air rolled his hips and declared that he had been happy when drunk but was now miserable? He had a suit jacket on and a floral shirt and what appeared to be a fox's tail or something similar hanging behind him. Moreover, this guy looked like a skinny reject from an Elvis impersonating contest with his quiff and fluid gyrations. His louche movement seemed to mimic a very bendy tree in the wind. He had bad glasses and a pocket watch swinging around his tackle area which, thought Kelly, could be dangerous but more than that he had no microphone? The guitars weren't plugged in, either and it all appeared as though this lot decided not to go with the playing live façade, of which everyone knew anyway, and portray the truth, as it were. As he listened and watched he caught some of the lyrics, most of which returned to this chap being *miserable now,* but he concurred entirely with *Bendy Elvis* about giving up his time to anyone who didn't give a monkey's about him and was introduced to the notion that Caligula could actually be embarrassed. What did resonate with him was the misery endured by *Bendy Elvis* when looking for and actually securing gainful employment. The guitar seemed to be omnipresent with all of this but independent of the lyrics, yet fitted. It wasn't the usual chords tripping along underneath it all but *something* other. Beyond this, *Bendy Elvis's* avowed philosophy concerning finding a job in Thatcher's Britain was both public and brave with implicitly more productive ways of spending one's time, most probably writing songs in this quartet's case and drinking beer in Kelly's. He was intrigued and not a little captivated but didn't want to appear too interested in guys younger and more talented than himself. Kelly, despite himself, was drawn towards this quite tall and pretty young man with the tonal value of a goose farting in the fog and fixed his gaze on the TV until they were applauded off and some vapidly smiling DJ introduced the next act.

"Didn't think we'd see you tonight, Kells. Dead on your feet at four." Joe called across to him.

Kelly made his way to Stan and sat. Joe discreetly dropped an envelope into his hand as he sat and Kelly pressed it into his pocket, albeit his wages were a day early, but Joe often displayed a trust in people that was often unwarranted, whoever they were.

"How much are ye, payin' him!" May abruptly spat.

"None of your business, May, none of your business." Joe said with surprising candour and honesty.

"What's the big secret? Tell us!" she bleated, again. "If he's minted he's in the chair! Times past, I've been flush and stood him a few, so let's hear it!"

Kelly smiled at Joe. Joe returned the smile knowing that Kelly was up to something.

"Actually, I don't mind, Joe, but let's keep the government money under wraps, shall we?"

May bit immediately as her eyebrows went north and even Spider desisted from his grin to make an *oooohhhh,* sound.

"Government money, eh? Sounds tasty." said Spider.

"Shurrup Spider! I'll do this. What fuckin' government money?" The hook was securely barbed into May's lip.

Joe contributed, "Really shouldn't've mentioned that, Kells."

"Don't give me that *shouldn't've mentioned that*, shite! Out with it!"

"Out with what?" Bullet said.

"These two are working on that new office block in The Cowgate, and the government are gi'in' them money for something!" May openly accused.

"Which Cowgate?" Bullet enquired.

All looked blankly.

"There's only one Cowgate, I know." said Spider.

"There's two" Bullet confidently replied. "We stopped there for our break an' a cup of rosy tea just this mornin'."

"It's *Rosy Lee*, Bullet. You don't say the thing you're rhyming with! How's there two?" Joe asked.

"There's a bend in the road when it gets to The Grassmarket, right?" Bullet said. "Well, as it turns the bend there's another sign that says the road heads to the *Cowgate*. So there's two. Cowgates. Two Cowgates. Different streets."

Bullet almost smugly took a pull at his pint and wiped his mouth with Spider, who wasn't smiling, trying to work it out.

"It's just two signs for the same street." Joe said.

"But it bends away from the first Cowgate, doesn't it? They

Newtonchange." Bullet said.

"Sorry what do they do?" Joe was becoming exasperated.

"*Change*...you know Newtonchange." Bullet looked pleased with his chance to clarify.

"*Newton* friggin' what? You've just been told, when you use rhyming slang you don't say the'actual word you're tryin' to rhyme with you dozy fuckwit!" May affectionately offered.

Bullet was emulating some of his wittier workmates who used this for a laugh on the bins but Bullet never quite got it, not even with a mining village outside of Edinburgh called Newton*grange* which was, in fact, their own local version for *change*. Likewise for Cowdenbeath which substituted itself for teeth, but Bullet had invariably been known to say, ...*and that's when he got a smack in the Cowdenteeth.*

"Okay,....", Bullet said, "... but it's a different street."

May was incensed.

"It's not two different fuckin' streets at a' ye' thick prick! One o' them is The Cowgate*head!* It isn't a sign sayin' it *leads* to *The* Cowgate, dipshit. It's the Cowgatehead! They're different streets! Two fuckin' Cowgates! Are ye blind to where they put the word *head*? It's where we keep oor brains an' you keep budgie food and dubbin" quipped May in her best conciliatory tones.

Kelly and Spider quietly laughed.

"That's right it is The Cowgatehead." said Kelly.

"Niver mind that! What's this money frae the government?" May delved.

"Can't say and now I'm sorry I said anything." Kelly manipulated the hook further into May's flesh. "Suffice to say that all those working on that building are in the confidence of the government. Had to sign an official secrets form and other stuff. They know they don't get a confidential workforce for free. Hush money."

"How much hush money? What's in there?" May was now a ball of frustrated inquisition.

"Look, I'll get this round, if it'll stop the questions." Kelly said.

"Two o' these an' a nip." May said pointing at her stout bottles.

"Spider?"

"A pint please, Mr Bond."

"And Joe can't say anything either, so leave him alone. He's got more to lose than me if he blabs." he said as he got up to go to the bar.

"Four figures?" asked Bullet, letting Kelly go and with a quick look to Joe who feigned awkwardness at the question and darted a look to Kelly who feigned a need to extricate himself from the interrogation and went to the bar.

Joe shouted to Kelly, "I need photos!"

Kelly was actually lost on this aspect of their slippery tale and looked back to Joe.

"For my book. Samples. I keep a book of my work. Good work. Samples. There's a forty-foot stairwell, six lengths, I papered with an alternate pattern with a nine-inch drop on each length that I didn't let stretch at all when it reached the skirting."

May was suspicious. Spider was with the concept. Bullet couldn't begin.

Norrie decided there wouldn't be a need for him to help Megan so removed his polypropylene trousers from in front of the unlit John and disappeared out the back of the pub. The Brylcreem Boys drank steadily and left around ten o' clock. Megan cleaned and fussed around tables wiping and arranging the lost causes. DI McQuarrie folded his newspaper on tomorrow's racing page and put his notebook back into his inside pocket, stroked Lenni and left. The fraternity at Stan, drank heavily, Kelly moreso, until Megan insisted they leave.

Kelly had drank much more than he should have. He sank several nips of whisky, courtesy of Joe, and north of at least five pints but did well to keep it together in front of Megan and remain apparently erudite and well-read to her as the evening moved to an end. He was really feeling it as he hit the night air. He'd made up some Shakespearean quote she would never have known was verbose Elizabethan tripe with the words *verily* and *forsooth* included, which apparently celebrated her constance and beauty. This, she just about got and giggled girlishly that suggested to Kelly she was still corralled in his web of words, wit and sexually motivated deceit. However, he knew he'd outstretched himself when he declared loudly that he would compose a sonnet to her on these very qualities and present it to her in a scroll. That had been a bad move. That would require thinking, time and probably talent and he didn't want to have to do the first, give the second or wrestle with the latter. A discussion for tomorrow, he decided, so tottered drunkenly towards his door and into the common stair.

Ascending the stairs he thought he heard some noises and looked back down the stairs to the door. Nothing? Then he heard a woman's voice. It was above him. He cautiously climbed the stairs and reached his landing in time to see the young lad that had the top floor flat *in-flagrante* with the woman who had the flat above him. This lad was about twenty and a leading beacon of the track-suited, Adidas wearing generation who had, ironically, little or no palpable skill with sports or muscular carriage to suggest otherwise and he'd suffered with acne late into his youth bearing the vestiges of his affliction sporadically on his cheeks and forehead.

They were up against the wall right next to his front door and taking up much of the space across the landing and so he couldn't get past and he didn't want to politely excuse himself as if there was nothing unusual or marginally embarrassing about this situation, however, the voyeur in him denied voice to alert them to his presence, at all, and so watched for the next few moments as she uttered,

"That's it, son...oh yer gettin' there.... don't stop...ooo yer so big." as he hammered youthfully away at her pelvis and grunted with every thrust. She continued, "That's it, Graham..."

"*Jason....*" he breathlessly corrected her and pushed his tracksuit bottoms further down across his bare arse.

"*Jason*...keep it goin'...that's it....oooh...."

She seemed quite bereft of any passion, just the need for him to *get there* and dishonestly coax him towards it. Her skirt was neatly tucked into her waistband and a pair of black knickers stretched widely taut from ankle to ankle.

Kelly never knew any of the two of them that well beyond a courteous nod and surmised that she was probably mid-forties but had *seen a lot of life* and here probably confirmed just that. The Pumping Tracksuit began to groan.

"Aww.... fuck....yes...aw yes..."

"Let it go, son! Rinse me oot wi' that big hose o' yours! C'mon, son!" her encouragement most likely quite indifferent to the dimensions of his member.

He moaned louder. "...Awww..... Yessss.....Yesss.....here we go..." Even louder and quite uncaring of any other residents who might be enjoying *Newsnight*. "Yessss!!!"

"There we go..... c'mon, son...gi'e me it!!" she shouted as he thrust forward and remained there lifting her slightly up the wall and she checked her watch. It was then that she saw Kelly, first naturally alarmed and then she smiled at him as The Pumping Tracksuit relaxed and withdrew his *big hose* from her and she slid back down the four inches or so to take her weight again. The Pumping Tracksuit immediately pulled up his trousers and looked at where she was looking. He grinned at Kelly and said,

"Top notch, man. Your turn."

Then he went quickly upstairs. By this time she had used her knickers to dab and wipe herself clean. Kelly, drunk, mildly excited, and a little bemused said,

"Just need to get to my door......"

She looked at his door and said,

"Zat where ye live? Didny ken which door ye were. I'm the one above ye." as she used the hand in which her glistening knickers were being held, to point upwards"

"Yes.. I know..."

"Well if ye ken ye should've knocked on ma door afore noo. Widna' cost ye much. Special rates fur ma nee'bours, ken?"

The penny dropped. "Right....well....thanks.....I've just got to...." pointing at his door.

"Sorry, son. There ye go." as she moved out of his way and then began to climb the stairs. "See ye again, eh? Dinny be shy!"

"No... I won't...knock....err.. you know? For..*something*... just say *hello*...you know?"

Drunkenness and an endearing inexperience had confused him.

"D' y' need *something*, son?"

"Sorry?"

"D' y' need something? A smoke? D' y' smoke, son....*herbals?*"

The thought of trying to get a hairball into a cigarette paper confused him and the conversation further.

"Sorry....*hair*...?"

"Herbals! Weed! I can sort ye oot."

The penny dropped.

"Right...right! I see......No! No, I don't ...erm..wee bit pissed...sorry..."

"That's a' right, son. if y' change yer mind, y' ken where I am.."

She made to go upstairs.

"An' if y' get a wee bit lonely an' the sap's risin'.... couple o' shillin'll see ye sorted."

Presented with such a matter of fact tone that sounded as though he was being given advice on a bus timetable caught any worldliness he thought he had, completely off guard. She went upstairs. Kelly opened his door and went inside and staggered to his bed..

It was in the pub, alone after she had locked the front door, that Megan noticed Lenni still under the table where Eric had been sitting and his stick still hanging there. She pushed Dick ajar and called into the toilet. Nothing. She went in and found Eric in the cubicle, dead.

Chapter 3

Undercover

Friday, 8th June

He hadn't pissed the bed for at least a year, now, however it had been an unexpected yet particularly heavy session last night. He woke but didn't move but then sighed knowing he had to go. He made his way to the toilet and removed his three-day sodden underpants dropping them in the basin and splashed his face with water, realising he had occasional smatterings of piss still on his fingers. He made an entirely new sound of disgust that echoed his distaste but through completely weary lips and sounding akin to a plughole sieve jammed with corrupting matter finally allowing draining water to escape. He plonked himself down on the toilet. He could feel a draught coming through the door that had always annoyed him and he had recently stuck black duct tape untidily around the edge of the door to keep it out. He pulled the door closed which rendered the windowless toilet into total blackness. He stayed there for a few moments, naked and blind. He was enjoying the cool feel of the porcelain and decided to splash his face with water again, so he slipped his hand out of the toilet door and flicked the light switch. He forgot he'd lately replaced the spent bulb with a red one he'd liberated from an old electric-fire while trawling around a second-hand furniture shop and this somehow made him feel really queasy, but also a little ridiculous.

He returned naked and sat on the edge of his bed and breathed heavily realising he couldn't get back in and then looked around the room. The place was a mess and understood that sometime, this year if possible, he had to get it organised. He'd lived in this flat for five years, now, and still it looked like someone had moved in yesterday. There were a few boxes punctuating the scene and books on the floor and whichever ledge could support them. Over time he'd amassed a collection of very worthy titles that he'd never finished, which he knew was a nagging trait of his. He never finished anything. They were in small piles against a wall, stood erect on a window sill or were an unorthodox plinth to a mouldy, unemptied tea-mug and they hung around him like children awaiting attention, looking up at him with big eyes that craved his returning consideration.

He turned and studied the bed in the darkness but he couldn't see that of which he was ashamed but pretended to himself that he didn't care. He felt for the wetness and quickly caught the shoreline and followed the turning arc trying to gauge the circumference of his urinary tsunami, which finally, discerning with a groan, understood that it was considerable. He renegotiated his way across the hall into his living room and lay down naked on his couch. His internal thermostat was fucked and it was still quite warm outside. He felt the lovely cold air around him but was cooking inside and his head was getting decidedly painful. He began to think of various excuses of why he shouldn't go and sign-on later that day and an excuse he could give Joe for non-appearance. However, he knew he couldn't let Joe down. A quiet sadness, unexplainable but certainly apparent, hovered in his thoughts. He farted a slightly wet one but dried it with a cushion corner, lowered his head down and fell back to Nod.

Retribution came in his most private of moments. Morning. He couldn't remember the last time he had shared it with anyone. He winced at the pain in his right lower back but decided that was down to the exertions of painting for Joe, not his alcoholic consumption. He rose and sat on the edge of the couch, still naked and now quite cold. These were the moments when he'd like to have had a body like Richard Gere in *An Officer And A Gentleman*, and be wearing a vest like Bruce Willis does in ...well all his films, actually, and get up, gently take the mousy brown flick out of his eyes, check his six-pack stomach and put on some eggs while piecing together the face and frame of the Broad he was with last night. So he clawed his nads, farted and moved a half-full beer can out of his footfall. It was ten thirty. He was late. He hadn't meant to sleep so late but as he'd missed his signing-on day, ironically because he was working. It seemed to matter little to him now what time he presented himself but there was Joe to consider, too. On his way out he picked up a handwritten note at the door and read it. It was from his Aunt Peggy who lived across town. Obviously she would have knocked but he missed her. His mother *wasn't well*. He should *go to see her*. He immediately wondered what was amiss, slightly worried of what could be wrong. Later.

He had this to do, first.

It was June, although he couldn't have told anyone the date. He hated this time of the year because the sun shone and hinted at a very un-Scottish and enduring month ahead. Strange to think that impending heat and languid evenings of summer were so unappealing to him but it made him feel guilty for some reason. He hated the smart students who crowded the Edinburgh streets at this time of the year, with their middle-class ripostes and pretentious little liaisons *accidentally* bumping into *Alasdair from Philosophy* or *Chloe from Lit*. Truth was, his extensive but shallow smattering of unfinished literary knowledge was threatened by them.

He crossed The Meadows, a green and level swathe of parkland adjacent to the university sprawling across the south side of Edinburgh's old town and headed to Tolcross. His coat was flapping and he could smell that he needed a bath. His heart was flapping a bit, too. He was two days late to sign-on and needed an imaginative excuse this time, or they wouldn't come across with the readies. He needed *Personal Issue*. That would be a tough one to swing.

The sun was getting warmer, he thought, and he was getting a little breathless. He sat down on a bench and cut the natural figure of *wino in the morning*, so much so that another of that fraternity decided to swanee along-a where he was and see if there was a drop to be had from this brother of the gutter that he didn't quite recognise, but did acknowledge the uniform.

"What about, ye?" he spat as he slid his rancid arse onto council green pine.

Kelly turned in his pain, drew a hand abruptly across his face and considered the ruddy visage confronting him. He faced a large man of a brown and wrinkled aspect with long unkempt hair flattened across his head in a vain attempt to induce order. The *what about ye* gave away his Irish descent. He immediately saw this fellow in better days drawing a plough across a field with a large horse.

"Fuck off." he tiredly said and turned away again and let his head fall backwards over the bench, which really began to nip and his lower back was beginning to ache again.

"Gies a wee swally, son. I'm strugglin', t' day an' it's no one o'clock, yet."

Kelly didn't move. The wino stank. Stale piss and sweat.

"Ach, go on, son, I've days tae go 'til I get ma money, ma mooths dry 's fuck! Jist a wee blast...?"

He really couldn't be arsed with this. His dignity was somewhat compromised as well. This fucker believed he partook of Chateau Brasso and was much aggrieved at the slur.

"Ma pal's been lifted, ye see and he usually sorts me. Put a Merrydown bottle through a winda, so he did....so gies a wee shot, son?"

He'd heard frequent stories of the homeless fraternity perpetrating such acts whilst *in their cups* and brought his head forward again and considered this unfortunate for a moment, just looking at him, and understood his aching need as he shaded his eyes from the sun. This was indeed the remnants of a man of the earth wasted by the sauce.

"What's your name?" He heard himself ask.

"Driscoll. What about that drink, son?!"

"Mr Driscoll, what would make you think that I have something for you to drink?

"What?"

"Drink? Why do you think I have something for you to fucking drink?

His delivery confused Driscoll as it was quiet and almost friendly yet he knew he was being swore at. And again.

"Who fuck do you think I am, you rancid old shite?"

He now heard himself lose the rag, slightly and didn't quite recognise this tempestuous aspect of himself. He did, however, enjoy the apparent bravery of the outburst in the face of what might be a dangerous and unpredictable foe but beneath all of this he recognised within himself the actions of a bully. Winos were renowned across the south side for their very public disagreements and the ensuing, yet often entertaining, conflagrations that ignited at the refusal of a drink or accusations of questionable parentage or personal hygiene. The indignance was obvious in his voice, but decided to go with it, sure that Driscoll's discomfort and inferiority was increasing with the tenor of his delivery.

"I don't care who you are, son.... I just need a drink. If ye have a drink and you're happy to give me a drink, well then I'll take a drink from ye and then shake yer hand, but if ye don't have a drink, well then say so...."

Driscoll looked at him, his green teeth drizzled in saliva. Kelly stood, drew his coat across his knees and wandered off without a word to the big Irishman. The pride of The Driscoll was somewhat dented by this silent rebuff, which to him was worse than someone actually berating him.

He was ailing now. His head was really starting to throb. The dew on the grass was starting to let into his boots, as he walked away, which he knew would make them uncomfortable and also smelly in the process of drying, but he just wanted to get this mission over with.

The dole office was packed, of course, with some quite forlorn attendees waiting to make their signature and secure another fortnight's money. There were mostly men who seemed to have dressed down for the occasion sporting ill-fitting jeans and sports tops hoping to declare their remaining interest in *something* and some women who'd patently made the effort to retain their dignity during this ordeal and were discernibly smarter. There were also the perennial baseball caps in their track-suited uniforms whose body language and volume amongst others of their fraternity told the state and all its minions to go and fuck itself and he'd passed a pit-bull terrier tied to the railings outside who probably would have shared its master's opinion, could it talk.

One particular claimant replete in jogging bottoms and polo shirt with a horsehead logo on the left breast was in full voice as Kelly dropped his arse onto comfy section number-one. This was where those who wish to make fresh-claims, those not yet fully prepared for the social ignominy that comes in platefuls from the civil-service manual of how to be a cold-hearted harridan and look as though the funds dished-out came from their own pockets, sit waiting to be called. Kelly recognised him as The Pumping Track Suit of the night before who politely addressed the fearful young man who was sitting opposite him behind the desk,

"I jist want ma fuckin' money man! I'm no fillin' in any mair fucking forms, either. I fuckin' filled in forty-fuckin thousand last week, man. Jist gi'es ma fuckin' cheque! Fuck!"

Such erudition. Such semantic bravery in the persistent use of an expletive to drive the meaning home and illuminate the sub-text of *Frustration*. No doubt there were other adjectives in his armoury but nay, he thrust his linguistic cutlass into his cephalic thesaurus and drew it back to find *Fuck* firmly skewered on the point. Quel langue! Kelly sensed an opportunity to aid this profane waif *and* himself. He stood up and approached the desk just as another tirade was winding up.

"Jason? Alright ma man…"

Well, he had to adopt the tongue if his ruse was to proffer.

"Heard the stramash fae the seats there an' jist realised I hud the same problem as yersel a while back. Widnae come across wi' the cheque unless ma B1 wiz tickety. That it?"

The Pumping Tracksuit slightly caught off-guard by this interjection, looked up, recognised the face as the scuzzy guy that has the first floor flat beneath their streetwalking neighbour, who was watching his thrusting manly moves with her last night. He stared for a second, then nodded.

"Aye…aye. Cunt wants mair stuff aboot me, n'that. Goat ma fuckin' shoe size n' evrithin, man. Dinny ken any mair!"

A slightly portly *British Home Stores* shirt opposite, pulled at his damp seventeen-inch collar and heaved a sigh. To him, Kelly was a most unwelcome addendum to all this, figuring he was The Pumping Tracksuit's cavalry and his nemesis.

"I'm guessin it's a' the stuff about getting the stairs cleaned, and bulbs changed? Am I right?"

"Bang fuckin' oan, big man. Fuck dae I ken aboot that, man?"

He turned to Shirty just as he looked across to a security-guard trying to read the *Health and Safety* poster near the door. Apparently oblivious, the guard read on. For three quid an hour he fights nobody.

"I'm gonna take ma china tae one o' yer wee desks there and fill in the blanks for him. I live in the same block and know his story. Grab yer form wee man and pit it oan one o' those desks an' I'll skate across in jig time. Jist gauny hae a wee word wi' this fine gentleman, aforehand."

The Pumping Tracksuit deferred to this obvious authority and immediately lifted his form and slouched across to another free desk. Shirty was now in a mild panic about the certainty of what was about to come but was addressed in an entirely different voice. Edinburgh middle-class.

"Don't call security. Please. "

48

He leaned in to the desk and scoured the room as if checking for eavesdroppers, and began in confidential tones.

"We've been onto him for weeks now. He's trouble. Right?"

Shirty frowned as if puzzled at this metamorphosis and confidentiality then looked from left to right for potential assistance, of which there was none close, but then came back to Kelly and nodded.

"He's been fencing burgled goods about the area and also acting as an out for most of the drugs that come into this town. I'm nearly at the zenith of seven months activity watching him and others…."

He threw in the *zenith* just to try and nail his blag.

"….and I don't want it messed up now. Are you with me? Good. It's no coincidence I'm in here behind him, today and I think he's beginning to trust me. My actual signing-on day passed two days ago but there was too much happening. There's one other person in this building knows about me and my activities, and shall, for reasons of security, remain nameless ….and now *you*. Quite frankly I'm sick of living like this but if you blow my cover now my Super will not be happy. Now listen, I'm going to say a few choice phrases to you then go and join my little troublesome friend at that desk, okay? Then you are going to go into your little room back there and get me a personal issue cheque. You ready?"

Civil-service training courses never ran to undercover Bobbies who smelt like Gorgonzola. However, the change from scuzzball to middle-class Drug Squad officer was too much for him this early on a Thursday. So he nodded and said,

"What's the name?"

Completely absorbed and alive to the scene, Kelly now dropped in,

"Campbell. Detective Camp… *Kelly*. Forget what I said first. Kelly. Leonard Kelly. It's *Leonard Kelly*. Okay? Now go!"

Shirty scribbled down the name and stood up quickly. Kelly had enjoyed the narrative corpus and proceeded sharply to a voluble epilogue.

"…jist dae whit the guid taxpayers o' Scotland pay ye to dae, ye chinless fuck-up! Many times've I got tae say it tae ye, I know the wee mans sticky-point an' I'm aboot tae git it sorted fur 'im. Noo jist git in there an' git the wee man's claim or I'll claim you!"

He knew he had an approving audience, who understood his thick vernacular by this time and rounded off the performance with a slight dip in toward Shirty's name tag,

"Douglas!"

Mr Douglas Shirt pulled the sweat stain from his back and disappeared with said scrap and name while trying to take his name badge off. Some smiles, nods of approval and much respect came from many of the baseball caps and tracksuits in the queue as he withdrew back to where TPT had tried to understand the difference between *Do you pay your landlord for cleaning the common stairs?* and *Is this service included in your rent?*, on his B1 form. He, enjoying his moment despite the violin concerto in his napper, sat next to TPT.

"Magic man. Need ma cheque…know" revered TPT.

He did indeed know very well the necessity for funds. He thought about augmenting the performance with a few more untruths to gild TPT's particular little lily but realised that his scene with *Dougie-Boy* had drained him and he had in fact nothing left to give....*darling.*

"Mr Kelly."

The voice came from a large cheeseplant with *Good luck, Irene* carded onto one of its leaves. He looked toward the plant worried that the DTs had finally arrived and that he was about to discuss his personal finances with a houseplant that wished Irene, *all the best*. A thirty-something, bespectacled, side-parted, polyveldt-wearing, paunchy man stepped from behind the plant holding a piece of paper and scanned the waiting area.

"Mr Kelly? Leonard Kelly?"

Too quick, he thought. The jury's brought in a guilty verdict. No enjoying the hotel and the break from work for a few more nights at the expense of the public purse. Much too quick.

The room was small and had magnolia walls and white glossed doorframes. Table and chairs fixed to the floor. Douglas Shirt had let him down badly. He looked at his adversary across the table and studied him for a moment. He knew him, he thought, but couldn't quite fix the face.

"You're three days late with your signature, Mr. Kelly. Have you been working?"

Monosyllabism was required while he gained valuable thinking time.

"No."

Had Douglas bought the story? If so had he conveyed it to this....*person?* Assessment of the situation said *no* judging by the tones opposite.

"Have you done any work at all since you last signed-on?"

"No." He lied.

"Have you been ill?"

"No." He was today.

"Well if that's the case, Mr. Kelly, and you don't have any mitigation for your lateness in signing-on then I'm afraid that we will have to deduct three days from your claim for this fortnight which will be apparent in your next cheque."

Well that was it. Dougie-Boy had obviously not bought the story but claimed a piss-break and gave the case over to this face that he couldn't quite place. However, he decided to test the water because in truth he was a tad excited by his quite public performance and new identity.

"Erm…I was just wondering if …*Douglas*... who dealt with me out there, mentioned anything about a certain situation that I am in fact not really supposed to disclose, for fear of public safety, to you regarding the circumstances of my tardiness relative to the said signature, Mr…."

He looked up from his file through his thick specs.

"What, all that bollocks about you being an undercover cop? Yes, he mentioned it."

See… without the insertion of the phrase *all that bollocks*, he could possibly have had room for hope in this situation, however….

"Zuckerman. My name's Zuckerman and I'm guessing you're trying to place my face, right? Well cast your mind back to 1965. Techy department. Boroughmuir High School. Screwdrivers? Ring any bells…*Kells?*"

Kells! Who was he?

"If I lift my shirtsleeve up you can just about make out the scar among the freckles."

He rolled his shirt cuff up to the elbow and started to fish among his arm-hair.

"Some people say that you can be scarred by your time at school if you don't quite fit in. But me, I took a permanent reminder with me of the bastard that made my life a living hell when I was there.

There it is *at perfect right angles to the line of the forearm* you said, just as you laid the red-hot rod onto my arm."

The smell of solder-flux and melting brazing-rods assaulted his nostrils as *The Last Time* by *The Rolling Stones* struggled to be heard above the lathes in the technical workshops of his old school. He focused in to the braze in the corner where 4F6 were heating metal rods to a glorious orange hue so that they could then batter the end flat on an anvil, force the other end into a six-inch length of dowel and call it *screwdriver*. He now saw the image of himself with Zuckerman's hot iron held in a pair of tongs while Zuckerman wiped down his anvil in preparation, then Zuckerman turning back to the braze and his jaw dropping at the sight of Kelly brandishing his hot rod. In truth it was a blank. Not only until this moment here in the dole office but also then. He couldn't articulate it at the time but understood intuitively that he was about to do something forced out of him by the education system. Make a mark. Literally. A reflection of history. He had been moved by the holocaust story in History, but also in a voyeuristically fascinated and ashamedly sadistic way and avariciously absorbed every detail. He just knew at the time it was what he had to do and laid the glowing red rod across the arm of Zuckerman.

"Threeby?"

He realised he was now at the mercy of Threeby Zuckerman. The Jewish kid he branded. His name was actually David but he didn't know this. He never had. He only knew that he had given the moniker of *Threeby* to Zuckerman inadvertently because he mentioned Zuckerman's name at home once and his uncle Gerry had said, *he must be a three-by-two,* and took this to school the next day. To Zuckerman's dismay, *Three-by-two* caught on with the fuckwits, and got shortened to *Threeby.* Of course, Kelly being the architect of Zuckerman's misery had to ensure that his authorship was acknowledged abroad across the school as it was a means of a) deflecting any flak that might come your way by targeting another, and of b) appearing to have fuckwit tendencies that kept that particular fraternity at length looking non-conformist, cool and witty. Compounding Zuckerman's misery further, Kelly also sadistically alerted the aforesaid cohort to other gatherings whereby he could humiliate David Zuckerman, with the obvious homosexual undertones in the syntax of his name, suggesting male fellatio. Zuckerman endured homophobic physical attacks from said fraternity and when he pleaded his heterosexuality under a rain of slaps that often occurred as he walked home, a verbal delivery of well-rehearsed anti-semitism was often led by Kelly....until the fuckwits all seemed well-rehearsed enough to dispense with their director.

"David. It's David. I'm thirty-three years old….."

"Same age Jesus died." He couldn't believe he'd interrupted him with that.

"…..and it's started to stop now, but all through my twenties I dreamt of meeting you in a pub, or on the street and just walking up to you saying... *David is my name. I am a proud Jew and I am not nor ever was gay...* and then flattening your nose to your face with my forehead."

He thought of saying, *well you couldn't do it with your foreskin,* however felt a pang of shame and decided this wasn't the time to pick up the baton of a bully and run with it.

"Can you believe that, Kelly, you evil shit? Me wanting to hurt someone?"

To agree or not to agree. That is the question? To agree might be considered tantamount to an admission of guilt but not to agree might just rub Threeby up the wrong way in a situation where he's holding all the aces. The rhetorical stance looked favourite and so he just half-smiled, insipidly.

"So ...how are you…*David?* You haven't changed, a bit." He blatantly lied.

"Really? I haven't changed?"

Threeby leaned in and said the following to Kelly, quietly and with a well-deserved hint of aggression.

"Something wrong with your eyes, *Kells?* I'm carrying two stone I don't want and got psoriasis all over my legs. I can't socialise very well now or keep a girlfriend and I occasionally meet ex-school....*people*...couldn't say *friends*...could I... who have a vague and entirely misplaced memory of me being jewishly gay. You throw enough shit, Kells, and some of it is bound to stick, eh? Speaking of shit, you look fucked, Kells. You're dressed like a tramp and you smell like a camel's arse *and* you're signing on. Things not work out for you, then, I'm pleased to see?"

He now understood that Threeby did indeed, not only have the moral high ground, but more importantly, all the power, and any retort questioning the proximity of camel's arses and their particular smell, would sensibly be considered misplaced in these circumstances along with any foreskin jibes. Threeby's arse had to be well and truly wiped, powdered and kissed before this meeting was concluded or this may not go well.

It didn't.

He was promptly enrolled onto *Theatre Skills*, a course to help with communication and interview technique, apparently, which Threeby pleasingly knew would be a nightmare for Kelly. He'd argued the toss with Threeby and accepted that he was going to have to attend some sort of course and tried to swing *Starting a Business* but Threeby knew that the thought of flouncing around on a theatre course would crush him and so told him *Starting a Business* was full. Then smiled.

What a fucker! Kelly thought and nearly let himself fall into a torrent of anti-semitic profanity but consoled himself with another seat on a bench in the June sunshine. The sun was behind him and he could feel the heat warming his shoulders. He thought of the gross imposition to his lifestyle that this *Theatre Skills* course would have and sighed heavily. He put his hands in his pocket and realised that he's buried *The Good Soldier Sveyk* there before he came out. He liked to have a book with him going to sign on just in case anybody wanted to get into conversation with him, and literature, *of any sort,* usually saw most of them off. He dipped back into the introduction he'd started earlier and read how Hasek got his first story published by Narodny Listy, a Prague newspaper, but anonymously and it was when he went for what turned out to be one of his regular jaunts into Moravia, Galicia, Slovakia and Hungary without a bean in his pocket but just hooked up with a few gypsies and vagabonds and lived by their wits, thievery and off the land.

Kelly liked the sound of Hasek. A kindred spirit. He did what he wanted when he wanted and he liked the sound of these gypsies and vagabonds, too, and thought that *vagabond* was a great word. So much so that he said it out loud. Then smiled. He could imagine Hasek up to no good, *gypsying and vagabonding* deep in the heart of Eastern Europe probably, robbing and defrauding anyone gullible enough to be robbed and defrauded, or selling palm-readings and clothes pegs. He imagined Hasek was happy when he was with them, free and roaming the land to their heart's content. *What a way to live*, he thought. Exciting. Free. Just taking whatever from whomsoever, whenever they needed it. He could do that, he thought and instinctively looked across the green parkland for a victim. He saw a man of about fifty walking a dog and wondered how much money he was carrying and imagined robbing him, a quite Romany preoccupation, apparently. At first with violence and threats, which didn't suit him at all, so he then morphed his daydream into his bumping into him as he passed on one of the paths and deftly removing his wallet from his jacket pocket. Which would require skill and years of learning! He audibly groaned. Even his dreams disappointed him. He wondered who the man was, his name, if he was married, single, got kids, rich, poor and imagined himself being him for a while. Being someone else. Fooling everyone. He could do that, he thought. Go to his bank and empty his account. Easy. Drive his car away and sell it. Job done. No Threeby, tattooed fuckwits, personal issue or Theatre Skills.

Chapter 4

Czech Mate

His horse ran well in the 1:35pm race at Haydock. Very well. It ran so well that it romped home by four lengths and DI McQuarrie was sure that when *Czech Mate* roared passed the line it smiled up at the TV cameras which beamed the races into the bookies shops. This was a 13/2 punt but he'd been watching it for a while, diligently noting its improving form but in this race it was considered by the pundits a step too far and too much of a rise in class for it to make any impression on this race. DI McQuarrie thought differently. He thought it was time, thought its elevation was deserved and laid two hundred quid for it to win on the nose.

Big George, the rotund, five foot two Bookie, was sorting out the winning bets behind his old fashioned desk and ornate brass grill. This was Pilton in the north of the city and he had been done over a few times so now stayed behind its safety glass with a stout and bolted door behind him. Big George's shop was one of the older independent bookies shops that were gradually being subsumed by the big chains but George was hanging on, admirably resisting the temptation to sell out or sell up.

The only member of staff he had now was a local retired fella, Charlie, who looked so thin he might blow away if the door opened and he sported a greased quiff haircut twisted at the front to remain in place. He was cardiganned with shirt, tie and suit trousers covered in white chalk and moved with the alacrity and verve of one several years his junior. Charlie was a known Elvis fan and reputedly a great jiver often showing his moves at the Pilton British Legion and thoroughly enjoyed his current job on stage in Big George's bookies. Locally, it was suggested that Elvis, seeking a more normal existence, faked his own death, chose Pilton in which to disappear and was now in partnership with Big George listening to the tannoy for untelevised meetings and *marking the board*, a tremendous skill of concentration, scrawling incoming betting prices at top speed but legible enough for the punters to understand. This was his job. A huge blackboard was fixed to the wall above a two foot high raised plinth underneath a crackly tannoy speaker that incoherently sparked and hissed what seemed like indiscernible info into the small shop.

Before DI McQuarrie went to collect he shuffled near to the door and lifted his coat and covertly spoke into his walkie-talkie on his suit jacket that none would have heard even if they were two feet away. A couple of punters who saw this but heard nothing quickly disappeared out of the door realising that Plod was present. This cleared the space nicely for DI McQuarrie to broadly beam a smile over to Big George as he approached the desk.

"Yes, I saw, Jack! Couldn't kick the smile off your face now, could I?"

"No, you couldn't. May I present you with my winning ticket, please Mr Turf Accountant."

He slid the slip under the grill.

"We'll just wait for the result in stone, Jack. You know the score."

Big George shouted across to the board,

"Charlie, soon as you like with that result." and Charlie gave him a thumbs up and then flattened his greasy hair above his ears as he marked up the next race from Fontwell."

Gettin' a wee bit back then, Jack?" George said.

"Is it not about time, George? I've kept your motor on the road for a few years, now; you surely can't begrudge me the odd wee win here and there?" McQuarrie hit back.

"I'm a bookie Jack, you know every pay out hurts a bookie and when you get to know your punters it becomes personal but they don't know it's personal. That's the difference."

"Ach well, I'm sorry if I've hurt you George but I have to say I love you and hope you'll be here for a long time, but right now, I don't care."

George, leaned to his left as if looking for something and came back quickly.

"Actually Jack, you're into me for just over a grand on tick, mate. Black and white in the book. would you care to make a deposit to reduce the hit later in the season?"

McQuarrie knew Big George was going to raise the question of his debt and really wanted to skedaddle beforehand.

"Sort of a crucial win, George. It's dug me out a bit. I'll square you later like you said later in the season...if that's okay?"

George shrugged, "I'm not starvin' Jack and you're Plod so I guess I'm good for a week or two yet but I have to close your book until we're square. Sorry mate."

A different voice interrupted the current one on the tannoy. Charlie looked over to Big George and threw another thumbs up to him.

"Reeshult!" His Elvisian qualities never ran to diction but then he threw up the piece of chalk in his right hand, caught it with his left and spun a one-eighty back to face the board.

Big George counted out McQuarrie's winnings who said nothing and went to leave. George stopped him.

"Actually Jack.... you know us bookies we talk to each other?"

"Wouldn't imagine otherwise, George."

"I know you have a slate with three or four of us across town."

"Get to the point, George!"

"The natives are restless. Think you might be abusing your position as Plod. They'd all really like you to square up at the earliest, if you could, Jack."

DI McQuarrie never thought he'd ever receive a veiled warning or threat from Big George.

"Including you?" McQuarrie said bluntly.

"Who doesn't want to be square, Jack? It comes between people, starts to smell."

"What 's starting to smell is your lack of trust, George. How long have I known you?"

"How long have you known Dixie McCandlish? He inherited your debt from Bob Casey when he bought the business. You knew Bob well but McCandlish doesnt give a flying fuck about who you are, Plod or not and he's connected, Jack."

DI McQuarrie didn't feel like laughing but affected one for this conversation.

"Connected? This is Edinburgh, George, not New Jersey. You sound a little pathetic when you start to use language like that, so don't. Not to me."

George was now a little more resolute having been described as pathetic.

"Yeah, that might be, Jack but you know what it all might add up to. It's happened before to a couple of the town's more eminent personages, so a promoted flatfoot won't worry them much. Let's face it there's been a few months where you couldn't pick your nose, never mind a winner, Jack and we all know you've been spreading the cost among us. Not a warning, Jack just a heads up on *something* that could become a little tense."

DI McQuarrie was about to say something to redeem his position when a younger female officer ran in and urgently said,

"They've found the car, Sir! We have to go." and then ran straight back out.

"Well thank you for the conversation, George. Most illuminating and I'll consider what you've told me and your application for a licence renewal when the time comes."

He knew this was underhand and a tad desperate and that Big George didn't deserve that from him but he always had to leave every conversation on a winning footing. It was in chapter one of the CID's manual.

He went outside where DC Jones was waiting for him. She was dabbing her skirt with tissues. McQuarrie grimaced at her in reproval.

"Sorry Sir. Spilt tea on myself. Couldn't get there bang on sixty seconds. Everything okay?"

"Hunky bleedin' Dory, Jones... just dandy. And don't keep using *they've found the car,* one. Bit more imagination, required, *Clare.* Use *Key witness turned up at the nick, only speak to you* etc. Okay?"

"Okay, Sir." They walked over to their green Cortina. "Where to?" Jones asked.

DI McQuarrie lowered himself into the passenger seat with a sigh.

"Dalkeith."

Chapter 5

Picture a Totem

The sound of laughter and van doors slamming could be heard coming up through the open window as the tradesmen all went home for the weekend. He hadn't got to the Cowgate office block until two o'clock because he was still feeling rough. He'd gone back to his flat after his eventful morning with Threeby intending to get his overalls together and get there sooner but sat down and laid his head back on his couch and fell asleep for an hour. Despair engulfed Kelly. He just wanted this week to be over. Everything had seemed to him to have conspired against it ever coming to an end.

Joe came into the room carrying his overalls rolled up under his arm and started packing away his flask, cup and newspaper into his tartan shopping bag.

"There's just these room walls to second coat with Maggy, okay?" referring to Magnolia emulsion. "All the cuttin'-in to the ceiling is done. You just have to do the internal corners and avoid the skirting."

Joe's tools started going into his bag.

Kelly sighed looking at the size of the room. "Where are you goin'?"

"I told you, I have to go and price another job. That's the van packed. I'm away."
`
"The two of us on this will get it done in jig time if you stay?" he pleaded.

"No can do, son. Another office across town. Got it organised with the caretaker who also wants to get home. By the way, don't leave anythin' cos' this is shut from the moment you leave tonight. All work stuff has to be out. Big opening on Monday."

"Lovely."

"Now, now son. Don't be like that. This is the last hurdle. I'll see you in the pub tonight. Actually, there is one more wee job I need you to do for me."

Kelly's jaw dropped.

"Don't panic! It's not a big job. I mentioned it in the pub."

Joe pulled out a plastic bag from his bag and carefully brought out a camera. This was a good one. A *Yashica* with a lens requiring manual focus. Little specks of paint sullied its shiny exterior telling tales of other jobs it had graced.

"What do you want me to do with that?"

Kelly acted outrage because he knew he'd be challenged with this task. It wasn't point and click.

Joe lifted his hand in mid-air trying to interject and becalm Kelly.

"It's easy son. Just turn the lens until it's sharp and click."

"'Til what's sharp?"

"The picture!"

"Of what?"

"The stairwell I papered!"

Joe looked at his watch and moved over to the window gauging the increasing rush hour traffic.

"There's a scaffold still there!" Kelly appealed.

"It's comin' down and goin' onto the back of a lorry as we speak, Kells. Just do it last one thing for me before you go. I need it for my samples book, my brochure of work. I'll get the camera bac whenever."

63

Kelly attempted another get out clause

"Wait 'til the scaffold's gone and you do it!"

"There's nothin' to it! Just point, focus and click. Help me out here, Kells. Fuck sake!"

Joe rarely demeaned himself in displays of irritation culminating in profanity and Kelly knew this. Shoulders slumped as Kelly relented.

"If I mess it up don't be havin' a go at me. I'm not David fuckin' Baillie."

Joe pulled on his worn tweed jacket and picked up his bag.

"Good man, Kells. I've got to go. Two hours max in here if you tank it. I need you to take the roller and bucket back to my place, Kells. Sorry mate."

"What!" Kelly wasn't happy.

"I need it for the next job and I can't leave it here because we won't get back in after tonight. My place is just a wee detour. It won't take you long. Take my spare key."

Joe gave it to Kelly.

"Just put a plastic bag around the roller-head and leave it in my hall. I wouldn't ask but I really need the heavy pile on it for an exterior rough-cast wall in Kirkliston for Sunday. I'll bung you an extra tenner and get the key back sometime. Thanks, Kells. I have to go. See you later."

Joe exited hurriedly and the door squeaked to a close and silence but for the noise of the traffic rising up and humming, distantly. Everyone going home except him. He looked around at all walls to paint and picked up the roller on the end of a broom pole and plodded across to the starting point near the door. He noticed a white mark on the wall as he got closer. Filler. Joe had sneakily flushed a few missed dents sometime during the day. Kelly knew there would have been no need to have filled them because nobody would have mentioned it but he knew Joe was a proud tradesman and often quite meticulous. Pedantic, Kelly would have said. Now these would need sanding flat. More work. Kelly then realised that he would probably be there until at least seven-thirty and thought there was no use in killing himself to get it done. He put the roller down and opened the window and leaned out watching the cars pass each other below knowing most of them were returning home to wives, husbands, mothers, fathers or kids. Dinners warming in ovens, beers cooling in fridges, all delighted with the prospect of the weekend. He imagined girls of sixteen practising to be women arguing with their mothers about the amount of make-up they were wearing and the entreaties to their husbands to *have a word!* Young lads that were getting ready to go out bedecked in their latest acquisition from *Top Man* and the smell of pizza wafting through their living room, a TV in the corner with *The Tube* on, the current barometer to cool with Jools Holland and Paula Yates presenting and interviewing bands and singers after they'd played their latest compositions, all being slightly too loud. Dad sitting there after his week's labours and the first beer of the evening being raised as his wife sat down on the couch next to him and he, automatically, putting his arm around her. Then he imagined he was that man. He leaned forward in the vision to get the bottle of beer but couldn't reach it but then his teenage son passed it to him as he was walking to the mirror to check how his new shirt was hanging. And he smiled. And he smiled back. He then secretly dropped a twenty into his son's hand as he walked back across the room but his wife had seen him do it and mockingly reprimanded him for it but then smiles at him and kisses him on the cheek. His son then kisses his mother in this vision, who tells him to be careful and not be too late and he, his father, winks at him and hears the front door slam as he leaves.

For those few moments he was content and able to be that fictional man but something, somewhere distant, a voice, his voice, the sound of his uncle Gerry, his mother, his dead father, reprimanded his lack of structure, his haphazard and accidental life and there, elevated in that solitary box, removed and above the vortex of life, he watched the rest of the world, doing something, going somewhere and trying to be happy.

The slamming of a door in a corridor somewhere in the building wove itself into his vision and shook him out of this reverie. And then the building was quiet again.

Then Kelly felt lonely.

He then lifted his eyes and gazed across some of the rooftops and realised he was looking out towards the street he grew up in. It was a small street of tenement blocks and he remembered playing there as a child. He smiled inwardly and thought of the mates he'd had and had since married with their own broods knowing not where most of them were now. He remembered Thomas Alexander's mother standing at the stair foot and loudly, quite unembarrassed, shouting his name at the top of her voice, him needing to return home for his insulin injection. He saw his own mother cleaning the three steps into the common stair. He remembered the note from Peggy. He knew he would have to go and see her soon.

He sighed and returned into the room and began to sand the filled patches on the wall.

Kelly worked on as the traffic died and a deafening quietness grew in the room. He'd closed the window and every noise of the roller squelching across the walls was magnified in his solitude. There were distant occasional bangs and thuds from the building that made him start inside but he realised that there had to be someone to lock up. The room felt different, as if he was now trespassing on a time zone that belonged elsewhere. He began to hum a tune to break the silence and realised he was dripping out the tune he had heard by The Smiths on Top of the Pops in the pub. Then he started to add a few words to it of his own. He didn't know the lyrics....he had to, but he applauded the sentiment Bendy Elvis proclaimed vis-a-vis finding a job and being miserable. He got louder singing the same thing over again and enunciated the guitar part where he thought it should go and then realised.... he quite liked it.

Three hours later he finally reached the point back where he'd started and stood the roller up in its tray.

"Thank fuck!" he exhaled, tiredly. "Ten to eight. Never again."

He cleared the dust sheets and wrapped a plastic bag around the head of the roller and carried it out to the hallway with the tray then removed his overalls and went back into the room to pick up his bag. Joe's camera was revealed as he picked his bag up and took a step to leave. It sat there tiny in the large empty office but grinned at him, teasingly. Kelly thought about making up some story about getting hurried out by the caretaker but ultimately realised this would just disappoint Joe and he would have let him down so he picked it up and made his way across to the other side of the building to the large stairwell Joe had papered.

Thankfully the scaffold had been removed. The stairwell spanned two floors with refurbished offices on both levels. Chrome banisters now adorned the scene and an abstract painting that Kelly was immediately struck by, had been hung on the wall opposite. He never imagined he'd ever like an abstract. Kelly thought that this area might be where the opening ceremony would take place as it was directly above the main foyer. He looked down to the large foyer and then up and saw the glass roof that changed colour as he moved and couldn't deny it was spectacular.

Looking up at the forty-foot stretch that Joe papered with a sweeping grass-like pattern, he remarked that it was indeed a decent job well done but it was time to get out of there and so he put the camera to his eye and began to view the wall from the bottom but it was too close to a large subject, so he went up to the next floor and leaned over the chrome banister trying to get it all in. The light was better but the camera was still too close. Office doors were behind him stopping him getting the whole wall into the shot with the banister giving it size and perspective so he leaned on a door with his back and tried to frame the picture this way but it still didn't get the full drop in.

Surveying the shooting areas, he realised that if he took it from the office door last along the landing which was in the corner, he could get the stairs, banister, and the whole wall all into shot so moved towards that office door. He framed it up but knew he needed to move further away so he felt for the handle on the door while still framed up and eased it gently open and moved softly backwards into the open doorway. Perfect! Everything was framed. He switched the flash on and clicked, levered the film forward and clicked again then did one more for luck. Light bounced into the darkened office behind him but threw back noises so he turned around quickly.

Before him, deep into the office space was a suited forty-something large man with thick, black hair sitting in a swivel chair with his trousers at his ankles and a shocked demeanour coursing across his visage. Sir Clive's large erect penis craned northward and was silhouetted perfectly against a distant window with the blinds drawn. On his knees before this huge totem, his face inches from it, was Mr. Immaculate of the stairwell smiles and wanking filling-knife encounter, still with one hand on his recipients knee, the other wiping his mouth and occularly recovering from the camera flashes. Kelly remained there holding the camera up at his chin until he realised what he was watching before quickly panicking, picking up his bag and Joe's roller and then descending the stairs to the large foyer. He ignored two tall men wearing black coats standing in the reception area and rushed towards the main door.

A voice shouted to him.

"That you square, up there?"

Kelly turned to see a bald head leaning out of a hatch with a sliding window.

"Aye. Done." He said after his momentary hiatus in his panic and he opened the door and hurried briskly past a large black Bentley parked arrogantly on the double yellows.

Chapter 6

Global World Theatre

Monday 4th June

Kelly had not risen at eight o' clock in the morning for a long time now, especially a Monday, but the threat of impending poverty had made him set the alarm clock. Poverty was indeed a growing cloud having caned away his earnings and his extra tenner from Joe at the bar of *The Old Duke* over the weekend.

He resentfully gathered himself together without a thought for breakfast and pulled his Crombie coat over his unwashed shirt and jeans and heavily dropped his boots down a stair at a time and out into the street. It was drizzling but bright. He had to stop to think about where he was walking to but then turned right and headed out for the old primary school on The Canongate. He checked in his pocket for some change that was rattling around hoping there was some silver there or maybe a pound note and pulled out a few coppers of little value. He looked across the road at a little coffee shop and heard the loud voice of the vendor sharing banter with what were, most probably, his regulars, workers heading for the nearest offices in town. He wondered if he could do a job in a café like that? Get fed and watered for free and be that someone who shares daily badinage with the office lemmings, or maybe he could get some of Joe's paint dregs he never uses and create some piece of *Art*, abstract, naturally? He could punt it to café's and pubs, put a signature in the corner that sounded like a current artist or just make one up? *R.L. Forsyth?* No, that sounded too much like *The Glasgow Set* from the turn of century. Something a bit foreign sounding? One name. *Carlucci?* That's it. *Yes, this is actually an original Carlucci from the late fifties,* he imagined saying to his victim. *His magnolia period.* He realised that would take time, effort and commitment as well as plenty of shoe-leather and that his imaginary efforts to defraud publicans and coffee-wallahs into buying original art was flawed. As he crossed a road to the next block he saw two large men smartly dressed men in black coats standing on the corner and one of them was holding a large thick book. As he neared them they looked his way and smiled. Kelly realised they were holding a bible and sighed heavily.

Bit early for Jesus, he thought.

Their smiles got larger as he arrived to the corner,

"The Lord God wishes you a fruitful day, Sir." said the first one holding the bible.

Kelly had risen much too early for an appropriate riposte so dipped his hand into his pocket and grabbed the coppers and then dropped them into the hand of the second man, whose smile dropped from his face as Kelly ambled by without speaking. Maybe they were at it, he thought? Maybe they couldn't give a monkeys about God, Jesus and whether or not we were all to be saved? Maybe they weren't collecting for anyone but themselves. He could say *God bless you*, no problem. He could say *Most generous, Jesus be with you,* while gullible or embarrassed punters pay ten-pence for him to fuck off out of their faces? He could make up a fund to be raised to save a church roof somewhere. Every church roof in Christendom seemed to need work, these days. Why not? Maybe he would go to jail if he was caught? He just made his way on towards the venue for *Theatre Skills* and decided that any ruse to defraud the world of their livery and coin would require a much better morning than this drizzly dreich affair and with a much clearer head. He walked on accepting that this current mission had to be the source of any meaningful income in his life. He plodded forward as if walking to his own execution.

Rodger was a large man. Tall. Rodger was tall and fat. He sported a checked shirt atop a white tee shirt, but the buttons on the shirt were taut and desperate to free themselves of their snares called *buttonholes,* and he had on a pair of *Wrangler* jeans secured tightly around his waist by a metal buckle of a bowlegged cowboy carrying a saddle. This buckle dug into his belly when he had to bend over but Rodger was keen to just deal with the discomfort because the buckle, he thought, was cool. He was forty-six and quite keen not to be, so he worked quite diligently at creating a look that he considered a ubiquitous male presentation universal to all ages and since he had started this job he had begun to moisturise. He had recently separated from his wife and was now exposed to many young women, far too young for him, of whom he thought might be dazzled by his expertise in theatre and his tales of when he toured across the whole of The Lothians, with *Lear,* as he casually called it, and of the TV ads he had been *up for*, shot, but never made it to the screen as they were too *out there,* wacky or a little risqué and he always made sure he told anyone who was listening as to his input and consultation with the director, who had *missed a trick* that made the ads *much more dynamic* and immediately *watchworthy,* this being a favourite word of his. He frequently used it to try and impress in the right situation.

He was busying himself with a toaster and some white sliced bread in a small office that was decorated with theatre posters and some postcards which were fixed on the wall behind his chair, seemingly from a copious amount of people he appeared to know who either lived, were travelling, or engaged in *the biz,* in far off places. There was a postcard of a massive park in Madrid with a skyline of classical sun-bleached buildings across the back of the park with the word *here* handwritten on it and an arrow pointing down to a beautifully porticoed frontage of a white-stoned building. A kettle purred next to the toaster.

His work colleague arrived. Katherine. Her name was Katherine but insisted on *Kat*. Kat with the K, if anyone had occasion to write it in a friendly, informal, easy-going, *what the hell*, manner. She had within the last year changed her name by deed poll to Noh. Katherine Noh. Kat Noh. It had been Grimley. Katherine Grimley was perfectly serviceable as names go, but she let it be known with friends, colleagues and family that she had become so enthralled with the Japanese form of theatre, *apparently,* that she felt she must do something to acknowledge this damned compelling attraction but more importantly, place herself within the milieu of Edinburgh theatre and all its acolytes who would remember her name.

She said nothing to Rodger but went straight to a shelf with a large double cassette player that had APSS, (Automatic Programme Search System), the latest gismo to make the theatre practitioner's work so much easier as it would find the track a busy theatre practitioner needed by pressing fast-forward and stopping at the requisite place. In this case it was *Ethnic Echoes*. A sound of a gentle wind breathed across the office as a rising Arabian pipe settled on the breeze and a haunting female voice began to hum and lah and shift in a skewed breathy noise offering a vision of sand dunes and a caravan of camels leaving the still palms of an oasis. Then Rodger's toast popped. Kat looked across at him and then to her desk which had a burgundy *Gibson SG* electric guitar laid flat across it.

"Could you move this, please, Rodge?" Terse Monday tones.

"Yeah, cool Kat. Sorry. Had a gig last night. Need to fix one of the songs. Brought it with me."

Rodger periodically brought his guitar to work with him in the search for chord sequences that *eluded him*. He played in a trio who gigged in pubs and everyone who worked or attended Global Theatre Works, knew it. Often a GTW attendee would enter his office and begin to speak as Rodger, gazing past them, stopped them holding up his plectrum indicating they had to wait, played a couple of chords before finishing on a tricky B7th and letting it ring as he smiled and assessed the sound then said,

"Couldn't find the seventh at the end of the bridge. Annoying! *Do You Feel Like We Do?* Peter Frampton. It's on *'Comes Alive.'* Seminal work."

Attendee replies, "There's a pigeon in the studio, again."

The building was a former primary school that was culled by the council and given to the government as a day centre for dole-ites who, having been unemployed for a length of time, were helped to find work by attending a course ran by *industry professionals*. It was a tired old building and a blessing to the council that they could give it away, requiring much maintenance and did indeed have the odd window devoid of glass.

Rodger buttered his toast.

"Toast?" he asked Kat.

"I can't eat bread. Bloats me. Just coffee." she said as she tied a scarf of green taffeta around her head and adjusted her flowing terracotta full-length dress.

"Instant?"

"No. Don't we have a cafetiere?"

"A what, sorry?"

"A cafetiere. For coffee. Good coffee. You know...." and her mime skills kicked in with one hand on an imaginary pot as she pushed down towards it then started to arrange some papers on her desk.

"Oh yeah..." Rodger said, "....a plunger pot. Up there. Behind you. Shelf."

Kat took down a dusty cafetiere from the shelf. "This is a prop."

"I'll give it a wipe and a rinse. No probs." And with that Rodger rinsed and cleaned the cafetiere and put in three good sized heaped spoonfuls of instant coffee and poured boiling water into it.

Kat observed the creation of her hot beverage in its unnecessary housing but just went with it. She was much more comfortable pouring her coffee from a French named vessel and anyone coming into the office would assume it was good coffee, so she let it go. She sipped the mix and Rodger tore into his tea and toast. He, having seen off the toast in seconds and slurping his tea, loudly became thoughtful and quiet as Kat sat back in her chair with her eyes closed occasionally lifting the coffee to her mouth. The caravan of camels had faded out by this time and Namibian drums began to thump the relative peace out of Monday morning when Rodger spoke to Kat.

"Kat?"

She was somewhere else. Namibia, presumably?

"Kat." he said louder.

She opened one eye. "Yes, Rodge?"

"Can I turn this down, please?"

"Is it irritating you, Rodge?"

"No! I like it." he lied. "Just want a word about today, if poss?"

Kat stood up and silenced the Namibian Cozy Powell.

"What is it, Rodge? What about today?"

Kat knew what the subject of his discussion would be but put him through it, anyway.

"It's the Stanislavsky workshop, this afternoon...."

"Exciting isn't it!" Kat enthused. "If you're worried about it Rodge, you won't have to stay in the room, you know. It a very powerful method which can be disturbing and upsetting for some people. Even just watching."

"No..no...I'm cool with it all, Kat, it's cool. I'd like to lead it, if I could?"

Kat, who was the course leader, was about to dangerously overstretch their charges, of which none of them had ever engaged with Drama beyond school or ever took seriously and now after a few months of the course's sporadic comings and goings of her *students,* as she liked to call them, she had thought them experienced enough to engage in Emotion Memory, an exercise formulated by probably the most famous practitioner Theatre had ever produced, in order to accurately engender the required psychological disposition of a character and the prevailing emotion present to get to *the truth.*

The truth was she wanted to do this because she *wanted* to do this. It wasn't anything to do with providing a learning experience for their often disinterested charges but creating a talking point for her in the social circles of theatreworld, trying to validate a piss-poorly funded course populated by characters who had been coerced into it, at risk of the withdrawal of their dole money should they refuse. And she wanted to be loved. Celebrated. Told that she was fantastic, be considered interesting for wearing Moroccan sandals and Toledan jewellery, feted and notable, renowned amongst her peers and was not going to let the opportunity to introduce *The Method,* that which will get her students talking about it, and of her, to so many other people at parties, at home, within and without of theatre circles. Oh yes, they would all remember the taffeta headscarf which she wore whenever *teaching.* She widened her eyes and tried to look sorry.

"Can't let you do it, Rodge."

Rodger frowned. He also knew of the unspoken kudos acquired from a Stanislavsky workshop.

"Why not? I know the routine. I know the formulae. I've read up. I can do it. I *want* to do it!"

"And I love you for it, Rodge. I respect your drive, your learning..." Pause and eye-contact for dramatic effect. " It's the insurance. You don't have the certificates. You think you can do it and I harbour no reservations that you could, I trust you, but you're not qualified, Rodge. Base camp one, love. What if we meet a monster, this afternoon? What if we dig up the dead? Conjure the past? Reveal that which should never have been revealed? What if you were really good at it, Rodge and we sent home a quivering melon..."

"Jelly..."

"That's what I meant. What if, Rodge, what if? We'd be closed down. Out on our ears. Ran out of town. Stick to this morning's Impro workshop, it's just as valid. Just be there for me this afternoon, Rodge. I know I'll need you. Rodge?"

Rodger looked downhearted.

"Rodge?....."

"Yeah, okay.

There was a knock at the door.

"Come." Kat quickly said and was grateful for the interruption. Kelly stood there holding the letter he received and unenthusiastically said,

"I've been sent to the Theatre Skills course. Is this it?"

Kat was in the process of getting up to greet him when Rodger leapt up and took the letter from his hand officiously, then studiously slowed down reading the info.

"Yep.... this all looks in order..... Rodger Hampton." he said quickly without introducing Kat and holding out his hand. They briefly shook hands.

"And you are....?" Looking at him and pretending to search for a name on the letter.

"Leonard Kelly."

By this time Kat had reached Kelly and took the letter from Rodger with a sarcastic smile and said,

"Kat Noh. *Course leader.*" and she offered her hand out to Kelly who really didn't get the name.

"Sorry.... *Catno...?*" as he took her limp grip.

"Kat!" she quickly replied before any descent into explanation and spelling was forthcoming, "Just *Kat* will do. Sorry what did you say your name was?"

"Leonard Kelly."

He hated having to say his full name. It confirmed something about him he had never been able to pin down. He really didn't like being Leonard Kelly. Never had.

"Kelly....just *Kelly* will do. Nobody calls me Leonard."

Rodger burst back into the conversation desperate to gain implied authority.

"Maybe you could start now? Why not? New beginnings! New people! This could be the start of a new journey as *Leonard!* Or Len? *Lenny? Leo*! Whatever you'd like? This course is all about trying to use drama to find out who you are. Discover parts of you had no real idea existed!"

Rodger beamed at Kelly and Kelly thought.....*What the fuck!!?*

"Smidgeon early for any existentialist discourse, Rodge. Let's just get *Kelly* into the register and we'll take it from there, shall we?" Kat smirked.

And with that Kelly was registered onto the Theatre Skills course, briefed as to *where they were* in the course and all the problems of continuity with people arriving and leaving and the gratuitous absences and of how difficult it was to remain on top of each and every one of her student's *personal development*. However, her labours were *her pleasure*, she said, and then asked Kelly not to be too disappointed if there wasn't a big end of course production, which he assured her he wasn't. Then Rodger told him about the plan for that morning's impro workshop, which would be *tremendous fun,* and then said *over to Kat* for an outline of the afternoon's activities. Kat asked him to *trust her* in all things as an opener, stating she was *a safe pair of theatrical hands,* and she ran through her verbal CV, which she always did, to reassure any latecomers to the course of her abilities and experience that had shaped her *current being,* which she thoroughly enjoyed as *Rodge* had to just sit and listen. She embellished a description of her honours dissertation on Noh Theatre, in hope that he might make the connection of name and theatrical form, gained one glorious summer at Doncaster College of Higher Education and then she described numerous TIE (Theatre in Education) companies she'd been *overjoyed* to have worked with. At this point she giggled slightly as if a fond and distant memory had just arrived from the past. She apologised and explained that it was such a tour, *Smell the Bully*, devised by *We're On It!* Theatre Company*,* that had brought her, eventually, up to Edinburgh, fallen in love with the city and the *Fringe* and *just bloody well stayed, thank you very much!* Kelly had to reply that he hadn't heard of the play or this company and then asked her where the toilets were.

Kelly actually considered escaping through the window whose aperture would have allowed such desperation but would have had to stand on the toilet cistern which looked as though it might collapse from the wall if two toilet rolls were laid on it, then he thought of the loss of his dole money, of having to work for Joe, or his inability to devise a dishonest enterprise with which to dupe the world, so he checked himself in a mirror, took a deep breath and went into The Studio, which was the old primary school games hall, painted black and with a few donated lights on tripods at one end. There were a few other attendees sat along the edge of a small stage near the lights, quietly chatting. Most of them were younger than him and mainly female. Rodger was there by this time and was expending a lot of energy in trying to be bright and funny. He cracked the odd punned gag which was poorly received and then saw Kelly.

"Girls and chap," he said doffing his metaphorical cap to the only male amongst them, this is Kelly. He's new."

Kelly walked over.

"A'right." he said.

A collective, *"A'right."* came back.

Silence. Rodger then tried to break it. "Did you find the err....?"

"Yes thanks."

"Always good to lighten the load, as it were, before our exertions. Right girls?"

The girls, of which there were three, all of around their late teens, did that inward huddle accompanied by a giggle that was young girl code for *what a prick, isn't he embarrassing, he's talking about peeing, Maybe sex!*

Then the young man sitting near them threw a look across to the girls and came to Rodger's rescue.

"No, you're right, Rodge, I always go before we start." Then he stood up and approached Kelly who was also still standing and offered his hand.

"Steven."

Kelly understood what Steven was doing and gladly saw the possibility of an ally should the future ever require one. They shook hands just as a further group of girls and a very thin tallish man wearing nylon shell suit bottoms and an Adidas top entered loudly. Rodger immediately went over to them.

"Mornin' Jane."

"Morning Rodge."

"Mornin' Rodge."

"Morning, Sammie. Liz, you can't smoke in here! We've told you."

"Morning Rodger."

"Yes, good morning, Darren. You'll have to put it out, Liz!"

Liz was a flame-haired custodian of denim, freckles and expletives.

"Ah'm no puttin' any fuckin' fag oot! Ah've only goat twa left fur the rest o' the day! I need ma hit Rodge and a've goat tae spread thum oot. Dinny be a big gay cunt!"

"Go outside then! But don't be too long. And stop using that language, Liz, please!"

"Whit...gay?"

"No! Cu... just take it outside!"

"Ha Ha ya big shitbanger, nearly goat ye!"

Liz spun around to leave and nearly walked into Shell Suit Bottoms.

"Fuckin' shift ya stalkin' weird bastart! Mind ma fag on yer guid breeks there, Pisspot, ye'll go up in seconds. Where'd ye git thaim, oot a skip? Me an' ma Ma ur gaun shoapliftin' oan Thursday night. Want tae pit yer order in noo?"

Rodger hated Liz. She was quicker witted than him and had what seemed an innate and quite talented ability to offend everyone.

Amongst her peers, there was a broad acceptance of the scallywag, the loveable rogue who, very often just said what the others were thinking but resisted from saying, even though social etiquette suggested that it be withheld, shelved for a more appropriate moment but she had no compunction, or perhaps ability to gauge the room, but more to the point Rodger couldn't control her. Threats of dismissal came back with threats of his car being burnt-out should he ever be the architect of her poverty. He believed her.

"Just go please, Liz!"

"Ah'm gaun, ah'm gaun." She spotted Kelly. "Wha's the new cunt in the Crombie?"

Rodger thought he'd get her onside with an introduction.

"This is Leonard..."

"Kelly." Kelly said

"Kelly. You can say hello properly when you've had your cigarette."

"Kelly no' a burds name? You a burd, Kelly? You hidin' a big pair o' tits under that coat?"

Kelly was taken aback by this hurricane of profanity, so just said,

"No."

"C'moan ootside Kelly and ah'll show ye *ma* tits fur a packet o' ten. Benson and Hedges, tho', nae fuckin' big girl's Silk Cut."

The room had started to laugh and Rodger knew it wasn't the best start to his impro workshop.

"Liz!!"

"Ah, fuckin' relax, ya big Bozo, ah'm gaun. ...'.kin 'ell, man!"

Liz exited blowing a puff of smoke back into the Studio accompanied by a cheeky smile.

Rodger decided that this would be the best time to get the workshop started. There seemed enough of a quorum to begin and if any stragglers arrived late they'd soon pick it up. Rodger looked at the boots of Kelly.

"I think tomorrow you might think about wearing something lighter? Training shoes, maybe?"

Kelly was starting to panic inwardly. This was quite a shock to his system. Unfamiliar surroundings. Characters he knew very little about. Being called a *cunt in a crombie* before ten o' clock in the morning. And now being asked to wear trainers.

"I don't have a pair...?"

"Anything, sand shoes, rubbers of any description for tomorrow." Rodger said and frowned.

Then it dawned on Kelly, thankfully, that he was going to Eric's funeral tomorrow but knew if he opened his mouth now how it would look and that *I have to go to a funeral* would appear as a lame excuse and a puerile attempt to extricate himself from this looming hell. He had nothing else.

"I can't be here tomorrow. I have to be somewhere else." That was enough. Embellish only if necessary.

"Really? Not the best of starts, *Leonard*." Rodger beginning to enjoy his show of authority. "Why not?"

"It's *Kelly*." Kelly tiredly reminded him "I'm going to a funeral." He knew how this sounded and that all in the room were now quiet and listening. "A friend....*colleague.*" Colleague sounded better.

"That was quite inconsiderate of your *colleague,* Leonard,

shuffling off just as you acquire commitment to this course. From where was this colleague?"

The flock of hair bobbles suppressed a collective but quite nervous chortle.

Telling him Eric was an old fixture from the pub wasn't going to swing it in this context and with the gaggle of gigglers present, quick thinking was required.

"He was someone that used to do the accounts in a business I used to work in. Got quite close, actually."

Steven became quite attentive to the quiet exchange.

"And now he's *dead?"* Roger blurted, knowing he would exacerbate the tension and get a reaction from bobble city, who poorly stifled another audible grunt and *Oh my God*'s which was really beginning to annoy Kelly. As was Roger.

For the first time in years Kelly felt the surge of an entirely justified wave of anger. This fat prick was implying from the way he said *dead* that Eric's demise was nothing more than an excuse to alleviate himself of the requirement to engage in all this shit, and all these little gigglebags who obsequiously snort at his pathetic joke and at his expense. He was just in the door and being told he was a *cunt in a Crombie,* albeit from someone who had the social skills of a dog licking its arse at a wedding, what to wear, and having the piss, *apparently,* ripped out of him by a witless wannabe teacher using shit gags to get the approval of wee girls. Kelly flattened his tone and steeled his gaze at Rodger,

"My *friend* Eric has died......", embellishment came sailing quickly into view..... "...which was years before he should have. Whatever this new disease is, he had it, died a horrible death and his funeral is arranged for tomorrow and I would like to go, preferably with your approval....*Rodger?"*

Silence descended and Rodger knew that he'd been confronted and called out by another man and to engage in any fracas would see him probably crumble because he knew that he wasn't good with confrontation and recalled the time an advert director asked him to wear a dress. However he did want the last word,

"Whatever. Could you just do something about the footwear, please, they're not appropriate."

"And what about tomorrow?" Kelly continued in the same tone.

"I'm sorry, I don't follow?" Rodger frowned.

"Will I lose a day's money?"

"Well compassionate grounds for absence do exist....so I can put that in the book....
I suppose...." Rodger using the *I* to reassert his authority. "Just try to lose the boots..."

Then Steven stepped up.

"I have a few pairs of trainers I don't use anymore. What size are you, Kelly?"

Kelly turned and looked at this quite clear-skinned, healthy and unassumingly stylish young man that was courteous, confident and now helpful. He wore a brown cardigan with a khaki tee shirt underneath it and a very well fitted pair of Levi jeans and smart pair of soft-soled suede shoes. His hair was quietly quiffed, not declaring it's quiffitude, but just there and held together with some product or other that allowed its odour to be extant around him. *What is it with quiffs?*, Kelly asked himself realising he'd seen a few lately.

"Erm... nine... but you don't have to do that, I can sort something out..."

Steven now smiled at him, "I'm a nine. No problem, Kelly, I've got a few pairs I won't wear again. You're welcome to them. Dunlop

Blue Flash? Not that exciting but good enough."

"Well, yeah....okay...thanks. Be Wednesday. Thanks."

Kelly had forgotten his name and was aware that this was all too public a show with him not controlling the action, so made to show willing and took his coat off and placed it up on the wings of the stage with the bags and coats of everyone else but also to close this little spectacle.

Rodger called everyone to the floor and asked them to form a circle. He then told them to turn and quickly look at the person who was on both sides of them, which they all did. Kelly was next to a small girl on his right that had been peripheral to any conversations before the activities began and was very dour looking with bad skin but also painfully quiet and looked like she'd rather be back home hugging her mother's skirts than here in this dangerous crazy place. Steven was on his left. He was fearful of all of this and expected embarrassing moments in the post. Rodger then asked everyone to say something positive about how both of the people next to them looked.

Something collapsed close to Kelly's arse or around that vicinity. *What the fuck do I say or get back!*

He dropped his chin down onto his chest and sighed. Steven was busy with the girl to his left so Kelly turned to his right. The small girl was turned to her right. He looked the back of her up and down and found nothing about her in the least bit appealing so checked out the back of her hair. The she turned around. They both stared at each other for seconds that dragged on quite uncomfortably and then with very little enthusiasm said to Kelly,

"I like the way you look."

Fair enough, he thought. Decent approximation that gets you out of the mire. He replied,

"Your hair's nice." and with that a moment passed and then a broad beaming smile coursed across her face revealing her stained and misshapen teeth. He knew why she looked so dour.

He felt a tap on his shoulder and turned to see Steven looking at him and smiling. He could smell his pleasant odour and quickly thought that just about every part of Steven was pleasant to the eye. Steven held his smile and nodded to Kelly, indicating that Kelly should commence. Something flustered Kelly so he said,

"Your cardigan is smart." Then Steven flattened the sides of it and looked at Kelly as if to say *why thank you, kind Sir,* then Steven said,

"You have very strong cheekbones."

Kelly was taken aback, somewhat, but flattered. He'd never considered his facial bone structure before or given it any thought but now was glowing in the flattery of another man.

Then the door burst open.

"Huv yez a' startit wi'oot me, ya shower o' fannies! Rodge, ye coulda gi'en me a shout, ya fud! Whit ur yez dae'in'?

Rodger was annoyed at her entrance, language and disrespect but really couldn't take her on so just said,

"We've just started, Liz. If you stand here beside me and Sophie on the other side of me we can demonstrate the kind of thing we're after in this exercise. Okay everyone?"

Liz stood beside Rodger and he started by telling Sophie her hands were elegant. Sophie told him his shirt was nice. Rodger turned and told Liz her freckles were delightful. Liz said to Rodger,

"Whit suits you totally, man, is bein' fat."

Rodger explained that he wasn't offended but that using an inverted negative as a positive was still alluding to the negative and that any negative inversions like that shouldn't be used. Liz was lost but thought she got it and had no problem with getting it wrong again in front of everyone so she was determined to have another shot at it.

"Right, goat it this time.... Rodger, you are *not* a vaj." she said sincerely to Rodger trying to maintain an intense look that augmented the intended sentiment and hoping her powerful acting skills were being absorbed by all.

Rodger moved quickly to the next exercise which was walking around the room and filling the space.

"When we are improvising we have to be aware of the space that we can use and of how we are going to *fill it*. We have to ask ourselves what is going to be *watchworthy?* Am I watchworthy and is the scene I am creating watchworthy?"

Everyone was asked to walk around the room and to fill a space wherever they saw the space and then to move to the next space and so on. Kelly got breathless in this exercise and started to feel like a bit of an arse, which he'd expected and decided to play the asthma card. He nodded to Rodger and made a gesture around his chest area and heaved a little heavier for good effect.

Sitting on the edge of the stage getting his breath back gave him a chance to have a good look at everyone. Apart from Steven they were a pretty hopeless lot who didn't appear to have much about them at all, never mind any semblance of talent that would lead them to greater fame or riches when they left clasping the government certificate of *General Competence and Ability in Theatre Skills*. Darren *shell-suit* Bottoms thudded about like a club-footed giraffe from space to space periodically hauling his trousers up over his arse-crack, which obviously wanted to see what was happening, too. Liz swore at others and told them to *fuck off out of her space cos she was there first* and the giggly girls moved everywhere not far from one another sharing the odd word that kept them amused. Steven neutrally shifted with quite feminine grace avoiding Liz whenever he saw she was near.

There was one girl, Sophie, who Rodger had used in the demo with Liz that did appear to have genuine desire to act. She was dressed with loose clothing and baseball boots that allowed her movement to be quite fluid and he watched her for a while as Rodger encouraged and barked out observations to make as they moved, with what seemed to Kelly, a pointlessness, around the room. Sophie had obviously decided that neutral movement didn't get you noticed and so she moved with the mien of a dancer between spaces but when she got to a space she *arrived* quickly then slowed quickly with arms outstretched. Having arrived in the space she had an urgent look around her as if she was being chased by something and her facial expression declared loudly that *she was acting* and then moved in large steps to the next space and did it all again. Kelly suppressed a smirk as this continued for a few moments more and then Rodger told them to stop and think of another person in the room but not identify them or look at them. Then he told them that they were to stay a reasonable distance away but secretly follow that person. Rodger called Kelly, *Leonard*, and asked him if he needed a few more minutes and of course he did because he wanted to watch the antics of Sophie which were becoming cringingly pretentious but entertaining. This was a girl that wanted to be noticed and felt she was destined for the stage.

Sure enough, Sophie now had her *dynamic to work with*, her *actuality of motivation* giving her an *emotional focus* to push her or pull her whichever way when she intuitively felt her pursuant was near. Amid her determination to consider all of the above, because she read the manuals did Sophie, she forgot to follow someone herself and so all of her energies went into the crescendo of fear that was now apparent on her quasi-thespian grid. She occasionally slowed and dramatically turned as if to catch the culprit but then surveyed the room like the lead in a bad Hollywood, straight-to-video film collecting two stars from the critics on the way. Sophie was now in every sad, bad, low budget horror movie she'd ever seen and was having a great time.

Rodger announced that if anyone, without turning around to see their following presence, could identify them then all they had to do was stop and let the room know who they thought it was. If Kelly had been a betting man he would have thrown his shirt on Sophie being the first. This hard-working attention-seeker was a gift to any gambler and sure enough his horse shortly came home thundering past the post with a few lengths to spare. However, Sophie didn't announce that she had stopped, she just froze with her eyes shut in a tight scrunched-up vision of concentrated tension.

Rodger loved Sophie. She was twenty six and beautiful, he thought, and bloody talented! She just needed a break and an experienced hand to guide her and why should he not be that man? It was only twenty years difference and society was changing its mores with every year that passed. This was the eighties. He knew lots of people that had had children out of wedlock and some that just lived together, so what the hell! Mary Whitehouse would be dead soon and they'd all be free from her horn-rimmed morality. He enjoyed any chance to say Sophie's name out loud or make her feel that she was special and now there was one thrown before his size tens and he took it.

"And let's stop there, everyone....and freeze. *Sophie* has stopped. Sometimes we know things intuitively or we just feel things, what's going to happen next, who's going to call, or maybe someone who's following you? So, *Sophie, Sophie, Sophie...*" getting his daily quota in early,

"Who's following you?"

Sophie's eyes were still clenched closed and she still said nothing.

"Sophie....?" One more, what joy! "Earth to Sophie...!" Rodger was inwardly melting with pleasure.

Kelly had decided minutes before she was a pretentious wanker but was loving the show. A few tuts broke the silence and Rodger was forced to get an answer from her.

"Who's following you, Sophie?" Orgasmic. Then she made noises as if to speak. The giggly girls were embarrassed for her and muttering, *Oh my gods,* to each other and then Sophie said,

"She's close. It is a she...." Not great prescience given that there were only four males in the room and one was sitting on the stage and another wasn't in the exercise.

"I can feel her..."

Liz joined in, "Whit bit o' her are ye feelin' ya carpet-muncher?"

"It's Sammie!" Sophie shouted."

"Sammie..." Rodger asked, "Were you following Sophie?" another just to get him through to the afternoon.

Everyone looked across to Sammie who seemed quite surprised.

"No." Sammie said, flatly.

"No no... it was Mhairi!" Sophie shouted again, her eyes closed again in profound engagement with her intuitive female spirit.

All looked at Mhairi, the small, quiet girl with nice hair and bad teeth, who hated the attention, and had said Kelly looked nice.

"Mhairi?" Rodger enquired,

Mhairi was frozen with fear with everybody looking at her.

"What....?"

Liz had had enough. "Wur ye stalkin' Meryl fuckin' Streep, there, or wur ye no'?"

"No!" Mhairi frustratedly said.

Sophie saw the opportunity for an emotional fracas with poor little

Mhairi who would never fight back with her at the centre.

"Mhairi, I know it was you! I could sense your quietness, your soft steps, your gentle mind! It was you! I know you're shy but don't lie! Tell them the truth, Mhairi! It was you, wasn't it? Tell them!"

Sophie was now, as she wanted, at the heart of a real drama. Mhairi was in the witness box being hotly pressed by the prosecution and she tried as she might but could not stop the tears from beginning to well up in her eyes. Then Kat, who'd heard the noise, eased out into the doorway that linked their office and the studio.

"Mhairi...." Rodger intervened, "Who were you following?"

The tears fell like rain. "Nobody!!" Now properly upset and bubbling, openly.

Liz began to laugh loudly and Rodger became irritated with both Mhairi and Liz.

"Liz! Please! Mhairi, you were supposed to be following someone. Why weren't you following someone?"

Crying intermingled with snot and the words, "I don't knowwww!!" were just about discernible through the bubbles. Rodger then asked,

"Well who *was* following her!" really frustrated.

Silence as everyone looked about the studio. Kelly sensed an opportunity.

"Actually.... it was me." he said quietly. "I have asthma but I wanted to contribute."

All eyes in the room fell on him.

"How the fuck does that work?" Liz actorially enquired.

"Yes how the f.., how does that work....erm..." Rodger had forgotten if it was *Leonard* or *Kelly* he had to call him.

Kelly knew this was a chance to ingratiate himself with Kat who he knew was the boss and had seen come out of the office, which would be handy if he ever needed to be absent again and so he became enigmatic and interesting. He adopted quietly solemn tones and the occasional pause.

"I followed her with my mind.... I watched her and I tried to project a sense of myself walking closely behind her..... I imagined drawing close and falling away from her just to let her get a sense of the psychological perspective needed to receive the picture of me in her mind. I imagined being malevolent and dark and then warm and inviting. In short, I sent my spirit out. Or tried to. The shaman leaders of the Potomac Indians used to do this to spy on their enemies and secure warning of an attack. I'm not really sure if she sensed my spirit close to her?"

Sophie was miffed not being the centre of the conversation now and glowered at Mhairi. Kelly continued with his bullshit.

"In Potomac Indian lore their enemies believed they could do this so their enemies would offer the nether world the soul of their purest heart to try and absorb the Shaman's spirit and stop him from seeing their dark plans. They did this because their purest heart had so much goodness and beauty to spare that the Shaman spirit would have thought them all pure and good, too. In this case the purest heart seemed to have been, Mhairi."

The whole room turned to Mhairi. Mhairi slowly began to smile at the public declaration of her being the purest heart of goodness and beauty. Then she wiped away a loose dribble of silver snot from her nose.

Liz quietly muttered, "Creepy Crombie cunt."

Rodger was about to try and restart the session when Kat walked further into the studio.

"That was really interesting, Kelly. This is exactly the type of mysticism that should be informing theatre in the west. Their mysticism and rituals are their theatre, so why shouldn't we have our theatre include theirs?"

Kelly knew that if the conversation was to enter into a territory that he'd have to validate, he'd be rumbled and the powers that be were dropping into his lap and offering ambrosia. A short burst of cod-humility should gild the lily enough to retain believability, so he just said,

"Maybe, but I don't know enough about theatre in the west to make any real observations. I guess that's why I'm here."

Kat was beaming now at the thought of having this older chap, in touch with the mystics and ritual of our forebears, and his desire to be taught. By her! She asked Mhairi to go and wash her face and compose herself and spoke with Rodger supposedly close and confidentially but deliberately in earshot of their students.

"Look, Rodge, it's first thing Monday morning and the reason I want to do the Stanislavsky stuff is because I don't want them worn out because they're going to need a bit of staying power thisafto. Got me? Emotional fireworks and flames and for a change and we might have someone, now, who can really make a contribution. This has all gone a bit pear-shaped as well, Rodge so if you don't mind, I'm going to make an executive decision and put them straight onto the texts we'll need them to know and we can maybe talk a little later about your workshop management. Just a few little hints about *what and how* and *when to reach, stretch for gold* and when to *crank the pace* or *feed the scene*. Okay with you, Rodge?....... Rodge?"

It was far from okay with Rodger and he knew he was being patronised and that *the students* could hear her and he didn't really understand all the reaching and cranking and when and how stuff, which was actually bollocks, but didn't want to appear as though he didn't know and he also knew he was being put in his place. Whatever affection or regard he had from any of the students was most likely lost now and he knew it. Kat touched his shoulder a few times as if in care for him but was outwardly signalling to the room that Rodger was a prick who didn't know what he was doing, but *she* did. She loved working with Rodger.

A break was announced by Kat and they all spread to the toilets, outside, off to the shop or to make tea in the kitchen. Kelly stayed where he was sitting on the edge of the stage. Steven came over and sat down beside him.

"That was all quite cool, Kelly. How'd you know all that stuff about sending spirits out?"

Kelly instinctively saw another felonious embellishment come riding over the horizon but there was something really cool about this guy that he seemed and wanted to respect.

"Books. Just books."

"So you read a lot, then?"

"Yeah, suppose I do but it creeps up on you, you know. I sometimes don't realise some of the things I've read about and then something in a situation, or something someone says just triggers off the knowledge, and then bang, you're suddenly talking. *Weird*."

Much of which was actually true but he couldn't help himself and began to use an oral landscape and tone of voice that wanted to connect with the cool that Steven effused. When had he ever said *weird* like that at the end of a sentence and stared into the floor with the apparent detachment of a soul troubled by his immense knowledge and continual cerebral expansion?

"Do *you* read?" he heard himself say.

"Well... yes, a bit." Steven didn't sound so sure. "Probably not as much as you, Kelly. I mean I'm only twenty-three and you're....?

"Ermm... thirty three..." He felt uncomfortable giving out his age. He wasn't sure why? It might have been because it was to Steven in that context. It seemed as if he had been manoeuvred into giving it out.

"Thirty-three. So you've had a bit more time to trawl the bookshelves of life. I've just read *The Picture of Dorian Gray* by..."

"....Oscar Wilde. Brilliant isn't it? Why did you go for Wilde?"

"I guess I was recommended it by someone."

"Did you read the prologue?" Kelly asked.

"Ermm...yes I think so? The very first bit?"

"Yes."

"Well then *yes*, I guess.?"

"Do you remember the bit about Caliban staring into a mirror?"

He was just showing off now.

"Of how Wilde compared it to the Victorians inner dislike of themselves."

"Who's Caliban?"

"A monster in a Shakespeare play."

Kelly couldn't remember which one so quickly moved on.

"Oscar Wilde was saying the Victorians were monsters?"

"Not quite. Just that they didn't like to look at themselves too closely because they knew they wouldn't like what they saw."

Kelly stretched minutely as if this was a small and tiresome percentage of his knowledge, and then said,

"Who recommended it to you?"

Ever heard of a band called The Smiths?"

"No...? The Smiths?"

"Yeah. They were on Top Of The Pops on Thursday night with their new single, *Heaven Knows I'm Miserable Now*. Their singer is right into Oscar Wilde."

"Good for him....." Another phrase he rarely used. "I saw Top of the Pops last Thursday? Who are they?

"The Smiths. *Heaven Knows I'm Miserable Now?*"

Eliminating Madness, there was only really one other contender

"Oh yeah....Bendy Elvis."

Steven and Kelly talked a little while more but mostly the enthusiastic Steven who effused obvious admiration for this new font of erudition and rattled on about this new band and of their singer and the songs that were so current and didn't follow formulaic patterns and sang about The Moors Murders, charming men and someone called William? Kelly was happy to let him ramble on and enjoyed his youthful exuberance and determination to proselytise on behalf of these messianic musos and understood something unassumingly innocent and joyful in Steven and let a smile curl honestly onto his face.

"I'm going to get a band together." Steven said.

"That's great. What do you play?" asked Kelly.

"Nothing yet. Guitar probably. Might take a while but you've got to do something with your life, haven't you?"

Kelly smiled and nodded and wished him good luck, then Rodger came in and started to arrange small piles of excerpts from plays onto the edge of the stage into labelled categories of Fear, Love and, Hate. He was followed by a young woman who was smiling broadly. Rodger turned to see who had came in.

"Oh, hello Kerry." He said, "Busy?"

Kerry nodded and said,

"I'm *very* busy, Rodge. I'm busy showing two new students onto the course. Would you mind very much if they came in to see the studio. Kat's busy so I'm showing them around."

Rodger perked up at an opportunity to impress without Kat there to undermine him.

"Of course not, Kerry. Please...bring them in."

Two old ladies both wrapped in broad shawls of black allowing only their heads to be seen walked in to the studio and stood there looking at Rodger. Kelly wondered what the hell was happening. Surely they didn't recruit these coffin-dodgers who'd be on the state pension not on the dole. He didn't say anything. Rodger paused looking, too, but then a smile broadly coursed across his face, as did Steven and then several small chuckles occurred around Kelly, from Rodger, Steven, back to Kerry and the two old ladies had a little gurgle too.

Rodger stepped forward smiling and held out his hand to the first old lady.

"Enchante, Madame. You're very welcome. And who is your friend?"

He took the hand of the second who was laughing quite loudly now. Everyone had apparently decided to have a good laugh except Kelly who knew he was out of a loop, and tried to work it out. Who were they? Previous students? Surely not. They would still have been nearly-fossils ten years ago. Somebody's granny? And friend? Bemused.

Rodger blew away the fog. "Terrific work Kerry! That is very, very, impressive. How long did it take you?"

"Hour and a half for both. The new stuff is great." She beamed back at Rodger.

Kelly leaned into Steven, who caught a whiff of his prominent pheromones and pulled back slightly, and quietly said,

"Who are they?"

Steven smiled and said, "These? Well....these two ladies are the girls that give us all the money to run this place and sometimes bring scones to us on a Friday. If we're good little boys and girls. They're eccentric millionaires."

Kelly looked at them again quickly evaluating whether one of them was young enough to fall for any of his flannel.

"Absolutely amazing!" Rodger goo-ed standing back and peering at them both in a kind of studious fashion. "Knock out! Top of the Pops, that is!"

Kelly tried Steven again who was still smiling at him. "Sorry...what's so amazing?"

"They're just two of the girls from the make-up course! Kerry has just had some donations from The Lyceum Theatre and a film company who were having a clear-out. She's really good isn't she?"

Kelly's jaw dropped and turned to look at them again. He remained transfixed. Then he said loudly,

"Fuck me!"

Rodger with everyone else turned. "Not today, Leonard! I'm washing my hair!"

Kelly smiled and inwardly said *Shut up, you big luvvie quilt! Bet you've used that one a thousand times!* Which he had.

"That's the quality of what we can produce here at Global Theatre Works with the right attitude and investment, Leonard. Stick in and you might achieve something equally as good on the acting front. Might take some time, though."

Kelly wanted to punch the self-important arse but his mind had already started to tick, so he smiled at Kerry and said,

"Hi I'm Kelly, Leonard Kelly, but everyone just calls me *Kelly...*" throwing a glance Rodger's way. "That is....astounding! I was completely sold! These were two old ladies...the hair, the wrinkles... brilliant!"

Kerry was smiling, as were Donna and Julie, her charges. Kerry said,

"Thank you muchly, Kelly. Nice to meet you. And now the big reveal girls! Shawls off, just to prove you're not two old dames."

They pulled away their shawls revealing jeans, a pair of Adidas training shoes and trendy t-shirts.

Kelly smiled, genuinely impressed for the first time by the skills of someone at this institutional imposition to his liberty.

Then thought.

Chapter 7

A Red Descent

Tuesday, 12th June

Lenni knew nothing more than the pain he felt just missing his master. He was sitting at the edge of Eric's graveside with mourners, of which were no more than a dozen or so, arranged around the graveside. Spider stood there, with Lenni on a leash, dressed in a long black coat that confirmed his demonic appearance. Joe was there, in a very smart dark suit and black tie. Bullet carried his overalls and also in a black tie and May dressed in a black twin-set but with a dark headscarf around her fixed locks. What was left of Eric's family, which was no more than six or seven, an older couple who needed help walking on the grass and some scruffy looking nieces and nephews next to some middle-aged women dressed in variations of man-made fibres all gathered together in a clutch across from Eric's pub mates who they eyed in a quite unfriendly way. It seemed to Kelly that the world had made their mind up about anyone that crossed the door of *The Old Duke* and it wasn't flattering. There were two sombre looking men who stood away from the graveside at what appeared to be a respectful distance and were very smartly dressed in black suits and long black coats. Most present would surmise that they were connections from his past or old workmates, rather smart but, nevertheless, anonymous. Opposite them were two old men that Kelly never knew. One of the men wore a very old duffle coat over a well worn suit and the other wore a dark suit with a little red star on the lapel. Both wore black armbands.

DI McQuarrie stood alone close to the minister at the head of the grave and Kelly knew he was fielding the loss of someone he seemed to genuinely have had respect and affection for. Kelly stood there unaware of the rituals of death and burial and so retreated a few feet from the graveside designed to appear as though it was respect for those closest but was actually afraid he couldn't join in with any closing ritual because he didn't know what happened at a funeral and didn't want to look like an unworldly arse asking someone. He was thirty-three and he knew he should probably have known more than he did, so he just stood with head bowed waiting for someone to throw soil onto the coffin. He'd seen that loads of times in films, usually cheesy American ones where lots of people did that and uttered some clichéd goodbyes but, ironically, was quite unsure of a good dour Calvinist affair that was closer to home. No, play it safe. Head bowed. That was enough, he thought, a universal show of grief and respect. Thankfully, no arcane practice came with the ministers close to the eulogy and finished with his last words, *go in peace,* which everyone unfamiliar with the ritual knew meant *we're done, It's all over, go and get your cup of tea and sandwiches.*

The various factions began to gather together with pertinent hugs and attempts at comforting mourners who probably didn't need comforting but went along with the required display of apparently mild distress in order to look like they gave a fuck as hankies were handed out among Eric's family and arms went across shoulders. Joe approached the two old men and shook hands with both. Spider took Lenni across to the familial clutch as they made to leave and offered his careful sentiments and then engaged in what seemed to be a quizzical and unsure discussion about something. Megan approached Kelly.

"Where'd you get the suit?" she said sidling up to him but retaining her gaze on the grave.

Kelly waited as people drifted away before talking.

"Cowan Tailoring on The South Bridge." He lied.

Megan had another quick look and then a look back at Kelly with apparent doubt on her face.

"British Red Cross. Fiver."

"Looks made to measure." Megan observed.

"Really?" Kelly now forgot Eric and enjoyed Megan's compliment.

"Very sharp. You should make an effort more often."

"Sorry Megan. I just need to..."

He hurried across to Joe before he left with his older friends and gave him back the camera, pulling it out of a plastic bag. Joe thanked him and asked if he had his spare key on him. Kelly apologised and said he'd get it back to him soon. He returned to Megan.

Mourners drifted away with the minister as two very keen but rough gravediggers waited with spades behind a mound of earth covered in a green tarpaulin. One tried to conceal the cigarette he had sparked up just as the minister had left and looked over to Megan and Kelly. Kelly's ego couldn't help but allow him to bask in yet another quasi-affectionate/flirtatious observation from Megan, so he wanted to extend the contact.

"That's it then?" he offered trying to appear philosophical.

"Suppose so. We better go. Those two vultures look like they want to get an early dart." she replied nodding to the gravediggers who were fixed eagerly on the pair of them.

They began to walk off and hadn't got ten yards before they heard the first shovelful of earth hit the coffin behind them. Kelly was actually hoping for a sentimental discussion about the brevity of life and about who actually cares when you're gone etc; and then offer advice about enjoying life while you're there but throw in the caveat, *if there's something in life you want you should just ask for it or just take it*...knowing it was despicable of him to use Eric's funeral as the context of, ironically, doing the spadework with a potential suitor. So he used,

"Are we all dressed up with somewhere to go?" hoping for more sugar from Megan.

"Where do you think?" She brusquely returned. "He spent more time with us than with any of that lot who turned up."

"I didn't know much about him. He never spoke about his family. Sad really."

He had stopped caring about Eric five minutes after the coffin was lowered and knew that he had entered Clichéville but….. *Carpe Diem.*

"You look nice." Struggling a bit now.

"Black suits me, then?" Megan retorted, humorously.

"It does." He said. "Very slimming." Not a good extension. When in doubt, say nowt.

Megan looked quizzically at him which he clearly understood.

"You're not fat. Chubby. Curvy…. or anything like that…. you're just right….actually. You actually don't need to wear anything slimming….black, actually… because you're actually not *fat*…at all."

He knew this was piss-poor overuse of the adverb, *actually,* but realised she was beginning to smile at his bumbling attempts to dig himself out of the hole and so laid it on thick, to which she bit and smiled more.

"Speaking of black." Megan looked ahead.

Spider stood there next to a large gravestone with Lenni sitting next to him. *Beelzebub and Familiar.*

"They don't want the dog." Spider said.

"Why not?" Megan barked back.

"I don't know. *No space. Working. No one to look after him. Too expensive*. Lots of excuses."

"I'll speak to them!" Megan strode past Spider.

"Cars have gone." Spider quickly said and Megan stopped abruptly.

"They're coming to the pub, though? For a drink? Right? I'll speak to them there."

"They said they weren't going to go to The Duke. They're going to The Southern Lounge."

Kelly saw the implied slur darken her face.

Spider knew as well as anyone why they weren't going to *The Old Duke*, but had learned years ago to remain passive when danger threatened. Megan was beginning to wind up a tirade on uncaring families and the demise of society when Kelly saw an opportunity to solve the problem and rise further in Megan's estimation and so he *Carpe-ed* another *Diem* and said,

"I'll take the dog." and as he said it immediately saw a vision of himself walking endlessly in the park waiting for it to..*go*, feeding it, having to rush home early from…. wherever and a forever gaining dissolute effect upon his meagre income and then added,

"Until… *something*…. better is sorted for him."

Megan's face lightened visibly and smiled. A moment passed while she studied this heroic and misunderstood man. Then she tiptoed upwards and planted a small kiss on his cheek. Kelly was surprised but pleased and realised he had to contain his glee and use affected modesty, therewith, and so came out with,

"Steady Martha. Not in front of the servants."

Spider was smiling too… unsurprisingly, and then with a definite thrust forward with his hand offered the end of the leash to Kelly, who then realised the magnitude of the false gesture and further quipped,

"Married so soon? Tongues will wag…. errm…?"

"…Lenni." Spider quickly said.

"Lenni."

Then came man and dog bonhomie as he ruffled and patted Lenni enthusiastically.

"Come on, you big soft lump. Let's get you home and get you fed and watered."

They were all carless and began to walk towards the gates. Megan gushed inwardly and maternally at this act of communion and dusted off some of Lenni's hair that had stuck to Kelly's Jacket.

"Make sure you keep his hair off your new suit, Kells. You'll need it soon."

"Will I?"

"Yes. You're coming to a party with me…and some friends. Next weekend."

Kelly's heart discernibly heaved, and he hoped it hadn't been that obvious and offered,

"Well, I suppose I'll have a gap somewhere in my extensive social calendar that might fit you in. Party? Whose?"

"Uni friends of mine. Giving up the flat. Just doing their finals now and then heading off to Europe. Having a last bash before they go."

And with that Megan strode off in front with Spider and May trying to look cool and urbane with talk of her Uni friends. Potential adversaries, Kelly thought, with impressive credentials and realised his best references may be required to bounce back some nuggets of learning that will keep him knickerward.

His amorous cogitations were broken as the frame of DI McQuarrie leaned over his shoulder.

"Seven and six for the licence, you know, Kelly?"

"I know, Mr McQuarrie...I've got the time and the space...I suppose."

"That's nice. Will you have the time to explain to the dog how Eric might have lasted a wee bit longer without that shoutin' match you started across the pub the other night?"

Kelly was shocked. He didn't expect to have to answer for the death of Eric.

"I don't think that's fair, Mr McQuarrie...."

"That right, Kelly? Well life's far from fuckin' fair, and if I don't know that, nobody does. Let me tell you what I think of you, Kelly. I think you're a workshy, egotistical smelly no-user with little respect for yourself or anyone else and who's more concerned about how you think the rest o' the world sees you than what you actually are. Am I right?"

Kelly said nothing.

"You have lots of loud things to say in the pub but you'll only ever be heard in there, nowhere else. The rest o' the world don't give a fuck or know you exist. You're nobody, son. You could tell most o' them practically anything you want, but not me Kelly. Nor now Eric, who was ten times the man you'll ever be. Nice to see you bothered to shave."

And with that McQuarrie walked away. Kelly smarted at this public castigation.

They all went back to *The Old Duke*, sank a few pints and ate limp sandwiches with salmon spread and square cheese slices.

Kelly made his goodbyes and had the pub door half open when a voice asked him if he'd forgotten something. He turned to look at Spider who nodded towards Lenni lying under the table where Eric used to sit. Fortunately, Megan saw none of this and thankfully DI McQuarrie had made his excuses earlier saying he had to visit someone, so he quickly picked up Lenni's leash and trudged across the road to his flat.

He opened the front door and ushered in the dog and took it into the living room then filled a bowl with water and put it down for the dog. Lenni sat down in front of it and looked up at Kelly who also sat down and the two looked at each other.

"I'm sorry about Eric… your Dad...but it wasn't my fault…was it? I just wanted to wind Norrie up. This isn't forever, you know. It's just a favour. You can stay just until you've found somewhere better…. And I'll help. I'll help you find somewhere. Soon. We've known each other for quite a while now but we don't really know each other that well and we haven't really been thrown together like this before, so don't get any wrong ideas. I'm sleeping in there and you can stay in here on the couch. It's not the best but it's quite comfortable. Let's face it, you loved someone else and don't imagine you feel anything for me….. which is good! Which is what I want, actually. I have my life and you have….I mean, I'm not sure you can come to the pub with me, you know? We don't want anyone to get the wrong impression that this is a permanent relationship. You understand, don't you?"

Lenni stared back at him undoubtedly missing Eric beyond all feeling with the inability to express it beyond his doleful large eyes and slumped wearily to the floor.

Chapter 8

The Mother of All Bus Trips

Wednesday, 13th June

DI McQuarrie's words had hit home thinking about what he had said to him as the night had grown longer and he fell asleep with his words trapped in his head. He wanted to be angry. He wanted to feel a deep indignation. How could he be responsible for Eric's death? He imagined a scene in the pub where he confronted DI McQuarrie and set him straight telling him that he knew nothing about his life or what he did with his time. And as for workshy….well! Work was tough to find and he was turning a shift with Joe, here and there. However, he found it difficult to run to a satisfactory ending, one without questionable veracity or preserving his pride, which was difficult with the stink of stale piss curling around him lying on a rough blanket on a sheetless bed, which did enough to echo McQuarrie's opinion of him and he knew it. He resolved to do something tomorrow and straighten himself and his life up but then realised he had to attend the theatre skills course. *Shit!* he thought….he wasn't in the mood for fat Rodger, Kat Noh, or the clutch of inane giggling girls so decided that tomorrow was the day to go and see his mother. He'd tell Kat he was still upset from losing his friend and the funeral. Another lie.

The Glasgow Express was a bus service, something of a misnomer and a hugely ambitious statement. It was supposed to have limited stops but these were limited to every other bus stop as it trundled west out of Edinburgh past the airport and towards the M8.

He gazed out of the widow watching trees, fields and villages pass and wondered what he would be like if he lived in a small village. How would he function in a small community? Could he survive growing vegetables on an allotment and sitting in a hut with a fictional older chap called Bert and frequenting The British Legion for a pint? He came from the south side of Edinburgh and he had grown up there walking through traffic, and blanking every face he passed in the street. He knew every shop, street, pub and lamppost and decided that he really didn't want to go to a village, small town or with his mother to the new town of Livingston when she decided to spend the insurance money she received when Kelly's father died but the alternative was homelessness at the time, so he spent a few years there before returning to the city.

Livingston new town was no longer embryonic in the planner's minds but he still couldn't view it with any warmth. It had become something akin to a town but was difficult to embrace with any affection because Kelly thought West Lothian was not a pretty county and the housing stock in Livingston looked, to him, ill-conceived and impermanent. Either small wooden clad bungalows with concrete slabs as a gable and flat roofs which reminded Kelly of nothing more than garden huts, or flats that he called *The Filing Cabinets* appearing as though the drawers were open at the bottom with the next floor's drawer a little further closed until the top flat was entirely shut. These were finished in bright colours which fought the grey skies and hard, seemingly cheerless faces of all that stepped abroad there. He shook his head at this maze of slip-roads, thoroughfares with names declared in large plastic lettering that led to industrial estates, of footbridges and either dour or wacky houses that led to roundabouts with installation artworks, usually abstract, in the centre of them and looked largely similar to the previous one. Livingston was dreamt up by planners who laudably stuck their heads above the parapet and *took a chance* but should have known they were dicing with the Scottish Calvinist psyche, the lives of people that didn't want or need wacky or colourful or imaginative, strange or *interesting* but serviceable and psychologically secure. Needful people organised and filed away. Housed nominally. This was where his mother lived. Kelly had never been across The Iron Curtain and very unlikely that he ever would, but imagined that this was a close run thing to the Eastern Bloc.

He took out *The Good Soldier Sveyk* and began to read more of the life of Jaroslav Hasek and it turns out he was a right pain in the arse for the police, too. He was an anarchist and a hoaxer. Even when he was a kid he'd taken part in some anti-German riots, trashing the emblems of the Austro-Hungarian monarchy and smashing the windows of some government offices and as an adult joined the anarchist movement and spent a bit of time in jail. What a guy! Kelly chuckled audibly and let the smile remain on his face as he then read how Hasek pretended he was going to commit suicide by throwing himself off The Charles Bridge over The Vlatava and then the police carted him off to a mental home and he'd only done this just to get some material for the part in the book where Sveyk spends time with the lunatics. Then he opened a shop which he called a Cynological Institute which was a grand term he'd thought of for what was a dog-fanciers shop, but it was here he forged pedigree documents and made up names for the breed and sold them for a tidy sum and declared he like being the owner of *an institute.*

Apparently this all went tits-up when he met a girl called Jarmila Mayerova. Lost his shit over her, wrote her love poems, got married and got a job in a bank. Kelly frowned and shook his head at Hasek's decline, but then read that he got sacked because he was still disappearing for weeks at a time with his gypsy mates in deepest Moravia, came back looking like a tramp and then she left him. Kelly smiled again. He knew he should have known better but smiled anyway. Obviously a *fuck the system* type of chap. He searched in his pocket for a pencil but had to delve into the lining of his coat. He brought it out and underlined the bits he wanted to remember. He marked the bit about love poems he wrote for Jarmila and thought he should give that a go with Megan. Might grease the wheels a bit.

Kelly's eyes began to droop and struggle with the small print and the movement of the bus and he wasn't used to such early mornings and the exertions of walking Lenni and waiting for him to *go,* but he'd had a stroll around the bowling-green, not far but seemed enough for the ageing mutt. He rested his eyes but couldn't drowse with the movement of the bus so he picked up a discarded newspaper from the seat across the aisle from him and started to flick through it.

The Daily Mirror's front page had a picture of Arthur Scargill, leader of the National Union of Mineworkers wearing a baseball hat and what looked like straw descending from its interior down and across his ears reminding him of The Scarecrow in *The Wizard of Oz*. Kelly had been aware of the strike but knew little about the reasons why and there was only Joe who wanted to discuss it in The Duke but he seemed to wear people down with his vitriol and hatred of the Government. So people tended to nod and be non-commital, humour him, quite frankly and change the subject when they could. He leafed into the paper and much more was written further into the next three pages but he didn't have the resolve to read and understand but guessed that money would be at the heart of the dispute. Then he caught a small paragraph written boldly at the end of all three pages;

More closures originally listed but hidden.

Kelly had a moment of clarity, a minor political awakening. He read the first few paragraphs and realised that money had never been the primary cause but closures of mines, ergo money of course, but that men had decided to withdraw their labour because their fellow miners were threatened with their loss of work. He knew there was something admirable, selfless and comradely about all of this big mess that seemed to be occurring, something he felt he would never feel or be a part of in any situation as he meandered aimlessly through his life of unsecured hedonistic and superficial friendships that bordered on mere acquaintance. He didn't have the answer nor would he ever try to suggest that he had any idea of what that might be the solution. Intuitively he knew there was something bigger than the ostensible conflict out front, imagined that there were underhand political manoeuvrings involving government and secret machinations by the police but didn't really know what that was and hated himself for it. He knew it was about power and that it all seemed to be thundering to an inevitable destructive conclusion but the facts eluded him. Actually, they didn't because it was laid before him in newspapers and television news every day he took breath but indolence, as always, became a bedfellow. He wanted to know more but not to be socially or politically aware but to be able to superficially talk about it with the aggrandizement of himself as others see him. This, he knew was shameful and shallow using these people's struggle, thus, but he couldn't help himself and then heard the voice of DI McQuarrie at Eric's funeral, again and felt....*something*.

Facing that page was the entertainment section which had a picture of *Bendy Elvis*, the chap he saw on the pub TV with the bunch of flowers in his back pocket. Kelly realised this was the fox's tail he thought he saw. He was walking towards the camera with his large quiff leading the way and a comment below saying he was non-committal about his apparent deafness, which confused Kelly. If he was deaf how could he hear himself sing? Then he saw the small plastic kebab behind *Bendy Elvis's* ear. Definitely a hearing-aid. However, he was *non-committal*, it said? A tabloid paradox. His eyes didn't look as though they were in the best nick, either, with his glasses which looked as though the optician had picked the worst set out of a drawer last opened in 1972 and given them to him for free then asking him to leave before he started to sing. The song was tuneful, as he remembered, but this deaf, blind florist wasn't, if that made sense and he was singing about being miserable but it was catchy and despite himself, he had become intrigued. Not a great start to his pop career but then again, he wasn't as bad as many of the punk bands that had reached the dizzy heights of Top of the Pops, whom he found to be quite alarming and violent. He cringed at their ridiculous antics accompanying their ditties but knew there was an inherent anarchic demonstration of anger at work, with them and their fans. That said, he understood the disgust that was universally felt for Bucks Fizz, Racey, St. Winifred's School Choir and the fucking Worzels, et al and that an enema was required to purge these insipid, saccharin, abominations from the music scene and flush them into a sewer pointed at the Atlantic, clear the decks and start again at musical year zero. Something like that. Something was changing. Something had to fill the void left by *Racey* and *Genesis*. Punk was merely the enema and maybe *Bendy Elvis* and his mates might just be it.

He put the paper down and shoved his hands in his pockets and nuzzled himself into his coat, looking out of the window and trying to remember exactly where he was. This seemingly directionless bus paralleled his existence and knew the questions about work and love would arise and that he had no real or substantial answers and certainly couldn't declare that he was painting for cash in hand with some crony from the pub and that he currently was working hard to get into the knickers of a barmaid with little future beyond that. He could tell another lie but he'd learned in the past that they sometimes grew arms and legs and sometimes heads with savage teeth that could bite and spit back if you weren't careful. Too much like hard work. He heaved again in his frustration and sunk further into his coat. He considered reading some more of *Sveyk* as he felt the book in his pocket but felt paper between the pages sticking out and for a second thought he may have happened upon a rogue fiver but recognised quickly enough the feel of buff manilla with its little plastic window and drew out the envelopes from his pocket. He'd forgotten he'd stuffed his mail into his pocket carelessly upon leaving his flat. He knew the look of the DHSS communications and opened that one first. Confirmation of his *Theatre Skills* course. Bit late. A five day week was outlined with the penalties of non-attendance typed in bold as if they expected these misdemeanours from the great unwashed, and for the first time it hit home that his life was to be controlled entirely by this nonsense, which formed a twisted, belly-aching desperation within him. If he could think of something, anything to deflect this abomination he was now ready to meet that challenge. He muttered loudly and a woman with bags of shopping turned to look at him. He looked back and held the gaze. This trifling and pedantically untrusting bureaucracy had put him in no mood for niceties. She turned back unsure of this tousled and unshaven character in his long Crombie. His pheromones had radiated about the bus interior by this point in the journey and declared his social status so she refused the option to engage the beast.

Money was the answer. With money nobody bothers you. With money work is a pastime. With money the world smiles and you smile back. He pulled out the other envelope. White. Worrying. *Who do I owe?* fizzed into his head. Inside was an invitation to apply for a credit card. Immediately laughable. He'd love to apply and be accepted and then hammer it for all it's worth then disappear off the bureaucratic radar. The limit was £2500! *Are they stupid?,* he thought, and then saw the application process asking for confirmation of bank, work and personal details all of which would have to be verifiable. The two and a half grand was already being pulled from his hand by the wind, as he imagined it, holding painfully on to the bunch of tenners but with his arm fully extended out of the bus window and an inability to retain his grasp on the glorious cash. He looked at his paper again and he, ironically, opened it at the adverts page where he saw lots of other ads trying to induce people, anyone, it seemed, to re-mortgage their house or take out a loan. Apparently, in this time of mass-unemployment and hardship, money was for sale? He read another sparklingly, upbeat introduction to an offer of a loan of up to £20,000. He felt the humorous and ridiculous cruelty contained, therein, but this time declined to laugh. He read the table outlining the amount, time and eventual return of the borrowed money. The time was detailed in months rather than years. A ruse to psychologically shorten the perceived span of the loan in mind of the borrower. *Bastards!* he thought, or thought he had thought, but then realised he had unknowingly given larynx to this thought out into the bus. Madame Shopping looked across again. This time Kelly smiled a broad stick-on smile at her.

"Not you." He said holding the smile.

She uncomfortably turned back with a quick look down the bus to possible allies should this deranged individual decide to act upon his unstable cerebral activities.

He looked at the table and ridiculously gauged an amount he thought he might manage. A few days with Joe, here and there. Maybe Norrie would give him a shift or two when Megan couldn't do it. Free beer, as well? Add on the dole cheque and...... no. It was academic, of course, as verifiable income and bank statements would be required.

The thought occurred that he could create a false identity and take the fuckers for all they were worth. That would be nice. *Farquhar de Quincey* was a good name. Smacked of aristocracy and money. However, Farquhar's identity would require bank details, verifiable residency, work record, blah, blah....

Maybe someone could borrow the money and he could pay them back? Then he thought that if he were them would he agree to borrowing money in their name and give it to him? Really?

What if they were mentally retarded? Mentally retarded but worked? Worked and had a bank account? Some of them do, he thought. Special places where they make..... zimmers and metal walking sticks and wheelchair parts.....and stuff like that, he thought but wasn't really sure. *They'd* have a job. An address. Long standing address, too. Unless they'd been shuffled from institution to halfway house and foster homes, etc. He could fuck off with the money and they would be left to carry the can but who would throw a mentally retarded retard out of their home because they defaulted on payment of a loan? Bad press. Public reaction. Universal public disgust. Everyone's a winner. They don't get humped by the loan company and he gets the money. That's what he needed. A retard, he thought but his time knew it was more than a thought as he heard himself audibly say *retard* out into the bus interior.

Madame Le Shop was now decidedly uneasy and fearing for her safety.

This unworthy train of thought had made him inwardly froth, somewhat, getting excited at his ridiculous plan to entrap a mentally disabled victim into taking out a loan and giving the money to him. Or a credit card. That would do. Then he had visions of himself engaged in voluntary work lifting them onto buses and wiping shitty arses and the drool off their faces in order to get close enough to garner their trust and then, boom, off with their cash and into the sunset but didn't really relish the thought of working for nothing never mind wiping arses.

He sighed at the realisation of his destitute state and the irrationality of his thought processes and it occurred to him, uncharacteristically, that this plan was nothing short of abhorrent, however, he consoled himself with the fact that he didn't even know anyone mentally unstable, slow of thought or anywhere near trusting enough or where to find them. Except in The Old Duke.

He turned the page and another less showy ad said, *Small Business Loans* and outlined how easy it would be to acquire a loan assuming you had a small business. Maybe Joe would be interested? He'd show him later in the pub, maybe.

Unfortunately for our fearful shopper, Kelly had got off at the same stop as her but was rescued by the presence of an acquaintance that was waiting at the same stop for another bus. Kelly heard her animatedly describing her experience with someone who obviously had either eluded his carers for the day and in need of psychological and hygienic aid as he walked away towards his mother's house. Fifty yards ahead a large black car pulled in on the other side of the road. As he walked past he saw the two men who were at the funeral. He realised it was the God-Squad who had spoken to him on Monday morning and thought it coincidental that they had decided to bring *The Word* out to the great unwashed of Livingston.

As he turned the final corner into her street he groaned in despair at the sight of an eighteen-wheel articulated lorry parked in her small street. This belonged to her brother. Her right wing ex-army brother who Kelly disliked, intensely, his uncle Gerry. His ego, manhood and substantial gut were carried in this leviathan and imagined that when others saw him they bowed in awe. This was the equivalent of a trusty steed for Gerry. A muscular stallion tamed beneath his genitals which he tied up for all the townsfolk to see and admire whenever he came a-calling. *What a prick*, he thought but knowing that he was going to have to fend off hard-pressed questions and opinions or contest them at the risk of the local Sheriff being called to keep the peace.

His mother was in the same armchair she always used facing directly to the television. There was no fireplace in this house for the chairs to assemble around, just a massive radiator that was clinging to the wall tenuously as the brackets had come loose due to the constant presence of someone's substantial arse leaning against it. The particular large arse on this occasion was Uncle Gerry's.

"Alright Gerry." Kelly offered as he came into the room.

Gerry said nothing but tilted his head in acknowledgment.

"Saw your horse tied up outside." A genial attempt to start the next hour.

"How did you know I'd be in?" His Mother asked.

She was small and wore cheap clothes, brown of hue in every guise, that didn't fit her properly and that she'd had for years. Her hair was thin, grey and wispy and flattened to her head when she brushed it suggesting that any more brushing might reveal a shiny scalp sometime soon.

"You're always in." Kelly said, nonplussed.

"She might've gone shoppin'." Gerry growled across.

Here we go, Kelly thought. No *good to see you, son, how're you doin'?* or some such, just an obviously low opinion and judgemental attitude of him getting lasered across the room.

"She hasn't, has she?" still friendly enough but pointed.

"I went this morning. I needed tea bags. Do you want tea, Gerry?" His mother talking but Gerry still nailing Kelly.

"I'll make it." He returned. "I suppose you'll want a cup?"

Kelly already felt like telling him to shove it as far he could up his fat arse for he did indeed have a corpulent carriage. He was short and bald with a pelmet-like overhang drooping over his belt and wore, ironically, a sporty Adidas waterproof that suggested weekend training, bright complexions and glossy, healthy, white-toothed athletes. This waterproof couldn't be closed under any amount of pulling, zipping and coaxing but Kelly restrained himself and said,

"Just milk." And then Gerry exited to the kitchen.

"You look terrible." His mother said.

"I'm okay."

"I didn't mean *are you ill?* I meant you look terrible. I don't know why you wear that coat at this time o' the year. Heavy in this heat. Too hot for a coat. Why d'you wear a coat like that at this time o' the year? Have you got holes in your shirt?"

"No."

"Well take it off then. Or are you not staying for a cup o' tea?"

"Yes."

"Well take it off then."

"I like it." Tetchy.

"Not in the house. Take your coat off."

Kelly reluctantly acquiesced knowing that his coat did conceal clothes that either needed a good scrub or needed mending. He took off his coat off and removed it to the hall, came back then sat down on the couch. His mother watched him as he did this.

"You should shave. Get your hair cut. Sort yourself out." Two specifics and then a general as openers on the critique of his lifestyle and appearance. He was used to it and really didn't need this right now but chose to deflect rather than engage.

"This is new." He said.

"What's new?"

"This couch."

"The *sofa* isn't new. You just haven't been here for a long time. It might be new to you but it's certainly not new to me."

The battle lines of the conversation were now well and truly being drawn. Every opportunity for a negative response or observation intended to gain the higher moral ground or demean your conversational adversary were dutifully and quite Scottishly apparent. It seemed as though they had both picked up from where they had left off at the last argument the last time they had met and here, unspokenly, accepted that this was the way of communication between them with no other alternative considered. He wanted to say something positive.

"Well, it's quite comfy." Bouncing slightly to illustrate the point.

"Comfy is not a word. The word is comfortable."

He died a little inside. He said nothing, just as his mother did and settled on the comfy new *sofa* awaiting the tea. The television was on in the corner and his mother stared across to it as the news came on. Images of the striking miners, pickets and lines of uniformed police were beamed into the room compelling all to watch. Kelly seemed to have a new perspective on the dispute borne solely of one headline on a discarded newspaper on the bus, a perspective he had never really considered before or, in fact, wanted to have and he understood some sort of remote shame he should have felt at pulling the blinds down to absolve himself of any need to care or have an opinion.

His mother tutted loudly as a policeman was forced over and his helmet spilled onto the ground nearby and a miner booted it away like a football.

"Look at that. Bloody hooligans holdin' the country t' ransom, again." She quietly said.

Gerry came in with three mugs of tea and placed them on his mother's side table at her chair, took his mug then retook his position, strategically, on the radiator higher ground and assessed the battlefield.

"Should be bloody grateful to have a job! Lazy buggers. Want more money, again!" Gerry growled.

"That's just what I was sayin', Gerry. Holdin' the country t' bloody ransom, again. I mean where'd they think the money's comin' from. There's near enough three million on the dole...."

"Three million and one!" quipped the ever ready Gerry looking across to Kelly.

Although he knew that he knew very little about the strike he did understand that his mother and Gerry's rhetoric was a two-dimensional and uninformed view and he did know an element of circumstance that they did not and couldn't let this pass, however, he chose to try to offer a by-the-way remark in the hope nothing became too inflammatory, because he just couldn't be arsed.

He stood up and went to get his tea from the table and said, "Actually, I'm not sure it's entirely about money."

Of course, the immediate turn of Gerry's head towards the insubordinate Kelly indicated that, whether Kelly liked it or not, hostilities were about to commence.

"What the bloody hell do you know about it? You been listenin' t' those jakies you hang about wi'in town?"

"Actually, no. I read about it." Which seemed to incense darling Uncle Gerry even more.

"Read about it? I didn't know you could read? Did you know he could read, Kate?"

His mother declined a reply but allowed an upturn at one side of her mouth as loyal corroboration without turning from the TV.

"Actually, I can and do read, Gerry." A little more pointed and an indication that hostilities will be returned should no aspect of détente soon occur. "I read books. Mainly classic novels, actually…"

"My, you're fond of the word *actually*, this mornin'!" Beamed Gerry, thinking he'd scored ridicule points and was therefore now considered a wit as he looked across to his sister who allowed the other side of her mouth to rise.

"Which classic novel are you reading just now, then, Bamber?" Again ridicule. Bamber Gascoigne. University Challenge.

Kelly rose and went out to his coat in the hall and brought back in his thieved copy of *The Good Soldier Sveyk* and held it up.

"A Czechoslovakian novel by Jaroslav Hasek. A classic anti-establishment discourse and I read about the strike in the paper and they aren't asking for more money. They're striking because Thatcher is trying to close some of their colleague's pits. So what they are *actually* trying to do is help their fellow miners and, in course, their families, too."

Kelly knew that to keep it brief was the way forward and include an aspect of human goodness that would be difficult to refute. Take that, Michelin Man!

"They're helpin' nobody actin' like that! Carry on like that an' it'll be the army they're up against, then they'll know they're in a fight." Gerry returned.

Kelly saw an opportunity to make social and political comment and position Gerry as oppressor.

"Once more, I *actually* wouldn't be surprised if this government turned its armed forces onto its workers." Which he knew sounded as though he had a lot more in his ideological armoury with the use of *this government* and the word *workers* as a political indicator to his knowledge and as if it was beyond him to engage with their plebeian analysis.

A lull ensued. Gerry wasn't sure if this was all bluster. However his sister saved him.

"Do you want a biscuit, Gerry?" she said.

"No. I'll have this and get going."

You don't need any more biscuits you little fat fuckwit. They just hang around on that excuse of a moustache for the rest of the day and goad your belly into debate with your belt about the use of another notch. Fuck off back into your dick extension and deliver your little load off to whoever can be arsed looking at you, you horrible little cunt, Kelly thought but said…

"I'll take one."

"I don't remember asking you? Ye'll wait until you're asked. Did you learn nothin' growin' up?"

Gerry enjoyed this maternal rebuff as compensation of his previous loss, smirked and then added,

"Still looks that way."

Kelly's mother made a small grimace of resignation in acceptance of the remark. Gerry enjoyed the direction of conversation returning to the personal demeanour of Kelly.

Gerry wanted to even the score, somehow, before leaving the fray and so he added,

"Am I still keepin' you, then?"

To bite or not to bite. That is the question. An obvious reference to Gerry's employed state and his unemployed state and his receipt of a social handout. He was now tired of the fat little twat. Sometimes a roundly delivered *fuck off* could suffice keeping it simple with little scope for political and social debate that could trip one up with a paucity of facts. However, the ability to make up facts that can't be corroborated is always a tactic, sometimes used by politicians, themselves. What to do?

"Actually, no, Gerry. I've just got a job with the BBC."

And he left it there sipping a mouthful of tea and allowing Gerry's curiosity or disbelief to subjugate himself before the temple of Kelly.

"Well there's a lot of windows at the BBC." Gerry bounced back.

"Not all need cleaning. Some are for speaking to people through."

"Learned to speak have you."

Really poor comeback, Uncle Gerry, he thought. First I can't read and now….Tssch!

"No need to when you do it all with images." Lovely! *Images* is a good word.

"Your *image* can't have got you anywhere near the BBC!"

Ha! Kelly could tell Gerry was unsure but his pride precluded him from grovelling for anymore info.

"I've been freelancing as a photographer, *actually.*" Kelly quietly said as though at a dinner party for young professionals. "I intend to present some pictures of some theatre work in rehearsal and of current decorative choices within public buildings to the BBC as a commentary on current cultural perceptions."

His mother looked over to him unsure but hopeful that her son might be engaged in something productive, however, skilfully never letting the hope rise on her face.

Gerry understood his sister's hope and roundly extinguished the prospect of a rising Kelly.

"That's a load of shite for a start!"

Kelly had had enough.

"Why? Why does it have to be a load of shite? Do you think I'm utterly incapable of turning a shilling by my own wit? You haul that monster out there because you can drive. That's it! Someone asked you to *drive* it for them. Did you form the company, advertise for labour, buy the truck? Did you fuck! You pull your fat little carcass into the seat and press the pedals. You're not so high and mighty. You don't earn thousands or have found a cure for cancer, or invented the everlasting loaf, so don't try to run me down when I tell you I'm doing something with my life! Alright."

Gerry didn't expect anything other than a passive retort and was mildly surprised by this controlled outburst. Dramatic exit to return a hit.

"That's enough for me, Kate. I have to hit the road back to Glasgow before the traffic really starts and I can't stay here and listen to any more of this guff."

With that he took a deep draught of what was still hot tea as though he was John Wayne downing a whisky and leaving a saloon to confront some Mexican bandits and burned his lip. Kelly laughed audibly. Gerry saw this and felt suitably embarrassed.

"I'll warm yer jaw so's you canny laugh again, ye worthless wee prick!"

"It'll not be as warm as yours is, right now, though, will it?" and laughed again.

"Right! That's enough! The pair o' ye!" Kelly's mother barked.

Gerry turned to his sister. "I swear, Kate, one o' these days, I'll throttle this wee nyaff wi' the way he's treated you o'er the years. Turnin' up when he wants somethin' an' suckin' the life out o' the system, him an' his other lazy mates. I'm tellin' ye, it's hard t' watch when I'm up at five every mornin' to put food in the kid's mouths!"

Gerry was struggling now and playing an emotional card which he knew few can deride for fear of appearing thoughtless and uncaring and is obviously a tactic of the desperate. Nevertheless....

"*Actually*, do you know what's difficult to watch, Gerry....you tryin' to get your outsized gut into that cab and haul your big flabby arse onto the seat. Really, there shouldn't be any children allowed to watch something like that, well not until they're eighteen, at least. It might disturb them for the rest of their lives or cost them a fortune in therapy bills! And while we're speaking of kids, did my cousins Jack and Maureen not move out of your place the minute they could, which to my reckoning must be around five years ago? They put food on their own tables without any help from you, anymore. So don't give me the working-class martyr who's up with the larks every day. You sit down all day and push pedals for a living!"

Gerry threw down the *indignant and hurt* card and approached his sister placing his hand on her shoulder. God forbid he should do anything as affectionate as kiss her.

"I'm off Kate. Might drop by this time next week. I'm on the same run. M8, Forth Bridge, M90, Perth, Aberdeen and back."

He didn't have to name the roads, thought Kelly but he knew it was a description of his territory that Kelly knew little of not having passed his driving test and was Gerry's final parry before leaving. Last word prick.

"Last thing I'll say to you today is think o' your mother *before yoursel'* like you usually do. It'll not be before time. I'll see you Kate."

And with that Audie Murphy's underpants strode out back onto the dangerous streets of Deadman's Gulch and mounted his trusty steed.

An uncomfortable silence was left in the room, just as Gerry hoped and Kelly and his mother could hear him rev the engine a little more than he needed to, which Kelly chuckled inwardly at. He knew he'd be on the small road outside trying to reverse the truck into a position to get it back onto the main road and quite enjoying creating a little queue of traffic that could do nothing but wait for his manoeuvre to be completed but more importantly to Gerry, watch and commend his skill. Sad attention-seeking behaviour from a man that wanted to be loved but had not the balls to say so or do something less embarrassing to achieve it. After thinking this, however, he recognised that idiom of hypocrisy in himself, heard McQuarrie again, and he knew that selflessness wasn't high on his list of life's considerations. One of Gerry's arrows had found its home when he spat out the fact that he turned up on occasion, ostensibly to see his mother just to garner a little more immediate wealth. She was a widow and on a widow's pension, which really wasn't much but he knew she had something tucked away and would rarely refuse to help him. He began to feel slightly shameful realising that he hadn't enquired about his mother's health in the light of receiving the note from his Aunt Peggy and of the nonsense he had spouted about freelance photography and the BBC. Again, an arrogant and self-aggrandizing augmentation of the truth which, in essence, was just as sad as Gerry parking an eighteen-wheeler in a small road.

He looked across at his mother drinking tea, taking a biscuit from a tin and pointedly putting the lid back on sending the message out that these were her biscuits, then said,

"I got a note from Peggy."

"Wasn't a ten-pound note, was it?" she quickly darted back. Kelly understood the implicit barb.

"No!" instinctively playing one offended,

"She said you weren't very well?"

"Did she?" Again, he wished every conversation wasn't an exercise in pulling teeth.

"Yes she did! Are you ill? Can you just tell me if there's anything wrong. If I have any need to worry."

His mother drew a disbelieving look across to her son that needed no explanation to Kelly and he felt another barb hit home before she continued.

"Since when did you start to worry about me or anyone else for that matter?"

"Look, Mum…"

He had never been comfortable as an adult using that word. It was always used in the context of conflict as a child and now as an adult he found it difficult to place it into the milieu of apparent care or affection. His frustration and discomfort was visual as he sat forward on the *comfy* couch.

"Doctor sent me up to the hospital." Another sip of tea.

"And?"

"Done some tests."

"And?"

"Well, what do you want to know! They did some tests! Now I'm waiting for the results! That's it"

"What do I want to know? What do I want to know!! That's it? What do they think is wrong with you?"

His mother, despite offering occasional observations designed to demean, was and always had been a terribly shy woman at heart and was never comfortable talking about herself. As a child, Kelly occasionally saw her metamorphose into sycophancy, laughing in conversations at things that just weren't funny when she met people that weren't close enough to either ignore or scoff; the insurance man, the pools collector, a neighbour that wore a suit to go to work and required her attention. He knew she laughed because she enjoyed the contact, the human exchange, but he remembered liking it most because his mother was laughing and he recalled the uplift he felt within when she did this and would begin to smile himself, and then try to laugh at the same things just to be a part of something good happening when he didn't understand really what they were laughing at. He was laughing because his mother was laughing. He was uplifted because there appeared to be a semblance of joy that could be carried from this scene back into the house which might glow for a while sending communion into the space between them and for a while feel as though affection filled the rooms of where they lived.

"Are you in any pain?" Kelly said to her.

"It's just the doctor needs to know that, not you!"

"Could you please just tell me!"

"My lungs are sore. That's it. When I breathe or laugh."

The irony of what she'd just said was not lost on him. She had smoked since she was a teenager, although hadn't laughed nearly as regularly, and tried a few times to give up but inevitably the craving would demand satisfaction, and then she relented and once more filled the house with a fug that remained, perennially.

Inappropriate to say it. The word. Not required. It was painted large across the psyche of all concerned. So he didn't. Even to himself but heard it being said in the corner of his mind somewhere by someone else. A doctor.

"When do you get the results?"

"Next week. They have to send them somewhere. It's just a cough. I had bronchitis. I took a mixture and some anti-biotics when I had that. Went. It's just a cough."

Kelly remained with her for the next hour and didn't force out any more from his mother. They talked of his Aunt Peggy who lived in Edinburgh and of whom he saw little and of how he'd walk to her house some Saturday mornings as a child just to get the wrapped chocolate biscuits and cakes she bought for her husband, Uncle Tommy, who had a ridiculously sweet tooth. Occasionally, his mother would, chuckle, wince and then quickly drink tea to indicate it was a throat irritation and nothing else but largely they spent the time in unacknowledged comfort with each other talking about relatives and stories of past Christmases and of the time Kelly decided to climb Arthur's Seat, Edinburgh's small mountain in the centre of the city, as a nine year old and disappeared for seven hours only to be picked up by the police and returned to a very angry father who died shortly after that episode and at a very young age. They both allowed this nostalgia to waft over them in a silent agreement of *something,* knowing the difficulty of openly expressing their love for each other had been skilfully circumvented. They changed the channel on the TV and watched a programme about saving animals together and then The News came on again and, to Kelly's surprise, his mother asked him about the reason for the strike. Kelly, for once, offered no more than he knew but offered up his opinion that to selflessly put yourself and one's family into hardship and privation to help colleagues one had never laid eyes on was achingly noble and maybe economically rash but in this big mess of humanity, the right thing to do.

And Kelly meant it. And he liked that he meant it.

Shortly after this, he donned the Crombie and made to make his farewells when his mother stopped him and asked him to wait as she went into the kitchen. The sound of a tin having its lid popped off echoed out into the hall. He immediately knew what she was doing and in times past he had felt overwhelming relief and joy at the sound of the popping lid secure in the knowledge that a few days revelry would, henceforth, be on the cards. He didn't feel like that this time. She returned with a small bundle of folded bank notes and pressed them into Kelly's hand. Previously, he might have asked her for an advance he knew he probably wouldn't be able to pay back but this time heard himself say the word *no*, frequently. As much as he did, his mother fought back refusing the word. She made paltry excuses of her inability *to spend it, not need it, he need it more,* and then that she couldn't *take it with her.* He began to realise that to refuse was the more inappropriate thing to do, that something akin to *I love you, I care about you*, or some arcane method of Calvinist delivery of a similar expression was being said and so he relented feeling something quite alien akin to shame and let the money slide into his hand as the cold grip of his mother's crept around his fingers. She walked out to the front door with him and watched him walk down the path and onto the street. He looked back at her and she attempted to smile, which she never did. Kelly knew this was an extension of ...*something*... and smiled something back from the heaviest of hearts and felt the inability to not let it drop back into a dolorous look. Just as he turned to leave, his mother called to him and said,

"Do something."

Back on the bus to town he held onto the glow he still felt but felt relief to see the concrete disappear behind him. He fished around in his pockets looking for his folded Daily Mirror and realised he had the wrong pocket but felt the small wad of bank notes. He took it out and realised he hadn't counted it, something which he usually did as soon as propriety would allow, however this time a very steady but detached disinterest had coldly enveloped him as he walked from his mother's house and toward the bus stop. He had a quick survey of the seat behind him and then slid the notes surreptitiously out into daylight and peered down. A zero appeared. Then a five. In the knowledge that there was quite a tightly packed wad, a flutter was experienced in Kelly's stomach that wandered up into his throat and had to cough. As he did so he turned his head to check who may be watching but then knew this would appear somewhat shady and felt immediately guilty of something, and saw that a middle-aged chap in a flat cap, two seats behind him, across the aisle had clocked him but then perhaps realised he was staring and returned to his gaze to the underpasses and footbridges weaving through the concrete vista, away from Kelly.

Kelly looked down into his lap and counted the corners of twelve fifty-pound notes. Raised his head. Counted again. Looked up and across the bus. Counted again. Back to the bus. Caught the eye of the man across the aisle. Looked down at his pocket where the money was tucked away. Suddenly he had a tremendous and quite demanding itch in his balls and he reared up in his seat and thrust his hand down his trousers and clawed for Scotland, apparently uncaring of any audience making a suppressed grunt and sighs of delighted satisfaction.

Flat Cap, two behind across the aisle, watched this and decided that, to reply with a noise of affected offence and self-righteous disgust was the appropriate reaction. Having watched the surreptitious descent of Kelly's eyes to said crotch area and then up again to survey who may or may not be watching, at least three times, and looking impressively guilty of something, not sure what, he decided that an untoward act may well have occurred, or at the least had his cock out, waving it about on the bus as an expression of his obvious deviance. He was now in something of a moral quandary being burdened with this knowledge and pulled a stern look at Kelly and his attire, coat and tousled hair deciding that the circumstantial evidence was enough to convict. He looked up to the driver and then back to Kelly. Kelly was genuinely unaware of any potential offence that may have been given, so he screwed his face into an expression of *What's your problem?* and returned to face forward. He let go a few mutters. Not really helping.

He pulled The Daily Mirror from the other pocket and unfolded it and flattened it in a display of irritation designed to be heard by Flat Cap and began to scan the pages. He read a little bit more outlining the miner's strike, wanting to take it in and know more, but there was an antagonised kernel deep in his core that wanted to spit vitriol that stopped him from concentrating. He was angry, not least because the judge and jury behind him had him on death row for publicly scratching his balls, but remarkably and probably with himself and he knew it. He'd shamefully made up some cock and bull story extending to freelancing with the BBC just to assuage the condemnation of a judgmental relative that should offer affection instead of bile and his mother had the temerity to come right out of left-field and *smile* at him, moreso, share a pleasant couple of hours with him and then give him six hundred quid. *Six hundred quid!,* with the caveat of having to *do something*, and all this while she had ripened his conscience with the news that she was quite unwell.

As he read on it seemed as though the news had been intentionally created that day to wind him into a frustrated knot of impotence.

The world seemed to Kelly to be racing towards an insanity of conflict, anarchy, greed and violence and he knew the nauseous rag he held, and others like it, used its permanently sensationalist bent to pump this out to any who would part with coin and this made him angry, too. Ireland was in turmoil and the hunger strikers had recently departed, all during a recession, of which, there were a couple of million on the dole. Everyone hated Margaret Thatcher, except the Tories and police on overtime, and The Cold War internationally gurgled on in its tension and ominously dangerous quietude. A detachment seemed to remove him from it all, from anything that offered any sense of belonging to all of this monolithically impervious substance and all obviously there but quite beyond him.

He flipped the pages of his newspaper which opened up once more to the adverts selling money. It all seemed ridiculously and apparently easy and this prole rag was allowing it to happen to other proles as long as they got their fee for the ad, and he wrestled with this conundrum of being enticed, as it were by one of their own to jump into flagrant debt but were most likely to fuck up in their obligations to return it with interest, probably expected it, and yet nobody was saying the Emperor was naked and neither the money-sellers or the newspaper seemed to care. He smiled as he surprisingly realised he might be thinking ethically or feeling moral outrage.

The rain started to smear across the bus windows and his quiet anger began to find, unbeknownst to him, public audibility, as he let a few more subtle social observations fly into the void around him. There were a few more passengers on the bus now that he hadn't noticed get on and a few looks were cast across in his direction and then to each other and particularly to Flat Cap, who now had a woman of similar middle-age sitting next to him and was in muffled conversation with her as Madame Shopping, who was on the bus to Livingston with Kelly, now got on to make her return journey.

Kelly had decided that he'd had enough and snapped back through the pages to the cover as if to review all he had read and he landed on page three with a model in tight hot pants pressing out a globulously magnificent set of breasts with nipples like two football studs and pouting ridiculously at the camera just as this fearful small woman was about to sit next to him. She recognised the smell and then looked at him and then the page he was on, ejaculated an *Oh!*... and then quickly moved down the bus to the seat next to Flat Cap's companion, of whom she thankfully knew, there to re-tell of her frighteningly previous encounter with Kelly.

* * * * *

"This is the arsehole of fuckin' Broxburn!" Kelly shouted as he was guided out into the rain by the driver.

"I don't care. I'll be reporting this back at the depot and they might report it to the police. Dirty bastard."

"Dirty bastard? What're you talkin' about? And reportin' what?"

The driver, larger, stronger and older than Kelly, had managed to get him from his seat up to the front and out onto a grass verge with Flat Cap ably defending the rear somewhere between the towns of Broxburn and Newbridge, notably none of the two and adjacent to fields of unripened Oil-Seed Rape. The interior of the bus had now become a gaggle of opinion and unison as to the danger and unwholesome demeanour of Kelly and were standing and straining to see the ejection, and any other welcome fracas, from their seats. None came. The bus doors closed and thirty-one heads collectively turned to eyeball Kelly goodbye as the bus pulled away.

"Bastaaaard!!!........." erupted from Kelly and into the grey skies and growl of passing traffic.

He looked back up the road and saw nothing but a factory in the distance and the disappearing carriageway. He pulled up his collar and hunched his shoulders against the rain and raged internally against those that had conspired to have him removed from the bus. His rage then extended somewhere into that great greyness of deceit, evasion and dissatisfaction that was his life and he let a rising, guttural roar howl out into this void of a place that was nowhere, between nothing and far from the place he wanted to get to and his eyes welled up into red puddles of sadness.

And it was then he then decided the *something* he was going to do.

Fuck the world. Why should he care? He was going to do something, alright. He felt his mother's money and the letters he'd received that morning in one pocket and the Daily Mirror and *The Good Soldier Sveyk* in the other. He took out the newspaper looked aggressively through the pages and tore out one and stuffed it back in his pocket then threw the rest of it down onto the sodden grass verge.

This day had given him clarity. He had perspective and an ostensible method. He wasn't exactly sure yet how he could make it work but if it went wrong....so what!. He didn't care anymore. Why should he? The world obviously didn't give a flying fuck about him, or ever did. He felt as though a weight had been lifted from him. He had a plan. Of sorts. A project with an end result worth working for, worth using his ability and wits to achieve.

A ruthless determination from somewhere coursed through him. He secured his coat, tightly and began to walk back to Edinburgh.

Chapter 9

Sophie's Voice

Thursday, 14th June

Liz was sitting in a quite grand and ornately carved wooden chair on the stage and facing her was the rest of the group sitting facing her in rickety steel and canvass chairs on the floor. Rodger was somewhat aerated. He was rolling his eyes and standing behind her trying to get the rest of the group to ask Liz questions in a hot-seating exercise but Liz was being far too honest, apparently, and answering the questions as herself when she should be answering the questions as a character she has chosen to be, who was apparently the lady who delivered the Littlewoods catalogue and subsequent purchases to her and her mother, whom Liz was convinced was a lesbian and *cookin' the books and puntin' gear that was 'lost in the post.' Dodgy hoor!*

Liz had been asked what her favourite pastime was and scurried gleefully towards vodka and fighting with her neighbours but Rodger then tried to bring her back to the fact that she should be her character, the Littlewoods lady, which at one point she had been, but became enthusiastic and *lost her focus*, as Rodger said, and then Liz declared that all of this was *a load of shite* and that she *didn't get it* and Rodger should show everybody and be a better teacher, quite frankly.

Kelly liked Liz. She was endearingly, but brutally honest, seemingly unable to be anything but herself. She was free, uncaring of what disparaging others might think and would speak to the high-born as she would the working man. He wouldn't say it but there was an element of respect for this smoking ball of shoplifting talent. Liz said what she wanted and took what she needed in this world and he really liked her for that. At the same time she seemed friendless among her peers and spoke a lot of her mother and he was very wary of her visceral propensity to confrontation, of which she was remarkably well-practised. He sat quietly and watched as Rodger's entreaties fell on misunderstanding ears and loud exhortations as to his corpulence as a defence, which never was one, merely an attack to repulse a pressing demand upon her intelligence and to mask her own insecurities, of course. Nobody's perfect.

Much of the watching audience became a pressuresome factor for Rodger because there were many open gurgles of pleasure as Liz jousted with the rules and Rodger in her own stark way, and Kelly, who had been late this Thursday morning, also let a curling grin announce his quiet enjoyment of the edifice that is *Theatre Skills,* fall down around Rodger's head. It was becoming embarrassing for Rodger but nobody else had wanted to be first to volunteer for the exercise except Liz whose initial enthusiasm and badgering insistence to participate couldn't be ignored.

"Look….Liz! You have to remain with your character! You just can't switch back and forward. You are either the Littlewoods Lady….

"Lesbo…."

"….or you are Liz! But you can't be Liz because if you're Liz you're not doing the hot-seating exercise properly! Do you understand?"

"Aye …..ah've goat it. An' dinny git in such a fash aboot me no daein' it right or talkin' aboot lesbian's Rodge or ye'll pop yer buttons again!"

Liz's reference to an actual occurrence when Rodger's shirt decided to shed two buttons from his midriff area when demonstrating *stretching* and *cutting shapes* in an expressive movement morning, reduced the group to an open laugh that

Rodger should have laughed at, also, but decided to change the volunteer, to whit, Liz was offended and publicly told him so. Nevertheless, a change was made and Liz dismounted the stage as Graham and his shell-suit bottoms ascended to the world of otherness but Liz held things up declaring that she wasn't going to sit in the now empty seat where his *Ronson Lighter* had been and went to get another chair from the back of the hall. None of the group except Kelly understood her rhyming slang but Kelly held in his laughter, not wanting to appear too comfortable with the course because he had other plans, but then he heard his name being called by Kat who was leaning out of the office door.

Kat poured instant coffee from the cafetiere. Kelly sat across the desk from her and she lifted the cafetiere and looked at Kelly offering him some to which he declined. She then went to the cassette player and turned down the soundtrack of *Gypsy, The Musical,* and returned to her seat opposite Kelly. Kat made as if to speak twice before saying anything just to get her audience's attention and curiosity, which was a technique of hers she had developed playing a headmistress on the *Smell the Bully* tour, which she had assimilated into her teaching to great success, she thought, and then said,

"Leonard....

"Kelly!"

"Yes, sorry...Kelly...I was really impressed with your contribution on Monday. Really interesting...from a theatre perspective for me....you understand ritual and symbolism.... cultural metaphor.... and such."

Kelly made a face as if to say *ok, thanks* and tried to work out what a cultural metaphor might be but said nothing in reply. Kat obviously had an agenda but was treading carefully for some reason. Kelly offered nothing.

"Yes really interesting and good to have......*someone* on the course with …. depth...*experience*..."

Kelly understood the reference to his age and wondered now where she was going to go with this.

"So.... good! Good start! Very good start. Couple of other issues....."

Aha, Kelly thought. To the point.

"Erm... Rodger has mentioned to me that a couple of the others.... *girls*... have mentioned to Rodger that you have a very particular and quite earthy... smell ....which I am personally cool with! I'm ok with a man smelling as a man should smell, which is.... however, here.... well here it is not for me to selfishly enjoy that *manly aroma*.... But to ensure that ... my *bright young things,* as I like to call them, are....ok with whichever grooming products you like to use, too. *Or not.* Yes?"

Kelly knew he was remiss on the hygiene front and despite this was a tad miffed. He decided to rescue her.

"Which girls?"

"Well initially, there were.... but then ....*all of them.*"

"All of them?"

"Yes."

"But you like it?"

"I wouldn't say *like* it but there is something about the natural smell of a man that is quite..." she struggled for an adjective and settled for *"...male...* and you being a little more mature than the rest of them, well…"

At this point her eyes dropped with a smile to the desk and she became fifteen years old again. Kelly recognised the signs and remained outwardly the same in appearance but there were guns going off in his head. Was she declaring an attraction to him?

"...and I see from the register it's your birthday in a few weeks? We usually *do something* when a birthday comes up. So….? However, on the original tack, maybe you could spray a little longer in the mornings, with…"

"Sure." Kelly cut in.

"Yes that's a good one but maybe something with a heavier perfume…..?"

"No…. I mean ok. Yes. I understand.

Kat, who was at least ten years older than Kelly, nodded said *of course* and poured herself more coffee and, this time, Kelly accepted a cup of the weak tepid brew and stayed a little to chat with Kat, whom he knew was laughing a little too easily at anything he said but he also knew with her in gurgling mode she would be easier to manipulate. Nevertheless, she did say that she *had to mention* yesterday's absence to which Kelly outlined the pain he had felt at saying goodbye to his friend and colleague….*Eric*…..and found it difficult to swing his mind toward Stanislavsky et al, despite rising in time to get to *get here* but just lay down for the day to remember his friend.

He told Kat he spent an hour yesterday framing a photograph of the two of them together on the beach in East Lothian on a warm summer's evening last year which made her nod all the more seriously mentioning it was important to cherish the good times because hard times were always in the post, whatever, because *that's just how life is* but also made her think that Kelly might have been gay? Kat nodded with a quite serious face just as she was sipping some coffee that dribbled down her dress and to deflect the attention from her embarrassment asked Kelly if it was actually *the virus* that had taken Eric. Kelly had no idea which virus she was talking about but said that it was and then Kat skirted around a story of someone she had known in theatre who had been gay, *funnily enough*, who was *taken* recently. Kelly then understood her reference to AIDS having quite forgotten he'd used it with Rodger and so changed the subject as if it was all too difficult for him, explaining to her how Eric had been a make-up artist in the film industry and had become quite familiar with some of the techniques that Eric used as he had shown him on a few evenings over a cold bottle of Chablis but he had kept his secret for years tragically denying himself the succour of love and that if only he had known he might have been able *to have helped him.*

Kelly told her how he was now charged with the care of *someone* that had been close to Eric who would need daily consideration with regard to exercise and *getting out* a bit more but didn't mention anything about not shitting in the street. More serious nodding from Kat effusing how noble and decent it was to be entrusted with the care of someone that was loved by someone close but Kelly reassured her it was just moral guidance and love required and then asked her if she had a family, which she hadn't, alas, but held out hope as her ovaries *weren't dry yet.*

A natural hiatus occurred at that moment. Kat rescued it by telling Kelly she had deferred the Stanislavsky workshop until he returned as she was sure he would bring a lot to the table. Kelly told her he was glad she had done so and thanked her for that to which she smiled broadly. Kelly would rather have licked shit off a nettle and realised that he had to do something that would get him out of the acting bollocks but keep Kat's allegiance. He stepped up a gear.

"You know I love the honesty of those actors who use Stanislavsky and don't think I'd like to see it *misused*, Kat? Eric took me onto set a few times and I watched a few actors try to apply *The Method.*"

"No, no! I agree." Kat blurted out, "The Method unearths the truth and uncovers liars."

"I hope so but I've only read about it and watched others, you know, and hope you'll *look after me*, Kat and not allow any fabrications to facilitate egotism?"

He realised that was twice he'd used her name in two sentences and told himself not to lay it on too thick. Nevertheless, she beamed broadly at the thought of becoming his theatrical guardian for the afternoon, and later, perhaps more.... *if* she could definitively ascertain whether or not he was gay?

Grasping opportunity again he asked if he might be allowed the time up until after lunch to try to put Eric *somewhere else* for now and prepare for the afternoon with a quiet time feeding the birds, to which Kat enthusiastically assented.

He went for a pint on the High Street.

He rolled in at ten minutes late, three pints to the good. He took off his Crombie, and sat down on one of the available chairs. Rodger made a great show of looking at a watch that wasn't on his wrist and tapping it as Kelly did this. Rodger was an arse. Kelly didn't care. Kat was the power in this crew and it was just then that she came in. Rodger was distributing script excerpts and there was a little chatter about them between the group. Kelly got an excerpt from *The Crucible* by Arthur Miller. He'd heard of it but never seen it or read it. This was act two with a chap called Proctor and his wife, Elizabeth. Steven sidled over to him and presented him with a plastic bag.

"What's this?"

"The trainers? Just a pair of Blue flash I bought to wear in the flat but I don't, so..."

Kelly peered into the bag.

"Yeah... thanks. That's great.... thanks. I'll try them on in a bit I think Kat's going to..."

Steven nodded and smiled and gave a thumbs up. He really was a lovely chap, Kelly thought. Kat made a bit of a sound to get everyone's attention and then made two false starts which drew a silence across the room. Kelly smiled inwardly. Kat started,

"We are….about to go on a journey together, or perhaps *alone* this afternoon….a journey that takes us to who knows where, who knows when or knows not where the destination ends…."

Rodger was rapt, already.

"….which station or town you end up in…could be Happytown, likewise could be Sadsville….I don't know but the most important thing is that you take the journey and you learn something…something about yourself, The Method, and then how to use the experience of that journey with your character. If along the way you decide the journey's too bumpy, heavy, or just plain rough…get off the train! Get off the train quickly! To go back to somewhere you've been that wasn't good for you can sometimes be dangerous." She paused, then lifted her hand to her heart and earnestly said, " I'm here for you. So is Rodge…."

Rodger beamed but then quickly dropped his expression to one of *done it all before got the t-shirt mate,* and made some eye contact around the room and nodded reassuringly as if to say, *I'll be here.*

"….and don't be shy in asking some of the older students for help if it gets rough."

Looking across to Kelly who was clenching his bum cheeks trying to stifle the inevitability of a fart arriving. He nodded *a la Rodger* who drew a dark look his way, patently miffed at his inclusion.

"First thing is we have to pair up. Make it someone you feel comfortable with….."

A large space quickly grew around Liz. Kelly felt a tap on his shoulder. Steven was there smiling and shrugged as if to say *it has to be me and you, pal…*. But then Sophie spun Kelly around much too quickly for his liking.

"Steven, let me work with Leonard! I want to use the experience we shared on Monday."

Steven relented with a smile and a shrug then sought another partner. Most of the group had paired up. Three of the giggly girls asked if they could work in a three which Kat said wasn't possible. Liz was paired with Mhairi who appeared distraught and already glassy-eyed at the prospect of what might come. Kelly made another diversion of going over to his coat as if to put something in the pocket which got him away from his cloud of noxious gas. As he did this Rodger walked through the place where he'd been and gradually got the message, contorting his face, gagging and moving quickly to another part of the hall.

Kat spoke. Only one false start this time, but she had a thoughtful little walk to compensate.

"Whose life is perfect? Not mine, not yours either, I imagine. We all suffer. Pain. Tragedy. Loss. Heartbreak… Tragedy……Loss….. Pain. Your first task is to first of all relax in the company of your partner. Both of you sit and close your eyes and let me…."

Rodger was purposefully eyeing across to Kat,

"…..*and Rodge* ask a set of simple questions while you relax that may be quite searching. All you have to do is answer the questions in your head and let your soul absorb the …*the feeling.*

With that the group settled down except Liz who complained about the chair and the fact that she had Mhairi as a partner who couldn't or wouldn't talk and *what was the point of that, man!*

Kat slid off her rope salopettes and quietly padded barefoot around the room. She wanted to be connected to the earth, apparently. Rodger saw this looked at his tightly laced shoes and so started to walk as though he had a full nappy. Kat frowned at Rodger and looked at his creaking shoes and then raised her eyebrows indicating she was about to start. And off Kat went into who knows what. And she loved it.

"You're young. …

"Young." Rodger said immediately securing himself into the process. Kat darted a look at him.

"*Very young*. This is your first memory. Go back. Melt back into time and see yourself. What are you doing, saying? Who are you with? What time of the day is it? What season? Take your time……take your time…."

Rodger looked across to Kat and smiled and nodded as if to say very good and then pointed to his chest hoping it was his turn to ask the questions. Kat shook her head, Rodger deflated like a child.

"You're older now. Perhaps at school. Things happen at school. We remember them. What do you remember? Remember that boy, that girl, that teacher, that class…..that boy…

"…or girl…." Rodger sneaked in.

"Remember *that situation?* Unfair wasn't it? See the faces, hear the sounds, smell... *the smells*. Were you ever in a fight? Why? That question the teacher asked. You couldn't answer that question could you, *could you?* Remember how you felt... Keep thinking…… thinking ….

Rodger, "..thinking…."

At this point Liz was heard to mutter something with the word *fucker* in it but the group kept it together with the help of Kat moving on to her next part, to the consternation of Rodger who wanted a turn at delivering the mood. However…

"You're older again. You decide. How old are you? Are you at the age where pain and heartbreak invade your being? It is your first time of real suffering…go there…"

Rodger was looking across to her wanting to chip in! He was determined to be a leading part of this. Kat started to raise her voice. Kelly opened one eye. Rodger tried to signal. Kat ignored him.

"...go there! Go there now.... Go on!. Go there!....."

Rodger couldn't help himself. He joined in.

"Yes go on.... go there!....Yes, there...just go...*go now!*"

Kat scowled at Rodger. Rodger pretended not to see this. Kat got louder all the time killing Rodger with her eyes,

"It's your first life's loss, a pain...

Rodger crashed in, louder.

"It's sore!...Sore!!...."

Kat tried to top him again.

"A heartache. Understand the hurt! Count the tears!

Rodger again, louder,

"A hundred...a thousand!!...."

Kat was determined to remain the lead practitioner, the volume became absurd,

"Streaming into your heart....!! Feel it! Feeeel iiiittt!!

Kelly, now bemused had both eyes half open and saw Sophie wetting her eyes with her saliva in readiness for an Oscar performance as she delighted in writhing openly determined to be affected by their clumsy and amateurish technique. No doubt she'd *found her centre* and was warming to the coming performance. Kelly now had two objectives: one, be removed from the acting course and shifted on to make-up, and two; to expose Sophie, this pseudo pretentious knobhead and it was then he realised he had the opportunity to kill two birds with one stone.

Kat told the group to open their eyes and each other was to tell their story not missing any details. Kelly insisted that Sophie unburden herself first as everyone else in the room began their stories.

"Well…. when I was growing up I never had a good relationship with my Mum."

Kelly made a conciliatory expression which encouraged her.

"….and it was only later when I got to about twelve or thirteen that I found out that my Mum wasn't my real mum…."

Here Sophie paused in amongst all of the quiet and meaningful hubbub and looked around the room as if to be using that as a means of taking a break because it had already become too intense for her. Kelly wanted her to continue.

"Go on." He said with a soft reassuring tone. She half smiled and took a dramatic breath that fought the oncoming pain.

"It was near the end of term before we broke for summer. It was a golden summer. 1972…..every day was so hot and sunny it felt like it would always be that way. That was the summer I had my first boyfriend…."

Sophie laughed a laugh that was straight out of *The Painful and Ironic Laughs,* manual that was used in poor American dramas.

"…..George was lovely. We kissed that summer…..my first kiss…"

Kelly wanted her back on the quasi-painful path trodden by her and her adopted mother.

"You were talking about your Mum…?"

"Oh…!" She quietly erupted, dragged from her deliberate reverie.

"Yes. It was nearing the end of term and there was a fair that came to town…I grew up in Whitburn, out west and everybody from school said they were all going that night and I said I'd go too, and Mum told me to wear my blue Farah slacks, high-waister, nine inch flares, … 'cause they were nice, and then my Mum…huh….*Mum*…. said she was going to come along *just in case*…..Just in case! I mean just in case of what? She knew about George and knew he'd probably be there……. And it was as if she wanted to embarrass me…..laugh at me….All my friends would be there…. I don't know….*hurt me*….?"

Sophie got louder to encourage an audience. Kelly knew it because she raised her head as if to take a breath but then assess who was aware of her performance.

"She wanted to hurt you?" Kelly pulled her back.

"I didn't *really* think so….but something happened that night…something that made me wonder and remember other things that had happened along the way…when I was younger…"

Kat was patrolling, deftly creeping around soft-footedly and purposely stopping and craning to hear snippets of the recounted heartaches and Rodger had seen this and tried to emulate this with all the poise of a hippo on a tightrope but had managed to reach *his girl*, Sophie. He outwardly remained professional and apparently objective but secretly wanted to hear her tale that might reveal something that he could use later to *connect* and he stopped but looked away from Kelly and Sophie. He listened as Sophie cranked up the intensity in the knowledge of his presence and got to the meat of the tale.

"It was The Chairoplanes! I went on The Chairoplanes and George sat in the swing next to me. I didn't want him to be so close to me when my Mum was there but he just smiled and did it anyway. The seats were hard wood and very slippy, like really polished and I had on my blue cotton slacks, *Farah* that my Mum told me to wear! George said they made my legs look really long… and then the chairs started to move and we got higher and higher and faster and faster and I could see my Mum every time we went around….."

Sophie cranked up the pace here just as she'd seen witnesses under severe interrogation do in courtroom dramas. Kelly nodded and suppressed another fart.

"…..and all there was to keep us in the seat was a small chain. The chain was too loose. It couldn't stop me from slipping as the ride got faster. I realised then that I was going to slip off the seat under the chain and be thrown onto the ground if they didn't stop and every time I went around I knew my Mum could see that I was slipping but she just smiled and then the man with the microphone shouted *do ya wanna go faster?* and everybody shouted *yessss!* And I just wanted it to slow down but I saw my Mum looking at me and smiling…..smiling!!......and she knew….she knew!! I was slipping…..slipping off….as if she wanted me to be hurt….to be killed…I looked across to George and he knew I was in trouble…..and then the man said again *do ya wanna go faster?* And everybody shouted *yesssss!* And then I saw my Mum shout *yes,* too! I couldn't believe it! She could've told the man with the microphone to slow down and let me off… but she didn't and just kept shouting *yesss* and smiling and looking right at me everytime I went past. It was then that George reached out for me….but I couldn't reach his hand…we were too far apart and the speed of it stopped us from touching…..he wanted to help..save me……he knew I was in trouble."

Rodger couldn't move on to the next pair as much as he knew he should and he made an outward show of feeling her pain with a little grimace designed to be seen by Sophie and for later reference on the connection front.

Kelly nodded and frowned sincerely, begging her to continue. Sophie dramatically reached out into nothingness. Kelly suppressed a laugh and nodded.

"At one point the tips of our fingers touched but we couldn't hold hands… and it was then I slipped under the chain….I was very slim…… a little bit slimmer than I am now.... I was so scared I thought I was going to die and my legs were dangling…I held on to one of the chains that held the chair up and someone shouted…."

Here, Sophie stood up and loudly shouted across the room, which had her desired effect, halting the other tales and offering visual testimony to the horror of her tale

"There's a girl gonna fall! There was a scream…"

Kelly knew she was a pretentious mare but couldn't believe it when Sophie actually screamed the scream of the imaginary crowd watching her fall. He found it hard not to slap her let alone encourage her to crack on to the climax. However, this was all grist to the mill as his ruse would be all the better for this performance.

"…and then the ride slowed down and I held on. The ride stopped the opposite side to where my Mum was as the man with the microphone asked me if I was alright and if I was there with my Mum or Dad and I said my Mum and expected her to come around from the other side and give me a hug but she didn't…she just put her head out enough to see me and beckon me over. She just looked disappointed. I couldn't believe it! George wanted to talk to me but my Mum started to walk away and out of the fairground and I had to catch her because I knew she'd be angry if I didn't follow her."

Rodger acknowledged Sophie's decrescendo and moved on.

Then Sophie progressed to her denouement which outlined various tales of being unaware of hot custard her mother gave her as a child, and being encouraged to ride her trike down a steep hill near traffic and other anecdotes of food mixers and sharp knives followed by a tearful rendition of the discovery of her adoption and now estrangement from her Mother.

Having taken a discernible time beyond that which is necessary, she composed herself and asked Kelly to offer his contribution. The group were now tailing off as both in each pair had delivered their stories to the time it took Sophie to recount hers and Kelly now had the floor which suited him well. Rodger had crept across to Kat to commend Sophie's story and the telling of it louder than required in order for the rest of the group and Sophie to hear the word *Sophie* and *tragic* amongst his apparently covert discourse.

"Well….that was harrowing, Sophie. So dramatic and painful!" Kelly said.

Rodger shook his head and repeated the word…*painful*. The class began to listen. Kat focused on him. Sophie suppressed a smile. Liz made a small mime of being sick. Steven straightened his cardigan. Mhairi looked frightened. The giggly girls looked at each other in embarrassment and Graham pulled his shell suit bottoms over his bum crack.

"I used to sail. Out in the West Indies. Back in the seventies. I was younger, fitter and had my whole life in front of me until one fateful day when I decided not to take the advice of Buckshot Billy the local shark fisherman who had been sailing for years. He said there was a squall coming and not to go out that day. But I did. I went out. Alone….."

He paused to think realising he had to improvise nautical terms, then realised he owned the room. Tension crackled.

"… I took my forty-foot schoonermaran, *Saucy Lady*, a boat with three gibbet arms, a topside fonsackle with a portside turret, two spinkers and a deep but narrow sharp rudder. My god she was fast! Well, this day I took her out into deep water where the ocean can kick up white horses larger than a house….."

Liz was told he meant waves. Sophie nodded and frowned with fraudulent deep interest.

"I was skiffing broadside to the south-west over Danniken's Reef and well…. I should've known better. The reef threw up a wave that I couldn't hold, I couldn't ride out to safer water and it flipped the *Saucy Lady* a whole one-eighty, totally upside down and it threw me up into the squall. It was then ...that moment that *changed my life* forever...."

Another pause to let the tension grow. The room was rapt.

"I was coming down as the rudder was turning to the sky and as I fell it caught me. Hard. On the legs. Cut them both off clean as a knife through butter......."

Everyone looked at him with a shared intake of breath, frowns and a few head shakes but as he paused they all, in collective bemusement, then looked down to his legs. There were some quizzical expressions and looks to each other as Kelly held the pause. Rodger then said,

"But....?"

Kelly took to the big space on the middle of the floor,

"What? My legs?"

"Well, after I got home I went to see a wise-woman who told me to rub my stumps every day with a cold cabbage and after a while they grew back bigger and stronger and lovelier than ever!"

He jumped and spun around like a demented child.

"....and now I can run and dance and leap around just like I used to! I went back to ballet class and started training for the marathon and life is beautiful and wonderful again! Woo hoo!"

Bemusement stuck to their faces, initially but then Liz broke the silence and started to laugh a laugh that would be heard throughout the building. Kelly bounded around Sophie, the butt of his lampoonery, and grinned inanely, until he ran out of breath. Then farted the fart he'd been holding in for ages. What the hell. No need to withhold his bowels now. The rest of the group started to laugh as well. Rodger didn't and took his opportunity to comfort Sophie, who didn't need comforting until she felt the humiliation then anger kick in and pushed Rodger away. Liz shouted above it all,

"Fuckin' ripped! Meryl Streep totally fuckin' ripped, ya *up-yerself drama hoor!*" She laughed. "Nice one Crusty Crombie! Ye might stink but that's a doozy! Legs grew back. Ha ha!!"

And she continued gurgling as Sophie marched out of the room close to real tears. Kat went after her but threw back a scowl at Kelly. Rodger was livid.

Stanislavsky never meant it to be this way. Emotion memory was a technique worthy of a better response than this, surely? The workshop ended there and Kelly had a tete-a-tete an hour later with Kat and Rodger, who insisted he be there, and was decided that Kelly be moved to Make-Up and that there were a lot of make-up specialists that were men so he shouldn't complain and there was a very good instructor and a space for someone and as he'd had experience watching Eric in the past he might be very useful when the time came for any big extravaganza that GTW might undertake.

Kelly had planned to ask to be put onto the make-up and prosthetics course and used the Eric story to grease the wheels, however, it had all worked swimmingly, but was warned against openly farting in a group context and he had to attend to his personal hygiene *a little more diligently*. Kelly wanted to make a point of order that women were blessed with the fart gland too but withheld his observation and enjoyed the glow of having gained access to that which fitted his project.

He started that very afternoon with the small group of three other girls and Kerry. He'd dropped in to the course just as Kerry was taking the girls through blending in the skin tones with any prosthetics, like scars or false noses and how to age someone. Kerry explained that she had worked in film as well as theatre but that the level of work necessary to satisfy the camera was much more demanding, and she showed them how to make a complexion a little more sallow and how to grey up someone's hair, impressing Kelly, no end. Kelly listened and watched as Kerry wove her magic creating additions to her volunteer in the chair which were practically indiscernible from the real thing, and when there was a break for tea in the afternoon when the other girls had gone down the street for coffees, Kelly helped himself to a small selection of wigs, beards and moustaches of which there were many, and some basic foundation greying powder and spray-dye that wouldn't be missed, secreting them in the lining of his coat then wrote a message saying he had to get home to feed his dog, and left. On the way he bought The Daily Mirror and passed the two chaps in the black coats holding bibles, again. They smiled and said *God bless you* to him. He nearly said *God bless you, too,* back to them but felt silly and so just said *thanks,* and walked on.

Chapter 10

The Death of Lenin

Nobody ever knocked on his door. He stopped studying the adverts page in The Daily Mirror, put his pen down, went to his door and opened it. The two black coats were there, bibles in hand.

"Good afternoon, sir. Have you ever considered the current state of the world? The wars and conflict? Famine. Drought, and the role that Jesus Christ might have in all of this?" the first one said.

"Err…no! Sometimes?…." Kelly was wrong-footed by this.

"We'd like to talk to you about it if you have five minutes?" said the second.

"Not sure I have…. I'm a bit busy just now."

The first one moved back into the stairwell and looked up to the next landing and then leant over the banister and looked down to the floor below and then nodded to the second man still in front of Kelly who then pushed him inside with alarming strength and up the hallway as the first man entered Kelly's flat and shut the door quietly behind him. Kelly was efficiently forced onto his couch and each of the men sat next to him with the second man placing a leather-gloved hand across his chest.

"You're alarmed. Don't be."

Kelly *was* alarmed. What was happening? They weren't the usual type of housebreakers or robbers, he thought *God doesn't do things like this* and he could smell a discernible whiff of *Hai Karate, Denim* or a similar cologne from one of them that was very pleasant but nevertheless, more confusing. They were the most well-groomed thieves he'd ever met.

"What do you want? What's going on? God wouldn't approve of this, you know!"

He then thought back to last Thursday when he pretended to be an undercover CID officer when he signed-on and imagined he had the situation sussed with Threeby blowing him up to his manager who'd then felt it his duty to report that one of their signatories was impersonating a police officer.

"Really?" said the second man. "You haven't done anything?"

"Okay….okay…..I'm sorry. I just didn't want to lose a couple of day's money. I'm sorry! There's no need for all this."

"You needed some more money?" Number One quietly said to him. Number Two joined in as they went into a well-rehearsed delivery.

"There are ways of making money that don't drop you in so much shit, *Leonard*…"

"…..Kelly. Leonard Kelly. Thirty-three. No real education and been unemployed for…"

"....ever! Well, since you gave up that job turfing gardens in Livingston in 1975..."

"....and been in receipt of government assistance since then....."

".....but have been working on the black, occasionally for Joseph Delaney. Small time painter and decorator...."

"......and spending much of your time drinking in the pub opposite called...."

".....The Old Duke...."

"....and not cleaning this place which smells like an arab's arse-crack as do you.....*Leonard...*"

Kelly thought his penny had dropped with the mention of Joe and working on the black. These were investigators from the dole office, obviously. Bit extreme but...?

"I just needed a few more quid. Everybody is at it. There're no jobs that pay enough! Joe just gave me three days. I haven't killed anyone. Just charge me and take the money back. I don't care. But don't hammer Joe!"

There was a pause as they looked at each other. Number Two appeared to think deeply and then looked across to Lenni slumped near the door.

"Is it the dog?" asked Number One.

Kelly looked over at Lenni who was lying near the kitchen door apparently unaffected by this melee and utterly disinterested with Kelly's discomfort.

"The dog? Yes *it's a dog*. What about the dog?" Kelly went to get up but was pressed firmly back on the couch with a look from Number Two that read *don't be silly*.

"Is it the dog that makes this place smell so bad? But then again you've just acquired the dog, haven't you? At the funeral of…."

"…Eric Jameson. Friend? Acquaintance? Political instructor?......Do you need more money to keep the dog in the manner of which it's become accustomed?"

"I need more money, yes….but not for the dog!" Kelly was panicking and losing any sense of where this was going.

"Then for what?"

"You gave a camera to Joseph Delaney at the funeral. Why?"

Kelly's head was in a spin. "Yes…. I gave it back to him."

"…because you'd borrowed it?"

"He gave me it! For the paper! Look, who are you? What's all this about?"

"For the paper? You've been scanning The Daily Mirror regularly for a few days now. Why? Expecting to see something interesting?"

"It's not a crime to read a paper, is it?"

With that Number Two looked at number one and then stood up and turned his back. Then Number One laid a right hook onto Kelly's jaw. Kelly reeled at this very practised deed and then felt the hand of Number One grab his face and force his head into the back of the couch. Lenni raised his head as Number Two turned back to Kelly.

"How long have you known Joseph Delaney?"

"I don't know…I can't remember…."

Kelly felt the searing pain revisit his face as his jaw shifted to somewhere it had never been before. Kelly regained his vision and caught a trickle of blood seeping from a gum.

"I don't know what you're talking about!! I don't know!!"

"Well….we'd love to believe you…Leonard…" Number One said, "but you appreciate we have to be sure, so this nice man is going to ask you some more questions and you are going to be a good little smelly person and do your best to tell him the truth because if you don't…"

"Joseph Delaney was on a miner's picket-line recently and talking to people we don't like very much. Why? He's a painter and decorator." Number Two continued.

Kelly was now scared. "I don't know! I don't fucking know!!"

"Again….., said Number One, "….we'd like to believe you, Leonard but it's just the whole business with the camera." Number One smiled at him.

"Yes…the business with the camera and Joseph Delaney on the picket-line speaking to the wrong kind of people who would have a real interest in embarrassing the government at this time … if they could. Did you plan it in the pub?"

"Plan what? I haven't planned anything with anyone!"

"Did you hear anything being planned in the pub? At the funeral? Eric Jameson was a known Communist and associate of Monsignor Bruce Kent of the ANC campaign and not averse to occasional bouts of political violence, in his time. You didn't know? Every man has his history, Leonard, and it's our history that makes us, is it not? Yes, he was a Communist. Quite a committed commie, actually. Well he's a dead Commie now….*fortunately* and this was his only real friend in the world."

He walked the few feet over to the dog and began to stroke him and make reassuring little noises of; *there's a good boy...where's your master gone... has he left you?....yes he has, hasn't he?,* type phrases that Kelly knew probably were a softener to some other imminent attack. Then he started to laugh out loud. Number one smiled. Kelly frowned.

"The dog's called Lenni! That's two Lennies. Two Lennies and a red collar!"

Number One started to chuckle. Number Two addressed Kelly with much condescension,

"L-e-n-n-i, Leonard! It's an anagram of Lenin!"

Kelly was disappointed that he'd never worked that one out. But why should he, not knowing that dead Eric had been a known enemy of the state?

Then Number Two let the smile drop off his face replaced with a large-eyed possibly psychotic one, that Kelly knew was probably designed to scare him,

"We realise you're just a pawn, a patsy, as our colonial cousins say, ...an Oswald that pulled the trigger in this little fracas but if you heard any conversations in...."

"...The Old Duke."

".....about anything politically treasonous or plans to embarrass the government or any government ministers you'd be advised to let us know now."

And as he spoke to Kelly he quietly padded around the room with practised ease softening his footfall and lightly lifting the occasional item from a shelf or from on top of the TV. He had much to choose from but mostly it was books and the odd sock which had been utilised as a cloth to mop up from a tumbled beer can. His professional eye was taking in information but also looking for signs of evidence with which to corner Kelly.

Kelly was beginning to realise that these well-spoken English gentlemen were more than any DHSS investigators or CID and had an agenda currently beyond his ken but he was beginning to piece together the gravity of his situation. So Joe had gone to support the miners. So what? Kelly knew he had mates out in Bilston where there was a pit. That he was speaking to some of the union leaders wouldn't have been unusual. Joe knew a lot of people and was well-known in the south side. That Eric was a member of the Communist Party of Scotland and Ban the Bomb crusade was more than a tickle to the underside but why should he have known that? It was the camera bit that these chaps wanted to know most about. It was then Kelly realised they thought he had taken photos of Sir Clive Harrow and Justin, late of Magdelene college, Oxford, securing his career in MI6 that Friday night in the offices of the new government building and that they thought he had been put up to it by his leftie mates who wanted to attack Maggie Thatcher and her regime. As ever, despite himself and his situation, Kelly sensed an opportunity, a chance to be a part of something exciting or a chance for material gain, which would appear to any rational person a tad masochistic given the predisposition of these large chaps to their precise and well-rehearsed violence. He couldn't help it and put himself right at the centre of the drama.

"I knew they talked." He flatly said, instinctively hitting a lower register in his voice and getting eye-contact from both of them.

"That's better, Leonard. You'll feel so much better getting this off your chest. What did they talk about?"

"They always made sure nobody could hear. I knew it was politics."

"Did they change the subject when you came close?"

"Always"

Kelly had the feeling he was talking himself into a deathly spiral. But it was they who wanted something from him and he guessed that given this was the strong arm of government security pressing him and anything they would do to Joe could never be laid at his door and so he wrestled slightly with his conscience but consoled himself with the fact he had taken two decent pops to the jaw and deserved something in return.

"So you heard nothing? No talk of miners or pickets or police chiefs?"

"No."

"Union leaders?"

"No."

"That's really quite convenient, Leonard." Number Two said, then paused thoughtfully.

"What do you fear most, Leonard? That we may hurt you?" he said.

"No."

"Then what? We have no real interest in you. You're nobody. In fact, now that I've received your hospitality, in your own home, I feel sorry for you. You are a quite sad little man, aren't you? What happened that it all came to this when you squandered away the best years of your life on welfare and beer? This flat looks like you. Pathetic. Spent. Noxious. Quietly ridiculous, given that you've got yourself involved in this little episode. Where did they intend to sell the pictures? The Mirror? Did they approach you knowing you would be in the building? Was the late shift a set-up? The Sun wouldn't buy them and they are far too tawdry for The Express. They support the government. They like Maggie. Or was Delaney going to overstretch himself, pay you and dabble in blackmail, himself? Because that would be overstretching, Leonard, you know that don't you? He might yet, have to have an accident driving to work, one morning. A hit and run. The driver never found. Gone. Delaney gone. Is it political, Leonard or do you just want a few shilling for your trouble? Which one is it Leonard? Let me guess. Money? Right? Your money could be stopped indefinitely with the stroke of a pen, little man….you fear that, don't you?"

"Poverty's a great motivator. Ask my mother."

"Then we should talk about money if money is all you want. You can be the architect of your own wealth if you play ball with us and lose Delaney as a partner. After all, he didn't care about you did he? He just used you. He wasn't big enough to get the shots himself, was he? He put you in danger, though. You, Mr Kelly....*Leonard.* Why should you do anything for him?"

There was a knock at the door. The two men looked at each other and then Number One put his finger to his lips instructing Kelly to be quiet.

"Expecting anyone, Leonard?" said Number Two, gently.

"No."

"We'll just wait, then. Let them go. Be very quiet Leonard..." Number One said visually tightening the glove onto his hand.

Another knock. Number Two indicated that he would creep to the door. He put his ear to the door when a voice said,

"It's Justin."

Number Two turned the latch and pulled him in. He indicated he should not talk and pulled him into the living room where Kelly recognised him as Sir Clive's cock-sucking consort and he returned a dark look to Kelly.

Number Two leaned into his ear and threateningly growled, "Say your name again and I'll cut your tongue out."

Justin, aggrieved yet still deferential offered, "We have other places to be."

Number One drilled his eyes into Justin who knew he had acted impulsively in leaving the car and coming up to the flat when told to stay where he was. A silence dropped into the room as Number Two considered his next move.

"You never offered tea, Leonard…. but we'll take the negatives and be on our way…"

"Please…" smiled Number One creaking the leather glove and then said looking at Justin, "Which head looks best in the snaps. There's three to choose from?"

"Negatives?" Kelly knew what they were talking about but wanted to continue the deluded patsy act entirely in the knowledge that they didn't exist anyway.

"Yes the negatives. We'll take them now."

"I don't have them. You don't think I'd keep them here, do you. I saw you at the funeral. You were in Livingston when I was. Do you think I'm an idiot?"

Number Two considered Kelly for a moment and then saw *The Good Soldier Sveyk* on the arm of the couch. He leaned over and picked it up.

"Sveyk. He was an idiot, wasn't he? Declared his idiocy and avoided going to the front as a result. Right? Very clever. Very clever self-preservation. Do you read much of this *fuck the establishment* shit, Leonard?" and with that had a look around the room with a slow wander looking at other titles scattered around.

" Jaroslav Hasek was a waster, too, wasn't he?"

"You mean as well as me?" Kelly said.

"Well if the shoe fits….?"

Kelly had begun to warm to the role and ironically began to feel quite alive, however narcissistic, being compared to a European writer of great renown, albeit in not so glowing terms, however a famed author, nonetheless and now, with one knock on the door he was now negotiating with the British Secret Service, probably MI6 if they think he'd photographed the Defence Secretary delivering his seed to his nepotistic new intern, and he was deep in a mistaken mire of a potential scandal that could rock the British Government, which he ridiculously refused to clarify. His ego flared.

"Hasek was very good one according to the preface." Kelly sneered.

"Oh you read the preface? We read what we need to just to get the overall traitorous evaluation of this type of excrement. Who gave you this? Jameson?"

Kelly was enjoying jousting with the obvious superior in this double-act,

"Yes. Eric. You can have it after me if you want. I'm nearly finished and I'm sure you'd identify with the protagonist."

That was a mistake.

Number One's leather glove bounced off his jaw in the same place as the other two.

"We know you still have them, Leonard. The Negatives. We've watched every significant move and rendezvous you have made since you took them and they weren't in the camera you gave to Delaney at the funeral. Yes, we had *the gasman* visit him looking for reported leaks the minute he got back from the funeral. Don't worry, he'll never know. Unless you tell him, Leonard? That was your Mother you went to visit. I don't imagine you'd like her mixed up in all this?

"She doesn't know anything. She's not well."

"Really? Pass on our get-well sentiments, next time you see her, then. What idiot parks an articulated lorry in a side-street?"

"That was my uncle Gerry...."

"Malone...." Number one said.

"Yes. He's an arse, Ex-army right-wing knob. Don't worry he's on your side."

"Yes, we know. Done the checks." Number one said, again. Number two continued,

"You didn't meet your rendezvous when you got off the bus, yesterday in the middle of nowhere. Why didn't they pick you up? Did they see us? You did have a rendezvous? Did they tell you just to walk and they'd stop for you?"

Kelly rubbed his face and played the resolute suspect very well, saying,

"I don't know if they saw you. Maybe. The negatives aren't here."

"Have you developed them? Are there prints?"

"No."

Another right hook deftly bounced off of his jaw. He turned grimacing to Number One.

"What the fuck was that one for? I just said *No!*"

"Well… it's because we know you're lying to us, now. Why is there a red light bulb in your toilet and the door edge taped up? That your little developing room? Really Leonard? You're not very good at all this are you?"

Kelly began to wonder if there was some other unknown power of coincidence working for him, here. Either way, his fatalistic ego was glowing amongst all of the imminent danger and smell of espionage. He decided to preserve his face, which was beginning to swell up, and he could feel his eye closing over, so passively said,

"Okay, Sherlock....you got me."

Justin stood at the living room door quietly observing.

"We have a mole at in Fleet Street Leonard. We will know if they ever get near publication.... by any paper." Number One said.

"Number Two asked, "What did they offer?"

Kelly's head, at the mention of money, leapt into action, "I don't know. Joe was talking to them."

"But you still have them?"

"Yes. Not here"

"We will strike a small bargain with you Leonard. You *destroy* the negatives and we won't *destroy* you...*and* we might give you some money. In the meantime you destroy the negatives and any prints you've already made. Yes?"

Kelly looked at them and said nothing. Number two looked at number one then back to Kelly.

"Yes?" he repeated.

A silence hung for a few seconds as Kelly apparently mulled over his options. Then Justin went over to Lenni and started to stroke him making small noises of affection. The other two shared a look of disbelief at the timing and both knew would entail a discussion later.

Kelly wasn't sure what the reference to *destroy* actually meant here? Actual death or the ruination of one's health and wealth. He asked,

"…by *destroy me*….I presume you mean…"

The discussion was interrupted by Justin getting the dog to its feet and then putting the leash onto Lenni's choker collar, one that tightened as a dog pulled, and threw the the other end of the leash over the top of the door and then started hauling Lenni slowly up the face of the door. Lenni found a vitality in his movement that had rarely been seen of late as his legs paddled, flapped and scraped the paint on the door, his paws scratching and the sound being subsumed into a loud gulping and discernible whine as the dog struggled to find air. Justin held the dog halfway up, one hand holding the leash and addressed Kelly.

"If those negatives and photos aren't destroyed, you unseemly pile of crud, then I will personally ensure that *this*…." throwing his eyes to the gasping dog " ….becomes *your* end. Do you understand, shithead? I do not want Sir Clive's pictures bandied onto, of anything, the *tabloid* media. For me, I have a congenital disposition toward outlandish and quite dangerous behaviour, whereby it would be rude of me never to one day grace their slovenly seedy rags but it seems this isn't my time, but Sir Clive, who is now *my friend,* I will protect with every fibre of my very being….. do you understand me, you odious little rat?"

Kelly watched horrified as Lenni stopped struggling and his tongue lolled sideways out of his mouth.

Justin looked over at the other two men and then to the stillness of Lenni. Kelly's, jaw despite the swelling, drooped open as he tried to comprehend what he had just witnessed. He looked at Justin as if he wanted to say something. Nothing came out.

"I think he understands!" Justin said and let Lenni drop to the floor in a lifeless heap. "Shall we *go* now?"

The three of them started for the door and Justin led the way. Kelly played one more desperate card.

"Two thousand pounds!"

Number Two wheeled around.

"That's my price to destroy the negatives. The prints! I have them. I can tell Joe they were exposed and failed! I'll destroy them for two thousand pounds!"

Number two looked at Kelly and then to the unsightly and disorganised nightmare that was his flat and thought Kelly's price very cheap.

"We'll be in touch. Don't do anything *rash*, Leonard because we know where you go and what you do, which really that isn't interesting, but unfortunately our boss insists. Oh….. and find out how Trotsky died."

Then he turned and left, almost silently closing the door.

Chapter 11

Top Chairs

DC Jones dropped some coins into a vending machine and selected black coffee with three sugars. The machine hummed into action while Jones had a look at her watch and then had a look down the carpeted corridor with several rooms on the right side and a big communal room on the left with a loud TV playing the sombre tune of *Crown Court*. She retrieved her coffee and sat down on a soft chair opposite a reception desk and smiled at the young girl on the desk wearing a blue tabard, who then spoke to Jones.

"Do they know you're here?" she smiled again offering a little frown with it designed to indicate sympathy.

"No, no…. I'm not…..I mean yes. Yes. I'm with someone who's visiting. I've just come in to get a coffee."

The girl smiled and went back to writing in a large ledger book occasionally checking it with a pile of small hand-written dockets.

Jones was clearly unsure about something and flicked a look to the door here and there as she looked at her watch. She then made a decision and stood up and walked towards the double doors of the front entrance ten feet away and spoke to the young girl.

"I think I'll just….." and she pointed out into the well-maintained front garden.

"The roses are out by the side wall. There's a lovely bench we put there for some of our residents there if it's too warm in here? You can smell the roses." the girl said.

Then a voice behind Jones abruptly broke the horticultural lesson.

"I think we left the car on double yellows, Jones. Maybe you should check that we don't have a parking ticket!"

DI McQuarrie gave Jones a look that could melt bricks and she walked out onto the path and out of the arched gate. McQuarrie then turned to the girl on reception, immediately morphing to genial besuited professional and began quietly to ask about monthly outgoings as the young girl turned the ledger book around to let DI McQuarrie clarify his inquiries, and then he took out his wallet.

Jones got into the car just as the radio hissed a message, which she took and told the person at the other end that they were on their way to but had met heavy traffic. She put the coffee on top of the dashboard and put her head against the steering wheel in apparent exasperation. She stayed there for a few moments and lifted her head just as her boss was crossing the road towards the car. He got into the passenger seat and stared out of the front windscreen. He was obviously wrestling with a negative conundrum and sighed just as Jones said,

"We have to get over to Leith pretty quickly, Sir. There's been an incident at a scrapyard. They've just called asking how long before we get there?"

McQuarrie turned to her and quietly said,

"I asked you not to come in there."

"I was getting you coffee, Sir. I know they have a vending machine."

"Aren't there other shops here?"

"We parked on the main road! You don't want to walk far, you said? I didn't know how long you'd be! Sometimes you're in there for an hour or more. If I'd gone to get you coffee at another shop and you came out you'd have bollocked me, sir. I can't win!"

McQuarrie looked at the coffee on the dashboard and held out his hand to Jones who then passed it tentatively over to McQuarrie. He took a sip and sighed again then flicked his other hand in a tired forward direction and said,

"Leith."

McQuarrie and Jones made their way across town to what appeared to be an accident but had undertones of disharmony among the business partners and one accused the other of deliberately trying to hurt him with a huge mechanical grab that lifted scrap cars onto a pile and shouted *attempted murder* loudly. There were some other accusations of fraudulent bookkeeping, to which McQuarrie feigned professional interest and got Jones to do the interviews while he busied himself with the sequence of facts that occurred. *She had to learn,* he thought, which excused him from dedicating his disinterested self entirely to the situation. They remained there for much of the afternoon and close to the end of their shift, to which McQuarrie gathered and collated the requisite information and assured the rebellious partners that a follow-up investigation would happen at some unspecified time later in the week and that they'd be in touch. He then tiredly told Jones to take the car home that night and pick him up in the morning.

Before that, Jones dropped McQuarrie off at The Old Duke. It was Friday and he needed a drink.

It was now nearly six o'clock and The Duke was empty. Norrie was behind the bar as McQuarrie entered and sat down at his usual seat. He looked over to where Eric used to sit. Norrie poured him his pint and lifted it signalling to McQuarrie as he placed it on the dark, flecked grain of Hector. McQuarrie heaved himself up and over to Norrie and sighed with little apparent energy to make the return journey.

"Cheers Norrie." He said and took a heavy draught of the dark liquid. He then looked at Norrie as if to survey him and then turned to look at the room taking in the rough boarded windows with the flaking paint, the tall wooden seats fixed to the wall, the nicotine stained ceiling and back to Norrie and his beer-stained Farah slacks with a final look to the old wooden shelves behind Hector, dustily bedecked with bottles of whisky, which nobody ever bought, to the optics and finally back to Norrie. McQuarrie let the philosophical expression drop off his face and forced a beaming smile at Norrie which he held for a few seconds whereby it became uncomfortable and not a little unnerving for the usually dour and stolid, Norrie.

Then McQuarrie spoke.

"This is easy, isn't it Norrie? All this. Not much to it is there? Order the beer. Sell it to the proles and pocket the profit. Clean up the shite they leave behind, run the floor over with a cloth and give the bogs a quick skoosh with Domestos. Open up and do it all again. Easy."

"Bit more than that…" Norrie said, "….but more or less, aye."

Norrie was never inclined to be inquisitive but he detected a sea-change of some description in McQuarrie. Something at McQuarrie's core, possibly philosophical, life questioning or some sort of territory like that and really didn't like those conversations that forced meaningful opinion out of him or maudlin sentiment. Far too un-Scottish, but he felt that to retain the presence of Plod in *The Duke* was always a bonus when the locals went native, so he squeezed out a,

"Feelin' the pace?"

McQuarrie looked at him as if to say *really?* and then just started to laugh which unnerved Norrie but he also felt somewhat offended because nobody ever gets to laugh at Norrie because it's his pub, he's the boss and much as McQuarrie was an apparent ally, this was still his place, however, he didn't say anything and let McQuarrie's rasping cackle disseminate into the silence of the room. Then McQuarrie said,

"I'm barefoot, Norrie and my shorts are arseless, I've still got a few laps to go ..and it's hurtin'! Does that help?"

It didn't help at all, actually but Norrie was happy because McQuarrie eased himself back over to his table and became absorbed in his little black book. He studied it appeared to think and made notes for the next hour without a word or acknowledgement as one by one the Brylcreem Boys arrived and took up their positions at Hector. Bullet came in still dressed in his overalls and looking dusty but incorrigibly content went straight through Dick, into the toilet, washed his face and took off his overalls, came out, bought a pint and took the centre seat at Stan. Twenty minutes later Spider arrived, naturally dressed in black, and smiled up at Bullet and got himself a pint and joined him. Time passed and the pub filled up with regulars. McQuarrie drank heavily. Sasquatch arrived and did no more than he usually did dropping a substantial area of the room into shadow. Joe came in shortly after in a paint-flecked shirt and old suit trousers and joined

Spider and Bullet at Stan.

"Where's May?" Spider asked.

Bullet said, "I'm not long here. My usual lift didn't come to work today, so I had to come across town on the bus and it was packed solid, so it was. I had to sit next to a big fat guy. He just had a white shirt on and you could see his tits inside his shirt. They were like really big for a guy. Really big. But hairy. All around his nipples……"

Joe cut off Bullet's digression.

"Okay, Jackanory, ye'll be makin' May jealous, Bullet, with all this talk o' tits…if she was here."

"….massive so they were….for a guy. Why do guys have tits, Spider?"

"Keeps the heart balanced and stops the lungs from gettin' too heavy on one side." smiled Spider.

"What d'you mean? That right, Joe? How do they balance the heart?"

"They don't Bullet. Spider's just ribbin' you son. Wake up."

"You just messin' with me, Spider? Was that just a pig-in-a-joke?"

"Yes. So where's May, Joe?"

Joe was still shaking his head at Bullet but turned angrily which surprised everyone.

"What you asking me for? Who am I? Her brother!"

Bullet's standard response for confrontation kicked in,

"Whooooaaaahhh……"

Spider was just as surprised and held up both of his arms

"Alright mate...just thought you might know...that's all. Not noising you up, or anything...just asking...."

"I don't know!" Joe spat in finality.

An entirely new conversational stimulus entered the pub in the shape of Kelly. He walked in and looked up at Stan from the door. His left eye was slightly closed, reddened and he had a puffy jaw. DI McQuarrie had a double-take at this but then smiled and went back to his newspaper, notebook and whisky.

Kelly went over to Hector and looked at Norrie who looked back and said nothing but let his eyes momentarily betray his determined disinterest flitting to the area of Kelly's face. They just looked at each other. Kelly knew that his face was worthy of inquiry and that Norrie was never going to give way to a dishonest interest as to his well-being but just wanted him to ask, let alone politely enquire what he would like to drink. It was at that moment that Kelly became uncomfortable in the groin area and squirmed slightly. Then he knew it was going to have to be a full on bollock-shift from present discomfiting position and reached down and made a quick movement to a satisfactory end all the while retaining his eye-contact with Norrie. Norrie's eyes dropped south for a second taking in the shift, which confirmed his disgust for Kelly. However, Kelly was in no mood to jibe with the brickbat exterior of this miserable example of humanity and so stood resolute in front of him with Hector separating them and only their individual determination not to wilt to the ridiculous notion of common courtesy.

One of the Brylcreem Boys arrived at the bar to get a new round and observed this stand-off which had apparently arrived from nowhere but in truth was the culmination of years of Kelly's cutting remarks, superior detached distaste and mutual loathing. The Brylcreem Boy craned his neck slightly and noted the swelling on Kelly's face and the reddened eye and then looked to Norrie and wondered if he'd walked in on the quietest fight in history. He looked at Norrie, bemused, and then to Kelly. Norrie broke the eyeballed exchange and turned to the Brylcreem Boy and asked with a nod what he wanted, who was about to speak when Kelly abruptly said,

"Pint!"

Norrie continued serving the Brylcreem boy.

"Pint, please, Norman! I believe you were serving me?" Kelly was obviously in a state of irritation at Norrie's contempt.

At that point Megan came into the pub with some young and very fashionable friends. There were two young men dressed in charity shop baggy trousers and old suit jackets with short back and side haircuts, one with a quiff and two other young women wearing 1970's dresses of gaudy colours. Megan was laughing much too loudly at the quips of the young men and told them to take a seat, which they did at Eric's table, much to the chagrin of DI McQuarrie, now four pints and whiskies to the good, then went to the bar and stood beside Kelly. She didn't recognise him at first but as he turned to look at her she gasped and asked what had happened.

"I'm sorry Megan, I was in the middle of retelling that very tale to your venerable father, here, as he was serving me a pint of my favourite brew. Weren't you Norrie!!"

Megan immediately discerned a tension and went behind Hector and got Kelly his pint and the drinks her friends wanted and took Kelly back to their table.

"Kells.." she said, "....this is Annabel, Luccia, Tom and Jericho. What the holy hell happened?"

Kelly knew they were some of her new varsity chums who he acknowledged were very well turned out, quite, quite healthy with middle-class clear skin complexions and smelled delightful. Megan had obviously begun to use the linguistic idioms of her new acquaintances, *holy hell happened* etc., which was alliterative, he noted, so he guessed there was part of her that was still with him and not entirely with these sparklingly shiny people she had recently found.

Jericho spoke,

"Did you have a fight with someone, man?"

Kelly racked his brains quickly and concluded that he had never been in a conversation before which included the syntactical addendum, *man,* and smiled inwardly and considered whether to adopt said idiom, to whit, he again concluded that it might be construed as ridicule, embarrass Megan, which may inhibit the potential of them wrestling in drunken coital union at any chosen point in the future and so just said,

"Yeah…well sort of….erm…sorry, what's your name again?"

Megan quickly blurted out, "Jericho!" patently pleased with her new friend's moniker.

"*Jerry's* cool, man." Jericho said in his southern English accent.

"You shouldn't boast….like that!" Annabel clumsily threw in and they all chuckled at her witless joviality.

It then occurred to Kelly that he was now in a conversation with Tom and Jerry and as that bizarre fact lodged in his head, the past week of events in his life rounded on him, gathered in a ridiculous pose of lunacy as he imagined the Glaswegian plumbers, Driscoll the wino, Joe, Threeby, MI6 One and Two, Floppy-haired blondie, Lenni, Kat Noh, The Pumping Tracksuit, the prostitute and his sad fat uncle, all formed in a semi-circle blankly staring at him as if in a scene from *The Village of the Damned*. Then he started to laugh. He was aware that Jericho might think he was laughing at him and imagined the vision of a quite cross Megan refusing his sexual advances, so he said….

"Sorry, man….. I'm not laughing at you…."

Man! An involuntary sidling into a verbal niche that has patently pleased Megan because he saw the edge of a smile curl onto her grid as he said it. Megan was indeed delighted at Kelly's attempt to fit in with her new chums and was even more giddy when Luccia said,

"I love your coat. They are right back in and you can't find a good one in the second-hand shops for love nor money, these days."

"What happened?" Annabel frowned caringly.

Kelly went to work.

"I was out on The Meadows with Lenni…..my dog…and he was attacked by a very big Alsation….

"Alsation?" Luccia seemed confused.

"German Shepherd." Tom said.

"Got you. Thanks T." she bounced back.

"This thing was massive….I mean it had muscles on muscles and teeth like Alpine peaks….."

Alpine peaks! Where did that come from? As it turned out, they'd all been skiing. He thought it interesting that he could drop into the contours of *theirspeak*, almost at will and continued,

"It got Lenni down on the grass and started to really have a go, biting and trying to get Lenni's neck and I tried to get it off but then it started on me and I had to get away. Then I ran at it and tried to kick it and then right out of nowhere I felt something smash into my face and I fell onto the ground. As it turned out it was the Als…*German Shepherd's* owner who was a most unsalubrious Bill Sykes type of chap, a version of the dog actually, and he'd hit me with a small branch of a tree that he was throwing for the dog right across the face."

Megan affected a quite dramatic open-mouthed gasp for the gathering and said,

"Kelly! A branch of a tree!"

"Yeah...it wasn't nice. When I looked up, when I could see again, he'd got his dog back on the leash and was high-tailing it away over the road and into the streets. He knew he was wrong and just took off."

Jericho piped up,

"How's your dog, man?"

Kelly went right into Sophie mode and just looked at them and pursed his lips and then shifted to the middle-distance as if struggling with the narrative and quickly appeared to extricate himself from the painful memory by taking a mouthful of beer.

Tom said, "No way, man! Shit that's rough. What a bummer."

Megan, however, looked like Megan again when she said quite honestly,

"Lenni's dead?"

Kelly nodded, "He made it home and I tried to give him some milk and something to eat but he just refused. I sat with him for a while, just stroking and talking to him and then he just...slipped away."

"Fucker should be in front of a magistrate by tomorrow morning!" Jericho offered.

Then a rasping voice entered the fray.

"I quite agree! He should be hauled up and publicly flogged, put into the stocks in the village square and pelted with terribly rotten vegetables."

McQuarrie was now liberally sauced and in a real *what-the-fuck* mood.

The small assembly straightened at his sarcasm.

"Did you get a good look at this fucker? The fucker that hit you? Did you see his face?" McQuarrie slurred.

Kelly groaned inwardly at the arrival of McQuarrie to the conversation thinking back to what he had said to him at Eric's funeral and the fact that he was well lubricated.

"No. I just saw him walking away."

"Walking? Walking? Who walks away after committing an act of Actual Bodily Harm and having, having…..his dog kill another dog in a broad public….space….? Who….eh?"

Kelly considered placation the best form of parry.

"Walking….hurrying…. I was dazed…. Lenni wasn't killed there…"

"What was he wearing…?"

Kelly just made up, "Checked shirt and jeans."

McQuarrie's delight in the description and in pressing Kelly was written all over his now attentive but still drunken face.

"A checked shirt…..great, now we're getting somewhere! Blue check? Red check?"

"Red."

"Witnesses?"

"I don't know! I was busy being hit by a big bit of wood and lying *out of it* on the grass!"

"But there must've been someone there who saw it…..the attack….or you lying there *out of it?* People use The Meadows. Joggers? Other dog walkers? Nobody helped you or the dog?"

"No! No! Nobody helped me! I just wanted to get home…ok!! I was sore and bleeding."

"Did you get medical help? Go to the Doctor? A and E?" Where were you bleeding from? I can't see a cut?"

Kelly knew that McQuarrie was, ironically, a dog with a bone, drunk and harboured much antipathy for him.

" I….was bleeding from my mouth. From my mouth."

Tom leaned over and said, "Come on fella! The guys obviously suffering. There's no need for all this, you know. I mean who are you, man, the police?"

Megan's head dropped. McQuarrie smiled.

"Well actually… yes I am, young chappie ma lad. I am the police. DI McQuarrie at your service." And with that he flashed his ID.

"Look….Mr McQuarrie…..", Kelly said

"DI McQuarrie. Detective Inspector…"

"I was hit on the head…across the face… I was in pain. I just wanted to get me and the dog home."

McQuarrie eyeballed Kelly, "Lenni….the dog's name is…*was* Lenni."

Jerry backed his bunner, "Tom's got a point, you know*, Detective*

Inspector, maybe this isn't the right time to be *helping him*." making the quotation marks with his fingers in the air.

McQuarrie laughed. More sarcasm, "Helping him? No, no, no, no, no.... you frightfully freshfaced boy with nice hair and perfect teeth.... I don't want to help him... I just want to get to the truth! I don't think he knows what the truth is."

McQuarrie then leaned in to the table and put his finger over his lips to indicate their silence, beckoned them to lean in, which only Annabel did, looked around as if to check there was nobody listening and then covertly said,

"He tells stories. No, no hear me out, he does. Makes things up. I've heard him. He thinks I don't listen…but I do. It's my job! It's my job to listen in pubs. People get drunk and say things, things that might be useful to a listening secret policeman or they pretend to be people that they're not and do things that they shouldn't and I can see them, I can see them not being them…"

Then he winked and threw a pointed finger into the mix just to nail his point.

"Whatever, man. You're drunk and Megan's friend is suffering!"

"Yes but tomorrow I will be sober but you will still be a middle-class, posh English prick…..*man*!"

McQuarrie inwardly reprimanded himself for the racism, classism, xenophobia, whatever it was and for appropriating Winston Churchill's riposte to an ugly woman who disapproved of his drinking and it quickly saddened him. His father would never have condoned that attack and this also in shadow of his old friend, Eric, a man of that generation who refused to be taught to hate. That thought of Eric and his father and the alcohol changed his mood. He also saw Megan openly embarrassed by his behaviour, who didn't deserve this.

"Tell me son…..what's your name…?"

"It's Jerry, actually!"

"Well, *Mr Actually*...tell me what Tom knows about suffering, if you would...*please?*"

Luccia to the rescue.

"Everyone suffers. It's part of the human condition."

Kelly squirmed and put a hand over his face. McQuarrie homed in on her.

"Where are you from, you lovely little ball... of lovely *bally* things...?

Kelly said to himself *don't* but Luccia, in proud defence of her regionality said,

"Chester! Why?"

"Chester!!.....Chester....a stronghold of the Roman empire in Britain for a hundred years. You could be Roman, my pretty! A daughter of Mithras. You could be descended from the rape of a Cestrian goose-girl by a penurious patrician senator! How about that? You like the thought of that don't you...don't you? Your middle-class English accent gives away your breeding like an advert on the side of a bus. But I don't hate you for it. What's your name?"

Luccia maintained the façade of hostility to the nasty drunk man but glowed inside at the description he made of her potential heritage and so couldn't resist the fact that she had a very Italian name, and so said,

"Luccia."

"There you go!...There you fucking go!! Was I right Kelly Redface? Was I? I was right wasn't I, Megan? Your posh English friend is a fucking Roman goose girl humped by the nobility and descended down to us, here. Tell me little goose girl, did you suffer when the big Roman Centurion thrust in his salty sword? Did the bastard slide out easily. Or did you suffer? Was the midwife good?"

"Just ignore him, Luccia." Jericho said flatly.

"I've got it Jerry, don't worry." She replied.

McQuarrie started to chuckle.

"Am I in a cartoon, here or an episode of Jeeves and fucking Wooster? Tom and Jerry? Luccia? What's your name, love?" he asked Annabel. "Portia? Rosalind? Jocasta?"

Annabel, Luccia, Tom and Jericho all looked at Megan in unison to either blame her for bringing them to this nicotine-stained wooden box of confrontation, which was somewhat hypocritical of them having previously assured Megan it was a part of Edinburgh's old town that was *real and alive and most probably nothing short of bloody charming, thank you very much!*

Megan settled for,

"Maybe you've had too much, Mr McQuarrie?"

"You reckon, Megan? Too much of what? The shit life throws at you? Or trying to keep body and soul together surviving on thin memories and unfulfilled dreams."

McQuarrie went silent for a moment or two as did they. He stood up, put his notebook in his inside pocket at the third attempt and picked up his newspaper. He held the newspaper like a torch in the middle of their table and said,

*"Tomorrow and tomorrow and tomorrow…*I'm going to ask some questions and make a few notes when I have sufficiently regained my sobriety and if I find out that dog died in any other way than

you say it did, Kelly, I'll make you the sorriest man in Scotland…and then you will know *the truth* about suffering….."

McQuarrie left the door open. Megan got up and shut it. Annabel said,

"Well that was a bit heavy."

"Sorry, I've never seen him drunk, before." Megan said looking at the door.

"Well he's gone now." Annabel said brightly. "Let's have a good drink. You need a good drink don't you…erm.."

"Kelly." Kelly said.

"Don't get pissed, Anna! You know what you're like!" Tom growled.

"Bloody well will if I want to! I don't have to revise tomorrow. One more final next week then it's all over for me."

Kelly thought this somewhat ironic knowing that her life was far from over and only just beginning and he wanted to change the subject and garner favour once more with Megan and he had a bit of a mission tonight, if it worked out.

"What are you studying?"

"Politics! Bloody boring! Wish I'd done Phil. What do you do Kelly?"

"Well, nothing, just now, I suppose. I'm one of Maggie's chosen few."

"I'd love a year on the dole!" Annabel said, who was quiet when McQuarrie was there but had a *Bright Young Thing* joie de vivre bubbling beneath that shy exterior.

"Really?" said Kelly, "It's not that attractive, you know. Food and rent, bills. All of the stuff that keeps us in one piece." Hypocrisy radiated through him.

Annabel then said, "I'd stay at Dad's place in the Cotswolds and write a fucking bestseller."

Then Megan realised she had to big up Kelly a little to fit in more.

"Actually that's not entirely true is it Kells? I mean you do a bit of work for Joe, now and then, don't you….?

Kelly smiled and shushed her, mockingly at the danger of being overheard.

"….and you now do Drama stuff as well, right?"

Kelly knew he had to maximise the material.

"Yes. I suppose…." Cod modesty.

Tom offered, "I'm in the Drama Soc. at uni. Doing an Aristophanes piece just now. Fucking shit. I don't like the Greeks. Got a production on the go, just now?"

"Scheduled for the autumn. Working on a bit of Stanislavski, just now."

Luccia gurgled, "Wow….I know about him! If you're going to play a farmer you don't wash for three months. Right?"

Kelly took the opportunity to smile as if humouring someone he didn't want to offend and Jerry picked up on Kelly's affected care.

"There's more to it than that Cheeya!! Don't be so fucking thick! Sorry Kelly, man."

"No, no…it's cool…."

He never said *cool*.

"…..there is a bit more to it, yes but essentially Luccia has it right. It's all about preparation for the role."

Something akin to jealousy occurred in Megan when Kelly said Luccia's name and she wasn't expecting it. None of this group were attached to each other and she realised that Kelly could possibly be a potential mate for one of these girls who were younger and prettier and brighter than her. Megan heard herself say,

"Why don't you show us some of the things you do, Kells?"

She made much of the contracted version of his name, which was *hers* and hers alone. There was then general approbation and approval with some *yeahs* and *it'll be a blast, man* and *I'll give it a go*. Kelly explained that there wasn't a great deal of room to do anything physical, where they were and so decided to offer a session of Hot-Seating, which required chairs and talking, only. Luccia enthusiastically declared that she wanted to do it and decided that her character was a Cestrian goose-girl who had lately been raped by a Roman Centurion and was fighting to stop her brother going on a quest to kill the Centurion as a matter of family honour because he was likely to get killed, himself.

Kelly outlined the exercise and offered to start the process by asking her name. Luccia loved this and declared her name was,

"Boudicca Postlethwaite!" and all her yah friends nodded approvingly at her choice of name the first being *bloody lovely* and the other *sooo common*.

Jerry asked, "What's your job?"

"I'm a goose-girl. I'm a very good looking goose-girl, bare-footed in a rough muslin dress just above the knee but the sunlight makes it near bloody see-through but I wear a flower which pokes out from under my tresses of long hair. I take the geese out onto the stubble fields and there they all feed *on the stubble*....obviously.", Luccia gurgled relishing her fantasy.

Annabel joined in, "Why do you say you are good-looking, Boudicca?

"Because the soldiers all want me to polish their swords! They've all seen me stroking the geese…"

Kelly smirked at the euphemism and her description and felt a stirring in The Trossachs.

"…which all the geese like very well and they all thought that someone who's generally good at stroking would be good at stroking their swords and keeping them nice and sharp."

Jericho snorted, " You are such a tart, Cheeya!"

"I know but I love this. Let's do it some more! Oh fuckage! That's me out of character now when I didn't want to stop!"

"Is that what the Roman soldiers say to you, then….too…as well…?" Annabel awkwardly trying again to be a wit.

Just then Joe was walking back from the toilet and he asked Kelly what happened to his face to which Kelly made an approximation of the story he told earlier to spare his new friends. Megan decided that he needed a whisky, on her of course not her Dad, and went to fetch one from the bar. Kelly introduced Megan's friends while Joe looked at him quizzically wondering what the fuck he was hanging around with these for? Kelly got the message and told him they were Megan's new chums from uni and what they were doing was something that he'd been doing on his drama course to which Joe told him that it was *lovely darling* and that if it was that good he should try it out on Spider because if he could make Spider talk about himself it would be a minor miracle and that he'd furnish Kelly with one of The Old Duke's finest whiskies. Kelly picked up the gauntlet but said that he had to go to the toilet first and got up and pushed his way past Dick and into the loo. He went quickly into one of the cubicles and tried to lock the door which was unlockable because…..well… it had no lock. He remained standing and undid his trouser button and slid down the zip and then started fumbling in his underpants occasionally looking down. It was dark in the Duke's toilet and he struggled to see what he was doing. He had another look down and there was a very obvious click.

The sound of someone coming into the toilet made Kelly immediately alert and he went still and quiet. He could hear them approach the urinal and unzip their flies.

Then he heard a strange hissing noise at which he thought was the sound of the urinal user sending a steaming spiral onto the porcelain but was quite unusual for a piss and then suddenly from nowhere he heard his own voice say,

"Testing, testing…to be or not to be that is the question….testing testing….one two three….."

Panic! He thrust his hand into his crotch and another click was heard and silence set itself suspiciously across the void of the toilet. Kelly held his breath. Stillness and quiet resumed. He waited for three good breaths and a count to three in his head and pulled the overhanging chain to flush.

He pulled the cubicle door open and slowly leaned out. He looked to the urinals to his right. No-one. Relief. Turning to his left would take him back to the bar but towering there was Sasquatch. He had a fixed stare on Kelly. Kelly stared back. His trouser arrangement dropped an inch. He quickly adjusted it. Sasquatch looked at his crotch then back to Kelly's gaze. Kelly, presented with this anomaly of humanity was quite unsure of how to continue with this non-conversation, so he just started to conduct voice warm-up exercises,

"Testing…, testing testing tsss….tsss kcha, kchuh, kchoo, kcheh …niminy piminy….. mmmnaa….mmmnaaah…"

Which he had seen Kat do at *Theatre Skills*, once before she addressed the group.

"Got a big show in a few weeks. Shakespeare. Just taking a moment to enjoy the acoustics in here. Got to sort out my diction......you know? Doing a bit of *Bottom*. Midsummer's Night's Dream. Not like that... *Bottom*... I mean gay....just the play...character....*Bottom*... I expect my *Bottom* will be truly outstanding." Kelly chuckled to try to get a response from Sasquatch.

Nothing from Sasquatch, just a heavy stare into Kelly's eyes. Then he looked down again at Kelly's trouser department waited a moment and then ducked under the doorway and back out into the bar.

The bar door opened at that point and a head tentatively peered into the room. A very pretty face and gay party dress leaned around the door and made eye-contact with Annabel, who loudly said,

"Juicy!! Come and join us. We're having a game of *Top Seats*...or something? Cheeya is a Roman tart!"

Their friend, Lucy, sent a brief look around the bar and the distaste was more than apparent.

"Don't think so. Not sure I'd speak the language. We're on the guest list at *The Ice Box* but I told you we're going for cocktails and coolers at The George Hotel, George Street, first. Jonathan's parents have organised this and I don't want to be fucking late, okay!"

Lucy was obviously someone who was used to being obeyed and her authority was broadly accepted by the group who started to finish their drinks. Annabel shouted,

"Megan! We have to go now?" who was still at the bar getting Kelly's whisky and talking to one of the Brylcreem Boys. Kelly came out of the toilet at that point and closed Dick firmly shut. He saw that they were in conference with this new addition to the group so stood away as they spoke.

Lucy leaned over their table and spoke in hushed tones.

"Look...I told you, earlier...we can't bring her...*Miggy, Muggy... whatever...*I can't just bring *anyone....*"

"I like her! She laughs at my jokes!" Annabel cooed in mock disappointment.

"Well... you can fucking introduce her, because I won't!" Lucy sharply said.

Megan arrived with Kelly's whisky and smiled. Kelly smiled back and looked across at the huddle.

Tom audibly spoke up, next, "Look it's not a black tie do, Juicy, for fuck's sake, anyone can attend the cocktail lounge! It's open to the public. It's a fucking hotel for fuck sake!"

Megan stood with Kelly and listened to the urgent conference.

"I agree with, Tom, Juice. We can introduce anyone we like, can't we? I mean, having someone new who is *actually Scottish from Edinburgh?* would be the ratherest thing....." Luccia simpered.

"It's not just that..." Lucy hesitated, "....somewhat *vulgar...* but there's the money?"

"I'll step up if it's an issue. Got my American Express card, last week. No problem."
Jericho said.

Megan picked up the central discussion. Kelly saw her face drop.

"What about the varsity issue, Jerry?" Lucy countered, "I mean, could it be said a real course was ever attended at uni?"

Kelly, from nowhere, turned to Megan and said,

"Well, it looks like I won't be going for cocktails tonight!"

Megan frowned quizzically at Kelly.

"They're deciding whether or not I'm dressed to go out with you all, tonight. They know I'm your friend and didn't want to offend you, but let's face it; it's been a while since I sipped a Manhattan wearing this outfit and with this face!"

Megan's smile betrayed her relief and delight and then her expression turned to consolation for Kelly.

"Ohhhh… another time?" Megan said with a droopy sad face just as the group disconvened.

They started to leave led briskly by Lucy.

Annabel was last to leave and blurted out halfway through the exit "Come to our *End of Finals* party on tomorrow night, Kelly! Megan's coming. You come too! Eight for eight-thirty. Bring a bottle!"

Megan looked at him with mock expectation and a hopeful smile on her face.

"Yeah……cool…. " Kelly said,

They made their goodbyes and *see you tomorrows* to Kelly and Megan grabbed her bag and squeezed out the door and got sandwiched by Tom and Jerry, which she made much of, smiling and rolling her eyes at her clottishness. Tom and Jerry held the door and Megan left as they followed. Three seconds later the door quickly opened again and Megan poked her head in and said,

"Seventeen Marchmont Road. Top flat! And I haven't forgotten about that sonnet you promised!"

Kelly smiled reassuringly at her and tapped the side of his head as if to say *it's all in here,* then she left and he was still looking at the door and wondering where his altruism arrived from when May burst in and met Kelly blocking her way. She was a little bemused with the guard of honour.

"Fuck you gawpin' at, Kells? Ye niver seen true beauty before? Fuck happened to your face? Fuck it, I don't care!"

Kelly was struck dumb for the first time in a while and May burst past him and marched up to Stan where Bullet, Joe and Spider were sitting.

"Who's shout is it? Two stout an' a nip for me!"

"Spider smiled, genuinely pleased to see her and said,

"Late tonight, May?"

"I am that, Satan, but ah've had a wee situation to sort but noo it's sorted, so git them in if it's your shout."

Bullet said he'd got the first round and then Joe said quite flatly,

"You're on your feet? Bullet'll take a Special, Dracula a Bloody Mary or whatever he wants and you know what I drink."

May dropped her face and looked coldly at him. Joe added,

"Kells! May's in the chair. Get your order in before she forgets where the bar is. We're alright for the minute....I've drawn her a map."

May held her stare but then breezily elevated her stance and visage.

"That's right Kells, I'm getting' them in, so stop droolin' efter Megan an' her pretty mates and git over to the bar and gi'e Norrie a great big kiss an' me yer order!"

Kelly joined the group at Stan and May duly did buy her round and brought it over and unusually sat next to Spider at his end of Stan. The five of them drank and talked and Kelly told the story of how he had acquired such a bruised and reddened face and of his conflict in The Meadows with the German Shepherd, because that was their proper name, until the conversation came around to Megan and her new friends. May declared loudly that she would have *got a hold of the dog's nuts* and not let go and that Megan's friends were short-term acquaintances and far too posh to be seen in the Duke and that she had heard their English accents as she came in and while saying hello to Megan. Spider smiled and said nothing. Bullet asked which university they went to. None answered but just looked flatly at him. Joe then offered that they might well not be short-term acquaintances, at all and that it was good to see Megan expanding her social circle and that when anyone met others in higher education it was usually a relationship or friendship for life and that it was premature to say that they were plastic when one didn't actually know them, which was quite hypocritical given his first response when Kelly was at the table with them. May then said that it was obvious that they were middle-class posh kids and that Megan was just trying to impress everyone by bringing them in there when they had no business coming into a pub like The Duke, in the first place.

Sitting at Stan and facing the rest of the pub with Joe at one end and May at the other and the others in between it became the debating chamber all the regulars knew it to be.

The discussion ensued with a quiet determination in Joe and a resolution in May to counter anything Joe offered. Not much but a murmur of agreement or few words of disdain came from Spider. Bullet asked what *Bourgeoisie* meant when Joe explained that although Thatcher had said that *there was no longer such a thing as class,* he thought that, paradoxically, the strength of the ruling classes was, in fact, being embedded further into the British class system by the erosion of the working-class and all the rights they had fought hundreds of years to secure. The Establishment were more established than they had ever been, he said, as the *trickledown effect*, so said by Thatcher to enliven the economy among the working-class, was also enlivening the petit-bourgeoisie in their aspirations to achieve real personal power and wealth akin to that which The Establishment enjoy, thus precluding the proletariat from acquiring the wealth required to live without struggle or privation.

Bullet was lost at *paradoxically.*

Spider smiled, keen to avoid taking sides.

May pursed her lips and appeared not to listen.

Kelly tried to change the tone and get the conversation on to his project. He then offered that they, the posh kids, had been very keen to engage in his Hot-Seating exercise which he had been learning at the Theatre Skills course which he said was absolutely fascinating and he was learning so much and enjoying enormously.

"So…how d'you do it?" Bullet asked.

"Do what?" Kelly replied being purposely evasive.

"What you said. The Top Chairs thing you did with Megan's ….?"

"Oh, right….Hot-Seating? I could show you, I suppose?"

Kelly then tried to organise their wee group into a semblance of chair and audience with Bullet in the chair. He also knew that he had to garner a better atmosphere between Joe and May if his plan was to profit. He hoped May would bite because she was inquisitive by nature, some would say just plain nosy, either way a few well-timed jokes would grease the wheels, not least a few drinks,

"Okay, Bullet, in a minute I'm going to ask you some questions and you have to be someone that you know very well. Your dad, Grandad…."

"Granny!" May shouted and Kelly smiled.

"Granny is allowed. Sex doesn't matter."

"That's a matter o' opinion." May sarcastically said.

"We'll get to that, May, if Bullet knows anything about his Granny's sex life, that is." Kelly said trying to keep May onside.

Kelly smiled at them all and then to Bullet who was beginning to look a little perturbed at the thought of his Grandmother in coital union. A loud laugh broke from Spider and Joe chuckled with him.

"Have a think, Bullet, while I get the round in."

Kelly went to the bar but heard May ask Bullet when the last time he watched *his Granny jump on his Grandad's cock* was, and a loud laugh come from them all. Bullet was genuinely disturbed.

Kelly watched them do this from the bar, content that they were on the edge of his web and then turned to face Norrie, who just stared at him.

"Good evening, Norman. Three Special, a lager, two bottles of stout and a nip, please Mr Purveyor of Mirth."

Norrie began to pour and continued to watch Kelly, which was unusual and Kelly felt it as he gathered the pints and bottles onto Hector. Norrie dropped May's nip next to the assemblage of drinks and as he did so coldly said,

"Stay away from Megan."

"Sorry? Not with you, Norrie."

"Yes you are. She's easily impressed and likes all the shite that you spout. That's why she's knocking around with them...."

Kelly adopted a posh English accent. "*Them* being Cheeya, Anna, Tom and Jerry, Norrie?"

"I don't care what they're called but you stay away from her."

Kelly handed over a fiver to Norrie,

"By *away from her,* I think you may be under the misapprehension that there might be a romantic bent to your observation?"

"Close enough."

Kelly had never shared such a detailed and expansive conversation with Norrie.

"Fear not, for the Landlord's daughter's virtue is built on solid stone, Sir. There be no connivance or underhandity from this mere onlooker."

Which was a barefaced lie. He was biding his time to assault the gullibility of Megan and enjoy the fruits of something which he had not tasted for more than a year now and would be made all the better in the knowledge that it was into Norrie's wee girl he would plunge. Nevertheless, there was more than an apparent fear in Norrie that this low-life would seduce his daughter with his verbal and quasi-literary dexterity and so for Kelly's continued attendance in *The Old Duke* and to assuage the fears of he that would compromise Kelly's current ploy, he said,

"Look Norrie….I know we don't exactly see eye to eye, but don't worry on that score. I know she laps up all my drivel and tries to join in but ….well to be honest she can't keep up…."

Which was a subtextual slap in the grid for Norrie via his progeny,

"….and she's really not my type, plus the fact that my current girlfriend whom I've just met at my Theatre Skills course would have a hissy fit if she found out I was sharing my attentions with another woman. *Yes*…..I have a girlfriend….*woman*…a very experienced and respected theatre practitioner of some note in this town, Norrie, which I know you'll be surprised to hear but there does exist in me the sensitivity, care and depth to maintain a relationship, you know, despite this rough exterior. So Megan...? She's an acquaintance, nothing more. You know, Norrie, I don't think we've ever shared such a detailed, honest and expansive conversation, before. We must do it again."

Norrie leaned in.

"If I find you sniffing around her, anymore, we will....*Kells*."

Norrie served another customer. Kelly could feel the presence of Sasquatch along the bar from him, looking at him. Kelly turned to face him knowing he had likely heard this exchange, however, not knowing what level of comprehension or interest had lodged in him.

When he got back to Stan May was still pressing Bullet on the sex lives of his grandparents which had now extended to sado-masochism, his Grandad in a gimp mask and his Granny in a dominatrix role-play scene much to the horror of Bullet whose open-fired, scone-scented, grandparent's knitted world of homely innocence was being ravaged into a mess of leather, handcuffs and whips. She then loudly described a quite unnecessary vision of the flagellated and dripping, bloodied back of his Grandad.

Sasquatch could hear this and started to breathe heavily. Nobody really noticed.

Kelly distributed the drinks and organised the arc of chairs facing Bullet, who announced that he couldn't be his Grandad anymore because of May and someone else could do it. Kelly needed someone to reassure Joe.

"What about you, Spider?" Kelly said.

"You can be Dracula!" May exploded.

" I don't know anything about Dracula." Spider shrugged.

"Satan, then! In hell and fire everywhere! You fuckin' look like him!"

Sasquatch threw a Bushmills down his neck.

"Just be youself for now….? Kelly said, "How about that?"

Spider didn't look too sure.

"Okay…go on then."

Kelly told him to take the seat facing them all and then took a mouthful of beer of which some dropped onto his lap.

"Oh shit sorry…. Let me just clean…"

He stood up and turned his back to them to wipe his crotch area and sent a hand down the inside of his trousers and then coughed loudly as something clicked.

"Sorted." He said as he sat back down.

"I'll start if you want. What's your name?" asked Kelly leading the way.

"Spider." Spider said.

"That's no yer real name, ya quilt!" observed May shyly, "Did yer ma christen ye *Spider* for fuck sake? Tell us yer real name!"

"Oh right…."

Joe and Bullet leaned in realising they had never known Spider's first name.

"John…"

"Ohhh..John, eh?" May was in a mood to take the piss whatever his name was. *"Dear John, You look too much like a vampire. Yer chucked, love Marion!"*

Joe tried to get it back on track.,

"Do you have a middle name, *John?"*

"…errm…*Mickleover….*" Spider meekly intoned.

"Micky fuckin' what!!" May disbelieving.

An abashed Spider said ,

"*Mickleover!* What's so bad about that? It was my mum's maiden name."

Kelly tried to summarise to keep it on track.

"So your name is John *Mickleover* Blackwood?"

"Yes."

"What's your starsign?" said Bullet.

"Scorpio."

May animatedly leapt on this.

"The deathly sting of the scorpion! Look oot, everybody! I've changed fae a vampire tae a scorpion an' I'm gonnae sting yez a' tae death!"

Kelly remonstrated with her.

"May! So you were born in the month of *September*…? Kelly asked.

"October. The 21st."

"1724!" May gurgled at her jibe, "Or whenever the fuck yon fella wrote ye! Whasisname, Kells? *Barn Stormer*…some fuckin' thing like that?"

"Bram Stoker, May!" Kelly said.

"Fuck kinda name is that tae gi'e a kid?"

Then she did a sinister minister's voice at a christening,

"I name this child… Bram… which is a quite shite name but you will go on to write aboot Dracula, vampires, scorpions and shit, what suck blood an' drink in The Old Duke doon by the Meadows!"

May chortled delightedly at her obviously witty addition to the exercise and shouted aggressively across the pub,

"Lookoot evr'ybody!! There's a vampire here's gonna bite yer neck squirt yer blood everywhere an' suck it 'til ye've nae blood left! Ha ha ha ha!!" she shouted demonically and made a move as if to swish a cloak around her shoulders and began to laugh in a manic way looking at everyone in the pub from the elevated position of Stan.

Then Sasquatch began to moan. He let the moan get louder and then screamed twice in succession. All in the pub covered their ears. He settled again. Spider shook his head at Kelly and waved his hand.

"No, no. That's enough. I don't think I'm the man you want."

Joe stepped up. Kelly was delighted.

"I'll do it. I've got nothing to hide" he said pointedly looking at May.

"I'll start if you want. What's your name?" asked Kelly leading the way.

"Right…I'm Joseph James Connolly Delaney, aged fifty-two and live here in the south side of Edinburgh. I am a painter and decorator to trade and I own a small business. Anything else, you'll have to ask. Go!"

May made some disparaging noise and turned her back to have a drink.

Kelly was delighted at Joe's enthusiasm and looked around them all as if to say any questions? He didn't want to be seen to be pushing this too much just in case anyone starting putting two and two together. Spider decided he'd like to ask something.

"Have you ever been married, Joe?"

Joe adopted the semblance of a tone of regret.

"No…no. Never happened for me."

Bullet said, "Why not?"

"Because…other things got in the way, I suppose?"

"Other things?" Kelly said.

"Yes.. you know… circumstances… other loves."

"Starting to sound juicy, Joe. Tell us more." Bullet said.

"By other loves, it's not always the love of *someone else* that I mean. A man can love his work or *something* else that he decides to do."

Kelly couldn't have agreed more and there and then decided that he had to *love* this project and see it through entirely, do it properly and then his mind went back to the soiree he had with MI6 who mentioned Joe's involvement with the Union. He expected Joe would expand on that but he knew it might take up valuable time before May decided to ridicule again and waste opportunities. He also thought rescuing Joe from this line of inquiry would look thoughtful and caring trying to spare Joe the narrative of a painful tale. He said,

"I think we should leave that there before we get to know Joe better, folks. Ok?"

May arrived. "Fuck d'ye mean, know him better? I know him! We all fuckin' know him!"

"Really?" Kelly said. May had thrown him the chance of appearing helpful and considerate, which he wasn't expecting from May, at all.

"Aye…Really!!" Indignant and apparently offended.

"May…this exercise is an opportunity not just to question Joe but to question what you think you know about him, or any other character but in this case it's Joe…"

Kelly decided flattery would grease the wheels very well, here,

"….and the point is to question him, *Joe*, the character, the man and our relationship with him. Dig beneath the surface and you often find aspects of the *person* you had no idea existed, people they *know*, exploits kept *quiet,* places they've *been*….impressive things worth knowing and *talking* about."

Kelly realised he had just started speaking like a theatre practitioner and emphasised four or five significant words and could quite easily have dropped into a generic southern English accent, in this case Kat, but was fulfilling the role quite well, he thought, but he knew if he went too far, and he knew by May's face that she had picked up on the role he was playing and if he kept it up before long she would start to mimic him in ridicule and he would lose his audience and his objective, so he pulled up a little and brought Bullet into the fold.

"Bullet! Come on, what do you want to know about Joe? You can't know him completely, can you?"

"Ermm ok....ermm… right...."

May audibly sighed.

"Errr...what's yer favourite drink?"

"Vodka." Joe said immediately.

"Never see you with vodka, Joe?" Spider looked puzzled.

"Not the slop they serve you in the pubs here. The real stuff that slides down like clear oil. Made in Russia and Poland. The stuff they send over here is like the worst whisky we make and punt out to…. well *we* drink the rough whisky in our pubs…..you know the stuff I could use to clean my brushes but they don't over there. The vodka is rich and thick."

"Sounds like Bullet!" May barked.

"How d'you know about this? Have you been to Russia?" Spider asked.

"No, I haven't but I know people that have. Brought some back."

"Have you still got some?" Bullet asked.

"No. Still got the bottle though?"

Kelly gripped the baton.

"Sounds like there has been a chance in the past for you to have gone to Russia, Joe?"

"There was. I didn't go in the end. Eric did."

Spider was wide-eyed for the first time in years.

"Eric? *Just died Eric?*" he asked

"Yep."

"Went to Russia?"

"Moscow. Eric was CP. They organised trips. I was an organiser in the Union and was offered the chance cos' someone dropped out."

"Why didn't you go, Joe?" Spider asked.

"Had to get the visa quick but …work got in the way."

"What's CP?" Bullet piped up.

"Communist Party." Joe smiled at him.

Kelly, of course had been illuminated as to the political proclivities of Eric by MI6's men in black, but decided to appear surprised,

"Get to fuck! Eric was a Red?"

"Through and through, mate." Joe nodded with a small smile.

Kelly looked across to May,

"There you go, May! Never knew that, did you?" who just raised an eyebrow.

"What was it about work that stopped you from going, Joe?" asked Spider who was really becoming interested in this story.

"1972. Three day week. Lights were out. Business was struggling. Couldn't afford it. The Party paid for Eric. So he went, instead."

Spider leaned in and changed the subject, "What's your favourite type of music, Joe?"

"Well...." Joe seemed reluctant to divulge. "..... you won't know it...I don't think... bit..."

"A bit what?" Kelly asked.

"....unpopular I suppose you would say."

"Just tell us!" Bullet blurted.

"Ermm..." Kelly was intrigued. ".... classical...."

"I love the classics!" Bullet enthused. "The Beatles, The Stones. Brilliant."

Kelly interjected, "That's not what I think he means, Bullet, is it Joe?"

"No...no. Ermm... Debussy, Eric Saty, Berlioz. Classical."

"Sorry, Eric sat where?" Bullet was confused.

"Saty. Gymnopody."

Bullet quite prided himself on his musical knowledge but was thrown at this.

"Jim Nobody? Never heard of him."

Joe didn't like revealing this part of himself. " They're French. You won't know them. Vaughan Williams! There you go. He's English. You'll know him?"

Spider, Bullet and Kelly sat quietly looking at each other and shaking their heads. May looked away quietly scowling. Joe tried again.

"The Lark Ascending. My favourite piece. Amazing. Listened to that in the bad old days when I thought the business was going under. Really lifted me. Special tune."

More blank looks. May said nothing. Kelly rescued the situation.

"But the business survived, Joe?" Kelly asked.

"Just. I started on my own the year before the *winter of discontent* and picked up work here and there but nobody had the bunce to afford a decorator. It was hard and the bank didn't help. I was running on fumes and just getting there at the end of every month for a few years."

"I know where you're coming from, Joe,..." Kelly encouraged, "....the banks are all sweetness and light when you're in the black but they're bastards when you're not. Take my bank, The Clydesdale, when I'm overdrawn they send me a letter and make me pay for the letter as well making the situation worse!"

"I've had a few of them, mate" Joe said, "Had a blazing row in The Midland on Hanover Street with a big queue behind me about that."

Lovely, Kelly thought. Maybe just a bit more required.

"I've done a few days for you on and off for a while now, Joe but I've never actually known the name of your company? What is it?"

Joe said, "It's not a company. I'm not limited. I'm a sole trader. J.J.C. Delaney. Tax is easier."

"Why was Eric going to Russia?" Bullet looked genuinely perplexed.

"Let's just say…*Education*, Bullet." Joe replied.

With that Joe seemed to have drawn a line under that area of discovery and concluded the drawing of that line with the drawing of a large gulp of beer. Spider was surprised by all this information about Joe and was contemplative. May was quiet. Bullet was still trying to recall where Russia was by imagining the big world map they had on the wall of his primary school classroom. Kelly was fidgeting around his crotch.

"You got crabs?" May smirked at him.

"No, May just not hanging right. Us lads have to get that right before we can relax into a conversation."

"Well I'm sick o' this one. Theatre shite."

Kelly knew that he'd probably got everything he'd need and didn't want to be caught. He then explained that that was the sense of the exercise and that there was no need going on and anyway May was pissed off with the serious tone and obviously something else but Kelly knew not to go there, not to ask.

Kelly was very pleased with his night's work and as it wore on he drank some of the bad whisky Joe had spoke of and quite a few more pints of Special. Sasquatch looked over at him a few times which was a tad unusual for the big lump and Kelly clocked this and wondered what was going on in that head so mysterious and large but was becoming more than a little inebriated and thought little of it.

Home was what Kelly started to think about, then, too. He'd had a good night. He'd got everything he needed, he hoped, from Joe, met Megan's friends who'd invited him to a party that Megan was going to and he'd noticed how she had become mildly jealous when Luccia became interested in him, which was all good and as he walked back across the road towards his stair doorway he imagined kissing Megan at the party. He decided that a slow kiss, initially, was the best policy if he was eventually going to get to the moment of the moon and stars with her. He was wearing the suit he got for Eric's funeral in his lusty imaginings and had shaved and had a splash of *Denim,* because he'd got some of that somewhere in his bedroom. He knew this because he'd spilled some on *Persuasion* by Jane Austen, which was quite ironic, he thought but he didn't like Austen much and every time he tried to get back into it he was accosted by the powerful whiff of *men not trying too hard* and eventually gave up and let Austen's giggly girls and frustrated women negotiate their matrimonial aspirations to ridiculous lengths, without him. He was handsome and well-groomed in his vision and allowed himself the vanity of Megan dropping her hand towards his tackle area as they kissed, which immediately stirred the central character between them into doing a bit of stand-up, replicated reasonably successfully in real time as he reached his stairway door and entering. Coming down the stairs was the working girl who lived in the flat above.

"Alright son. That's me back in uniform and back on duty for the next few hours and I think it looks like rain. You been out, son?" She smiled at him.

She was wearing a blouson-type top, pink, very loose and unbuttoned down to her cleavage which was exposing the top of the cups of the safety net of a substantial black bra supporting what Kelly guessed, left to the vagaries of physics, were quite pendulous breasts. This bra was bedecked with a little pink bowed ribbon which drew Kelly's gaze quickly set against the black background. Below that was a short black skirt with a pair of thighs of sizable dimensions trapped tightly in fishnet stockings underpinned by a pair of pink high-heeled court shoes to top and tail the assembly. Her hair had attempted to emulate the bigness of any of the girls in *Bananarama* or *Duran Duran's* bassist and was fixed stiffly by copious sprays of *Ellenette,* which Kelly could smell but mixed in with a powerful odour of a middling-priced working girl's perfume which would be undoubtedly perceptible but in no way subtle but enough to let the punters know that her business was open for business, which Kelly noted.

"Yeah…yeah.. just been across at The Duke. Had a few you know." He inconfidently slurred back at her.

"That's nice son. With your girlfriend, were you?"

"No. Don't have a girlfriend."

"What's a good lookin' fella like you doin' wi no girlfriend, son? You must get weary sortin' yersel' out when the sap's up, d'ye no?"

Her very direct reference to masturbation and sales pitch took him by surprise and he stammered a little knowing what she was about to suggest but said,

"Yeah…. Yeah.. bit of a drag…"

However, at this current moment, with his sap very up, he felt unusually brave, which he never was with girls. He could never ask because he feared rejection more than anything else. Something resided in him after rejection which took him days to recover from, something quite painful and dark but in this fortunate liaison which would be contracted verbally, he actually felt more aroused knowing that the conversation would be a discussion of what would occur when the contract was concluded. He'd never been with a prostitute before not having the bravery to approach one even if he did decide to avail one of their wares and was generally very clumsy with the whole seduction process, which he inwardly acknowledged, and knowing, hoping, that there was the chance of bedding Megan, soon, he opted to ignore the crackled skin on her face and her slight turkey neck and get a bit of practice in.

"I never usually do home visits." The Prostitute said as she walked into his hallway.

Kelly had baulked at the thought of humping in the common stairwell with the possibility of anyone seeing them and them knowing he was paying for it, so suggested they go into his flat.

"This is exactly the same layout as mine." She said. "Is that your living room there? Aye…same as mine. Tenner to suck it and twenty a fuck." She flatly said changing the tone.

"Right…ok I'll try option number two, please..if that's ok?" He said as he guided her towards the living room and then stopped her quickly. He remembered he had a dead dog in there.

"Wait here…" he said to her, "….just got to tidy up a bit."

He hurried into the living room and grabbed the corpse of Lenni, which was a considerable weight when not on his paws, and tried to push it into the kitchen, which was just off the living room. It didn't work very well and he had to pull Lenni by the neck which became a drunken and surreal replay of his death.

"D'ye need a wee hand wi' somethin' there, son? Whit are ye doin' movin' a dead body, or something? She shouted from the hallway.

Kelly came back out and guided her into the living room and onto the couch.

She looked around. "Did ye rob a library, son?" she said looking around the room. "That was a big book I heard ye shiftin' was it no?"

Kelly was alarmed that she heard.

"It wasn't a big book.." he happily and drunkenly smiled at her, "… it was a dead dog…."

She looked puzzled and then saw Kelly's smile. She began to smile with him and laughed at the ridiculous suggestion.

"Dead dog!" she laughed, "Got the cash, son?" He went into his coat pocket a drew a twenty out and gave it to her which she put in her small pink handbag. She then smiled at him as he concluded she didn't look too bad in the darkness of his flat.

"Now…lets get you ready for action, big boy." And she opened his coat and ran her hand down onto his crotch.

"Well well, well, no need to get you all steamed up. That's the hardest cock I've felt since I started, hookin'. You take yer coat off son and I'll free up this big fella down here."

Kelly sat forward and removed his coat as she undid his trousers and slipped them down onto his thighs, then looked up at him smiling and pushed her hand up over his balls and then into his underpants. Her smile then dropped off her face.

"What the fuck's this?" She said and then pulled out a small hard plastic device out into the darkness of the room and strained to see what was written on the side.

"Tashika E14 Speakeasy?"

"Sorry….forgot about that. It's a dictaphone."

"A phone for yer dick?"

"No…no ..it's for recording stuff. When you talk."

"Recording me?"

"No! I was using it earlier…and I've got a hole in my pocket…" he lied, "….and it slipped into my Y's. Gimme it over."

And he took it from her putting it on the side of the couch.

She shook her head and muttered something about getting this over with as she climbed onto Kelly and slipped him inside of her and she started gyrating on top of him. She decided to work at this one diligently in order to conclude business with the thought of big books, dead dogs and dictaphones and considered the scruffy guy from downstairs to be a wee bit weird. Kelly watched her bouncing around on top of him and reached out to touch her right breast.

"No touching! That's extra."

she said and Kelly drunkenly thought it quite churlish and pernickety in the circumstances and not really a good business move. It had been a long time since Kelly had spilled his seed and it didn't take long for him to start making the right noises that encouraged her to bounce ever more robustly. Kelly started to groan still in his alcoholic haze, leaned his head back and shut his eyes. She bounced away on top of him and started to encourage him to get there, all the while looking around at the books and for the corpse of a dead dog and eyeing the dictaphone next to Kelly and feeling a little unnerved about him. He was pissed and it was all taking far too long so she went in to fifth gear and enthusiastically went about her work. At last, Kelly started to let it be known that an eruption was somewhat imminent and fought to move more underneath her but couldn't shift her weight and so started throwing his arms about to support him and get the right position to maximise the sensation. He started to feel the pleasure and threw his arm to the right of him and a click was heard.

"There ye go son, that's it, yer getting' there, c'mon, give me it"... she encouraged just as May's very convincing Hammer House of Horror voice joined in,

The deathly sting of the scorpion! Look oot, everybody! I've changed fae a vampire tae a scorpion an' I'm gonnae sting yez a' tae death!

"What the fuck?" she said looking around her quickly.

Kelly hit a random button trying to quieten it.

1724! Or whenever the fuck yon fella wrote ye! Whasisname, Kells? Barn Stormer...some fuckin' thing like that?

She was becoming quite alarmed and so rode harder and ignored whatever the voices said thinking this was how he got his kicks and knowing that he was close, just wanting to get out. Seconds later,

....I name this child... Bram... which is a quite shite name but you will go on to write aboot Dracula, vampires, scorpions and shit, what suck blood an' drink in The Old Duke doon by the Meadows!.....

He thrashed about trying to orgasm and reach the dictaphone at the same time and moaning louder. Then she nearly left thinking she was in mortal danger with a deviant weirdo when she heard,

...Lookoot evr'ybody!! There's a vampire here's gonna bite yer neck squirt yer blood everywhere an' suck it 'til ye've nae blood left! Ha ha ha ha!!.......

Kelly was as close and closing faster to the finish. He tried to find the stop button but pleasure misguided his reach and turned up the volume to the max, instead.

She rode faster than ever but had a look around just in case a dark-cloaked figure should emerge from the shadows or from through the wall to bite her, "C'mon son, that's it, let it go, let it go, for fuck sake!!" as she got more and more breathless.

"Kelly shouted "Yessss, yesss....!!"

The sound of Sasquatch started to moan loudly and then two fearful screams united with Kelly as he orgasmed for the first time in years and let it be known,

Yeaeaaaaarrrrrghhhh .... aarrrrrghhhhh ....

The timing was so good the hooker thought it all pre-arranged and having never had to deal with such a fetish before became positively unnerved by him and started to look around the room for darkened accomplices approaching to kill her. She just wanted this assignation over with. This was his first ejaculation in a long time and had never really taken the time to drain his spuds, manually, being either too drunk or disinterested. He actually went a little light-headed as a tremendous rush coursed through his stomach and a pleauresome pain enveloped his torso. Then she stopped and went into her bra and took out an inhaler and sent a blast into her tubes. Kelly pawed about on the couch for the stop button and clicked it off.

She leaned forward, exhausted and breathless. Kelly slumped back onto his couch and she dismounted, slowly, tiredly and pulled down her skirt and then went into her bag and took out some tissues and a clean pair of knickers. She dabbed herself and then slid the new pants up her legs quickly and took another blast of her inhaler. Then while Kelly was lying back, sexually spent and pissed she went into the kitchen to get a drink and found a dead dog on the floor.

Chapter 12

Well-Appointed

Kelly slept until 4:08am when his bladder woke him up. His head was fuzzy and he leaned a bit as he went to the toilet. Then an overpowering, really shitty smell made him gag. He thought it might be the drains, again, but they'd been fixed. He wandered up to the kitchen to check if anything had become detached under the sink. He opened the door and a thousand flies took to the air. He closed it quickly again. Lenni. He forgot about the dog. He went into the living-room and tied a random sock across his nose and mouth then burst back into the kitchen and opened the window. Many of the flies were quite happy where they were, *thank you very much,* and he had to give the corpse a kick to disturb them. Lenni was buried in a shallow grave without eulogy or ceremony in the back drying green behind a bush and next to a wall down the bottom, away from prying eyes. Kelly looked back at the grave and convinced himself it was a good spot. Shaded. Peaceful. Well away from the washing poles. Just what Eric might have wanted for him.

He crept quietly upstairs and went back to bed and slept away his hangover. He ate toast and then went out to the nearest phone-box with plenty of change.

Monday, 11th June

Early on the Monday morning, Mrs June Ducketts, the business manager at The Midland Bank, took a call from a Mr Joseph Delaney who would like to apply for a business loan of ten thousand pounds. Being a client of The Midland Bank for some years now and with a current business account, Mrs Ducketts afforded Mr Delaney an appointment in five days time and advised him that he should bring his books showing last year's tax return, overall profit and his passport as ID, however, everything else required to facilitate his application would be apparent in the bank's records. Delaney thanked her, confirmed the date and hung up the phone.

Chapter 13

The Tale of the Tail

Friday 15th June

Marchmont was a very smart part of the south side. Stone built tenement flats with carved stone on the exterior and salons of stucco moulded coving, grape and cherubim-clad centre-pieces and enormous mantle shelves of marble and painted tile. They had begun to price themselves out of the market for ordinary buyers in the early eighties and gradually it became more profitable for owners to rent them out and students were popular clients. This particular one was five bedrooms, a lounge, large old kitchen and a drawing room. The view from the corner bay window had a view over The Meadows and to Arthur's Seat, Edinburgh's city-centre small mountain, that would have commanded a pretty price on the market but it suited Megan's four friends admirably who had just finished their last final exam and were about to celebrate so they were busy making punch for their party guests. It was closing in on 7:30pm and Tom kept berating Annabel for sneaking in too much vodka who repelled his arguments with another that claimed there could never be too much vodka in punch. Luccia was cutting up fruit and Jericho was loading the cassette that he had made especially for the party. He had loaded it with all the good tracks from *Big Country's* new album and a few standard *Abba* floor-fillers but also a bit of *Japan* to mix it up a bit.

Jericho had a mate in London called Dante who had given him a demo of four tracks but he'd included one he loved most on the *Marchmont Flat Anthems* cassette. The band was called *The Dressers* and the track they all loved was called *The Madness of the Biggest Brain*. It was their *Top Flat Anthem*, they said and they all agreed that one day it would be a hit if the band could get a decent deal. Jericho talked about his talented mate, whenever he could to whoever he could.

He was busy rewinding and fast forwarding trying to locate the start of the track without giving away his jape to the rest of the gang in the kitchen. He wanted to play it to his jolly flatmates before all the guests arrived to surprise them all and get the party going for them and they all had a routine *that just bloody well bonded them all, as well, I'll have you know!* But what they all liked the most was that it was theirs, exclusively. Nobody else knew it but when they played it to their various gatherings, they all could sing along with it and it elevated them, they thought, above the oiks that had made it to Edinburgh on an A and two Bs with a scholarship from West Yorkshire Council thrown in to grease the wheels of their education. This separated them. This made them cool....*they thought.*

He found it and set it at pause and turned the volume up. He straightened his new shirt almost giggling to himself at the wheeze they were about to have and pressed play and walked briskly to the kitchen and stood dramatically leaning against the door frame. The drums dramatically rumbled in and the others all looked at Jericho and realised what he was doing. They all laughed and came in together with the first line and sang loudly,

I thought of the heroes but then I felt so disappointed,

Jericho moved in towards their big wooden dining table and they all met there on the lyric *disappointed* with a deliberately dramatic and frownful face. Obviously something they had done before. Then:

Plato pushed the bar, told his stories but then he thought "I Kant,"......,

a double entendre they all elevated their volume for just to emphasise the philosopher's name and broadcast their learning.... and loved doing it, dearly,

And so insanity has me, tears me, shakes me, and then......,

musical pause....,

I explode......,

which saw the drums emulate an explosion and they all burst away from the table as if a minor eruption had just happened in their heads,

And wonder at the madness of the biggest brain......,

and here a nauseating display of various interpretations of how their physicalities would be affected by their minds being so negatively impaired, occurred;

The madness, the madness, the madness...... .

Tom took his hands and put them to his temples and simulated a searing pain coursing through his cranium, Annabel rolled her eyes upwards until the whites were only apparent and stiffened her body and jerked,

The madness, the madness, the madness.....

Luccia engaged in some sort of fly catching exercise of invisible chimeras and Jericho pretended to head-butt the wall. Then they all turned as one to face each other just as the singer cried out at his debilitating but cephalic brilliance,

Arrrrghhhh!!......,

And loosely fell to the floor in unison.

As the band prepared to surge into verse two the doorbell stopped them. Tom ran to turn down the music and Luccia ran to the door.

A huddle of six massive young men entered through the door and Annabel ran towards them all and tried to collectively hug them in one go. She kissed them all enthusiastically and grabbed one by the hand and dragged him into the lounge. The rest of them went straight to the kitchen and deposited a large amount of beer onto the table.

"What was the score, today, Nick?" Tom smiled.

Nick was enormous. Probably six feet four.

"Slammed it, Tom! Four tries. 37-12. Hugo got them all."

Nick pointed at Hugo. Only a six-footer of sculpted muscle.

"Yeah….Hugo drawled. "Managed to get over the line, once or twice." he smiled taking off his jacket.

"And what about Crispo?" Jericho asked. "Was he….?"

Crispin, a heavier and stockier rugger chappie with a shock of blond hair, stepped forward and grabbed a can of beer from the table, aggressively.

"Fucking right I was. Bar-stard tried to gouge me in the fucking scrum. Caught him square on the jaw. Had to break and he came at me with a haymaker! Stupid fucking attempt to punch anyone. He was wide open so I warmed his ribs!"

"Jupiter's cock, Crispo!" Tom blurted out, "Every week!"

"Relax, Tomster! I bought him a pint after the game and gave him a free midriff swing at me in the clubhouse before we left. Not a problem. All muscle down there. Bar-stard probably hurt his knuckles! Where's all these fillies from Philosophy Annabel promised? Annabel!"

Crispin strode out of the kitchen looking for Annabel and he found her in the lounge kissing *her* member of the rugby team.

The doorbell rang again and Crispin shouted that he would get it being so close. He strode to the door and opened it briskly letting it swing into the hall and without looking who was there and said,

"Come in. Booze on the kitchen table and don't shit on the floor!"

A gaggle of students of both gender entered and one ran up to Crispin walking away and kicked him in the arse and shouted, "Three points!"

Without turning Crispin said, "Hello, Polly! Where's my fucking essay you copied?" and went back into the lounge.

Gradually the party filled up with their friends of varying student-types and the music got a little louder.

Megan arrived at nine o'clock wearing a frock she's bought in a charity shop on Nicholson Street which was full of them and which many of her new friends did, ironically. It was delicately floral and augmented with a thin leather belt around her waist. She wore brand new black Doc Marten boots which were nipping her feet and chafing at the ankles and had her hair plaited in two very Scandinavian looking pig-tails, which was the current postmodernist look, ironically worn as inversions of wealth and style with the student sororities. She had to go into *The Old Duke* to tell her dad not to wait up and that she was only a mile away in Marchmont and she got a few chuckles from the Brylcreem Boys and a head shake from her dad.

Megan went into the kitchen and found Luccia. She put her bottle of expensive red wine down on the table as Luccia gave her a hug and then said,

"Meggy you absolute fucking star! Chateauneuf du Pape! This is too good for the shitheads coming here tonight. I'll put this in the cupboard and we'll crack this over some crispbread and cheese, sometime soon. Yeah?"

Luccia secreted the bottle in a shadow at the back of a cupboard. Megan was delighted but had never been called *Meggy* before?. She'd managed to sail through the cocktails on George Street the night before without fucking up or making any contentious quips that gave away her prole origins or grated with the parents of her friends and now had acquired more amiable capital in the purchase of a top shelf red.

"You look cool, Megan! Watch out for the rugby team. They have eternal erections and don't mind where it goes!"

Megan wasn't sure about what she actually meant by that but let it go and so just giggled a giggle that stopped as soon as it had started. She grabbed a bottle of lager and started to mingle with the rest of them, mainly in the lounge. She wasn't entirely comfortable and knew it as she saw some faces she nodded to and smiled at but none brought her into the conversation.

Kelly was making his way up the stairs after having a few in The Duke. He fielded a few questions about where he was going to in the suit he'd bought for Eric's funeral but remained enigmatic. He was suffering a bit from the night before and his exertions with the asthmatic dark lady of the night from upstairs and disposing of Lenni's body but he'd gone back to sleep and woke up around two o' clock and had a bath. For the rest of the afternoon he'd sat with pen and paper trying to compose the sonnet that Megan reminded him of, wishing for once he'd not tried to impress. So he wrestled, slapped, stroked, prodded, and licked Constance and Beauty all afternoon until their cerebral writhings ejaculated a sonnet that he thought might do the trick and seduce Megan. Although it was much of an alcoholic blur, he'd enjoyed what he remembered of having sex with the prostitute from the flat above. She was very enthusiastic as he recalled and gave him every encouragement, which to be fair, was her job. She reminded him of a supportive mother at a children's football match with her *come on's* and *you can do it's* until they hit the back of the net and yelled in joy, which amused him a tad as he sat in front of a small mirror he had leaning up against his bedroom wall, applying base make-up foundation to his face and trying to get the hang of blending it in to his natural skin tone. He could still see obvious areas around his eyes where it was still apparent it was make-up and he got annoyed at his inability to evenly weave any magic such as Kerry had demonstrated, so he had a go at the greying powder on his hair. This seemed easy to him and he gave himself a streak in the centre of his head inwardly remarking that he now looked like a skunk and smiled at the irony that he honestly had to acknowledge vis-a-vis the relative pong that skunks could throw out, reminding him that he needed a bath before venturing out tonight. Her enthusiasm had chafed him, he thought, on his foreskin because it burned a little in the hot water but he glowed inwardly at his reintroduction from a lengthy hiatus to adult activity beyond merely drinking and felt quietly smug and wished he had a mate he could tell. He had thought of not going to the party. He thought of not going because he felt rough, he said to himself, and the easiest thing to do was have a night in The Duke and maybe he could get a bit more information out of Joe to use in his underhand dealings, or stay in and read for a while finding the excuse that he hadn't read nearly enough of *The Good Soldier Sveyk*, however the truth was that he felt quite nervous about having to mix with more of Megan's smart young set who knew much more than him and were a potential inconvenience with regard to his being exposed. Throughout his life had never put himself in situations that might reveal his weaknesses and often found reasons not to engage, thinking *if you don't run the race you can't lose*. What actually did motivate him was something a little deeper that he didn't recognise, initially, but then understood that since Megan had shown him some attention and flirted with him it had created a longing or a need that couldn't be quelled by alcohol and a desire to be closer to her, something simmering and visceral within him and he knew that her exposure to new people might see her gone forever if he didn't do something soon. He articulated to himself that he had bought a suit, had a bath, fixed his hair, without the skunk stripe, into an arrangement that suggested he cared what others thought and dared to wear the cheap canvas Dunlop trainers Steven had given him with the suit, which he quietly considered could be a game-changer if Megan approved, met her friends and delivered the sonnet. Hell, he was even going to find the remnants of that bottle of *Denim* and dab his erogenous zones just in case any erogenous activity was in the post. So he'd sank a draught of Dutch courage at The Duke and arrived before the door of the top flat of 17 Marchmont Road. Music was coming from within as were a hubbub of voices and laughing. He straightened his suit, checked the sonnet was out of sight in his inside pocket, took the dozen cans of McEwan's Export from the plastic bag presenting them as though it was a ticket to be checked and put his hand down the front of his trousers and shifted his chafing cock into a different, more comfortable, position and pressed the bell. He heard a voice say *I'll get it* and the door opened. A young-looking fat girl with big hair opened the door. She had dark eye-shadow and dark lipstick and was wearing a Ra-Ra skirt, which Kelly thought looked ridiculous on thin girls but did absolutely nothing for this portly party concierge.

"Hi" he said.

"Hi." She said back to him and smiled.

"I'm Kelly…..? Megan's friend? Err…Luccia and Annabel were in the pub with Megan and invited me to the party….?

"Oh..okay. Cheeya and Anna! Yeah, come in…..?

"Kelly."

"Cheeya!!" The fat girl shouted, "There's someone here you met in a pub."

Which Kelly thought a tad oblique.

Two rugby players were wrestling in the hall as Kelly stood there waiting not really knowing where to look. The fat girl ignored them. Luccia arrived, ignoring the coil of grunting muscle on the floor.

"Hi…..?" She was obviously tipsy, or forgetful not recognising Kelly, who realised it might be the suit distorting her memory.

"Kelly? Megan's friend from The Old Duke, last night?"

Luccia apologised and took Kelly into the drawing room where Megan was standing on the edge of a conversation listening in and occasionally laughing. When she saw Kelly Megan lit up and Kelly was delighted. Megan took him to the kitchen to deposit his beer and he asked her if it would be alright there because most of the parties he had been to one often kept one's beer in sight. She reassured him it would be fine where it was and that there would be plenty of anything he'd like to drink available for the entire evening, as if she had arranged this herself. Kelly grabbed a beer and opened it

"What's that smell?" Megan asked him.

Kelly panicked.

"I've had a bath! And changed….*everything*….you know?"

"It's a nice smell, Kells! Easy tiger!"

"Oh..right? Erm….Denim,…it's *Denim.*"

"For the man that doesn't have to try too hard, eh"

"Well…. I might put a little effort in."

"Maybe you're trying too hard with that suit. It was good for Eric's funeral but maybe not for a party?"

"What d'you mean? All the best parties I ever went to were in my Sunday best. My mum insisted!"

"Really? What was the last party you went to?"

"Finlay Robertson's eighth birthday. I looked superb in my pressed shorts and matching jacket and tie! I gave him a kaleidoscope and he was delighted with it because they'd just taken the patch off his specs that covered his lazy eye and I kissed Debbie Robertson, his big sister, so don't mess with the man that doesn't have to try too hard. Okay!"

The Megan saw the white canvas shoes. "Oh....I see!"

Kelly was none the wiser. "See what?"

"It works now. I get it. The subverting of the formal with the informal which creates a fashionable postmodernist irony."

She was pleased she'd learned and parroted that just as a student passed them both.

"Which is exactly the effect one can achieve with...*ironic wit...* when trying to....you know.."

Megan laughed and put her arm through his as they walked into the lounge. Two trendy looking girls were singing to each other and cutting disco shapes as *Abba* belted out *Dancing Queen*. Kelly thought they were very sexy girls and took in more than a passing eyeful and said to Megan,

"They're happy."

"Do you want to dance?"

Megan knew the answer to that. Kelly gave her a look as though she'd just asked him if he'd like to be beaten with a rubber hose and have his fingernails pulled out with pliers. Megan laughed. He realised that it was the first time that he'd ever heard her laugh as loudly and gave her a second surreptitious glance, enjoying her smiling face. He took a swig of his beer and squeezed past some chaps that were also laughing but far too loudly and stood by the massive bay window overlooking The Meadows and then to Arthur's Seat and Megan followed him.

"Beautiful view. They gave the landlord more money just to get this place, you know?"

"Did they?"

Kelly had the inclination to start a discussion about the ability to do something like that, the nature of class and the relative wealth required but decided against it. They were her friends and he knew he would piss all over any chance he had of this being his night with her and would only be seizing on an opportunity to appear principled when he wasn't. Just full of shit, as usual, which he heard him say to himself in his head.

He had a good look around the large lounge and the nineteenth century décor of cornice, dados and stripped wood shutters. Then at the rugby team and girlfriends, that smart set of people that would soon travel the world and move on to glorious new lives in chambers and surgeries, archaeological digs in Mesopatamia and a world of stocks and shares and then he looked out to the view that he lived in, but was then entirely taken by surprise when he understood that he meant it. Maybe he was principled? He knew he was in their ivory tower that overlooked his world that was safe from the sweat and stress required just to ensure his next pint or dodging around the world of signing-on, getting rent cheques on time and buying stodge to eat from the stack'em high *Presto* supermarket. He realised he was above it all there in that flat, out of it and seeing another more privileged view of where he lived. It might be pleasant to look at but wasn't the countryside of Dorset also pretty? Thomas Hardy's characters fought the land and Tess fought an arrogant distant wealthy relative who could have helped their family. This lot didn't have to see the winos fight or piss against the trees in their beautiful view or see the *Young South Side* gang fight *The Young Niddrie Terror* with a violence they would have never witnessed before, on the swathe of green they so admired. They could ignore the failing sandstone on some of the older tenements and the rat-infested back greens. Their stay was ephemeral, finite and ultimately pleasant. They just used the town for what they needed, took it and left. Maybe he should become one of them? The rewards would probably be so much more enviable, perhaps. An unusual sense of injustice welled up within him and he had felt disinclined to be amiable. However, he shook it off as Megan smiled at him and rejoined his current project. Bedding her.

"I'm just going to grab another bottle, Kells. Want one?"

"Not yet." He quietly said.

Megan went to the kitchen. Kelly had another gaze on the view.

"Which faculty do you teach in?" A voice said.

Kelly turned around and the fat girl who opened the door to him stood there. She looked more ridiculous to him up close with her New Romantic make up and big hair.

"I don't teach anywhere?"

"Why not? Your suit says you do."

"Does it? I told it to keep quiet before I left my flat tonight, as well. You can't trust suits, these days, can you?"

She laughed and held out her hand.

"Rebecca. Becks. Like the beer."

"A distinctive taste!" He didn't know he would say that but enjoyed it as she laughed again. "Kelly."

He shook her hand.

"You at the Uni?" he asked.

"No. I'm going next year though when I get my results in August. Thought you might be a lecturer or professor there. They said they'd invited a couple."

It dawned on him then that she was a few years younger than the rest of them and the adherence to the current popular fashion of big hair and shoulder pads, a la *Duran Duran* should have given it away. He quite liked that she would buy it if he had said he was a lecturer but then knew he'd be rumbled at some point.

"Well good luck on your results." He just said.

"Thanks!" and she smiled delightedly at his interest.

"What do you do?" she asked him.

Despite his earlier dalliance with class struggle and hope for the redistribution of wealth and income he didn't want to admit to his dole-ite status and heard himself say,

"I'm a writer."

"Wow! Really? Fantastic….!" She glowed, trying far too hard and making far too much of this revelation. "What do you write?"

He considered journalism as an immediate and convenient career but then the conversation might take an unwelcome turn towards politics and he might offend someone should they sally into the conversation and so thought that novelling would be a good starter with a bit of poetry thrown in to sauce it up.

"I'm writing a novel but I write poetry, too."

"A novel? That's a long grind. What's it about?"

Shit! He forgot she'd ask that. Remain enigmatic. Keep it broad.

"Love. Loss. Tragedy."

"Just read a love story. *The French Lieutenant's Woman.* She was waiting on a harbour for him to come back since he'd fucked her and then fucked off. I love Love Stories. Do you? Well of course you do. Stupid! What kind of poetry?"

"Mainly.... observations.... of feelings.... all the stuff we can't touch but feel...."

"Metaphysical? I really like John Donne."

"Yeah... he's good....*metaphysical.*"

"I like the one where his mistress comes to him in his chamber and they *lie together* but he describes untying her bodice! Really lovely but like, well *dirty* as well." She excitedly giggled

Chamber....Lie together... bodice? He hooked the period and took a punt,

"The *seventeenth century* had its style and social and sexual taboos, of course, so one had to be careful what one said, as a poet, unless you wanted to lose your head!"

"I know!"

Score. Becks continued in her salacious mien.

"....but Donne more or less tells you they're going *to fuck* but doesn't and it's more exciting that way. Real turn on, don't you think? Do you ever write about fucking? You know ....? Do any of your characters ever have a really good fuck?"

What!! She looked so earnest when she said that. That was three fucks in the same sentence.

"I have done....before....in another novel I abandoned."

"Why did you abandon it? Was the fucking no good?"

"No…..the fucking was good….the best bit… actually… very good….err.."

"…..fucking."

"…..just that the plot was wrong… that's all."

"Was there too much fucking? Was there the wrong fucking? It has to be right, doesn't it? I mean if your characters are on a train to say… Milan in a sweltering hot summer they can't just get to it banging up against the buffet car seats when the rest of the passengers are taking dinner, can they?"

He was getting flustered by an eighteen year old who was far too graphic for him but sensed she was trying to be shocking….or *something?*

"No it was just….*fucking wrong*…I guess." He half stammered out.

And he laughed at that but then, quite alarmingly, stopped suddenly and said,

"Was that your girlfriend you were with before?"

"What... no! No, just a friend."

"Lots of people fuck at parties."

"They do. Do they?"

"Yes."

There was another intense stare from her and Kelly rightly suspected that this was an act of desperation from a hefty lass that had been ribbed constantly about it by bastards like him at school, which earmarked her out as an untouchable among the boys at the expense of severe ridicule being heaped upon them should they ever plough that field, and she had listened to all the other girls describe their fumbles at bus-stops and liaisons with their paramours when their parents were out wishing her turn would come soon but it never did. Kelly then understood that she had singled him out as one who might oblige and possibly be equally desperate, which didn't please him much, at all. He then had a mighty irritation in his y-fronts that needed rearrangement and excused himself trying to covertly have a claw as he left the room. Rebecca saw him do this and concluded he had an erection with all her *fucking* talk and decided that he, a man of an experienced age and possibly unattached or desperate, could be the one to break her hymen once and for all this glorious summer's evening and that her brother, Crispin, was not going to get in the way this time.

Rearrangement successful, Kelly talked with a few people as he mingled around the flat for the next few hours steadily drinking. He was aware that wherever he went Becks wouldn't be far behind, which he found mildly amusing but egotistically flattering, also, which he enjoyed even more as the alcohol took a good hold of him. A stream of people arrived as the night wore on. He drifted into the kitchen around midnight where Megan was in a group around an older man who was drinking whisky from a cut crystal glass with two large ice cubes clunking around in it. They were assembled around the table with him firmly at the focus and two very studious chaps with long hair, beards, t-shirts and jeans. One t-shirt declared that *Led Zeppelin* had toured extensively around the UK, recently, and the other had *Dissident Aggressor* starkly printed in white letters across the black front. An assortment of young women stood and sat at the table listening, of which Megan had managed to position herself at the centre of the huddle and was nodding at the voluble and passionate rant being made by one girl who seemed to have been rattling on in her southern English accent for quite a time.

"Look.....I'm not saying that Jane Austen was a raging revolutionary, for Christ's sake! I'm not saying she was a female writer who wanted to bring down the government and install another woman just because she had a pair of tits and a flange, all

I'm saying is that her observations and analysis of the world that she had to tolerate, let me repeat...*tolerate*....was short-sighted patriarchal shit designed to control and curtail the ambition of women, any women, to aspire to anything other than a simpering, low-cut, tits out, trophy wife who said the right things at dinner parties......"

She took a breath at this point which was a good thing because she was becoming red-faced in her ardour for the defence of Jane Austen as a subversive critic of The Establishment. Some other girls around her nodded their approval. As did Megan.

Kelly looked over to Megan who smiled back. Kelly reached onto the table for another beer.

The *Led Zeppelin* acolyte spoke.

"They were *part* of The Establishment, weren't they? Women? All across Europe women, of that petit-bourgeois and bourgeois class, not to mention the aristocracy, were busy either supporting Napoleon or knitting socks, or getting their servants to knit socks for our boys out in Crimea and seemed happy to do it as far as I could see. What did you expect them to do? Their job was to support their men and get their legs open when they were told to."

She stupidly chomped right into the bait.

"Well if they were anything like you Don, they'd be lifetime members of the two-up-two-down club and just spunk without any thought for their women's pleasure......"

Kelly opened his can which hissed out its gas loudly and spurted a white foamy froth onto the kitchen floor. He apologised to Robert Plant's underpants, whom he was standing close to, with non-descript mumbles and went to the sink to fetch a cloth. Megan squirmed. Kelly's interruption had stopped Jane Austen's vociferous minder from unleashing her eruptive tirade back on Zeppo, who sported a tiny smirk, which was noted by the whisky drinking professor who made an attempt to quell her fury.

"Emma,, Emma... take no heed of this right-wing rock n' roll ruffian. He does the same thing in my seminars, don't you, Donald? He is a philistine quite unworthy of your cerebrally delicious analysis of Napoleonic and Georgian womenhood."

"You fucking prick, Don!" One of Emma's mates said.

"Oh, loosen your bra-strap for fuck's sake, Julie! And it's Mr Prick to you! Anybody want to talk about *In Through the Out Door* and drink shit loads of beer."

His mate, the dissident aggressor, threw up his hand and smiled broadly at the chance to talk about Led Zeppelin's album. So he did.

"*In the Evening* is a turd of an opener to this album and I move that we petition Zep to have it re-pressed with that track as track three on side two and that we, by law, drink copious flagons of beer!"

Kelly thought, *what an absolute knobhead* as he dabbed the floor with a cloth. *He couldn't take one night in The Duke.* He looked like he weighed eight and a half stone, wet through.

Emma wasn't finished.

"She was subversive because she quietly lampooned the characters, culture, society and protocols in her sub-text and narrative voice. All I'm saying is this made her a feminist and anti-establishment. So you can fuck off, now, Don!"

She took a celebratory swig of her bottled cider physically issuing a full stop. Professor Whisky, however, took a sip and offered his opinion using a tone that sounded guarded and perhaps a tad condescending,

"Whereby, it may be reasonable to say she was subversive in a closeted way, it can't be ignored that she was also enjoyably gossipy for her large readership of *other women,* Emma? And she was a sad little stick herself, wasn't she. Spinster? Virgin? Her themes hardly wavered from *Prejudice* to *Northanger Abbey;* love, marriage, social stratification, money, relationships? If you want to talk about the early more overt anti-establishment stuff, one could argue Robinson Crusoe was an attempt by Defoe to use the trials of Alexander Selkirk to offer a new model of society, perhaps a *let's go back to Eden,* sort of discussion……

Emma wasn't having this,

"Oh come on, Arthur! Crusoe adopted every convention he could learned at the knee of his beloved England that retained his civilised status and eventually Defoe threw in a class system when Man Friday arrived! He didn't even give him a Christian name the hypocritical shit!"

Zeppo chimed in,

"…and he prospered and survived, did he not? Class happens. Nobody designs it.....and it was *Man.....*or Mr Friday to you!"

Prof Whisky continued,

"Yes but the reaction to those stratas that evolve are also important in literature. Bit obvious but we have to put Dickens up there. The bearded adulterer was a noted champion of the underclass. Moving on; *Germinal, Josef K, The Iron Heel,....*"

Kelly had an out of body experience as he heard himself quietly say,

"The Good Soldier Sveyk."

Everyone turned around and looked at him. Megan panicked just in case Kelly had made an embarrassing addendum to the list and her association with him.

"Quite so…thank you….." Professor Whisky returned and then Megan beamed a relieved smile out at Kelly

"…..however, the geography of Europe is covered in that particular tome and the examples of *affected* idiocy as an *effective* undermining of establishment hegemony, possibly surpass it in the landscape of stupidity both in the emblem of Sveyk and in the folly of The Great War. Very good example….ermm…."

Nobody really knew the man in the suit with too long, slicked back hair. Again, all turned to him to find out.

"Kelly." Kelly quietly said.

Professor Whisky studied him.

"A man of knowledge, I presume?"

"Some. I just read."

"Those who *just read* see a melange and confusion of letters that create sounds in the density of their profound dullness. Those who *read* hear our universe of ideas, our human limitations and our need to improve. I presume you *read*, sir? Delighted to share your company in cups, Mr Kelly."

"Likewise….?"

"Millington. John. Prof Lit."

The conversation then took a turn towards whether Led Zeppelin should split and call it a day because they were now just producing shit that wasn't even sellable shit and that Punk had shifted the goalposts of rock music which now must harken to the body blow that had been so soundly delivered. Megan had only heard of them and so ducked the issue and quickly twisted through the thronging kitchen to Kelly and took his arm.

"That was nice of Prof Millington to say that to you, wasn't it?" she said to Kelly cosying into him and the reflected approval. "I knew you read books but I didn't really expect you to have known one of the books that professor Millington wanted to remember. Aren't you clever."

"I suppose so." Attempting to apparently dismiss it and sound cool and sophisticated.

Kelly noticed the display of physical contact that Megan was apparently beginning to enjoy but he knew she was marking her territory when doing this which gave him great hope of the next few hours and Kelly enjoyed it and considered it perhaps a time close to the appointed hour to deliver the sonnet as a coup de etat that would finally see him meet Megan in a twelve round clinch of sweaty enmeshment. Where and how was his next consideration but he didn't want to rush things and really wanted to get a glassful of the whisky that Prof Millington was slurping. He had noticed that there was quite a superfluity of various bottles and blocks of canned and bottled beer arranged around the flat which suited him perfectly giving him scope to wander from room to room and attack the said grog without looking as though he was an avaricious alcoholic to the attendant throng. His timely interjection into the conversation had increased his stock with a few of the silent observers of the debate who now gave him a smile as they passed across the large hallway.

Megan guided him into the massive lounge and they sat down with their drinks on the sofa. Kelly wanted to start a discussion with Megan that was in relationship territory but not to get too heavy either. He tried,

"I don't think your Dad was very keen on me coming here with you."

"What's it got to do with him? You're my friend, aren't you?" she glowed.

"Well…yes but I don't think he wants me to be any kind of *special* friend?"

"What, a mentally retarded one!" she giggled

"Not that kind of special! You know what I mean. Don't you?"

"Well, I might know what you're talking about, I might not. Nobody has asked me to be their special friend, lately, that I can remember?"

Kelly then, quite inappropriately, did an imitation of someone with a speech defect and keening head and said,

"Will yooo….will yooo beee my shpeshull fwend please Megan?"

She said "Not cool!" and gave him a playful dig in the ribs and she heard the sound of paper being crushed.

"What's that in your pocket?" she said craning her neck to try and see inside his suit jacket.

"Oh that's just my seduction manual. I've just completed section C sub-clause four. *Remain enigmatic and interesting while talking to pretty girls.*"

"The only pretty girl I've seen you talking to was Crispin's younger sister when you first arrived?"

"Who? Oh the fat kid! Yeah she was a bit obvious about it and a smidgeon graphic but I managed to get out of her clutches unscathed."

"Maybe you should hang around until she *scathes* you, then? She's got a pretty face."

"Well….I can't say I'm fond of *fulsome* girls, you know……"

And then he looked Megan up and down as he leaned back on the sofa.

"……I like them trim and pretty all over with pigtails and Doc

Marten boots…. Oh look! You've got pigtails and you're wearing Docs! Well I never….who'd've thought it….what a coincidence….!!"

Megan laughed and told him that she was going to get herself another drink and asked Kelly if he wanted another, which he did because he wanted to make alcoholic hay in this situation while the sun was distinctly shining, but he coolly refused adopting an unhurried lie and held up his half-full can of beer and checked out her shapely arse as he watched her go.

Seconds had hardly passed as Becks circled her prey and plonked herself where Megan had been sitting in what was an uninhibited predatory move. Kelly knew this immediately as his masculine ego swelled again, quietly delighted that he was being hunted. She stared straight at him as if she was going to declare something or stab him. He knew not so just smiled back at her.

"Hi, Mr Writer." Becky said drunkenly. "I was just thinking that if you wanted, entirely up to you of course….if you wanted….you could write me a little love poem, nothing too big, just a ditty, just a few lines declaring your lustful intentions to me and I would rebuff your advances for ten seconds, just to preserve my unblemished reputation and then the verse, hugely romantic would overtake me and I would then fall into your strong arms and then you'd take me to a bedroom and shag me?"

"Hi….?" He returned. "Good party."

"Is it? There's lots of people kissing each other all over the place and nobody is kissing me. Do you want to kiss me?"

As she spoke the alcoholic source of her hard stare and bold approach became apparent. She was slurring a little and had the head wobble of imbiber close to the point of inebriation. Kelly didn't want to be rude to her or hurt her feelings despite the admission that his quest for Megan was not currently in full flow, or if it was but he was being rejected, there was every chance he would accept her less than timid advances and make the best of a heavy load, however, Megan was his quarry with every possibility of future returning fixtures should he get his tactics right.

"Err...that is a lovely offer but I don't think I could do that this evening...Becks."

"Why not? I mean we're in the same league aren't we? There's nobody else at the party that will kiss me tonight. They all think I'm too young and most of them know my brother so they won't and you aren't, like, in the rugby team or anything and you're wearing that shit lecturers suit and your hair isn't cool...just a bit long but, like, not rocker long, just *shit* long. You know?"

Kelly's ego had just been pricked by an eighteen year old. A fat one that couldn't get a boyfriend, so he'd do. Apparently? His attempts to smarten up for the evening had fell on barren ground, it seemed, with this rejected, big-haired, third female backing singer from *The Human League*, the one that didn't get through the audition, the one that sweated too much under the studio lights and spread her pheromones in a light haze over the rest of the band, but would take pity on him and snog him when times were tight. Despite this, which irritated him, he decided to remain diplomatic.

"I can't.... I have another...*friend*. You know."

Becks then looked at him and then to the door.

"Not Meggy McMiggins, the thickest whore in Whitechapel!"

"Sorry?....Who?" Nonplussed.

"Meggy McMiggins. The TEFL girl, Megan, who thinks The Great Barrier Reef was a huge fence in Australia? The girl that thinks Alan Bennett was Gordon's brother?"

"And you call her....?"

"Meggy McMiggins. Well I didn't but I do now. They all do. She's nice but dim. They all made up a Dickensian character for her because she was so dense and *sooo* desperate to be cool. Everybody laughs at her behind her back and says she's the whore that Jack the Ripper turned down. Is she your girlfriend?"

"Well….no…?"

"Good! Now listen to me…listen…this is very important... to me…you…as well…also…..erm…"

"Kelly."

"Kelly! Here's the deal… if you kiss me tonight…and not Muggy McMikkens it doesn't have to be here, because my stupid big brother would see us, anyway, if you kiss me tonight…. I guarantee I'll let you feel my tits. That's on the table right from the off. That is a guaranteed opener. If that goes well I'll let you rub my pussy and I'll play with your gearstick and then assuming there's a bedroom free we can go and have a really good fuck, after that. Wha'd'y'think?"

For so long Kelly had dreamed about such a girl but he was still smarting from the description of him and the collective, two-faced humiliation of Megan, who at that moment arrived at the lounge door and saw her place was taken. She smiled and indicated she was going to the loo which was at the end of a long part of the hallway secluded from elsewhere and thought he could catch her there and deliver his *piece de resistance* that had taken him all afternoon to write. After all it was well past midnight now and the move had to be made soon. However, he felt a greater affection and need to protect her, whatever they thought of her and it wasn't for ever. They'd be gone soon and she'd never know what they thought of her. He liked her. That was all that mattered and he knew that tonight was a future investment that could possibly pay back dividends for some time to come so this short adventure would have to be refused.

"Well…as I said.. I think it is a terrific offer but I have other interests and have already made some investment of time into the venture, which I'll never get back and have drawn up a small inventory of the goods which I intend to present at the next fortuitous meeting....so....?"

Becks threw herself back into the couch in a petulant display of disappointment as Kelly was about to get up.

"Why can't I lose my fucking virginity! None of the boys at school wanted to shag me and I even put it on a plate for Nigel Dankworth *Wankworth* the school dickhead, and he didn't even want to shag me! I'm eighteen for fuck's sake. Why won't anyone shag me?"

She was tipsy and speaking far too loudly for Kelly's taste and he met a few eyes looking back at him. He half smiled as if to say *what can you do, eh?* and went to get up. She grabbed him on the shoulder and gave him a healthy thrust downwards and he plonked back down again.

"Listen....." she slurred, "....think it over! The offer still stands, Mr Writer.... *Kelly!* If you change your mind and Mickey McMiggins won't shag you, I will do the decent thing and step up. No....I will... if you write me a poem. You could just pretend you were reciting some of your work to me and I'll pretend that it *was* good or interesting. You don't have to say *Okay, Becks get your drawers down. We're on!,* I'll know because of the poem."

Which, again, was a little too loud for Kelly's comfort? More glances over to the sofa which made him even more uncomfortable.

"Back soon. Don't touch the prawn vol au vents. I've had seven of them and I don't think they were defrosted right. They're dodgy. I'll go and see if there's any more ugly boys arrived."

She tottered away and Kelly was keen to catch Megan in the hallway corridor to the toilet but didn't want to appear as if he was chasing a drunk eighteen year old so he stayed where he was for a period that was politic and of good sense before he left the room but when he did he took the time to study a picture that was on the wall moving his gaze to detailed parts just to gild the lily.

The corridor to the loo was more or less empty. A few people crossing at the top of the hall but not so close that they would hear if he delivered his opus there. The bog door was locked and he could hear shuffling and the tearing of loo-roll. He checked the hallway again and got a little anxious of the inevitability of someone having to use the toilet pretty soon. He decided that it would be quite romantic if he delivered the sonnet through the toilet door to Megan, almost like the distant sound of Romeo below the balcony and reciting up to Juliet. He had another glance down the hall and took out the paper and unfolded it. He spoke the first lines:

Why should the sun deceive the world this way?
Why should the moon beguile with lighted face?

He got the depth of voice bang on, he thought, as he pressed his face up to the door. The sounds within then ceased. He knew then he had her attention. He pressed on;

Here lies unfettered loveliness each day,
Here on this earth is bounteous light grace.

Then into the meat of the subject he said he'd write of;

Constant is thy charm, endless is thy poise,
Thy Beauty doth anoint the smiling globe,

He'd decided to use the *thee's* and *thy's* to give it a more classical feel which he knew she'd melt for;

Mute radiance assures thy greatest noise,

A quite discernible farting noise echoed from the chamber within and then some muffled sounds again. Nevertheless he continued;

And acolytes of thee do fall to touch thy robe.

He took a big breath knowing he was driving dramatically toward the big finish which would send the thunderbolt into her and he imagined her face smiling as she hugged him and then the sound of Marvin Gaye singing *Let's Get It On;*

Like faithful dog I wait the love of thee,
Like lovelorn youth, I crave the lovers dance,
While giving Zeus adorns thee in Beauty,
And Jove attends the time of thy Constance.
If I could kiss the lips that speak my poorest name,
Then happy is my heart and thus begins the game.

He knew he'd broken some of the metre of the sonnet but *what the fuck*, he thought, it had a job to do. This was Megan, not F.R.Leavis. He held the sonnet out and stepped back as the toilet was flushed. The jolt of the bolt opening thudded and the door began to open slowly and light emanated into the darkened corridor and then onto his beaming face losing vision for a moment or two. His broad smile couldn't have been any broader and his sense of self-satisfaction was at level ten.

Becks, the fat girl, stepped into the light with a visage of girlish joy. She stepped towards him and lifted her hand to take the sonnet. Kelly's smile dropped off his face and ran back up the corridor and out the front door, leaving him there, mouthless and dumbfounded.

"That was beautiful!" Becks, said and put her hand to her eyes as if to stop any more obvious emotion from embarrassing herself any further.

"No....no..it wasn't....erm..you know....?" as he pulled back the sonnet.

He was about to say *for you* when a heavily methaned shitty smell from the loo hit him and he gagged a little. He stepped away from the toilet and she placed herself slightly up the corridor between him and the exit back into the flat. He panicked as he saw one of the big rugby lads turn into the corridor obviously to come and use the loo and so he darted into the toilet and locked the door. The smell was thick but he had to stay there to assess the situation and what to do next. As he was there he decided to have a piss, mainly to authenticate him being there because the big rugby player would have seen the lovelorn joy on the face of Becks, and so he unzipped and fished about for his cock. He located it tucked well away against the top of his thigh and pulled it to extract it from his trousers but then a stinging pain shot across the top of his foreskin.

He carefully dragged it out and looked down at yellow pustulating sores adorning his glans and foreskin. He dropped his head further down to get a better look and then understanding what he was looking at felt the rush of shock create a light-headedness and he nearly swooned. Regathering his senses, he put his hands on his head and turned as if to travel somewhere but the confines of the smallest room stopped him going anywhere and then he looked down at his infected penis which looked even worse on second glance. He delicately pulled back his foreskin and revealed even more wet sores underneath. And then the gravity of the situation began to unveil itself. *Her upstairs,* he audibly said and looked down again. He actually needed to piss so he dangled his penis over the bowl and began to pee. The urine caught one of the sores and he winced as a hot stinging pain radiated through him, so he pulled his foreskin back as far as was needed to let him piss. He stared at the wall above the bowl and anger began to rumble somewhere within him. He knew what this meant. He had no idea what the infection was but either way sex with Megan, with anyone, was off the table. He then began to feel ridiculous having read the sonnet out to the wrong girl, at having ever written the fucking thing in the first place. He dabbed his cock with tissue and then turned to open the bathroom cabinet hoping that there might be something there he could use to appease the infection. Nothing.

A thudding on the door gave him a start as a middle-class accent forcefully said,

"No fucking wanking, please. *Hugo Hurry-Up,* here! My back teeth are floating!"

The irony of what was said was not lost on him and he carefully zipped up and exited the toilet.

"About time, mate. Fuck me you're not well!" he said as he caught the smell.

Kelly's mood was now entirely flat. He didn't care. He turned to look at the rugby player who was smiling in apparently masculine bonhomie at Kelly. Kelly said,

"Fuck off....*mate*."

There was a drawing room in this massive flat that he noticed nobody was going into much so he thought he could hide for a while in there as he decided what to do and avoid Megan and Becks

There were a few people in there. Mainly young students who'd had too many lemonades. They were sitting in a circle with a lighted candle in the middle and quaffing beer and sharing jollity about their youth. Kelly walked across the room to an old oak desk that had a bottle of whisky amongst other spirits placed neatly on it and unscrewed the cap and looked for a glass. He took a swig from the bottle uncaring and unable to locate one as the gaggle of young students laughed collectively. He turned to look out of the window.

"Do you remember The Woodentops!" one excited young girl said.

"Yes I do!" said another, "Do you remember the dog? What was he called, again?"

Two other young girls and a young lad, all patently varsity friends, all shouted together,

"Spotty-dog!!" and gurgled like drains! *Oh how they laughed,* thought Kelly.

The solitary lad offered an excited contribution,

"I have to say I loved Andy Pandy. Mum used to watch it with me.

One of my earliest, and I have to say, my most cuddliest memories!"

Kelly retched, inwardly and took another swig and checked the label. *Glenlivet.* Decent stuff but what else would you expect of Britain's future?

"Yes, Andy Pandy was really good but I was a little unnerved at Mr Benn." A girl said from across the main huddle."

The door opened and Becks came in. They all shouted *Beeeeeccckkks!!!* together and she sat down in the circle with them and looked across to the anonymous suit by the window. Kelly caught her watching him. She smiled and struggled to focus. He returned to his blank gaze out of the window.

"Which was your favourite kids show, Becks?" said a girl dressed much the same as she was.

"I quite liked Hector's House with the nosy cat who always put her ladder up against Hector's wall...."

"And that's not a euphemism!"ejaculated the young lad and everyone laughed loudly, again. Becks continued,

"..... but I reckon my favourite had to be The Magic Roundabout."

Everyone shouted *yes* and then a general discussion ensued about stoned guitar-playing rabbits and a moustachioed thing on a spring that always ended the show with the phrase *time for bed*. Kelly had had enough and wanted to offend them. He wasn't really sure why because they were really quite harmless but there was undoubtedly an otherness to them, a distance of language, demeanour and culture that he had been forced to understand as a child but knew that the gesture had never been reciprocated and he wanted Becks to fuck off and stop chasing him, as well, so what the fuck? He took another swig and adopted their excited tones and exuberantly crossed over to the circle and kneeled down with them all. Becks was delighted. They all shushed each other as Kelly said,

"Yes.....yes....I loved The Magic Roundabout, too, it was great, wasn't it! I have to say that I quite fancied Florence's pants, she was well fit with that little skirt! But the best bit was when you'd watched it and you'd got all tucked up in bed and your Dad would then come in to say goodnight and you'd give him a kiss and then he would slip his hand underneath the top sheet and slide his hand carefully under your scrotum and then give it a little tickle, a little stroke, which made you smile...... and go to sleep...quite quickly.....No?"

Kelly watched the jollity dissipate amongst their dropping faces and affected a tone of bemusement and then said,

"Just me, then? Oh well...."

Then he got up, picked up the whisky bottle and walked out of the room. Becks hurried out after him.

"What was all that about?" she slurred to his back. He turned.

"I'm sorry, Fatty. Were you speaking to me?" He took another slug of whisky.

"There's no need to be mean, you fucker! You were mean to them in there and you've been mean to me leading me on all night!"

"Leading you on! Leading *you* on? I can see that your delusions stretch further than the reflection you see in a full-length mirror. You practically talked your knickers off to me on the couch and put a ribbon around it and you were terribly, terribly mean *to me* leaving that fucking stink in the bog, earlier, *Darling!*"

"You read me a poem! I thought you wanted to kiss me....and *all that*....you know?"

"Did you look out of the window in the lounge?"

"Yes...why?"

"Because not so long ago there were cattle that used to graze on The Meadows. Big, fat, ugly-faced, stinky-arsed cows that just pissed and shit where they stood and then ate the grass next to their piss and shit. Right next to it! I would rather kiss one of those cows that used to graze out there than kiss you, you fat, sweaty, lump of desperation. I'd probably have a better conversation as, well! A lot better than, *why won't anyone shag me, sob, sob, sob,* they'd just say *moo* and I'd prefer that to you, *Dumpy.* Now fuck off and find a fellow tubster and get yourself a skirt that doesn't accentuate your girth, pie-arse!"

Tears welled up in her eyes and then a torrent of sobs blurted out and she turned and went back into the drawing room. Kelly went to the kitchen and kept the whisky close, surreptitiously swigging then dropping it under his jacket. One of the Rugby team had his friend by the waist and was showing some girls how to bring down a player with a tackle.

Kelly stood for a short while watching this great show of bravado, loud voices and rutting males vying to impress anyone who would listen or watch and found them ridiculous. Then he began to hate himself for being at the same social event as these arseholes and then began to chuckle, inwardly at first, but as their descriptions of holds and grips and underhand methods, like flicking bollock areas or seizing a handful of thigh-skin, to bring an opponent down became more graphic, all interspersed with the cracking of a few beers that were fed to them whilst in a ruck or scrum position, which Kelly noted they thought *a terrific wheeze*, he began to audibly laugh. Laughter that morphed with the laughter extant in the kitchen but then it became a solitary cackle conspicuous by its singularity. Then Megan came in. Kelly didn't see her. One of the rutting rugger chappies addressed him whilst in a head lock and wiping beer from his face.

"So...do you play, mate?"

Kelly laughed louder.

"Good god, no. I'm straight."

The two rugger chums released each other and looked at Kelly.

"Straight? What exactly are you saying......?"

Kelly sprightly marched up to them and offered his hand and lampooned their southern tones.

"Kelly! Reading Shite in the university of life. How very spiffing to meet you....?"

The room had gone quiet and some sloped out feeling the tension rise. Crispin flatly spoke as he squeezed Kelly's hand, tightly.

"Crispin Douglas. Scrum-half reading Physics at the University of Edinburgh. This is Peter Oswald. Front-Row reading...."

"Mathematics at ditto." Peter Oswald growled.

"Ditto?" Kelly said. "Is that the bar where you all sing *I Will Survive* and pour buckets of champers all over each other?"

Crispin rose to his full height.

"You must be either very stupid or very brave, chum. Which is it?"

Kelly was in no mood to be cowed by this buffoon.

"Well......I know I'm not stupid so I reckon I must be being quite brave, Crispin. Sticking my head above the pink parapet you hide behind, and all that, what ho!"

"What pink parapet?" Slugger Oswald asked.

"Oh come on chaps. It doesn't take much analysis, does it? Wearing tight shorts and chasing each other around in the mud, grappling one another tightly around the thighs, and using the need to have possession of *the ball*, which, let's face it, looks like two bell-ends that have been grafted together, as a pretext? Then you all jump naked in a bath together and drink beer and sing songs. Songs about young ladies of questionable reputation. Misogynistic songs basically denigrating womanhood thus confirming your hatred of them and reinforcing, let's face it, your love of each other. Methinks the lady doth protest too much, there, n'est pas? You even have two big H's at each end of the field declaring your homo-erotic need to hold other men tightly. Freud would have called that a turkey-shoot of a psychoanalysis! It's more than apparent to me that you're all quite, quite gay!"

At that moment one of the young girls who'd been in the drawing room hurried in and whispered into Crispin's ear. He drew a dark look across at Kelly and rushed out the room.

"This isn't finished!" he snapped at Kelly.

"Oh, I do so hope not! We could be super friends and get on famously if we'd just give it a shot!" Kelly threw back increasing the volume as Crispin left to attend to his wounded sister.

"What do you think, Petey? You don't need back up from your boyfriend, do you? Could we be friends?"

"I very much doubt that, you shithead. You probably like that girl's game football, right?"

"At least the ball is the proper shape, Peter Rabbit."

"The shapes they make are the ones where they roll around like idiots pretending to be hurt? Fucking girls!"

Kelly sighed and spoke flatly,

"Look, Peter, I am working-class as are most of the lads that play football and because we're working-class we don't have that, what do all call it... *Corinthian spirit,* you know that fallacious stiff upper-lip shite that makes you herald three cheers to the plucky opposition and all that bollocks. They roll around because they're trying to get the fucker that decked them booked so that the next time they come near him they won't be so keen to upend him just in case there's a second booking in the post...and then the little shite of a yellow card turns red for the tackling chappie and then he's off!! Gone! Down to ten men and defending like demons for the rest of the game! They're trying to influence the referee to help them *win the game*, you posh streak of piss!"

"Yes, bloody unfairly!!" Petey returned quickly.

"Absolutely fucking bang on, Petey boy. Completely unfairly. That's right, we cheat and scrap and lie just to try and get an advantage, just to get a break, just to stay ahead in the game. Just to feed the striker. Just to score. Once! Just once because we don't know where the next one is coming from if at all or if we do score it'll be taken away, something good removed, because those in authority say so. Because they deemed us offside, outside the rules, possibly dangerous and then, ironically, they fuck us right up the arse and then we have to pick ourselves up, dust off the shit that has stuck to us and go again. Over and over and then sometime near the end of the game we'll realise we're too tired. Too beaten and worn out. Fucked, Petey. Down, out and fucked. Dead. Sound familiar? A view of life from the gutter....*mate*. Three cheers for Crispin, Petey and all their fruity rugger chums! Hip hip!...."

Nobody shouted *hooray*. The room was silent.

"Oh come on everybody! It's not like you're cheering The Miners on to a glorious victory or anything like that! Give it another go!! Hip Hip....?"

Nothing.

"Oh well then, I'll just settle for a big wet kiss, Petey, but no tongues yet. I'm not a slut. Come on, big fella, bring it home!"

Kelly held out his arms to Peter. Peter seethed.

Megan darted forward as Peter Oswald tightened his fist and

glowered at Kelly. She took him by the arm and led him out into the hall. She was astounded by his outburst and the metamorphosis from sober boyfriend material to this slurring suicidal lush and didn't really know how to deal with him. The whisky had rushed to his head but was no excuse for insulting her friends, she thought, and she didn't really understand what Kelly was actually saying but knew something implicit, maybe a metaphor, she thought, but wasn't sure. Megan told him it was late and maybe it was best if he left on his own, to sober up and get out of what was most likely, imminent danger. Kelly knew that she was embarrassed by him and suddenly felt resentment course through him at her toadying to these alien yahs. The truth was he hated himself, also for the unclean state he now found himself in and the humiliation that was to come, medically, and for ever having chased Megan, whom he had started to love, and knew it, but now couldn't and he decided there and then he didn't want her to like him anymore, either.

"You think I should leave, now, *Meggy?*" he cruelly jibed.

"What?" Megan said.

"It's what they all call you behind your back, you know. All of them. Meggy McMiggins. A thick bitch who can't get far enough up their arses and is really dense. Some shite about a Dickensian hoor and Jack the Ripper. They all laugh at you, *Meggy!* They think you're a joke!"

Megan looked around to see who had heard and met the eyes of whispering faces and smirking onlookers. Then she walked away from him into the lounge. Kelly jammed the whisky bottle into his jacket pocket. Then he left. He quickly descended the old stone stairs out into the night air and crossed the road onto the grass and into the darkness of The Meadows.

It was quiet and although it had been a warm day a shower had occurred while he had been in the party and the grass was damp so he got himself onto one of the tree-lined paths and realised his anger was driving his pace and so he slowed down and caught his breath. He adjusted his infected cock which was bothering him and which made him think drunkenly about his evening's sex with the hooker. He pictured her on top of him and heard her voice encouraging him towards orgasm and his face tightened into an expression of deep regret and anger. He took a healthy swig from the bottle and tried to replace the cap three times each time failing to get the threads into the right position. He managed to replace it but then thought of everything his life had lately been and a surge of rage, pain, humiliation, despondency, rejection and loneliness then erupted in him and he threw the bottle into the air behind him and he let loose a roar that cathartically reflected everything inside him and his eyes welled-up with tears. There included a minor dance of frustration and heard his feet hit the tarmac-ed path, however, confusingly to him the sound of feet on tarmac didn't stop when he did. He realised it was from behind him and turned to see Crispin, Peter, Hugo, Robert Plant's Underpants and the Dissident Aggressor running towards him.

When he'd absorbed the gravity of what he thought was about to occur he just shouted,

"Fuck off, fuck off!! Leave me alone!"

They caught up with him and Crispin spoke first as they surrounded him.

"You said some bad things to my sister, you weird twat!"

Kelly appeared as though he was about to say something when he felt a slap connect with his face. He recovered to see that Hugo, the super try-scorer had delivered the first blow. Then he spoke.

"She's really fucking upset. She's just a kid. You've been trying to get her into a bedroom, all night. That right?"

Kelly, understanding and imagining her spinning her drunken fabrications to these lumps of maleness, experienced a voice-removing swoon of injustice., then found it again, somewhat enraged.

"What! Is that what she told you?"

"You calling her a liar?" Big Peter said.

"Yes, I fucking am! She's been trying to get me to shag her all night! It's the other way around. She's fucking desperate, you big posh tool!"

Another slap came from his left.

"She fucking must be if she was trying to get off with the boyfriend of Meggy McMiggins!" Peter said flapping his warm hand in the air.

The right-wing Robert Plant's Underpants has ostensibly come for the jaunt as a gesture of support to his varsity chums but the truth was he saw a possibility of exerting some physical pain on someone socially sanctioned or at the very least witnessing some, which he quite liked and was thinking of something to say to appear offended whilst saying it, to justify the assault. He decided that a tangential approach would be clever.

"Am I overweight?" he said.

Kelly knew where this was going.

"Yes you are. Haven't you seen what you're carrying around? If it's a fact and the evidence backs that up then it's the truth, isn't it?"

RPU swung a haymaker of a slap against Kelly's face that sent his head into orbit and he fell to the ground. Crispin leaned over him and shouted down at him.

"The truth is you're a weird bastard that's been harassing my sister all night and you called her fatty, and said she was a shitty cow when she told you to fuck off! She told me about the little love poem trying to get her into a bedroom and talking about tickling your scrotum or some shit like that. The truth is you're fucking toxic, mate. A strange bastard that shouldn't be near us or my little sister, you cunt!"

Kelly lifted his head and had a vision of clarity and met Crispin's face nose to nose as he leaned upwards.

"The truth is I'm not weird, strange or fucking unusual Crispin, Old Boy! I am the one here that represents the majority! The schlepps that empty your bins and clean your streets and fix your fucking plumbing! I'm the one that digs the roads while you lot nance about in your seminars and applaud the closure of the mines and watch kids starve as you stare into your filofax looking for another chance to shuffle some numbers and screw a few shilling from wherever you can screw it from, doesn't matter who suffers! That's who I am!"

He should have stopped at the *kids starving* bit. He had given them more than enough to justify beating up the lefty socialist that he really wasn't....*or was?* He wasn't sure but the correct rhetoric fell out of him. But even in these circumstances, he found himself unable to resist playing a role and in this case it seemed somewhat masochistic, however, he was past caring, past the point of any self-preservation because he innately felt he was unclean, lazy, manipulative, deceitful, dishonest, deluded, loathsome and apparently unworthy of love.

Crispin laughed in his face.

"Yeah...? That right, Mr Marx? Who do you think creates the fucking wealth to install my fucking plumbing or build the streets you clean? Not fucking you for a start."

Crispin made a fist and tightened to deliver the blow until The Dissident Aggressor spoke up.

"Crispin! Gentlemen! States rise and fall not by strength alone but by knowledge and wit....or the lack of it? I propose a form of retribution equal to the humiliation suffered by Becks which circumvents the necessity to imperil our own personal liberty....

and *immediate futures*...of which most would be compromised by the bloodying of this fucker, turd that he is, which let's face it, he does deserve...but perhaps an eye for an eye....something thereabouts...much more profound and damaging. Thoughts?"

Peter was bemused.

"What.. we tell him he's fat and I want to shag him?"

The Dissident Aggressor laughed.

"No, no, no...my enormous cherub. Has not this repulsive Trot revealed himself to us?"

They looked baffled.

"I will answer that for you all. The answer is *yes,* and now some parallel metaphor seems appropriate? Keeping up everyone? Take off his trousers. Use them to tie him to a tree. Relieve him of his underpants and then his shoes, of which, they will be trophies we can then present to Becks as honourable redeemers of her reputation and continued maidenhood. This way he will be revealed, exposed, humiliated for who he is to a degree that will deter any future ventures of revenge on his part at risk of having to recount his humiliation to the Scotch Constabulary, possibly the local rag. Everybody wins and nobody is hurt.....*except turdface."*

It took seconds before all, except The DA who conducted and supervised the debagging of Kelly in a dispassionate and distant fashion, grabbed and held him down while his trousers and trainers were removed and his hands were tied together with his socks that were themselves conjoined to make one large tether and then he was pushed up hard against a tree as his trousers were wound around the area of socks between his wrists and were tied securely around the tree so that Kelly, anticipated by The DA, couldn't rip the trousers from the tree. Then they poured a beer over his head and the knots in the socks and trousers to ensure a tight grip and left laughing and playing rugby with his second-hand Dunlop Blue Flash.

Kelly was left there. His man-tackle was inches from the bark of the tree and he had to arc his back to keep them from chafing an already irritated penis. His arse was exposed to the world. His most private of bodily parts was naked and he was unsure of who or where his saviour would come from. He had decided halfway through The DA's description of his proposed punishment, that he had not the energy, strength or sobriety to fight them. He didn't have the resources and knew that any verbal importuning to assuage his situation would fall on deaf ears and so he resolved to suffer. He was relieved that it was dark and that they had not seen his shame, his pustulating *end* or abraded it in any way in their rough handling of him. He couldn't have felt lower. He had not the will to shout for help and he accepted whatever fate, shame or ridicule was now about to befall him. Something welled heavy inside of him and as much as he would like not to have, he cried. Alone. In the obscurity and gloom of the night, tied semi-naked to a tree surrounded by a sea of darkness, cold and with no other soul in sight.

An hour and ten minutes had passed and no-one had ventured along the path in The Meadows. Some minor assaults and drunken altercations had occurred recently in the early hours of some Sunday mornings and people generally gave it a wide berth because of it. There was a line of trees running parallel to the line of trees he was at and occasionally he thought heard some distant shuffling and a small cough. However he wasn't sure. If it was a shitfaced wino lying on a bench and he called out to him for help he couldn't be sure what else might befall him in this state. Kelly's legs and backside were very cold and his feet, despite the summer months, were freezing, too. He had to keep changing position to stop the stress on his body which had become very tiring for him. He had tried to pull and rip at his improvised manacles but they had tied him so close to the trunk of the young tree he had no space or leverage to make a tear in any of it. He leaned his shoulder against the trunk and stared into the darkness. Then something moved in his eyeline about two or three hundred yards away. A lone figure was wandering across the grass and towards the road. Kelly shouted,

"Hello! Hello, there! Can you help me, please!"

The figure stopped. Kelly saw it turn in his direction.

"I need help please! Please, help me!" he shouted again but with a non-hysterical tone.

The last thing he wanted to do was frighten whoever it was away. The figure changed direction and walked unsurely towards the voice in the gloom. The streetlights from the road stretched their dim reach just enough to discern a silhouette.

"Who's that? What's wrong?" A male voice shouted back.

"I'm... *stuck*..." Oblique enough to retain interest. ".....to the tree."

The figure crept towards Kelly like a cat pawing a dead animal unsure that danger may still exist. He was now only about forty yards away and peering at Kelly in the dark whilst looking around perhaps expecting this footpad's accomplices to burst out at him as he fell into the gang's trap. He came closer and as he did so his features became apparent in whatever light there was.

"How are you stuck to the tree?" the now clear face said.

As Kelly went to explain that he was getting married soon and his mates had pulled a stag-night prank, he saw the face of Threeby. Then Threeby saw him and his jaw dropped. Threeby looked him up and down and from the way he did so Kelly knew Threeby was a bit pissed, too. Then he stood back and looked around again for signs of life elsewhere. Then he smiled.

"Bit tied up there, Kells?" Threeby gloated.

"Look....Threeby, could you just....."

"That's not my name! I told you in the dole office. My name's David!"

"I'm sorry...*David*...could you untie the knot for me ....*please.....?*"

"What knot?"

"The knot in the trousers. On your side."

Threeby then realised in his semi-pissed state that Kelly had no trousers on and went around the back of Kelly and observed his bare arse. Then he started laughing.

"You've got no trousers on, Kells! Did you know that? No trousers. Or shoes."

"Yes, I know, Threeb....*David*... just untie the knot..." Kelly said trying to remain friendly.

"Your feet are getting very dirty as well, Kells. Where's your shoes?"

"They've been taken."

"Who took them?"

"Some rugby fuckers. Untie me!"

He let a spurt of emotion dart out and Threeby knew this fully aware of his position of power and decided that to let the moment pass without entirely milking it of any opportunities would be quite remiss of him as a montage of scenes from school flashed through his memory.

"Some rugby fuckers? Why did the rugby fuckers do this to you, Kells?"

"Because they're fuckers and they play fucking rugby! Now untie me you...!!"

".....you what? Jewish cunt? I haven't heard that one for a while. It was always three by two...you know...*Jew*.... or big nose....not that mine is...or ever was....but you said it and everybody laughed. You were always a good laugh at school weren't you, *Kells?* Not to me. I knew exactly who the cunt was, and it wasn't the little Jewish kid."

"I'm sorry David. I'm sorry......"

"Are you?"

"Yes... yes, I am...the knot...."

"You're sorry now,...yes...you're sorry now because you *need me.* You need .me to do something for you and that's why I think you're saying you're sorry. Why did you piss off the rugby players, Kells? I'm guessing you were being a prick and you said a few things. Right?"

"Yes!! I said a few things..."

"What....like you were an astronaut, a racing driver, or *something?* You were a fucking undercover cop in the dole office, remember?"

"Yes..yes! I remember!"

"Why?"

"Why what?"

"Why were you pretending to be an undercover cop? I don't remember you in any of the school plays?"

"It just came to me...I was late....needed an excuse....look can you just untie me and then we can talk..."

"But that's your problem, Kells....you always said too much. Just opened your mouth and fuck the consequences or who you hurt or what lies you told. I'm guessing you did that with these rugby fuckers. Right? Had a few too many, said some things, and you were being a prick."

"Yes!! Yes!! I was being a prick!! I was being the biggest prick on the planet! Untie the trousers!"

"Slow down there, Kells. We finished with the bit when you were being a prick but we haven't finished with the bit when you were saying sorry!"

Kelly considered telling him to fuck off and that he didn't need his help because he sensed that Threeby wasn't going to yield this situation without further discomfort, physically or otherwise to him, but making a few admissions might be easier than another hour exposed to the elements.

"Okay...*I'm sorry.* What more do you want?"

"I want you to tell me what you are sorry for. Tell me."

"And then you'll untie me?"

"Yes."

"First...I want you to look over there on the grass..." Kelly nodded towards where he'd launched the whisky bottle. "....there's a bottle of whisky. Give me a drink."

"Magic word?"

"Please. Fucking please! Give me a drink!"

Threeby went onto the grass and found the bottle and brought it back to Kelly but then he looked at the label, made some comment about the quality and made a big deal about taking a big mouthful, himself.

"That's a very good malt, Kells. Would you like a drink?"

"Yes."

"Would you like me to untie you?"

"Yes!"

"And you want a drink?"

"Yes!"

"Yes....?"

"Please!"

"Here you go..."

Threeby lifted the bottle to Kelly's mouth but then withdrew it as quickly.

Forgive me, Kells, how very rude of me to interrupt. You were saying you were sorry....?"

Threeby took another very deliberate mouthful. Kelly seethed but had to play the game and knew it.

"I'm sorry...."

"....for...?"

"For bullying you!"

"Because....?"

"....you were Jewish."

"...and...?"

"And that's it! Fucking untie me!"

"No....that's far from it, Kells. You're sorry also because it made me feel....?"

"Sad?"

Threeby stepped in and shouted inches from Kelly's face, "Too easy. More! More you heartless cunt!"

The whisky was recycling whatever Threeby had drank earlier.

"Very sad. Hurt. I'm sorry!"

"Try nervous, afraid, embarrassed, ashamed, fucking worthless, different, yes you made me feel like I was from another fucking planet! Like being Jewish was like being an alien! And then you capped it all off when you put that hot iron on my arm! Fucking branded me! Then half the school pointed at me or wanted to see your handiwork. I was a freak. I was your trophy, you cunt and you loved it! An accident you said to Mr Dawson. An accident my fucking arse."

Threeby took another gulp. Kelly could see that he was downing it far too fast and that Threeby was becoming dangerously drunk and emotional.

"Look...David...."

"Sukerman! And I've never sucked off another man in my life! That was another arm to your skills, pun entirely fucking intended!"

Kelly saw Threeby was churning himself into an angry, emotional mess with the memories of school and for the first time had a moment where he understood the longevity and pain that Threeby endured but he had to deal with the immediate problem.

"......David... It was a few years ago now, not that that excuses...*what I did*...but I'm not the guy that I was then....I understand your pain, now.... I want you to know that I'm *ashamed* of how I treated you, yes ashamed....of how sad I made you feel, as you say, so *different*... and that, given the chance I would make it up to you....I would try to understand how you felt....if I could...but you'd have to untie me first....

Threeby listened but stared into the darkness slurping the whisky. Then he had an idea.

"I can help you with that."

Threeby became purposeful and walked across to the next tree and looked at the lower branches. He grabbed a bushy thin branch and snapped it off. Kelly became justifiably alarmed.

"What are you doing, David? No need for that."

Kelly was just taking a guess at what *that* was but he became quite nervous at the apparent imagination of a drink-fuelled, angry and emotional Threeby. He took the bushy thin branch around to Kelly's face.

"You want to know how it feels to be different? Other fucking worldly? Like I said I can help you out. I saw a programme on the telly about a man that had a tail. A tail! Imagine that! He felt like me. I'm going to give *you* a tail, now! How about that"

Kelly's blood drained from his face as Threeby went behind him with the branch.

"Threeby, no! No, you fucking maniac!"

"Come on Kells help me out here, you need to stick your arse out for me."

Kelly did the opposite and clenched for Scotland as Threeby tried to drunkenly find his arsehole with the pointed end of the branch. Kelly felt the missed arrows jab at his arse and the top of his thighs. Then Threeby made some demented noises about Kelly *really not helping much* and Kelly understood the bizarre and frantic attempts for recompense and began to loudly scream for help. This unnerved the already frantic Threeby and he stood and punched Kelly in the side of his face and put his hand over his mouth. Kelly couldn't resist as Threeby's now crazy, wide-eyed face lay inches from his. He manically whispered,

" Do you believe in fate? Destiny?"

Kelly was bemused and said *Ow* against Threeby's hand but relieved the focus had shifted, He nodded and breathed through his nose.

"Good! So do I. Tonight is fate. You have been *presented* to me by destiny. Yahweh has given you to me and... I've just realised that if I can give you a tail.. make you feel as I did, things might change for me. If the bushels can be balanced... I will find a wife, be funny, have friends, children, die with the contentment of a life that was lived. Help me?"

Threeby, tentatively, took his hand away from Kelly's mouth.

"You are not sticking that branch up my fucking arse!"

Threeby gagged him again. Quiet determination characterised his delivery.

"I have to. The vision came to me. I am being guided. I have a proposal. I will say my proposal and then I am going to take my hand off of your mouth. Then you will say yes or no. Do you understand?"

Kelly nodded.

"Tonight you will have a tail. For moments only. But you must comply. Help. You must help me. My life has to change. I can't find a girlfriend. I'm very needy. I want someone to say they love me. I want to be married and have a family but I have no confidence. I think little of myself. I wear unfashionable clothes because I don't deserve to be smart. Because I'm not. I'm not smart. I'm well educated but don't have the balls to tell the world.

I've been passed over, excuse the pun this time, at work for promotion five times. I don't cover the scar you gave me. I wear it openly. I feel guilt. Unworthiness. It has to change. Help me, Kells. You owe me!"

Kelly had thought of an alternative to a sycamore branch being shoved up his arse. He realised Threeby was drunk, had become ridiculously philosophical with a good dollop of insanity thrown in and would not be dissuaded in his desperation or vision of ridiculous retribution. He nodded to Threeby who took his hand from Kelly's mouth.

" Okay, okay...I'll help you...David....I'll help you...but you *cannot* put that branch up my arse. What I *can* do for you...for merely moments only.... is hold the branch between my arse cheeks so you can see what a tail looks like on me..."

He couldn't believe he was saying this.

"...and you can have your revenge. Hurt me. Humiliate me...it's okay...but then you have to untie me? Yes?"

Threeby nodded and took the branch around the back of Kelly and lined up the branch with his arse.

"I have to break off some smaller twigs....be right with you...."

Kelly, at that moment, wondered if his life could become more bizarre as he leaned forward on the tree.

"I'm placing the tail between your cheeks now. Clench!" Threeby told him and Kelly duly obliged.

Threeby sat back onto the path and looked at his work. The leafy bush hung from Kelly's arse as he clenched with all his might.

"How is it? Is it what you wanted to see!!" Kelly desperately asked him. Threeby was silent.

"Threeby! David!"

Threeby looked at Kelly with his tail with obvious dissatisfaction and drank more whisky. Then he stood up.

"No!...No it's not, you fucker, Kells! It's not a tail! It's still a branch! Leaves and twigs stuck between your arse! I want you to feel bad! Strange!"

"Oh I do, I do, David!!...Right now I feel really strange.. *very strange*...now untie me!

"It hasn't worked! It hasn't fucking worked, Kelly you cunt!"

Threeby ripped *the tail* from Kelly's arse cheeks as Kelly winced as the chafing wood tore his flesh, and started a hysterical thrashing of Kelly asking God when he will be free, when will he be loved, why He was making him suffer in this way? Kelly took the first few whips to his bare legs and backside groaning at the pain and took a whip across the swollen part of his face courtesy of Her Majesty's Secret Service which made him wince. Then Threeby lost his grip in his frenzy and the branch flew out of his hand so he started to slap and throw pathetic punches at Kelly who tucked his head down near the trunk of the tree. Threeby was throwing ever-weakening blows, gasping for breath and crying. Kelly had to try another route.

"David! Stop...stop!! God has not forsaken you! He has not left you! He *has sent me* to you! To *you*, David. *Love thine enemies as you would love....those who are not thine enemies...*" he improvised having a go at Judaic scripture.

"Can you not see?...I *was* your enemy but now, if you will let me....*I* will be your friend. *I* will be your friend and we can have a beer together, watch the game together, and *I* will introduce you to *lots of women*..." he lied, "Lots of women! All looking for husbands. We can even go on holiday together...make memories before you settle down with a beautiful girl and have kids. Kids, David! You will be a father! Happy with a wife. Let me guide you...you will be my saviour now....*if you untie me*....and I will be *yours*....later on....n'that..."

Threeby seemed to have an epiphanous moment of light rising on his little horizon as he looked into the dark and then to Kelly and slowly said,

"Yes...yes....I see, I see!!", drunkenly acknowledging Kelly's rationale.

"This is the most unusual of meetings, David. He has had me tied to this tree for *you*, David....so that I can help *you*....and then *I* become a better person...."

"You're right...Kells! This is fate!"

"Exactly.....I know you see and when you *free me* ......from my old ways....and from *this tree*...and let me help you with *your life* we can both be better people. Happier people!"

"Yes!! I want to be happy.... find a wife...."

"...have kids!"

"Yes, have kids!"

"...and by untying me our new lives begin, ...David."

"Yes, yes! I have to free you to free me! It's a sign. A sign! I am being watched I should have realised! It was a test! You have to be free and then I will be!"

Threeby untied the trousers and freed the socks from his wrists whilst telling Kelly that he knew some good places they could go to together. Kelly affected a smile and nodded at Threeby only focused on the task being done and done he quickly pulled on the trousers and buttoned up. He then snatched the bottle from Threeby who was looking at him with a deluded hopeful smile of better days to come.

"What now?" Threeby smiled at him.

Kelly held the bottle up to whatever light he could find and checked to see what was left and took a swig of the three inches, or so, remaining. He had never broken a bottle over someone's head, before and the first time seemed to take an age as someone else inside of him swung the bottle towards Threeby's head as he heard a gutteral shouting noise come from deep within him. What he also didn't expect was that it didn't break only catching Threeby on the side of the head with the thick part on the bottom of the bottle. Threeby crashed to the ground and Kelly landed several emotional punches to his face whilst calling him *a sad weird bastard* and every pejorative anti-semitic name he could remember from school. Threeby cried out and when Kelly stopped he lay whimpering. Then he pulled Threeby's Hush-Puppy shoes from his feet aggressively, while listening to his sobs. He looked at the size. Eight. Big enough to get him home, He jammed them onto his freezing feet and picked up the bottle considering another slug but was stopped by the familiar howl of Sasquatch in the dark. Everyone in the pub knew he didn't stop at closing time and often took himself into the darkness of The Meadows to drink away his pain. He strained to see in the darkness. He'd had enough whisky and dropped the bottle and made out towards his flat across the grassy parkland. The sobs of Threeby were eventually lost to Kelly, fading as he shuffled homeward. Threeby's shoes started to really hurt after about half a mile and decided he'd manage the last quarter mile in his socks. Threeby's shoes hit the fence of the tennis courts and dropped down behind the hedge surrounding it.

He went home and straight to bed and lay in an exhausted stupor until the sunlight stung his eyes into waking through the uncurtained window and church bells declared its Sundayness. His head hurt nearly as much as his lacerated arsehole, sore face, broken heart and his dignity. His squelching sore cock reminded him of that.

Kelly sat naked in the darkness of his toilet getting respite from the light and from the heat in his flat exacerbated by the malfunction of his physical thermostat whenever he was hungover and chose to sit on the cold porcelain. His head was a myriad of thoughts. He could feel the discomfort at the end of his penis and was scared to look in the daylight at what he might see but he knew it wasn't going to be good, whatever he saw and he had started to feel the swelling of the glands in his groin which were becoming sensitive to the touch. Then he remembered the party. Blackness enveloped him. He needed to drink water so he got up and made his way to the kitchen past the door with the paw-scratches. He drank a glass of water and winced as he moved. His head was throbbing and his cock wasn't much better. He knew it was time to take a look. He pulled back his foreskin and beheld several yellow sores. Small blisters seemingly full of glistening...*something*. He became quickly sad and angry at the same time. Everything that happened the night before had been precipitated by this. It was her doing upstairs! She could have told him to use a condom. He was drunk. How was he to know what to do in that situation? He'd never been with a prostitute, before. She was diseased and needed to know it. Then he thought that every one of the punters she serviced last night might have caught whatever it was that he had. A selfless instinct from somewhere saw him resolve to make sure it didn't happen to any more faceless guys he would never know and pulled on his trousers and a t-shirt, splashed his face and went upstairs. He had ran up in his rage and was now out of breath but he wanted to look and sound angry, aggrieved, and that helped. She had to get the message. He thudded the door three times. Nothing. She might be out, he thought. He hammered again three times. This time he heard the movement of someone and a door creaking inside.

"Who's there?" her sleepy voice said.

"It's Kelly!" Kelly said.

"Who?"

"Kelly. Downstairs!"

"It's too early, son. Ah'm no open for business 'til nine o'clock the night. Gi'e me a knock then."

He thought of shouting *open the door you dirty fucking diseased hoor or I'll kick it in!* however, he knew that wouldn't really do the trick, so he just said,

"I'd just like to speak to you for a minute."

The door began to unlock. It drew ajar and the face that appeared was far from the one that he remembered. A grey-faced, wizened, unmade, skeletal visage peered at him.

"What is it, son? Ah'm no at ma best this time o'the mornin'"

Kelly looked at her knowing that he had to say something but was quite unsure about his opening gambit, never having begun a conversation with the phrase *you've given me the clap,* and he saw that she was becoming irritated with the hiatus so he said,

"You've given me the clap!"

She straightened up in the doorway and glanced down at his crotch and said,

"No me, son. I'm clean! You've got it frae someb'dy else. Ye need tae talk tae yer girlfriend, no me!"

And then she went to shut the door. Kelly knew from his long absence of *a plunge* that her defence was ridiculous and so reacted with angry indignation and then a determination, apparently, not to let this happen to any more men, kerb-crawlers though they were, and he had another rush of selflessness, which quite caught him on the hop because it morphed his emotion from anger to the disappointment of a customer returning a defective jacket to the tailors.

"I won't be fobbed off with that!"

he said knowing how stupid it sounded in the circumstance, hearing his other self repeating the phrase *fobbed off* with much disdain, and pressed his weight against the door to stop her pushing it shut but leaned forcefully and then she fell backwards into the hallway, her dressing gown falling open and revealing her bare legs. She started to shout at him to get away and get out as Kelly went in to try and pick her up, and then she started to scream at him,

"Git away frae me ya weird bastard!"

which was now really loud putting Kelly into a mild panic because he didn't expect a flailing, noisome banshee to be the one of whom he had words with and all adjacent to her open front door for the rest of the flats to hear, however a flailing, noisome banshee it was. He realised that this could get way out of hand if she continued in her attack. Kelly realised it was her means of rebuttal. Her defence to act as though she was defending herself against a pushy punter who'd now become her assailant but in full knowledge that it was she who had delivered Kelly of the clap.

He didn't want anyone to hear her shouts so he closed her door merely with the intention of starting a lecture that began something like, *now listen here...* however, her angry defence had genuinely turned to fear as she saw her front door close and started to scream very loudly. Kelly panicked and walked quickly towards her, saying,

"No...no...you don't understand...you have to know that you have .....*something*....and now I do.... it's not nice...pussey yellow things."

She backed away from him and began to shout and scream expletives at him and told him to get out and then turned a doleful shade of grey and started to struggle for breath. She staggered into her living-room and started hunting in her bag for her inhaler and while she did so she pulled out an assortment of items that every hard working girl would need, paper knickers in case the punters liked to rip them off her, some of them liked that, make-up, lipstick, tissue paper and a half-loaded toilet roll, condoms, which Kelly ironically noted, a silk scarf and then a large bundle of money, loosely spreading around the carpet next to the bag on the floor. Twenties and tens fell with abandon around her floor. She found the inhaler and sucked in its relieving cloud of goodness and staggered to the kitchen, which was just off the living room like Kelly's place, and filled a glass with water. Kelly walked up to her and stood diagonally two feet away genuinely concerned that she may choke to death. She gathered herself and started to breathe easier as she inhaled again. Kelly saw a slight turn of the head as she heard Kelly breathing She held the full glass in her hand and threw a sideways look to Kelly and then to her draining board which had a short sharp knife lying alone on a chopping board with the detritus of some greenish matter attached to it. Kelly saw this and had a vision of her using this in her panic on him and met her eyes knowing they were both thinking the same thing, so he said,

"Nothing stupid, eh?"

She glanced at it again so he picked it up holding it close to him and then was confronted by a horrifying vision of her turning and screaming and trying to hit him with the glass. Her face was pale with dark areas around her eyes and Kelly saw for the first time some of her blackened teeth in her opened mouth which, with the lank hair around her face, completed the picture of mad sorceress. She bounced off him and he was pushed away further down the kitchen towards the door.

"Get out!! Get the fuck out!" she shouted at him.

"Look I will if you just calm down! You have to do something about whatever it is you've given me....."

Kelly was looking straight at her as she looked down to her midriff with a frown feeling her ribcage and then touched her dressing gown. A small crimson patch began to form on her robe and then she looked up at Kelly with a look of shock across her face. Kelly, disbelieving at first, shared her shock and then saw large drips of blood fall at her feet from inside her dressing gown and realised he was holding the bloody knife, which he then dropped as if it was smelly end of a shitty stick.

"Oh shit....No! No no no, he said and rushed towards her. "Lie down!"

He had some idea that you had to put pressure on the wound. She lay down on the floor as the pool of blood became a torrent seeping amongst his fingers as he tried to stem the flow. She looked up at him with a face that was now much paler than before and started to make gasping noises as her punctured lung denied her the oxygen she needed. Kelly watched her fade away, her eyes rolling upwards, and he cried,

"No! Don't do that, please! Wake up! Wake up!" slapping her across the face a few times.

He laid her head down on the kitchen rug that was sopping up the blood and watched her eyes settle to a half-shut position and then became quite still. He stood and walked away from her body to nowhere in particular and put his hands to his head which smeared his forehead and the side of his face with some of her blood, which threw him into another panic, making some noise of horror and distaste. He had the inclination to cry out as he walked about the living-room in random directions occasionally looking into the kitchen at his handiwork and trying to take in the event that had just happened but he knew that if he made a noise it might wake the other flats or they might hear something so suppressed his noises of horror and stayed quiet until he decided what to do next.

He, too, became still and ironically noted that he was hyperventilating. His chest heaved as he stood looking down at the dead woman. He looked at his bloodied hands and realised that whatever he did next he shouldn't touch anything more with them and he went to the kitchen and rinsed them under the tap. She'd had a good view from her kitchen window, he thought, and Kelly could see over the trees and to the rooftops across the south side and acknowledged the ridiculous tangential observation given the circumstances. His head still hurt and so he picked up a cup and rinsed it. Then he stopped realising that he couldn't leave fingerprints so he wiped the cup with a cloth and set it back where it was. He took a tea-towel that covered his hand and turned on the tap with and let the tap run gently. He filled up his cupped hands and drank from them. He had a moment where he gathered his thoughts as the tap splashed water into the sink letting it run as he considered the prospect of prison should he come clean about this but understood early on in this new dilemma that it would be a difficult defence that would probably require a lot of money and therefore little chance of coming out of this unscathed and probably devoid of his liberty and knew that the time to act was now.

He sat down in a chair in the living room and looked at her feet protruding out of the doorway to the kitchen. This had to look like it was a punter who maybe robbed her. Or just a plain old robbery. No, a punter. A punter who got violent. A dissatisfied punter who wanted his money back and it all went wrong. He stabbed her. She didn't want to give him his money back, there was a fight and he stabbed her. And robbed her. Robbed all her money. *No... just the money he wanted back.* Kelly realised he was imbuing this fabricated punter with an ethical sense of propriety, which was ridiculous. He took all her money. Well he would, wouldn't he? All of it. He....*the robber,* would've taken all of it.

He knew he had to eradicate every indication that he had been there and checked all of his clothes for her blood. He'd seen implicating clothes being burnt in some American murder stories and thought he should do that. But where? He'd take them all off and dump them. But not now. Not here. He had to make it look like the robbery first.

He went to her bag on the living-room floor and started to pick up all of the money that had fallen out when she retrieved her inhaler. He reckoned it to be just over two hundred pounds. He went into the bag and dug around looking for more and pulled out another sizeable wad which was much more than two hundred, he reckoned. He had to go into the mould of a thief that would go through the flat and so he took off his shoes and left them in the living-room and went down the hall and into her bedroom.

What he saw next was not a matching dressing table and wardrobe but her bed against the top wall and two rows of finest quality compost grow-bags, numbering about twenty, against the remaining three walls with tall plants at varying stages of maturity that gave a quite pleasing impression of a verdant small forest scene. In the bay window were six, large, fresh unused bags of compost. She spared no expense with this venture. He looked closely at the plant nearest him and rubbed the leaves. The sweet smell of marijuana accosted his nostrils as he held his fingers to his nose. Obviously this was her sideline to scoring punters. He decided to avoid the plants, not getting any of the vegetation on him that would place him at the scene of the crime further down the line and just hunt for whatever money she may have had in her bedroom. There were a few of her outfits on hangers in a rough old wardrobe he looked through. Nothing. He lifted the mattress off the bed being as quiet as he could checking for any signs of a stash which yielded nothing at all ends and then behind the headboard. There was nothing else in the room to check for so he went back into the living-room trying to get into the mind of a professional thief. He sat back on the chair and decided that he had the money she had on her and that's all that a thief who had just killed someone would take in his panic to get out. So he now wanted to get out. He pulled himself to the front of the chair to stand but then noticed a piece of skirting board under the window was loose and poorly fitted. Maybe? Another six hundred pounds in twenties was secured in a plastic food bag just behind the wooden board. He was close to a thousand pounds the better for alerting the hooker to his ailment but had to remove himself from any suspicion when she was found. He was fearful that he'd have forgotten something that would put him there at the time so he took her key, which focused his mind onto the new task, and quietly left her flat with the money.

Chapter 14

Greyfriars Body

Saturday, 16th June

DC Jones didn't like having to work weekends because there were always domestics and conflagrations occurring inspired by over-consumption of alcohol. Women made calls about husbands that were abusive and details were required about the circumstances of some drunk trying to take on a bouncer in town who got the wrong end of a knuckle-duster. It was tawdry saddening work made all the more enduring by the presence on-duty, this particular Saturday, of her boss DI McQuarrie, who also felt as she did but had the cable to vent his dislike unlike her who just had to suffer him. He had become more and more introspective recently, she had noticed, dealing with his frequent attempts to try to meet the financial demands of having his father reside in that nursing home in Dalkeith and desperation to meet those demands via the bookies. However, he never shared anything with her although the weight was fairly obvious as she drove him from investigation to investigation. His father was eighty-one and suffering from Alzheimer's Disease, which quite ironically, removed him from any of the stress he should feel for his son. Frequently he thought he was getting a new visitor whenever DI McQuarrie went to see him and liked to talk about the Scotland he used to live in which was populated by neighbours *wha' wid come ben intae your hoose* and talk the night away or on occasion a bottle would be cracked and a few drams shared. He'd regurgitate the songs of the music hall and Harry Lauder to his son and lately had taken to singing the popular songs of any of the contributors to *The White Heather Club*, which was a TV show in the late fifties, of which, McQuarrie had been known to call the *bastard child of Scottish culture,* and which he really disliked, moreso, because, as a boy, he had it shoved down his throat and all through his youth but he knew it was popular and he preferred to keep his own counsel about what he thought were populist attempts to fulfil the broad perception of Scotland, beyond the shores of Scotland. And he thought it a little pathetic and privately despised his *ain folk* for ever having paraded such shit. But he didn't have an alternative. He didn't know if there was one. He just keenly felt the superficiality of it all, cloying nostalgia and desperation to be unique and an attitude of *wha's like us?,* which he was quick to consider, might also be said in variation in Bolivia, Greece, Iceland or some other shore, equally distant.

His father often now asked when *The White Heather Club* was coming onto the TV which left that generation of nurses and carers bemused and unable to help.

These visits wore DI McQuarrie down. He thought frequently of the big questions in life but was neutered by the effort required to debate them with anyone, especially down at the station, and the immediacy of that which was required to keep body and soul together to ensure the commencement of a tomorrow. Like most people, despite his salary, he always seemed to be *just getting there* every month by the skin of his teeth with a few shilling left for life's libations.

Nevertheless, he listened to his father and smiled knowing he was occasionally a stranger, a stranger that had to be paid for, maintained, fed and watered in *Woodlands Brook Care Home*, this grey world of broad deceitful smiles, of untruthful colour strategically placed to give the lie that the darkness was happily deferred. He wanted to say that, confront them about it or *something* like that, something honest, but he never did, or could to anyone knowing that the indignance of the righteous would be returned in spadefuls. What did inspire DI McQuarrie were tips on horses and a good murder enquiry to get his teeth into. This Saturday morning the sun shone bright for him. DC Claire Jones walked into his office and delivered the news.

"We have a corpse, sir."

He visibly brightened up as he lowered his Sunday paper and peered over his glasses.

"Excellent news, Jones. Beats football violence hands down! Where?"

A good murder allowed him to assert his intelligence and rank over most others involved

"The Old Town, sir."

"Well we won't be hammering the petrol bill for this one will we, Jones?"

"No sir." She was pleased that he now had a professional distraction from his other worries, which cut her a bit of slack, as well.

"Warm up the car and I'll be right with you. And Jones?"

"Yes sir?"

"Details. Times. Names. Reporting officer and a nice sharp pencil."

"Of course, Sir!" and she ventured a smile and was delighted that the semblance of a smile reshaped her boss's face.

Chapter 15

The Key to Everything

Sunday, 17th June

He'd turned the place upside down. His plans couldn't be scuppered by this! He knew it was here. He forced himself to stop and think but it was at least a week previous, more, and a few slakeworthy sessions to the good which entirely would disorientate any memory of what he did with it. He didn't give it back to Joe. He knew that. Any ability he had to focus was being coloured by the fact that he couldn't stop thinking about the corpse upstairs and the finite amount of time that was now ticking away before the shit hit the fan. Joe gave it to him on the Friday, then he dropped off the sheets, roller trays and paint, just as Joe asked. He came home....or did he? His place was such a shitstate that he knew he might never find it this side of Christmas if he continued randomly throwing couch cushions across the room. He had to stay calm and move methodically. What did he do when I came in that Friday after the pub? He knew it was a moment of a tree falling in a forest where no-one was there to witness it so did it actually happen and even if it did, would he remember? What was he wearing? His coat. He grabbed the big Crombie and rifled through the pockets and then the lining feeling around the bottom seam hoping the firmness of metal would smile on his groping fingers. Nothing. The hooker had gone nowhere except the kitchen and the living room and with the hammering the couch had taken that night, if it was in that vicinity it may well be deep in the stuffing or down an arm, cushion or down the back.

Approximately twenty six minutes later the lining on the underside of the couch was strewn about the room and the padded arms were detached and lying like haunches of meat on his floor. The material on the back was slashed open in two places and torn to the stapling. A small cloud of dust hung in the air and he stood sweating and breathless in the streaming summer sunshine beaming onto his desperation. The two government monkeys in black had a scout around when they were in. Think! Where did they go in the room? One sat and one wandered taking in information about the place, he guessed. He stroked Lenni. Then he had a stealthy shufti around the room. He lifted things. The old sock. It was still where it was last left. Kelly lifted it, sharply. Nothing. Then what? The book! *The Good Soldier Sveyk.* Had he taken it out since then? No. He didn't think so. He relived that moment in his head and turned slowly to look at where it was left by Number Two. It was still on the side table by the couch. He took a moment and then walked across to the table and lifted up the book. Beneath it was nought but a ring-stain on the varnish of the ugly little table. Kelly sighed deeply and went to place it back down but stopped, feeling something solid between its pages and opened it up at page 231. There it lay. Bright silver and shining almost as bright as Kelly's smile. The smile dropped as he heard the door opposite him on the landing being knocked and then silence. Shortly after that his door was knocked. Probably just someone selling something. Maybe. Or was it a neighbour from upstairs asking about a funny smell? Not yet surely? He had to answer the door to find out.

A uniformed policeman stood in front of him. Kelly shit a brick.

"Good morning sir. We're making house to house enquiries about an unfortunate incident yesterday night where a crime, possibly a murder, occurred...."

Oh my God, he thought, *are they psychic?*

"...and would like to ask you if you were out and heard anything unusual or saw anything that might help us in our investigation. Were you out last night, sir?"

Kelly stammered a little, "Errrr...yes. Yes I was. Why what's happened?"

"Where did you go out, sir and did you hear or see anything unusual or untoward?"

"No..no. I didn't see anything. Nothing out of the ordinary."

"Where did you go out, sir?"

"Err.. The Duke. *The Old Duke.* Across the road."

"And did anyone in *The Old Duke* speak of anything they might have seen or heard?"

"Not that I heard. Why....what's happened?"

"As I said sir, a crime has occurred.....possibly a murder."

There was no earthly way possible that they could know already! He had a vision of himself crying out *It was an accident. She walked into the knife! I'm sorry!* but he kept it together

" and a man has lost his life on or near Greyfriars Kirk and we are trying to identify anyone who might have information....."

A man! He nearly leapt for joy.

"...that could help us in our enquiries. Could you tell me how your face became reddened, please, sir?"

"I walked into a door.... bit pissed...y'know."

"Thank you Sir. Can I leave this with you, sir..." handing him a flyer with a number on it "....and if you do recall anything or know of anyone that could help us please call us on this number."

As the Policeman left, Kelly saw him clock the couch hanging in pieces and had another look at Kelly that rang of professional acumen or plain distaste before he left. He wasn't a good advert for domestic organisation. He retreated back into his mess and looked at the flyer. They didn't say who it was. Greyfriars? Probably winos fighting again. Anyway, with plod knocking on doors, now he had to move quickly. Then he had a thought that sent a wave of panic through him as he realised he could hear him knocking on the doors upstairs. He went to his door and quietly opened it as he eavesdropped the uniform go through his spiel with The Pumping Tracksuit and thankfully heard that it didn't last long but then listened to the knocks repeatedly made on her door. He held his breath. Three knocks again. Then footsteps. Kelly exhaled relieved but then heard The Pumping Tracksuit's door being knocked again.

"Sorry to bother you again...*sir..*"

Kelly heard the disdain and mild sarcasm in the policeman's voice. TPT must look fucked, he guessed, still full of beer and whatever else he grazed on last night.

"....could you tell me if your neighbour across the landing is usually in on a Sunday morning?"

"Dunno...." he muttered back. "...might be in bed. She works nights....y'know?"

The uniform understood him at once, as Kelly yelled *shut up!* to him in his head, knowing that working girls out late are often the eyes and ears of conflagrations or crimes and a valuable source of information, at a price, apparently, he'd heard from CID, though never willing witnesses in court.

Now that Plod knew she was a hooker there was less circumspect knocking which turned into the flat of his hand thudding her door.

"Hello...Police! Could we have a minute of your time please?"

The uniform knew that she would be unwilling to talk to him now that he had revealed he was police.

"Hello? Police. Can we have a minute, please?" He waited again. Nothing....*naturally.*

A thought sent panic through him. Could she be seen from the letter-box? Was the living-room door closed? Could her legs be seen? It was a narrow hall with the light at the top end where she was. He had to act. He quickly, making as much noise as he could, hauled an arm of his couch out of his front door and shouted up just as the uniform was bending down to have a look.

"Leave a flyer with me and I'll make sure she gets it, if you want?" He abruptly said, dropping the butchered couch-piece and running halfway up the stairs to arrest any interest in letter-boxes.

"I usually hear her when she comes home. I'll give her one.....*a flyer.*"

Plod smiled at Kelly's verbal faux pas and said, "I'll put one through the door for her, anyway, and you can take a couple."

It was interminable for Kelly as Plod fiddled with the stiff flap and occasionally bent a little to look at it and re-thought how to fold the flyer to get it through. Kelly sharply spat out,

"You must be roastin' in that uniform, today?"

Plod looked down at him and said, "Yeah...might lose the jacket if it gets any warmer." As he forced the folded flyer into her hallway. Then he walked down the stairs to Kelly.

"We'll call back to see if her or her..*colleagues*... heard anything. All confidential, let her know?"

"I will. But like I said, she disappears for days at a time. More than a week, sometimes. Away doing something, no doubt?"

He knew was talking too much. Plod shook his head slightly.

"Whatever. We'll call again." He looked at the couch arm on his landing.

"Couldn't get it out myself in one piece. Tscchh..." Kelly said as casually as he could. "....getting a new one......G-Plan...McKay's have got a sale on. Don't suppose you've got ten minutes to help me....?"

The uniform frowned at him and looked up his hallway at the mess and then sardonically just said,

"Busy." And held up his flyers, then squeezed past trying not to be infected by touching it.

Kelly leant on the banister, relieved as he heard his footsteps walk back out into the street. He knew that if he was going to get this *thing* done, it had to be soon. Too many things were closing in. Suddenly the sound of the policeman's heels were heard again urgently returning. His heart leapt and he held his breath. Plod's face was at the bottom of the stair and shouted up,

"Hey! Just one more thing!"

Kelly leaned out and smiled. " Yeah...yes?..."

"That can't go on the street! This is Sunday and the council doesn't pick up on a Sunday. Do it tomorrow!"

His footsteps faded. Kelly went upstairs and looked through her letter-box. The living-room door was open and her feet were clearly visible.

Chapter 16

Mayday

Monday, 18th June

May was rarely seen by anyone from *The Old Duke* outside the confines of that hallowed refectory but this Monday morning was walking with intent down towards Causewayside. Monday morning's she liked to do her shopping on Clerk Street because *it was full of real shops*, she often said, shops that had real people behind the counter that would offer a view of the weather or whichever local aspect of tittle-tattle was current on the High Street. But she wasn't this morning. It was a drizzly scene of cloud with a definite sun somewhere behind it threatening to burn the cloud away but it was too early, still too cold and it made May pull her collar up and tighten her headscarf around her well-built hairdo and tighten her hands around her tartan shopping bag which allowed a little trail of black plastic bags to poke out of the back of it and swish about in the morning breeze.

Kelly had a bath that morning, which he needed and because it allowed him to check the progress of the infection on his cock. It had been two days now since he discovered his ailment and he had noticed the swelling of the glands in his groin. He knew that was the body trying to fight off whatever he had, which was good and he'd decided to wait and see what happens before he took his gloopy bell-end to see a quack, because, quite frankly he was embarrassed and didn't hold the prospect of some knob-doctor swabbing and applying whatever medicinal compound onto his old man, as a good opener to his day, especially as he had to play this day with a deft hand. He lay in the bath and stared at the ceiling knowing that there was her corpse roughly about twenty feet away and wondered when the smell would start to pervade the common stairwell and questions start to be asked about its source. He reckoned on being able to parry any questions that might lead to his culpability with the obvious explanation being she was robbed by a punter who got angry or desperate. Maybe a junkie. A user targeted her. Yes, that's what they'd think. Maybe the junkie knew she was punting hash on the side and guessed that she would either have lots of gear for them to steal and sell or maybe lots of cash?

May turned her direction away from Clerk Street and marched resolutely up onto Causwayside, a quite narrow thoroughfare known for its antique shops with flats above. Her beige raincoat flapped as her knees pushed it rhythmically forward and back to the sound of her small-heeled shoes thudding on the pavement. About half a mile further down she turned into a vennel, a small tunnel underneath the buildings, which led to the back of the flats above and climbed an old wooden staircase leading to a residential door.

The knife! Kelly slapped the water and sat up in the bath. Where was the knife? Did he leave it at the scene or did he bring it with him? He has a key, too. If the police came in to his flat and found those two things he was dead! Then as the doubt started to fly around his head he started to put together the time frame he needed. Panic began to embed itself in his head. Did he wipe the skirting board where he found the money? No. He couldn't remember doing it and he still hadn't done anything about the clothes he was wearing. Truth was he wasn't dealing with this very well from a murderer's point of view, at all, as he'd seen all the baddies at the start of Columbo meticulously eradicating every possible shred of evidence that point to them and he just wasn't up to their level and had to do something that would give him time to get his plan moving. There was no point in running away now because that would point to guilt or culpability and he wouldn't get far without the necessary funds so he had to stay and buy some time. Somehow. And there was still the issue of the inevitable smell?

May entered the flat above *Shrove Antiques* and sat in an armchair in the living-room. This was a tidy space. Well decorated. Quiet. She began to pull out the black plastic bags from her tartan shopping bag but less with the resolve she'd had. There seemed to be something other obviously weighing her down. She stopped pulling out the bags and looked around the flat and then down to the array of dark plastic that to her, ironically, looked something like the shape of a nest. Then a quiet sob dropped from her mouth into the silence around her and she heard it as if it was someone else's sound, not hers. She rarely heard herself cry, which made her worse and a steady flow of salted water rolled down her face. Moments passed before some stoic Scots emotion arrived from somewhere shortly after this as she regained her determination, straightened herself and started to open up the bags and lay them on the floor ready to accept whatever she was going to fill them with as she wiped her face dry with her sleeve.

She lay there on the floor her eyes half open. Kelly thought. She was there where she was left but the pool of blood on the kitchen floor was horrendous. He had to do something.

A picture of Joe with a group of friends were assembled under what was presumably a red flag, as the photo was black and white, and they held their fists aloft, smiling broadly. This was taken obviously some years ago but had pride of place on the wall next to an armchair that flanked the open fire, now bereft of flame, with grey ash lying in the grate. May looked at it for a short time focussing on Joe, his fist raised and his smile broad and then she picked up the first bag and walked into the small square hall and into the flat's only bedroom.

Her door opened a couple of inches and Kelly peeked out onto the stairwell. His vision struggled going from the brightness of her top floor flat to the relative darkness of the stairwell. The skylight had been scheduled for repair some time ago and corrugated plastic sheets had been placed over the broken glass to keep the rain out by the housing association that owned the flats but this also blocked a lot of the light that came into the stair and they had never quite got around to fixing it, which Kelly was reasonably happy about on this occasion. The only person he had to worry about was The Pumping Tracksuit exiting his flat but it was early. Too early for him Kelly thought. Nevertheless, he crossed the landing quietly and put his ear against his door. Nothing. No sounds of movement. He was out late most nights, Kelly guessed, and so slept late. One flight of stairs was all he had to manage with her and then safety.

She was heavy. Heavier than he imagined she would be and so he decided to get her in a position whereby he could perform a fireman's lift on her but then he saw the bloodstain on her white towelled dressing gown. He grabbed a large towel from the bathroom and wrapped it around her at the wound to keep the blood off him.It took him three attempts to get her in a sitting position and haul her up onto his shoulders. Even though she was slight and smaller than him this was a dead weight and his lungs and excuse for muscles were pointedly reminded of this as he manoeuvred her into a position so he could open the door and see out to where he needed to go. Still quiet. He leaned out as much as her weight would allow him to and peered down into the darkness that was his landing which was quite dark when the scheduled lights were off. He decided that was the time to just go for it and he counted a one, two, three and made to rush with her into the stairwell but her head swung around and banged loudly against the door and slammed it shut. *You dick, Kells* he chastised himself, standing back in her hallway, not so much about the poor positioning of her head but more about the noise he'd....*she'd* made. He had to take a rest but he didn't want to go through the rigmarole of getting her back over his shoulder so dropped her back onto her feet and leaned her against the wall with both hands on her shoulders to keep her upright. He breathed heavily and regained his composure but in the position he was, he was compelled to look at the dead human being in front of him. The magnitude of what he'd done and was doing began to find a morality somewhere in a corner of his conscience but he knew that if he dwelt on these thoughts and allow that morality to affect his plan then he may as well go and jump off The Forth Bridge because his liberty and reason to leave was now acutely compromised should he fail.

Bright colourful dresses lay spread on the double bed in front of May. Occasionally a tear would roll down her face and drop onto the bedspread but she rolled up the dresses and placed them carefully into the first bin-bag. Others followed, just as feminine bright and gay, some with floral patterns and quite modern but some that were retro harking back to the fifties in cut and shape and it seemed with every one she had a memory that elicited an occasional smile but then the dress would be carefully rolled and bagged. She continued until the wardrobe that held them was empty and then she pulled open the lid on a large old chest of drawers and began to empty that, too.

With each step downwards his legs were shaking and his descent with her on his shoulder was taking a lot longer than he'd anticipated. He had no idea he was so unfit. At thirty-three he imagined he would have been fit and strong, no less a definite babe-magnet of rippling muscle but there was, *had been,* more muscle on Lenni. It was an inconvenient time to be reminded that he was less of the man that he thought he would have been and so he dropped carefully onto each step with wobbling knees. *Ironic,* he thought, *not the first time she'd made a man's knees tremble.* A noise from below! The street door slamming. He held his breath and her tightly as he heard the inevitable footsteps ascending. He listened to hear the steps walk onto the first landing hoping he'd hear them stop and then the jangle of keys. No jangle and slow methodical footsteps ascending further. Shit! He gasped to himself. Then the recognisable sounds of The Pumping Tracksuit muttering narcotically induced gibberish as he climbed higher. Kelly had brought her down to a dark angle on the stairs and hoped that with the darkness and his residual effects of what seemed to have been another ribald evening, The Pumping Tracksuit. might just buy his next move. He dropped her down against the wall and leaned his head against her to try and hold her up as he undid his top button and belt on his trousers and dropped them down revealing his bare white arse. Then she slipped down the wall. The Pumping Tracksuit had almost reached his landing about eight feet below.

He pulled her back up with a strength induced by his own drugs called *adrenalin* and *fear* and got an arm underneath hers and with the other grabbed her hair at the back and used that to hold her up. The Pumping Tracksuit was walking across Kelly's landing and past his door still making his little noises. Kelly parted her bare legs and started to dry hump the corpse. Vigorously. He thought he'd need to act breathless but there was no need for any acting on that score, but what it did require, Kelly realised, was something of a soundtrack to the ruse just to ensure the wool was well and truly blinding this unwitting audience, so he opened with,

"I know it's early but I'm horny...*bitch* so just get on with it!"

The Pumping Tracksuit now had stopped and was looking up the ten or so steps to the dark turn in the stairs and at Kelly's bare arse. Shitfaced...*again*...he was, or off his face with whichever illegal substance he'd lately ingested, and it took a few seconds for him to absorb and understand the sight before him. Kelly added,

"....yeah, that's it....nearly there....no let me do the work....."

and then turned as if surprised to see The Pumping Tracksuit and said....

"Alright, man. Just had to get the day off to the right start, know worra mean?"

And humped on with the odd groan of felonious pleasure and smiled at him. Then TPT smiled back and began to ascend the last set of stairs past them both and up to his flat.

"Totally man!" he replied and wobbled slightly with unfocused bloodshot eyes, drugged and tired as he climbed the stairs watching the thrusting but achingly weary Kelly.

Kelly said, "See ye later, man." by way of a *Get to fuck you addled tosser and let me stop this macabre necro nonsense, please!*

But then TPT stopped and fished around in his inside pocket and pulled out a little plastic bag of pink capsules and took forever to extract one from the bag. Then he leaned down to Kelly who was only about four feet away but held onto the banister so that he didn't have to do any more stairs and held it out to Kelly.

"Nex'...time......nex' time....*man*...take one o' these... jist before ye ...ye shag her... totally.... 'mazin'..temrindus....'tastic...n'tha'"

Kelly leaned harder against her to hold her up as he took the pink pill from him and smiled.

Still humping , he said, "Cheers. Any chance o' letting me get there, today?"

Then he directed his next words to her as if she'd spoke to him.

"I know!! I know yer busy and got things to do...and places to go.....I know that! But I'm tryin'!" Then he looked up at TPT and apologetically said "Any danger...?" implying he needed privacy to complete their apparent contract.

Then TPT released his grip from the banister and held out his open palms and said,

"Sure...yeah..." Then he fell headlong past them both and onto Kelly's landing where he appeared to be temporarily unconscious.

Kelly seized his moment and let her slump down on the stairs and pushed his key into his door and kicked it open. He grabbed her under her arms and pulled her letting her feet thud against each step and dropped her into his hallway. Then he pulled the door shut and got TPT to his feet and helped him up the stairs and into his flat. He'd started to come round and was thanking Kelly profusely saying he was *a top man* but that he had to get to bed, which Kelly helped him to. TPT climbed into his bed fully clothed and fell immediately into the blackness of his mini death. A terrible thought accosted him. It would be easy. He was a pest. Always there when he shouldn't be. Just jam a few more of his pink pills into him and leave. He stared at this young man prostrate and already deathly before him. He walked towards him and took the small bag of pink pills out of The Pumping Tracksuit's pocket.

May now sat before a row of binbags neatly gathered on the bed. She sat down on the corner and gently pushed one up to the pillow and leaned it where a head would be. She pushed another to make a neck. Gradually used more bags and formed a human shape on one side of the bed, as if it was sleeping.

When Kelly went back downstairs the Policeman that was there yesterday was on his landing and that is where they both stopped. The policeman looked at his door.

"Left your key in the door" he said looking at it.

"Yeah, thanks, I'm an emptyhead." He replied trying to look as natural as he could.

"Have you heard your nightwalking neighbour come in yet?" he said throwing his look upstairs.

"That's just what I was trying to do, actually. Let her know the flyer was there and tell them you'd like to speak with her. No answer. Like I said, you see her regularly and then she's away for days at a time."

"I thought I heard a door close?" the uniform said.

"Yeah...that was my other neighbour. He thought I was knocking on his door."

"So he's in?"

"Yes..but he's just come in...*apparently*. Totally off his head on something and pissed, as well. Tscchh...kids eh."

The policeman went up to TPT's door and gave it a good rap. Kelly wanted this diligent plod to not be so diligent and leave and he knew that he couldn't go back into his flat with *her* still lying on the hall floor. Kelly went up a couple of steps and craned out to speak to the policeman.

"Like I said he was off it. Probably just crashed into bed?"

The uniform came back down to his landing and said nothing appearing to think. Then he said,

"Don't forget your key."

Kelly acted as if glad to be prompted and said thanks and retrieved it from the lock and just smiled back at him. The policeman stood there and said,

"Well, cheerio for now." And just stood where he was.

Cannons were going off in Kelly's head and his stomach was turning inside out. Think!

"I was just off to get a pint of milk. Can't get started without a cup of tea....." he said and then couldn't believe the bravado of what came out of his mouth next,

".....if you hang about I'll do you a cup when I get back?"

Some other Kelly deep inside of him was screaming *what are you doing!!*

The policeman declined in a tone that spoke volumes about the potential risk of infection should he ever use a mug from Kelly's hovel, and left. Kelly followed him out of his block, onto the street and towards the small shop around the corner, his heart thumping in his chest and shouted a goodbye to the policeman.

After hanging around in doorways watching where the policeman went next because he didn't have any money on him for a pint of milk he made his way back to his flat and slammed the door shut with a massive sigh of relief. He grabbed her by the arms and dragged her up to the kitchen, got a roll of plastic bin bags that he'd liberated from Joe while on the Cowgate job and managed to get her into an assembly of plastic and sellotape. He then realised he only had this window of opportunity that morning and had to get going.

May sat on the bed in silence looking at the human sculpture of bin-bags. She then lay down on the other half of the bed with her head on the pillow looking at the black plastic opposite her. She closed her eyes and gently fell into a reverie of thought and eventually, a deep sleep.

Kelly's chest was heaving at the pace with which he arrived at the window of *Shrove Antiques* and looked at the time-flecked stock. There was a grate for a fire that looked Victorian and some brass tongs and shovels as companion pieces next to it and a small wooden table atop a pine sea-chest. On the floor of the window display was a chess set of carved pieces, however, the black king was short of a head, which Kelly thought might be a prognostication having never allowed himself to be superstitious, previously, and had a 'talking to' with himself about *bucking up* and *being resolute* and *this will work* and other fleeting thoughts convincing himself that what he was doing would be profitable in the end. He'd stopped to look in the window to ensure there wasn't anyone around to see him slope through the vennel and up into Joe's flat.

He opened the door as quietly as he could and closed it as softly. Paint, dust-sheets, roller trays and brushes were stacked in an ordered pile in Joe's hallway. He was getting heart sick of creeping around other people's flats but knew there were neighbours that might hear or see him so he had to be shady. He knew Joe was meticulous with his work so it wouldn't be hard to find his ledger and passport. In the living-room it was quietly morgue-like with a distant sound of traffic from the front of the building. There was a table set up at the window with an array of business papers, receipts and ephemera which, thankfully, faced the back-greens of washing-poles and tussocked unkempt bits of grass that someone had once called a garden but had been abandoned to the care, or not, of next owner of the patch and Kelly doubted that anyone who saw him would bother, so he lifted and let fall some of the papers looking for Joe's big ledger with his accounts and tax details. This was something that Joe wouldn't have out and use infrequently and knowing Joe he would have it in a cupboard or something similar. Kelly turned and looked at the rest of the room. There against the opposing wall to the fire was the prime candidate, an old oak sideboard of sizeable dimensions with a few photos in very tasteful frames accompanied by a small brass cast bust of Karl Marx. These few items formed a symmetry, a discernibly considered arrangement around a centre piece that was a beautiful silver tray kept stoutly in place by a half-full bottle of eighteen year-old *Glenlivet* malt whisky and two cut crystal glasses. Kelly was tempted but the photos drew his attention. Joe was in one of the pictures with whom he thought must have been a family member. The family member or friend was in an open-necked shirt, bald and shaven-headed had his arm around Joe. Both were smiling and patently in happy times, together. Kelly thought he had seen the bald-headed man before? He knew the face but couldn't place it. Nevertheless, the organisation and tidiness of the flat was reflected in this small display on the sideboard, typical of Joe he thought. Typical that he has a photo book of sampled work, proud and methodical. Joe was never late for anything and Kelly had noticed that over the years whenever he'd done the few bits of work for him if Joe said he was going to be somewhere at a particular time, he was there. There had never been any question that Joe would be anything other than scrupulous and honest when it came to money, in fact Joe had, on occasion, given Kelly a few quid more than he'd said he would when it came to paying Kelly and Kelly knew his skills were limited and Joe could easily have found another more skilled Painter to help him in these straitened times of laissez-faire politics, but Joe had always, quite altruistically and loyally, offered Kelly the work first. Then Kelly had a dichotomy of thought knowing he admired and respected Joe but was about to become him for gain. Again, Kelly rebuked himself and denied anything moral was welling in him and opened the sideboard doors beneath and there it was alone on its own shelf, big and bold.

This sideboard seemed the hub of Joe's organised world and Kelly guessed correctly that his passport would be in one of the drawers.

Nothing in the drawer was randomly placed and the passport was underneath a small pile of notebooks tucked into the right-angle of the back of the drawer. Kelly drew it out without disturbing anything else. Both would have to be returned as soon as possible before Joe noticed. Kelly checked he still had Joe's key and put the ledger down on the floor leaning against the wall so he could get the passport in his pocket and crept into the small square hall past the bedroom door.

He froze in panic as the bedroom door abruptly opened but nobody came out. He looked at the front door and thought of running but who ever had opened the door would have heard and then seen him. Then a black bin-bag filled with something came sailing through the air and landed on the wooden floor. What was happening? Then another. Kelly felt sick. Into the hall walked the bald-headed man in the photo with Joe. Noticeably older but definitely him. He stopped. He was naked but for his y-fronts but with obvious lipstick smeared around his mouth. They both looked at each other disbelieving of what each was seeing. Kelly spoke first.

"Hi..... ermm....I'm Joe's.... *friend.* He gave me the key. I'm just.....bringing him.....some paint."

And nodded at the neatly stacked tins against the wall.

"I....don't think we've met....and I'm...err...I'm sorry I didn't know you were here...." he stammered on.

Kelly offered his hand. The bald-headed man didn't shake his hand but Kelly could now see into the bedroom where a woman's wig was lying on the floor next to a skirt, tan tights and a beige raincoat. Kelly then clocked the lipstick and looked harder at the man and then two and two became an arithmetically precise four and the penny dropped companioned by Kelly's jaw.

"May!! *May?* Fuck me! May? You're May....The Man! A *man!* You are a ..... you're a man! That's...your *hair...* Shit!! ..... here...Joe's flat...how...??...."

May walked past him without saying anything and into the living-room.

Kelly found May in an armchair.

"I'm sorry.... May... I had no idea... obviously....I mean why would I?"

"Nobody does!" May barked without looking at him.

"I was going to say I had no idea *you were here*...but the other...*thing*.... as well, I suppose...?"

"Well now you know!" May spat again.

"Yes...I do...*know* that you're actually....."

"A man."

"A man...yes.. but here? Erm...why? I mean...Does Joe...know...?"

May looked up at him with profound disdain. Kelly openly corrected himself.

"....yes of course Joe knows because you're here.... in *Joe's flat.* So...Joe has......what?... has been putting you up?.... Helping you..out?....Actually you're a tra..."

"Transvestite! Well done, Kells."

Again Kelly rebuked himself for appearing so unworldly and apparently naive. He'd never had the pleasure of meeting a transvestite or their convivial company but his impression had been one of flouncing colours and heels of ridiculous heights augmented by shimmering bewigged tresses and dresses pumped full of mamarian hills and make-up, so unsubtle, that a circus clown might have been proud of it, but here was May, quite deliberately dowdy and unspectacular for one of that tribe.

"Ermm....what are you doing here in Joe's place, May...if that's not too personal a question?"

"It is fucking personal, Kells but I'm guessing you've put two and two together...right?"

Kelly had some inkling, which he first considered so outlandish that he threw it away into his cerebral dustbin, but May was hinting, or expecting, Kelly to have made some assumption. He had seen the photo of them together in former times, so there was an element of *something* to be deduced from that and the fact that she ...*he* ...was here in his flat plainly busied with a task of some description that implied a familiarity with the place. Despite more disdain that would come from May at the obviousness of his projected question, he felt he needed absolute clarification of what was occurring, here.

"So....you and Joe are...*together?"* he tentatively ventured and then the disdain arrived on the express from *Disdainville* with a large package for Kelly marked *Thick Prick.*

"Well done, Kells. That rapier mind of yours hitting top speed again, eh?"

"Yeah..sorry...I just wanted to be....so Joe is actually...?"

"For fuck sake, Kells! Yes! Yes Joe is gay. I am gay and a crossdresser. Joe and I are both gay, love each other, or did, and have been together for years! Is that clear enough or do you need me to draw you a picture?"

"But... nobody would ever have...I mean in the pub.... you're so...well....*rough*...and you dress the same..all the time..and swear and drink stout...."

"You're such a cliché, Kells. You talk a good game in the pub with all your book titles dropped in but you're just like the rest of the fucking world. You think transvestites and gays are just so raging and out there, don't you? Like some cartoon drawn on the Dick Emery show. *Ooh you are awful, but I like you* and all that shit. Is he dead?"

"Sorry...who? Dick Emery?"

"Yes. Him. Is he dead because if he's not me and a few others would like to kill him. I'm hiding, Kells. I have to be someone else that I can comfortably be, someone I know. Do you really think that I could have been me, openly in The Duke, without a ton of shit hurled from on high? Do you think Joe would still have his business, do you think other straight painters or joiners, plumbers, whoever, would have worked alongside him? Do you think me and Joe could have led the life we wanted to being openly gay and drinking in The Duke? I'm a working class guy who had no hope of being anything but, just like Joe and we wanted to stay just a pair of regular people but they're a judgemental lot the British workers and those of their class. Narrow-minded, scared of anything that isn't meat and two veg. And judgemental, by god they are!. Judgemental and quick to dish out the shit despite their poverty. The arrival of AIDS isn't helping, either. You get the picture, Kells?"

"Errr..yes, I do..." he said knowing that he would most probably have been the first to throw a stone at the expense of someone's soul just to aggrandize himself amongst his peers. "You sound so....different, May. And not so...aggressive." He offered, hoping to assuage some of the guilt he was feeling and change the subject away from bullying.

"Well, like I said, I play a part and it comes easy to me. Nobody asks questions and me and Joe are free to be *normal* people and function. I'm not quite the thick whisky-soaked bitch you think I am."

However, Kelly inwardly opined that he had seen many evenings that would herald a proliferation of testimonies to the contrary but declined to throw this into the conversation.

"You said before that you and Joe..err..." Kelly had real trouble saying this, "..erm *loved* each other... but then said *you did*...past tense...and all that..?"

"We've had a row. A big one. We've had them before but this was huge." May said.

"Well...maybe it's really not as bad as you think it is. Can't you talk to each other? Sort it out?"

Despite his intentions to defraud, Kelly had quite naturally become *thoughtful friend.* His enquiry was heartfelt and he'd got over the initial jolt of May's big reveal and now was beyond any distaste or shock he felt and trying to bridge the chasm that had become a breach between two people he realised he cared about.

"This will take a helluva fixing." May snorted.

"Really? What's the problem.... if you don't mind talking about it that is? Totally understand if you don't."

"It's that bastard, *Money!*" May had started to sob openly in front of Kelly and every teardrop burned a hole in him as he sat and watched her bare her soul.

"He's been giving it away! Every week for the past six months! Giving it away! Working long hours and weekends to get paid for the job and taking on too much the very next day. And he never told me! Not a word. I feel so betrayed! And when he comes home he's knackered and all he's been doing is fixing the books. Ignorin' me and sortin' his tax!" and May sobbed loudly again.

Kelly was delighted to hear that Joe was being Mr Assiduous with his bookkeeping but didn't quite understand the part about giving his money away? He knew Joe was as open-handed a man that he had ever met and always had treated him well but he tended to agree with May that actually giving it away might be a smidgeon more open-handed than most.

"Who's he been giving it to?"Kelly asked.

"The Miners! He's been giving nearly half of what he makes to The Miners. I know they're on strike and it's hard going but nearly half! What about me? Us?"

At that moment, everything Kelly had recently learned about Joe, the Socialist connection, his private dignity and silence regarding his sexuality, his relationship with May, his gentle insistence of his shout at the bar and his meticulous organisation and pride in his work, all crystallized for him there and then before his nearly naked, sobbing, lipsticked, bald, transvestite, partner. Some things in life you just don't expect. Kelly was actually knocked out by Joe's solidarity with that which he held dear and envied him the depth of conviction he felt but that wouldn't sit well in this scene right now and he knew he should just let May have her say. Something general and unpartisan was the way forward.

"Nearly half....phew..that's a lot!" He couldn't remember the last time he'd said *Phew*.

"It's not just the amount...it's just that he didn't tell me. The mortgage was shy last month and I saw the letter. Then it all came out. The pits in Bilston and Monktonhall. He said that if he'd have told me I would never have agreed. Fucking right I wouldn't, I said! Then he started all his political talk about comrades and their kids, losing their houses, eating grass, which was a bit fucking far! Eating grass! *It's true,* he said*, there's families in Yorkshire eating grass because there's nothing else.* But what about me, I said. I'd been with him for years, watched when he struggled and got him through that and I loved him whatever, and we were goin' to retire to the south coast two years ago, open up, come out and be honest but that came and went and we only get one go at life, Kells, just one, right?"

Kelly couldn't disagree in light of the reason he found himself there but couldn't help but understand the hurt May felt but also, despite wanting not to, held nothing but admiration for Joe and his display of humanity.

"All these times I would sit in the pub close to him but I couldn't touch him, love him, kiss him, could I?"

"I don't think so, May.....*not* in The Duke."

"I wanted to but we had to hide. We didn't want *the scene* so I did it for him. For him! I hid for him!"

"I think you did the right thing....might have got a bit of flak, ..you know..?"

"Exactly! We had to wait "til we got home, closed the door and then opened up. I have nearly twenty dresses he loved to see me in. Twenty! And so pretty. Well they're in bin-bags now! Just like our fucking lives!"

Kelly was honestly moved. Something akin to *care* rode over the horizon.

"Look, May...do you think Joe wants you to leave? I mean...honestly?"

She paused, wiped her face and then said, "Prob'ly not. No."

"I'm guessing that underneath it all, you feel the same. And this? This is a gesture. You're drawing the battle lines but maybe diplomacy can avoid the war? Don't do this. Does he know you're doing this?"

"No."

"Then there's no need for it. This is an emotional over-reaction, which is understandable, of course ...but....you're *a team*....you love him.... he loves you....right?"

May had burned out the rage and sat listening, for once quiet and unemotional. Kelly seemed to being doing a decent job of helping a friend.

"Yes."

"And at the end of the day, and I know he should have talked to you about it, but he was doing something that is so.....*good*. I can't find any other words to say about it other than it came from his ....*goodness* and care for others, May. That makes him *a good man.* Why lose a good man just because he was doing good?"

May couldn't argue with Kelly's unusually honest speech and decided to parry.

"You don't half talk some shite in the pub but that makes a bit o' sense."

"Actually, May....I think I might have just surprised myself, too."

May straightened her face and wiped her eyes. Then said,

"Joe sent you to get paint?"

"Err..no May....Joe gave me his key to take home the kit, rollers and stuff, after the Cowgate job...."

" Yeah...he would have... I wasn't here. Stayed with my mum. She's dyin'..."

Kelly immediately thought of his own mother and considered saying something but just said,

"Really.. that's shit..May, sorry...."

"S' a'right."

"Well, I *forgot* to give him the key and he *forgot* to ask for it....so I thought I could *borrow* a drop of paint to do my flat..."

"Fuckin' thieve it ye mean!" and May was back.

"Yeah... sorry... I'm.."

"...a theivin' bastard!"

"If you like but he wouldn't have used the dregs, would he? You know what he's like, May."

"So do you! You should've just asked....but what ye've just said was really nice... so ye're a *nice* thievin' bastard. Take the paint. I won't say anythin' You weren't here."

"Thanks, May."

"And you won't say anythin'... about us. Me and Joe. In The Duke?"

"Deal. Talk to him. Work it out. He's a good guy."

May gathered herself and stood up in her saggy Y-fronts.

"Fuck off now, Kells. I'm goin'to have a shower and hang my dresses back up."

May went out and into the bathroom snapping the lock behind her.

Kelly grabbed the ledger, checked he had Joe's passport, and left.

Chapter 17

Uncle Joe

Wednesday, 20th June

On Tuesday he'd spent all day practising, he told Kerry. He experimented with hairpieces and adding wrinkles. That sort of thing. He'd really started to get the hang of it and when Kerry helped him *it looked bob-on,* he thought. But it had to be perfect.

Kerry was parrying girlie gossip.

"So did ye snog him?" a young girl in a bright checked shirt said to Kerry but giggled at her mate also wearing a large man's shirt with flecks of colour and smudges all over it.

Kerry was holding court with her make-up girls as they were being taken through wigs and hairline-blending and the use of spirit-gum and regaling them with tales from her career. She'd told them about a few actors and actresses she'd had to prepare for ageing or scenes where they had injuries but the girls were more interested in Kerry revealing more of her fleeting but torrid affair with a scenic artist on a feature film that didn't get a deal or released, so they wouldn't know it, she told them.

"Whit wiz his name?" Julie, the girl in the checked shirt asked.

Kerry smiled and said, "Torquill." Much giggling. "....I know, I know...it's a strange name but he was from Cornwall."

The other girl, Donna, in the big shirt offered some cultural clarity at a hundred miles an hour.

"He was Welsh? They talk total radge. I canny understand a word they say. I talked to some Welshies when they were here for the rugby and they were like...*sooo*... like...I canny even dae their sound... coz... it's just like... *sooo*.... and they had a big green thingy... but it was white at the bottom....an' they carried it..n'that... an' they hud a great big floo'er. Yelly.", she eloquently offered

"Leeks and daffodils. He wasn't Welsh."

"How come he hud a Welsh name, then?" Donna rejoined.

"Cornwall isn't in Wales. It's in England. Down in the south west. Of *England.*"

"I thought it was in Wales." Donna clarified again. *"Did* ye snog him?"

"Well I said earlier I had an affair on set with him, so....."

Much more giggling. Julie then shushed the giggling from Donna and circumvented another question, they both wanted to know.

"So...you snogged him... *but*...." she asked

"Yes?" Kerry said correcting the work of Donna's hairline-to-wig on a manikin head.

"Wuz he a guid kisser?" Donna blurted out.

"Shurrup, Donna! Ah'm talking tae Kerry!"

"You need more gouache, Julie...." Kerry pointed to her manikin head.

"Aye, aye...in a minute.."

"Did yez dae tongues!" Donna again.

"Donna!" Julie trying to appear shocked.

"Whit? Ah'm jist askin' if they did tongues!"

"Ah ken whit ye said! But ye butted in oan me askin' Kerry if....*did* ye dae tongues?"

"Well what do you think?" Kerry shook her head and smiled.

The two girls made a big and silly wooing sound but Julie shushed Donna again, who told Julie not to shush her like that and Julie complained that she was trying to ask Kerry more stuff about Torquill but couldn't because Donna was continually interrupting Julie whenever she was about to ask *the big question* and then Donna asked Julie what *the big question* was going to be to which Julie made noises of exasperation and said that she was thick and

Donna told her to shut up but then Kerry sharply said,

"Yes, I shagged him!"

Just as Kelly walked in. It was pretty obvious to him what the topic of conversation had been and just wanted to get to his agenda. The room went quiet and Julie and Donna suppressed their juvenile mirth while Kerry made her greetings. Kelly said,

"I'm a little late, sorry, but I'm trying to plan something."

"Sounds mysterious?" Kerry said back.

"You might be able to help me, actually?" he said and looked at the other two, who contained their embarrassment, further.

"The thick plottens..." Kerry said to the room. Julie looked puzzled. Donna looked blank.

"How can I help?" Kerry asked,

"The family are having a surprise party, which is why I'm late...*sorry*.... and I have to look like ...*my uncle...*"

"Photo?" Kerry asked.

Kelly drew out the passport.

"Ohh...I think we could do that, easily enough, couldn't we girls?"

"Could you? Really?" Kelly said with a smile and sycophancy dripping out of him. "That would be marvellous!"

Donna grabbed the passport and looked at the photo. "Huh! That's no even a challenge! Half an hour max!"

So he sat down in front of the mirror and let the girls work their magic on him while he attentively watched what they did. Where and how they applied the make-up. But then the hair seemed to be a problem because his was thick and unkempt and so he agreed to a haircut. He thought he was going to get a trim but the electric hair clippers came out and he was given the shortest of cuts at the same length all over his head. Then the hairpiece was attached. He made sure he feigned wonder and obsequious disbelief at their abilities until there was a very obvious and remarkable resemblance to Joe in the photo.

Chapter 18

Borrowing from Buggles

Miss June Duckets was a small figure of about fifty years and dressed from a bygone age. She was the archetypal sister to Mary Whitehouse. Tweed twin-set, blouse done up to the neck, string of pearls and American Tan stockings stoutly supported by small-heeled sensible brown shoes with the extravagance of a gold coloured buckle. Her short hair was swept back over her forehead under which was a pair of spectacles where perhaps a pair of horn-rimmed frames should be but had lately allowed herself a nod to a notable fashion the eighties had to offer, plumping for large oval lenses and mauve frames, as she'd seen a pop music video with two chaps singing about the demise of radio caused by the upsurge in these video whatsits and to which, she quite agreed, having grown up in an era that venerated the radio and its radio stars. Anyway, she opted for those spectacles but fretted privately the previous night about whether to take this brave and outlandish step. They did, in fact, cause a murmur in the office with the younger set, knowing they laughed at her behind her back but her secret attraction to a younger, forty-something man in *Mortgages,* who was tall, wore pinstripes and smoked a pipe, convinced her that this was a good move and would be a certain talking point with him. Her only engagement that day beyond the mundane slog was at 12:30pm with a Mr Joseph Delaney.

He sat impassive wearing a dark suit and had his overalls rolled up and on the desk.

"Would you mind.....ermm..." Duckets said nodding to his overalls.

"Oh yes sorry!" He replied taking them off the desk, "I'm going straight to a job right after this."

He tried smiling but got nothing back from her. She opened a large card wallet marked *app 13 Del* and took out some documents and perused them in silence for twenty seconds that seemed a lot longer to him.

"You'd like to borrow ten thousand pounds Mr Delaney?" she sternly uttered looking up and pushing back her mauve shop-windows.

"Yes that's right." He tried another smile ".....you see I'd like to extend my busin...."

"Yes we'll get to that in good time, Mr Delaney. *Business plans* are always good when applying for *business loans* but there are a few preliminary formalities we have to observe before we get to that."

And it was here she smiled an acidic stick-on smile that dissipated as soon as it had arrived.

"The first thing is that I have to warn you that any information you give today has to be truthful at the time of offering that information and that if any information, of which you give is latterly found to be inaccurate it will invalidate the application or any applications in the future and may lead to criminal prosecution. Do you understand?"

He nodded and went to say, " Yes....I..."

"That's lovely.....Mr Delaney..." she acidly interrupted scanning more of her documents.

"Now...you have brought identification?"

He reached down into a leather satchel and fished out a passport and handed it over to her. She then checked the address matched her documents and the passport number which she wrote down. She went to hand it back to him but stopped correcting herself, leaving his empty hand in the air.

"I suppose I have to have a look to see if work is taking its toll on your good looks Mr Delaney!"

She thought this was good practice for when she flirted with pinstripe pipe man, however, quite against her nature and really didn't want to die alone.

He sat unmoving. She pushed her new specs up and had a good look at the photograph.

He held his face still. She looked up at him. Then down at the photo. Then back up to him. Then back down to the photo.

"You're looking very well, these days, Mr Delaney. Work is making you younger!"

And she smiled again. More practice.

"Actually, I had just had a terrible bout of flu when that was taken. I wasn't well at all."

"Well Russia is a cold country, Mr Delaney?"

"Sorry?" Wrong-footed.

"I'm sure you'll catch the flu going to those kind of countries."

She was smiling and looking down at the passport at the same time.

He just said, "Sorry?" again.

"There is a Russian visa on here? Not that it is any of my business where you go, Mr Delaney, just an unusual destination. Mr Breznhev......or whoever they have in charge just now, are not exactly best friends with Mr Reagan....who *we* are friends with."

The royal *we* most probably included her adoration of Thatcher, no doubt, he thought. She looked like a Maggie disciple and he consoled himself imagining Duckets in a sweaty clinch with Norman Tebbit who was wearing a bright red leather posing-pouch and a dog collar and leash and being paddle-whacked on her bare arse by him. He remained apparently upbeat but self-effacing with his next observation.

"I didn't get there, as it turned out."

"No?"

"No. It was a cultural exchange and someone else took my place."

"Ohh....that's a shame ...." she insincerely said, "Money?"

"Sort of. I had a few jobs on and couldn't make it."

"So business got in the way of something that is none of *my business,* you might say, Mr Delaney?" and curled another smile around her mouth. "....and that is what we have to talk about next, Mr Delaney."

He was relieved to hear it as she put the passport on the desk but remained looking at his documents and said,

"Do you have any distinguishing marks, Mr Delaney?"

She dropped that in very well under the cover of normality. He racked his brains and paused unsure of what it said on the passport knowing he should have checked it. This was a fifty-fifty. A *Yes* or a *No.* However, if he said *Yes* a new line of authentication might ensue and he might find himself baring his inner thigh or his third nipple to this tweed-clad Buggle. He had to brass out a *No*.

"Err....no. No I don't. A few scars on the heart in times of yore but no other marks." he said.

Flouncing romances of the past in her face wasn't a good idea with Duckets as she'd a real paucity of activity on that front, deluding herself that she much preferred a good crossword, and was never inclined to be pleasant to anyone parading their amorous successes, especially when she held their financial well-being in her bony grip.

"Quite, Mr Delaney but it's not that *sort* of business we have to discuss now, is it?"

Bitch, he thought, but smiled.

"I've looked through the activity on your company account and you have been banking regular sums of money each month, some greater than others but regular nonetheless and I note that you have not used your overdraft facility on your current account for over two years, now. Which is good. May I look at the records and tax return you have kept and perhaps compare your figures with ours on last year as a working example."

He passed over a big black ledger to her and she spread it across the desk and ensured what Joe had recorded was what she had. Duckets tutted here and there and pointed out that there were a few anomalies regarding dates but told him it may be the banking system slow to react or the ineptitude of a new clerk, or some such and then made a muttered comment about illegible handwriting. She asked him about his orders which were full for the next five months with projected dates and contacts written in with the word *confirmed* next to them and he explained that with the loan he would be able to take on another tradesman and create more profit but he needed ladders, another van and the money to kit it out. It was as simple as that. During some of this time, which was a good twenty five minutes, her eyes occasionally drifted to the passport adjacent to all the other papers and then back to her task. After she had made detailed comparison to her documents and written down the phone numbers of all the confirmed contracts she excused herself and took his passport with her. This didn't look good. Behind the desk there was an internal window from which the whole office could be seen so he stood up to see where she was going. She stopped at a desk where another smartly suited manager-looking type in a pinstripe suit, about her age or maybe a bit younger, was seated and spoke to him quite covertly nodding towards the private room and showing him the passport. The other worker studied it and looked at particular aspects of it turning it over. What was happening? Was there a problem? Maybe he was in too deep. He considered leaving quietly but realised he would have to leave via the main office. He could go to the toilet? A simmering panic fluttered in his stomach as he watched her. Then she addressed a young man in a smart suit that was worn in a quite dishevelled way and gave him the passport. *This was it,* he thought. He's been told to go and fetch The Flying Squad, who will cuff him and read him his rights. The young man disappeared around a corner and then Duckets returned to the other chap she had spoken to before him, said something and smiled, no less laughed, and pushed up her new glasses and flicked an imaginary tress of hair from her shoulder as he laughed back. She pulled up a chair as he retrieved a pipe and a penknife from a drawer in his desk and began to scrape out its interior with gentle but firm thrusts and he could see Duckets remaining with the conversation but entirely enjoying his manly display entitled, *The Pipe Show.* Nevertheless, maybe she was just waiting for the young man to come back with a constable? He waited another few minutes until the young man came marching towards the interview room and abruptly burst in. *Ah well*, he thought. Prison dinners.

"Mr Delaney?" He said and sat down.

"Yes? Everything okay?" he tentatively said.

"Actually, no. Mr Delaney. It's not." was the rejoinder as the young man sat then stood up to look back into the office at where Duckets was and then dipped quickly back down into his seat.

His stomach twisted into a knot knowing he was just being occupied by a young blood in the bank who could tackle him before the law arrived should he make a desperate bid for freedom and he heard the rush of blood in his ears as adrenalin and panic was pumped into his bloodstream.

"That witch has been on my case all fucking day. I'm hungover and haven't been home yet. I had to come straight to work from wherever the holy shit I was last night! She suspects I'm hungover, I know she does and is just being a shithead to me. This why she's given me this to do, with you....." and he held up the papers he was carrying. "I've been drafting and copying this stuff for your loan all mornin'. I hate havin' to work wi' her! Mind you she's happy now. She just wants a bit of time to flounce around Basil Fawlty and his smashing big pipe, there!"

He looked up and out into the office and sure enough the chap she was talking to did hold a reasonable likeness to the mad hotelier. However, he was ecstatic with relief and thought that if he doesn't pull off the loan then at least he's out of here with his liberty intact. Meanwhile, the young man had pulled a cold can of coke from his jacket and efficiently searched his trousers and pulled out two white pills.

"Paracetemol. Got them from a girl on the front desks. She understands. She's young."

He went to open the can, rising up slowly to watch Duckets who was still in the open office flirting around Fawlty, but decided to hold it against his head for a few moments.

"Awww....that's good..." he said with his eyes closed and then cracked open the can and popped the paracetemol nearly finishing the entire contents in one go. Then he burped loudly.

He was slightly taken aback with this change from twin-set school mistress to suffering youth with a hangover and it was written on his face. The young man saw this as he gasped for air and burped, placing the can on a space on the desk between the documents.

"Sorry mate, I saw the documents you've got to sign and could see you're a painter and if you're a painter then you're a man of the world. Guessed you'd be okay wi' me slakin' my drouth. My Dad's a painter and when him and his mates get drinkin' they can drain the pumps in any pub and have a proper chuckle."

He smiled back and nodded, "Yeah, it has been known in the trade that we get the lunatics, now and again. Drinking the turps." He said, keen to appear jovial and keep him onside but delighted with the turn of events.

"Sorry, Mr Delaney, I'm Angus...*Gus the gopher,* fetch this, bring that, photocopy this pile of shit, et cetera, you know the score. I'm nineteen going on fuckin' fifty workin' here. I really hate it. Drew the line at makin' the tea. They can fuck right off! Should've gone to work wi' my dad but my mum wanted me to try this first."

The sound of the door handle being turned was heard and Angus immediately changed into functional office clerk.

"......and so these are the terms and conditions of the loan with repayment details which you can have longer to read if you need to......"

Duckets leaned in and dropped another sheet of paper onto the desk and said to Angus,

"Two signatures and explain the colateral." And then smiled her special smile to Kelly. "Approved on verification of the future contracts, which Angus will do, forthwith."

She was about to leave and saw the can of coke on the desk and glared down at Angus, who, to all ends, appeared busted. Kelly saw this and saw an opportunity to make a friend for life....well as long as this meeting took, and leaned over and swigged the last of the coke.

"Practically addicted!" he said to Duckets and smiled then returned to Angus who went back into his spiel.

She appeared disappointed, closed the door and returned to Basil and his gloriously elegant pipe. Angus exhaled and smiled across at him.

"Aww...thanks mate! Now I know you're a painter! Brothers o' the brush an' a' that. Wait 'til I tell my dad. He'll laugh."

However, Kelly was keen to garner progress while he was on his side.

"Approved?" he said to Angus.

"Oh aye. I do all this borin' shit all the time. Approved. Take five workin' days after I make the calls. You're flat is the collateral. We presumed it would be as you've got your mortgage with us, as well?"

He realised that was a glaring oversight on his part and never even considered the issue of collateral and was delighted that the issue had resolved itself. He nodded sagely as if it was a natural presumption by all.

"Of course....yeah. Just assumed you'd .... do that, you know....."

"We could actually put it on your mortgage? Might be a bit cheaper in the long run but we'd have to start the application again?"

"No......no, really need to get this sorted...... soon...." he mumbled with mock disapproval.

"Good man! Didn't want to go there with my head full o' pigshit. I'm sure you understand, Mr Delaney."

"Oh, completely."

Gus the gopher organised the papers in front of him and he knew he was close. He signed as best he could with Joe's signature, which happily was a scrawl, where Angus indicated and then he leaned back in his seat and felt a surge of excitement course through him and also one of fear. He was now in this up to his neck which would snap should any untimely rope to trip him up or hang him be presented but it had gone well. However, he had one hurdle left to get over.

"Ermmm..... Angus......"

"Just Gus to you, Mr Delaney."

Could I..... erm... put the loan in a *separate account......Gus?* A new one. A cheque book has gone missing on the business account and I'm not sure if it was taken or lost."

"No sweat, Mr Delaney. I can do that for you now, if you have the time? I see you've got your ovies with you so if you need to go, I can send the details on?"

"No, no! Lets do it now. Set it up and I'll have everything I need to take with me....right...*Gus?"*

"Right, Mr Delaney but we'll post the cheque books to you. Do you want the plastic?"

"The.??....*sorry*.....what?"

"Cashcard. Hole in the wall machine."

He was unfamiliar with all of this but had seen the new ATM machines which all looked complicated to him but he realised this would be instant access, so...

"Yes I think so...*Gus....*"

"Good choice. My dad loves it. Great for cash purchases. You'll get the cheque book, card and number in separate letters in about five days, so you're lookin' at ...*Monday* at the earliest. Safer that way in case anyone tries anything, you know, steals the card or cheque book and tries to use them pretending they're you."

He genuinely chuckled with Gus at that observation, nodded and made some noises of approval and considered asking Angus for more information about how the cashcard and machine all worked but understood he would look far from someone who runs his own business, so Angus concluded the meeting and shook his hand telling him that his dad was bound to know him because he knew everybody in the trade in town. He then asked him if he knew his Dad, the firm's name and a description of what was an apparently large man, to which some acting was required pulling faces as if scouring his memory for a face or name he knew when he was just desperate to get out. Eventually, Angus shut up and allowed him to march down the open office and nodded to Duckets on the way past and smiled a smile that he honestly enjoyed as she inspected Basil's pipe. He reached the double doors leading into a larger foyer of marbled floor and walls. He was nearly out and onto Fredrick Street, then it would be Princes Street up the North Bridge and home, safe, out of reach, when a voice shouted his name from the double doors with more than a hint of urgency. He turned to see a uniformed security guard hurrying towards him and he thought the worst and so just remained where he was gazing out into the street. Obviously a discussion and an agreement about him and the veracity of his identity had occurred and, naturally, his fortune was about to plummet, once more.

"Mr Delaney, Mr Delaney...." a breathless guard said, waving something in his hand, "Your passport."

Chapter 19

The Unusuality of Death

"So... DC Jones, might I and the rest of the team have your

considered opinion and summary of where we are with this unfortunate young man?"

The office all turned their heads to Jones and she shuffled a few papers before clearing her throat. There were two other male detectives and two uniforms.

"Well, sir....the victim...."

"Victim? Have we decided that?" McQuarrie had a little look around the room. One other detective smirked knowing McQuarrie was deliberately pressuring Claire leading her first case conference.

"Well some of the circumstances seem to lead us to that, sir. The most post-mortem says that he died of an aneurism on the brain located just under the cranium where he had received a blow to the head. The wound was fresh, less than twelve hours old when the body was reported."

She'd started confidently

"......the presumption was he had either been in a fight, which none of the door staff on any of the pubs around the High Street or around Greyfriars Kirkyard reported neither did we make record of any of the public out that night reporting any disturbances."

One of the male detectives, Watson, spoke.

"A Saturday night in Edinburgh without a fight? In summer when lads are thirsty and the blood's up? Unheard of."

A few chuckles went around the room. Claire continued,

".....and there weren't any reported assaults anomalous to those that occurred on the night club doors. Even then, they occurred around closing time in the clubs and the time of death was placed between one o' clock and three at the latest. We have considered that he might have got drunk, and he was or certainly had to be because the amount of alcohol recently ingested would have *floored a horse,* apparently. Pathology's words not mine."

"He got drunk decided to have a kip in the Kirkyard, slipped and fell against one of the headstones?" said Watson.

"We considered that..." Jones said, "...but there was small pieces of what turned out to be brick remnants in the wound and there are none that match in the Kirkyard."

"So he's been bricked on the head. Somewhere else, presumably?" Fenlon offered.

"We think so, but we traced the victim's movements to the bars he went to and it seems he was alone. He drank beer and offended nobody, apparently. Never spoke to a soul but to order his drinks. Sat alone and nobody joined him. There are two unusual aspects to this, however, the last bar he was reported to have been seen in was *The Old Golf Tavern* by Bruntsfield Links...."

"And before that?" McQuarrie tested her, "...*Bennets Bar* next to the King's Theatre, where he drank copiously according to the barmaid."

"Was he gay?" asked the first detective. "Theatreland. You never know."

"He wasn't married nor did he have a girlfriend, but his parents said they would've known if he was gay and didn't think this likely?"

"Maybe they didn't want it to be true?" said the second detective, Fenlon.

"What do his friends think?" McQuarrie barked.

"Well...sir....he appears to have had none. Not one."

"Get to the pubs? You were talking about the pubs, Jones!"

"Yes, Sir. *The Old Golf Tavern* is a good hike from Greyfriars and not on his way home. We think he might have gone to try to report the assault...."

"If there was one?"

"If there was one." She conceded.

"And the unusual aspects, Jones?" McQuarrie asked seemingly weary already.

"He was shoeless, sir." Claire sharply said to McQuarrie and McQuarrie gave her brownie points and a grain of respect.

"No shoes?"

"No, sir."

"Thoughts?"

"Maybe.."

"Not you, Jones." And he looked around the room.

"They were new and hurting him, so he kicked them off? Drunks do strange things." said Watson.

"Possibly but not very likely."

"Stolen?" Fenlon offered.

"My...we're on fire this morning, gentlemen.....*and Jones*. Stolen because what...? They're so cool...trendy..."

"Just a bunch of lads, pissin' about with a loner. Students. Drunk students are worse. Drunk students studying law are worse than worse!" Fenlon said.

"Possibly and it has happened before, Fenlon, but they, assuming they took the shoes, are not necessarily our culprits." McQuarrie condescendingly said.

"There was other unusual stuff, Sir..." Jones chimed in.

"Well, bring forth more unusualities, please Jones. We like unusual!"

"He had small bits of foliage on his clothes, Sir and tree bark under some of his nails. There's no trees in Greyfriars Kirkyard."

"And there is your next task, my lovelies. Identify the species and find that tree then locate the type of brick that matches the crumbs in the wound! Fenlon, family and work colleagues, you know the drill*"*

Fenlon hated doing family questioning. He had to be so sensitive and he just wasn't.

"Re-assurance and accompanying the grieving process from a discreet distance. Public image of the force dictates that our presence must be around. Shoes Jones. Style, size etc. Find these shoes, wherever or whoever they may be with, and find out if they fit and if he was going to the ball! Do you agree Jones?"

"Yes, sir."

McQuarrie turned to address the Sergeant in uniform.

"Bruntsfield links, The Meadows, and Tollcross, George....."

Claire Jones interrupted him,

"They've been briefed, Sir. A dozen uniforms are set to go...on *your word* of course, Sir?"

The rest of the room smiled but suppressed their chuckles. McQuarrie noted their mirth and said,

"You have the word, George. Go."

"Are you coming with me Sir?" Jones asked.

"No, but you can drop me off where I'll make my own enquiries."

Chapter 20

Planted

Across his arms were three bags of compost. This was a good idea, he thought and he quickly padded downstairs and into his flat and turned sharply into his bathroom where he emptied the compost on top of her, now lying in his bath. He hurried back upstairs and did the same with fifteen of the compost bags but ripping out the marijuana plants and throwing them across her bed. He then went into her kitchen and spent the next half hour cleaning the blood from the floor and checking the room for any signs that anything was unusual or untoward and gave every surface a good wipe down.

He stood in his bathroom and looked at the level layer of compost. He flattened an area that he wasn't so satisfied with and then felt the need to pee. The toilet bowl was immediately next to the top of the bath. For some reason he had decided that her head shouldn't go at the taps end, even though her face would be under a substantial plot of earth and he had these stupid ideas about her face popping up out of the soil. Possibly, he'd watched too many horror films. His glands had swollen up in his groin recently and thankfully he realised that the pustules on his cock were reducing. He knew this was happening because his glands were doing their job and the fact that he wasn't pissing broken glass meant that the infection was subsiding. Nevertheless, the discomfort and tenderness in his groin was much noteworthy and felt it as he'd lugged the bags of compost down the stairs. He finished peeing and was giving it a shake, looked across at the bathful of soil and then audibly spoke to her,

"Look....I'm sorry, okay. You came at me. None of this would've happened if you were clean. I mean look at it..." and he turned his dick towards the bath. "You should've been clean. Rule one in the prostitute's rule book, right?"

He had no idea which rules were up there with the *rub yer tummy guv'nor* sorority but he felt the need to say something. He felt guilty. Sad. He was now starting to feel hunted, too. He switched out the red bulb, darkly ironic, he thought and said into the darkness,

"Sorry." Then closed the door.

He covertly made the trip to and from her flat with all of the compost bags available and made a tidy grave for her in his bath.

The remnants of the broken-up couch were strewn around his living-room, a stark emblem of his life. He sat on the floor leaning on the wall and thought of the events that were overwhelming him. There was a mirror against the wall opposite. He stared at himself for a while considering the face looking back, which all seemed new to him despite the very short hair. He was changed. Doing something, as he had done, changes people. Not the outward signs of recognition but the perception of those that see. Those who see and judge. A monolithic silence filled the space around him. He didn't like him. Him in the mirror. He wanted to be someone else. Close by on the floor was a plastic bag of liberated make-up and the hairpiece he wore to the bank.

Chapter 21

A Racing Cert

It was now ten o'clock and *The Old Duke* was quite busy. There were a few faces he'd not seen before, so that was good. Other strangers were decent cover. Spider and Bullet were up on Stan passing the time in occasional exchanges.

He wore a checked shirt and an old pair of jeans. He went to the bar and noticed that there was a new face behind the bar, too. A prettier version of Megan busied around the customers serving and wiping slops. He waited until Norrie came close and held up a one pound note. Norrie looked at him and nodded as if to ask what he wanted. He paused and feigned a cough to give himself time because he'd forgotten to consider the voice. A middle English accent required a pint of lager. Norrie complied not batting an eyelid at the new face in the pub and poured and delivered the pint, took the money, issued the change and moved onto the next customer. He smiled and remained at the bar. Ten minutes passed and no-one had spoke to him or looked at him with anything other than the norm; nods, *excuse me's* etc. Then a voice behind him said,

"Sorry mate can I just squeeze in there."

Kelly turned. Joe was smiling at him. Still in his overalls and spattered with white dots of emulsion all over his face and hands, he spoke again,

"Busy night. Just grabbin' a swift one before the late shift!"

Kelly smiled back and laid on the accent, "Of course, dear fellow! Not many things more important than the swift one before the late shift. Sustenance from the gods!"

Kelly shifted to let him to the bar. "Thirsty work, the laying on of paint?"

Joe didn't really want to talk but was polite. "Very much so. Especially in this weather."

"Yes, dries remarkably fast." Kelly said and Joe did a double take at him before his pint arrived and said,

"You're a painter?"

Kelly flushed internally realising he had quickly become too smug. As usual.

"Landscapes." He quickly replied. "Occasionally portraits. You?"

"Nothing quite so artistic. Walls, windows and doors!"

"And *you!*" Kelly laughed, indicating his face and hands. Joe weakly smiled back.

Joe's pint arrived and he squeezed away from Hector and started to make his way across to Stan closing with his own witticism, "Yes, it's my white period!"

Kelly watched him go laughing at his retort and raised his pint in acknowledgement. He remained at the bar for the next quarter of an hour watching the room ignore him until he decided to go back to his flat before anyone decided to find out who the new face was. He was passing McQuarrie's table and couldn't resist.

"Soldier Sveyk." He said leaning in over the table and nodding down at his paper spread out at the horse racing.

"I'm sorry?" McQuarrie said remaining quite still and lifting his eyes to Kelly.

"He's getting out soon. Within the fortnight, I would imagine. *Soldier Sveyk.* I have friends at a stud in Oxford. Showing remarkable form."

"*Soldier.....?*" McQuarrie said lifting his pencil.

"Sveyk." Kelly spelt it out for him. McQuarrie wrote it into his little book.

"Young horse. He'll be running soon. Don't miss him."

Kelly left tapping his nose and pointing at McQuarrie's paper.

Chapter 22

Revelations

Half an hour later Kelly arrived into *The Old Duke*. Bullet gave him a nod and Spider raised his glass and beamed his yellow teeth at him. He passed DI McQuarrie who gave him a cursory glance and returned to his notebook.

"Any big results, lately, Mr McQuarrie?" Kelly knew the answer to that one as McQuarrie returned to his paper without replying.

The new barmaid approached him but Norrie sidled into view and stood in front of him. Unusual?

 "Special, please, *Norman*... New girl?"

Norrie nodded and began to pour.

"Megan won't be pleased." Kelly ventured at humour and smiled.

"Megan's friend." Norrie said and then did something Kelly had never seen him do. He smiled back.

Kelly was astounded. Norrie gave him the pint, took his money and held the smile for the next customer.

Kelly sat down next to Spider.

"You look tired." Spider said.

"I was gonna say that, as well." Bullet also said.

"Thanks lads. Always rely on your mates for the truth." Kelly said and then swigged.

"Not sleepin'?" Spider continued. "Got lucky wi' one o' Megan's new mates, eh?"

"Really, Spider? Do I look like a catch for some middle-class bint ten years younger than me?"

Spider shrugged and smiled. A moment elapsed and all in the company accepted that that aspect of their conversation was done with and they quietly sipped their pints.

"No." Bullet said.

Kelly was confused. "No what?"

"No...you don't look like a catch...for one of them." Bullet said quite earnestly.

"Thanks Bullet...like I said...mates and all that. Actually where is Megan? She not working?"

"She's got an interview. Norrie said. Earlier." Spider nodded over to where Norrie was.

"Did she not like workin' in here then, Spider?" Bullet asked.

"What interview?" Kelly sat up.

"London." Spider was being annoyingly vague for Kelly.

"London? What about London?" he pressed.

Bullet offered his view. "Must be a top bar. A good rub-a-pub. Top money for her to go that far. But she's a good barmaid." he said, comprehending at his usual pace.

"Spider! Where's she gone?" Kelly said ignoring Bullet.

"She's got a Teflon interview. In London. To do the English."

"English! Teflon! London! Try harder to be clearer and less fucking annoying, Spider!"

Bullet looked like he was thinking and said, "That's not very good."

"Actually, no it's not, Bullet!!" Kelly spat back.

"Terrible name for a pub."

"What!!" Kelly turned on Bullet.

"Teflon. I know it's an English pub, like Spider said but I think it's a bad name."

Spider started to shake his head.

"No, no, no... Bullet...it's for the err ... it's for the err..abroad.....malarkey. *Teachin' abroad*...English. Spoke to Norrie earlier. He told me. He's dead pleased...." and Spider nodded across to where Norrie was at the bar and caught him looking across.

"There ye go! Look." Spider said pointing to Norrie who knew they'd pass on the good news and was looking directly at Kelly and smiling. Spider and Bullet raised their glasses. Kelly stared back at him Norrie held his smile.

An internal and quite schizophrenic discussion occurred within him.

She's gone then, eh? What the fuck are you so bothered about, you couldn't shag her anyway, you clapped up piece of dirt! I loved her! Well you fucked it up good and proper at the party, didn't you! She wouldn't want you now even if you could do the nasty. She didn't tell me she was going. Why the fuck should she? What are you to her but a source of literary amusement and quite interesting facts. I was more than that. She felt it too. I know she did. We could have maybe given it a go. What with Norrie as your father in-law? Are you fucking nuts!! And by the way, you're a thieving fraudulent murderer...and a bad friend. I'm not bad!! I'm sorry but the evidence says different, chummy me lad-ee-o!

"You liked her, didn't you?" broke his thought. Spider was leaning in and smiling in a confidential and conciliatory way. His breath was bad.

"No...no! Well, yes...as much as anyone liked her...in here. She was okay... but I didn't *like her*, like her....like that. Not really my type....n'that."

"Remember that Queen in the Shakespeare play you told me about?" Spider smiled

"No? Which one?" Kelly was astounded he'd remembered

"The one where she says, *Methinks the lady doth protest too much,* when she's a lyin' bitch. That one."

"Hamlet."

"Can't remember which play ye said, but that's you...."

Kelly really wanted to change the subject. Megan had left. Not a word or goodbye. That's it. He was patently unaware of how he felt about her and the intensity that arrived when confronted by a world without her. He knew that when his plans all came to fruition that he couldn't stay, anyway, so what was he bellyaching about? He'd made a choice that was going to change his life forever and knew there was no going back, now. He'd decided that to lead a life devoid of labour that he would sacrifice the chance of love and the contact of his family. He'd killed someone. What more reason to run? But *to where* was a consideration entirely missed in his machinations of fraud and deceit. Down near the door DI McQuarrie had stood up and Kelly, knowing he was hiding the corpse of his neighbour in his bath, was glad to see him ready himself to leave. He picked up his paper, downed the last of his pint and then put his paper in his pocket and lifted his notebook but instead of leaving, walked deeper into the pub up towards Hector and started to speak to The Brylcreem Boys and the other customers and occasionally making notes. Kelly was mildly alarmed but had no need to be, he assured himself. *He can't know about her already. She can't be missed yet. It'll be something else.*

McQuarrie made his way around the bar with apparently the same spiel, some punters nodding, him making a note, then the punter shaking his head. He reached Stan and climbed onto the platform.

"Evening." McQuarrie said to them.

"A'right." Bullet said and Spider nodded and smiled. Kelly said nothing.

"Had a death round here, recently. You might have heard?" McQuarrie looked at Kelly. Kelly froze. *What?* he thought. *How can he know?*

"Greyfriars murder?" Spider asked. "Saw it in the paper."

"That's right. The Kirkyard. Wondering if any of you were out on Saturday in that area? Might've heard something? Seen something? About midnight? Maybe half twelve to three o'clock?"

"Tucked up in bed, Mr McQuarrie." Spider said. "I was in here all night before that."

"Ford?" Bullet reddened at hearing his name.

"No. I was in here, too." He said. "With Spider."

"Have you heard of anyone talking about a fight or disturbance? Anything at all?"

"No...sorry Mr McQuarrie." Spider said and Bullet shook his head with him.

"You're quiet, Kells? You okay?" McQuarrie smirked and Kelly then knew that he and Norrie had discussed the leaving of Megan. *Pair of bastards* he thought. However, Kelly, was relieved at the news it was another murder and breathed easier.

"I'm a quiet man, Mr McQuarrie. Just doin' away. Getting by. On my own."

"Wasn't that quiet for you on Saturday night, I hear? Party wasn't it? Marchmont. I hear you were a tad offensive to a few of Megan's friends. That's no way to get the girl, is it, Kells?"

So she'd come home and cried on her dad's shoulder and he'd blabbed to McQuarrie. What did he expect, none of the two of them liked him, he knew that, and now that Megan had left without a word to him, it added humiliation to his pain and in front of the audience of Bullet and Spider.

"Just didn't share the same view of the world, Mr McQuarrie. What can you do?"

"Accept that others might not feel as you do but respect their opinion, whatever. How about that for *something to do?*"

Kelly knew that anything he said was going to be met with sarcasm and possibly a greater wit and learning so he just took a pull at his pint.

"Wino was it Mr McQuarrie?" Spider asked by way of digging out Kelly.

"Sorry?" McQuarrie said.

"In the kirkyard?"

"Young fella. Loner."

"What was his name. Might know him?" Bullet said.

"Sukerman. David Sukerman. Thirty-three. Too young." McQuarrie said.

Kelly felt the heat as his face reddened and he heard the blood rushing in his ears. Adrenalin started to surge around his body and his face visibly flushed and he had an immediate inclination, stupidly, to run out the pub. His heart started to pump and his breathing became erratic and he had a wave of nausea, unfortunately that was when McQuarrie turned his head to look at him.

"You okay, Kells? Looking a bit green around the gills, there."

"Yeah, I'm fine. Just got a cold coming...or *something*. Felt the draught when the door opened."

Kelly referred to the arrival of Sasquatch who came in and took his usual seat by the bar. The new girl breezed up to him with a smile and asked him what he wanted. Sasquatch stared at her and then frowned looking behind the bar for a familiar face. Norrie was busy and so she asked him again,

"What can I get you?" remaining just as breezy.

A few of the regulars had noticed this and turned with curiosity and a modicum of trepidation to see how it would pan out. Norrie heard the noise level drop and looked to see what the source of it might be and saw the non-verbal stand-off with the new girl. He left who he was serving and went into cavalry mode, however, a deep, slow drawl emanated from Sasquatch, which stopped him in his tracks.

"Guinness."

Everybody who knew Sasquatch was astounded by this new aspect of this dark character. The new girl naturally grabbed a glass and began pouring the Guinness with a look of bemusement as to the silence. Norrie rescued her and took over the pouring and took his twenty and put it in the glass behind the bar. She was confused but deferred to the authority of Norrie and began wiping the slops off of Hector.

McQuarrie turned back to his audience on Stan. "My, the world is in flux. Actually, Kells, cold coming and draughts aside, I thought you looked a little shocked when I mentioned the victim's name. Did you know him? David Sukerman."

McQuarrie said his name again, deliberately to try and get another reaction from Kelly, but he managed to keep a straight face but then thought it might be best to give McQuarrie something. A reason as to his flushed reaction, a reasonable but tenuous offering that kept him at a believable distance.

"There was a lad at school in the same year as me called Sukerman. I never knew his first name, though. Might not be the same one?"

"But it might be?" McQuarrie said. "It's an unusual name. Jewish. Which school were you at?"

"Errr.... Boroughmuir." He mumbled knowing that this had been a mistake and McQuarrie would become the proverbial dog with a bone, even if it was just to make him feel uncomfortable. McQuarrie had told him face to face that he didn't like him, threatened him if he found out anything untoward occurred with the death of Lenni, so Kelly expected more in the post from him.

"You don't sound so sure, Kells....." Kelly wished he'd stop using his name. "...how old are you?"

Spider and Bullet had now become engrossed in this and looked at Kelly in expectation.

"Thirty-three." He resignedly said knowing that McQuarrie had given Threeby's age to Bullet and Spider nodded and smiled as if to say *there you go!*

"Probably the same fella. Our man went to Boroughmuir. What a coincidence, Kells. He worked at the local dole office."

"Did he?" Kelly said acting none the wiser.

"He did. You're *on the dole,* Kells...right?"

"Yeah...."

"Never seen him up there? Never stopped to relive the japes and teachers?"

"No."

"Not in...how long?"

"What do you mean?"

"How long have you signed on up at the dole office that David Sukerman worked at?"

Again, his name and McQuarrie's tone became a tad more direct.

"Seven. Seven years." Kelly was patently uncomfortable and but McQuarrie had nothing more than that. A man uncomfortable at the death of someone he used to know.

"And never seen him? He didn't socialise with his workmates so he needed some friends, maybe? You never saw him? Said hello? Talked? How's life? What are you up to? Are you married? Kids? All the usual stuff."

Kelly did his best to appear to think and then just offered a shake of the head.

"No."

McQuarrie paused, appeared also to think and then brightly said,

"Ah well.... thanks anyway, Kells.." and smiled, "....that's a shame. If you remember anything about him that might help us ...I'll be at my usual table!"

Kelly just smiled insipidly, understanding the quiet malevolence and McQuarrie went off into the other punters and asked the same questions. Spider and Bullet talked loudly about the case and Kelly watched as McQuarrie reached Sasquatch. Sasquatch looked emptily into his face. Kelly saw McQuarrie pitch his questions at the massive man who had for the first time that anyone had seen in this pub, decided to use the spoken word, only one admittedly, however speech it was. Sasquatch appeared to listen but said nothing back to him. McQuarrie shrugged and moved on when he realised he was going to get nothing and then Sasquatch slowly turned his head and stared across the pub for the next minute, without blinking. At Kelly. Kelly broke the stare and relived the howl he heard soon after he left the bleeding Threeby holding his head and getting to his feet. Something was unspoken but undeniably, said, and understood by both in that moment.

Kelly went back to his flat as soon as he could excuse himself before closing time, which was noted by Spider, Bullet and Norrie, however Norrie was happy to think it was because Kelly was too upset at the leaving of Megan without a word or goodbye and inwardly glowed at his discomfort and unhappiness. Kelly strode around his living-room in and out of the bits of broken couch and piles of books and beer cans with a charged movement akin to panic. He tried to digest the news that he had killed Threeby and emanated the occasional *shit, shit!* and then his thoughts went to Megan, Sasquatch, McQuarrie and then a look down the hall to the occupant of his bath.

He had to stop because he was breathing heavily. He stood in his living-room amongst the detritus and mess of his world and head. The arms of his broken couch lay forlorn, like two dead children robbed of breath and meaning, the main stretch of the back support of couch-padding was pushed and contorted until its wooden struts had snapped in his desperate hunt and was now reshaped into a deathly pose of dysfunction with the intestinal stuffing strewn across the floor. Books formed rectangular structures, open, closed, on end, crushed, abridged snapshots of a greater knowledge and experience denied by his inability to complete anything in his life. Randomly distributed socks found resting places behind shelves and in corners with a layer of dust across the top marking time for him beyond any timepiece, and a TV, monochrome and colourless in its transmission into his world, sat noiselessly in the corner. A fridge in his kitchen left by the last tenant seven years ago, held onto its skewed door, struggling with the uneven floor and bereft of any sustenance worthy of the word *food*.

He imagined Threeby's last stagger from The Meadows up to Greyfriars Kirkyard, the looks he would have received from those on their way home. The assumption that he was a drunk that took a sore one in a fight, a drunken brawl outside some nameless pub. It was also likely that at that time of the morning he could have struggled unnoticed up to his final resting place, perhaps having stopped the flow of blood and deciding that he should walk into the darkness of the kirkyard to rest? To quietly and perhaps thankfully accept his end? He could have cried but he didn't. Kelly understood that he should feel something more akin to remorse having been the tormentor of this unfortunate in his youth and now the deliverer of his final moments on earth but the sordid melange of everything that he was, murderer, fraudster, liar, egotist, thief, drunk, all swam around his head and he imagined these visions of himself now swirling in shades of grey, external above his head in scenes of shame and the isolated image of Threeby was now only another portrait of his innate wrongfulness.

It was then a switch flicked in his head. A sullen coldness crept softly over his body and enveloped him and then an acceptance of who and what he was with no likely hope of change. He was drowning in his wrongdoings and was now easier, it seemed to him, to be that which he was than to make some sea-change of self. He caught himself in the mirror leaning against the wall and was stopped in his tracks at the vision he saw. He took in the sight of a someone that he knew had always been there, hidden behind the egotist and the actor, someone he knew, someone there within but now just plainly there. The painting in the attic had come to him.

Lack of sleep and alcohol had drawn deep shadows beneath his eyes and the still pinkish flecks of previous cuts and bruises to his face drew a mottled effect sometimes catching the light through his three-day growth. The whites of his eyes were now minorly, but permanently, bloodshot and his hair could no longer hide them. This vision depicted the anarchic, disorganised, dissolute, selfish and dangerous man that had squelched out and forward into the world in sickly, stinking yellow juices and then, maintaining eye-contact with this *Mr Hyde*, quite naturally, he tipped his head forward allowing a shadow to drop over his face, his undernourished cheekbones becoming quickly apparent and as sharp as the yellowing teeth behind his thin lips and the reddish tip of his nose, a beacon, warning those that may cross him of his black-hearted iniquity. He chanced the curl of a smile and watched the immorality before him grin back.

He pulled quickly away from the reflection and turned to face the room. Clarity and simplicity of thought galloped through the throng of other useless ideas that made up the monolith called *Contrition*. It was simple. Follow through with the plan. Be there at Joe's in the mornings to watch him go and wait for the post to arrive. Get the card. Draw the cash. Then leave.

"Hello, Mr Kelly." A voice behind him said.

He spun around in fright.

"Now that's what you call a party!"

Number Two stood before him large and imposing in his long black coat. Kelly looked at him and then fired a look down the hallway to the front door where Number One was standing and looking back at him.

"How...?" Kelly stammered.

"…..did we get in? Really, Mr Kelly? We have skills. We know things. Lots of things. We told you that last time we saw each other did we not?" Number Two sarcastically said.

"Yes... what do you want?"

Trepidation coursed through him at the thought of the gloved punches he took, the last time and the dead woman in the bathroom.

"Well... we'd like to congratulate you first of all."

"Would you?" Kelly looked suspicious and fearful.

"Yes. We would. It looks very much like you have made a very good decision which makes us very, very happy, and Sir Clive? Well, he is *very happy,* too, over the moon!"

"Very." Came the first word from Number One down the hall who was standing far too close to the bathroom door for Kelly's liking.

"It looks as though you may have been having a good time in here, as well, Mr Kelly? Didn't you like that sofa?" Did the colour clash with your overall theme of...." He had a quick scan about the room, ".....dusty, shitty grey?"

"I'm moving flat." Kelly snapped out at him, braver, harder, seemingly in no mood for his sarcasm. "I've had to break it up to get it out."

"I can't see why you want to move, Mr Kelly? You have a beautifully appointed place, here. We think it's really you!"

"What the fuck do you want?"

Number Two smarted a little at the expletive and sent a little glance down to his accomplice. Number One then slowly walked up the hallway and pulled his leather gloves tighter onto his hands. Kelly backed into the room finding a spot between his TV and some books.

"....and we started so well." Number Two sighed and held out an arm to stop his mate from approaching Kelly further.

"I'll shout out! I fuckin' will!" Kelly warned them.

"And then we'd be forced to silence you, Mr Kelly. Possibly for good. And that wouldn't be good. For you. Or for us, quite frankly. It's messy. Gets headlines and nobody wants headlines do they. We don't. Do you?"

"No."

"Unless of course you like headlines? Do you like making the headlines, Mr Kelly?"

"No of course I fucking don't!"

"No you don't! Who would? I mean.... take this little local rag..." He pulled The Evening News from his coat pocket. "....look at this headline....I can't think of anyone that would want to be associated with such an unfortunate headline as this. Not a one. Tscchh...."

He held up the front of Monday's Evening News which had the headline,

Shoeless Greyfriars Murder.

Kelly looked at it and then, suppressing a new found rage where fear should have been, he flatly returned a steely stare.

"What about it?" Kelly wasn't sure if they knew anything or if it was coincidence.

Number Two sighed again and looked at his watch. Pragmatism won.

"It's late. I'd like to go to bed and I'm sure you'd like to....if you have one.... and I'd also like to progress to whichever measures are necessary to conclude our association on behalf of Sir Clive and stop watching, or having you watched. Or watching the people that may be complicit in your tawdry sad activities concerning the negatives or prints, whichever of them currently exist, of Sir Clive *in flagrante* with our now loyal colleague who hung Lenin....*Lenni...* the dog. I'm sure you remember. Now, with regard to the headline, here displayed, it seems the worm has turned for us and not for you. Shame, but there you go and now you are in the desperate situation of...well... *murderer....*Mr Kelly."

"How did you know?"

"Oh we have friends everywhere. In pubs, in the streets, in workplaces, *universities,* watching and listening for treachery that may undermine the state wherever it may lift its ugly head. You shouldn't be surprised Mr Kelly. We also send them *to parties* to ensure no exchange of information or materials occur and to seize opportunities that may present themselves."

Kelly smiled at them now, accepting of their opinion of him and now apparently comfortable and inured into the world of espionage. And he liked it. His egotism suppressed any fear and roared forward, once more

"Who was your man? One of those university rugby-playing fuckheads, right?"

He loved using the phrase *your man* and said it as though it was a covert meeting in a public park somewhere in Budapest, Prague or Sofia.

"Wrong. But you must be quite careful with *dissident aggression* in any of your future dealings."

Kelly flashed back to the T-shirted MC of his humiliation and shook his head and smiled.

"Come, come, Mr Kelly you shouldn't be surprised. You're a thespian now are you not, and was not Christopher Marlowe, a renowned playwright that rivalled The Bard and a thoroughly applauded, Cambridge varsitarian, atheist, sodomite and spy?"

Kelly curled his mouth downwards and slightly frowned.

"You didn't know?" Number Two said in mock shock. He turned to Number One, "He didn't know! You must read more, Mr Kelly. More of the right sort of reading."

Kelly fished around for a comeback to save his face but had nothing, so he returned to the Threeby story.

"Now what?"

"So now......we have noted that there appears to have been nothing in the tabloid rags, nor the suggestion of any impropriety reported vis-a-vis Sir Clive's short hiatus in Edinburgh, fun though it was for him, and that is *good* Mr Kelly! Very good. For us. For you. For Sir Clive. Everybody seems to see the sense that those negatives, pictures, however many copies there are, *or aren't,* never reach the light of day. Ever. *You* make sure that they are destroyed, Mr Kelly. You are now *our man*. You work for *us*."

"Why haven't you just asked me for them?"

"There would be no point in you giving them to us when we just couldn't be sure however many copies have been made, which is, unfortunately what usually happens in such cases. But now, thankfully, we have you, Mr Kelly. We have you to ensure that our wishes are observed, for the good health of all concerned, and we trust you, we trust you to do the right thing, to preserve the good reputation of our beloved Defence Minister. We observed you visiting the abode of Delaney when he was at work, the other day? That large book wasn't a photo album was it? Just a joke, forgive me. And he left your theatre building, *old school place* whatever it is, and went to the bank the day after with the big book, but as far as was apparent, we didn't see him arrive? Did you tell him we were watching you? And him? Did you tell him to use a back door?"

Kelly realised they'd swallowed the disguise and make-up, entirely, and quietly began to chuckle and then it became a louder manic laugh. Kelly had duped them, too. He laughed on, which displeased Number One enough to tighten his gloves once more and silenced Kelly's laughter.

"I didn't tell him about you and I don't know which door he used. Maybe you just missed him? Maybe you're just not as good at all this as you think?"

His laughter waned seeing they didn't share his levity. A harder tone came back at him.

"Our intention is never to bring our knowledge of this to Delaney's notice and you should do the same. We still have to keep tabs on The Trots and all their red friends during this season of political unrest, so should he ever become aware of our presence, or those negatives fall into the wrong hands, we will assume that you are the agent of revelation and distribution, and then, miraculously, evidence that marks out the perpetrator of the Greyfriars murder, will come to light for the fair constabulary of Edinburgh. Do you understand us clearly, Mr Kelly? My colleague doesn't have to convince you again, does he?"

Kelly paused. Number One stared unblinking at him.

"No."

"And you do understand? Everything?"

"Yes."

"Good. And if that day should come where we drop a subtle hint to the police and you somehow wriggle your shiftless carcass out of culpability, then the fate of our friend, the Greyfriars Body, will become yours."

Kelly smiled.

"What? You're going to hit me with a bottle?"

Number Two turned to Number One who was shaking his head and said,

"Oh dear....he hasn't put two and two together has he? Your branch-whipper was bleeding but not so much to imagine it was more than a surface wound and it didn't persuade any passing Good Samaritan to come to his aid and so he merely took himself into the churchyard to sit on the nearest slab and attend to his bleeding head, and as I said before, we have those among us who would seize opportunities wherever they may present themselves.....and so in order to effect your culpability for more than GBH... which we all agreed, at the time, would be a paltry charge and not one we could attain any *leverage* with, so... we befriended him, offered him copious amounts of vodka to assuage the pain and.....a swift knock with a stout half-brick to the same wound *helped* him on his way...."

Kelly was dumbfounded. He took this in but couldn't believe it.

"It wasn't me? I didn't kill him? You pair of murdering cunts!"

Number One, quiet through all of this, walked toward him leaned in and spoke to Kelly nose-to-nose. Kelly withdrew against the wall.

"No...the only cunt I can see in here is you, Cunt! And as far as the law is concerned the only murderer in here is you. Okay? Cunt!"

"I think he is quite clear with the situation and his future duties.." Number Two said defusing the tension. "...Oh dear....I seem to be caught short, as it were, Mr Kelly. Would you mind if I use your facilities before we go? I wouldn't ask but when needs must, and all that..."

Kelly had to think quickly.

"You can use it but I've had a shit about an hour ago and it wouldn't flush. Sometimes happens. I've told the landlord. He doesn't give a fuck. Piss in the bath. I don't care."

Number Two considered his options and then said,

"On second thoughts...I won't, thanks. This will do."

And then he extracted his penis and began to piss on Kelly's floor just in front of his feet all the while looking at him and smiling. Number One, meanwhile, made his way to the front door and gently opened it and looked out. Number Two gave it a shake and then said,

"Won't make that much difference, will it?" throwing his eyes in all directions, indicating his flat, and then zipped up and made to leave. Halfway down the hall he stopped.

"Oh...I nearly forgot! We saw that you liked reading and didn't want to come empty-handed. So..."

He reached into his coat and took out a black bible.

"Sir Clive thought that this might tidy things up. Something he wanted to do *before* our branch-whipping Greyfriars chum met his end, however, we feel your face deserves it. Be good, Mr Kelly, and good things will come your way. Revelations. Bloody scary. Give it a read."

He placed it on a small table and then left without a sound.

Kelly flicked piss off of his foot and looked at the bible. He looked down the hall to where they were no longer. He opened it up at the start of Revelations. A rectangle had been cut out of the previous chapters to house a brown envelope in which was two thousand pounds. A typed note read,

Revelations? Shew not the image of thy master nor reveal thy wits, else timely, wilt thy fate descend. SCH.

He stared down the hallway at the empty space where they had been and at the surreal way in which they had melted quietly away. No noise of footsteps on the stairs outside. No creak of door pulled home nor latch-snap. Then he looked down at the wet patch of piss before his feet like a moat he was not to cross until they left. He thought about how they said they wanted to conclude their business with him and the two grand seemed to put the full-stop where it should be but he knew he was stringing them along allowing them to believe that there were negatives or photos and if they should find out they might not be too happy. He was shaken. All the bullshit bravado when fielding their enquiries was not him. And now that they were gone and no performance was required, he was himself. Kelly the boy that never grew up. Kelly who never meaningfully jumped into society or made a contribution. Kelly the deluded liar. Kelly who was becoming scared and wanted to have somewhere to run away to. As usual. The mess of imagery that was his approaching nemesis swirled faster around his head and the colours became more vibrant. The green of The Meadows contrasted with the blood in a pool upstairs. The walk from Broxburn under, what was now, a shower of crimson drops in his visions pushed his adrenal gland to secrete its familiar liquid into his bloodstream and a realisation of what he had to do next fell like a brick from a navvie's hod on a high scaffold into his head.

He had to think. Where? There was nothing to sit down on and he put the moneyed bible on top of the newspaper on a side-table and leaned his back flat against the wall and slid down sitting on the floor next to it at nearly eye-level. He looked at it for a moment and then as if to prove the money was actually there put his finger as close as he could to the end of the book looking for the start of *Revelations* and lifted it and let fall the pages of the apocalyptic chapter until the envelope appeared out of the darkness. He gazed a moment on the brown envelope inside. Then he let the book fall shut. The headline was blocked by the bible and he pushed it across the front page and out to the edge. He pulled the paper from under the bible and looked again at the headline. He wanted to sigh, which is what he would usually do and then walk away from anything that presented a problem or the prospect of hard work but a state of alert was now permanently extant within him, courtesy of his adrenal gland and he knew he now couldn't walk away from this....yet. His eyes flicked quickly across the report picking words out that screamed out his need to do something. Soon. He knew McQuarrie sensed an anomalous deceit within him and that he would press him further about Threeby and however much he knew or didn't know about him, hoping Kelly would make a mistake. The shoes would be found, no doubt, with a whisky bottle nearby and his prints on it, pointing in a direction from Greyfriars towards his place. He knew that *she* would be missed by someone soon. A friend, relative? A punter? He had her key. He had the knife and he guessed that however much he had cleaned her flat that there would be a lone print on a cup, door-handle, a fibre from his clothes....something. And Sasquatch? That long and sustained stare at him from Hector up to him on Stan. What did he see? Everything? Nothing? Why did he howl? He only did that when there was confrontation, an altercation or aggression afoot. Kelly had to assume that he saw or heard what occurred. He spoke in the pub for the first time, too. One word but it was something. McQuarrie heard him. What if he decided to speak more? His mind was racing.

He let the paper fall onto his knee. There was a short article on page two about an Olympics for maths? The word *Edinburgh* leapt out at him. He lifted it and began to read and pulled it closer to his face absorbing the details, avariciously. He finished it. Lifted his head, eyes up-left, and thought for a moment. He quickly began to read it again and got to the end. He let it fall, thought again and then looked out of his window to the dark sky outside.

Chapter 23

If the Shoe Fits?

Thursday, 21st June

"Hello! Is this the abode of a Cestrian goose-girl?"

McQuarrie stood on the threshold of the flat looking at Luccia who looked bemused.

"DI McQuarrie. I had the pleasure of your company for a short time in The Old Duke pub a few days ago? You're Megan's friends."

More bemusement, then,

"Oh...yes. Meggy McMiggins! Ermm..*Megan.* Yes. She's not here. She's gone. Got a job....somewhere. London agent, I believe. Abroad. She might be abroad by now."

"Actually, I'd like to speak to you and your friends if that's not too inconvenient? I can see you're about to disappear soon, yourself? Anywhere nice?"

"Well I'm going back to see my parents in Cheltenham and they're all going to see theirs and then we're meeting in London and flying out to Italy next Monday for the summer...if we can get flights in time." She half smiled.

"Italy! Molto bene!" McQuarrie threw in humouring her along. "They look heavy?"

He nodded to the boxes in the hallway.

"Oh, yes" Luccia said. "Charity boxes. Books are so heavy. Can't take them with us. They're collecting."

"Which charity? He asked her with a smile. "Can I come in for a few minutes?"

"Yes...sure. Not sure." Luccia shouted into the flat. "Jerry! Which charity is coming for the boxes?"

Jerry's voice boomed from the kitchen.

"Fucked if I know, Cheeya! What fucking difference does it make? They're collecting aren't they? Skin problems with kids...I think? Dermafuckingsomething or other....oh hello."

He said, walking into the hall and seeing McQuarrie.

"Hello.....*Jericho*? Right?" McQuarrie said pointing and smiling.

"Yes....*Jerry's* good. You were..."

"....drunk! And I offer my profuse apologies. To you both. And your friends. I have to drink to switch off from work, and it turned out that the switch was rather a big one that night and I have recently lost a good friend. You were sat where he used to sit."

"Oh we didn't mean to offend....it's just that Miggy...*Megan*...asked us to sit there..."
Luccia said.

"No...no...don't worry. How could a mere goose-girl offend?" He smiled again.

However, Luccia didn't smile back and McQuarrie knew he was exhausting his armoury of ingratiation so he cut to the chase.

"You had a party on Saturday night?"

"Yes....?" Jerry stepped forward implicitly confronting McQuarrie. He'd seen his father do this when dealing with potentially nauseating *Oiks,* but his way was blocked by a large cardboard box which he was glad of because it made it look as though he would have kept this irritating raincoat in his place but for the annoying obstruction.

"Were we too loud? Sorry! Has someone complained?" Luccia said.

McQuarrie noted Jericho's haughty approach but reassured them, well.... because he wanted something.

"It's nothing like that, don't worry....*Jerry...*" McQuarrie flatly said meeting his eyes. ".....I'd just like to ask you a few questions about someone who was at the party, if that's okay? Actually, you met him that night I drowned my grief in The Old Duke..."

McQuarrie played the grief card very well, he thought eliciting hopefully a helpful response.

"......you remember Kelly?"

Chapter 24

The Last Post

Monday, 25th June

Kelly hadn't been up this early for years. It was 6:30am. He strode towards Causewayside past bus-stops with workers queuing, silent and miserable despite the summer morning. Nobody was talking. Newspapers were read and watches were watched and the impending gloom of another day on the grind was coursed across the lemmings faces. He saw this and allowed himself a note of vindication for his deceit and abstention from it all. He reached the antique shop beneath Joe's flat and tucked himself into the doorway of an unopened shop at a corner a hundred yards down the street. If Joe left before the post, great. If the post came before Joe left....well, another convincing enactment of identity would be required with Mr Postman. He'd foreseen this eventuality and had brought rolled up overalls and a bag as if he was about to go to work and hoped the postman didn't know Joe. He wrapped his coat closer to him and waited.

Chapter 25

Sticky

The Pumping Tracksuit was trying to fix a poster of that vixen of punk, Siouxie Sioux, to the wall directly facing his bed because it had fallen forward and hung with the blank side of the poster facing out to the room. He's fixed it with drawing pins a few times before he rushed back to lie on his bed but the breeze from his open window had blown it until it wrestled its corners free every time and drooped this way and that, but the corners had been punctured and torn repeatedly until there was nothing left of their paper right-angles. It was 9:20am and he hadn't had the funds to go out the previous night or go to see his streetwalking neighbour that insisted on calling him *Graham* but hadn't seen for a while. This was a dilemma because his sap was up, being sober the night before, and he needed some fantasy material to accompany his engorged penis and he's already lined up the seven-inch single *Hong Kong Garden* on the Dansette turntable he got from his Granny with the feeder arm pulled back so it would repeatedly play the song and the sight of that beautiful spiky-haired goddess of punk completed the arrangement but he was becoming increasingly frustrated because he really worked hard orchestrating these mornings when he was lucid, wakeful, rested and horny. An event to welcome the day. He decided that sellotape was what he needed.

Kelly was coming up the stairs carrying a clutch of envelopes and a plastic bag and heard some echoing shouts and banging. He immediately panicked thinking the worst. Then he recognised the dull tones of The Pumping Tracksuit and craned his neck out to look up but could see nothing.

"Urr ye in...err.."

Apparently he didn't know her name. *Should've fed him the pink pills*, Kelly thought.

"...it's Jason.....err.... *Graham*....frae upstairs, n' that... ah'm no wantin' a shag or nuthin' I ken it's early but I jist want a wee bit o' sellotape.... sticky tape.... huv ye got any?"

Kelly had to do something to stop this idiot from drawing any more attention to the scene. He went halfway up the stairs to the next landing.

"Jason, ma man! Whit's the story? Whit's a' the noise aboot?"

"Jist tryin' tae git a wee bit o' sellotape.... no got any."

"Sellotape?"

"Aye."

"Whit fur?"

"Stickin'. You goat any?"

"I think I might have, Jase. Gimme five and come doon tae the door."

Kelly disappeared quickly and into his flat and shut the door before TPT could follow, put the plastic bag and letters down and got the sellotape from his kitchen. Shortly there was a knock on the door. Kelly had the bits of sticky tape individually stuck on his fingers.

"There ye go, Jason, man. Whit's it fur?" he asked.

"Pittin' a poster oan the wa'. Corners are fucked." He said taking the bits.

"Right....bastard that when the corners go. These wee bits should git it oan the wa' 'n that."

"Cheers." TPT said and went to go back upstairs, then said, "Huvny seen her for a wee while noo...?" pointing up at her door.

Kelly replied, "She's a busy girl, Jason. Got tae bring the bacon home."

"She wiz busy wi' you the other day oan the stairs. Looked a bit out o' it, tae me?"

"Err..yeah, but so were you mate. You went straight to sleep. I think she'd had a smoke o' the other stuff. Reckon I could smell it oan her."

"See...that's jist it, man..."TPT said a bit desperately, "....I git ma smokin' stuff fae her, as weel an' I've been needin' a good hit and she's cheap. Huz some guid stuff. Huv ye no seen her?"

"I havny, Jase..err.. I'll let her know ye need a smoke...or *somethin' else,* if I see her."

And with that he went into his flat and shut the door waited a few moments for some sounds of footsteps then opened it again slightly and watched him go back upstairs. Then he heard his door shut and he heaved a sigh of relief.

He went into his bedroom and sat on the edge of his bed and pulled his trousers and underpants to his ankles and then gingerly pulled up his cock to face him, eye to eye as it were. He revealed his glans and his heart began to beat faster as he anticipated bad news in the sight he thought he may shortly see, however, it was good news. The pustules were certainly still there but had definitely receded in size and were now more red than yellow. He didn't want to have to see a knob-doctor if he could avoid it and today's news vis-a-vis his genital health was encouraging, no doubt about it.

The first envelope he opened was junk. A company punting life insurance. Ironic. The second was from the bank. He read it and then did what the instructions asked and peeled away a little window which revealed a four digit number. He tore open two more letters. None of them had a bank card in it. There was a second post later that day. He was going to have to go back. Shit! He was stupid enough not to have realised he could have felt the envelope for a card before some rushing home so he pulled his underpants and trousers back up, lifted his coat and hurried back out.

He'd walked up and down the street five times. He'd stopped to look into *Shrove Antiques* at least three times and the old lady who was the proprietor smiled a beamer at him with what appeared to be a terrific set of ivory worthy of Spider, hoping he'd go in and buy whatever it was that he had to keep returning to look at, but this obvious antiques buff was considering other items which resided in the other antique shops along Causwayside, she thought. He'd returned close to the window and she decided to grasp this particular nettle and secure a sale.

Kelly was looking up and down the road with his back to the window now but then heard the tinkle of the shop-bell behind him and spun around as he heard,

"Was it the chess-set?" said a very refined Edinburgh lady's voice.

She was in front of him flashing what had to be a new set of sparkling false teeth that nearly blinded him. Her grey hair was tidily arranged and she wore a dark blue dress and cardigan of cream with a string of pearls around her neck and she spoke with the accent of the Edinburgh petit-bourgeoisie, apparently polite but using the occasional syllable to send out barbs of condescension.

"Sorry…what?" he said, mildly surprised at her bold approach.

"I've noticed you keep coming beck to look and I'm presuming you're perheps a dealer as you keep coming beck to view the display we have arranged here in the window."

As she said window her top set dropped down and clacked against the bottom row of imposters.

"…..Yes…actually, yes!" he said seizing the cover. "Yes it is the …errr…" he looked back in the window, ".. chess set… and the ..the.. fireplace…things. Metal whatsits…"

She'd reattached her top gnashers and appeared slightly disappointed at Kelly's description of....

"The faresaide bressware? Well if you'd like to come in I could give you more information rether then heggle here like pair of gypsies selling clothes pegs."

Patronising smile.

"What do you think?"

It was the letter *W* that had her in a pickle. As she said *what* the top-set dropped again but she made a big show of opening the door to him and furtively sent a finger into her mouth which quickly pressed north.

Kelly had a look up and down the street before he decided to enter the shop thinking he could see the postman coming from either direction as the said items were in the window.

"I cen just lift the chess-set from the window for you..." *window* foxed her palate suction again. Clack. The door tinkled shut and she leaned into the display. Kelly scoured the street looking for the tell tale uniform of red and black. Then,

"No!" he snapped and she halted herself halfway up as the black bishop fell forward and took out three pawns in front of him but she balanced the rest of the board and managed to replace the pieces back to their squares.

"....I err...need the light on the pieces...to...to..assess the....*carving*... I want to study the carving...." Keeping his direction facing the street.

She replaced the chess-set

"Es you w....*choose.*" she said and rescued herself from the W "....but I have to polish the bressware, anyway so I'll lift that out ..."

Her salesmanship made much of the effort to lift it and threw a couple of glances to Kelly who was still scouring the street. She wanted him to touch the merchandise, feel the weight, get to know it, become attached. Tactility sells in the antiques trade she was always told and then made a little noise of *damsel requiring saving*. Kelly looked down at her travails and understood the protocol but didn't really want to engage. Nevertheless, he lifted the heavy portcullis-looking frontage of what was a weighty piece of brass.

"If you'd just pop it on the counter for me, please, thenk you Mr...?"

Spotaneously and without thought he said, "Kelly." And wished he hadn't as he carried it to the broad wooden counter and placed it down.

"It's nenteenth century, probably Grays of George Street, Mr Kelly, solid bress through and through.." she began, launching into her sales pitch, "...the accootremon's err also bress, if you'd care to lift them ecross..."

Kelly turned to look at the window and saw a flash of red and white uniform disappear past the window. His eyes widened and he went into action. He wanted to catch the post before he reached Joe's door or he'd have to use the key again and didn't want to go in if he didn't have to, now that he knew May might be there.

"Nooo!!" he shouted as he tore away from the counter pulling the firegrate behind him thudding loudly onto the floor and rushed out of the shop and caught up with the postman.

"Mate!!...." The postman turned. "Anything for Delaney? Number one five two? I'm in a rush."

"Sorry mate. Just put it through your door."

Kelly watched him go and marched up towards the vennel and

passed Mrs Shrove Antiques at the door watching him.

"Fortunately... thet didn't break, Mr Kelly....."

She didn't get much further as Kelly loudly said "Fuck!" as he passed and turned into the vennel.

"Well!" she exclaimed as her top set dropped.

Kelly was peering as quietly as he could through the letter box trying hard to look down and see if there were any envelopes worth taking the risk of entering the flat and being caught by May. He listened for sounds and none came. He took out the key and pressed it slowly into the lock and turned it. The latch clicked and he gently pushed the door forward. A white envelope was the only one on the floor so he quietly leaned forward and picked it up and pulled the door closed with the latch turned ready to slot home without noise and gently closed it again with a solitary click from the latch. He looked at the letter and felt the outline of a card and smiled broadly. He opened it and sure enough there it was gleaming before him with *Mr J Delaney* written across the bottom. At last he had the card and the number and access to ten thousand pounds.

From nowhere the door opened and he quickly stuffed the letter into his pocket. May was looking at him, the May that he knew, bewigged, headscarfed and beiged. They looked at each other in silence.

"Kells! Did you just knock? I heard somethin'."

He improvised quickly.

"I did, May."

"What is it? More paint? He'll notice if ye take anymore. Severe haircut?"

"Yeah...summer cut. Actually, no May. I came around just to drop this off." He pulled out the key. "I was going to put it through your letter box but I heard you coming. I forgot to leave it with you last time I was here. Thanks for not saying anything to him."

"Aye...whatever. How's your flat lookin'?"

"My flat? How's it looking?"

"Aye. Yer decoratin'?"

He completely forgot.

"Oh...right..yes it's....err lookin' .... magnolia!" He smiled with open arms.

May just looked back at him and caught sight of the white envelope sticking out of his coat pocket. Kelly saw her looking. He pushed it back in the pocket mildly panicked, which he couldn't hide.

"So.... how are you and Joe getting on....better? Did you talk?"

May didn't really want to talk to Kelly about her relationship but conceded that there was common ground and didn't want to tell him to mind his own business because as much as she wanted to he was involved and had appeared to care.

"Yeah... we spoke. Had a good chunner. About stuff. That mattered. To me. To him."

"Well that's great, May. Money is a bastard. Trust me, I know too. So...sorted?"

"Aye...I think so."

"So, you might still be heading to the south coast then?" Kelly ventured with a smile using this only to keep the conversation away from white envelopes.

Then May dropped a semblance of a smile to Kelly.

"Actually....aye. That might happen yet. He said he's got somethin' goin' on that could make us some money quite quickly and get us there after a'. So watch this space."

Kelly was intrigued. Mildly alarmed, too. For what reason he didn't know but he didn't want Joe doing something that would throw a spanner in his plans because he knew time was running out.

"That's great!" he feloniously enthused. "What is it? Pools win? Inheritance? *Business expansion?"*

A hint would be good to quell his head.

"Don't think so.." May said, "He'd've' told me if it was somethin' like that. *Surprise,* he said. Better if I don't know."

Come on May, ya big cross-dressing moose! Give me more than that. Just tell me he's not going to the bank for a loan, for fuck sake! He could hear his aggression in his own cerebral delivery. He had to push a little further.

"I've always thought Joe should go bigger, you know....."

May interjected with a grin. "He has his moments!"

Kelly really didn't want to picture Joe and May *backscuttling* and was far too early in the day and too much information for him but he had to keep fishing while she was smiling.

"Now now, May....don't be giving out all your secrets..." was all he could manage with a stick-on chuckle. "I meant a bigger *business*. He could do it. He has the work. And the contacts.... do you suspect he might be going *that way*.....May?"

"He went *that way* a long time ago, Kells! I've got the bruises to prove it!"

And another cheeky smile. Kelly realised May was quietly pleased at the liberation of having someone know about them and was enjoying something cathartic in the process but Kelly hadn't time for this *gay abandon.*

"May....you old tart!" he joined in, however, with the badinage of *the boys,* "No really, he should..."

"He has!" And another. Kelly laughed but really didn't want to.

"Well...whatever he does... at least he's doing something, May. And if you ever get to the south coast give me a call."

Are ye fuckin' kiddin' me Kells? We're goin' tae get away frae smelly, shiftless, scroungin' scruff like you! I'll no be handin' my phone number out so a set o' dirty tramps can follow us for a free holiday!"

Smelly? Fair point. *Shiftless?* Well he was doing something now, wasn't he? *Scrounging scruff* was admittedly in the ball park but *dirty tramp?* A tad excessive, perhaps but it was hard to deny the progression towards that impression the rest of the world probably held, so he just said,

"Need to go. Theatre course. I'm already late. See you in the pub."

Chapter 26

Harrowing Headlines

Tuesday, 25th June. 7:00am.

Joe Delaney pushed his way through the sea of men in the opposite direction to which they were all looking which was at the road into the pit head at Bilston Colliery. A few men nodded to him and he smiled back at them. They knew Joe only as the Union man that had brought out some of the trades to back them on the picket lines and organised the food donations in the South Side. Joe pressed though until he reached the gate into the pit head. These were the gates that would be opened only when the buses arrived carrying the non-striking miners into work and would then have to be barricaded by the line of uniformed police as they tried to shut the gates again. A sharp ring made Joe look up but he was now used to the occasional stone rattling against the galvanised steel posts of the fence and pressed on trying to look above the heads of the throng of men now blocking the expanse of road where the gates will open. A few random shouts were the barometer to the increasing tension and one miner barked,

"Criminals!" to the police line behind the gate so loudly that Joe had to shift his head away from the man's mouth.

The anger in his face was apparent to Joe but he also saw the disbelief at how he, and by proxy, his family and community were being treated by the state but more than anything was the sadness there in his being.

"Fuckin' Criminals!" he shouted again through the mesh into the line of uniforms only this time louder and to one policeman who had caught this miner's eye and returned a smile goading the man. Joe looked at the young policeman who seemed no more than twenty-five, and knew this lad knew nothing more of this conflict that what he was told by his superiors.

"Yeah, smile and enjoy your overtime while you can you little cunt but I never forget a face!" the miner snarled.

The Policeman now freed his smiling teeth into the summer morning air, leaned towards the mesh and replied,

"This face has just got his double-glazing done, shithead. Why would I not be smiling?"

And then straightened back into the line as a few chuckles from the uniforms adjacent riled the miner into a rage that saw him punch the mesh and shout,

"Got kids yet, have you! Got kids? No? Well I have and they're hungry! How'd you fancy watchin' that, eh? Watchin' your own bairns starvin'! You can do this but could you watch your kids starve, ya fuckin'...."

He punched the mesh at the level of the policeman's head repeatedly until Joe stopped him. He put his arms around the big miner and used some of his weight to lovingly get him away from the mesh.

"Mate....mate....*brother*....stop....stop. It's what they want. They've been told to...don't...don't ....save it for when we might need it most.... don't rise to it. There's other ways."

The miner's knuckles were bloodied and he started to feel the pain and stretched his hand as another stone flew across the fence. Joe went into his pocket and pulled out a pound note and covertly slipped it into the miner's jacket pocket. Realising what was occurring the miner wanted to be noble and refuse. Why should this good fortune drop upon him and his family and not his mates? He shook his head looking at Joe and then his unwarranted shame pulled his eyes towards the tarmac.

"Get them a loaf and some jam on the way home. Take it. You're not a criminal. What we're doing is not a crime. This is an injustice on a national scale. You're not to blame. What you're doing is something selfless and noble. Not many people in their lives get the opportunity to be afforded that dignity. Don't forget it...*brother*."

Joe patted him on the shoulder and turned to the mesh looking the young policeman in the eye and quietly spoke through the gate.

"One day, probably years from now, you will be older, hopefully wiser and you will understand your part in this national crime. And feel nothing but shame."

He held eye-contact for a moment then headed towards the gatehouse which was on his side of the fence, and craned his neck about as if looking for someone. A waving arm summoned him.

Next to the gatehouse were the two older men who were at Eric's funeral minus the suits and black armbands but the duffle coat was present, as was the little red star on the lapel of the other. Joe reached them and nodded.

"Not here." The duffle coat said and they turned and walked to a set of brick buildings that had alleyways between them and stood in the shadows. Red Star was about to speak as a miner ran past them through the gap in the buildings towards the gates. An angry roar filled every space between them as a bus pulled up and onto the road to the gates.

Red Star spoke. "This is everything." He said pressing a brown envelope into Joe's hands. "Put it away now."

Joe slid it into the inside pocket of his jacket.

"The name to ask for is there but the phone number is a general number. Use a street phone. Insist you speak only to the name written for you. They're one of ours. Do not reveal your name. If they say you have to wait, stay on the line for no more than forty seconds. Hang-up then wait two hours and call again. We can't do it. You can, brother. If their phone is tapped, and it will be, they'd know our voices. Former campaigns."

Duffle coat continued,

"When you've spoken to the name they will call you from call-box to call-box. Them there and you here. They will tell you where to be and at what time and the password your meet will use. Only then do you give them it." Red Star quietly said into his ear as the howls and shouting at the gates got louder. "Then you will be given something for your *trouble,* Brother."

"Got it." Joe said.

The two old men turned to leave.

"One question." Joe said stopping them, "Is it all true?"

Red Star shuffled back up to him. "Does it matter? This is war. We are burgling each other's houses, *they* say, eating dogs and turning on each other. Losing our humanity, *they* say. The working-class are no more than an expendable workforce to create a wealth that only *they* enjoy. Uneducated scum who deserve no more than the living they decide that we can have. A few embellishments of the truth, in the right hands, might redress the balance and *his* head might roll, until their propaganda team dreams up another untruth to discredit the honesty in us. Why should we care? Harrow has been bouncing little boys for as long as I can remember and mainly in the east. Our little dossier in the right hands will hit the mark, you'll see."

The two old men left. Joe turned just as the sound of bricks and stones rattling off the barricaded windows of the bus and the miners shouts of *Scabs* hung in the air.

Chapter 27

Stroking Jones

Tuesday, 26th June. 11:17am

McQuarrie sat when he heard the news. He didn't say anything but walked backwards to the soft seated area which faced the reception desk. The girl on the desk made a quick call to someone and within the minute there was a nurse there.

"Mr McQuarrie?"

She was young. *She was far too pretty to have to deal with this shit*, McQuarrie thought when he saw her. He looked up and threw a weary smile to her.

"Where is he?"

"He's been taken to The Western General. We thought you might get here before the ambulance, but...."

"I didn't....."

"No."

"So it's a stroke?" McQuarrie said as a resident walked past.

"We can go somewhere else more private, if you'd prefer, Mr McQuarrie?"

"No it's fine. Stroke?"

"Looks like it."

"What happened?"

"He collapsed. He was in the communal room and collapsed. He was singing some old songs just before that. He looked quite happy."

"Yeah...I bet you're sick of hearing those songs, as well as me, eh? How'd you know it's a stroke? Might be his heart?"

"He was awake, one side of his face fell and his mouth was drooping too. Speech was gone. That's a stroke."

McQuarrie stood. He drew his hands down his face, tiredly and said,

"So what happens now?"

"He didn't lose consciousness. That's good. He appeared to know that he wasn't well when we spoke to him. That's also promising. His right arm hung loose as well, though but he'll be in hospital for a while."

McQuarrie tried to digest the description *promising* from the nurse as he thought of his right-handed father with dementia, aged eighty-two requiring help as an able bodied resident despite the cerebral diminution and now having been hit with a stroke there seemed to him nothing *promising* about any of the situation. He couldn't help it but he also thought that it would better if he just let go....shuffled off...died, there was no sanitised way of putting it but something deep within him still saw the man he grew up with and dismissed the notion. The thought that while he was in hospital there might be some sort of hiatus in the fees from the care home but knew it might be the wrong time to broach it.

"For how long?" he said to her.

"Well it's hard to say. Depends on the intensity of the stroke. The next few days are critical. He'll be diagnosed and medicated. Definitely Aspirin.

"And he'll come back here?"

"That's up to you as next of kin. You don't have to come back here. You might want to have him cared for at a more specialist home...or *you* might want to care for him now?"

McQuarrie couldn't say the words that exploded into his head at that point. The word *specialist* probably indicated a lot more money for the care and there was no way on earth that he was going to look after his father at his place. Life over.

She continued,

".....but if he stabilises quite quickly and responds to the prognosis....he could come back here? We *could* hold his room....."

"But it will still have to be paid for?"

She made a conciliatory turn of the head and *sorry* facial expression. McQuarrie sighed.

"And if he needs more help...more people, time..and...?"

"I think you'd have to talk to the manager's about that, Mr McQuarrie but, off the record....yes, there's a high probability that...*further expense* is likely."

She looked at McQuarrie and knew the stories of bundled notes and sometimes a bag of coins that would arrive with him when the fees were due. He held a flat, tired gaze for a few moments and she understood the hard work and heartache in front of him, to say nothing of the graft to meet the fees. McQuarrie thanked her and asked which ward at The Western to which she replied reception would tell him, and he left.

DC Jones was in the car waiting for him. He got in and said nothing. Uncomfortable moments passed for Jones.

"You okay, sir." She tentatively asked.

"Dandy. Just dandy, Jones. I'm in the pink. Flying!"

She got the irony. "Sorry sir.....your dad..everything....you know."

"Up to The Western, please, Jones. Don't spare the horses and you can put the flashers on, if you'd care to. Try not to kill us both but if you do I'll mention you in despatches on the other side and write a decent recommendation to the big fella."

"Yes sir." She said but didn't want to joust with his dangerous sarcasm.

Jones hit the flasher switch and then the accelerator.

"Uniform have found the shoes, sir." She said rounding the cars at a red light.

"Have they? Where?"

"Between the hedge and the tennis courts fence at The Meadows."

"So what do we assume now, Jones? What do we consider?"

"That whoever took his shoes would travel home in roughly the direction of a straight line between Greyfriars and The tennis courts, sir."

"...and if they were removed, stolen, abandoned while he was travelling in that direction?"

"Which direction, sir?"

"To Greyfriars, Jones! *From* the tennis courts up *to* Greyfriars! Keep up and bloody learn will you!"

"Sorry sir."

"And stop bloody apologising and creeping around me like a coorin' wee mouse! It's unnerving Jones! It bloody unnerves me! You're with me to learn not to scurry about fetching the worst coffee Edinburgh has to offer! Shape up Jones!"

Just then a bus pulled out in front of them turning right as they passed a junction and Jones had to swerve and put the car back into the road but between a stationary car and a lorry but she did so with confident and remarkable skill but then pulled in quickly and aggressively switched off the ignition.

"What are you doing!!" he barked.

She'd had enough. Jones looked him squarely in the eye.

"I'm shoving your rank, your condescension, your petty observations about what I am doing or not doing right and your attitude that I am some wee tea girl and driver at your beck and call right up your substantial and unfair arse....*sir!* Ever since I started with you I've had to lie about where I've been, cover up visits to a shitload of bookies that all seem to know you better than I ever will, and I'm sorry about your dad, I really am, sir, but there's another diversion to our time that I have to forget and say nothing about when we get back to the nick. And d'you know what, sir, everyone knows your dad's not well. Everybody knows about your gambling debt and the trawl you do from one tick book to the next trying to make the care home fees and pay your mortgage! The whole nick knows but *nobody* says anything! There's mornings when the car stinks like a distillery but *I* say nothing. I have to, just to get through another day with you sitting there giving out your orders as if I'm some irritating wee annoyance you have to put up with. But me, *we,* the rest of the nick, cut you some slack because they know you struggle, because they actually *like you,* God knows why, but I'm guessing it's because they know you're good at your job and knew you when you were a better man than the misanthropic shit that you are now. Now get a grip of yourself...*sir* and stop treating the rest of the world with the contempt that you think we all merit and use whatever's left of *you* to shape up and stop feeling sorry for yourself and your life and *do something*! Fix it. Be the man you once were. Witty, I believe? Knowledgeable, too, someone who cared about lots of things and was known to be a very decent bloke and shit-hot at his job. Right now, I don't know that man and unless you find him again you'll be no use to the team, me, your dad, that lad found in Greyfriars. Or yourself...*sir."*

Jones turned back to face forward and started the engine but McQuarrie leaned over and turned it back off. He leaned back in his seat and looked forward into the street. Silence hung.

"I'm sorry." He paused. "You're right. Thank you....*Claire.*" He turned his head as if to look at her but never managed to make the turn enough to look her in the eye. "Now....The Western General Hospital, please, Claire and after that we can get on with the business of catching our villain that left us the Greyfriars body. Right?"

Claire smiled at him. "Right, Sir."

"Out of hours...it's *Jack.*"

Chapter 28

A Calculated Gesture

Tuesday, 26*th* June 2:20pm

The official observer of the British team for the 25th International Mathematical Olympiad, John Gunn, strode purposefully along a corridor in the Maths department of Edinburgh University, towards the office of Dr David Hunter, the official leader of the party that would represent Britain, early July in Prague. He had a few sheets of paper in his hand and used the other to knock and then open the door. Dr Hunter stood at a bookcase and had a large tome of leather-bound mathematical theory in his hand and a pipe supported in his teeth.

"Ah, John... just wrestling with Euclid. He really was an awkward but brilliant Greek twat, you know!" Hunter snorted.

Gunn sat down on a beaten up old couch. There was something petulant about him. There always was.

"He's not the only one, either, David! Have you seen the flipping accommodation arrangements? The Reds are at it again! I bet it's those flipping Bulgarians, *again!* I bet it's them."

Hunter plonked himself at his desk and spread the book pushing an ashtray to within centimetres of falling. Gunn leaned forward quickly and caught it and delivered it to an enclave of pinetop as yet unused by Hunter's ephemera. Hunter cast a look across to him.

"Something of a footnote in the two big European fist-fights were the Bulgars, John. No real involvement. Probably the Reds. Who have they annexed now? Aren't they too busy in Afghanistan to be bothered with unheard of arctic islands...... or wherever?"

"Flipping wouldn't surprise me, at all. Not at all. They never fight a fair fight."

"What about *the accommodation,* John?"

"Oh flip, yes! We're across the other side of the flipping city from the venue. Half of flipping Prague will be between us and it!" And he waved the documents and dropped them on Hunter's book.

Dr Hunter was tired of Gunn. He was appointed official observer of the team because everyone else in the department that had been asked had either family holidays to arrange or fictional conferences to attend and Hunter then had to defer to the irrefutable truth of numbers. Ironically. He was the only one left. Gunn was far too energetic and conscientious for Hunter. He railed against undergraduates that applied for extensions to assignments even when Dr Hunter explained that it was all wasted energy, that they were young, getting drunk and having lots of sex with each other, which was just as valid a pursuit, in his opinion, in the great tapestry of life, as was The Finial Inaccuracies of the Logarithmic Sequence of Numbers. He also found problems where none were apparent and the irony of *finding solutions* in Mathematics was not lost on Hunter. Hunter lifted the papers and really didn't want to read them.

"So the problem *is*....John?"

"Well it's flipping obvious, isn't it?"

"Is it? Just *tell me*, John."

"Two trams and a ten minute walk! Every other team without a tram ride and with just a five minute walk will be in prep and discussion while we will be making our way across flipping Prague in a pre-war street-trolley!"

"We could always leave a little bit *earlier* than the rest of the teams and rendezvous at the *same time* as them.....*John?* I wouldn't mind a view of the East from the perspective of the workers off to their factories and Bloc Offices for a couple of mornings. See the world from the bottom up, as it were, and a snatch at the city, too."

Gunn saw the big needle arrive gleaming and bright about to puncture his self-importance with a bang if he didn't have a comeback to this unpredicted logic.

"*True...* quite true... but flip me, it's the blatant temerity of it all, isn't it, David? We'll get less sleep. Be up with the flipping Czech larks, we will! Tantamount to flipping cheating, some would say!"

He was trying hard to appear offended to Hunter, thereby demonstrating his verve and commitment to the team and the excursion and about to launch into another validation of his loyalty when a knock at the door and the head of Josephine from the faculty office invaded Gunn's next tirade against the commies.

There's a journalist down at the office outlining his interest in the Maths Jolly to Prague, David. I can tell him you're busy, if you and John are doing something more....?"

Hunter seized the opportunity to relieve himself of Gunn's affected vitriol.

"No...no! Of course not. Send him up.....if that's okay with John. John?"

Gunn was delighted at being consulted and Josephine awaiting his assent. He milked a moment and then said,

"Yes...go on. Why not? Another thing to think about won't muddy the waters any flipping further, will it!" he said covertly delighted at the thought of more coverage of the event and him in the newspapers.

Before long there was a knock and Josephine opened the door.

"Dr Hunter, Mr Gunn, this is Mr Delaney" Josephine withdrew and closed the door softly leaving a very scrubbed up, smart and shinily besuited Kelly, with a pair of brown brogues he picked up in a charity shop. He presented himself as Joe but without the disguise.

Hunter stood up and shuffled around his table and held out his hand to Kelly then Gunn did the same.

"Delighted, Mr Delaney. I believe you are a journalist interested in our forthcoming jaunt across the iron curtain?" Hunter said. "This is John Gunn, the official observer for our team and I am the leader. Will you sit, Mr Delaney?"

They shook hands and Kelly sat at the desk across from Hunter who had retaken his position whilst Gunn sank into the couch significantly lowering himself to all in the company, which didn't please him at all, so he quickly sat up and onto the edge of the settee and looked alert, ready for the hack who'd come to see them.

"How can we help you, Mr Delaney?" Hunter said.

"I saw the article in the Evening News about the Maths Olympiad...." Kelly offered,

"Yes, sadly not a great deal of detail." Gunn chirped in.

"Well, I have to say that I was intrigued when I read it, with or without the detail. That there would be such an event behind The Iron Curtain in this climate of political tension with Reagan's Star Wars programme and the SALT treaty at the heart of much discussion.... well it fascinated me and got The Soviets attention, I would think."

He'd consulted the papers and mugged up on a few phrases.

"I'm a freelance journalist, I've delivered articles and news to all the big hitters, *The Observer, The Guardian, The Times* and I just think that this is, could be, social, cultural and political dynamite, depending on the outcome, of course, and not a great deal of people have heard about it. I hadn't, nor had any of my hack friends, so my question basically is this... would there be room on the trip for a journalist to chronicle and document this event? Possibly raise the profile of the university and your department, of course?"

Kelly used his hands a great deal looking very animated and apparently excited at the proposal he made, mainly because he was nervous. This was a performance he'd worked on and he knew would solve his immediate problem and get him out of Edinburgh and Scotland and who would ever think to ask the university if a journo had joined their entourage to Prague?

Hunter sat back in his seat.

"John?" he looked over at Gunn who, again, didn't expect this public show of trust and was slightly taken aback.

"Well... I must concede that the department would enjoy a little more of a higher profile. We do well enough but the Rector and Chair would flipping well applaud some positive publicity at such an international event. We might win too!"

Hunter took a deep breath.

"Yes there is that...*John*, but might but I suggest we exercise caution before we know enough to assent. I'm not sure it would be *dynamite*, as you say either, Mr Delaney. We numbers geeks are a common breed all over the globe and seize whichever opportunities there are to convince other fellow geeks from other countries of our geeky prowess, wherever it might be. In short, we like it and really don't care a great deal about the political capital to be made. We do it for us, not for the state."

Kelly nodded.

"That may be.... but I'm not sure the Polit-Buro would agree with your geeky hand of brotherhood extended across *The Curtain*, Dr Hunter? Their need to declare and validate their ideology is painted large, just now and they'll take whichever opportunity to say so. Won't they? Especially if the USA are entering a team. Are they?"

Hunter thought for a moment.

"Can I ask, Mr Delaney, if there is anything else in this for you other than selling copy? Which aspect of the competition do you envisage covering at length? You mentioned the political angle...and we all know that The Russians are in Afghanistan, currently uninvited, and if, for instance, you made journalistic capital from that... via this competition....well the university wouldn't appreciate being at the centre of a diplomatic shitstorm, assuming this was reported the wrong way? And besides, I expect Reuters cover this? A page-filler admittedly, but it will make print."

Hunter was playing hardball. Kelly had rehearsed.

"There is the cultural and social angle, Dr Hunter. Reuters will report the facts as they are widely given but how will this be reported in the East? Will they sell it as a great victory of a Marxist society over the decadent West if an Eastern Bloc country should win? What will they do to ensure they win, is a question I'd like to be answered? Will the people of Czechoslovakia give a monkeys about a Maths Olympiad when all they've been eating is cabbage for the last three months?"

He'd mugged up on a few of those phrases before coming and had a copy of *Das Capital* that he'd stolen from the local library. He was expecting a few tough questions and had to sound like he knew what he was talking about and was surprising himself at how much he didn't realise he knew and a twenty minute discussion ensued about East/West relations, The Cold War, militant activity in the Miners' strike with broad generalisations from Kelly that didn't press for detail too much and so made immediate application to the Maths Olympiad. They asked him where he *went*, to whit, he was lost before he realised they meant which university and he said Aberystwyth which brought a few raised eyebrows, tilts of the head and exchanged looks that smeared derision across the face of Wales but he knew there was little chance of either of them knowing the recent lecturing staff which he obviously couldn't corroborate.

Gunn, throughout all of this seemed quite taken and quietly keen for a journalist's inclusion which would allow his academic ego to fly and he wanted promotion because his wife wanted a bigger house but equally insistent on not appearing to give away his hand, which Kelly plainly saw, but he managed to hold back his enthusiasm except for the part where Kelly, again, mentioned the prospect of anyone cheating.

"They've already started their flipping shenanigans having us billeted one end of the town from the other, you know!"

Kelly seized the sword by the blade.

"That's before any of us have even got there." he said using the *we* to cement himself as much as he could into the party and minds of them both."...and of course I would never lose sight of the fact that this is a Maths challenge, the language of science that may well be the glue that brings like-minded people, however geeky, together, whichever ideology they've been told to uphold?"

"Ohh...well played, Mr Delaney!" Hunter smiled. "Curry favour to that which defines us all. However, assuming we agreed to your attendance there would be the re-submission to the organising country of an addendum to the party that would require practical measures to accommodate. Frankly, another headache, Mr Delaney. All the hotels, flights and visas are made via the faculty and university office and a list has been submitted, already. And then of course there would be your nominal title, required by the host country. What would that be? *Freelance Reporter* would not go down well with the Czech authorities, I would surmise."

Gunn saw his photograph on the front page of all the country's broadsheets fading before his very eyes.

"Perhaps....*independent observer?*" Gunn ventured. "Our party is small compared to the Hungarians. They have always had hangers-on, no offence, Mr Delaney, who are obviously there for the gastronomic rewards and The Farewell Ball. Surely it's not beyond the flipping wit of the faculty to add *a-n-other?*"

Kelly could have kissed him if he wasn't such an obvious knobhead and played his joker.

"Naturally, I anticipated that there would be a modicum of disorder thrown into the pot at my inclusion at this period so I have taken the liberty of offering to make a *contribution* to The University....*your department,* perhaps... that will *offset* the unavoidable cost and turmoil to flights and visas... and suchlike...."

Kelly produced the brown envelope delivered in *Revelations* from his inside pocket, but a thousand pounds lighter, and laid it on the pages of Hunter's large leather-bound tome straddling his desk.

"...in the hope it may shine favourably on my inclusion on an excursion that would see my standing amongst my peers....*elevated...* somewhat."

Silence roared loudly in the room. Gunn looked across to Hunter who was staring down at the heavy brown envelope. Kelly held his breath waiting for Hunter to do something. Then he stood. He stared down at what was obviously a sizeable wad. Then he looked at Kelly. Moments passed and he looked down again. The stillness deferred to his authority. Then he spoke.

"Would you excuse us for a few moments, please, Mr Delaney?" he said flatly and then closed the book over the envelope.

Kelly waited outside in the corridor. He heard muffled mutterings and sharp stabs of words and then silence followed by more of the same. There was the sound of a drawer sliding open and shutting, and then the door opened. Gunn held it and gestured he should re-enter. Kelly walked back into the office and the door closed quietly behind him. Hunter stood in front of him large and imposing, studying the contents of his pipe. Kelly feared the worst. Gunn leaned against the door.

"Mr Gunn and I have *discussed* your proposal of journalistic inclusion to our party and feel *comfortable* that your donation has not come from one of the leading houses of hackdom and their declared allegiances therefore acknowledge no favouritism to Murdoch, Beaverbrook, Maxwell et al; *and* believe that many international events as these, go largely *unreported* to any meaningful depth. *Therefore...* the requisite arrangements will be made for your visa, travel and accommodation as a member of the university party and as a *second observer* reporting to Mr Gunn, here. We will be leaving for London and then Prague on the morning of the 24th of June, a Thursday, methinks, however Josephine in the faculty office, whom we will advise as to your imminent inclusion, will furnish you with specific dates, times and requirements, so you should liaise with her before you leave here and all should be well. What you will have to do tomorrow is take your passport to the Czechoslovakian Consulate, which is along Atholl Place at the west end, with an official letter of inclusion into the party stamped and ratified from The British Council, copies of which we have here ...*somewhere...?*"

Hunter pulled open a drawer.

"John?"

He looked over to Gunn who already had a cardboard folder at hand and was flicking through various papers. Gunn handed Kelly a letter-headed document from the university to The British Council with areas with which to fill in details. Hunter asked him to do it there and then and complete the passport number later.

"They will issue your visa. As it is under the auspices of The British Council jollies tend to be processed post-haste as is passport control at the airports. Minimal waiting and all that, priority boarding. Celebrity status of sorts, eh John?"

Gunn smiled back. "Flipping right!"

"This will be sent back to you within twenty-four hours. Welcome aboard, Mr Delaney." Hunter said.

Kelly beamed.

"That's great news, gentlemen. Thank you very much. Just one other thing, Professor Hunter, I'm a little dubious about the postal service these days. Would it be possible for me to nominate a trusted person to pick it up? I'll be down in Yorkshire covering a *minor event* that's making the front pages the next couple of days and I really don't want to miss an opportunity to travel behind The Iron Curtain. I don't want to leave this to the vagaries of chance or the whim of the post office."

"With identification, naturally, I see no issue with that. Write down your trusted colleague here for me, please, Mr Delaney.

Kelly took the pen and paper, made a little show about deciding on a trusted colleague and scribbled the name.

"I will make sure that this courier.... *Leonard Kelly*...is expected by the consulate. Make sure he takes ID with him, won't you or they might not release."

"I will. Thanks again, gentlemen and I will see you at the airport on the morning of the twenty-fourth."

Dr Hunter opened the office door as Kelly shook hands with a delighted Gunn who said,

"Make sure you paint us brightly and in a flipping good light, won't you?"

"Of course! Right then, faculty office!" Kelly enthused and raised an arm in goodbye as he walked down the corridor.

"Oh, Mr Delaney?" Hunter said looking up and down the corridor. Kelly turned. "You don't have any criminal convictions, do you? Banks you might have robbed... murders we don't know about, have you?" he chuckled, however patently interested in the reply.

Kelly frowned and smiled back as if to say *tssscchh, perish the thought!* And then said, "Nooo..." as if pouring derision on the ridiculousness of the thought but then got cocky,

"I've just buried my dog, though? Does that count?"

"What would that be?" Hunter said searching for the descriptor, "Caninicide?"

"Possibly? Don't worry, I'm not a dogicidal maniac, however he has just died but not by my hand. Mistress fate decided his end was overdue and greater powers than ours exerted their supremacy over my mortal mutt."

Hunter chuckled again and said in mock condoling tones, "I'm sorry for your loss, if there's anything I can do....?"

"No..." Kelly returned, pretending to shed a single tear, "No flowers and all donations to the kennels in Seafield."

"God speed, Mr Delaney." Hunter said and went back into his office.

Josephine was expecting Kelly and gave him the itinerary.

This was happening. His arse was close to melting but his was definitely happening.

Out on the street he was still vibrating with the nerves he'd generated in his performance in the meeting. He was having a natural high. No alcohol, just a polished and confident presentation worthy of any show at The Lyceum but was now racking his brains trying to remember whether his passport was at his flat or at his mother's house as he walked back across St. Patrick's Square and towards home. That aside, he was relieved and very self-congratulatory at his ability again to morph, act and lie again and strode past a cafe which emanated a delightful aroma of fresh coffee, which stopped him. He looked in the window. There were plenty of seats. It had been ... *forever*...since he had last taken himself into a coffee house, forever since he had drank a cup of coffee and as he was now so smart, so journalistic, so connected with academia, so urbane and about to be a European traveller he began to believe his own press and decided that coffee would be the correct beverage for one of such a cosmopolitan milieu and stepped in. He walked up to the counter which was arranged with pastries and muffins of various flavours and colours and wondered how they managed passing hot coffee across this mountainous range of cakeware?

"Jist take a seat, son and I'll be richt across tae ye, the noo." Said a loud female voice said with the shyness of a horse pissing in the street.

A very thin woman with greying hair and sporting a newly formed fug around her head from a lit cigarette eased into the scene from a beaded curtain. He took a seat. He sat facing the large window and stared out into the street thinking about what to do next. Passport? Phone his mother? She'd know if it was in the house and if it wasn't he must have it. But then she'd want to know where he was going? He was approaching the endgame and had to play this right.

"What cin I git, ye son?" Stick Woman had arrived wound in an apron his mother would call a *pinnie*. It was floral and stained with days old slops of coffee and tea. The bones of her hips and shoulders were marked out against this covering of flowers.

"Coffee...black." He'd never drank coffee without milk before. He wasn't aware he was going to do that, order black coffee. But he did, which drew a frown from Sticky when she realised he wasn't a tourist and certainly not one of the local shopkeepers from warmer climes.

"Ye sure son? Colombian. 'S gey strong."

He was affronted that she hadn't acknowledged his urbane appearance and obvious daily convivial Colombian ritual and just looked up at her and flatly said,

"Yes!"

She shrugged and drew her parochial carcass back into the gleaming world of hissing chrome and steam and began to expertly attach and turn then pull levers, of which, he had little idea of how they worked. He heard his fingers tap the table and felt that he should be reading something. Something worthy of being in a cafe, drinking black coffee and wearing a suit having just come out of a meeting with two academics. There was an abandoned copy of *The Scotsman* on another table so he took himself across there and withdrew back to his table with the worthy broadsheet and checked to see if Stick Woman had seen him do it. She hadn't, so when she brought the coffee she would think this is the regular custom he had. Coffee and a broadsheet.

He turned to the headlines but didn't take it in as his eyes fell on a picture he first thought was a scene from a Napoleonic war. A mounted cavalryman in helmet and stretching out his sword to slash at a man turned towards him with every crease in his fifty-something face declaring his fear. This man was in a hedgerow behind a low brick wall and had an arm raised in a vain attempt to protect himself. There was another horse and rider following up to make certain the demise of their quarry if the first attack failed. Then shock dropped into his stomach as he made sense of the image before him. He saw the word *Police* written across the helmet and the Perspex visor and then stayed with the image of the man and felt.... *something*. This man had nowhere to go, literally and most probably metaphorically. There was a wall in front of him and a hedge at his back. Kelly imagined the following seconds after the camera had clicked. What happened to this older man he could clearly imagine, and then a desire to stop the clock, go back just one day and help him out of that horrific scene, welled up in him. And then anger. He turned the page and a collage of black and white pictures fell before him as he realised this was reports of the miners' strike. There were more images than print. One picture showed a collapsed town-sign of broken concrete pillars with protruding steel rods and the now upside down sign which read, *Orgreave*.

"There ye go, son."

His coffee arrived. Black, rich and steaming with a delicious smell. She leaned over him.

"Bloody sin, so it is. Those lads jist want to work and that bitch in number ten'll no let them!"

Kelly looked up at her. He understood the crystallisation of the conflict that had come from someone he thought uneducated and quite simplistic in her assessment but couldn't disagree.
He softly said,

"Yeah..." which was nothing against the weight of her stark statement and wished he had more to say, but he couldn't find the words to honestly give an opinion of something that was occurring *now*, current and real. He didn't know how to. Something descended over him as he peered at the picture of what was obviously a claustrophobic seething sea of humanity swaying and shifting despite the stillness of the photo and the difference made apparent by the line of dark helmets, shields and uniforms against the t-shirted and barehanded defiance of the miners. Suddenly he felt ashamed. He didn't know why. He wanted to feel something like kinship with these men but he understood his privation compared very little in any actual, philosophical or ideological sense. He heaped three spoonfuls of sugar into the black brew and stirred. He lifted the coffee to his mouth and sipped. He expected a sourness and distaste that demanded milk but as the brew slipped over his tongue a sweet, hot, newness broke into his mouth and into his head. Then he sipped some more.

"Black coffee, a broadsheet, suit and a haircut, Kells? My we are getting uppity."

He looked up. McQuarrie stood before him.

"What's happening in the world, Kells, anything I should know about?"

Kelly looked shocked to see him...which wasn't good. McQuarrie noted this.

"Errr...no I don't think so..."

McQuarrie called across the shop, "Coffee, please, Joyce"

"Righto Jack. Ye takin' it wi' ye?" she rasped back.

He addressed Kelly, "I usually do but now that I have some company....? Not this time, Joyce. I'll sit in with *my friend,* here." He said smiling and lifting his voice up and over the counter.

Kelly groaned inside and managed the butterflies below. He had to appear relaxed and uncaring of his presence. McQuarrie slid onto the seat facing him blocking his view out into the street.

McQuarrie sighed. "Big mess all this, eh?"

Kelly paused and echoed his sigh.

"Yeah I guess so? I don't know anything about it though." He said quickly.

"Really? I think you know more than you think you do." McQuarrie said to him and shrugged.

"I don't. I only know what people are talking about in the pub, n'that. I only knew him from school." Kelly opened a hand upwards on the table as he said this.

"What? Oh I see, Kells. You're talking about...the chap...*The Greyfriars Body* as the papers are calling it. Nice to know you're thinking about him, though. No, no...I was talking about the strike.

The miners' strike, Kells! The miners' strike! I just noticed what it was you were reading, there. Terrible. And sad. What have we become?" McQuarrie laughed a laugh that wasn't a laugh. More of a forced throatal ejaculation of air.

Kelly looked across at him. "Is that rhetorical?"

"Is what rhetorical?"

"The question."

"What question?"

Kelly sensed the game McQuarrie was playing and doubted that he had happened along coincidentally.

"The, *What have we become?*, question."

"Oh, I see. Yes... I suppose so. It was just a thought...you know? You're doing a lot of thinking with that big beast of a paper, though, Kells? What are you thinking? Looking at that, I mean. Messy."

"Just trying to take it all in, that's all." Kelly remained as neutral as he could. He really didn't want to encourage him to further sarcasm. McQuarrie chuckled and said,

"Clever that though, isn't it?"

"What is?"

"Greyfriars Body. *Bobby*. Greyfriars *Bobby*. Get it. Body...*Bobby?* They always do something like that, the papers. Do you get it Kells?"

There was patently no need to ask that but McQuarrie used it as another chance to say his name and annoy him more. Wind him up. He knew Kelly would know the pun on the faithful mutt.

"Yes I get it. Not really that clever though is it?"

"Actually no... What about yours?"

Kelly was lost. " Mine? My what?"

"Faithful mutt."

His heart missed a beat but he rose to the challenge, "Oh yes. What about him?"

"Well I don't think you put him in Greyfriars with Bobby, Kells?"

"No, I phoned up the Seafield dogs place and they gave me a number and a van came and took Lenni...away...to be hygienically *disposed of.*"

"Oh that's good....that's good. What were they called?"

"I can't remember."

"No?"

"No. The word *pets* was there somewhere, but I can't remember the exact name."

"Ah well...you did the right thing though, didn't you. Eric would be pleased."

Joyce arrived with his coffee. "Thank you, my radiant Cherry Blossom."

Joyce was unmoved by his sweet talk.

"Aye....that'll be runnin' in the two-thirty somewhere this efternoon, Jack! It's no me yer talkin' aboot!"

She left chuckling.

"Sheesh! Everybody knows me!" he smiled and took a sip of his coffee. "Mmm...lovely. How's yours, Kells?"

"Very nice."

"You take it black?"

"Yes."

"Have you always taken it black?"

"No. Thought I'd give it a try."

"Quite right, Kells. Ye've got to open yourself up to new experiences in this world, right? Try different things. Different food. Different drinks. Different people. Yes?"

"Sure, why not?"

"Well, actually not everybody is as progressive as you and me in this world, Kells. Most people don't like change. Most people are fearful of the unknown...and it's a reasonable thought. I mean why would anyone want to put themselves through a journey into the unknown when what they have is safe and secure? Comfortable. Why change? Why give yourself the hassle?"

Kelly tilted his head as if to question McQuarrie. "Rhetorical?"

"Oh yes. Absolutely. Just shooting the breeze." He paused and took another sip of coffee. "I have to say though, Kells, this miners' strike looks bad now, though. Looks like the face of the British worker might not be so black with coal dust of home in the very near future. I mean metaphorically..... you know the coal industry serving all those other... they don't *actually* have coal dust on..."

"I know what a metaphor is. Like I said, I don't know much about it. If I read about it I might have a different opinion from you? Maybe they're being unrealistic? I don't know."

McQuarrie flatly said, "My father was a miner. Bilston. Forty-six years. Fucked now though. Bent back and arthritis everywhere. Feet, shoulders, hands. Painkillers for the last ten years. Now his stomach is fucked with them. It's okay now, though..."

Kelly genuinely was surprised at this upbeat tone. Then McQuarrie said,

"...he's got Alzheimers so he doesn't know he's fucked!"

A pause occurred while McQuarrie's face lit up at his dark humour and began to laugh loudly. Kelly actually did find him funny, black and *gallows* though it was, he laughed with him though he didn't want to. McQuarrie's laughter subsided nearly as quickly as it had begun.

"Anyway....you get the picture, Kells? Of course you do. Sorry Kells. I've heard you talk in the pub. Well-read aren't you? Clever."

Kelly caught his eye and held it for a second just as he raised his cup to his mouth and then appeared to think before completing the sip and lowering it on to the saucer.

"Actually, no Mr McQuarrie. I'm not so clever. I haven't finished a book...ever. I just enjoy knowing the characters and situations and what their next move in the plot might be. I just can't seem to finish any of them. I just use that to look clever in The Duke but I've decided that from now on, I'm going to finish things, tasks, books *projects*..... see them through to completion. Know what I mean?"

Kelly almost had an out of body experience with this honest revelation.

"Really?"

He knew McQuarrie wasn't surprised.

"Yes. *Really.* But you knew that. You told me what you thought of me at Eric's funeral."

"Yes, I did, didn't I? Emotional moments often bring out the truth or what we really believe to be the truth. I've seen it before a few times over my years on the job. People often realise that there is an inevitability about truth that will emerge at some point when all the indicators point to that unavoidable beacon in the distance and then they let go, open up and free themselves, sometimes uncaring of the upshot. Seen the biggest of men liberate themselves at the cost of their liberty but they knew, at that moment, they were genuinely themselves. Finally honest even though they were guilty of a crime. Do *you* know what I mean, Kells?"

"Very much so, Mr McQuarrie. I'm being honest with you now. I've hardly finished a book in my life. I just let people think I have and that I am well-read and enjoy the glow that comes with it."

They shared a moment of eye-contact and silence that spoke of much more. McQuarrie broke first but back to the former state.

"Ah, well... maybe you'll finish one soon. Change. Enjoy seeing it through to the end. Finding out who the winners are. Actually, I've seen a wee change in you recently, Kells. Suit and tie. Clean shaven. Short haircut. Less of you in The Duke. Black coffee. Reading the broadsheets. What's going on?"

And the fishing begins.

"Been papped onto this course. Theatre Skills. Complained about my boots and aftershave. Can't do the nights in The Duke I used to."

"Not there today though?"

He thought quickly.

"No. Interview. Hence the suit.."

"Oh very good! Good for you, Kells! Where?"

"Seafield Dogs Home. I really enjoyed the time I had with Lenni so I asked them if I could volunteer. Had to have an interview first, though. Seems you just have to be keen and good with the dogs. Not rocket science or much learning at all required."

"That's terrific. Speaking of rocket scientists, I saw some of your new friends from the university, recently actually. You know the very lovely Luccia, Jerry.... you know? Them. The ones I was unfortunately a little offhand with. And Megan."

Kelly expected the bait. "They're Megan's friends. Not mine."

"Of course they are, but what with this business of your old schoolfriend..."

"Again....He wasn't *my* friend."

".....acquaintance, I'm obliged to follow every line of enquiry that might throw some light onto the situation. Family are devastated. Anyway, I spoke to your ..*Megan's* friends and they told me you were at the party?"

Kelly was about to ask.....

"No not rhetorical." McQuarrie said, sharply.

"Yeah. I went with Megan."

"Good time?"

"Okay. Not really my kind of people."

"Is that why you said a few things to some of them?"

"What do you mean?" Kelly had to try to ascertain what he knew.

"You weren't very nice to a few of them, apparently. Started a class-war, I heard. Told someone your dad sexually assaulted you and then you insulted a fat girl?"

"I was drunk...funnily enough. They were middle-class posh kids that had a rake of top labels knocking around the flat. *Glenlivet* being one, I remember. I *capitalised* on the situation. Excuse the irony and the pun!"

"Call of duty? I didn't realise you were a class-warrior, Kells?"

"Neither did I."

"And so you put them straight?"

"Yes. I put them straight!"

"Then they put you out?"

"Yes."

"Maybe you're a shiftless no-user with a conscience?"

"Maybe I am."

"With Megan?"

"No. It was her suggested I leave, actually."

"Then where did you go?"

"Home."

"Time?"

"Don't know."

"Still drunk?"

"Very."

"See anything?"

"Like....?"

"Oh you know.... anyone else. Noises? Shouting?"

"You asked me this in The Duke."

"True, but you didn't tell me you were on The Meadows at the same time our man met his end."

"He was killed in Greyfriars wasn't he?"

"I don't know but he had to get there from somewhere. Bennets Bar by The King's."

"And?"

"And that's a line across Bruntsfield Links across part of The Meadows and up Middle Meadow Walk. Forest Road. Greyfriars."

"I didn't see him."

"Megan's friends were a little nervous about something?"

"Like ...?"

"That's twice you've said that and it's beginning to piss me off a bit....*Kells.*"

"Well if I don't know anything, I don't know anything!"

"They know something that they're not telling me. I know they do, and I think you know what that thing is. That thing might well throw some light onto the enquiry. Am I right?"

"Why would I know something that they know? I went to their

fucking party got drunk and insulted a few rugby knobs and a fat girl. Then they threw me out and I went home. Pissed!"

"Did some of these rugby chaps go for an impromptu game onto the grass, into the park? I mean ...it's just across the road? You know the thing. Drunken high jinks.

"I left. Drunk. I went home. I've told you!"

"Did they have a rugby ball with them at the party?"

"I didn't see one."

"But they might have had one with them? In a bedroom? The boot of a car? I mean they're that type aren't they? *Japes* are what they like to call their tom-foolery, don't they? An impromptu game? Perhaps saw other people, *our man*, crossing The Meadows and made him join in? He didn't want to join in. Also pissed. Which he was. Words exchanged. Drunken bravado. Our man boots their ball away and tells them to fuck off and our front row of the first eleven dish out a few over-exuberant slaps and our man has a go back, to whit, they are astounded that a member of the serving class would have the temerity to dare to strike back at those who dine in the big house and they consider it their duty to teach the prole a lesson he will take to his grave. Literally."

"Possibly.....I don't know!"

"But you were there at a location on the route that our man might possibly have taken. You could have heard or seen something?

"Maybe."

"*Maybe*...or yes?"

Kelly saw the possibility of gaining valuable time while McQuarrie focused his efforts on the muddy thigh gropers but didn't really want to get into any discussion with McQuarrie that put him at his disposal.

"Maybe....I told you I was drunk. Maybe he didn't cross The Meadows?"

"Grass, dust, mud, tree-bark under his nails and seeds on his socks. He lost his shoes there."

Kelly wanted to close this and leave.

"Mr McQuarrie...I was drunk but I would have remembered a staggering shoeless man!"

McQuarrie's body language released the rigidity from his core and let his shoulders relax and studied Kelly and then spoke quite matter-of-factly,

"Correct, Kells. You would've.... and maybe you did but you won't tell me. They're Megan's friends and you *like* Megan...and I know you know more than you're giving me. Protecting her while she protects her friends, who are preparing to leave the country, as we speak. Coincidental? Maybe desperate? If it so happens that you withheld information that would have led to the conclusion of this sorry business earlier... well.... I won't be able to help you."

Kelly stood and made an effort not to rush. He lifted his cup and drained the coffee, pushed the chair away from the table to allow him to go. McQuarrie spoke.

"Oh...I nearly forgot, Kells. When I was up at their flat They had a piece of paper with a shield drawn in black-marker pinned to a door, one of the reception rooms, I believe, and nailed to that was a pair of white training shoes. I know! It's becoming a bit of a theme, eh? Written underneath in Latin was the phrase *Quoniam Ultio.*"

McQuarrie made him ask.

"What does that mean?"

"For Revenge."

"Really?"

"Vengeance? Shoes? McQuarrie said wearing a mock frown.

Kelly held together an internal flush of adrenalin. He had to enquire to throw him off the scent.

"Are they........?" he asked, knowing the answer.

"No, not our man's. He's an eight. We've got his. Hush puppies. Very him, apparently."

"Well.... there you go..." Kelly struggled.

"There you go?.....What's that, Kells? There you go?"

"Coincidence...japes...jokery...having a laugh....*there you go...*"

"Most people only say *there you go* when they've ran out of conversation....*or answers.*"

He had to brass it out so looked McQuarrie straight in the eye and said,

"Really...well *there you go.* And here I go. See you in the pub.....or whenever." And he headed for the door.

McQuarrie shouted after him. "Oh...Kells!!"

Kelly turned and just looked at him.

"What size are *your* feet?"

"Nine. Why?"

He knew why.

***

He slammed the door and caught his breath leaning against the front door. He turned his head to the bathroom door and his face squirmed into a contorted vision of concern as he caught a semblance of the smell of decay. He had to do something about...*her*, and soon. He had five days to kill before leaving for Prague. His next move had to be *his* passport. His mother. He nearly made it into his living room before there was a knock on the door. He froze. He listened hoping to hear footsteps leaving. The door knocked again. He thought it might be TPT but he really didn't want anyone gazing into his mess before he could leave with the money. He turned and looked at the door breathing heavily. Then the letterbox opened and a pair of eyes appeared. The voice then followed.

"There you are, Kells!"

The voice of McQuarrie reverberated its felonious bonhomie.

"My you got back home quickly. Did you run?"

"Yes. I needed a shit."

"Is that what that smell is? It's not a shit you need, it's a drag through with a Christmas tree! Jeez that's rich Kells."

"The drains back-up as well in this block."

"You forgot your paper! I've got it here. I was passing in the car anyway and couldn't not do the decent thing."

The letterbox shut before Kelly could say anything. Tentatively, he opened the door but kept it close to his shoulder only putting his head out.

"It's not my paper. It's the cafe's." Kelly flatly said knowing this was another angle McQuarrie had with which to press him.

"Is it? Joyce doesn't usually have such weighty material lying around. Are you sure?"

"That's where I got it. I don't want it. You can have it."

McQuarrie effected a chuckle. "Well someone must have left it there. Actually I noticed that the crossword was half done. Tsccch...I should've guessed. Well....I'm here now, why don't you put it in your bin for me?" he said handing it to Kelly who paused before reaching out to take it. Kelly grasped it and pulled as McQuarrie held tightly to the other end.

"I'm parched Kells, any chance of a wee glass of water while I'm here? It's a warm day, again."

Kelly met his eye knowing he wanted to come into his flat and knew that if he did he would manufacture another reason to hang around snooping and Kelly knew the inevitable questions of broken furniture and piss stains on the floor would occur. Added to that he had a dead body in his bath.

"Wait here." He said. "I'll bring it to you." And went to close the door.

"Well that's not very sociable, Kells." said McQuarrie, "I won't spit on the floor."

Kelly stopped and held the door ajar, again.

"Place is a shitstate. "Kelly said.

"I'll be gettin' a complex. Don't you *want* me to come in, Kells?"

"Like I said, it's a shitstate. I'm in the middle of changing furniture and decorating....so..."

"So no?"

Yeah...no."

"Well....I'm hurt, Kells so I'll forego the glass of water and go and see if I can figure out how our man met his end, eh? Really is a bit of a conundrum. Just like this crossword."

"Yeah...good idea." Kells said, implicitly telling him to fuck off.

"I'll take off then unless you've remembered something you forgot to mention in the cafe?"

Kelly looked him in the eye and said "No. Don't think so."

"Ah well... that's a shame. Don't forget your paper, Kells." He said pushing it into the gap below Kelly's head. McQuarrie turned and walked to the top of the stairs and smiled back at Kelly throwing a glance into the gap between door and jamb and into the smallest area he could see of Kelly's flat secure in the knowledge that Kelly was uncomfortable about...*something*... and was sure he knew more than he was letting on"

Kelly watched him descend the first steps and went to close his door as McQuarrie called up to him.

"It'll be alright if I call back when you've tidied up a bit, okay?"

Kelly didn't know he was going to say,

"I'm going to stay with my mum, tonight... *for a while.* She's not well."

"I'm sorry to hear that." McQuarrie said.

"Yeah...she's ill."

"Oh yeah, that as well. Just sorry you have to leave us *for a while.* Anyway, the break might jog your memory? *You know*....drunken flashbacks?"

"No...doubt it."

"I thought you were decorating?"

"I am! Her being unwell won't wait for that, though, will it?"

"Livingston. Right?"

"Yeah. How would you know that?" Kelly frowned.

"Oh you know...you hear things in the pub. Don't be gone too long now, Kells, I've started to quite enjoy our little chats. We'll speak again, soon, eh? Give her my regards from a stranger."

"Yeah." Non-committal.

Kelly closed his door to the rush of blood coursing quickly around his head and the thumping in his chest.

McQuarrie got into his car and looked across at Jones.

"Any joy, Sir.....*Jack?*"

"Nothing solid, Claire, however confirmation that he knows more."

"How'd you know that?"

"Just the human stuff. Body language. Tone of voice. Evasive. Where his eyes go when you mention particular parts of the investigation. Really didn't want me to go in."

"What do you think he knows?"

"Those students. They're getting off to Daddy's villa in Tuscany soon...quite conveniently. That's what he knows more about."

"Those shoes might be his, Jack? The ones on the students wall."

"Yes, maybe......*I think*. I'm not sure. What do you think, Claire?"

"I think we could just go and get them and make Cinderella try them on!"

"What do you think would happen, then?"

"Then we'd know if they fit? If they're his or not. "

"They might fit. But he could say they weren't his....even if they were. He knows something. He's connected. He's protecting someone. Right now he's where we can get him and turn up the heat if we need to. If we drop him into the fairy tale he might just do a bunk and Prince Charming might still be single and utterly free as a bird...whoever that is? Erm...Claire...?"

"Yes?"

"Erm...I'm *sorry*...I asked you to wait in the car when I spoke to him in the cafe....for all the reasons I have just said... I didn't want to scare him off...you know.... sorry?"

"It's okay, Jack. I get it. It's fine. The paper thing was a good idea."

"....and I meant to bring *you* a coffee... but I wanted to beat him home in the car...you know...?"

"Like I said. It's fine."

"Yeah....thanks."

"Actually, Sir....Jack. You seem so sure he's hiding something, so why don't we just get a search warrant and go in there? Something might turn up."

"What might he be hiding do you think, Claire?"

"I don't know. Physical evidence?"

"Possibly. And if not?"

"Then he knows something?"

"Which is what we both surmised, anyway, before wrecking the China Shop and scaring our other customers away. Slow, constant pressure, Claire. Let him know we're there. That's enough...for now. Actually, he's going to see his mum today, stay tonight, so he says. Not well, apparently. So if we jog along and she's in the pink, or he's not there, he has some explaining to do. Maybe he didn't kill our boy but he knows who did."

"Why would he protect strangers, if it was the students, I mean? He doesn't know them. Why should he care?"

"Protection by proxy."

"Megan? The girl?"

"He loves her and she adores them. Possibly."

"She's gone to..."

"....London. I know."

"TEFL job. Convenient?"

"Seems so but she *was* doing something at the uni to get a teaching job. Not the type to fly. Nice girl. Not the sharpest tool in the box. Like lots of teachers, know more about their subject than the world they're in. We can locate her if we need to."

"Okay Jack. How's your dad?"

"Stable. Apparently. Bit of occupational therapy then going back to Dalkeith if he stays like that. Which is *wonderful!*"

The ironic reference to the fees wasn't lost on her.

Meanwhile, Kelly strode through the mess of his flat in a panic knowing he had reached the point where he had to go and get the money from the bank and make preparations to leave and for the first time he properly confronted the idea that he was about to leave for good. He knew he couldn't do anything with the body in the bath, which had definitely begun to disperse its pungent fumes of decay, and now he had to pour more of her compost over her but it was already at a level that reached the top rim of the bath. First things first he had to go and get his passport.

He put the bank card in his pocket with the PIN code and left to go to Livingston.

Chapter 29

Ticket in a Tin

Wednesday 27th June 1:15pm

Kelly knocked at the door. No answer. He looked in the kitchen window. Nothing. A door opened from across the road. Alice, the neighbour shouted across to him

"Yer Maw's away tae the hospital, Leonard, son. Took her this mornin'. She's gone tae Bangour General. Ah've a key if ye need tae git in. 'Spec ye want tae make a call?"

Kelly felt a rush when he heard this.

"Aye...aye, thanks Alice."

"Hing oan the noo, son. Ah'll jist be across."

She went in and a few moments later came across the road. She was a trusted neighbour and friend of his mother's. A few years older than her and one of that generation that still wore a pinnie.

"There ye go son. Did someb'dy call ye?" handing him the key.

"Actually..no Alice. Nobody called me....I just felt like I should come....you know?"

"Well ye did right, Leonard. Git in there an' gie them a call. Find oot whit's happenin'. I widnae mind callin' masel, but ah'm no family, an' I didnae want to be botherin' the nurses an'doactors......"

Kelly spoke across her abruptly, "What happened, Alice?"

"Weel she come across here fur oor wee cuppa in the mornin' and she said she didna sleep weel, wiz strugglin' wi' her breathin', know? Then she wiz hauf ways through a buttered digestive an' sippin' her tea when she went a rare colour o' blue, scared the life oot o' me so I goat richt oan the blower an' an ambulance wiz here in jig time, mind they;'ve no goat faur tae go fae Bangour, have they? I mean hospital's jist a mile or twa wi' nae traffic..."

"Thanks Alice. I'll call them now. Do you have the number?"

She went back into her house and left Kelly standing in the street numb and not knowing what to feel but the truth was, he was shocked. His mother was a distant but perennial and comforting figure and the thought of her not being there was too much for him to think about.

"Here it is Leonard. Mind gi'e me a wee update before ye rush doon there, noo. Away in son."

Kelly assented and went into his mother's house. It was a strange feeling without his mother there. He'd spent some formative years here but never without the presence of her and now he felt like an intruder. Excluded and unwelcome. He took the number to the phone and dialled. He got a switchboard that put him through to the ward his mother was in and told she was breathing bottled oxygen through a mask, was to be given a sedative to help her sleep with tests occurring in the morning which would be the best time to see her. He didn't argue. He hadn't the focus to gainsay them and so he passively said *yes* a couple of times and repeated the time to come, *eleven o'clock, eleven o'clock...yes...yes...* As they were making their goodbyes Kelly shouted into the phone,

"Tell her, tell that I called! I'll see her tomorrow! Tell her that. I'll see her tomorrow. Eleven o'clock!"

The call ended. Silence enveloped him at the dreary foot of the stairs. Greyness, heavy and sad, sat on the first step with him. He listened to his own breathing for a time, thought of his mother again, then stood up. He looked upstairs, knowing that was where his passport would be. He went into his old room which had since been badly decorated with a gaudy green and orange wallpaper and had nothing but a table and sewing machine in it now. Not even a bed if he wanted to stay the night, which he was going to now, but he saw and felt the reduction in care and desire for the baubles in anyone's existence in this spartan reflection of how his mother felt about her life. He looked out of the window to the back garden and the row of houses opposite and saw the door of Rhona Collins, the girl next-door, whom he secretly thought he should have courted and married, certainly loved her at one point in his youth but he told the world and Rhona he had things to do and places to see which might have been a vague notion at the time but was, of course, self-deluding bullshit.

He searched in a box in his mother's room which held a mass of photographs, birth, marriage and death certificates of various members of the family, his father being one. He picked it up knowing he'd seen it before and read it again but this time with the eyes of a man. His dad had died at the ridiculously young age of thirty-four of a massive heart attack and he had never known him properly. He just held on to some memories of him in The Meadows taking photographs of him and his sister and then he realised he'd be thirty-four in September. Meaning what? The thought troubled him.

He delved for the passport It wasn't there. He rummaged around in the wardrobe and on shelves becoming more frustrated pulling out shoe boxes which held jewellery or papers referring to insurance policies and wedding invitations that had been saved, each place yielded nothing. He messily dumped them on the bed behind him and kept searching.

A voice behind him spoke.

"Couldny wait till she was dead, eh?"

Kelly spun around. His Uncle Gerry stood there in his usual garb and corpulence glowering at him.

"No...no, it's not like that....I just had to find something, something that's mine...."

Gerry cut across him, "I know exactly what it's like, ye selfish fuckin' leech! I know exactly what ye'd like to find, unless you're into wearin' womens dresses, now, and that widn't surprise me!. She keeps no money in the house. I sorted that for her a while back but ye'd settle for her jewellery, would ye!"

"I'm not taking anything!" Desperation and frustration raised his voice. "I'm not after her jewellery....." He realised that phrase made it sound as though he was.

"I'm just looking for something that Mum would've kept here....."

He couldn't tell him it was his passport

".....it's mine. I need it...now..."

"That's a pile o' shite! Yer mother get's taken ill and it so happens you need something from her room now? You always were a shiftless low-life without a day's work in you but I never thought you'd stoop as low as this!"

"I've told you....stop saying that about me....I just have to find something...."

"Go on then! Tell me! What is it you're lookin' for?"

Now, normally, Kelly would have a decent yarn to colour the scene, however, as this was indeed an honest situation and a misrepresentation of his character by the moustachioed Michelin Man, whom he disliked quite a lot, but was probably quite entitled to conclude the worst of him seeing what he was seeing. Kelly's frustration rose up into the red and entirely inhibited his creative juices finding nothing to go with that might have sufficed and satisfied his audience of one. Frustration elevated and so came volume.

"I can't tell you! I can't fuckin' tell you! It's private! Private business! Mine!" he yelled.

"Private business? You? The only business I see here is plain thievery. Thief! You're no more than a bloody thief! From your own, ill mother! You make me sick!"

Gerry turned and made to descend the stairs and Kelly panicked knowing that if that was the last word on the subject he would very much be vilified by all but he also knew that Gerry had found the material with which to crush Kelly now and forever and so it was in his interests to appear as disgusted with Kelly's behaviour as he could. Kelly ran after him and stopped him halfway down the stairs.

"I'm not a thief and don't you dare say to anyone that I am, you...you....!!"

"What? What am I?" Gerry challenged. "Your mother's brother. An honest family member. Certainly not a thief!"

"I'm not a thief! Stop saying that!"

The irony of that statement hung around in his head for a second as he considered the reason why he needed his passport but he didn't feel like a criminal. He didn't feel as though he had done anything wrong, just stolen his friend's identity, defrauded a bank of ten thousand pounds, was complicit in the death of an old schoolmate and a pubmate's dog, killed a prostitute and kept the body in his bath. At that moment the gravity of his situation hit him hard.

"Are ye not? It's what it looks like to me. Have ye been around the rest of the house? Found anything else?"

Kelly became immediately tired. The will to live drained from him in a second.

"No." His weariness apparent.

Gerry saw Kelly's resolve was wilting and sought to drive the blade home.

"No? Well let's have a look shall we? I know your mother kept some money in a tin in the kitchen. She didn't know I knew about it so I let her keep that in the house. There should be a decent wad in there."

Gerry strode down and into the kitchen and Kelly knew that there wouldn't be any money in the tin but he couldn't find the will to fight him and so just followed him, let him go through his charade and sat down on a chair under the shelf Gerry was bringing the tin from. Gerry strove to make a big show of placing the tin on the table. Alice entered.

"Whit's happenin', Gerry? Are you's two a'right? Whit's a' the shoutin' about?"

"Ah, Alice, I'm glad you're here! I came in an' found this one riflin' his mother's wardrobe takin' out boxes and pocketin' jewellery..."

Gerry, it seemed, had discovered the family gene for drama.

"Away! Ye niver did, Leonard! An' yer mithir no weel!" Alice turned shocked to Kelly.

"No.. I didn't...I wasn't...I was looking for something that is mine....that's all... I was lookin' for something!"

"And I think he'd more than enough time before I came in to rifle elsewhere, an a'!" Gerry added trying to get the evidence around to the tin. "She kept some cash in here for rainy days. So there should be a good amount in it."

Kelly knew the outcome. Gerry opened the tin and spun around like an Edinburgh Advocate at the high court nailing the case.

"There you go! Not a penny!" Gerry beamed.

"Leonard!" Alice put her hand over her mouth in disbelief.

He knew he was hung. Condemned because whatever he said now there was enough shit that would stick to him. Gerry gloated waiting for his response. Kelly had a go.

"She *gave* it to me last time I was here.... when you'd gone....she gave it to me....told me to *do something* with it..." He was tired. The explanation didn't go far.

"Aye...an' I'm the King o' Siam!" More evidence of Gerry's bent for impro.

Kelly considered defending himself, again but didn't have it in him. Instead something began to well deep within him and start to rumble. He seemed not to have much control over this. He found himself rising to his feet as a guttural roar, a la Sasquatch, broke free and filled the air. Alice screamed and declared she was *going to get Frank* and ran out. Kelly swung a hate-filled punch at Gerry's jaw and sent him sprawling across the kitchen lino. He then leapt on him and started to slap, punch and shout every colour of profanity at him as Gerry shouted at him to *fuck off* etc. with equally determined expletives. Frank arrived moments later. Sixty-one, cardigan and slippers, and tried to ungrip the clawed hold

Kelly had on his uncle's throat. Alice added a few *Oh my God's* and Frank tried to reason with him with lots of *Come on now, Leonard's* and *Let him go's.*

"Right that's enough!" Came the voice from the doorway. DC Claire Jones leapt into action, loudly declaring her membership of the Edinburgh Constabulary and eventually becalming a rabid Kelly with promises of handcuffing if he didn't desist, to whit Kelly stood but remained above his cowering fat uncle until DC Jones told him twice to sit at the table and not move.

Gerry got up and straightened himself, nursed his bloodied face and held his ribs in pain assuring Alice and Frank that he was okay. Frank closed over the kitchen door as there was now a small gathering of passers-by and neighbours aware to the scene inside. Alice delivered her version of the tale as did Frank and lastly, Gerry, who swore he was going to have him *done for this* and that it had been coming to him for years. Kelly laughed openly.

"Yeah just like you and you got it today, *Chubster!*"

Jones took the details from Alice and Frank. Uncle Gerry did likewise assuring Jones he needed no medical attention and that if it had lasted thirty seconds longer it would have been Kelly that needed medical attention, not him. Jones smiled inwardly and saw them all out to the door.

Kelly breathed heavily and lowered his bruised hand onto the table but caught the edge of the tin, so he stood up and put it roughly back on the shelf but knocked another tin down and onto the floor. The lid fell off and revealed a few newspaper cut-outs of his mother's friend receiving an award for the Womens Institute of West Lothian and beneath that was his passport. He grabbed it quickly and slipped into his inside jacket pocket next to the bank card and letter addressed to Joe with the PIN number on it

"Shit!" He whispered. He knew this might involve an arrest and emptying of his pockets before some cell-time.

Who was this plain-clothes plod that arrived like the fucking cavalry just when Gerry needed her, anyway? He thought.

Quickly, he pulled out the sheet, looked at it, tore off the part with the number, then dropped it down his shirt, then he quickly took the card out, slipped off his left shoe and slid it under the insole. The noise of Jones ensuring Gerry left could be heard outside and then the neighbours being assured all was well. He leaned back in his chair and made much of stretching his fingers and leaning against the table as if he'd never moved.

The kitchen door's hinges groaned as it slowly opened revealing McQuarrie who looked down at Kelly. Then he smiled and said,

"Lovely."

*****

Wednesday 27th June, 2:00pm

"Don't you think DC Jones is a very good driver, Kells?

McQuarrie leaned across the passenger seat looking back at Kelly in the back seat. They were driving down a country road.

"I think she's a very good driver. Some men think women are bad drivers. I don't think that. I think women have just the same ability to drive a car, control the vehicle, as men do. I think the difference is all about confidence. Confidence, Kells. Women don't have the same confidence as men. Men are full of shit, really. Bluster and bravado. Ego's as big as their balls...however big they are? See, my point is that if you browbeat and deride someone for long enough, they lose confidence. Lose that ability to tell themselves that they are good and that they can succeed...drive a car as well as anyone else, in this case. That's men for you, eh?"

Kelly craned his neck to see past McQuarrie. "Where are we

going?"

"I'm getting to that, Kells."

Jones smiled. She enjoyed seeing him work.

"Where are we? Where are we going?"

McQuarrie looked nonplussed. "I'm not driving. DC Jones is driving. I'm not in charge of that part of this...this.. erm....what is this? Jones?"

"I think this is an arrest, Sir."

"And *where* are we going, Jones?"

"Back to the station, Sir. That's where we process arrests. Just thought I'd take a more scenic route to let Leonard calm down a bit."

McQuarrie sighed contentedly and looked out of the window. "Isn't that thoughtful of DC Jones, Kells? Uniform would never have done something like that for you. What do you say, Kells?"

Kelly shook his head and looked out of the window. Jones joined in.

"Oh, that's not really necessary, Sir. I know you and Leonard already know each other so I thought a bit of time together to chew over things might be a good idea?"

"Well that is very thoughtful of you again DC Jones, however, I do think acknowledgement of your kind-heartedness is required on this occasion. Kells? Go on do the right thing.!"

He didn't like being part of anyone else's charades. He preferred to make the rules. McQuarrie dipped his head and lowered his voice to Kelly.

"Kells?"

"Yeah, yeah...Thanks!" he blurted out and then looked back out of the window like a petulant schoolboy.

McQuarrie noticed this.

" Ahh...Scotland is a minx of a seductress in the summer, don't you think, Kells? It is lovely around here when you leave the towns behind you. Peaceful. Unhurried.....oh look... a horse....*aaaand...gone."*

"I don't give a fuck about the scenery and any fuckin' horses! What's happening?"

Jones tutted. "Language Leonard!"

"Oh.. I should have told you, Jones..." McQuarrie said leaning across to her, "....he doesn't like to be called *Leonard*. Do you Leonard? He likes to be called *Kells...* just like the holy book of Kells in Ireland. Right Kells?"

No reply.

".....although I don't think Kells is as holy as that particular book, eh Kells? Keep a few secrets you do. *So*......just before we actually reach the station and we're all together in here we'll call him Kells. Ok Kells? After Jones reads you your rights and it'll have to be *Leonard* again. Sorry."

Kelly sat up. *"Reads me my rights?"*

"Oh, just a formality, Kells. Happens with every arrest. Where was I? Kells?" McQuarrie looked back at him again.

Nothing.

"Jones?"

"Women drivers, Sir." She really started to enjoy her work.

"Yes...yes...as I was saying..."

Kelly breathed heavily and sighed.

"....in a nutshell...if you give someone a hard time for long enough, harass and badger them, then they're bound to question themselves and break. Right? Don't you think? I mean everything they do never mind driving, will be affected and those effects can last a long time. Years in some cases."

McQuarrie paused as if to think and smiled looking out of the window. He continued,

"But DC Jones isn't one of them, thank the Lord! Jones is very good. Very observant. For example consider when she's in court giving her evidence about today's debacle? I mean families always fight when there's an older one not very well, don't they? Jones will be very particular about what she saw. Recall everything. Great memory has Jones. Don't you Jones?"

"Photographic, sir."

"Hear that, Kells...Photographic! Recalls everything. What did you see today, Jones?"

Jones picked up the baton. "Man being seriously assaulted, sir. GBH. Possibly attempted murder."

McQuarrie appeared shocked. "No! Surely not."

Kelly panicked. "Attempted murder! How's that. I just punched him a few times."

Jones dropped the bomb. "I saw a knife. Sorry..... *Kells*"

Kelly raised his voice. "What knife? What fuckin' knife!! I never had a knife!"

Jones sighed as if sorry to deliver the bad news, "*Well....* there was a knife on the kitchen worktop and when I came in it looked to me as though you were reaching for it....*Kells.*"

"Oh dear...." McQuarrie said shaking his head. "Could you have done it?"

Kelly was confused. "Done what?"

"Well...kill someone with a knife, I suppose. Could you?"

Kelly began to think McQuarrie had the gift of second sight. McQuarrie peered at him.

"And the time. Long stretch for *Attempted Murder.*"

"I didn't try to murder him! You know I didn't use a knife!"

Jones chipped in. "Maybe? Might be a discussion to be had there, though? Might not. But you did switch the tins."

McQuarrie was impressed with Jones, now. "Tins? What's all this about tins, Kells? Which tins?"

"Mr Malone...the assaultee... explained that they had looked in a tin for money that Kells had stolen, apparently. That tin was red. When I returned to the kitchen after taking some details from the witnesses the tin was now a different shape with a delightful picture of Lady Di and Prince Charles on it and the red one was back on the shelf. So if Kells has nothing to hide and he wasn't stealing from his own mother, I'd like to know, as would a jury, why he would want to switch the tins?"

McQuarrie looked quizzically at Kelly, "Kells what's all this about tins and stealing from your own mother? Tut tut."

Then he straightened up and enthusiastically said, "Oh look..there's the Forth Road Bridge! Are we going across the bridge to Fife, Jones? They have lovely beaches in Fife."

"If we have to, sir." Jones replied. "But could we get some petrol from the garage on this side first. Might need it."

"Certainly Jones. You're the driver! You're in charge."

Kelly was now in a state. "Why the fuck would we be going to Fife! Edinburgh's the other way! What's happening?"

McQuarrie continuing the mock enthusiasm said, "Yes let's get some petrol, Jones. And some coffee. Black, right, Kells? He takes it black, now, Jones. How very urbane."

"I don't give a fuck about the coffee. Tell me what's happening!"

Jones pulled into a parking space away from any other cars at the Petrol Station on the south side of The Forth Road Bridge. McQuarrie insisted that it should be he that fetches the coffees. Kelly spoke to Jones.

"He's up to something. He's working me. What does he want?"

"I think he'd like not for you to go jail, Kells, which I think is in his remit of power and influence. Theft? From your own mother. Ill in hospital, I believe? *GBH? Attempted Murder?* What jury could ever see anything but a conviction? Could add up to a hefty holiday in Saughton Prison, Kells. And if you don't play ball and we flush out who did for our man in Greyfriars without you and find that you withheld information, you can throw *Attempting to Pervert the Course of Justice* into the pot. Possibly a ten stretch. More. Have a think about what you know about the Greyfriars Body case and he might not tell me to drive across that bridge and into the heart of darkest Fife, remove your shoes and let you walk back to Edinburgh while you think about it, *Cinders*. They're your shoes stuck to that wall in that flat, aren't they?"

He said nothing. Jones just shrugged and said

"I'm going to stretch my legs. Have a think, Kells. Up to you. The car will be locked, by the way and anyway I could probably catch you after I saw your heavy breathing after the fight. Really not that fit are you?"

Jones left the car. Kelly hated that she was right, younger, than him, good-looking with a career. He had to buy time but if he did tell them the truth they'd never believe it. They'd think he was taking the piss. However, he knew he was up against a sticky wicket and had to tell them something. Then he knew what he was going to tell them although he spent the next few minutes trying to make sense of what his story should include. When McQuarrie realised he didn't have what he wanted, he'd come looking for him, again. And then it would get much worse.

McQuarrie came back into the car with two coffees and gave one to Kelly. They sipped it quietly for a minute. McQuarrie broke first.

"Jones spoke to you?"

"Yes."

"So....?"

Kelly looked at him. Now he held all the aces so took his time, doing an acting job, trying to look as though it was a difficult thing to do. It worked.

McQuarrie became impatient, shouted and filled the car with his voice.

"C'mon, Kelly! Talk to me!" I know it's not easy. The truth never is. Tell me what happened!"

Kelly was slightly shaken by his outburst although he expected it and he knew he was serious because he'd called him Kelly. He augmented his little charade with a very obvious deep breath and then, flatly said,

"I know who killed him."

Chapter 30

Fleeing and Flying

Wednesday 27ʰ June 3:00pm

Kelly had been driven back to Edinburgh by McQuarrie and Jones and told not to go anywhere because they might want to speak to him again soon. Jones had asked him if he wanted to be dropped off at the hospital to go visit his mother but said he'd go another time because he'd missed the early slot but honestly knew he'd most probably seen her for the last time in a long time and felt that something, quite heavy and black, was weighing him down into the seat of the car and without invitation, a globule of tears welled up in his left eye as they sped back to Edinburgh.

Kelly rushed up to the West End and found the Czechoslovakian Consulate, bought an envelope, posted Joe's passport through the door with the letter from professor Hunter. The least amount of people see him the better and he knew now the shit was about to hit the fan and knew he would have to travel as Joe. The itinerary said they were to be at Edinburgh Airport Saturday morning of Saturday the 30th. It was an 08:30 flight to London then an hour and a half before the flight to Prague. He had to get off the streets and out of his flat and lay low for the rest of Wednesday, disappear for Thursday and Friday but he knew he'd have a few hours before McQuarrie got to London and realised his information about who killed Threeby was a pack of lies.

He rushed into his flat and considered the task of gathering everything that he needed knowing his clock was ticking. It was then he discovered he'd no bag or holdall, anywhere, just a ridiculously massive suitcase that was old, battered, and had been used to bring all of his books into the flat when he moved in.

McQuarrie squared the trip with his boss in light of the new information, made the necessary calls and booked an evening flight. Jones remained in Edinburgh. Two hours later a group of friends about to fly to Italy were stopped by security at the Heathrow and held in airport security.

Luccia cried a lot. Tom was confrontational and Jerry discovered he didn't quite have the cahones his father often displayed with surly oiks, nor the gravitas that comes with age. Annabel thought the whole thing was a wonderfully exciting episode, loving the tension and tears and asked the security chaps, who were told to say nothing, if they thought she was a drugs mule or held vital information into an international arms deal, to which, they remained quiet, but she told them it might make it into her bestseller and could she use some of their real names?

McQuarrie had asked for the four of them to be taken to Paddington Green police station where he could formally caution them and organise getting them back to Scotland. This was the United Kingdom in many ways, but in some, only by name because Scottish law, different from English law, dictated that protocol must be followed to the letter so that no smart Scottish advocate could have anything thrown out of court because of technicalities that weren't observed.

He really didn't want to do this but he had no choice. He slipped her key into her lock and turned as quietly as he could. Everything was just as he had left it. Why wouldn't it be? He'd done a good job, he thought, because it did look as though she had been severely burgled, sure enough. The living-room had nothing like a bag in it so he crept into her bedroom, guessing she'd have kept luggage in there and scanned the place. The remains of the hash plants were brown and dried leaning limply in their death throes. He opened a wardrobe door. Nothing. He had to move shoe boxes to see to the back and there it was, a grey sports bag, which he hadn't seen when he fixed the place to look like the burglary, was tucked away in a corner. He grabbed it out and gave it a shake. He didn't think she was the sporty type but whatever was in it had to come out so he unzipped it quickly. He couldn't believe what he saw. Kelly stared down at a substantial amount of ten and twenty pound notes in small heaps and guessed that there had to be at least another grand in there. Possibly more. He lifted some the notes and some small amounts of silver and coppers sloshed around the bottom. He sat on the bed and took a moment to reflect on the amount of riches that were now at his disposal. He'd never been as wealthy before in his life. Most likely never would be again. He looked around the flat at the mess then thought of his own flat and the disarray it was in and shook his head. He regained his urgency grabbing the bag and went to exit the bedroom. Then there was a loud rap at the door.

Kelly could hear breathing close to the door. There was another knock.

"Sandra..?." the voice echoed in the stairwell and against the wooden door. "Urr ye there? Sandra?"

He was an absolute pest! The Pumping Tracksuit's voice was pathetic, bereft and somewhat lovelorn. The letter box opened.

"I don't know why you've gone away. And come back....n' that. I know yer in there. I heard ye an' just want to say I'm sorry....." Kelly didn't need this or for TPT to see him leaving the flat but he was intrigued to know what the sad sap was sorry about.

"....d'ye know what I mean, Sandra? D'ye know what I'm talkin' about? I know you do. You said I was stupid. I'm not. An' I'm sorry if I scared ye away cos ye've been gone fur ages, now..."

Kelly sensed that TPT was going to be a while. He was going to have to wait it out.

"...I said it because I meant it, Sandra. I did. I do. I love ye. I love ye Sandra. Talk to me. Please."

Oh my God, Kelly thought, *the lad's in love.* Kelly's initial reaction was to smile but this situation didn't require smiles, it required The Pumping Tracksuit to fuck off back to his flat and let him do what he had to. There was also something in his voice that was utterly and quite enviably, believable. His soft determination was something he'd never seen in him before....mostly because, well.... he never knew him very well and he was either shitfaced or narcotically vertical, *just*.... but this poor sap had indeed fallen for a prostitute. A now dead one, unfortunately, and he didn't have the heart to tell him that the love of his life was downstairs in a bath covered in compost. TPT then romantically alerted Kelly to part of his problem.

"I need ye, Sandra, I need ye. I haven't had a jump fur ages now, Sandra. I canny walk straight and my balls are groanin'."

Which isn't a quote from *Brief Encounter*.

Chapter 31

Checking The Mirror

Dorothy Dean, the fifty-seven year old sub-editor of The Daily Mirror was quietly chain-smoking her way long into the afternoon and in deep consideration of tomorrow's front page. Her door burst open and Stuart James, the red-haired political correspondent burst in. She jumped and hit the tall glass on her desk spilling it everywhere.

"Fuck me, you Scotch twat! I've just filled my fucking nappy and spilled a large G and T over a twenty pack with only one out of it. You owe me one pack of Marlboro for scaring the shit out of me and another one for being fucking ginger! What the fuck is it?"

"Listen DD.... I've never had the chance to say it but I'm saying it now!"

"Saying fucking what! Out with it you Jockanese fucking politico!"

"Hold the front page!"

"We don't have a fucking front page, yet! You're three hours early."

"Well, DD...we do now!"

Stuart James outlined a reliably sourced leak of information lately received about the sexual proclivities and affection for young boys of the Defence Secretary, Sir Clive Harrow.

She then excused him for bursting in, making her spill her drink and soaking her cigarettes.

Then smiled.

Chapter 32

Hitting the Road

Half an hour had passed. Kelly was becoming fractious. He didn't have this time to squander. He couldn't hear any noises coming from outside the door, anymore. Hopefully The Pumping Tracksuit had given up and gone upstairs. He crept to the letterbox and gently lifted the flap. Another pair of eyes stared back. Something of a retinal stand-off occurred for a few seconds. He stood up quickly and leaned against the door. He had no time for this. He had to get out and get gone. A decision was required. He grabbed the bag, took a deep breath.

Kelly opened the door quickly and nearly got it shut before TPT could get past.

"....yeah...right ..see you next week. Same time."

He got himself quickly out of the door and onto the landing just as TPT shouted into the flat,

"Sandra! It's me Jas....*Graham*. I need to see ye! Sandra!"

Kelly slammed the door shut. "She says she doesn't want to see you. It's because you said you loved her. She doesn't need that, she said. Too heavy. Gets in the way of business."

He took off down the stairs and ran into his flat just as he heard The Pumping Tracksuit banging loudly on her door, shouting her name, crying and declaring that he wouldn't care about her having to fuck other men for money as long as she came back home to him. So thoughtful.

He took a minute to settle himself, breathe and gather his thoughts. He looked into the bag again and at the array of cash once more dropped into his lap. The irony was ridiculous. He took the remaining thousand from out of the bible, gathered the money he's taken from her when he did the deadly deed and took the new stash from the bag. There was also the remainder of the six-hundred quid his mother had given him which he stalled at for a moment but then quickly laid it out before him on the floor. He counted it all as fast as he could being pleasantly pleased at the arrival of a roll of fifty pound notes from the sports holdall and then sat back against his wall looking at it all. £7027.13 lay before him. Riches beyond any aspirations he had ever expected to achieve. But for that he was also a thief and murderer. Alone. Running. Never himself. Pretending to be something he wasn't. As ever. With that thought he began to consider the array of evidence left in the flat and so he started to grab everything he knew had to go with him into the bag. Some clothes; underpants and socks. He ran to the bathroom and took his toothbrush and considered taking the gnarled and creased tube of Colgate but the smell that was now decidedly worse than before hung in the air, so he tried to rearrange some of the compost to plug any gaps but it seemed futile and too little too late. He saw the make-up, wigs and powders he'd lifted from Theatre Skills on the floor by his telly and put them all in a plastic bag and stuffed it into the holdall. He went through the itinerary every holiday maker goes through before leaving but obviously had to omit the *tickets* part of it. Money and passport. For some reason beyond his current rationale, he also put Lenni's leash, the one that had hung him, into the bag. Maybe because it was an accessory to a crime, but one he didn't commit just like he hadn't killed Threeby, but he knew McQuarrie wouldn't see it that way. He threw the Dictaphone and the hollowed-out bible both into the bag and looked around for anything else he thought might help McQuarrie guess where he'd gone. He looked down at the money on the floor and decided against putting it all in the bag which might be separated from him, at some time, and thought. He looked at his Crombie coat and had the bright idea to put the money in the lining but knew that McQuarrie would list that in any description of him, however the lining idea was good, he thought.

He hurried into the bedroom and searched a pile of clothes in a heap in a corner and dragged out an old Parka coat with fur-lined hood and heavy insulation in the lining and tore a hole into the inside pocket. The money, barring a hundred quid he kept for his three day expenses, was stuffed into the cavity quite easily. He tried on the coat. It felt okay. He went to his window and looked out into the streets. He knew he had to change his appearance.

The black dishevelled wig dropped onto his head quite easily. He stared at himself in the bathroom mirror then drew the hood of the Parka over his head and took in the view before him. He no longer recognised the man before him and considered himself quite changed. The smell drew him to the makeshift grave in the bath. He stared at the black compost and quietly said,

"...sorry."

He pulled the bathroom door shut tight and tried to re-stick the tape that was around it's edges.

The Pumping Tracksuit seemed to have quietened down.

The Good Soldier Sveyk was where it had been left my Number Two. He grabbed it and stuffed it in the bag. He took in the carnage that was his flat for the last time then rushed out the door closing it too loudly and rushed down the stairs and out into the street.

The Pumping Tracksuit, who'd decided to wait faithfully for his love, however long it took, was sitting on the first step on her landing and had begun to doze when he heard Kelly's door shut and caught only the shadow of him disappear.

Chapter 33

Goose Girl Got

"Now my little goose girl, do you have something to tell me?"

McQuarrie fixed Luccia's gaze.

They were in an interview room in Paddington Green police station.

"What's happening?" The tears arrived again. "What have we done wrong?"

McQuarrie knew she would be the easiest to crack first and after that it would be no trouble to let the others know this and soon after they would crack, too.

"I think you know very well, don't you? The night of the party. The night an innocent man died. On The Meadows, in Greyfriars Kirkyard, it doesn't matter. What matters now is the truth.. Don't tell me you don't know about this. Just give me the truth. Was it Tom and Jerry? They're big strapping lads. It might have been an accident, high jinks, but someone is dead and it has to be answered for."

"We didn't leave the flat that night! It was our party, we were the hosts. We couldn't do that!"

If she wasn't so middle-class McQuarrie would have been inclined to consider this a lie, however this frailsome little posh flower seemed not to have the gall to lie and to be honest, he believed that her breeding and sense of social decorum actually would have kept her in the flat, that night.

"So you stayed. Tom and Jerry went out onto The Meadows to play rugby. Right?"

"No!! None of us went. They did!"

"Who did?!"

"Crispin...Peter, Hugo...some others. It was them that came back with the shoes and nailed them to the door. It wasn't us!"

"What did they say they'd done.?"

"What you said. They messed around with him, played rugby with his shoes and hit him a few times..."

"....and it got out of hand. Right? He was just crossing The Meadows and he said some things to them, told them to fuck off and they hit him."

"Something like that but they said they tied him up?"

"Why did they tie him up?"

"They tied him to a tree! Took off his trousers and used them to tie him to the tree, they said. Because he was so nasty to Becky!"

"Who's Becky?"

"Crispin's sister!"

"When was he nasty to her?"

"At the party!"

"He was at the party?!" Who did he arrive with?"

"Nobody...but Miggy invited him."

"Miggy?"

"....McMiggins....*Megan*. He was Megan's friend!"

"The man that died in Greyfriars Kirkyard was Megan's friend?"

"No! No! No!" The tears came again.

"He wasn't *her* friend!"

"Then why did she bring him?"

"She didn't bring him! Not the man that died in the graveyard.....I don't know anything about the man in the graveyard...."

Lots more tears.

".........she brought Kells! Kelly! It was him they tied to the tree and slapped around. It was Kelly!!"

DC Jones was still at St. Leonard's Police Station late into the night in the South Side having a sandwich and a coffee when someone shouted *Phone!*

McQuarrie had taken the time to speak to all the others individually and corroborate the story as quickly as he could. There appeared no reason to doubt them.

"Jones?"

"Yes Jack, it's Claire here."

"Kelly's a liar! Find him! Find Kelly and hold him!"

DC Jones arrived at the stair door with a uniform and ascended the stairs to his door and knocked loudly. The Pumping Tracksuit leaned over the bannister again. Jones looked up.

"Have you seen your neighbour recently? Mr Kelly?"

"Ye've jist missed him."

"How long?"

"About ten minutes"

"Shit! Jones said imagining the chagrin of McQuarrie. "What was he wearing?"

"Too dark."

Jones got back to the car and radio-ed in to put a general description of him out to all cars and to apprehend if seen.

Chapter 34

Driscoll Done

Thursday 28th June. 9:37pm

Kelly'd been dashing about from doorway to doorway all evening afraid to go for a pint anywhere and now it was beginning to darken. He walked quickly up a main road knowing he had to get off it and so he turned onto a side street and made for The Meadows knowing its imminent darkness would shroud him. Another hour passed of him shifting nervously in the street and then walked up a path lit by a few streetlights and past the tennis courts but then made his way onto the centre of the unlit expanse of grass and sat down. From there he could see the road and the paths across the park and anyone approaching. Nobody was likely to cross the grass in the dark and for the first time that day breathed deeply and lay on his back and leaned his head against the bag. He looked up at the clear sky and the stars and felt as though he was part of that vast darkness, a darkness that had extended downwards enveloping him, removing him from the world. Lying unknown, unloved and alone. He'd spent most of his life avoiding the familiar paths that made any demands on him and now he felt entirely and utterly removed.

He fell asleep. He had no notion of how long he had lain there when he was woken by a rough Irish brogue and the terrible smell that accompanied it.

"What about ye?"

The wino Driscoll stood above him. He was dressed exactly as Kelly saw him a week or so before, however, on this occasion the summer heat had probably sweated away his choice of *Eau de Cologne* and what emanated from him now was *monkey cage*.

"Hey, are ye alright, son?" he rasped. "These summer nights I come for a lie down on the grass, meself, so I do."

Kelly sat up quickly in an unsure panic and looked around checking there was only him.

"D'ye mind me stretching out on the grass wit ye, son?"

Kelly didn't want to arouse any suspicion but he also didn't want any company for fear of attracting any interest from further brothers of the gutter and then the law.

"Help yourself." Kelly said. The big Irishman made a loud soundtrack to the act of sitting and then lying down. Kelly looked about. Still nobody else.

"Ah, that's much better..." he tiredly said, ".....I had meself a wee tussle wit Isaac One-Arm before. He can sure throw a decent punch for a one-armed fella, so he can. He's a southpaw!"

Driscoll rasped out a cackle and repeated the gag then said,

"He's no feckin' choice!" and cackled loudly.

"Need to rest me muscles, so I do and I could do wi' a drink. Do ye have a drink, son?"

Driscoll didn't take long to get to the meat of his reason for seeking out the silhouette on the grass, thinking it may be the source of a free fixer until morning. Kelly didn't want to annoy him but he did want him to go away. He'd had enough of this day. He did think about telling him to fuck off but there seemed a determination in him this time, whereas the morning they last shared banter there was a resignation about this big man. Maybe the sunshine had invigorated him with vitamin D? He did say he'd been fighting that day, albeit with a one-armed man. It did occur to Kelly that he'd like to know the outcome but declined the question not wanting to encourage any bonhomie, ergo further contact.

Kelly couldn't stand the smell of Driscoll.

"No. Sorry."

"Would ye have a wee smoke for me then son? Just a wee nipped end would be fine. A wee nipped end. Have ye, son?"

"I don't smoke.... *big man*." He threw that in to assure the Irishman of his ability to converse a la wino/working-class pub discussion groups.

Driscoll looked disappointed. Then annoyed. This assignment was yielding nothing.

"Holy mother of feckin' God...ye don't drink and ye don't smoke! What's happening to young people, today?"

Driscoll then dragged himself onto his side leaning his head on his hand like anyone would do on a summer picnic by a river and wiped his face while apparently thinking. It was dark but Kelly saw him turn and survey the space around them and lifted his head to the direction he had just came from.

"I think.... I *know* who you are?" Driscoll said. Kelly turned to him quickly.

"Do you?" Kelly said with affected doubt to try and convince otherwise.

"I do. You're one of dese fellas that like other fellas, aren't ye? Is that it? That's it, in't it? An' yer here hopin' another one of you fellas comes along an' yez have a wee fiddle wit each other an' then go on yer way? Right?"

Kelly flushed. "Wrong! I'm not one of those guys! At all. Actually!"

Driscoll wouldn't be put off. "Ahhhh...there's no need to be shy about all a' dat wit me, son. Some a' me drinkin' buddies are livin' down in the Grassmarket coz they're like that. Turned outa where de lived a whiles back because o' it. I help dose fellas out, now and again. For a bottle o' *King's Head* or *Four Crown,* a few packets o' fags an' a coupla shillin' here an' dere. So ..ye've nothin' to drink an' no fags but for a few quid...say a fiver... I'll pull yer cock for ye. How would that be?"

Kelly rounded quickly. "No...no! I don't want...."

Driscoll cut in. "...a'right you want more? I get it, make it a tenner...eight quid...ah go on I'll suck yer cock for a fiver as well. There ye are!! Do we have a deal?"

Kelly stood up at the thought of his green-slaked teeth anywhere near his tackle.

"No we don't have a fucking deal you stinking old fuck! I'm not one of those fellas! Get the fuck out of here and leave me alone."

Driscoll rose to his full height and towered above Kelly.

"Well what the feck are ye doin' here in the middle o' the night, then?"

Driscoll eyed the bag. Kelly saw this and looked at it too. A moment passed as each of them knew the next move. Driscoll lunged for the bag. Kelly dropped down on top of it. Driscoll pulled without much strength but his size and weight was pulling it from Kelly. The bag became the centre of a bizarre dance of turns and jerks *fuck offs* and *leave it alone's*. Kelly managed to pull it into his chest and get both hands on it and Driscoll came into wrench it away. They were, but for the height of Driscoll, nose to nose in a bizarre heaving desperate tango upon an empty parkland plain, however sans orchestra. Driscoll looked into Kelly's eyes and then surprisingly let go of the bag as a look of realisation swept over his face.

"I feckin' *do* know you! I feckin' saw ye, that night, you up against that tree an' yer bare arse out for all de world t' see and yer wee bumchum shoving' it up yer arse. I saw ye!"

Kelly revisited that night in his head and put two and two together hearing the howl of Sasquatch and the brogue of Driscoll muttering in the dark.

"But ye wasn't that happy wit him, was ye? Wasn't doin' it right for ye was he and so ye hit 'im wit that bottle, ye fecker ye, an' took his shoes!"

That was enough to hasten Driscoll towards his end. Kelly booted Driscoll squarely in the balls and watched the reduction in size as the big man fell forward, to whit, Kelly sent his left foot to his head. He dropped to the ground and Kelly sent another to his exposed ribs and booted him again on the side of his head. Kelly breathed heavily as he thought of his mother and his negligence over the years and disliked himself dearly. He sent another boot to

Driscoll's ribs and followed it up with another to his face. His face? He only relented when he broke from his frenzy of punches trying to compensate for his waste of years, his arrogance, his pretence, his denials, his indolence, his lack of love, him being unloved and sense of worthlessness that throbbed at his core. He was on his knees above the bloodied face of Driscoll. His heart pounded trying to pump oxygen to his unfit muscles. He looked at Driscoll knowing what he'd done then at his bloodied fists. He thought of wiping them on his jacket but realised the stupidity of that. He bent down and wiped them on Driscoll's jacket but as he bent down he saw his shoes. Blood filled the eyeholes for the laces and the laces themselves were sodden with it. He knelt down at the feet of Driscoll and began to undo the laces on his boots.

Chapter 35

Bootless Goodbyes

Thursday 28th June

Kids were crossing The Meadows walking to school and encountered the strange sight of a huge man carrying another man in his arms across the grass. The hulk of a man seemed to be crying.

Sasquatch had picked up his comrade, his best friend whom he went through many beer-soaked evenings, basic-training and now armed conflict and whose flesh he had watched being torn from his torso as an Argentinian shell's shrapnel ripped through his abdomen. They'd joined up together before the South Atlantic ignited but were happy to fight for the Falklands, Queen, Country and each other and grew closer as each political move brought the action closer to their regiment, closer to their arrival at Goose Green. He held his friend as the blood drained away into the South Atlantic soil and when he'd whispered his goodbyes and watched him slip away, cried and howled loudly in his pain reliving the noise and violence of the exploding shell and hail of bullets and seeing Argentinian boys wounded and crying for their mothers, fall at the behest of his automatic weapon knowing they were ill-trained and ill-equipped but had no choice but to end their lives on this barren South Atlantic sod, a last emblem of empire that, apparently, must be defended. Blood and death surrounded him.

Sasquatch saw the moment in his head, replaying his brother in arms being opened up in front of his eyes in a blaze of scarlet. He then carried him to a safer place and saw his blood on his hands and tried to wipe it on his trousers and cradled him again. Again his hands reddened with blood. Again he rubbed it away. He sat down with his friend across his knees. The howls rang louder than the crash of mortar and the crack of rifle fire.

Sasquatch sat on a bench on Middle Meadow Walk with the bootless Driscoll laid across his knees and cried. The prostrate heap went unnoticed until Sasquatch, who had been out all night himself, found his now expired drinking associate and regressed seeing the corpse. The tears of Sasquatch rolled down his face uncaring of the stream of morning workers passing closely on the broad pathway. Many thought this scene was two homeless drunks dealing with the arrival of another day. Then they heard him howl.

Chapter 36

Goose Green Again

McQuarrie arrived at the station at 9:30am. He looked over to Jones's desk which was empty.

He turned to Fenlon who was at his. "Where's Claire?"

"And a very good morning to you, as well, Jack. How was *The Smoke?*"

"It's still there. Jones?"

"At home sleeping I presume. I heard she was here 'til all hours last night co-ordinating a search you asked for."

McQuarrie picked up Fenlon's phone and dialled. Jones answered. He told her to get dressed and get down to the nick and pick him up, toute suite.

McQuarrie drank coffee and she arrived twenty-five minutes later looking tired and harassed.

"So which cell is he in?" No good morning. Jones frowned puzzled.

"Sir?"

"Which cell? Where's Kelly?"

"He's not in a cell, Sir. We couldn't find him. We'd just missed him, apparently. Guy upstairs saw him leave."

"I'm sorry, Jones? One more time, please. *You just......?*"

He wasn't happy. Claire groaned inwardly.

"....missed him, sir."

"Warrant?"

"Sorry sir?"

"Warrant! Did you search his place and not just take the word of a neighbour!"

"I was busy trying to find him if he'd just left! We put the word out to all cars. I was tired, Jack. I got caught up in finding him."

McQuarrie kept his temper behind a scowl. "Livingston?"

"Made a call to the nick there and they said there was no answer and that their neighbour across the road hadn't seen him since we were there. He hadn't been to see his mother in hospital, either. Maybe he's just on a bender somewhere?"

McQuarrie squared a fiercesome look at Jones. Fenlon, who was listening winced and removed himself back to his current workload.

"So.... he sends me to London with duff info, makes me look like an amateur in front of The Met.... meanwhile you *can't find him* not with every available car looking.... and you think he's just on a bender?"

Jones took a deep breath. She was too tired for this.

"Well what did you expect me to do, *Jack!* That's standard procedure isn't it? What would you have done differently? Driven around in the middle of the night when your eyes are shutting because you've had a shift that day and if you've looked a dick in front of the Met that's got nothing to do with me, has it! It was your man Kelly that sent you there, not me!"

Fenlon was inclined to applaud Claire while McQuarrie glowered at her but then his phone rang. He listened without saying much and then turned to McQuarrie.

"Ermm..Jack? Bit of twist on the Greyfriars Body story..... *possibly...*"

"What?" McQuarrie barked still staring down Jones.

"Another corpse. Badly beaten. Wino. Meadows.

"Why has that got anything to do with the Greyfriars case? It's tramps fighting. It happens."

Fenlon pulled a face that described his fear to tell him.

"Erm...two things. Uniform think the fella that did the deed was with him, local nutter, had him lying across his knees on a park bench....*crying*...so they say...and *shoeless*. Again. Seems to be a theme forming, Jack?"

"Where?"

"Middle Meadow Walk." McQuarrie marched out without another word. Jones sighed tiredly. Fenlon looked across at her suppressing a smirk.

"All the best...*Claire.*"

"Shut up!" she said to him then she jumped at the sound of her master's voice.

"Jones! Car!"

Chapter 37

Castle Dosser

Friday 29th June

Kelly tried to open his eyes but everything was black. He heard the sound of shuffling near him and then a terrible smell of stale piss. He pushed the black messy wig up and the light hurt his eyes. An old homeless figure passed the bottom of his steel framed bed and he tried to lift his head and look around but his neck was stiff because he put his bag under his pillow and rested on that all night. A brown overall-coat loudly called out a communal and unsympathetic message down the large hall which had beds lined up dorm-style along each wall.

"That's quarter to eight gentlemen. Time to go out and meet the day. Leave nothing behind you and please try to piss straight before you go. Anyone seen deliberately pissing anywhere they shouldn't piss will not be allowed back in tonight. Have a nice day boys....and try to get something to eat before you start drinking...*please..*"

This was Edinburgh's Grassmarket set beneath the east wall of the castle, a wide and cobbled market square with two exit roads at each end and former scene of many public hangings, and which now housed *The Castle Trades Hotel*, opened in the days of yore for Irish navvies and itinerant tradesmen looking for work. It was now an evening repose for homeless men so the *hotel* part was something of a misnomer. Every vagrant, tramp or wino could sleep their drunkenness away and take their hangover back out into the day for a quite reasonable and nominal fee. They were accepted after six at night and kicked out at eight in the morning.

"Let's be up and at 'em chaps." The voice cried again but getting closer.

Kelly could smell bleach now as well. Rough bearded and unkempt men, never usually less than forty summers, were rising and wandering out and away from their iron-framed beds. Another overalled custodian was behind our shouter with a mop, bucket and bottle of bleach. He'd squirt a splash on the floor next to each bed and quickly spread it out with the mop and then pull the single blanket back down to the reveal a sheet and then shout *Clear!* and move to the next bed. Some, however, were not clear. If any were splashed with vomit or circled with a piss-stain they were pulled off the bed and thrown on the floor to be collected and sent to *The Steamie*. They had a room detailed specifically for this job.

Kelly covertly rotated the wig and drew his legs out of the bed and pulled his Parka closer to him.

A southern English voice was raised down the dorm.

"You're not my Father. You're not my Father! You can't be tellin' me what to do and where to go. I'll be gone in my time! I paid my money. You're not my father!"

A small, bearded man was gathering himself as the overalled bleacher waited to check his bed and floor. He was pulling a pair of dirty trousers on top of another pair of trousers he already had on and trying to fasten his belt over the them and the large shirt flapping around his middle.

"A' right, Esmond...sort yersel' an' git oot . You've got two minutes."

Esmond then told the bleacher that his father was a Captain in the Belgian Army and that he would send for him soon and wouldn't have to stay here for much longer. The worker had heard it a few times before and humoured him having once learned that to gainsay Esmond about anything was grounds for a fist fight there and then, drunk or sober.

Kelly stood, stretched his back and lifted his bag.

Kelly could hear Esmond shouting that he was fixing his cravat and not to bother him until it was done and *what time was breakfast being served,* as he stepped across the threshold into The Grassmarket. Some of the ejected men were gathering around The Bow Well directly opposite the Castle Trades Hotel, an old street source of water that constantly ran in years previous and where the homeless fraternity convened to slake their drouth when nursing hangovers. A suitable meeting place for some and Kelly knew that he had to blend in, be invisible in plain sight. He pulled the hood around the back of his neck and shuffled over and sat down at the well. He was accosted for *a shillin'* by one and knew that other entreaties would follow if he remained and there had been a few curious looks to the bag. The wino fraternity never usually had a bag so he wandered along to the foot of the Castle Rock. Here the volcanic edifice climbed above him and a rocky steep slope up to the half-moon battery of Edinburgh Castle. He stood and felt very small beneath it but was wakened by the sight of a police car coming up King's Stables Road and lifted the bag so he could lean it against the fence but covered with his coat. The car passed. The bag was conspicuous. He was the only tramp on the streets carrying a bag. He had to secrete it somewhere. Left-luggage at

Waverley station was the obvious choice but reckoned there were too many police wandering about down there. He looked at the rock behind the fence and upward to the walls of the castle.

Down through Saint Thomas's church and graveyard, closer to the west gardens of Princes Street, he saw a couple of his temporary fraternity sitting on fallen headstones and quickly walked around the path which had no fence stopping anyone from climbing the castle rock. Tourist's kids often felt adventurous so he went off the path and started to ascend the grassy aspect further round nearer trees and he climbed up the rock away from the gaze of any passers-by. He turned to check he was out of sight and pushed the bag into a crevice, broke a large flowering buddleia from the larger bush and covered the spot. He dropped back down to the grassy slope and looked through the trees onto Princes Street's west end and marked the spot with a view to the Union Jack flying above The Overseas Club.

Kelly then spent the day blending in as much as he could with the other vagrants around the Grassmarket and occasionally sat on the ledge of the long window of *The Castle Trades Hotel* where others were whiling away their time. There seemed nowhere else to go for these men. Some of them walked the mile or so down through the Cowgate and into Holyrood Park and went to get a drink at Saint Anthony's well, a natural spring that drained through the volcanic strata of Arthur's Seat, so he decided to make that trip, too.

He took a drink but then walked past the well and began to ascend the grassy slope further up the hill. At around two hundred feet there was a beaten path locally called The Radical Road and after a few stops to catch his breath he reached the path. He was, ironically, feeling reasonably fit, no alcohol for days, a lot of running around and impromptu dance followed by a fight. He turned and sat on a rock, drew his hand across his face and forehead then raised his eyes and beheld the impressive vista that was Edinburgh before him. He picked out buildings close to his flat. Stared over to the Castle Rock and thought of his bag, what it contained; the wherewithal to leave this town and become someone else, someone new. It was the ticket to doing something that would change his life, start the new chapter.

Then he looked again and allowed the suggestion of a smile to upturn his mouth at the corners. He identified streets he knew well and then his street and then *The Duke* where he held court during evenings of revelry and long felonious, improvised deconstructions of notable works he had never read entirely, had occurred, but then the smile fell back to an impassive demeanour as he understood the fraudulent ramblings, the dishonesty that deluded and sustained, the essentially empty chimera, that was him. He had blustered in a small unchallenging pond and grown little within his thirty-three years, never engaged with the city and the intellect beneath the architecture as he knew he should have. Then he thought of that impulsive moment at the party where, for the briefest of seconds, his light flickered within the shadow of knowledge and learning and he felt the warm glow of respect in the room, but the truth was it was a moiety of substance, nothing more. He had hardly ever left the south side. Not met new people. Not had any discussions about the world or left an opinion hanging in a room that anyone ever listened seriously to, nor ever put himself in a position where he could patently be proved wrong.

If you don't run the race you can't ever lose. Right?

The rolling greyness which obscured the sun reflected his mood. He knew this was the only goodbye he could make and he knew he wanted to say more but something other told him that this thinness and distance would be all that the city would allow him.

He was hungry and so made to push himself up off the rock to descend but he caught the sight of a police car driving on the road below. He sat perfectly still and pulled the hood over his head. The police car stopped and pulled in. Kelly held his breath. The sharp focus of slopping out and avoiding sexual assault in Saughton Prison brought him back to his current dilemma. Two uniforms got out of the car and stood at the edge of the road and pointed at something. The hill slope blocked the view to all but the car and them from what they were pointing at. They then looked up and onto the craggy cliffs. Kelly guessed that he was all but a dot so stayed still. Then the two policemen waved their arms sharply, and walking forward toward a steep grassy bank.. About a dozen sheep appeared from behind a rocky outcrop and ran away from them. He relaxed. They got back in their car and drove off.

Chapter 38

Moving the Mountain

Friday 29th June 9:00am

"Look, big fella, if you don't want to answer any questions you just have to say *No comment.* That would be a start."

Nothing.

McQuarrie held eye contact on Sasquatch who seemed to be elsewhere. Jones leaned on the wall at the back of the interview room. A young uniform stood nervously at the door.

"That man you were holding was dead. He was beaten and bloodied badly. Why was that?"

Sasquatch, for the first time flickered. McQuarrie clocked this.

"Did you kill him?"

Nothing.

"A man is dead and it was you that was holding him. Did you kill him?"

Sasquatch twitched and looked into the middle distance somewhere near the floor. Remembering. McQuarrie saw the signs as Sasquatch began to heave slowly at first and then groan. McQuarrie got everybody out of the room. The bellows of Sasquatch were heard on every floor of the nick.

Jones approached McQuarrie back at her desk. "Maybe this is one for the shrinks, sir?"

"Maybe"

A voice from across the office called to him. "For you Jack"

He walked across and took the call. "DI McQuarrie."

The accounts department of Woodlands Brook had outlined fees outstanding for some of his treatment enquiring as to when they expected payment. He assured them discreetly he'd deal with it soon and call in, but everyone knew the probable subject of the call as they'd heard them before on a few occasions. He side glanced around the office but everyone had turned away from his discomfort back to their tasks and the discretion of camaraderie. He hung-up and began to think again.

"Did you see him react in there? Just before he started howling. What did I say? *The man you were holding was dead?*"

"Yes sir, "Jones said, "Maybe he just reacted to the word *dead?* There's no skint knuckles or bruising. Maybe he's not our man?"

"Maybe. If he's not maybe he saw something? So.... *thoughts* Jones?"

"He found him. He knew him and where he'd be? You said what he was like in the pub.

McQuarrie brightened. "Fancy a drink, Jones!"

"The pub?"

"Correct. Let the big man stew for an hour or two. Car please, Jones."

Chapter 39

Learning to Fly

"It's all about Roswell, really, you know. New Mexico. Crash. Chap told me when I was doing my Nash Service. Yankee chap. Met him in Germany. Fifty-three. Was there. They got the spaceship and they got the chaps that were flying it...well not *chaps*....ermm *beings,* space chappies...dead of course. Can't crash at several thousand miles an hour and not take a break or two, eh...even if you are from Zeta Reticulae?"

Kelly had been cornered by an obvious member of The Castle Trades clientele but with a surprisingly plummy, upper-class English accent. He'd introduced himself as Bartie. He'd sauntered along to Kelly when Kelly was about to launch into a sandwich he'd bought in a shop on the corner of Jeffrey Street, just off the High Street. Bartie wore a severely soiled suit and sported an unkempt thick thatch of hair and beard. They both leaned against a wall as tourists passed them on the pavement. Kelly gave him half. Bartie seemed glad to have an audience.

"....and they actually had the bodies. Said it was a weather balloon. Weather balloon! Ha! Absolute poppycock! But, you see... they'd already put out the word that it was a flying saucer to the press so had shot themselves in the foot, hadn't they just! Yes they had! Hadn't they just! Yes! Had indeed! This is lovely chicken! And so...you know....all this flying to the moon nonsense back in the seventies was just a charade, cloak and daggersome doings just to divert the attention from the truth. P'raps needs salt though? And there's the rub..*the truth,* the truth...what is the truth? Who knows the truth? What happened to them? The space ship? All the gubbins in the space ship. The *being* chappies were dead so they didn't know what they had. They didn't know. Ha! So what did they do? Gave it to the boffins. Got the boffin chaps to have a look, took a good long butchers at it all and didn't they just go and work it all out! Ha! They only worked it out! I'll have those crusts if you don't...ermm... worked it out and made their damned own flying thingies. Flying whatsits. Not the saucery type chaps but different with new propulsion. Not petrol...gasoline.... what they'd got from the space whatsit, thats what they used. Reverse gravity...millions of volts and then one can float..erm fly, actually."

Bartie looked around just to check the CIA weren't watching him. Then he changed his demeanour very quickly and seemed very sad.

"...and that's the thing, you see.... look around us at these contraptions that clog up our streets and contaminate our air...none of it is necessary."

Kelly jumped as Bartie then shouted violently,

"None of this is necessary!! None of it!" Kelly looked about as if to apologise for his friend and smiled at a few passers-by.

"We could live lives in comfort...free energy.... no pollution... ...televisions....light bulbs... radios....bacon slicers..... they know how to do it but they won't share it you see! Won't share it!"

Passers-by passed by as quickly as they could.

"If they'd shared it, if they thought of others, us, me and you, do you think I'd be hollering like a madman on the streets? Would I? I wouldn't be poor and I'd have a house. A house, damn you!!."

Two young female Spanish tourists threw fearful looks at Bartie and hurried past the *lunático apestoso*.

Kelly was still inclined to answer *yes*.

Bartie continued, "....but they don't do they? They hide it and use it for war. For war. And we know this. The governments of the world know this but they don't do anything. They pretend. Go along with the charade. They won't stick their necks out and say..."

And here, Bartie stepped into the middle of the pavement and spoke to a smartly dressed lady walking with her as she tottered by on her heels.

"Hey! We know you have the things we need to make our lives better, so give it to us. Give it to us!"

He returned to his previous tone as if nothing had occurred

"But they don't. We should stop wasting time and all get together and do something. Seize the day, carpe diem, and just do something. Well I'm the one that isn't going to waste any more time errr...sorry old chap I don't know your name....?"

"Giles." Lied Kelly.

"Giles. A sainted name! A cathedralic set of sounds! No I'm not wasting any more time and I'm going to *do something.* I'm waiting. Waiting for the right moment. The right time to reveal, myself. Reveal my secret, shock the world and make them listen."

Such passion and intrigue deserved the enquiry. "What's your secret?"

Bartie leaned in and scoured the street for any lurking spies in doorways, and then covertly said to Kelly,

"I can fly", and then nodded and smiled in confirmation to Kelly's raised eyebrows and shoved the rest of his sandwich into his mouth and quickly chewed then looked about again. This time as he looked down the street towards The Canongate and froze with a look of shock on his face. Breadcrusts hung from his mouth. Kelly turned to see what the source of such immediate anguish might be half guessing an apparition had arrived in Bartieworld.

Bartie grabbed Kelly and said,

"We must leave! They're here. They know! They know my secret and don't want me to reveal it to the world! They know I'm going to do something with my secret soon!"

Kelly went along with it but wanted to know more.

"Who are?"

"The tall men who have black coats and the book. My name is in it! Bartie Fortesque! They're here again. They're too close! Follow me, Giles!"

Bartie took off with surprising speed and agility.

Kelly chuckled. Then he saw Number One and Two looking around, carrying a bible and walking up The High Street. They ducked into a vennel between buildings and hurried down the hill to The Cowgate. He left Bartie cowering behind a large industrial bin who insisted that he *save himself* and made his way back to The Grassmarket.

Chapter 40

A Howler of a Name

"Sasquatch? I don't know." Norrie replied to McQuarrie, shrugging his shoulders.

"What about his name? What's his name, Norrie?"

"I don't know Jack. Not sure anyone knows. You know as much as we all do. He comes in here lays out a twenty and then drinks it. Why do you ask?"

"He was found on a bench in Middle Meadow Walk this morning with a dead man on his lap. A wino, apparently? Badly beaten. No ID and I can't get a cheep out of him. "

"Yeah...? That's not good."

"He was crying....and had a howl....*of course.*"

"You think it was him?"

"Well it's fair to say he's not stable so...."

"That's where you need to look."

"A stable? "I'm not looking for God, Norrie."

"Hilarious, Jack. You know what I mean."

"Where?"

"The Winos. They might know more than us. I've heard that when we shut he takes himself into their company. He doesn't look or smell like one of them so I'm guessing he lives..*somewhere?* Ask them. There's a fella with one arm you might look for. He might know."

"Name?"

"Isaac. Tries to get in here, now and again. Stinks. Ask him."

"*Where...* will he be?"

"They hang about on The Meadows..."

"I know that, Norrie! Specifically?"

"How the fuck would I know, Jack! If they're not there then try The Grassmarket. Fuckin' shithole of a place. Always has been and always will be. Do you want a drink?"

"Yes. But no. Work then play. What time do the ....you know....May and Spider....Bullet, come in? They're always here before me."

"Half six? Seven. Sometimes earlier. Depends how much money they've got."

"When was the last time you saw Kells?" McQuarrie said.

"Been days, now. You know why, right?"

"Megan?"

"Got it in one, Jack. Smart arsed-fucker was sniffing around her. You see him? I put him straight. Took great delight in telling him she'd gone."

McQuarrie was inclined to devilment and said, "Kelly's a nice lad, isn't he?"

"He's a shiftless no-user! That's what he is! You're not seriously saying I should've encouraged her to court that fucker?"

McQuarrie declined an answer.

"What was that fellas name?"

"Which one?"

"The one armed Wino?"

"Isaac."

Chapter 41

Headline News

Kelly sat in The Grassmarket in plain view but hopefully out of sight. His beard had naturally started to grow and now his rugged unshaven look actually matched the colour of the dishevelled wig he was wearing and began to appear entirely the part he was playing. It was a still morning and the traffic rumbled past on the cobbles as he sat on a bench in one of the fenced off green spaces that were strung along the middle of the wide thoroughfare. Only a few of his homeless comrades were dotted about the place. Some hung around in front of doss-house sitting on the window ledge and there was one sat at The Bow Well. He began to formulate his final his trip out of the *The Castle Trades Hotel* and out to the airport and then wished he had a watch. It began to drizzle, that summer fine rain that not many ran from or rushed to seek shelter from, however he pulled the wig covertly down a bit further and lifted the hood on his coat but he was partly under the shade of a tree in full foliage so didn't care that much. He was bored and wished he had something to do. He spun his head around and looked up at the castle and thought of his bag secreted in the rocks beneath it. He looked across to the large heavy doors of the doss-house and considered the irony of him having several thousand pounds in the lining of his coat. Then he sat up quickly and realised he'd forgotten about Joe's business bank card. He knew there was one of those machines outside the bank on The North Bridge. He fished around the inside pocket of his coat and took it out. It was wrapped in the piece of paper that came separately with the number he needed. He was nervous about this and wondered if the card would somehow alert the staff inside as to who was using the machine. He had another ten thousand pounds at his disposal and was scared to try to get it, however he knew it would have been a waste of energy and time having gone through the whole rigmarole of being Joe.

There was a queue. He didn't want anyone watching his inept floundering with this technology so he waited for it to die down. Someone handed him a ten pence piece, which he looked at for a second before realising this was a decent ploy while he plucked up the courage to try the machine. A few more people used the machine and he tried to have a look at how they did it, which buttons they pressed, where the money came from. He figured that one out because everyone bar none always held their hand at a slot on the right hand side waiting for it to come but before that they used the same hand to pull something above it. Maybe it was a lever you had to pull before the money could come out? He didn't know. Some people realised he was craning to see and covered their business from him. Then he asked them for ten pence. Most hurried past him. Some stood counting their cash and just ignored him. One old woman smelling of lavender and who seemed entirely *au fait* with the whole shooting match, blatantly counted her money in front of him, plopped it in her handbag and then squarely told him to fuck off. *Bit of a surprise* he thought. Nice old lady, looks nice, smells nice...mouth like a sewer. The world is changing. The street was quieter now and the machine vacant. He went for it and took out the card. He scanned the machine and saw where it went in and tried to push it into the slot. He couldn't get it in. He tried to push harder. Nothing. He tried turning it over. That didn't work.

"You have to put it in face up." A voice behind him said.

Kelly turned and Steven from the Theatre Skills course was there looking as neat and tidy and smelling delightful, as he ever did. He panicked slightly inside and then without thought affected a gravelly rasp to his voice, turned his face away and said,

"Oh right. Ah'm new tae a' this mate. Cheers. Which way?"

Steven, without judgement, showed him and then Kelly pushed it in and a motor from somewhere sucked it into the bowels of the machine. Kelly got a fright and pulled back his hand but then sighed, relieved. The screen lit up and asked him to enter his pin. He didn't have a pin? What the fuck did it want with a pin? Was this supposed to arrive from the bank, as well? They didn't send a frigging pin! Another flush of panic engulfed him as his head searched around for a pin that was perhaps lying around nearby the screen. He turned back to Steven, who had retreated to a respectful distance. A fat middle-aged business man joined the queue behind Steven. Steven smiled and stepped forward to look at the screen.

"You have to enter your number. Four digits?"

Kelly involuntarily said *yes, yes,* in his own voice and delved into his pocket and dragged out the numbers, checking nobody could see them. He hit the keypad four times and then pressed enter as he was instructed on the screen.

"Cheers...again." Steven retreated again with his perrennial smile and then discreetly had another look at the face at the machine. Kelly was looking non-plussed again because it now asked him if he wanted to change his number? There was a *Yes* or *No* choice.

Was changing the number the right thing to do? Did everyone change their number? If he didn't change the number maybe it wouldn't work? Arrgh!

"Oh for Christ sakes! Hurry up, will you!" the businessman shouted. Then in all calmness Steven turned to him and said,

"He's obviously new to this. Would you say that to me if I was struggling with it? Probably not. So what you're doing is judging him, mate. Give him some space."

"Well get in there and help him again, I've got a meeting in half an hour!"

"I will only if he wants me to." Steven said turning to Kelly who was already nodding.

Steven joined Kelly at the screen and guided him through the process of withdrawing the day's limit of £300 which was belched from the machine. Steven explained that he could only take that amount out each day which Kelly said he was ok with and then grabbed the cash and thanked Steven still in his raspy voice.

"About bloody time!" Said Fatso behind them.

Kelly glowered at him and intuitively decided that he was one of life's bastards, a money orientated twat who cared little for anyone but himself and his continuing corpulence. He counted out five ten pound notes from the wad, turned his face away and thrust them into Steven's chest and rasped,

"Thanks for helpin' me."

Steven naturally and vociferously declined but Kelly was already walking away, however stopped at the businessman, and brought out the ten pence piece he'd been given and thrust it into his hand and said,

"Thank you, Taylor. You can fuck off somewhere, have a heart attack and die alone now if the hearths are clean and the fires are set... *Fatty.*"

Kelly crossed the road and was halted in his tracks. The headlines on the day's *Daily Mirror* was written large before him on a board outside a newsagents.

Sir Clive Harrow in gay sex abuse scandal

Whaaaattt!! He was stunned. Bemused. What was this? He didn't need this. What happened? Who....? This wasn't him? He hadn't done anything. Instinctively he looked around expecting to see them, One and Two, across the road. This was bad. Very bad.

Chapter 42

Mac's Favourite

Jones pulled the car up outside Big George's bookies and McQuarrie got out. Jones stayed where she was but then rapped the window and rolled it down as McQuarrie was heading for the door.

"No routine today, *Jack?*"

McQuarrie turned and looked at her and said nothing for a

moment.

"No, *Claire*. Not today. Today is the day, for good or for ill, I do something about this situation."

He went inside. Claire smiled. It was quiet. Big George was almost hidden behind the grill. He stood up and saw McQuarrie.

"A'right Jack. Didn't think we'd see you for a while, not since you wished me well for the summer holidays last time you were in?"

"What's my tally, George?" McQuarrie by-passed the sarcasm.

"Well now....lets have a wee look..." he said lifting his large ledger. " Oh, it doesn'y make good reading Jack. D'ye want me jist to write it down for ye or shall I say it out loud?"

"Just tell me, please George."

"Just shy o' thirteen hunner. Twelve eighty one...*and.. let me see...seventy four pence.*"

"So two eighteen and twenty six pence takes me to fifteen?"

"Yer quicker than me Jack. It does."

"Give me that tick, George."

"Jack...Jack.....I would love to because yer a top customer and I have to confess that even though yer plod, yer a decent plod... but I'm guessin' yer chasin' yer losses....."

"Save me the sermon George. Yes or no? I need it. Now. Give me that tick. Give me that and then no more before I clear it. Do this for me George and there'll be no problems with any licence reviews. I'll sort it. Well? Don't make me beg."

"Actually, it might be worth the money just to see that for once, Jack. We've known each other for years but yer just a crabbit auld bastard these days and I don't recall your enquiries as to my good lady wife's health."

"You're not married, George." McQuarrie frowned bemused.

"I am now, Jack." He said flatly holding up his wedding band. "Nice wee do in March. That's how interested you are in me."

McQuarrie sighed. "Congratulations, George. How's your wife?"

"Ina ....is very well thank you for askin' Jack. How's yer dad?"

McQuarrie's dejected sigh was enough to answer George who got the story.

"Two eighteen and twenty-six pence, Jack? For old times sake and as ye were so nice askin' about ma missus! Then no more. Where's it goin?"

"Have you heard of a horse called.. *Soldier Sveyk?"*

"No. Got a tip?"

"Sort of. Can you check today's runners on the list please George."

George sighed heavily and returned after a few moments with the negative. " No. So...?"

"Favourite. Next race."

Chapter 43

Getting the Bullet

He dipped in and out of the vennels that fed off The High Street and made his way from The Cowgate back around to The

Grassmarket and sat back on the bench he'd vacated earlier. He was a bag of nerves. His insides were churning and he knew he had to get something to eat soon. He really wanted to get a room in a hotel but knew that was too dangerous and in his current state he doubted any amount of money would get him in even the worst. He reached down and picked up an empty brown bottle. It was *Four Crown,* a sweet but potent favourite of the vagrant chaps which saw off afternoons nicely until *The Castle Trades* would be open again at six. He held it close to his chest just as he'd seen others do in expectation of larceny. He was sweating underneath the wig but he looked the part and kept scanning the broad square for black coats and bibles, however it wasn't them but a green Ford Cortina he immediately recognised pull up just outside *The Castle Trades* doors.

McQuarrie, who looked patently upset about something, got out of the car quickly and crushed up a piece of paper and threw it away, followed by Jones. McQuarrie dished out some abrupt instructions and strode away from her into the broad square. Jones knocked loudly on the doss- house door looking back to McQuarrie striding purposefully away and seemed to expel a heavy sigh of relief. Then the door opened and she went in. McQuarrie turned to look if she'd entered yet and then stopped near a fence and moved uncertainly, agitatedly, seemingly not knowing where to rest his gaze or hands. He tapped the top of a fence post, turning again and also breathed heavily but then seemed to settle himself, deciding to focus and regained his resolution to the mission. Kelly wasn't in the broad cobbled square but under a tree, nearby and in the shade. He slowly started to lift his legs up and onto the bench whilst ensuring the bottle was in full view and pulled up his hood into the guise of recumbent piss-head. He peered out of the hood into the sunlight watching McQuarrie walk up to The BowWell and talk to a couple of tramps.

The conversation included McQuarrrie indicating an arm, to which a shake of the head was returned and then the vagrants shuffling off quickly. He saw McQuarrie go into *The White Hart* pub and exit after a minute. Then he turned to scan the area again. He saw McQuarrie shift his view down towards Kelly's bench and shade his eyes to see better, then shifted his head looking to the bench and then started out towards it. Kelly's heart began to thump. He didn't know what to do. Run? Stay and brass it out as a poleaxed wino? He'd see past the wig. He knew he would.

A bin lorry rumbled into The Grassmarket close to where Kelly was and a group of men quickly leapt from where they were hanging on to every part of it and began to lift the steel bins that were left on the street for them but now obscured McQuarrie's view to the bench.

A familiar face picked up a bin from the kerb twenty feet from Kelly.

"Bullet?" he said quietly to himself and then louder, "Bullet? Bullet!!"

He leapt up and stayed the other side of the slowly moving lorry from McQuarrie and ran up to Bullet.

"Bullet! It's me."

Bullet was a bemused and quite unsure of who *me* was?. The only place he was called Bullet was in *The Old Duke* but he didn't recognise this tousled, black-haired, unshaven, Parka-wearing man accosting him. He recognised the voice but couldn't place him. Kelly saw this and pulled the wig up and smiled.

"It's me...Kells, Bullet! Look." He said keeping up with the crawling lorry. Clangs of steel on steel and the roar of the engine made Kelly raise his voice. "Kells!!"

The penny dropped and Bullet looked him up and down. "Kells! What...? You look..."

Kelly spared him the burden of cogent thought quickly and urgently weaving another lie.

"It's a long story..mate, but the short of it is I've been asked to take the lead in a new film that going to be shot in the autumn and it requires some research, which is what I'm doing now and there's a couple of people knocking around with video cameras who are documenting my research as a homeless person, but I'm tired, hungry and really need a shower and a roof, mate and they won't let me go back to my place. They'll be watching it. But I've done enough research and just need somewhere to lay low for a couple of days. How about it...Bul...*Ford?* Just a couple of days and then I'm gone. Back home."

Bullet thought and picked up steel bins while doing so which impressed Kelly at this ridiculous moment.

"I don't know, Kells.....?"

"Hundred quid.....Bullet! I'll give you a hundred quid!"

Bullet suddenly brightened.

"It'll be the floor, Kells... I haven't got two..."

"Fine!! Absolutely fine! Where'd you live?"

"3 West Cross Causeway. Flat 6."

"Give me your key!"

Bullet spun the circular bin back onto the pavement with expert timing and jumped back onto the slow moving lorry clinging onto some part of its exterior while he fished around in his pocket and threw Kelly his key.

"I'm back at five!" He shouted, as the lorry pulled away and Kelly disappeared up the West Port and out of sight.

Inside the doss-house Isaac was delighted with the attentions of Jones.

"My...you're a pretty-faced lickle bit o' stuff and no mistake, aren't cha. Hiv ye got a boyfriend? Hiv ye?" He drawled salaciously at her whilst lookin' her up and down, groanin slightly and using his single hand to wipe drops of spittle around his mouth.

"I'm disabled so they let me in early for a wee lie down. I like a lie down. D'ye like a lie down yerself? Why doncha lie down here wit me, Pretty Face. The one arm I have left will cuddle ye as gud as if der were the two!"

He cackled like a villain from a dark Romanian fairy-tale. Jones had to play him.

"That's a lovely offer, Isaac, but I'll have to politely decline. I'm at work you see....difficult. In any other circumstances..?. Do you know the big fella I'm talking about?"

"I do but I'm tellin' ye nottin' until ye say me name again. G'wan say it again for me, Pretty Face. I haven't heard a soft word from a doxy like yerself for a long time, now, an' me name'll suit me nicely."

Jones mustered all the lascivious tones she could spare in the utterance of that one word.

"What..... *Isaac?*"

He cackled again and rocked back and forth.

"So...the big fella?"

"I'll settle for a kiss. One kiss. Den I'll tell ye!"

"Again....Isaac...I'm on duty but what I do have is a crisp ten pound note, instead. Will that do,.....*Isaac?*"

It did and a fleeting peck on a rancid, one-armed, dosser was professionally circumvented.

McQuarrie waited for the lorry to leave revealing an empty bench. He looked around bemused then met the face of Jones right next to him.

"We have a name and an address, Sir." She smiled, delighted to give him some good news.

"He was in there?"

"Yes, Sir. One arm, like you said." Still smiling determinedly.

McQuarrie turned sharply and strode back towards the car. He threw a few words of observation back to Jones as he did so,

"If he was a boxer I'd likely back him!"

Chapter 44

Along Came a Spider

Friday 29th June 5:30pm

Kelly sat down on a wooden chair at a large, white, plastic garden table in the kitchen area of 3F6 West Cross Causeway. This room was both kitchen and living area and guessed it was where he would be sleeping that night. Surrounding him were a varying assortment of things Bullet had apparently decided to fill his life with, things that nobody else apparently wanted, saving them from the fate of landfill.

A blue sequinned ball-gown hung on the back of the door suspended by a wire coat-hanger. Next to Kelly's feet was a one-eyed, stuffed fox with a semi-detached leg which hung on determinedly at a strange angle and only by the slight attachment of the animal's quite patchy pelt. He pushed the leg gently and it swung like a pendulum. Appropriate he thought. *Your time's nearly up.* Along the floor protruding from beneath the couch was a deep green leather-bound collection of *The Encyclopaedia Brittanica.* Again, appropriately ironic, given the cephalic inabilities of his host. He stood up and reached down to a stack of framed pictures leaning against the wall and pulled them forward to see. Gustave Munch's *The Scream* alarmingly accosted him, followed by the bare backside of a naked girl about to step from a paved seafront into the briny. The next one seemed familiar. There were cartoons in thick black lines behind the glass. Four individual cartoons. One of a tall-hatted moustachioed army officer complete with sword, looked like First World War or earlier, dressing down a very scruffy, unshaven and corpulent private in an ill-fitting uniform. There were three others all depicting this private soldier in varying situations but managing to smile inanely throughout his travails. Kelly looked at the back and tore the tape holding the pictures in. The backing came away easy enough but he left them in their frame. You never know, Bullet might have an appointed place for it on his wall. Speaking of Bullet, it was now nearly five o' clock. Kelly had had a look in his fridge beholding not much. He had the idea to suggest Bullet go for a take-away with himself bearing the cost, because he could. He very could. He hadn't eaten since his fling with Bartie and his aviatory secret and was hungry.

The sound of the door lock jostling with a key brightened Kelly no end and actually was looking forward to Bullet coming in and him treating him to a slap up meal as well as his hundred quid. He was tired of running and hiding, tired of waiting and this closed door was welcome respite. He stood smiling, glad of the arrival of the worker, drudgery done and a welcome face.

The door opened and Spider walked in.

Chapter 45

A Bloody Hero

Friday 29th June 5:30pm

Sasquatch sat in the seat at the table facing McQuarrie. Jones stood nearby and two uniforms attended the door. McQuarrie looked down at the information in front of him and looked up.

"Your name is Alexander Paterson, aged thirty-nine. Is that correct?"

Sasquatch looked at the table. McQuarrie had another go.

"19 Moncrief Terrace. Ex-Black Watch. Served in Belize and The Falklands. In receipt of a services pension. We've had a look around...sorry, however necessary. Correct?"

Nothing. McQuarrie was in no mood to pussy-foot around.

"You were seen carrying one Donal Driscoll over The Meadows and then seated on Middle Meadow Walk cradling him, to which two of our officers, when inspecting the situation, found that he was dead. Did you kill him?"

Still nothing. McQuarrie tried again. "Alexander? Alex? Lex...*Lexy?* Sandy?"

Sasquatch looked up quickly at McQuarrie and then back quickly to the table.

"Is that it? Is that what they called you in the regiment? Sandy? Sandy Paterson?"

Sasquatch seemed to draw his head from somewhere else and this time looked at McQuarrie.

"Sandy....listen to me..." Sasquatch tried to return his eyes to the table but McQuarrie rounded the table and met his eyeline, "....listen to me Sandy, Sandy Paterson, look at me, look at me, Sandy, my name is Detective Inspector McQuarrie and you are in

Saint Leonards police station....do you understand?"

Sasquatch looked at him for a few seconds, turned his head and looked at Jones,

"This is Detective Constable Jones and these are two officers of this nick...ermm..police station...now, Sandy... this next question is very important...listen to me, ... the man you carried in your arms, the man you cradled on the bench... did you kill him?"

Sasquatch started to twitch his face and then he started to rub and wipe his hands on the table as he started to remember. McQuarrie had seen this before and knew he was back wherever he went to. He looked across at Jones who quickly approached Sasquatch.

"Sandy! Sit still and listen. She put her hands over his to try and get him to focus but then Sasquatch envisioned something other and started to heave slightly. McQuarrie knew what was in the post immediately and leapt forward.

"Take your hands away, Claire!! Quickly!"

Jones drew back unnerved by McQuarrie's determination.

McQuarrie grabbed him by the shoulders as the heaving got deeper and turned him in his chair to face him.

"No! No! Not this time! Listen! Sandy! Sandy Paterson, listen to me!"

McQuarrie took him by the chaps of his beard and pulled his own face in to his.

"Mr Paterson! Paterson.... don't go there...stay here with me..."

McQuarrie had an epiphanous thought and his eyes went up left for a second then he stood back sharply from Sasquatch straightening his back and barked,

"Stand up Soldier! Name, rank and serial number!"

Sasquatch leapt up. His chair flew against the wall. He was enormous. The two uniforms shit a brick and swallowed hard hoping they didn't have to tackle him. Jones went back against the safety of the wall. McQuarrie was shaken at how quickly it worked.

"Paterson, A. Corporal, 2496725, Sir!" Sasquatch belted out.

"Stand to attention when you are addressing me Corporal Paterson!" McQuarrie barked again.

"Yes Sir!" Sasquatch straightened and hammered his heel down onto the floor.

"I spoke to you earlier, Corporal Paterson, I described to you a situation in which you were carrying a man in your arms and cradling his dead body. Do you recall, Paterson?"

"Yes, Sir!"

"That man, Paterson....did you kill him?"

Sasquatch fought the back tears and his desire to flee this dutiful request as his face began to contort. His words now twisted in his throat, dropping painfully into the room woven with sorrow.

"No, Sir...*yes*...yes! I did.... I moved the mortar...forward...we had to go forward....take it to them...*Jamie*..Private Caplan....was behind it....I didn't know sir..I never saw him in the mud...in the grass....he was exposed. I moved the cover. I gave the order. We left him there... it was me...me..*Jamie..Jamie...*"

Water now dripped into the big man's beard with cathartic regularity. Jones, now aware of his story and pain, professionally fought her own welling humanity becoming steadily impressed with her boss's abilities.

"What happened, Corporal Paterson? What happened to Private Caplan?"

Sasquatch was suffering, "He took one, Sir. Shrapnel. No cover, Sir. I moved it! It was me, Sir...I moved it....his guts were hanging out...I'm to blame, Sir....I killed him...it was me....Jamie...Jamie..."

"You listen to me, Corporal Paterson..." McQuarrie morphed into Sigmund Freud. ".....You did not kill Private Caplan. Did you? Who did, Paterson? Who was it that killed Caplan?"

Sasquatch bubbled like a child imperceptibly trying to say that he did but McQuarrie leapt in again.

"No Corporal Paterson! Not you. Who? Who were you fighting! Say it! Say their name!"

Sasquatch gurgled out something that sounded like *Argies.*

McQuarrie led the big man's head towards the light. "One more time, please Corporal Paterson, that wasn't quite clear?"

This time Sasquatch said it clearer, "The Argies, Sir." and wiped his face, quickly returning to attention..

"That is correct, Paterson. The Argentinians. The Argies. They killed him. Not you. And if you had not have moved that mortar forward many more than Caplan would have fallen. But you were in charge, weren't you Corporal Paterson?"

"Yes, Sir."

"...and you made a decision, you knew you had to do something, do something that would ensure the safety of the unit and the battle objective and in doing something you saved the lives of many more than Caplan. My god, you're a bloody hero, man! What are you?"

"A bloody hero, Sir."

"A bloody hero, Corporal Paterson! A hero that no longer has blood on his hands. None."

McQuarrie quickly dipped into his pocket and took out a white handkerchief.

"Take this, Paterson. Take it and clean your hands." McQuarrie held it towards him. "Go on, Paterson. Take it!"

Sasquatch lifted his hand and took the hanky.

McQuarrie quietly said. "Wipe them clean, Corporal Paterson. That's an order."

Sasquatch quietly sobbed and slowly dabbed and smeared the snot rag across his palms wiping away whatever imaginary blood he saw there, then held the handkerchief by a corner as if to avoid his scarlet visions once more befouling his soul. McQuarrie turned to a uniform who had a slack-jawed stare on Sasquatch, and told him to fetch a lighter from the front desk.

Twenty-five seconds later, McQuarrie set light to it and let Sasquatch watch as he dropped the remains on the floor and beat the remains under the sole of his shoe telling him that the stains were gone forever. Then he said,

"One more thing, Corporal Paterson, I've asked a couple of people to come and speak to me about something but I'm afraid I'm rather busy for the next few hours but I have recommended you as my first able man that I trust entirely and to stand in my stead. Can I trust you, Paterson?"

Sasquatch softly said that he could.

"Good man, Corporal. They're just going to ask you a few questions and I'd like you to tell them all you know, if you would Paterson. Do you understand?"

"Yes Sir." He said with increased volume.

"You will answer honestly and clearly, representing me and the regiment to the best of your ability, Corporal Paterson?"

"Yes, Sir" A quiet resolution.

McQuarrie looked at Jones. She braced herself for...*something?*

"This is Captain Jones. *Medical Corps.* I have to leave now but you will remain to attention and Captain Jones will stand you down and when she does so you will be comfortable and coherent.... and then you will have a seat and wait for the man I expect with the questions. He will be here shortly after. Remember, honest and clear. Good man, Corporal. Bloody hero."

McQuarrie then surprised the room in saluting Sasquatch who sharply saluted back. McQuarrie turned and left the room mouthing *stand down* to Jones. He indicated the two uniforms should follow him. Jones was left eerily alone with a mountain of a man awaiting her command. How she wished it would always be this way.

"Corporal Paterson......*stand down!*" she said as authoritatively as a Captain in the Medical Corps could.

Sasquatch thumped his heel on the floor again and spun ninety degrees and then relaxed, saw the chair and sat down.

The door opened sharply and McQuarrie came in smiling, in role, and this time without his coat on, greeted Sasquatch saying his name and shaking his hand and introducing himself. Sasquatch was haltingly communicative but there in the room, all the same.

"Sandy Paterson?"

McQuarrie maintained the smile as Sasquatch said "yes Sir" and struck while the iron was hot.

"Recently, a man was assaulted on The Meadows and died as a result, Sandy. Do you know who did this?"

"Yes Sir." Sasquatch slowly said.

Jones looked over at McQuarrie who understood her as she sat down at the table and gently asked,

"Was it you, Sandy?"

He looked at them both for a few seconds.

"No, Ma'am."

"It wasn't you, Sandy?" she continued, "We found you with the body. Maybe you can't remember....maybe...."

"Kells, Ma'am." Sasquatch flatly interrupted.

McQuarrie sat up. "Sorry, did you say *Kells?*"

"Yes Sir."

"Kells? From the pub? The Old Duke?"

"Yes, Sir."

Jones attempted to restore the gentle touch.

"He killed the man you were found with on the bench?"

"I don't know, Ma'am."

McQuarrie became patently frustrated. Jones arrived again.

"Then who did Kells kill, Sandy. You tell us." She softly said.

"The crying boy with the bush. He whipped Kells when he was against the tree. Kells hit him with the bottle. Then he took his shoes.....took his shoes, Ma'am... when he was crying."

McQuarrie had to push harder, "Our man...*the crying boy*...didn't die there, did he?"

"Walked away...like he'd been shot, Sir."

"Which direction, Sandy? Where did he go?" Jones pushed tentatively.

"Up..."

"...the slope?" Jones leaned towards him excluding McQuarrie who got the message.

"Graveyard."

"Greyfriars!" McQuarrie snapped. Jones's disdain was apparent and threw a look to McQuarrie.

She maintained her tone, "You followed him, Sandy?"

"Donal said he could take his money if he fell over."

"But he didn't fall over?"

"No. The men with the black coats helped him."

"Men with black coats?"

"Yes."

"How did they help?"

"Took him into the graveyard."

"Did you see them in the graveyard?"

"No Donal left. I went home...went home, Sir."

Just then there was a knock on the door and McQuarrie opened it gently and was told he had a call at the desk. No doubt another reminder from Woodlands Brook Care Home about the fees.

Back at the front desk he picked up the receiver and sighed.

"DI McQuarrie."

An urbane English accent said, "The Greyfriars Body? A name. Leonard Kelly. Compliments of Her Majesty's Government." Then it hung up.

He rushed back to the interview room and loudly said,

"That's enough, for me Jones. We have him." then went out as quick as he entered. Jones remained and gently said to Sasquatch,

"Thank you, Sandy....Corporal Paterson. You can go home now and if you think......."

McQuarrie's voice resounded from the front desk.

"My magic is spun, Jones, he'll be fine now. Car!"

Chapter 46

Dungeons...

Spider was as shocked as he was. There was something of an unspoken stand off until Spider decided to smile and say,

"Kells. Haven't seen you for a while. How are you?" he said remaining where he was at the door.

Nonplussed Kelly, said, "Yeah...good, Spider. Doing okay. You?"

"You know me. As even as the day is long." Spider replied.

Kelly was the first to address the fact that he had a key.

"You've got a key?"

"Err...yeah. He gave me it because I get home earlier than him so I can get set up."

Kelly nodded not really knowing what was to be set up?

"Set up?"

Spider lifted a box from the plastic bag he was carrying,

"Dungeons and Dragons."

Kelly turned his head to view the box a bit better and enquired,

"Sorry....Dungeons and....?"

".....Dragons. It's a new game. We play it. Me and Ford. We like it."

"A game?" Kelly asked.

"Yes."

"Board game?"

"Yes...well sort of. Erm....Did Ford ask you to come and play?"

"No. I'm...er...just going to crash here with Bull..erm, *Ford* for a couple of nights. Got a bit of a situation at the moment. I can't go back to my flat."

"Has it flooded? Burst pipe?"

He was tempted to say *yes* but he'd spun Bullet some research bullshit about being the lead in a film, which, of course, had an egotistical bent to it and that Bullet would swallow it quite easily, however it might be more difficult with Spider.

"Actually, Spider....I'm in a bit of soapy..."

Spider frowned.

"Soapy....?"

"Bubble. Trouble. Or *soapy trouble* as Bullet might say. He affected a small laugh.

"What sort of trouble, Kells?" Spider asked.

"Well, Spider..*mate*... a while back I was asked if I wanted to earn a few quid extra doing not much really, or so I thought. I was taking packages to a few places and coming back with envelopes....full of money. I was quite naive about it all, really, or more like I just buried my head in the sand because in my heart of hearts, I knew it was a bit dodgy. I was delivering messages and waiting for replies between business addresses, sometimes and then get paid for that, too and I was doing alright, you know?"

Spider nodded, pleasingly for Kelly.

"Well, a couple of days ago I was on down in Stockbridge coming home with a big envelope of money, early morning it was and I saw someone getting mugged by two junkies, well that's what they looked like to me, and I thought that if that ever happened to me there would be no way I could tell the police because they'd want to know where the money came from and all that, so I had this idea to tell the people that were sending me on the errands that I'd been mugged and keep the money. And I did. I kept it...."

"How much was it, Kells?"

"Five grand." Kelly quietly said.

"Five grand!!" Spider yelped.

"Keep it down, Spider!"

"Sorry, Kells. *Five grand?* he whispered.

"Yeah. I phoned them, well him..."

"Who?" Spider quickly asked.

"Dixie McCandlish."

Spider's jaw dropped. All of Edinburgh had heard of the exploits of Dixie McCandlish, however, not this fictional one.

"I know... I know... I put those marks on my face myself, Spider."

"So the dog, Lenni's alive?"

Kelly forgot about that bit. "I took him to my Mum's place in Livingston. She has the time...you know?"

Spiser nodded. "Yeah...I get it.... but what about McCandlish?"

"I told him I'd been mugged but he didn't care. He was well pissed off and then he told me that it was me who was now in debt to him and that he wanted his money or they would do something to incriminate me. Set me up. Frame me for something."

"Like what?" Spider was wide-eyed.

"He said, he'd get his mob to put a body, a corpse in my flat and then call the law. More than that, they had been paying off the police to keep them sweet, anyway, so they'd just do me for murder. They're all in on it together.....McCandlish and the police. They don't care as long as the money keeps coming in. They're looking for me, now as well, the police. You know Mr McQuarrie that drinks in The Duke?"

"Yeah?" Spider was hooked.

"Him."

"No!"

"Yeah. He's one of them and now he's looking for me, too. I know too much. I could put them away for years if I blabbed."

"That was what the wee book was, probably, the one he always writes in in the pub. Writing the names of the crooks who were to pay him." Spider excitedly said.

"Exactly that, Spider. But I panicked."

"How?"

"I got rid of the money."

"Where?"

"I gave most of it to charity. The Salvation Army."

Spider's eyes widened and said, "I've seen them! Black coats and bibles! Two of them."

Kelly's eyes widened. "You've seen them? Where?"

"I passed them coming here, Kells. Down on South Clerk Street."

"Well, I don't want them to see me either, mate because they can identify me."

"What are you goin' to do, Kells?"

"I have to leave, Spider. I have to disappear. But I'm going to lay low here until I can slope off.
Forever."

He enjoyed that dramatic one word addendum.

" Errm.. Spider...I couldn't tell Bul...*Ford* the truth. I reckoned it would scare him, so if he asks me about being in a film about homeless people just go along with it, will you?"

Spider looked sympathetically at him and then smiled and said. "Of course! You'll be okay here, but first you're goin' to play D and D with Ford and me!".

Kelly smiled. How hard could a board game be?

Chapter 47

Hot Bath

Friday 29th June 6:30pm

The door had been rapped a number of times and by now the presence of the police cars in the street and the amount of uniforms in the stairwell rushing up had brought out the neighbours. Two uniforms swung their battering-ram and the door crashed open and jumped out of the way to let other uniforms go in first but they were met by an unholy stink that had them all gagging. McQuarrie covered his mouth with a hanky and walked in shouting *Police, Mr Kelly, Leonard Kelly, Police* all the way to the top of the hall and then surveyed the carnage of his living room, abandoned clothes everywhere and wrecked couch. There was also a stink of piss. The stuffing of the couch was strewn around the room resting on piles of books as if they had just been freed from the straw softening their journeys in packing cases.

Jones called him back to the bathroom to make sense of a bathful of compost. McQuarrie didn't have to do much dusting away of the top layer before he felt the bin-bags and then the papable outline of a human form. He lifted a hand and dusted away the compost then tore the plastic from her head revealing first her forehead, then hair and at last her face was revealed, eyes half closed. A voice behind McQuarrie quietly said,

"Sandra?"

And then he got louder, "No! Sandra Sandra!!!"

The Pumping Tracksuit was forcibly removed by the uniforms and up to his flat all the while emotionally calling her name.

McQuarrie and Jones spoke to the desk back at the nick and a description was put out again. Then, somehow, as if they were expecting this, a couple of reporters arrived and so they fought them off for half an hour. They waited for forensics to finish and nosed around in the stairwell and back drying green, where they also found the putrefying remains of Lenni.

Chapter 48

......and Dragons

Kelly had insisted on paying for two dozen cans of beer and two bottles of whisky which had lubricated the early evening very well. They used these to wash down the Chinese food he had also bought for them and now Spider and Bullet were properly shitfaced and in the middle of the game. However, Bullet had a green velour, full-length hooded gown on with extremely wide sleeves and a pointed wizard's hat and was waving a wooden spatula from his cutlery drawer, which sufficed in the absence of a proper wizard's wand saying that at this point in the game he was going to cast a *dingly spell.*

Spider had a black cheap nylon gown tied at his neck and false black fingernails and had flattened his head with water. Not much more was required to create *The Master.*

Kelly had been furnished with a false ginger beard and a Noddy hat and something that was intended to look like a leather jerkin but was actually the tackiest of plastic which crackled when he moved, and then informed he was an Ork from Driddshire-in-the-Marshes who was on a quest to take a secret with him to another land but first was confronted with some ridiculous situation he needed to pass beforehand.

Bullet stood up and moved the floppy front of the hat out of his eyes.

"Safur the Ork...." he slurred to Kelly who had been secretly not drinking and pretending he was getting pissed with them and so unsurprisingly really didn't want to do any of this.

"You have entered a dusty old tomb and there is a sarc...scophaggy...stone grave thing...an' in it is the Lady Asdran who was put to sleep for a thousand years by ... him!"

Bullet pointed accusingly at Spider who raised his whisky, smiled and said *Sorry*.

"You must wake her to find out which way you should go because she has the second sight but you don't know the secret rhyme. But it is written somewhere near. But where? What do you do?"

Kelly had watched, Bullet, *The Dungeon Master,* take Spider through a situation earlier and then thrown a dice of many sides, which apparently had the number to an answer in a book, it was all a pile of shit, he thought, full of fairytale bollocks with gnomes and magic rivers and quite dark satanic undertones that no adult should be near never mind kids and besides, they'd made him dress up. Bullet was doing voices that quite frankly embarrassed Kelly, and he seemed quite uninhibited by it all but then that's what a lot of whisky can do for you. Kelly guessed these two had been doing this for some time, but quite frankly, should know better.

However, he had a chance to play the drunk card and slurred

slightly.

"I pull out my sword...."

"You're an Ork!" Bullet interrupted, "You can't have a sword....Sorry"

"Can I have a drink?" he asked.

"Yes. Drinking is allowed!" They all took a large draught of whatever poison they had.

Kelly continued, "I drink this which is a potion that gives me the power to make my hands as magic as....lots of magicky things and I magic myself a really big hammer...which is magic, as well."..."

"Check!" Spider shouted

"Hang on, Safur!" and he threw the many-sided dice, checked a book and then said, "Yes...you can! Carry on."

"....an' then I knock fuck out of her stone grave thingy and throw in an alarm clock that goes up to a thousand years, she hears the alarm go off, wakes up an' has a pot o' strong coffee. Bingo., she's up!"

"Ah, ah, ah....Worrabout the rhyme?" Spider smiled. Kelly sighed but humoured him.

"That's carved into the inside of her stone grave thingy? Yeah... it goes,

> *A thousand years is an awfy long time*
> *To be lyin' somewhere as dark as a mine,*
> *I'm starvin' hungry so brekky's a feast,*
> *Oh, an' by the way Bollocks, the best way's east!*

"There ye, go. Sorted." Kelly slurred.

Bullet shouted "Hang on!" again and threw the dice and paused as he checked the book.

"The rhyme's good! On yer way, Safur!" pointing dramatically with his spatula.

The evening progressed in this way with Kelly staying as sober as he could while cajoling Spider and Bullet into becoming as drunk as possible. They spoke in voices, flounced about in their costumes enacting a war dance that the elves of Marvache Dale had to do to frighten the forces of Blackturf Ironfist, some dude that was a bit of a shit to all the other elves in the dale. Kelly joined in. He had to. He felt stupid but played the part as best he could eventually feigning lack of breath and having *laughed too much* to continue. They got so pissed that Bullet fell asleep underneath his wizard's hat and then Spider announced that he had better go and had two tries at standing up before he corrected his balance. Kelly insisted he have one more drink before they go, which Spider did and sank a very large whisky. Then Kelly gave him the bottle with a quarter remaining in the hope that he'd quaff it all on the way home and then be so hung-over in the morning he wouldn't surface or go to work, thus reducing the potential of him blabbing where he was.

Kelly took him safely to the front door and gently guided Spider out onto the street.

"Remember, Spider...not a word."

Spider smiled and put his finger to his lips and made a *sshh* sound, then said,

"The fifth step of the dance is the key..."

"Not that. Spider! Remember, I'm not here."

Spider nodded and smiled then turned quickly and the cape, which he'd forgotten to remove, flew dramatically around him. Kelly watched the Prince of Darkness wander delicately down the road swaying uncertainly as the night traffic drove past.

When he returned Bullet had gone to his bed fully clothed....wizard clothed, so Kelly left him, ripped off the plastic garb and grabbed a sleeping bag and a couple of blankets from a cupboard and bedded down on the couch.

Bullet was expected at work the Saturday but didn't go. He asked Kelly to go down to the street and use the public *dog and phone* because he didn't have one and call in for him, say he was sick and then went back to bed. Kelly assured him he would after a cup of tea leaving Bullet time to get back to bed and back to Nod and didn't do it.

Kelly spent a large part of the Saturday peering from behind a dirty net curtain down onto the street. This period of time was interminable so he planned the time he'd get up the next morning in time to get to the airport but at some point had to retrieve the bag. He decided he had to do it that night because he had to be at the airport to check-in at 7:30am. *Who flies on a Sunday?* he thought.

Kelly spent the rest of the day watching an athletics meeting on TV but what he needed was local news, so he switched it off and listened to Radio Forth, Edinburgh's local station, listening mainly for his arrival on the bulletins. An unannounced record's sharp jangling guitar intro burst joyously over the airwaves and he recognised the voice of Bendy Elvis. The song, he thought was wonderful. The guitar ran its own chords but each note precisely picked out with a couple of sharp stops and then Bendy Elvis would come back in saying he would've went out that night but he hadn't a stitch to wear and then about something gruesome because someone was so handsome and cared, which was all a little incongruous for Kelly and then Bendy Elvis yelped, which he thought was funny, actually really brave, musically, but it fitted. It all fitted. He listened on to words of desolate hillsides and the hope of nature making a man of Bendy Elvis in a car with a pantry boy, which had smooth leather on the passenger seat, all recognisably homo-erotic but this lot didn't seem to care. They flagrantly ignored the disdain unarguably waiting for them and sang! Loudly.

The song was musically full of openness and honesty. Nothing concealed not even the atonal aspect of Bendy Elvis's voice and the guitar was ringing aloud, bright and out there, and the bass lived its own life pumping beneath, joining in with the drums as sharp and tight, being the beating stage, the public platform upon which they announced their views of the world. And didn't care what anyone thought of them. And Kelly felt something. Frustration, mainly. Conversely, to the title of the song disclosed by the DJ at the end, Kelly could dish out bucketfuls of apparent charm when he needed to but beneath this, was not *a charming man*.

He felt something was happening in the world, changing, but he was uninitiated, not invited, peripheral, even to the shit stuff, like the prospect of nuclear war. Nobody would ask him to say something, make a stand for someone else, sign a petition, do something selfless, for no reward or put his head above the parapet for the sake of *Right*. Then the news came on. The expected news of his *house guest in the bath's* discovery and his connection with the Greyfriars Body case was announced. And he was shocked at the news as much as an objective viewer would be. He had a head rush as his adrenalin pumped and the underlying sense of panic consumed him. A description of him was issued and the advice that he was not to be approached as he was possibly dangerous also sent into the ether. He then imagined his mother's reaction to this news and felt sick.

Bullet got up for a drink of water and Kelly pretended to be suffering, too. Bullet asked what the reaction was to his absence and Kelly lied, naturally, saying that they said *no problem* and that they'd see him on Monday if he was well enough. Bullet retreated to his lair and slept for the rest of the day.

Kelly had a look through some of Bullet's things. He looked at the framed cartoons again but this time took them out of their frames and put them in a leather satchel, which he decided he was going to take with him, too. He doubted Bullet would mind having retrieved it from the bins.

Chapter 49

Fear Amongst the Beer

Saturday, 30th June

That evening McQuarrie went into the pub at 6:30pm. One of The Brylcreem Boys was on his own at the bar and there were a couple of faces he'd not seen before who were probably lads just grabbing a pint after work. Norrie nodded to him. McQuarrie just looked around. He approached the Brylcreem Boy,

"Alright?"

"Aye. You?"

"Could be better. You know Kells?"

"Not greatly."

"Seen him lately?"

"No. But readin' the news, I wouldn't want to."

McQuarrie left it there and sat down. A pint arrived delivered by the new girl. He thought of asking her but he knew waiting for the usual crew might yield more. May came in and sat up at Stan. She had a copy of *The Evening News* and naturally was reading of Kelly's exploits. Spider shuffled in looking decidedly unwell, however pushed out a smile to May. She raised her glass and pointed into it indicating he was in the chair. He got himself a pint and a nip for May and delicately sat next to her.

"Fuck's the matter wi' you? No get enough blood las' night?" May flatly said.

"Blood's fine. Too much o' that, though." And he pointed at her whisky.

"Where were ye?" May barked, patently offended by her exclusion.

"Friends house." Spider attempted a smile.

"*Friends?* Get tae fuck, Spider! Now I know yer lyin'!"

"Okay." He hadn't the energy to joust with her.

She took a sip of whisky and pushed the paper in front of Spider.

"See Kells has been busy, lately."

Spider tiredly drew the rag closer and read and as he did so. He turned to May in disbelief. She pulled that face that says *I told you so*. When he got to the part about the body in the bath he began to remember the yarn Kelly had spun him and then flicked his eyes up at McQuarrie, apparently the corrupted arm of the police in deadly cahoots with the gang Kelly was working for, who was watching him read. Their eyes met. Spider flushed, panic setting into him and wondered if McQuarrie had seen him. He had. McQuarrie stood up and slowly walked across to Spider, who was now very still in his seat. The gang had made their move and set up Kells just like he said they would!

McQuarrie sat at Stan next to them both. Spider's heart was thumping.

"Mind if I join you?" he said.

"Fire in.", May said, "Yer a sight better lookin' than him!" she said nodding at Spider.

Spider effected a poor grin.

McQuarrie made a great deal of leaning close to Spider as he craned over the paper.

"Always thought it might end up bad for Kells." he said.

"Fuckin' worse than bad, is it no? Dead fuckin' wumman in the bath?" May blurted.

"When did you last see him?"

"Been a while.", May said. "Came up to my flat stealin' paint"

"Really?" McQuarrie said. "Why you?"

Then May forgot that nobody knew about her relationship with Joe and squirmed a bit knowing she had spoken too quickly.

"Err... he was wantin' a bit o' paint.... that *I had...* and he tried to get a tin out behind my back." She obviously stalled and tried to change the subject. "Have yez caught him, yet?"

"No.... but wee stories about him stealing paint and when he did this might help us, May."

"Aye...well...that's a' there is to it. He came up coz I had the colour he wanted and tried to get it oot without me seein' him...an' that." She took a quick, nervous sip of her whisky.

"But you *knew* he was coming to see you ?" McQuarrie got tactically quieter.

"Err... aye..."

"About what? Paint?"

"...aye."

"So you said to him you had some colour paint he wanted?"

"..aye..."

"And happy to let him have it.?"

"Aye...no..I canny remember."

"So why would he try and steal it?"

May erupted "I don't fuckin' know! How wid I know what a criminal like him does!" she lifted the paper for effect and announced that she *had to pish* and went into the ladies toilet.

McQuarrie knew that something possibly unspoken amongst them was afoot and turned slowly to Spider, smiled and said, "Got a bit flustered there, did May, Spider."

Spider smiled fearfully imagining his name being written into McQuarrie's little book and seeing himself tied up in a car boot heading to his certain death in the highlands, his two sons never knowing where he was.

"When did you last see him, Spider?"

Spider found it difficult to talk and just made a face that said he didn't know and shrugged then smiled.

"Easy question, Spider. Having trouble remembering or just answering?" McQuarrie knew that he was close to something. May was acting very strangely and Spider was reluctant to talk and so he pressed harder. "If you know where he is, Spider, it could be very bad for you, *very bad,* if you don't tell us."

Spider understood the euphemistic meaning of the phrase *very bad* and then saw his fingers being snipped off with wire-cutters and his nails being pulled out and couldn't contain the fear. After all, McQuarrie and a group of local villains Kells had been running errands for, were all in on this and bad enough to kill someone and put her in Kells's flat so he surmised he'd be nothing to them and could end up the same way. He started to bubble slightly making imperceptible noises and then a few tears started to drop from his face and he began to physically recede in his seat as much as he could from the imposing presence of McQuarrie and then through his fear he mumbled,

"Don't cut my fingers off....I need them... don't kill me....*please....*"

McQuarrie jolted out of his role as interrogator, pulled a confused face and said,

"What?"

Norrie was now watching the scene with the Brylcreem Boy from the bar. The new girl, now considering her position as barmaid in *The Old Duke,* watched horrified as a grown man began to openly cry.

"Don't kill me...please....I don't know where he is...I don't know..."

Then the door opened and Bullet walked in and over to Stan, oblivious of the situation and slowly picked up the silence in the room and then saw the blubbering Spider and the unmoving figures of Norrie, the Brylcreem Boy and the new girl.

"What's happening?" Bullet said.

McQuarrie said, "Spider here, seems a bit worried about telling me where Kells is and he's getting a wee bit upset."

Bullet smiled a big glaikit smile and said, "Sheesh, is that all? Don't worry Spider! It's alright. He's just hiding! He has to hide from the film company cos they're watching he does the research right. It's not a big deal."

Bullet smiled at the assembly in the room proud that he was assuaging what was obviously a bit of a conundrum that had boiled over, emotionally, and shook his head then smiled around the room saying, *Sheesh,* again. He sat down next to McQuarrie and took his coat off. All stared at Bullet, who was beginning to feel the tension. McQuarrie turned to him and quietly asked,

"Where?"

Bullet said, "Where?"

"Yes, *Where*....is he *hiding*......please, Ford?"

"Kells?"

"Yeeesss.......?"

"Oh aye.... great night, right, Spider, eh? Rough this mornin' though!"

Spider didn't smile back but stood up saying he had to go to the toilet and did walk in that direction, but past Dick, and then he quietly opened the front door and slid out quietly into the street as McQuarrie contained his rage with Bullet and quietly and clearly said again,

"So...*Ford*.... try to focus... you're feeling rough, okay....but just look at me and tell me...*where* is he *hiding?*"

Bullet now seemed to get the gravity of the mood and said,

"Awwww...yeah. In my *bowler flat.*"

McQuarrie grabbed him by the shoulders, "Address!!"

"Mine?"

"Yes yours, you microcephalic, pigshit for brains, fuckwit! Yours!"

" 3F6 West Cross Causeway."

May came out of the toilet fixing her skirt and closing her coat.

"Underrated, that. A good pish!"

McQuarrie burst past her, wrestled with the latch and flew out the door. May looked to where McQuarrie had left the said,

"Did he forget something?" And sat back down at Stan. All was quiet then Bullet said,

"No need for that... microcephalic!"

Chapter 50

Getting Leathered

Bullet had gone out around 6:00pm to the chippy, he said, and hadn't returned. He was becoming twitchy. At around ten minutes to seven that night he made a decision against the darkness as cover and didn't want to have to buy a torch to look for his bag which would just have every tourist and potential passing plod looking to see what the deal was halfway up the castle rock, and to just be a punter in the street but he knew he had to smarten up a bit so he decided to lose the Parka. He took the money out of the lining and put it all in the leather satchel, then picked out one of Bullet's leather jackets from his coat hooks and then flattened the wig with water. He looked at himself in a small mirror and was quite pleased with the result, then put the mirror in the satchel. He knew he'd need it later. The wig covered his forehead and eyes and he just looked like an unkempt trendy thirty-something guy who worked in a record store or a cool advertising business, something like that. Driscoll's boots were wrong though. He took them off and put on a pair of Bullet's black trainers. Much better. A size too big, perhaps, but what the hell.

McQuarrie called in the location and told them he and Jones, who was outside in the car, were heading up there. It would only take minutes with the flashing light on but got stuck behind a broken-down bus which was causing a bottle neck on Clerk Street. He leaned out of the window and shouted at the other cars to pull in but then told Jones to spin round and head down Bernard Terrace and go the back way.

Kelly descended the stairs towards street level and stopped to check the coast was clear to go. All quiet. He stepped out onto the street and then onto the main road with all the other pedestrians and he walked with an effected bounce to suit the role.

Jones raced along St. Leonards Street, turned left at West Richmond Street to turn back to the flat, the light still flashing.

Kelly saw the flashing light driving towards him a long way down the road and recognised McQuarrie's green Cortina. This was it, he thought. This was the end. He froze. Others passed him by and looked at him wondering why he wasn't moving. His breathing increased as the car drew level but failed to stop. His eyes looked up back to the street in front of him and he continued on with his bouncing walk and then looked back as he saw the car turn into Bullet's street. He turned off the main street and made his way down to The Cowgate which had tight vennels and alleyways leading up to the High Street.

Two uniforms, McQuarrie and Jones stood in Bullet's living room the lock smashed in behind them. McQuarrie looked incensed. Nothing of his remained. McQuarrie looked around for something, anything that would put Kelly here but couldn't find anything. Jones picked up the boots.

"These are a bit ...well...*fucked*... Jack. Could be his?"

McQuarrie spat out the word *shit* and looked at the boots.

"Size?"

"Ten."

"Too big."

"Driscoll was a ten?"

"Bag them."

Chapter 51

Being Bolivian

Kelly had to hang around for ages before the stream of tourists abated and was about half past nine before he could ascend the rock to get his bag. He was careful climbing up taking him a few minutes but reached the point at which he could reference the flag on the Overseas Club on Princes Street and pulled back the now wilted bush. He had a quick check down below at the path and delved in the crevice and dragged out the bag. To his relief it was all intact and dry. He needed a breather so he turned unsteadily and planted his arse down onto a rock and took in the view of the town before him for a good ten minutes, taking in all the buildings and shop-fronts and roads so recognisable to him.

"Hey!" a voice below him shouted, "Get down out of there! Did ye no see the sign!!"

A police uniform and a Park Keeper were looking up at him. *Where did they come from?* His heart began to thump. He thought quickly and just looked back and smiled inanely and lifted his arms as if he didn't understand.

"Come down!" The uniform beckoned to him.

"Jist be careful fur christ sake!" said the Park Keeper, "Ah'm jist aboot tae louse ma shift an' I dinny want ony mair accident reports tae fill in wi' fuckin' tourists fallin' oaf the rock!"

"It's alright, just stay calm and we'll get him down safely." said Plod.

Kelly pointed to the panorama in front of him and smiled broadly and spoke in a broken unspecific accent.

"Be-ootiful Citee. Beeg river. Far." And he pointed again for good measure.

The park keeper gave international relations a go, "Yeeesss...*very pretty*...but ye huv tae come doon oot o' there cos it's dangerous..."

He enacted a slow motion version of someone falling, taking a knock to the head and replete with a cry of pain, equally as slow. The uniform watched incredulously shaking his head.

"Is that the extent of training they give you at the council before you get this job? Brilliant. Which acting school did you train at?"

"Well he's' foreign, in't he, ya sarky fuckin...."

"Careful, Archie, careful. I'll sort it."

He used the universal language of patently being pissed off and pointed to the ground while looking at Kelly, who used the time to think slowly as he delicately searched for footholds of descent. He was about fifteen feet from the path below when the Parkie shouted,

"*You!* Throw down bag. It easier.....n'that..."

And again acted out the jettisoning of the bag. Kelly knew that if he made a big deal about it they'd be suspicious so he had to comply. He threw it down. The Parkie caught it and put it at his feet and spoke slowly, as if to a five year old.

"Noo ca'canny...wi' yer feet.. it slippy...." and he acted out losing his footing.

The uniform looked at him again and nearly laughed out loud.

488

"*Ca' canny? Ca' canny?* He's a foreigner! He doesn't know what ca' canny means? My English sergeant at the nick doesn't know what it means! How the hell is he gauny know what it means?"

"At least ah'm tryin'! An' ah dinny ken whaur he's frae! Ah'm huvvin' a go but you're jist standin' there like a big....."

"Careful Archie, careful."

Kelly dropped to the path as yet unsure to which country of the world he hailed from. He smiled as if he had done nothing wrong, but then didn't know he was about to introduce himself. But he did.

"Hagh lo. Mi Alejandro. Edeenboorha ver preety. Castillo forte." He gargled and made a fist looking up at the castle. Plod replied.

"Yes we know. Very pretty but..." he pointed up at the rock and made a stern face and shook his head, "No climbing? Climbing?"

He made a few imaginary grips above his head and steps that weren't there. Archie enjoyed watching him and they caught each other's eye and plod stopped the exhibition.

"No a lot better than I did! Whaur did *you* train?" Archie smirked.

"Tulliallan police college! That's where I trained!" He turned to Kelly, "Where are you from?"

"Boleevia." Kelly decided.

"Whit dae they speak in Bolivia?" Archie said.

"Well what do you think they speak, Archie? Bolivian!"

He addressed Bolivian Alejandro, "*Pick up bag and on your way.*" who then asked,

"Que?"

Archie took the reins in his patronising best attempt at foreign diplomacy.

"Gates shutting soon, Keep winos oot graveyaird."

He made a glug- glug sound and mimed drinking from a bottle and then lightheadedness. Kelly accepted the challenge of another quick improvisation.

"Si. Good. Dreenk. Weet me? We make dreenk? Now?" as he started to unfasten the satchel.

The uniform sighed in exasperation, "Archie can we just get the gates shut across the cemetery and off home. Please? No! No drink. Go!" and he pointed out along the path.

"Si. I go. Tomorrow."

"No not tomorrow. Now please!"

"Tomorrow...I go." Kelly made an aeroplane noise and put out his arms.

"He's awa' hame the morn!" Archie concluded excitedly in his thrill of deciphering Alejandro's acting and immediately thought he deserved a seat at the next major conference of The United Nations.

"Thank you, Sherlock! Just padlock the gate into the cemetery, will ye!"

They both ignored Kelly and walked to the graveyard gates. Kelly picked up the bag and walked along the path and past them and made his way out towards the street waving and smiling but Archie and Plod had already begun another friendly conversation.

"So, *Mr I ken everythin' aboot everythin'*, where exac'ly is Bolivia, then, ye grumpy fucker?" Archie affectionately enquired.

"Middle of Europe. Right next to Romania. Good skiing...*apparently.*" confirming the geographical acumen of Edinburgh's finest, of whom, ventured rarely beyond the by-pass.

Kelly flattened the wig and made a decision. He walked out onto Lothian Road and down towards the West End and there he entered a taxi waiting outside The Caledonian Hotel.

Chapter 52

Flying with Joe

At least it was warm. He didn't know if this was busy or not. He's never flown before let alone been to an airport. The thought of flying now a very real prospect made him nervous, however the alternative was quite undesirable. The flight wasn't until 8:30am the next morning so he had more than twelve hours to kill but one very important task to fulfil around 5:00am. The timing had to be right.

He tried to look as though he was a traveller occasionally checking the flight schedule on the boards because there was security around. He went for a coffee and got himself a large baguette sandwich which got rid of an hour and then went to check out the toilets. The cubicle seemed large enough. He was satisfied but he knew it would take a while so was a little dissuaded by the gaps under the doors. An easy viewing point for any security guard to check what might be happening. Nowhere else. No other choice. Then thought he saw signs directing anyone that wanted it to a shower, which upon a little more research corroborated exactly that and decided that was the best option. Privacy. No balancing mirrors on toilets.

Looking through his bag he thought he was a bit light on clothes to make it convincing as it went through the x-ray machine so he went out to one of the clothes shops on the upper level and bought some shirts, trousers, t-shirts and a tie, then a toiletry bag and some deodorant and toothpaste and toothbrush. He also bought a *Walkman* personal cassette player and spent an hour in a shop that sold tapes. He browsed and saw the throwaway *Top of the Pops* compilations, skating past them quickly, and then saw albums by *Frankie Goes to Hollywood* and *Howard Jones* but didn't really know much about either of them. A bare-chested young man accosted him on the cover of a cassette. *The Smiths* was written almost imperceptibly, as if they cared little if anyone saw it. Not a great selling point, which intrigued him, so he bought it.

As he was introducing his new attire into his bag he decided to put the tie in the satchel then realised that he had an enormous amount of cash in disorganised heaps strewn across the bottom and was just bringing out coins and note after note. He went to the toilets, ensconced himself in a cubicle and as quietly as he could began to arrange the money into piles, then his heart sank when it dawned on him that a large portion of the five grand was in Scottish notes. They were much of a mystery to anyone south of Newcastle never mind the rest of Europe. He'd have to change it at one of the currency exchange booths but then realised he didn't know what the Czech currency was? He had a look at the rates that were displayed on an electronic board outside an exchange booth but there was no mention of any Czech money. It was 1984 at the height of The Cold War. Why would there be?

He watched the process as customers exchanged various currencies, holidaymakers buying travellers cheques. A lot of dollars were being bought. Surely this many people weren't all going to America? He had to ask. He waited for a lull and approached the booth.

"Yes, Sir?" said a broad Scots accent, which he didn't expect and wasn't sure why but it felt a little more comfortable for some reason. A bald-headed, heavily moustached, middle-aged chap leaned towards the window.

"Ermm... I'm travelling to London and then onto Prague later today and just realised that I have no Czechoslovakian currency, at all. Is that something that you can exchange for me?"

"How long are you going there for?"

A bit abrupt, Kelly thought, but let's not rock the boat.

"Just for a few days. Maths competition and then back home."

The man in the booth lifted himself out of his seat and checked that there wasn't anyone behind Kelly waiting and then beckoned him to come closer to the window and then switched off the microphone he used.

"We've got a few Crowns...."

Kelly had a small explosion of happiness in his head as he heard the name of the currency, remembered and involuntarily blurted,

"Crowns! Yes that's it! Czech Crowns....." but regained his composure quickly trying not to look like an inexperienced child at the air travel lark.

"Aye, Crowns, like I said, we've got maybe a couple o' hundred quid's worth but no here. I'd have to go down to the office and git them or I could gi'e them a ring and say you were coming doon...."

He didn't like the sound of that. The word *office* indicated bureaucracy, which didn't sit well with him in his current situation. He made a *hmm* noise that gave away his obvious discomfort with that option.

"Hang on hear me oot..." the big moustache said continuing to check behind Kelly, "....if yer only there for a few days, and ye can be a wee bit shady...*dollars* go a long way across there. They a' want them. But I niver telt ye that, did I...?" Kelly shook his head and also started to look around him for eavesdroppers. "....so I could gie ye the Crowns and you could buy a few hundred dollars as weel? Ye'd have mair than enough for a few days. Ye could stay at The Ritz across there....if they had one."

He laughed out loud at his own joke and Kelly chuckled along to grease the wheels of the transaction.

"I have to meet someone here soon so I don't have the time to go to the office...." Kelly pulled a twenty pound note out of the satchel and slipped it under the window and said looking him in the eye with an almost indiscernible nod of the head,

"You've been a great help, mate and if you could find the time to bring those Crowns *up here*...... I'd be extremely *grateful?*"

Mr Moustache covered the twenty quickly and said, "Within the hour, sir. Happy to help." And then he winked at Kelly and readied himself for the next customer.

Kelly checked the time on the flight board above his head. Then he went to buy a watch, a wallet, sellotape and a new bag.

He took the original bag to the toilets and put everything into the new smarter holdall in a more orderly way, strapped on his brand new *Breitling* watch, and put two hundred in English notes into his wallet. He counted out the Scottish notes, which came to £1043.00, so put the £43 in his pocket and decided he'd exchange a grand, and then walked back out looking the part of international traveller with the two bags and a satchel.

He watched the booth waiting for Mr Moustache to retrieve the Crowns from said office and then went over and waited in the queue.

"Hello Sir..."he said, "How can I help?"

Kelly was bemused. He knew how he could help.

"Errmm....what we said earlier?" Kelly quietly said.

"I think that might have been my colleague you spoke with." Big tache said, lifting his eyebrows to the queue behind him.

The penny dropped. "Right! Yes...ermm I'd like some Czech Crowns please."

"Certainly sir. How much would you like to exchange?"

"A thousand pounds."

His head dropped. "I'm sorry sir. We only have *two hundred* pounds worth to exchange but I could make up the difference in *another currency,* which might help?"

The he mouthed the word *dollars* to Kelly.

"Oh yes... yes. I'd like American dollars, then. Yes them. Thanks."

"No problem sir. Passport?"

"Passport?"

"Yes sir."

He couldn't bring out two passports so he had to make sure it was his, not Joe's he brought out. He slid it under the window, relieved, then slid the grand to him. The passport came back and he put it away. Then came the Crowns, strange and large, then the dollars which he'd only ever seen on the TV. They went into the satchel and made to leave, then big tache said,

"Maybe they'll have more *in London,* sir?"

"Yes, right, yes.maybe! Good idea. Great idea! Thanks. Yes. London! Of course. Right. Cheers."

He took a step to leave and then came back and leaned back towards the window, pissing off an oriental chap in a sharp suit who had to retreat again, and quietly said to him,

"How, err..how *far* will that *go* across there? Got no idea. Never been."

He drew his fingers down his heavily forested top lip and quietly replied, "Six month's wages? The Crowns. Buy a house with the dollars. Next please!"

Kelly's mouth drooped but broke into a smile as he walked away. The potential wealth he had, in Czech terms, was ridiculous. He could live like a king until he could quietly slip back into Blighty. Wenceslas. He was a Czech king wasn't he? A good one by all accounts?

He waited until 6:30am and approached the information desk. A young woman in too much make-up and a bright red uniform spoke to him. He explained that he'd just made a call to a colleague of his that was due to be on the London flight but was at least an hour and a half away, was definitely going to be late but that he was part of The British Council party for the Maths Olympiad in Prague and could anything be done to help? She knew that the British Council parties were always ushered through separately and he explained the national importance of ensuring this maths genius called Joseph Delaney made the flight. A placard was arranged for the arrival of Joseph Delaney near the flight check-in from 7:45am onwards.

Then he went to the toilets and paid the attendant and booked himself a shower slot of forty minutes.

Thirty-five minutes later, Joseph Delaney, exited the toilets and out into the check-in area. He saw the placard being held up by a young woman of the same uniform near the desk, so he placed himself where he could see her and watched the time. At 7:50 am an announcement was made for passenger Delaney on the early London flight to make his way to the check-in as soon as possible. He went into the toilets and had a good look at Joe Delaney in the mirror. Satisfied, he went into a cubicle and locked the door then stood on the toilet looking over until it was empty and climbed over quickly, leaving the original bag sitting on the toilet. Then he tightened his tee shirt and shirt securely around his now portly middle, walked out onto the concourse and returned back into the building at another adjacent door running at full pelt, affecting breathlessness and holding the visa-stamped passport in full view.

He ran up to the young woman who'd seen him rushing in.

"Mr Delaney?"

"Yes, yes!! I'm so sorry! Traffic. Sorry. Sorry!"

"Don't worry Mr Delaney. They've not long all boarded. Just show your passport to the lady on the check-in desk and put your bag on the conveyor."

He did so. She took a cursory look at it making sure it was current with a fleeting look at the photograph discerning, apparently, the man before her now. Then she gave it back to him, wrapped a sticker with the flight number onto the holdall strap and pushed it through the hatch shouting,

"That's it. That's the late bag. Go!"

A pair of hairy male hands dragged it through into the darkness. The lady at the check-in hit a button on the desk which illuminated a *Closed* sign above her. Then she left exhaling tiredly and pulling off her hat and jacket.

"Thanks, Jackie!" The girl with the placard shouted as Jackie Check-in walked away, patently knackered, with a wave without looking back. Miss Placard ushered him towards the departure lounge giving him his boarding pass and tickets and took him straight up to luggage security, quietly saying *British Council* to the lady behind the monitor, much to the chagrin of those waiting in a massive queue. His bag went through and he went under the metal detector arch. A loud noise began to beep as he'd a pocketful of loose change. He gave it all to Miss Placard telling her to keep it. She gave it to an airport uniform who dropped it all in a plastic box and then she took him to gate thirteen and left him at passport control. He gave the officer the passport and deliberately retreated a few steps back towards her saying,

"Thank you. Thank you!" and he augmented the performance with a spontaneous hug, which conveniently took him out of view of the border control officer. Their faces touched. Too much. Cheesy. Miss Placard smiled and told him to hurry as the officer tried to look at him.

"British Council." She said to him. He looked briefly at the visa, closed it and gave it back to Kelly.

Then Kelly walked down a long flexible steel corridor with his heart beating and rounded a bend and beheld the anxious cabin crew waiting at the door. Then he boarded the plane. He settled into his seat but was quite nervous about the whole flying thing and really didn't look forward to the take off and decided to listen to his new *Smiths* album but he embarrassed himself trying to get the cellophane off and was completely un-au fait with opening a cassette tape. He slid the tape in and pressed play. A lonely drumbeat started and a lyric spoke of someone, probably a parent, taking a child in hand and ageing it prematurely. Familiar. A statement attributable to half the population of Calvinist Scotland. What a guy! He searched for the volume and hit fast-forward by mistake. The next track came on and now Bendy Elvis, prophetically had his attention singing about being at a grey school in the past, someone always being wrong with him always right and being his mother's only desperate son. He had the inclination to look around the cabin expecting to see Bendy himself seated close by who then winked at him. He listened on. A debate then ensued about which of them was rich and which one poor, culminating in Big Bendy declaring he'd made a horse's cock of his life and that he'd never had a job because he didn't want one. This time he did look around the cabin. Then Kelly had a terrible thought about fate catching up with him, some Karma shit deciding that this was the end for him and he pictured himself pulling small children over his shoulder and punching defenceless women in the face as he wrestled to get to the emergency exits as the plane plummeted earthward.

Back at her desk Miss Placard's mate told her she had a smear of something on her face and gave her a tissue to wipe it off.

Prague

Late June, 1984.

Prague was hot. He didn't expect this. He had a picture of grey miserableness for all countries in the Eastern Bloc so this was a surprise and not an unwelcome one. He'd sat in the allotted seat on the plane unrecognisable to Hunter and Gunn and heard them bellyache about the reliability of flaky journalists and considered this a tad hypocritical when they each had five hundred illicit pounds in their pockets, and they just surmised Joe Delaney, journalist, had found a better story to cover and had allotted the seat to a walk-up, London bound, latecomer. Either way, they didn't recognise him or venture any conversation which suited Kelly fine and he'd managed to exchange all of the rest of the money he had for dollars on the two hour wait in Heathrow and use the card to withdraw seven thousand pounds. His Delaney face was holding up but he had to go and do a bit of touch up in a cubicle just to ensure he was bob-on with the picture in Joe's passport. He'd asked a stewardess if he could sit in one of the many free seats on the Prague journey, to which was assented, and he stretched out and kept out of the way of that knobhead, Gunn. He leaned back, got comfortable and listened to more of *The Smiths*.

A very rough-looking airport transfer bus, patently fuelled by diesel which seemed to be leaking into the interior, was the mode to take them to the airport terminal building and when the doors closed the heat inside sent the mercury rising. He started to worry about his face and tried to get as close as he could to one of the small open windows.

Two minutes later they rolled into the bay by the baggage reclaim area and went inside. It was no cooler. There were lots of grey uniforms dotted around and one even had a large Alsatian dog panting furiously at the end of a leash. As the plane was from London he guessed this was a bit of a show for the decadent westerners. A chap in blue overalls appeared carrying a small painted white board, presumably from passport control at the end of the hall, and walked directly towards the carousel, still stationary, and climbed over the circulating bit that moves and onto the island in the middle. None of the assembled uniforms took much notice but it became the only focus for the arrivees from London who wondered what was happening? He used the white board to reach up and start to hit the side of the monitor, currently blank, which tried to show some spark of life, but stubbornly declined all cajolement, so he then turned the board and placed it in the middle of the island leaning against the pole that supported the dead monitor. The board read *London*. A few faces awaiting the carousel hid smiles and some openly smirked, much to the chagrin of some of the uniforms who took this slur as an insult to their national pride. The Alsatian must have because it barked loudly for no apparent reason. It was then that the carousel started. Kelly didn't smirk but quickly detected the inner snarl of the uniforms and clearly displayed seeming distaste at his fellow travellers to curry any future favour that might be needed in passport control. Then he went to the toilet, into a cubicle and took out the small mirror purloined from Bullet and checked his face. All seemed to be holding up well. He pissed, checked the stack of dollars taped to his waist was secure, took out the info sheet with the British Council letterhead and slipped it into his pocket with Joe's passport. He took a deep breath and went back into the arrival hall to see that there were only a few bags left on the carousel, one of them his.

The previous smirks at Vaclav Signplacer and Eastern Bloc technology had worked it's magic because a few of them had been pulled aside and were being questioned and having their bags inspected but not Hunter and Gunn who Kelly saw present their passports and letterheaded British Council info sheets to a sweaty face behind the booths, heard the word *mathematics* and were waved on after a ten second check of their, passport, visa and letter. Kelly rushed up to the queue while the border guards were inspecting the smirker's bags and got through without being questioned. He went to get to the same booth but not so fast as to let Hunter and Gunn overhear or see him do so. One woman was in front of him and proceeded to make some explanation on presentation of her passport, to whit, much checking and looking occurred. Kelly huffed and blowed tiredly as if he was a frequent flyer and just wanted to get this over with. He then leaned to the side as if searching for Hunter and Gunn and waved at nobody in particular and shouted,

"Hold the car!"

A small Czech man obviously waiting for an arrival was displaying a handwritten sign in what was presumably Czech, looked at Kelly, turned to see if there was anyone behind him, turned back and threw a bemused wave back at Kelly.

Eventually the woman in front was allowed back into her motherland and Kelly stepped up and presented his passport and letter. The man looked at the page with the visa for five seconds and then at some of the other pages but stopped quickly at one of them and peered at it. Kelly's heart began to thump and would have gone red if the make-up allowed. He thought this was it. For some reason the cat was out of the bag. He was rumbled. The man then said something to a colleague and leaned over to show him the page, but an obviously superior figure saw the discussion and intervened, taking the passport and drifted casually over to Kelly's window.

"Mr Dell Anny?" came the broken English.

No point in crumbling now.

"Yes." Kelly smiled.

"I must apologise for this very hot summer. They never get summers like this in Moscow." Mr Superior smiled back.

"No. I don't believe so." Kelly replied, still smiling and fanning his hand at his face.

"You have a previous visa. Why did you go to Moscow in 1973?"

Kelly's eyes widened and he started to bluster openly making noises while he tried to remember what Joe had said. And from nowhere,

"Cultural exchange!" filled the void and replaced his aura of panic.

"Ah, I see. And did you *enjoy* Moscow?"

Kelly knew there had been an uprising in the sixties here in Czechoslovakia which was brutally suppressed so guessed that they had long memories. Time for another punt.

"No. Not all of it, They took us to what they wanted us to see, I think. Saint Basil's Cathedral, Red Square. A boat ride on The Volga. Not the culture we wanted to see."

"No, I'm not surprised Mr Dell Anny. Who is... *we?*"

"Union. Trade Union. A couple. Trade *Unions.* Some delegates."

"Yes they do that, the Russians, whereas we Czechs have nothing to hide. Prague is beautiful. Czechoslovakia is beautiful. What is the purpose of your visit?"

"Ah yes...now...our visit..." he said trying to sound like a flustered academic. "....*Maths Olympiad.* Edinburgh University. British Council!" he proffered the letter.

Mr Superior looked at the letter and asked the man in the window something to which he nodded and replied.

"Yes he says that is the case, Mr Dell Anny. We have the honour of the tournament this year. Two of your colleagues have just gone through. Do you have a car waiting?"

"Yes..yes... I think so...yes. They have the car...*details*. I had to go to the err...."

"Welcome to Czechoslovakia, Mr Dell Anny." He said handing back his passport and letter. "I wish you luck but not so much that will beat the Czech team." He smiled. "Be careful of the Russians. They will cheat. Enjoy Prague."

Kelly smiled and hurried blindly into Czechoslavakia.

Hunter and Gunn were waiting outside the terminal. Gunn was looking at his watch. Kelly could hear him saying that this was *Czech shenanigans just to upset them and knock their equilibrium before the competition*. Hunter was sighing heavily; obviously sick of Gunn wishing he had one to shoot him with. Kelly got into a taxi and sat there, incommunicado, but with a Czech driver bemused and speaking to him. He had no Czech but turned his hands to the floor as if asking him to wait. The driver put the meter on. He waited for three minutes until Hunter and Gunn's car pulled up and they loaded their luggage, Gunn trying to make *very late* understood to a driver that didn't care.

Kelly then said loudly to the driver, "Follow that car!" Pointing at their car and waving his hand forward. The driver got it and their beige Lada roared into life, threw out a black cloud behind them and followed Hunter and Gunn's car out onto the road.

Half an hour later they pulled up outside a hotel. He told the driver to wait until Hunter and Gunn had entered then pulled out some of his Czech Crowns, looking at the meter intermittently to check the amount and gave the driver a healthy tip of two hundred crowns above the fare. He then smiled at the driver and put his finger to his lips and made a *shhh* sound. The driver nodded and smiled.

The hotel wasn't very big but there were plenty of people milling around and a few languages hanging in the air. This was the best choice for the present. Book into the room and take it from there. He waited until it was quieter and then approached the desk. All seemed in order and his, Joe's, passport was held in the office which was apparently standard practice.. He was expected and given the key to his room, no problem, after nearly signing the register with his own name.

The room was sparse. The window looked out onto a green swathe of grass beyond a busy road and in the middle of the park was a statue. Of whom Kelly could just make out the beard and bald head and see that it had been defaced with graffiti. Probably political, he thought. He was right. He stood there looking out at a Prague road full of cars that he didn't quite recognise and at a statue of Lenin beyond, somewhere in the middle of Europe, somewhere he couldn't quite picture on a map. He had no idea of the shape of Czechoslovakia or knew anything beyond that he'd read in *The Good Soldier Sveyk*, which wasn't much. A set of rooftops rose up and stretched further into the distance beyond the statue and parkland, smoke drifting from chimneys amongst a sea of TV aerials and he had the thought that he had seen something like this place before.

He heard voices coming through the wall and listened. The unmistakable whine of Gunn bellyaching to Hunter permeated the thin wall. He made a decision quickly and went into the dark bathroom. Five minutes later Leonard Kelly emerged and put the hairpiece in his bag and out of sight.

He figured the best way to play this was to be himself for the few days the competition was happening and to tag along with Hunter and Gunn which would buy him some time to familiarise himself with Prague, although he knew the risk was the picture on the passport, but he'd had enough of the make-up charade which decided would melt in the insane Czech summer heat. He ensured everything that should be was out of sight and retrieved the money from around his waist and laid it on the bed. The exchange in London was easier than he had imagined. The bank card had worked its magic .He was ridiculously wealthy but in a place where that wealth would become immediately conspicuous if he was to flaunt it. He looked around the room and looked for somewhere to stash it. The ceilings were high and in the corner above the door was an electricity cupboard about two feet square. There wasn't a chair or any furniture that looked like it would take his weight. He pulled the mattress off the single bed and pushed the frame longways towards the door until it nearly touched it. Then he gathered all the money but for a few thousand Crowns and put it all into a plastic bag then reached up from the bed on its edge and stuffed it into the cupboard and pushed it shut again. Then he put the room back together again. Sweat poured from him so he stripped and got into the shower which dribbled and sprayed intermittently, but it did the job. He unpacked walking naked around the room enjoying the breeze from the open window on his damp body. Fifteen minutes later he was in the suit he'd worn when he met Hunter and Gunn then he took a deep breath opened the door and checked the hall was empty and stepped out into the tiled corridor and stood in front of their door, took a deep breath, knocked and dropped into character.

Hunter opened the door, looked at Kelly, looked again and then smiled.

"Mr Delaney! Mr Delaney...how..?" he stuttered.

Kelly beamed back at him.

"Yesterday. I came yesterday. I sent word. Did you get it?"

"No...no. Nothing But why?"

Gunn appeared at the door. He was delighted Kelly had made it but wanted to be pissed off so said,

"Another thing we've had to worry about!"

Kelly spewed some bullshit about a news agency he worked for who wanted him to get there before the national representatives arrived to get an interview with one of the Czech organisers and had promised to cover his early flights and buy the story from him with huge coverings of the team from Edinburgh. Gunn knew the agency would sell it to the broadsheets and was delighted.

That evening they took a walk along the road which had metal dustbins on the edge of the pavement very similar to the ones he remembered from his childhood, with ridged lids and large handles. Kelly bought them dinner in an unassuming little restaurant with two rows of tables running up the long room and at the top a beaded curtain made little of hiding bubbling pots and gas flames and, yes, Kelly could smell boiled cabbage. There were a few Czech people already eating when they arrived who eyed them almost fearfully, yet desperate to stare.

Hunter spoke some words of Czech to the waiter and via pointing and smiling ordered three bowls of lamb stew with bread and butter. Kelly realised he hadn't had a beer for a few days and ordered three which came in large cold bottles with three unmatched glasses but Kelly thought the beer was incredible and he took a good look at the bottle almost involuntarily after he'd taken his first draught but didn't want to appear unworldly so said nothing and took in the room waiting for his meal.

"So what did you find out yesterday, Mr Delaney?" Hunter asked him. "Have we to fear anyone in particular?"

"Well actually..." He returned to what the border guard had said to him at the airport, "...the Russians are not very well liked by...."

Gunn blustered in, "Anyone!" delighted with his witty interjection.

"...yes.....yes, that became apparent with the residual resentment of the suppression of the insurrection of 68....but they cheat. Unashamedly. Apparently. However, ..." he began to improvise, "..... there are some officials that are either too frightened of the backlash should they confront the Russian delegation...."

"Or they've been bribed?" Hunter said just as the meal arrived.

"I knew it!!" Gunn said much too loudly, however Kelly noticed it was the existing Czech clientele that shrunk lower when they heard him. Gunn, acknowledged his social misdemeanour with an apologetic face to everyone in the restaurant but nobody met him eye to eye and Kelly saw this as well and wondered if this was their presence or a natural Czech reaction to public displays of passion? Minutes after a large man and his wife excused themselves from the restaurant leaving half a plate of food and some unfinished drinks and were followed shortly after by two thirtysomething men who settled their bill, quickly, and left. A couple of moments passed before Hunter said,

"Is it us, do you think, Mr Delaney? John?"

"Call me Joe."

"Thank you. David....and you know this is John. Well? Are we *persona non grata*, chaps?" Hunter quietly said whilst chewing.

"No. I don't think so. I mean they've seen westerners before, haven't they?"Gunn dismissed loudly.

"Well..actually, John.... probably not. This doesn't occur every year in Prague, so....?"

Kelly noticed one man sitting alone at a table further up the long room drinking a beer. He had a suit and tie on and was looking down towards them and caught his eye. Kelly effected a small smile. The man made no reply, took a drink of his beer and checked his shirt for drips. Then looked up again at their table.

"Seems we have someone quite interested in either who we are or how we look, gentlemen." Kelly said to them both.

Gunn spun around to look with the grace and subtlety of a club-footed dancer.

"Don't...John..." Hunter said but was too late.

Gunn ignored him and spoke loudly up to the man's table, "Good evening."

Hunter was cringing. Kelly watched with glances up from his stew.

The man then stood and placed a worn fedora hat on his head and walked up towards them. Gunn held a stupid grin and watched him walk towards them expecting to touch base with a local but the man strode past them and out into the street without a word or a look in their direction.

"Well that was a bit...off, wasn't it?" Gunn blurted out. "Hands across the ocean and all that!"

"I have been informed that to be seen consorting openly with westerners can be considered tantamount to treason, in some quarters behind *The Curtain*. People are fearful." Hunter quietly intoned hoping Gunn would do likewise.

Kelly leapt on this. "I've also heard something similar. Not just them but members of their families can lose jobs and such like. Extended punishment, if you like."

An older woman from behind the beaded curtain came down towards them. She had a careworn face of about fifty and wore an old fashioned smock. She walked past their table to the door to the street and looked from behind the glass up and down the road for a few moments then came back to their table and without a smile pointed at the food and enquired with a thumbs up to which Hunter said *very good* and returned the thumbs up. Then the woman asked with flattened hands crossed and then opened as to their need for any more.

" I think we might have outstayed our welcome at this establishment, chaps" Hunter said. "We can forego the Tiramasu for one evening, I think. This lady appears to be hurrying us out. I think we should finish and comply."

Nods of assent came from Kelly but Gunn, who was still eating, pulled a face that wanted to gainsay that opinion but was stopped with a stern stare and raised eyebrows from Hunter who smiled and agreed with her assessment of the evening and indicated that no more would be required, to which a bill was fished out of her pocket and laid smartly on the table. She departed for her lair behind the beaded curtain and then looked back through to the three of them.

Gunn swept the last mouthfuls of stew into his mouth while Kelly quaffed the last of his beer and fished around in his pocket for his wad of Crowns whilst stopping Hunter from doing the same. Kelly left four hundred Crowns with the three hundred Crown bill and stood up. Gunn had already abjured any responsibility of social decorum, having already made his way to the door and pulling on his jumper. Hunter followed him but turned to see her face watching them leave from behind the curtain. He nodded a goodbye and the slightest of nods was returned. Kelly was last out but turned and went back inside saying he'd forgotten something but then grabbed Hunter's practically untouched beer and sank it in one, wiped his mouth and joined them back on the street. They made their way back to the hotel with Gunn complaining of his likelihood of indigestion and of the twenty-seven minutes they'd spent eating which was an inhuman time to try and dine, apparently.

The next morning Kelly was awakened by a knock on his door and the voice of Gunn.

"Mr Delaney...Joe? We've had breakfast...if you could call it that...and we have to go quite soon."

The door knocked again. Kelly shouted back from the relative warmth of his scratcher.

"Yes I'm just getting dressed now. Be with you in five minutes."

"We'll wait for you downstairs in the foyer."

"Yes thanks! See you there."

He had no idea of what he was getting himself into but it couldn't be hard acting the journo, surely?

He bounced into the foyer ten minutes later with Gunn purposely looking at his watch and said

"Ready?" as if it were they who were the tardy culprits.

Hunter had a map and the instructions of how to get to the venue, which number tram to take and where to get off and the name of the building written down. He guided them like a schoolmaster with a couple of charges into the heart of the tram which was quite crowded, and sat down in free seats next to their Czech travellers. Gunn asked to see the directions and Hunter sighed and passed them over his shoulder and to the seat behind him without looking. The man next to him looked at him and Hunter smiled. The man turned away with no visual reply. Gunn made a big deal of standing up and craning to see the names of the streets fully in the knowledge that he was an unashamed spectacle for the quiet Czechs in the tram, quite enjoying being something of *difference* to them.

"It says about a twenty-five minute journey here. David?" Gunn said loudly.

The Czechs looked quickly then looked away. Kelly smirked to himself knowing what Gunn was doing and thought him to be a shallow sad figure craving attention and recognition for who he was, which was, in his opinion, a pedantic, egotistical, overbearing but quite insecure arse. He turned and smiled as he looked out of the window and caught the eye of a man looking straight at him with a an unremitting flatness that didn't waver. Kelly dropped the smile and turned his head away. Then he looked at him again, quickly and recognised him as the man who left the restaurant the previous evening. *Whatever*, he thought. *Some of them are bound not to like us. Don't blame them, either.*

They reached their stop and Hunter guided the other two off as if they were absolute novices at getting off a tram and then Hunter thanked the driver who nodded curtly back. Hunter got out the sheet of paper with the details and studied them whilst having a look up at the street. Gunn was about twenty paces already ahead of them and shouted back in his best superior arseholic voice,

"It's this way! All in here!" he said striding away pointing at his temple.

Kelly couldn't help himself and said audibly, "Yeah, that's exactly where I'd put the gun, Gunn!"

Hunter turned and looked at Kelly, who felt like a kid caught with his hand down his trousers, but then Hunter let a small disloyal smirk crease his face and Kelly got the green light to smile, as well.

"Thank god it's only a week." Hunter said to Kelly and stepped forward to follow him.

Kelly took a good look around and saw a street sign, *Skolska Ulice.* He set off to catch Hunter.
They stopped at a very grand white stoned edifice with arches along the front as Gunn announced the obvious pointing at a large blackboard with *Maths Olympiad* written on it in English but also in other languages. Kelly had a rush of panic from somewhere and really didn't want to get into situations where he had to sign in or get into conversations with anyone that might remember him.

"Listen... you chaps..." he said in his best varstarian, "....I'm not going to go in yet. I just want to wander around here for a bit...you know?"

Hunter was about to politely observe that they had better all sign in together and get badges but Gunn leapt in enthusiastically.

"Absolutely! Get a feel for the place before you commit pen to paper. Assess the lie of the land. I get it!"

Hunter sighed again. "Yes, alright. I'm sure you can manage a modicum of communication and a signature irrespective of where we are."

Kelly smiled, "I'll be fine, David. Just a quick scout around the place....like *John* said."

And *John* smiled at the approval of his idea.

"You'll miss the reception, actually. Just coffee and a few cakes and some dreary academic forcing a smile and a welcome speech out to all his adversaries. Good idea. Go and *scout,* Joe. See you in there."

Hunter and Gunn pushed a huge oak door and disappeared into the building but when it closed a bereft and solitary cloak descended onto Kelly. He turned and looked out at the increasing traffic and bustle of Prague beginning its day and then chose a quite random direction in which to walk and stepped onto the road and crossed over to the shadowed side of the street and turned a corner.

*

McQuarrie sat in his usual place in *The Old Duke.* He's had word that day that his father was being returned to the care home in Dalkeith. He wrestled with the news. Love and money got in the way of each other. Every available patrol car was out there looking for Kelly but none of them had had a sniff. This was why McQuarrie went back to his thinking den. They'd covered the train stations and the airport though he didn't think Kelly would have the wherewithal to skip the country so he concentrated on the side of town that Kelly knew. They'd been to his mother's place in Livingston but he wasn't there either, which would have been obvious and stupid. No, Kelly was in hiding somewhere and it was a somewhere he couldn't think of. And it bothered him. Was he holed up in a derelict house somewhere, under a bush on a golf course, hiding in a skip? It was obvious that Kelly had concealed the body in his flat for a couple of weeks at least and quietly commended how he'd stood up to the *friendly* grilling in the cafe and at that time she would have had to have been dead already. McQuarrie didn't like the fact that Kelly was out-foxing him and knew he had to think laterally. Broaden the thinking. He'd tried to find the two men in black coats that Sasquatch spoke of but to no avail. What he really hated was that he couldn't completely solve the *Greyfriars Body* murder but he knew Kelly was the bottle swinger and up to his neck in it but without Kelly he would never know. What bemused McQuarrie the most was the inclusion of his neighbour? Why did he kill her? He surmised it was a business liaison gone-wrong but couldn't deny that Kelly wasn't an idiot. Lazy, workshy, yes, but he wasn't stupid, so *what would, could, he do to evade capture?* Run? Yes but to where? Seek help? Possibly but all the friends he had were in here. Had he made any friends at the theatre place he had been attending?

*

Wenceslas Square wasn't really a square at all, Kelly thought. There were two lanes of traffic running both sides for a good quarter of a mile and a part in the middle that had a few roses growing in small plantations. At the far end was very gothic looking building with a large central turret that he'd passed under and walked the length of the square. It was all very impressive and thought it resembled a huge version of The Grassmarket in Edinburgh. Well, maybe not. He crossed to the middle and nearly got knocked over by the strangest looking little car painted in battleship grey that sounded like a souped-up lawnmower. He forgot that they drove on the right and looked the wrong way. A high-pitched horn which changed tone half way through its announcement broke the noise of the traffic which wasn't that much, either, he thought. Edinburgh could be a proper bastard at rush hour, especially during the festival because the council always have some brainiac who thinks they should introduce one-way systems and exclude the use of Princes Street or something similar and it always snarls up somewhere. This was nothing compared to that but then he thought that there won't be many privately owned cars? He actually didn't know nor had taken the time to find out. He sat down on a bench in the central grassed area of the square and felt immediately tired. This was the first time he'd had a chance to stop acting, drop out of character for at least thirty-six hours and was well and truly knackered. He knew he had to come up with a plan. Was he just going to skip out of the hotel without a word to Hunter and Gunn? Or should he go to the maths thing and drag up another performance? He decided on the second performance, his matinee, given that it was only nine o'clock in the morning. Maybe he'd meet someone there who could be helpful? The truth was he was entirely overwhelmed by the situation now that he had a chance to look at it from a distance. When he'd been in the mix, acting his way through scenes, he hadn't a chance to consider the enormity of what he was doing. What he had done. He thought of Spider, Bullet and May.... and Joe. Then he felt sorry for Joe. Sorry for how it would impact on his life and May's. Really stymie their plans for the south coast, their one chance for happiness. But he was selfish and he knew it... but had tasted the glow of being a selfless friend with May, which had arrived quite unexpectedly but he delivered it all, very naturally. Perhaps not a role? An indicator of who he could be. His mother. How would his mother react? It must have hit The News by now. She'd be the talk of the washhouse and probably be ashamed of him, too. All the neighbours would find it difficult to talk to her with that elephant in the room. *You son's a murderer*. His hunger dragged him from his reverie and he looked up, looked at the street trying to see a fast-food place or a shop among the magnificent architecture that enveloped him. There he was in the centre of Wenceslas Square, in the middle of Prague which was in the middle of Europe, with more money than he'd ever imagined he'd ever have. Alone.

*

McQuarrie and Jones had finished speaking to Roger and Kat. They'd told them of how he interacted with the other students, which wasn't much but that he had been encouraged to put his energies into *Make-Up* because of his personal hygiene problem and his lack of respect for the dramatic process, Kat said, with

Roger nodding in animated assent while the vision of Sophie in tears accosted his memory and made his bottom lip curl, slightly. Jones spoke directly to Roger.

"Are the Make-Up girls here?"

"Yes, they should be by now. Straight along the corridor and third on the right. It's quite a big room. Not as big as this, *the drama studio,* naturally..."

"I'll find it. Thanks."

Jones walked out into the corridor. McQuarrie went quietly around the students stopping to speak to them. He approached Mhairi who immediately burst into tears so he went over to Liz who was in full flow gabbling away at a few of the hair baubles and Shell-Suit Bottoms who was sitting a few feet away on the edge of the stage.

".....and that fuckin' coat! What the fuck was he hidin' in that coat. I reckon he was sellin' gear and jist got on this course so's he could ping a few out tae us! An' a' that shite aboot sendin' yer spirit oot! How the fuck does anybiddy send oot a spirit, fur fuck's sake! That bitch in the bath is just a spirit, now, n't she?"

"Hello." McQuarrie smiled at them.

A collective *a'right* came back at him and the involuntary fixing of baubles amongst the gum- chewing. Liz sparked up a fag. Roger saw this and was about to protest when Liz bellowed,.

"Fuck off Roger! Ah've been actin' my arse off in here wi' a fuckin' murderer. It coulda been me next, ya big cocksucker! I'm havin' a fag, A'right!"

Roger felt the hand of Kat on his arm. She looked at him and shook her head. He relented but didn't feel her hand removed. He looked at the hand, then at her, smiled and went to put his hand on hers. Then she pulled it away and said,

"Sorry Rodge....I'm ...err..just in the middle of... erm...*doing something*....erm", quickly picking up a book.

Huv yez goat him, yet? Shady bastard!" Liz quipped volubly.

"No we haven't yet. But we will."

"D'yez reckon he'll kill again? Is he dangerous? Fuckin' weird bastard. Knew that fae the start I saw him."

"How was he weird?"

"Said weird shite about spirits, d'in he?" Liz nodded at The Baubles who assented fearful of doing anything other, with a collective *yeah*.... though most were afraid to gainsay her.

"Spirits, eh?"

"'Kin right, man. Some shite aboot the Tarmac Indians and fightin'! An' he made Mhairi cry. Di'n he Mhairi? Haw Mhairi! Wake up dipshit. Creepy Crombie cunt made you cry, right?"

Mhairi felt the gaze of the room on her and her face scrunched up ready for the impending tears.

"Did you speak with him alone?" McQuarrie pressed.

A collective *Nuh*... came from The Baubles underscored by Liz shouting *Did I fuck! Him! 'Kin jokin' aren't ye!*. When all had settled, Liz offered, "Talked tae Stevie-boy though. Gave him his trainers."

"Sorry.... who gave....?" McQuarrie looked at Liz.

"Him. Stevie...."

Who looked up from the book he was reading.

*

In the Make-Up Department Jones was speaking to Kerry. Donna and Julie listened on.

"So he took an interest in all this." Jones looked at Kerry.

"Not at first but one day... he just turned. Couldn't get enough of it. He was a great student, actually. There are some that just want to make themselves beautiful every day with different kinds of lipstick and rouge." Looking over to her two charges. "He wanted to know more all the time."

"Like what?" Jones asked.

"Adhesives, spirit-gum adhesive, remover...."

"Which stick what?"

"Beards, moustaches, eyebrows... that sort of thing."

"Anything else?"

"Well you need a bit of that for prosthesis, too. You know rubber bits that reshape the face with wrinkles and moles. Something has to stick them on. And then you have to blend them in with your skin tones. He was good at it, actually. I can't deny it. Best student I've had for a while. He came in one day and asked if we could make him look like his uncle. A party joke, or something."

"Did he say the name of this uncle?"

"No."

"Could you describe the man he wanted to look like?"

Kerry pitched the description of Joe as Jones began to smile. Donna and Julie had started to whisper and then started nudging each other obviously trying to get one or the other to say something. Jones looked at them.

"You!" Donna said in a loud whisper.

"No you!" Julie replied.

Jones took charge. "If you know anything girls it would be a real help if you tell us. It doesn't matter how insign.. how *small* you think it might be., we'd like to know.

They both looked at each other and Julie stepped up.

"Well there was this one time when Donna was stealing black lipstick to be a goth at a fancy dress party..."

"I wasn't stealin' it. I wasn't stealin' it Kerry, I just wanted to borrow it. And anyway she was goin' to the same party as Snow friggin' White so she's just as bad!"

Kerry sighed, "It's okay girls just one of you tell the police officer whatever it is you have to tell."

"Nobody's going to get into trouble...*are they Kerry?*" Jones said and raised her eyebrows at Kerry.

"No." Kerry said shaking her head.

Donna took a deep breath, "Well when we were here that time borrowing the lippy and rouge an' some other stuff, we were just about to go in but Julie saw him... the fella you're after in there an' he was puttin' some of the new stuff from the Lyceum and film units in a plastic bag."

"What was it he took, Donna?" Jones asked.

"Dunno. Couldn't see coz we were hidin' too. We didn't want him to see us. We thought Kerry had said he could take it, or it was homework or somethin'. Dunno?"

"So you wouldn't know what was specifically in the new batch you got, Kerry?" Jones quickly said.

"Well, no, because it arrived in a big bundle. Bags of it. I don't know what he'd have taken."

Jones went quiet as she began to think.

Back in the Drama Studio McQuarrie sat with Steven. "....and you talked about reading....books mainly?"

"Novels. Classics. Yes."

"Can you remember which ones?"

"Oscar Wilde. I told him about *The Picture of Dorian Gray* and he told me about the one he was reading. A European one. *The Good Soldier Sveyk.* That was it. I'd never heard of it."

"*The Good Soldier Sveyk*?" McQuarrie said it to himself trying to remember where he'd heard that before. Slowly the picture of the man in the checked shirt giving him the racing tip came into focus. And two and two finally started to make four. He had a distant and quiet moment of realisation which Steven noted.

McQuarrie came to and *re-entered the room,* "The cheeky bastard!" he quietly let slip whilst shaking his head but didn't want to let anyone into any story of him being so obviously duped. So he said, "The red-haired girl over there said that you gave him a pair of trainers?"

"Yes. He didn't have any to do the workshops."

McQuarrie looked askance at Steven. Workshops to him meant industrial units of flaming welders torches and the noise of machinery.

"It's what they're called. Kat calls them workshops."

"Describe the trainers to me, please Steven."

"White. Dunlop Blue Flash. Size nine."

Jones burst into the room and beckoned him over. She looked elated, was smiling and was looking forward so much to offering the fruits of her deductive powers. McQuarrie, nodded his thanks to Steven and ambled over which threw her given her energetic entrance.

"Sir....Jack....I know why we can't find him....."

McQuarrie interrupted her, "He's made up, looks like someone else and is in disguise.....I know."

"Yes sir...but do you know who?"

*

Kelly was still in the Square. He'd bought a *sýrový sendvic* which he'd pointed at in the shop and was now chewing through some tough white bread and cheese. He found it all a bit dry. Her heard the shuffle of someone sit down on the bench next to him and turned. A heavily bearded older chap wearing some sort of ex-army cap nodded to him. He nodded back and then the man looked at his sandwich. Kelly looked at his sandwich then back up at him. Kelly couldn't work out if it was vagrancy, poverty or both that had painted this unfortunate.

"Uctivě můžete mi dovolte, abych si některé z vašich sendvic?" the man said.

Kelly didn't know he was asking for a piece of his sandwich but the tone was soft and sounded demure and respectful. He looked at the sandwich again. Kelly made some mime of the bread being dry and held it out to the man. He grabbed at it staying just under the line of disrespect and began heaving chunks from it with his teeth. He was clearly hungry and appeared as though life and fate had shoved it up him at sometime in the past. Kelly, of anyone, understood this but was still trying to find whatever semblance of saliva he had left in his mouth, when a bottle was presented before him.

The man nodded and shook the bottle. "Piti!"

Kelly displayed all the unsurety and suspicion of the Brits abroad. He didn't know what it was or if he'd contract galloping gumrot from beardy boy's big Czech kisser, however, he was in need of a slake so tentatively took the bottle from him and looked at the dark contents. *Hope he's not a plumber,* he thought.

"Víno! Piti."

Kelly got that it was wine and thanked him with a nod. Beardy went at the sandwich as though it was about to be taken from him. Kelly took a sip. Not a vintage but palatable enough. He took another belt and swished it around his mouth, then handed it back to Beardy, who'd demolished the tough bread in jig time and was now smiling with half of the sandwich hanging around his beard and then spoke.

"Děkuju." He said nodding to Kelly.

Kelly guessed rightly that he was being thanked and bravely made his first attempt at Czech.

"Děkuju....?"

Then he was surprised at the next exchange.

"You English?" The man said in a thick broken accent.

Kelly sat up, mildly shocked. "Errr... yes. No... I speak English but I'm from Scotland. You speak English! *You speak English?*"

"Yes." He said sending his index finger around his gums and sucking the soggy bread from it.

"Well... that's good. I didn't expect.... you know...?"

"My English not perfect. Speak softly...slow.."

"Ermm...thank you for the nice wine.."

Beardy laughed loudly. "Not good wine. Shit! But little money, Koronas... so ..shit wine."

Kelly smiled. "It was okay. I've had worse."

Beardy nodded knowing assent. "You drink with me."

"Well....not now. I'm just looking at Prague....ermmm *early*.... you know...?"

"No. Not understand. You drink...*with me!* Give me *sendvic*. Thenk you."

Kelly realised that he was saying he was *persona non grata* with most of the good burghers of Prague and not many would slake their drouth with him let alone give him something to eat.

"Errm...that's okay..." Kelly smiled but really wanted to say that he kept similar company back in blighty and how the fuck had the rest of Europe's vagrant fraternity got him on the wino radar despite the suit? So he just smiled and asked,

"Where did you learn English?"

"University."

"Ah.. you studied English, I see..."

"Professor. No study. Professor. *Filozofie*." He barked and took a swig of wine.

Kelly looked at him taking in he was being told this beardy semi-vagrant...*or not...* was... *had been* a university professor of Philosophy. Then he looked at the wine bottle and smiled then laughed as if he'd been the butt of a joke, until Beardy stared him straight in the eye with the sternest of central European glowers.

"Professor?"

"Yes. Filozofie."

Kelly frowned. "No joke? You are a university professor?"

"Now no. I go to jail. Prison. *Rusové*."

"Sorry?"

"Ruskis...." Beardy made the miming of shooting a gun. "....come here. Praha. *Revoluce.*"

"Ah yes. 1968! The insurrection."

"Ano! Yes. *Povstání.* Insur...?

"Insurrection."

"Wine?" Beardy held out the bottle.

"No. Thank you. Why are you..." Kelly didn't know if *in a shit state* was a universal term so he looked at his garb, unkempt face and moved his hand up and down. Beardy got it.

"Rusové take me. University then prison. Studenti bad. He say I bad professor. Studenti make with Rusové Rusové, make....."

Here Beardy went into an animated show of various means of torture and crying, so much so that Kelly put his arm on his and stopped him in case people were looking. He didn't want to draw any unwanted attention.

"Yes I get it. The student denounced you under torture, yes yes..."

"Yes! Studenti say Rusové I say studenti make war."

Kelly nodded and tried to look sympathetic but then seemed puzzled. "Did you?"

Beardy looked askance.

"Did you tell the student to make war?"

Beardy smiled, "*Ano!* Yes!" and then he spat on the ground and said *Rusové* venomously. Then he showed ten fingers to Kelly.

"Ten years?"

"Yes! *Deset let*. Ten years."

Kelly worked out he'd been out since 1978 and had been bumming around Prague for the last six years obviously excluded from any meaningful employment. No wonder he looked fucked.

"*Matematika?*" Beardy said pointing back towards where the Maths Olympiad was occurring.

"Yes...maths *thing*...olympics."

He decided that this was enough contact for the day and Beardy was about to talk again to him when he quickly fell silent as a grey-suited man walked past reading a newspaper. Kelly looked at Beardy and then to the man who looked Kelly in the eye for a second and walked on. Beardy got up and said thank you to Kelly and walked away looking back at the besuited newspaper reader. He lifted his arm to Kelly. Kelly lifted his and watched him go.

Back in the building where the Maths Olympiad was happening Gunn was poring over a paper at a large table when Kelly arrived.

"Ah Joe!" Hunter said and obviously pleased to see him "....we have been given examples of the kind of problems we are likely to encounter. Want a look?"

Kelly had to play ball and craned over Gunn's shoulder. Gunn was fixated.

"Looks very....*mathematical.*" he said and smiled at Hunter. Gunn took the opportunity to give him a withering look and then return to the paper.

"It's Geometry and Topology, Joe and I suspect our lads will have to deal with Mathematical Physics, too. Neither of these have occurred in the last few years." Hunter said.

Kelly looked at him intently. "Sorry....what was that? *Our lads?* I thought *you were* the lads?"

Gunn came up from his studies and smiled condescendingly. "Our team arrive later today. Four fourth year undergrads."

"Oh...I really didn't realise.... so it begins tomorrow?"

Kelly was taken aback by this new development to him. There was a chance that any one of these maths students had seen him at some time back in Edinburgh and certainly not as Joe. This wasn't a good development and then considered that hanging around here with his observers badge would only be more unnecessary exposure. He excused himself and headed for the toilets in the foyer.

He stood thinking while having a piss on the old ornate urinals. If he was staying it had to happen soon and while there was the maths event happening and a few foreign faces knocking around it remained less than unusual to any Czech observers. He took a deep breath marking some sort of resolution. Then someone came in and he straightened up fixed his flies and nodded to his fellow pisser and briskly left.

He returned to Hunter and Gunn at their table. There was a small card with a Union Jack printed on it which read, *Matematika Olympiády UK tým.* He spoke to Hunter.

"I'm going to have a walk around...*in here*... see what's happening, you know with the other teams..."

"Okay Joe, but don't expect to be welcomed by anyone. They're a very intense lot these maths bods." Hunter replied.

Kelly walked off into the busy room and hubbub of varying languages playing the part of *Observer* and meandered out back into the street without Hunter or Gunn seeing him leave.

He sat on his bed back at the hotel and gathered all his things together and then went into the electric cupboard above the door and retrieved his bag of money. He placed it all on the bed next to him. For all he knew these four students were going to be staying here. There were lots of students at the party, maybe Maths students, and he'd made his presence apparent. It was too much of a risk. He sat for the next half hour and re-made his face and hair to look like Joe. He was getting weary of doing this but becoming quite proficient, ironically. Then he went down to reception and waited for a young girl on her own to speak to, retrieved Joe's passport and left. Then he went to the nearest bar, ordered a drink took a sip and went to the toilets, took off the make-up and hair and walked straight out as himself again.

His bag wasn't so heavy and he kept the bag of money close to him as he made his way back into Wenceslas Square. He looked in every direction ensuring he looked like a tourist taking in the sights but couldn't make out anyone with a small peaked military hat. This was where The Professor found Kelly so Kelly decided to stay put and wait for him. Two hours passed and he'd lost the appearance of a tourist and had now become anxious foreigner obviously looking for someone. Then it started to gently rain and the cloud looked like it meant business so he went to find shelter, lie low and try again later. He rounded a corner where he knew the tram stop was and took a rest.

"Hello." A voice said.

Kelly turned and there was The Professor in all his scruffiest glory with a set of green teeth smiling at him.

"Professor! Great to see you again!" Kelly loudly spoke to him. Some passers-by looked at the unlikely duo speaking English and The Professor gestured at him to be a little quieter and took him by the arm.

"We drink coffee? *Déšť...* He pointed upwards and Kelly learned the Czech word for rain.

The Professor led him to a side street where they entered a cafe and sat at a table. He ordered coffee from a very thin middle-aged woman wielding a pungent cigarette. Kelly asked The Professor to order some food reassuring him that he would pay but The Professor countered his largesse. Kelly wondered where he'd got the money from because he was rooked only this morning but he accepted.

The coffee arrived first and they both drank in silence until both had savoured the heat and taste.

"Matematika?" The Professor pointed out into the street.

"Ah yes.." Kelly leaned across and spoke quietly, "...I don't like the hotel." And pulled a face universally apparent to all.

The Professor frowned. "Bad? Bad hotel?"

"Yes...*Ano*... I don't want hotel. Flat...ermm apartment...? Apartementi.." He said having a punt at the pronunciation.

"*Apartmán.?*" The Professor made a pillow with his two hands and rested his cheek onto them. "No hotel?"

"Yes exactly! I want to sleep in an apartment. You know?" Kelly asked with his hands spread out.

The Professor shrugged as if to think and then put his hand to his chest. "*Apartmán?*"

Kelly thought he was inviting him to stay at his place somewhat surprised that he actually had one, however, he had procured money from somewhere in the space of a few hours but he didn't want to doss with him. Two large sandwiches with a side of some cabbage-based dish and a brown condiment had arrived with it and The Professor tore into it all. He took a spoonful of cabbage into his mouth and chewed and swallowed while holding up the spoon and looking at Kelly.

"No my *Apartmán*.? Woman."

"I don't want a woman. Apartment."

"Yes woman!" The Prof insisted.

"No woman!"

"Dům! Dům!"

Kelly suspected this was an Americanism that he had adopted and was suggesting Kelly was stupid for not accepting the services of a Czech streetwalker but then The Professor held up his spoon again and drew an imaginary shape on the table.

"I not know word....?" He drew again. Kelly looked again the The Professor made a roof with his two arms over his head.

Kelly got it. "House! I see it's a house."

"Yes...house. *Dům*. Me...." He made a square with his hands while looking around the small space in the cafe. Kelly immediately understood.

He'd eaten his sandwich but not the cabbagey dish, and he felt better for it as The Professor led the way for five or six minutes out onto the edge of the city centre and into a side street with a row of tall houses. Some were grey and some had painted sills with window boxes of flowers. The one they turned into was sorely in need of some TLC. Rendering was hanging from the brickwork waiting to fall and the number 13 had been painted poorly onto the door. He wondered which street and looked for the name on one of the walls. *Toulovska* was given up by a faded sign.

The stairs were steep and creaked loudly then The Professor opened the door to his room on the second floor and beckoned Kelly to enter. It had bare floorboards, a large window, a small desk and a large double bed with an enormous headboard of dark wood and next to the bed was a set of bookshelves made from loose rough flats of wood with stacked bricks at each end supporting five levels all filled with what appeared to be text books. Kelly stood there and thoroughly approved. This seemed a quiet street and this house was in an unremarkable street.

The Professor held up a finger and went upstairs and knocked on a door. A smell of cooking wafted into the stairwell and a conversation with a woman began in Czech. This continued for another two minutes with the words *Matematika* and *Skotský* until The Professor beckoned him upstairs.

The room was exactly above The Professor's. Light poured in through the large window onto an old steel-framed double bed and a wardrobe. A painting of a rural scene hung on the wall and a threadbare rug attempted to grace the place with a semblance of comfort. The landlady stood with The Professor as Kelly made a big deal about apparently checking everything.

"Where's the toilet?"

"Toaletní." The Professor translated and the landlady pointed along the hallway. Kelly walked out and looked at it. Green painted wooden boards spanned the walls and a small tub with a primitive gas-heater above it had a steel tap connected to a hose which climbed up to an old shower-head held onto the ceiling with string. The toilet pan itself was cracked and without a seat and sporting the spattered remnants of somebody's breakfast.

"Yes this is fine. I'll take it." Kelly said, fraudulently, and gave

The Professor the thumbs up then listened to his debate with the landlady.

"How long you stay here?" The Professor asked.

"Two weeks? Maybe more? I'll pay cash." The Professor translated.

The landlady made a big deal about asking for the money and voices were raised. Then there was a period of quiet exchanges with looks down to Kelly. The landlady paused and then said something with a tweak of her head. The Professor translated.

"Six thousand Koronas."

Kelly pulled the money from his wallet, completely unaware if this was a good sum for the room, and climbed a few stairs passing it up to The Professor who gave it to the landlady. She counted it expertly then quickly looked at Kelly up and down before saying something to The Professor and nodding at the door across the landing opposite hers. The Professor turned to Kelly and said,

"Lady work...." and he also nodded to the door. The landlady waited to hear. "She work. Night. Maybe you hear...." he cupped his hand around his ear, then said, "...is okay?"

Kelly nodded and said, "Yes...is ok...err no problem."

The Professor then said something quickly to the landlady who nodded before sliding backwards like a spider into her flat and quietly closed the door. That wasn't too bad, he thought. He gave one thousand crowns to The Professor who initially protested but then took it also disappearing into his room below.

Kelly stood in front of the window and looked out at Prague, listening to the sound of the traffic from the main road. The smell of cooking wafted in from somewhere. He sighed pleased to be somewhere behind a closed door and felt something. Perhaps relief? The greyness of solitude? A softly churning panic? Or maybe like a small boy that had mistakenly stumbled into the ring at a circus.

A few hours passed between him unpacking his bags and finding another hiding place for his money which was down at the very bottom of the stairwell where he had to crawl to put it behind a wooden panel. He'd counted it and was currently sitting at approximately, two thousand dollars, nine thousand pounds, and twenty thousand Czech Crowns.

McQuarrie and Jones went to Joe's flat and naturally found May there. She went with them to where Joe was working but also took with her some letters from the bank that had arrived that morning. He was bemused when he was told his passport was missing but even more surprised when he opened the letters from the bank asking him to retain the business receipts for the recent seven thousand pounds he'd exchanged at Heathrow.

*

It was early. This bar was rough. But that was good. Inside was dark. A lot darker than the brilliant sunshine outside. There was a single stretch of sturdy oak running the full length of the room and behind it was a dark–haired small woman of about twenty-five. She wore a blouse that had once been white and a dark skirt. She had a careworn attitude about her but eyes that spoke of a resentment and anger at having to spend her life in this box of wood and plaster. There was a broad fireplace that had the remnants of a fire long left to burn out and on the hearth were the remnants of a broken bottle. Stains were sporadically a feature of this establishment decorating the unpainted plastered walls. An obvious golden beer stain here and there and further up near the ceiling were water stains that looked as though they had leaked in from the flat above but there were dark marks on the wall behind a long planken, backless bench behind a table that looked like one of those that were placed in parks for picnics but this was a lot older, rougher and had large cobs broken from it that spoke of either intentional vandalism or a violent act. Nobody else was in the bar. Kelly had chosen this street for its dowdy, crude exterior and apparently matching residents. Washing was draped from windows on the side that the early sun caught and naught but a few souls were on the street and those that were appeared to have somewhere to go and things to do. It was only ten-thirty in the morning. Kelly had checked the time just before he selected this street and quickly took off his Breitling watch stowing it in the pocket of his trousers. He was going to wear jeans but they didn't appear to be a popular choice of legwear here in Prague so he hauled on a pair of his old breeks he cared little for and pulled a shirt on. This was his approximation at blending in as much as he could. As he passed people who rarely made eye contact or let on in any way, he considered his efforts commendable which imbued him with a new confidence that was lacking before he spoke to The Professor that morning. He'd knocked on the door to get a quick lesson in the Czech language before stepping out abroad and managed to remember, *hello, please, beer* and *thank you,* in that order and he already had *yes* and *no*. He told The Professor that he was going to venture out and got a *good luck* from him before he left.

He stood in the doorway surveying the room for a second just as the woman arose from beneath the bar. Their eyes met and he smiled. Nothing came back. She put her hands on the bar as if to wait for him to approach and make his order, which he understood.

"*Dobrý den*", he said affecting the accent of The Professor, so much so that the woman flatly rattled off,

"Kávovar je rozbitý a pořád čekám, až přijede chleba!" throwing her hands up in the air and returning to whatever she was doing as he arrived.

Although her response had irritation dripping from it he was quite pleased with her quick acceptance of his garb and gab, however, really didn't want to give away too much of his insecurity so took a punt, guessing from the tone that something was amiss, so he just said,

"Pivo?"

A muttering ensued from beneath the bar and she rose and turned her back to him and pulled open the door on an ancient fridge and pulled out a large bottle of beer, snapped off the cap and placed it on the bar.

"Chceš sklenici?" she said loosely pointing at a row of glasses on a shelf behind her.

"Ne." Kelly replied and took a deep draught from the bottle.

There was a newspaper at the end of the bar and he concluded that it was low on her priorities as she returned to her task beneath the bar.

He sat at the rough table and opened it up scanning the indecipherability of the language, however, intrigued, as well, then gave up and pored over the pictures. What looked like a fat councillor was beaming on the steps of a civic building with a sash diagonally traversing his corpulence whilst receiving a framed certificate. The headline below read,

Policejní náčelník dostává město díky

The word *Police* was discernible. Czech plod winning an award, he thought and turned to the back page. Flanking everything was a large picture of a group of young and old men surrounding a gravestone with a large star on it. Fresh flowers were at the base. Kelly looked at the headline and was astounded to see the word *Skotský* written in the text. He looked at the article trying to find anything else that might indicate why there was the Scottish reference and he saw the words *Johnny Madden* written. Reading on he saw the words *Dumbarton FC* and *Celtic* further down the report and what he presumed was a date *Června 11,* and hardly able to believe the coincidence of his being there, but he had little idea who this Johnny Madden was, or had been and it was difficult to make out the writing on the gravestone. He looked over to the bar and saw that the young woman was still busy and tore off the back page, folded it and put it in his pocket. Then there was an angry cry. He jumped. Had he been caught? She stood up and kicked something at her feet, bent down again and seemed to be trying to lift something. An opportunity came riding over the horizon and he rose and walked to the bar. He realised he had nothing more than an English phrase as an opener,

"Can I help you?"

A frowning and puzzled face stood up and looked him in the eye.

He repeated, "Can I help you?....Lift something?" and he mimed the levitation of an imaginary box and pointed to where she'd been struggling.

She said nothing and then looked at the door then said, "Americký? American?"

"Ne...Skotsky." he quietly said.

"Skotsky? v Praze? Proč?"

Then she hurried to the door and closed it quickly. The room darkened. Then she said,

"Mluvíte Čechoslovák?"

Kelly shrugged and opened his hands. She spoke again, "I ask...you speak Czech?"

"Ne...erm, no. I don't. You speak English?"

"Yes. Little. All people young want English speak. But..." Then she put her finger over her mouth.

Kelly understood. Then he mimed the lifting and said "Something heavy?"

"Ano..yes." Then she beckoned him come around the bar.

Between the two of them they managed to pull a large wooden box full of empty bottles to her back door and then out onto the cobbled back lane. They came back into the bar and then she said,

"Thank you." and flexed her arm as if to tighten a bicep. Kelly smiled back delighted at her acknowledgement of his manly prowess and said *thank you* back to her but then she said,

"Ne... Mĕ!", then lifted her sleeve and brought a sizeable bicep into the discussion and smiled broader. Kelly liked her mock bravado and laughed. He went back to the table and sat down to finish his beer. She sat down next to him giving him a start not thinking she would follow him.

"Name?" she said and pointed at him.

"Kelly." Then he pointed at her.

"Irena" and she offered her hand to him. He shook it, smiled and nodded. Then a silence cloaked the mood for some moments as they sought the next topic over which to chew this international fat. Kelly then pulled the newspaper page from his pocket and flattened it on the table. Irena then looked at the rest of the newspaper, turned it to see the back page missing and made a big show of affected disapproval throwing her hands up but smiled. Kelly smiled back. He pointed to the picture and said,

"What is this?"

Irena leaned across him and started to read the gist of the story. Kelly could smell her sweat and the absence of any deodorant but didn't mind it or judge her. How could he? She straightened up and started to think.

"Fotbal...fotbal..." then stood up and mimed scoring a goal and celebrating.

He'd managed to work that bit out but said nothing and said, "Who is he?"

She read it again. "Johnny Madden. Skotsky. Here. Praha. Otec fotbalu. Otec českého fotbalu."

"A Scottish footballer? Here?" and he pointed to the floor.

"Yes.....but...." she mimed dying. Eyes half shut and tongue hanging out.

"Dead?"

"Yes. *Dead*....but Otec....erm....papa....old..." She used her thumb to point over her shoulder.

"Papa? Father?"

"Yes! Father football! Čeština! Czech! Johnny Madden! Skotsky!"

Irena went to the bar and brought back a pencil and wrote the years 1865-1948. Then an exposition of the story through a shared ability in broken English and the power of mime illuminated Kelly as to the story of an ex-Dumbarton FC and Celtic player who'd came to Prague in 1905 and managed Slavia Prague for twenty-five years and changed the face of Czech football, forever. Not only that but he'd married a Czech girl and had a son, Harry, and stayed there for the rest of his life. The story was Slavia Prague players and officials commemorating his birthday and laying flowers at the grave of Czech football's Scottish father.

Something warm welled up inside of Kelly. Something good had happened to him. A connection had been made, however coincidental. The subject closed and the uncomfortable quietness descended again. Kelly asked,

"Is this your pub? Bar?" lifting his arms up and looking around the room, then pointed at Irena.

She understood. "Ne. Otec. Papa...." then she said, "ermmmm.....*father?*" and smiled.

Kelly smiled and said, "*Ano...*yes, father."

He drank the rest of his beer and went to make his goodbyes and pay for the beer. Irena refused his money and pointed to the crate outside the back door and smiled. Then it dropped off her face as she tried to think of some words in English,

"...errm.... you... here...Praha?"

"Ano....yes." he nodded.

"ermmm..." was all that came from her as she looked at him trying to ask *how long?* rolling her hands and made her quizzical face. He got it, but didn't really want to give out too much, just in case of..... he couldn't say what but acknowledged the risk.

"Two." holding up his fingers.

"Dva? Dní? Týdnů?"

An exchange of fingers denoting seven and one occurred. Days and weeks were established.

"Tyd....?" he attempted *weeks*.

"Týdnů." Irena said smiling. He smiled back and said,

"Týdnů."

"Dobré! .... *good*.....yes?"

"Yes, good... *Dobré."*

Irena then appeared somewhat coy and asked,

"You come. Make speak. Mě?" Angličtina? English?"

He was pleased to be wanted.

"Ano. Yes. When? Tonight?"

She struggled so he took out his Breitling and pointed at seven o'clock.

"Ne! Ne!" Irena said quickly and put her finger over her lips making a *shh!* sound obviously not wanting her attraction to English publicised then pointed at the floor, looked at the watch and indicated ten o'clock then looked around the room and threw her hand between herself and Kelly and shrugged asking the question. Kelly smiled and nodded. She sighed and smiled relieved. Then she looked at the watch again and said,

"Pěkné. Krásné." And pulled a pose pouting her lips and drawing her hand across her face. Kelly laughed out loud and realised it was the first time in a long time that he'd laughed. Irena chuckled with him.

"Yes...*ano.*" he said then thought *what the hell* and said, "....you.." pointing at her, *"pretty...krásné..?"*

He could only remember the second word. Irena made a big show of probably saying *you silver-tongued fucking charmer* and mock-scolded him.

Kelly offered his hand to her and said,

"Goodbye Irena. Tomorrow?" pointing at ten o' clock.

"Goodbye Kelly." She smiled back. "Zítra. *Tomorrow.*"

Then he smiled, nodded and left. As he made his way back up the street he passed a suited chap carrying a newspaper who looked him in the eye as he strode on briskly.

He arrived back at the apartment and quietly crept up the stairs. He was getting used to creeping around trying to be anonymous. As he reached his landing the old wooden stairs creaked loudly, to whit the landlady disappeared quickly into her flat carrying a brush and shovel. Something about her demeanour alarmed him. He put the key into the door and opened it. He looked at his bags and surmised nothing was untoward but immediately felt like a fool. *Of course she had a key! She's the fucking landlady!* He muttered to himself.

He spent the next few hours trying to organise his things. He put the make-up and all the stuff he'd used to be Joe, into a plastic bag and then Joe's passport into the zipped pocket of a holdall and put the cartoon prints he'd taken from Bullet's flat along with *The Good Soldier Sveyk* and the bible into the main part of the bag and put it in the bottom of the wardrobe. Then he hung his clothes up in the wardrobe, something he never did at home.

He went out and bought some lunch and wandered through the streets of Prague until he found himself down near the river Vlatava away from the city centre and watched a couple of old men fishing. He went down to the bankside and sat down and felt the sun on his back and let it fall backwards. He lay there and breathed a heavy sigh of relief. He felt as though his presence here in Prague was accepted and also as if he'd put enough distance between him, Edinburgh and McQuarrie.

He thought of his mother then fell asleep. Fifty minutes later he woke and went home.

Back at the apartment he resumed his period of rest in the late afternoon lying on the bed and enjoyed the noise of the world outside passing him by and the welcome summer heat. He could hear the landlady going up and down the stairs and her talking to other people and again the smell of cooking wafted up and over the landings. He recognised the slow clump-clump of The Professor's feet climbing the stairs and the thud of him closing the door, below and before he knew it he was asleep again.

He woke at 4:15am to bright sunshine and silence but for the sound of twittering birds. He'd never felt so well-rested and took a while to shake off his slumber enough to get up and pee. He'd got to the toilet before anyone else being so early and was glad of it because there had been some shitty presents waiting for him clinging to the bowl any other time he had to go which offended his sense of decorum and vowed to begin the hunt for another place as soon as was feasible. Then the door handle rattled and a voice spoke abruptly in Czech. He opened the door to leave. A poorly made-up face with too much rouge and lipstick stared back at him, brown hair fell across her shoulders and grey roots sat atop of her head. She wore a large gabardine-type coat and carried a small bag.

"Kdo jsi?" she said abruptly.

He felt a little exposed standing in his underpants which she'd taken in, quickly and had no idea he was being asked who he was. She asked if he was deaf or just stupid and who he was again.

"Jsi hluchý nebo jen hloupý? Kdo jsi?"

He just smiled and went to squeeze past her. Then she saw the English writing on the waistband of his new underpants and smiled.

"Sloggi!" she said almost thrilled. "Velmi hezké!" Then she asked where he'd got them and if he had any more, "Kdes je dostal? Máš ještě?"

He really didn't want to broadcast his non-communist underpants and western credentials to all and sundry so smiled, nodded and went back to his room. She delayed using the toilet to watch which room he was going in to and smiled to him as he shut the door. He lay back on his bed fully intending to return to Nod but heard the toilet flush and the door catch. Heels deliberately thudded slowly on the old floorboards towards his door. He looked down at the dimly illuminated landing light creeping beneath the door until the heels stopped and a shadow blocked the light. He held his breath. The shadow stayed there until a quietly rapped knock broke the tension. He really couldn't be arsed with this. Then her voice said,

"Hey....*Sloggi?*" Then she said she wanted to show him

something, *"Chci ti něco ukázat"* said with a salacious undertone that didn't work for him in Blighty at 4:30am never mind behind The Iron Curtain.

"Chci ti něco ukázat" she said again but more softly telling him it was okay to open up and she wouldn't stab him or anything equally as undesirable. To relent seemed the only viable course of action in order to resolve this international standoff. He opened the door gently and smiled because he didn't want to speak English thus fuelling another discussion and questions.

Her hands were resting on both door sides of the frame as he opened up. *Oh good god* he thought *she's gone back to work!* Her eyes dropped back to his apparently desirable underpants and back up to his eyeline. Then in another attempt to appear seductive, she said, *"Hey Sloggi"* again but now took one hand from the door frame and placed it on the belt of her coat. With one sharp tug the belt was undone and the coat fell open revealing a pair of pink cammy knickers, circa 1952, and a non-matching white bra with a small knot on the shoulder strap where an adjusting clasp should be resulting in one boob further north than its lifelong friend. Between said knickers and bra was a flabby stretch of belly and discernible stretch marks speaking of childbirth past. All he could do was shake his head quickly and say,

"Ne... děkuju...*thank you*...shit!" his Czech slipped..

"Americky?" she quickly asked now very interested in more than his underpants.

"Ne! Ne..." he said then quickly shut the door. She didn't leave but spoke through the door.

"Hey...American *Sloggi...zitra*...tomorrow...yes?"

Her heels accompanied the sound of her coat being closed and then her keys rattling and the door closing. He sighed, lay back and looked out at the sunshine. He had to find another place.

At 10:30am he pushed the bar door open and peered inside looking for Irena. It was empty as predicted. He walked in and sat down at the same table. Then the babbling of voices was heard coming in from the back door and Irena arrived with a man in overalls clutching a spanner. He said something to her and took the spanner to a large nut on one of the pipes on what was the very old looking coffee machine. Irena saw him and quickly said she'd be with him in a minute as if speaking to a regular customer. Kelly nodded and smiled. Spanner man opened a valve on the top of the machine and then turned the last turn on the nut and shouted *ha!* just as a thick black soup of water and coffee grounds spilled from the blocked pipe and onto the floor. Irena reticently acknowledged that he'd been right as she spouted something at him whilst taking a mop to the mess. Spanner-man poured water into the pipe and tilted the machine so that all the water and grounds be evacuated. Then he tightened up the nut, again. Irena opened the till, passed some money to him then opened the fridge door and gave him a bottle of beer. He disappeared out of the back door shouting advice and *told you so's* as he left, all the while Irena talking back until his voice faded.

"Hello Kelly." She said and smiled at him. Then she said she had to clean up the mess. He understood as she held a mop up.

"Hello Irena." He replied and went behind the counter and started to use an old cloth to keep the black sludge in one place on the floor.

Irena protested saying *Ne, ne!* but Kelly made a quite European show of face-pulling and open hands, insisting he would help. They exchanged smiles as the coffee sludge was cleaned and dropped into a bin. Kelly was cleaning his hands at a sink when Irena spoke in English,

"I make practice with book." she beamed and lifted a text book from underneath the bar. Kelly smiled and gently took it from her.

The book was from the 1930s with pictures of very middle-class English families having picnics in a park or booking into a hotel.

Things English families used to do all the time, *don't you know*.

"Very good." He smiled at her. "Full marks."

She frowned. She didn't know *full marks*. Kelly changed the subject and said, "Coffee?" Irena smiled back and said yes and went at the coffee machine with the skill and speed of a seasoned pro. She brought two cups to the table then drew the lock across the front door. Kelly took it black with lots of sugar and he genuinely thought it ridiculously tasty.

Irena spent the next hour reading and being corrected by Kelly whilst randomly picking up items to which Kelly would say the name. And he felt good. For the first time he could remember he was doing something for the benefit of someone else for no reward but the pleasure of making someone happy. There was no room for his ego or improvisations because he had not the linguistic ability to go there but was merely in the room denuded of his bullshit but glowed with the satisfaction of his being needed and wanted. Irena was pretty, it was true but within him there was no desire to make the rendezvous anything but the innocent liaison that it was. He had something someone else needed and he liked it, wanted to give it freely.

A natural hiatus dropped into the ether between them and both knew that it was time to wrap up the English lessons but Irena spared their blushes by tapping her bare wrist as if a watch was there, indicating that she had to open for business, properly. Kelly smiled and nodded and finished his second coffee. Then he had a spontaneous and possibly ridiculous and risky thought, but did it anyway.

As he walked back into the street he couldn't stop smiling at her reaction, of the unadulterated joy she showed. The Breitling was a shade too big for her wrist but she wore it anyway. Then she offered him her hand when she had composed herself fully intending to merely shake it but spontaneously hugged him and kissed him on the cheek. Then she checked it in a very masculine way from different angles. Kelly beamed. He felt happy. He was about to leave when Irena quickly said to him,

"Kelly...you come ..bar. Tonight. Yes? But......*sshh!"* and she put her finger to her lips. This was progress indeed he thought and nodded.

As he walked up the street heavy footsteps clumped behind him. Then The Professor caught up with him.

"Kelly....Kelly...." he was out of breath. ".....you eat..make breakfast? With me..yes?"

He seemed to have arrived from nowhere and this was a good bit away from the apartments. People passed them and The Professor changed into Czech as they did so muttering something until they'd drawn out of earshot then dropped back into his broken English. They found a spartan looking cafe and ordered some coffee and bread rolls.

"You like Prague?" The Professor said between coffee slurps and vigorous moustache-wiping.

Kelly decided to be non-committal because there were areas beyond the city centre that could do with a coat of paint and some plaster patchwork.

"Yes. Beautiful."

"Why you Praha...erm...Prague?" He asked without looking away from buttering his bread roll.

Kelly's eyes widened. There seemed to be a subtext as he'd already explained that he was there for the Maths Olympiad. The Maths Olympiad was therefore the answer.

"The Mathematics Ol...."

"Yes...yes... Matematika! But you make apartment....with me. No hotel. Why?"

Without thinking much Kelly had to go to work.

"Okay...okay. I love football... I also love Celtic. You know? The football club. Glasgow. Skotsky. Scotland...."

"I know... make big win Europe Cup.. nineteen...erm...fif...ne.."

"Nineteen sixty-seven."

"*Ano*....yes, nineteen sixty-seven! Caesar!"

"That's right, Caesar!" Kelly didin't know a lot about football but he did know that Billy McNeil, the Celtic captain, lifted the European Cup and that his nickname was Caesar. "Well.... I want to write a book." Kelly said as if he'd been undone and opened his hands on the table in a *you got me* fashion.

"Write?"

Kelly mimed writing.

"Ah... *Zápis*. What book? Futbol?"

"Czech football....and Johnny Madden."

The Professor smirked and looked at him saying nothing for a moment.

"Yes....Johnny Madden. Skotsky. I know. Make Slavia Praha. Make Czech team. Write book. But...why?"

"Because I am a Celtic man and he played for Celtic...."

"Ne, ne, ne..... Matematika? Why?" he brusquely cut Kelly off.

"Because this is a communist country. Because there is a cowboy in The White House and his girlfriend in Downing Street that the Russians really don't like! To get a visa to come to Prague is difficult and if I said I wanted to research a book about *football* I wouldn't have got one. Simple as!"

Kelly loaded his reply with mock frustration which seemed to quell the curiosity of The Professor, who smiled his green teeth and said,

"Okay...Kelly..okay...you make book. Johnny Madden. Good. Very good. *Dobré.*"

Then The Professor flatly said, and waited for the answer before he bit into another bread-roll,

"You want I show? Slavia Praha. Stadium? Make photo. I come?"

"No...no thanks. I want to make this an adventure. Mine. No."

Kelly expected him to be put out by his response but he just said "Okay. I go now."

He finished his coffee and shook bread crumbs out of his beard, shook Kelly's hand and quickly left. Kelly thought he was just avoiding the bill but he was glad to be rid of him. Ten minutes later he paid the bill, did likewise and returned to his room in *Toulovska*.

He was getting used to taking a rest in the afternoon and lay back on his bed and slept until three o'clock. He wakened by the hushed tones of a conversation on the landing outside his door. He heard a male voice and that of the landlady. She didn't care who she disturbed, he thought. He went to the window and rubbed his eyes. Fortunately the sun had thrown his side of the building into shade by this time and was glad of the respite. He had no idea Czechoslovakia could be this hot. He'd been to Spain before and this was definitely on a par, if not hotter. About three buildings away a stork had made a nest on the roof and was sitting there sparkling white against the greyness of the tenement blocks in the distance. The nest was an artistic mess, however there was something of an abstract attractiveness to it, no doubt, said the David Bailey in him.

He pointed his camera at the stork and focused. It was more beautiful up close and he made an involuntary little appreciative noise that surprised him, too. The door into the apartments clattered loudly below. A grey-suited man exited onto the pavement and looked down the street then up to Kelly. Kelly clicked five times in quick succession, then looked down at the man. A second passed between them and then the man briskly walked away. Kelly had the inclination to take a photo of him as he walked away and gazed at him through the lens before he disappeared around the corner and out onto the main road. However, he thought he had snapped a cracker of the stork and decided that he should get a few more but not of the usual tourist stuff. He wanted to document a slice of the regular Czech people and places. Who knows, maybe it's shots he could mount in a frame and sell if push came to shove, he thought, and it would give him something to do. He had at least four hours before he was going to see Irena so he ventured out into the city and shot some pictures of mundane things like a shop-front he thought was particularly interesting, an old man sitting on a window ledge, a dog, and some graffiti daubed roughly on the wall of a stately looking building. He wandered around doing this for a couple of hours and returned to his room.

He took a shower, turning the water-heater tap on and a flame woofed into life. Eventually, however, he gave up on the irregular flow and settled for the tepid cold water with a better pressure. He soaped his body and shaved under the spray but then heard someone come into the toilet, drop their underwear to their ankles and proceed to sit down on the bowl while there was *patently someone having a shower*! Kelly put his head around the plastic curtain. Sitting there was his painted flasher from the early hours looking ito a small mirror and applying rouge and lipstick whilst a heavy deposit splashed below her. He'd had enough.

"Hey!!!" he shouted but didn't seem to make an impression as she continued with her artistry.

Then she looked up at him.

"Hello, American Sloggi...." she drawled unaffected with the scene.

Kelly thought of giving her a mouthful but English was all he had, so he just said *Hey!* again and raised his open palm to the shower.

"...eeessh...." and a roll of her eyes was all that came back. She ripped a square of newspaper from its string holder and began wiping her arse muttering all the while with the word *American* interspersed. Kelly squirmed and withdrew but beheld the shadows of her squaring herself to leave through the translucent curtain. Finally there was a flush but then a finger came around the curtain and pulled it back as her head came around, smiling. She looked at his body and then down to his tackle and said,

"Bye bye, American. *Tonight....?*"

"No! Fuck no!! Ne! Ne!" he growled. "Get to fuck....you old...."

She left laughing.

".....and I'm not American, okay!!"

He put his jeans on later and a white t-shirt, fixed his hair which had now grown to a length requiring shape. Then he splashed his face with *Denim,* checked he'd enough Crowns in his wallet and walked out into Prague. He felt good. Despite himself, and the clandestine regulations attached to the visit, he was excited at going to see Irena. He felt quite healthy, too. He hadn't had much to drink, of late and had put in a few miles walking, usually away from places but this had seemed to clear his head and his lungs and he'd noticed the sun had mildly tanned his face a little. The question of how long he could remain under the radar here behind The Iron Curtain was continually there, but tonight he was going to have a few quiet beers, be among people and enjoy the view called Irena.

It was eight o'clock on a beautiful evening in Prague as he turned into the street and wandered along. It was much busier now and he passed several people on their way to somewhere or talking outside the shops that were still open. He passed a massive display of courgettes outside a greengrocer's but not much else. Looked like courgettes were the veg to have this season. He approached Irena's bar from the other side of the street to see how busy it was. The door was open and from a distance he could see a couple of people sitting at the tables. He'd never bothered to ask or look at the name of the bar and from this side of the street he could see it was called *Bar Cerveny.* He didn't know what it meant. He craned his head to try and see Irena from where he was but there was no sign of her. He wasn't quite brave enough yet to go in and try to order from anyone else. Then she flitted into the scene from the back door and busied herself with a cloth. He walked across and into Bar Cerveny and immediately up to the where Irena was. There was an older man near the door with a tall beer in front of him and a man alone further back into the darker and cooler part with a beer and small glass of something.

"Beer please." He said quietly and Irena turned to see him and smiled.

"Dobrý den. Jedno pivo." She quickly said so the other two could hear and poured Kelly a large beer then wrote his tab on a piece of paper and put it on a shelf behind the bar.

Kelly took a huge draught of his beer and then smiled at Irena. She smiled back and flicked her eyes to the others. Kelly got it and spoke quietly.

"Hello. How are you?"

"Dobrý. Good. I speak now. Come my father. Soon...." then she put her finger to her lips again. He nodded.

"It is a beautiful evening."

"Me?" and she coyly smiled wider showing her perfectly straight teeth and pushed a tress of hair back over her ear.

Kelly thought of explaining but considered it unnecessary so just smiled back and said,

"Ano... yes."

Irena excused her quiet giggling and smiling self to the other end of the bar and took her cloth to a perfectly clean surface, all the while looking back at Kelly. Then the old man lifted himself out of his seat and walked to the bar next to Kelly. The smile dropped from Irena's face. The old man politely addressed him and Kelly could hear the humility in his voice despite it being in Czech.

Excuse my impertinence for addressing you sir, but I have recently lost my only friend in the world. I walked with him last evening in the park and I stopped to speak to someone and when I turned to see where he had got to I could see nothing of him. He must be lost and I fear that if he is lost someone might kill him and eat him, such is the price of fresh meat. I have been asking everyone and each time my sadness grows fatter and my hope thinner....

Kelly looked at him as blankly as he could trying to give out the impression he understood.

....if you see him sir he has a black coat and large brown eyes. I miss him so much and wish him to be found.

Irena rolled her eyes and said,

Ulrich! Your dog has died! You have to stop bothering people in the bar or you won't be allowed to come back in. Leave this gentleman alone!

He might have seen him! Sir, if you see him will you come back and tell me? His name is Havel.

Irena barked at him in, *He doesn't want to be bothered with any of your nonsense Ulrich! Do you, sir? No....no?*

Irena emphasised the *ne* and Kelly replied,

"Ne."

Ulrich muttered his way back to his table and sat down, Then he looked underneath his table at the bare floorboards as if the dog should be there.

A stout man walked in from the back door and behind the bar then walked up to Irena and, totally ignoring Kelly, brusquely spoke to her. He was in a blue shirt and well-worn trousers. Irena said something curtly back to him then he had a quick look around the pub then opened the till and appeared to count. Then Kelly saw he was wearing the Breitling he gave to Irena. He bristled doubting she had bestowed it upon him with a loving kiss. He guessed this was her father. A man in a grey suit came in and ordered whisky then took it to a seat in the darker cooler part of the pub and opened a newspaper. Irena's father shouted to her pointing at the front door. She sighed heavily, picked up a shawl from under the bar wrapped it around her shoulders and marched towards the door to the street catching Kelly's eye at the same time. She disappeared out of the pub. Kelly took another huge swig of his beer leaving a discreet amount at the bottom of the glass ready to finish when the time was right to follow Irena. He stood at the bar for a few moments longer and decided to stretch in a lame performance as if he was tired, then finished his beer and left Bar Cerveny.

Irena was waiting for him on the corner of the next block outside a tobacconists shop. She waved her hands at him to be quick and he hurried up to her.

"I make shop for coffee. Come you with me?"

She was even prettier in the soft evening light. "Yes. Okay."

They walked for a few blocks almost in silence for the length of time it took to reach a black-fronted shop. Irena indicated he was to wait for her outside. As the door opened the smell of coffee was nearly overpowering and he sneaked a look in and saw open sacks of coffee beans stacked against the walls. He felt quite vulnerable hanging around like this and a few passers-by noticed him somehow sensing his difference from all of them, but Irena soon came back out with a small sack of coffee beans. She said her goodbyes to the man who served her and then lifted the bag across the back of her shoulders and leaned forward. Kelly was mildly shocked by her rough but necessary and manly task so he insisted he carry her burden back to the bar. It was heavier than he expected but managed to lift it over his left shoulder keeping his left hand on it.

Irena had slowed the pace disregarding her growling father and asked,

"Come you tomorrow. Morning?"

Kelly's face was sore from smiling. She was lovely. "Of course!"

She frowned. She didn't know this phrase. Kelly just said, "Yes."

She smiled wider and asked, "We talk? What we talk? Tomorrow?"

"We talk about Prague. You teach me. Yes?"

"Yes I teach you but... tomorrow...bar no. Work no. I no work. Go Prague. Friend... Přítel."

"You have a pretty friend?" Lost in translation.

"Yes friend. Make coffee. Come you?" Irena said.

Kelly thought she was trying to set him up with a pretty friend, which was frustrating.

"I don't want your pretty friend you beautiful, strong lump of Czech loveliness! I want you!" said deliberately quickly, but he assented and asked "Where?" and held out his hands and looked around as if he was lost.

Irena took a pencil and pad from her pocket and wrote down an address and gave it to him. He put it in his pocket, quickly. Then Irena said,

"I go bar..." and she deftly took the sack from his shoulder and slung it onto the back of her neck and shoulders then held her palm face down. He understood to wait. "Come people...bar. No talk? Yes?"

"Yes. I'll wait." He said but he'd already made up his mind to go back into the bar because he thought the beer was fantastic. A slow walk took him ten minutes or so and then he walked into a now quite noisy space. Two men and a mouthy woman were at the back of the room at a table in heated discussion and it sounded like the fairer sex was winning. Ulrich was still alone at his table and two other working men in overalls chose to stand and talk. A black and white TV flickered on a shelf, its tinny sound filling the room and it all seemed somewhat familiar to him. Kelly had no need to order as his beer was already poured. Irena took his money and served someone else. The grey-suited man had had enough and folded his newspaper. He approached the bar and spoke to Irena's father closely. Her father looked down at the Breitling watch and shrugged his shoulders then pointed to Irena. Kelly guessed he was probably envious and quite liked the fact it was him that had sparked this exchange. Then the grey suit left. Kelly hated cigarette smoke, something that was never really a problem in *The Old Duke* but this place was beginning to look like a London smog. He hated the way it hung on his clothes, which just required that he resort to washing them, a task which he disliked and so rarely did it. He considered staying for one more but he couldn't talk to Irena and anyway she was busy and didn't fancy having to get over the language barrier with any of the assemblage of characters in the bar, so he caught Irena's eye, paid his tab and covertly motioned his head to the door. He took the note with her friend's address and lifted it so she could see. She smiled and nodded, then he walked out into the warm summer evening. He felt good. He'd made a contact, a pretty one at that and now he had something like a date. He looked at the address and tried to make sense of the words but he'd work it out tomorrow. Try to find it on a street map. He walked along the street turned a corner onto the main road and stopped at a shop and bought bread and butter and a few apples. That should keep him going until the morning. There was a spring in his step and awoke to the feeling that for the first time in his life he actually felt free. No constraint of work, form-filling at the dole office, pressure of money, fantastic weather even though he'd heard the winters could be brutal but that was months down the line. Here he knew he had enough to live on for years. The trick, it seemed,was to keep his head down and try to sail under the radar but learn a bit of the language to get by. However, he thought those problems insignificant compared to the enormous feeling of well-being and newness that enveloped him. He took an apple from its bag and bit into it. Even the fruit was amazing. The irony of this sense of freedom behind The Iron Curtain wasn't lost on him but he wanted to ride this pony for as long as he could.

He'd never been a lover of cars nor ever sought to own a licence but he knew true beauty when he saw it. Among the Lada's, Trabants and Yugo's that coughed out their fumes into the Prague roads a jet black Mercedes with the raised badge on the bonnet, or gun-sights as he liked to call it, gracefully cruised its way towards him, The radiator gleamed in the evening sun and he thought it was a good thing that a few of the good motors managed to get across the border for someone to enjoy. He even smiled involuntarily as its elegance purred down the road. It was driving much slower than the rest of the traffic, just as it should, he thought, and took another bite of the apple. Then the Merc suddenly growled and seemed to drop a cog reaching a quite ridiculous speed for the old street and cobbled surfaces of the city and then pulled in quickly with a screech of brakes. Kelly was outside a tenement block and a few people were gathered talking but then quickly dispersed indoors or elsewhere. He was bemused as it stopped where he was and the passenger and rear door opened quickly. Two large men in long coats came towards him. One grabbed his bag of apples and threw it on the street and grabbed his arm and shoulder as the other knocked the bread and butter from his grasp and did the same. His head was dipped into the car and an overpowering smell of old leather accosted him. Heads poked out of the tenement doors as the car drove away and gradually they emerged back into the evening sun and a small woman quickly gathered the bread, butter and apples and disappeared back into a door.

He sat between the two large men on the back seat of oxblood leather and looked at them both. Neither took their eyes from him. He suddenly felt something sink in his stomach and thought he might have a shitty accident but held onto his shame. He wanted to say something but he had no Czech.

"What's happening?" was all his trembling mouth could offer.

"Be quiet." A voice from the front passenger seat said and the grey-suited man leaned around to look at him. Kelly looked back at him then caught the eye of the driver in the rear-view mirror who outstared him for a ridiculous amount of time considering he was driving. He looked at Grey Suit again and felt his familiarity. The tram, the restaurant, the street, the bar. Kelly smiled and let a small chuckle out into the interior of the car. A gloved but cupped hand brutally slapped the side of his head. It had caught and covered his left ear and a pressure seared into his head as he lost his hearing then let out a delayed and muffled cry of pain. Then everything went black as a hood dropped over his head.

"Don't try to remove the hood. It will not be good for you." Grey Suit said.

Kelly travelled for twenty-five minutes in silence. Sweat ran down his face and neck. Thoughts of attempting a conversation in which he might improvise a character that might take the stinky smell of this situation away were all but forlorn with these quietly efficient men.

The car stopped. The doors opened and Kelly was pulled out and marched into a cold environment. A door slammed behind him then he was guided blindly forward on what he felt to be a concrete floor at a disturbing pace and then down some stairs on which he stumbled but held up by two pairs of clutching hands. He heard a door open, was pushed forward and then placed roughly in a chair.

Then everything went quiet and the door slammed behind him. It was cold. He turned his head quickly at every noise. Then footsteps on concrete steps faded and all was silent again. He didn't know whether to take off the hood. His sweat was beginning to cool and he shivered. He listened again. Nothing. He lifted his right hand up to the neck of the hood and started to lift it. The voice of Grey Suit said,

"Do not take off the hood."

"I can't breathe!" Kelly said which was a lie.

"Yes you can. We have hoods that are specifically designed for that effect. The one you are wearing is not."

"Still....can I take it off?"

Another heavy hand caught the side of his head and he fell to the cold floor.

His heart leapt. "What is happening!" he shouted trying to get up.

"Stay where you are. You will rise in a few minutes."

"I want to sit down. It's cold here! Let me sit down!"

A freezing shock of water soaked him.

"Arrghh!!" he yelled. "What have I done? What do you want?"

Another bucket of water hammered into him. He recovered and shouted,

"What the fuck is happening!!"

"Remain where you are. If you try to rise you will be punished."

"Why! What have I done!! What do you want." Snot ran from his nose. He was now quite cold.

He heard footsteps and the door opening and echoing as it slammed. He didn't know if anyone else was left in the room with him. He sat with his knees up at his chest and occasionally sneaked his hand underneath the hood to wipe his face. Moments passed. Silence but for his shivering and slapping of his arms as he fought off the cold.

"Hello? Who's here? Can I take off the hood!" Nothing.

He decided to lift the hood as he kept his head on his knees. He heard a foot move and turned as if he'd just been shifting for comfort. He was in the custody of the Czech StB, *Státní bezpečnost* secret police. He didn't know what they were called but he guessed right. He ran through the scenarios that might have dropped him in this mess but then considered that the whole entourage of any western country having a pop at the Maths Olympics would be quietly scrutinized and observed for signs of ....what? Doing something? Saying something to the wrong person? Appearing shady? Criticizing the government? He was guilty of being shady, that was about it, he thought and, hard to believe, started to fabricate a scenario that could attest to his movements since his arrival. He couldn't help himself.

He heard a shuffling, again and decided to test the water.

"What do you want from me? Why have you detained me.? My name is Kelly. Leonard Kelly. I am here as an observer of the Maths Olympiad which is currently happening at erm...."

He'd never known where it was happening or bothered to find out the name of the venue.

"I'm a journalist. Freelance." Then he realised that that was already a lie that he'd peddled to get out there. "Well....not exactly a journalist.....is there anybody there? Can I take off this hood please. This is all a big mistake..."

He got that one right. He decided to just take off the hood and deal with whatever was coming but try to explain first, before anything untoward might happen.

"Look...I know you said I'd be punished but I'm going to take this thing off and explain all of this to you, ok..."

He went to lift the hood then two pairs of arms grabbed him before he could get it anywhere near above his head. They lifted him by his legs and arms onto, what he surmised was a wooden table, and his hands were secured with a rope noosed around his wrists and going under the table. The rope was pulled tightly and he yelped feeling the muscles on his shoulders strain. He was now genuinely scared and deep from within him a guttural roar filled the room, echoing against the stone walls. He tried to say something but then the hood was pulled tight over his mouth and nose then a steady stream of cold water started to flow over his face. He blew out as hard as he could, trying to take in a breath quickly but it was a losing battle. He struggled for air for the next fifteen seconds, which seemed like a lifetime to him. Finally, it stopped and he gasped taking in as much air as he could. He lifted his head and shouted,

"Stop!! Stop, please this is all a mistake. Let me explain to you...."

The hood was pulled tight again. Another fifteen seconds of cold water. This time he thought he was going to pass out. It stopped and he gasped for air again. From somewhere he had a thought.

"British Council!" he said spurting water into his eyes, "I'm with the British Council! Please...listen to me..."

A voice flatly said.

"Are you cold?"

He was glad to hear someone speak.

"Yes.... yes I'm freezing! I'm very cold.."

Then the voice said, "That is good."

Then the hands grabbed at his shoes, socks, then at his jeans and ripped them off him. Then his t-shirt was torn from his body and finally his underpants were pulled off him. He lay there naked. Thankfully, the rope was undone and slipped off his wrists.

"Stand up." the voice said.

Kelly slowly got to his feet. He's started to shiver.

"When you hear the door close, you may take off the hood."

Kelly just stood there bent at the shoulders. By this time he was very cold. He waited for the door to close. He was desperate to get the hood off. Then a bucket of cold water hit him again and he gasped loudly in time with the door closing. Then he slowly, but now unsurely, lifted the hood.

Quite unusually, the first thing that he became aware of was his nakedness. He ridiculously tried to cover his man-tackle, realised he was alone and dropped his hands. Water was still dripping from him. He looked around the cell for his clothes. It was then that he became aware of the room. A dim, bare light bulb hung above him and threw its paltry beam onto the concrete walls on which there were red-spatterings across one wall. He knew it was blood. He looked back up at the ceiling across which an iron bar spanned the width of the cell. In the middle hung a fixed meat-hook. There was no window and in the middle of the rough concrete floor was a drain. The door was grey steel with an observation hatch at eye-level and it had a few dents and depressions, signs of former traumas, he rightly guessed.

The wooden chair and table were at the other wall. He shivered, slapped his arms around his torso and then desperately said, *fuck, fuck, fuck......* for the next few moments. His feet were becoming numb on the wet concrete. He climbed up onto the table and sat with his knees up at his chin. Then he felt a discomfort in his right groin and he dropped his hand down to feel whilst opening his knees slightly. Nothing appeared untoward. He felt his groin and immediately winced. His glands were starting to swell and with it came pain whenever touched. A small red lesion was also forming on his foreskin. He breathed heavily. Sadly. Naked, alone, cold and diseased the thought of ending it all flashed into his head. He probably deserved it, he thought. However, what could he do? Hit himself with the chair? He assumed this wasn't the end of the affair and that there was nothing he'd hold back from them when next he met his tormentors. The vagaries of Saughton Prison were probably far more manageable than this. He curled up on the table and put his head down hoping to maybe let sleep help him. The cold dug into him like a Cairngorms winter but occasionally he'd go under until the cold bit again. He managed to find a position on the table that supported him in a foetal position and he started to drowse. An hour passed.

Then the door burst open and one of the men from the car journey slapped him hard across his arse and sat him up, slapping his face then pulled him off the table. Then he picked it up and with practised ease guided the table legs through the door and out of the cell. Another man slammed the door shut. All completed in nine isolating seconds. He was awake again. The point of the intrusion. He felt like crying. Never had a wooden table been so dearly missed. Then he heard a strange noise. He realised it was his teeth chattering and himself making the sporadic moaning sounds of *the madman.* The cold bit into his feet again. He sat on the chair and put his feet on the legs of the chair trying to get some sort of support to keep him off the concrete. He sat shivering for the next four hours until his tiredness was greater than the cold and his chin fell onto his body. The second that happened the door burst open again and the same man slapped him around the face and head until he was awake again. No words were said. Then he took the chair away. The door slammed and footsteps faded. Then he heard the voice of Irena from down the corridor. Crying. It was unmistakenly her. She remonstrated with someone, loudly saying,

"Ne, ne! Potkal jsem ho teprve před dvěma dny!" declaring she'd only met him two days ago.

The voices dissipated. So Irena had been lifted, too. It was his fault. An innocent was fighting for her liberty now because of him. He had never felt lower. But he would explain. Explain? She had nothing to do with it all. All? What had he done? He'd done something. What? He turned and banged on the door and just shouted loudly and incoherently. The scene seemed to deserve that reaction but he'd been miles from conceiving this one. It just happened. Nobody came. He turned and let his back slide down the door until he was on the floor and just sat there until his chin once more hit his body. He became somewhat inured to the cold. For once, his mindset no longer cared too much about himself and cared little at this time for what could occur to him so he accepted that he wasn't in control and stayed there for the next three hours dropping in and out of sleep, hearing noises from along the corridor and from his imagination. He thought he heard a dog growl but he'd only seen the recurring image of his dreams, again, baring its teeth and breathing its foul and fetid breath. One small freedom he claimed in this scene was that he needed to piss. He let his bladder go and the ammonia stung his growing lesion, but he gathered the warm urine as much as he could into his two cupped hands and splashed it onto his body enjoying the warmth for the few seconds he felt it.

He had no idea of the time. The door burst open and the two large men came in. One of them threw a set of grey overalls at him. He pulled them on greedily and enjoyed the barrier between him and the air. A pair of canvas sandals followed and he put them on. The first man signalled that he come with them. Kelly was stiff but walked towards them. He could feel the imposition of swollen glands in his groin with each step. They marched him along the bleak corridor past other doors and he wondered if Irena was in one of them. They reached the foot of a staircase and went up. The noise of someone coming down the stairs could be heard above them and it was accompanied by the babbling pleadings of a man. He didn't understand any of it but he read the tone perfectly. They passed that party of two other men and an older bloodied man with a closed black eye and swollen face. Blood had congealed under his nose. As they passed Kelly realised it was Irena's father. He turned alarmed and watched them drag him down the stairs. Then they reached an open door in which was Grey Suit sitting behind a wooden table. He was placed in the seat opposite him then one of his handlers left and the other one sat on another seat by the wall, which had a smaller trestle table set up and upon it was everything he had brought with him. The Bible, The Good Soldier Sveyk, the camera, the Dictaphone, the make-up and bits of prosthesis, Joe's passport, his passport, the bank card in Joe's name, the cartoon pictures he'd lifted from Bullet's flat, the small note courtesy of Sir Clive Harrow that had accompanied the bible and money from Mi6 and a copy of The Daily Mirror with the headlines about Sir Clive, the and the note with the address he was given by Irena.

All was quiet. Nobody spoke. Grey Suit eventually said,

"Who are you?"

Kelly was delighted to be given the chance to explain.

"Kelly. Leonard Kelly...my name is Leonard Kelly." he quickly said, "...this is all a mistake. You see I came here with....."

"Be quiet." Grey Suit calmly said looking him straight in the eye. "I will ask questions and you will answer them. I will ask you again. Who are you?"

Kelly opened his hands and looked at him. "Kelly! Leonard Kelly. I've just told you! My name is Leonard Kelly!!"

Grey Suit looked across at the seated bruiser at the wall and nodded then calmly leaned back in his seat. Bruiser stood and drew a length of rubber piping from his trousers and walked across to Kelly. Kelly stood and moved away from him in panic but not quick enough to avoid the searing thud and following pain that coursed through his body, The pipe had hit him on his lower back. He yelled and fell onto the floor. Another one hit the top of his thigh. The pain was immense.

"I'm Leonard fucking Kelly!!" he cried again with his hands up

hoping to avert the third stroke.
"Leonard Kelly!"

"Who are you?" Grey Suit calmly asked again.

Kelly's hope collapsed at hearing the same question. He knew what was coming if he said his name again. He drew himself into the corner and put his hands over his head.

"Leonard Kelly......" he resignedly whispered.

This time the pipe struck him on his shoulder and a fire climbed up his face and into his head. He started to cry and let that shoulder drop to the floor.

Grey Suit nodded to Bruiser and he picked him up and put Kelly back in the chair.

"What are all of these things?" He pointed to the trestle table still looking at Kelly.

Kelly looked across and managed to reply, "My things. I just threw them in a bag before I came here. I was in a hurry."

"You entered this country as Joseph Delaney. Yes?"

"Yes."

"In disguise?"

"Yes."

"Why?"

"Because...." he paused increasing the doubt of Grey Suit as to what was about to be peddled.

Should he say he'd killed someone, was wanted for murder and was complicit in the death of a former schoolmate?

"I am wanted for the murder of a....*neighbour* in Scotland.... and for another murder that I didn't commit...but I was involved... I had to run....here."

Grey Suit said, "Really? There are many places someone from Britain would run to in that situation so you will have to forgive me if I tend not to believe your story. You are British...*perhaps*... and therefore a friend of our American enemy across the ocean, why not run to them? It must be easier than coming to Czechoslovakia?"

"It was the Maths thing, I used that...I gave them some money..."

He was still hurting. His tiredness didn't help his cause as the pace increased.

"You? Or the British government?"

"Me! I gave them a thousand pounds!"

"What is your occupation?"

"I don't have one. I'm on the dole. Unemployed."

"Where does an unemployed man get one thousand pounds?"

"They gave me it!"

"Who gave you it?"

"Mi6."

"Mi6? You work for Mi6? So you are a spy?"

"No! I'm not a spy. They gave me the money because of the photos......"

"Photos? Of what?"

"The Minister for Defence....but there weren't any photos.."

"You're lying. This is preposterous. You are a spy. An agent of the British government!"

"I'm not lying! There weren't any fucking photos, I keep telling you, you stupid fucking Czech twat!!"

Which initiated another rubber-piping massage of three good strokes again. He lay there crying. Grey Suit stood and walked over to the trestle and picked up *The Good Soldier Sveyk*. Bruiser picked him up and plonked him back in the chair.

"You have a copy of *Dobrý voják Sveyk?*"

"What?" Kelly said still half curled from his beating.

"The Good Soldier Sveyk. Hasek. Why?"

"Because..." He stole it? He bought it? Wanted to read it? What to say?

"Because...?" Grey Suit enquired. "....why do you pause?"

"Because it was recommended to me... someone said it was good..."

"You have some sentences underlined. Why?"

"Because I like them....I just liked them so I underlined them. I wanted to remember them so I could quote them...."

"To whom?"

"To the rest of the pub, to my mother, to anyone that would listen and be fucking impressed!"

"That is a poor answer and you know it! This is code. Each

sentence underlined has a meaning to those that would read it. Who were you going to give this to? Someone at The Maths Olympiad? For what? You enter this country under the guise of someone else with passport and bank card, a man that has recently been to Moscow, and you tell me you are given money by Mi6 for photographs. Why is there a space cut into this bible? What were you going to put into it? You leave the hotel you were at and try to merge into Prague as someone else taking a room. Did you think you would not be noticed? Ah yes, you met our friend, Professor Frantisek who showed you the room..."

Kelly's eyes widened hearing The Professor was partly his nemesis.

"...you are a spy and there is enough evidence here to prove it! We have looked at the photographs that were on your camera. An airport? Who is it that is in that picture? Who is of importance? Aeroplanes? Photographs of aeroplanes? Why? There are photos of quite unspectacular aspects of Prague. A shop. Why did you photograph a shop?

"I thought it was....interesting. That's all."

"Really? Interesting. Interesting for who? Someone who would require the picture to make a rendezvous?"

"No! Nothing like that. I just thought it was.... unusual. Not like the shops we have in Britain. I liked the colours!"

"I notice this shop has....how do you say...an awning?"

"Yes...an awning. Stops the rain. We don't have them anymore in Britain. I like them."

"This awning had red stripes."

"Did it? Yes...yes... I remember. I was just killing time."

"Do you remember what was on the window?"

"Erm... pretty things. It was a pretty shop. Arty...why?"

"There were blue stars on that window. Do you think we are stupid?"

"No...no, you're not stupid! You're not stupid.... but....I don't follow...?"

Grey Suit chuckled slightly, "Your performance is good but not altogether convincing... Mr Kelly, Mr Delaney...whoever you are. Good but not an Oscar performance. Stars and stripes? We will wait and see who will rendezvous at this shop and then we will have the truth. We will have the truth soon enough and it would be better for you if you tell us who you are and who you are working for." He paused "This is Alexej...."

He nodded to Bruiser. "..... he has many talents, some of which you have felt but he has not started to parade his skills that have made many men denounce their mothers to make the pain stop. If you do not start telling me the truth about whom you are working for and why you are here in Czechoslovakia your body will be broken and you will weep upon your knees like a child and cry for mercy before you leave here."

His threat was enough. Kelly roared, "I'm telling you the fucking truth! I'm telling you the truth!"

Grey Suit sighed and looked across at comrade Alexej Bruiser who made to rise. Kelly couldn't take any more of the pain. Once again from...*somewhere*... he didn't know the falsehood he would peddle next, and said,

"My name is John *Spider* Blackwood. I am seconded to the CIA but I am working for British Intelligence, you are right.

Grey Suit held up his hand. Comrade Bruiser sat back down.

"My code name is *Mayman,* and if you know the right people you can check this. If you don't you have to ask for *The Old Duke,* a weighty figure in the British Establishment but also Mi6. You might know him as Sir Clive Harrow. My identity will then be corroborated. I have been seconded to the CIA to try and help break the strike that is currently occurring in Britain. The strike has been used by many subversive entities and groups to undermine the government but beyond this they eventually want to create the circumstances into which civil war will ensue leading to a socialist coup d'état and much of their support is covertly coming from the Eastern Bloc. Why wouldn't they want to see a western power collapse allowing a power vacuum to create chaos? Britain cannot allow this to happen and their money and support has to be stopped."

It was a good start. Improvising for his life. Literally. His tone was also good, he thought.

"Why the CIA?" Grey Suit suspiciously said and not much liking saying it.

Kelly smiled and couldn't believe what he did next and haltingly said,

"The answer to that question will cost you a hot shower, some breakfast and a cup of coffee."

"That might happen with a little bit more Mr...?"

"Blackwood. Spider Blackwood."

"Why *Spider*?"

"Why do you think? I weave webs then crawl away into places where I can't be seen."

"Why the CIA?"

"The question you most want an answer to, I suspect. Coffee?"

"After. CIA?"

"America is not the capitalist utopia they would have us believe. There is a strong left-wing and trade unionist tradition that is kept suppressed for fear of the oxygen of publicity and it goes back for nearly a hundred years. Joe Hill. The Workers of the World. *The Wobblies* for short. Why do you think Jimmy Hoffa disappeared and why do you think, McGregor, the American, is leading the National Coal Board and working with Mrs Thatcher?"

He'd forgotten he'd read about all of this.

"The rich west scoffs at the tin-pot juntas in South America that have their enemies of the state disappear into the night but the truth is it happens under the nose of Uncle Sam, too. If the socialists see a world power like Britain topple they believe that it would incite nothing short of a mirrored uprising in America. Something I'm guessing you'd approve of? The CIA can't let that happen."

Grey Suit studied him for a moment. "Say those codenames again."

"Shower. Breakfast. Coffee."

"As things stand you are currently an enemy of *this* state, assuming we would not want our support for your Miners to be corrupted....."

Kelly pushed again like he was an equal. "Your English is very good. Where did you learn?"

"Cambridge. Foolishly, most things can occur in the west if you have enough money. Not much was practiced from any ideological conviction. It was full of traitors. Every college had them."

"And which was yours?" Kelly said.

"Enough." Then he gave some orders to Bruiser who looked bemused at first then distinctly miffed as he led Kelly out of the room.

Kelly took the longest shower he possibly could and drew out breakfast and insisted upon a second cup of coffee while he tried to make fit in his head all of the evidence laid out on the table, and concoct a suitable denouement to this most serious of situations.

Grey Suit looked over at him and sipped a cup of coffee. They were back in the interview room. Bruiser sat in his allotted seat with his pride still smarting and so eagerly awaited the call to deliver.

"What does the note mean? It is signed SCH."

"Yes... Sir Clive Harrow. I can't remember exactly what it says but it was a threat to keep my mouth shut. Read it to me again."

"Why can't you remember what it is written?" Grey Suit calmly said.

"Because I'm not James Bond! I'm just someone who knew someone who's taken the shilling to serve and now it's all gone tits up and Big Boris across there is champing at the bit to cut my balls off. I'm not a big fish, trust me!"

"Not yet. Trust will arrive when clarity has spoken...and you will speak. *Revelations? Shew not the image of thy master nor reveal thy wits, else timely, wilt thy fate descend. SCH.*"

Kelly effected a chuckle, "Well he's a bit of a bible nut, you know...or so I believe. I mean I never actually met him but what he's saying is...*don't do what I'm doing now, ...*blab....or he'll get his monkeys to cut my balls off."

"You are not a big fish, you say?"

"No."

"But you are seconded to the CIA?"

"Well, yes....that's the thing, you see, I haven't actually met anyone from the CIA but I know that it's them that are initiating this ...like I said they're a bit scared of..."

"Yes you said. The book? Hasek. The underlined passages?"

"I was given the book exactly as it is right now. I didn't underline anything. I was told to take it to Bar Cerveny and leave it there."

"With whom.?"

"Not with anyone. I was to put it under a newspaper and leave it on a shelf at the back of the bar."

"When?"

"Tonight."

"What time?"

"Nine."

Grey Suit spoke quickly to Bruiser who took the book from the table and left. Naturally, this would come back and bite him on the arse when nobody picked it up but it bought him time. Then he looked at Kelly and was obviously cogitating everything he'd told him, so far.

"We will take the girl back to her bar and she will open tonight, as usual. We expect it to be collected...*Spider Blackwood..*"

"Is she okay? She isn't involved in this, you know. She just wanted to practice her English. She knows nothing."

"Again...the truth will out with the correct methods.....*Mr Spider*. Why do you have prints of Josef Lada?"

Kelly was lost. "Of what? Who?"

"Josef Lada."

"The cars?"

"The pictures in your attaché."

"You mean the cartoons?"

"Yes."

"Who is Josef Lada?"

"The illustrator. They are prints of scenes from *The Good Soldier Sveyk*. Lada is the illustrator. Why do you not know this?"

"They didn't tell me."

"Instructions?"

"For the cartoons?"

"Yes!" Grey Suit was getting tetchy.

"I was told to take them to get framed and when I picked them up I was to take the back off the frames and there would be papers inside them. I was to take them back with me."

"What are the papers?"

"I don't know. I'm just the courier."

"Which shop?"

He was caught. Maybe not. Stall for time.

"To get framed?"

"Yes!" More ire.

"I was to await that instruction."

"When?"

"I wasn't told. It would get to me, they said."

Again, Grey Suit, with what seemed practiced ability, considered Kelly for some moments, silently. Then he said,

"The bible?"

"I was to go to any church in Prague. They would be watching me...apparently. Take the bible with me and sit and pray. I would be joined by someone who would also appear to be praying, place a large amount of money in the cut-out section and then I was to take it back with me to the UK."

"Why did you give your watch to the owner of Bar Cerveny?"

The truth this time seemed a reasonable punt.

"I didn't. I gave it to Irena...the girl. I tried to impress her. I'm guessing she gave it to him or he took it from her. I don't know."

"We will have it checked. If there is anything about that watch that links you to espionage and you don't tell me now, then you will disappear for a very long time... or worse, *Spiderman*."

"I know." Kelly said as gravely as he could. "There's no microphones or anything. They didn't give me it. They gave me a Dictaphone to record anything I might see that could be of any interest."

"Yes I listened to that. You were gathering information?"

"Yeah... that was a bit of practice just after they gave me it. Forgot to wipe it."

"An unfortunate oversight for a man seconded to the CIA, no?"

"Well yes....I suppose..." Not convincing.

"What about the airport photos?"

"Yes... they were just an accident. They gave me a good camera. I didn't know how to use it. I was experimenting."

"They can be confusing. Aperture, speed, light. It is a wonderful camera, Mr Spider. The technology is outstanding but perhaps the more the west improves their world the more it seems that something is also lost."

Grey Suit held his gaze on Kelly with a frown that expected an answer.

"Yeah...maybe. The world can be a convoluted place, these days." he unsurely offered.

"I have come to the opinion in my life and work that a certain vocabulary that includes words such as *convoluted* can sometimes mask a veracity in a quite *convoluted* way and often deliberately so."

Grey Suit held his eye on Kelly for what seemed an age. Then he smiled and lifted the copy of The Daily Mirror, looked at the headline and said,

"Sir Clive does seem to have other distractions to deal with at present. *Peccadilloes* I believe they are called. Many of the chaps in Cambridge seemed wilfully single-minded and quite determined to have a peccadillo that would mark them out from the crowd. A minor fame amongst one's peers, some would say."

He placed a pen and paper in front of Kelly.

"Write the codenames here."

Kelly complied.

"You will return to a cell until we have time to assess your information and the results of the assignations you spoke of."

Kelly was taken to another cell by another bruiser. He sat on the steel bed-frame but then seeing a thin mattress decided to avail himself of such small mercies. With a bit of luck he might just be kicked out of the country, he naively thought, but was so tired he didn't care. This last performance had wiped him out. His body had red weals from his beating and hurt him as he lay on his back. He turned quickly and winced with the pain of his swollen glands.

Gradually, sleep came down and he remained there slumbering on an iron framed bed for the next eight hours. He dreamed of *The Old Duke* and of his Mother who was, surprisingly, drinking in the pub with him and smiling at him. He tried to talk to his mother in his dream but all of his words struggled to sound coherent and she remained smiling, looking at him in askance and drinking. He became so frustrated at his inability to communicate clearly that he screamed loudly at her and the scream morphed into one of Sasquatch's top roars and then suddenly he was in The Meadows trying to stop a large Alsatian dog from attacking Lenni but could do little to help. He felt a thump from behind him on his head as a thick piece of branch hit him. A man in a check shirt was shouting at him but Kelly couldn't make out what was being said. The thump to the head was him turning on the narrow cell cot and bumping his head on the wall and he had woven it into the dream. From nowhere his Mother gently took his hand and guided him away from the scene of carnage and walked in the summer sun on the vast expanse of flat greenery. In the distance he could see the two black coats of Number One and Two walking towards him. He wanted to try to explain who they were to his Mother but she had gone. Vanished into the ether. In the dream the size of these men were massive and as they leaned over him the sun was blocked and gradually he was subsumed into the blackness of their coats until he could see nothing. He wrestled to try and free himself from their enveloping attire but to no avail and then he felt as though he was falling, descending into a void which had no bottom. Then he landed with a bump onto the compost which covered his neighbour and filled his bath. The soil began to move and he tried desperately to keep it covered but bony fingers protruded until they were hands and then arms. Then his pounding heartbeat woke him up. Food had been brought into the cell while he slept so he ate that and sat for the next few hours wondering what his fate would be.

Grey Suit entered the interrogation room. Kelly was already there. He was banking on their inability to verify much, in which case he could pretend to be the daft little boy. Grey Suit looked across to him and sighed. Then he said,

"Who are you?"

Kelly's heart sank. He planned on there being a discussion at least about his story. He stuck to his narrative.

"I told you...John *Spider* Blackwood..."

"We are many things here in the east but the one thing we are not is stupid. Your story is full of holes. Nobody came to collect the book, you say you will be contacted about framing the pictures, a task nobody can now fulfil, just as your story that you will be *watched* and allowed to enter any church in Prague to make a money exchange. The codenames *Mayman* and *The Old Duke* mean nothing to our intelligence although they obviously know of Sir Clive Harrow, formerly of Mi6, of whom you said originally you were given money? Then you change your story. I have listened again to the recordings on the Dictaphone and someone speaks of *The Old Duke*. They say, *in The Old Duke?* The Old Duke is a building, perhaps, a hotel, a bar, but it is not the codename for anyone. Let us return to the fact that you entered Czechoslovakia under the umbrella protection of The British Council but in the guise of a man who within the last decade had visited Russia yet you say you are seconded to the CIA? You have the passports of two men, Joseph Delaney and Leonard Kelly. You offer Leonard Kelly to us then come clean under very little pressure? The collapse of your first identity was too quick which makes us think that we are expected to be grateful for the following information about your *Spiderman* and swallow the story. We know of your strike in Britain and of the American, McGregor who is working for Mrs Thatcher, but as far as support goes, we know of no organisations here in Czechoslovakia that materially support the striking miners. Moscow, perhaps, is a far more believable proposition. So what do we have? We have three men, the first a lie by your own admission, the second offers freely his name and role, or fictional role, which brings us to the third man, Delaney, who is registered as an official observer to the British team but is, in fact, not Delaney. Unfortunately there are many inconsistencies that must be made clear. *So...*for the last time I will ask you again, who are you?"

The relative stillness and quiet malevolence of Grey Suit was much too intimidating for him. Kelly gulped and regressed twenty years in his demeanour and a frightened little boy said,

"Kelly. I'm Kelly. Leonard Kelly....I just wanted the beatings to stop...."

Grey Suit rolled his eyes and nodded to his bruiser who rose quickly banged twice on the closed door. Then it opened brusquely and the second bruiser came in and picked up Kelly and dragged him along the corridor. Kelly was shouting *I am Kelly, it's the truth*, repeatedly.

They took him back into the first room he was taken. He was sat down and his hands were handcuffed behind the back of the chair. Kelly saw a range of strange looking implements on the table and his arse turned to liquid. Grey Suit entered and sat in another chair away from the table. Alexej, the skilful painmonger went behind him and lifted his arms from the cuffs until Kelly could feel his shoulders about to dislocate. He screamed for him to stop, which Alexej did, then looked at Grey Suit.

"Who are you?" he asked again.

"I'm Leonard Ke..."

His arms were lifted again but a little further this time.

"This nothing compared to what you will have to endure if you do not tell us who you are and who you are working for. Tell me."

Kelly had never experienced pain like it. "I *am* Leonard Kelly...please...no..."

Alexej lifted a rubber pipe from the table and within seconds had taken it across Kelly's face. His teeth cut the inside of his mouth and blood began to drip down his chin. He was dazed and could still hear the thud as it had hit him.

"Please do not persist in your ridiculous story. Alexej will win."

Grey Suit held up a hand. Alexej stood away. "You really don't have to go through this, you know. Tell us who you are, who you are working for, why you are here and the contacts you have in Prague. I want names. Names that might be familiar to us. Really, it might not be a surprise to us if you tell us the truth."

What Kelly wanted to say was that he can't tell him any names he might know because he didn't know any, but all that he could manage was,

"I can't..."

Which preceded Alexej's next trick that involved lifting him onto the table. He was place on his back and the noosed rope held his arms down attached to each wrist and travelling under the table. The overalls were roughly opened revealing his torso. The second henchman held his legs down. Alexej had gone to his worktable and lit a cigarette. Grey Suit arrived looking over him.

"So....? Name? Paymasters?"

Kelly was petrified with fear. His mouth couldn't work. Grey Suit walked back to his seat shaking his head. Alexej then took a deep suck onto the cigarette then placed it onto Kelly's left nipple. The pain was excruciating. Kelly screamed.

Grey Suit's voice said tiredly, "Name?" Nothing. Another scream filled the room as the same nipple was burned. Then his overalls were pulled down revealing his cock and balls and as Alexej approached intending to administer another dose of sadism, he stopped and spoke to Grey Suit. Grey Suit walked over and looked at Kelly's foreskin.

"You seem to be already burdened with..... an *uncomfortable presence* on your member, my friend. Has someone got to you before us?"

The red lesion courtesy of his neighbour was glowing red and apparent. Grey suit told Alexej to use it and sat back down. Alexej took the cigarette over to his cock but leaned on Kelly's groin and the loudest scream yet filled the void. Alexej spoke to Grey Suit telling him what he had done and Grey Suit came across again. He looked at Kelly's swollen glands. Then he lightly tapped the right one. Kelly yelled in pain.

"You have problems my friend. Not of our making. I fear you are diseased. This hurts, yes?"

And he tapped his left gland. Kelly cried out again.

"Where have you been, my friend? Who have you been with? An experienced agent of espionage does not find himself lying with the wrong type of company. However, in these circumstances, it would appear a gift for us. If I was to slap you quite hard, like this..."

Which he did. Kelly cried out like a child.

".... on your swollen parts then it would exert a modicum of discomfort for you. Yes?"

Kelly moaned.

"I'm sorry, I didn't hear that. Did you want to tell me who you are, what you are doing in this country and who you are working for?"

"I'm Kelly..Kelly.." he was choking on his own fluids.

Grey Suit Slapped his groin again and then pressed angrily. Kelly screamed. Grey Suit shouted at him,

"I am tired of your stubborn attitude! Tell me who you are working for? What is your purpose in Czechoslovakia?"

Kelly hadn't the ability to form a sentence. Grey suit sat back down again irritatedly and lifted one finger up to Alexej.

Alexej's mate put a rope around Kelly's wrists as his overalls fell to his ankles. The rope was dropped through a hole in the table and pulled tight. Kelly's hands slammed against the table top. A chair was place under Kelly's arse. Alexej approached and opened a pair of pliers. Kelly couldn't believe what was happening to him and found his voice.

"No!!!! Don't please. I'm not anyone, I'm nobody!! Please no!!"

"Who are you? Who are you working for?"

"Kelly... I'm not working for anyone...no please...."

Alexej had a good look and selected Kelly's ring finger on his left hand, attached the pliers to the end of it and pulled. Kelly heard his own scream and felt a shudder run up his arm and into the side of his head, as he watched his fingernail slowly but brutally ripped away and then deposited onto the floor like some insignificant detritus. He cried loudly. Tears streamed out of him.

Grey Suit asked him the same question. Kelly tried to tell him his name again. Then, on the nod from Grey Suit, Alexej started to hit the end of his brutalised finger with the pliers as Grey Suit asked the same questions. Kelly cried out with every tap of the pliers.

"Would you like Alexej to even up the damage? He will, without thought, remove all of your fingernails on my say so. All you have to do is tell us the truth. No *Kelly, Delaney* or *Spiderman* stories. It is plain for everyone to see that you are an entity designed to act against the wishes and best interests of this country so it is therefore in your best interests to tell us who you are and what your intentions were and all this pain will stop."

Kelly rallied against the burning heat and throbbing finger and mustered another attempt.

"Please you have to listen to me... I really am Kelly... I have no bad intentions towards...."

Grey Suit nodded to Alexej and said "Změkni ho."

Alexej picked up his rubber hose from the floor. Kelly's wrists went tight again as the rope burned into his flesh. Alexej went behind him and kicked the chair away from under him and Kelly fell to his knees but his arms flat on the table. Then the hose caught him with a broadside on his ribs. The breath blasted out of his body and he gagged to get air. Then another hit his kidneys, then another to his right thigh. He thought he was going to die just as the fourth caught the side of his face and into his eye. Grey Suit nodded and Alexej stopped. The rope fell loose and Kelly dropped to the floor. He moaned in a foetal position half under the table and he felt his bladder let go of its load. A stream of piss filled the floor next to him, except it had apparent red colouring of blood in it. Grey Suit stood over him assessing his condition and saw the bloody piss. He nodded to the two henchmen and they picked him up and sat him back on the chair. Kelly was now beyond weeping. The breath returned to him and from somewhere and he managed to open his right eye. His left one had already started to close. Grey Suit, this time, lifted his chair across and sat opposite him. Blood ran from his nose and covered his chin and his lip had split. Kelly managed to lift his head and looked up at him through whatever gap was left in his eyes to see through. He took a breath and looked at Grey suit through a facial circus of blood, bubbles and snot.

"You must tell me who you are and why you covertly came into Czechoslovakia. This will continue and I fear that you might die, my friend, and if you die we will have learned nothing from you, but you will be dead, all the same and none of us will gain anything from this quite uncivilised, but necessary, behaviour."

Grey suit shouted loudly to Alexej,

"Pitná voda a uklízet jeho posraný obličej pro lásku Boží!" and got up and walked agitatedly around the room his heels echoing, loudly.

Alexej's mate disappeared out of the room and after a few moments returned with a steel bucket half filled with water. A tin cup was dunked in it and roughly place in front of Kelly. He drew it towards him and lifted it to his mouth, swilled it and spat out the first mouthful, then took another and swallowed this time. Grey Suit said,

"Vyčistit si obličej!" and a wet cloth was sloshed over his face, twice. Kelly gasped and Grey Suit leaned in and quietly said,

"For the last time, and it will be the last, my friend, I ask you again....who are you?"

Kelly looked him as best he could straight in the eye, took a breath and with limited clarity and as loudly as he could, he shouted,

"I am nobody! Nobody!"

He took a breath and managed to form his words through his brutalised mouth.

"Kill me and you will be killing nobody. I don't care anymore. I don't care about me, but let me tell about *the nobody* that I am. I have never worked or felt the satisfaction I believe is felt by those who have grafted and sweated to support their families. I have no family, yes a Mother who found fault with me all her life and openly declared all of the things that... *I couldn't do...* to the world, and an angry, right-wing, sack of shit she calls her brother but I have created nothing with my life. No wife, no kids, no love. It was all too much like hard work for me. I would have to be too *selfless*. At school. I was a bully but not the ones that just kick the shit out of someone because they don't like their fucking face. No. I used the intelligence I had to be a cunt and one day this cunt, who knew he was nobody and was angry about it, eventually did kick the shit out of a good person that I had made sad. Enter Mi6. I was asked to take some photos in an office block and mistakenly opened a door and clicked the camera at the wrong time and in there was Sir Clive Harrow getting his cock sucked by a very pretty young man. He sent his men to watch me thinking I was a journalist ready to sell them to the press. But they saw me hurt this man. I hit him with a bottle and I thought I had killed him. I hadn't. But they allowed me to think I had to manipulate me and get what they wanted and egotistically, I allowed them to think I did have photos. I hadn't. They gave me money to buy my silence but also threatened me with a phone call if the pictures, *that didn't exist,* were ever made public. Ask your monkeys to look at the Scottish press. *Greyfriars Body* story. That's me. Me that killed a school mate....."

Kelly started to laugh a little manically and said,

"... but I hadn't killed him! And there were no photos! They killed him and I was photographing wallpaper! Wallfuckingpaper, Mr fucking Grey Suit! And it was in that office block I stole the book, *The Good Soldier Sveyk*. I stole it from a desk when I was looking for water, took it home read all about the fuck-up that was Jaroslav Hasek and the fuck-up he created called *Sveyk* who lived in the fuck-up that is your country! I underlined the passages I thought would sound impressive and quote them to impress anyone that would listen. And I was glad. Glad that history had made more fuck-ups than this one before you now and declared it to the world. And I also tried to use this book and other classic yarns to impress someone...that I *cared* about. But I fucked that up, too. I decided the world didn't care about me so why should I give a fuck about the world and I hatched a plan to become someone else, a good man, a man that cared so much for the striking miners that he gave half of his wages to their cause....and I became him and stole from him. And in the theft of that man's name I had taken everything from him. His name was Joe Delaney. That is the cunt I am. Now you might laugh, Mr Grey Suit, but fate decided that because I was such a cunt, it would throw something else for me to wrestle with. I killed a neighbour. A prostitute.... and here is the truth...it was an accident. She gave me something. That sore on my cock, my swollen groin, was her. I hadn't had sex with anyone for years and that was a poor show, too, and here was this neighbour offering her body for a few quid. I tried to talk to her, tried to tell her not to give it to someone else but she fell on a knife *she drew on me.* And died. That is the truth. And I needed to run *somewhere.* Somewhere beyond the Costa del Crime and fate threw me a bone...or so I thought and I came here as part of the team for the Maths Olympiad. As Joseph Delaney. I learned make-up, prosthetics on a theatre course. It was shit but useful. Useful? Usefully used to extend my inability to do no good. To be a taker, to use my wit to do nothing, a fraud and in the end become nobody. Nobody of any worth. You and your sadistic minder have brought that home to me, now. I am worthless, beaten like a useless and vacuous piece of meat and I, as nobody, a nobody that has created anything of any worth in this life, no longer care. I don't care if you don't believe me. Kill me. I am worth nothing. Everything I touch suffers. That girl, Irena, is guilty of showing me nothing but friendship and kindness...and what does she get. Arrested for her trouble. I am shit, Mr Grey Suit. A mess to be flushed out of humanity. Do what you want. I no longer care but don't ask me who I am again because I have just told you. I was Leonard Kelly, I was Kells, I was a son, a murderer, a thief, an actor, I was Joe Delaney, but in the end...*I am nobody."*

Kelly stopped there. He was hurting too much and he'd struggled sometimes to make his words sound clear. He took another swig of water. Grey Suit looked at Kelly in his usual way for a few moments. Then he spoke to Alexej. Alexej stood and as he did so Kelly managed to stand, too. He refused to be fearful anymore. He turned and faced Alexej man to man. If his torment was to continue he would look at his tormentor, eye to eye, and whatever next it might be. Alexej hadn't moved and looked at Grey suit, bemused. He took one step towards Kelly, who felt a rush of fear and then an intense shooting pain in his renal area which flashed into his head. Then he fell to the floor.

*

Lenni looked young and fit. His black coat glistened in the sunshine and chased for a ball he threw for him on The Meadows. The grass was exceptionally green. Eric stood in the row of hundred year-old elm trees next to the road watching Kelly throw the ball for the dog, somehow removed but part of the scene. Eric appeared younger too and wore a different jacket. There was a red star badge on the lapel and he smiled continually at the dog enjoying the game. Kelly threw another one for Lenni and it bounced over to a woman with long hair sitting on the grass and enjoying the bright summer sun. Her back was to Kelly and Lenni but Lenni's enthusiastic panting and slobbering startled her. However, she laughed and turned and threw the ball back towards Kelly and smiled a beautiful broad smile and it was only as moments passed that Kelly realised he was looking at his mother. A younger woman. This was the woman he remembered from his childhood, although he didn't remember her smiling as broadly, but he immediately felt a wave of love wash through his body, a rush of love he was quite unfamiliar with but enjoyed, so much so, he didn't want it to stop. He tried to shade his eyes from the sun just to be able to watch her being happy but the sun shone brighter and so he tried walking towards her, but again he'd lost her in the glare. His walk got faster but the sun got brighter until it was nearly blinding him but he'd reached the place that she'd been sitting on the grass and tried to find her but she'd gone. He looked up at the sun until it hurt.

His eyes opened slightly and the glare of hard lights beamed uncaringly down on him. They were stark, circular white shades with a bright bulb which dropped its light onto his steel-framed bed of white blankets. He saw his feet poking out at the bottom and then took his head off the pillow and turned his head to the left. There was a door of arsenic-green chipped paint and through it he could see, although not clearly, a small corridor. It had a green dado, also of dented plaster. He tried to turn his head to the right but a pain ran down his right side and he winced. More gently he did turn his head to the right and saw an older man, grey-haired in a similar bed to his. His face was cut and bruised and he lay unconscious but notably he wore a black eyepatch. They were the only people in the room. The walls were white but also had the green dado. There was no window. He then noticed there was a drip into the back of his hand and the tube rose above his head to the right and a saline bag and whatever else they had decided to put into him. He didn't know, neither did he know where he was or how long he'd been there. He touched his face expecting it to hurt. He did feel a tenderness but nothing like he expected which made him think he'd been out of it for a while. Days? Probably. He tried to shift his body and he felt a dull pain in his lower back and remembered everything of his torture, his blood-filled piss and the cold concrete. Then he saw the face of Alexej in his head and lifted his index finger of his right hand. A bloody and tender mess befell his gaze. He started to piece it all back together and closed his eyes as each scene of his ordeal returned. Then he thought of what was going to happen to him now. What would they do with him? He'd entered the country fraudulently at the very least. Maybe he would get a stretch in a Czech prison? Maybe they'd send him back home? Back to a murder charge. Fraud. Theft. Maybe they'd do what they'd already done to him all over again? He closed his eyes again and definitely felt the effects of a sedative dull his senses. He tried to stay awake but dropped back into Nod and slept for another two hours.

When he was beginning to awaken he heard the voice of the man next to him saying something, however he thought it best not to declare his wakefulness to him until he knew more. He opened one eye slightly and looked across at him without moving. The man was incomprehensibly coming out of his imposed sleep and probably reliving some recent bad memories. Then footsteps briskly came down the small corridor and the door opened, quickly. Kelly shut his eyes again. A lone nurse entered, went to his bedside and clanked around on a small table against one wall. Kelly opened an eye just enough to see what she was doing. The man got louder then Kelly heard him start to plead with her. He couldn't speak Czech but he knew pleading when he heard it and this was pleading. He saw a hypodermic syringe being tapped and then plunged into his exposed thigh and the blankets being roughly thrown back over his leg. She went back to the table and put the needle back in a steel bowl. The man's gibbering gradually subsided and she went across to him and felt his pulse. Satisfied, she turned. Kelly went dead still. She gave Kelly a couple of rough pushes and said something loudly to him. Kelly held his inertia. She hovered over him for a few moments until, eventually, she went back out of the room, pulling the door closed. Kelly sighed heavily. He knew now how they kept their charges quiet. He took a couple of minutes to gather his thoughts but probably knowing what he was going to do next, then raised himself up into a sitting position and pulled the tube out from the back of his hand. A small pain went up his arm but it was nothing to him. Part of him already seemed dead and he cared little for any danger his next movements might entail then he swung his legs out of the bed revealing a cotton smock that didn't cover much. He placed his feet on the floor and took his own weight for the first time in days, expecting a wobble but he bore the burden well and walked over to the steel bowl on the table and lifted it to reflect his face. His hair seemed to be a little longer and his face was puffy and reddened with a cut across his right eyebrow that had some rough stitches in it. His left eye was still completely closed and his top lip was red and swollen with a cut inside his mouth nearly visible. He looked a mess. He lifted his smock and checked his body and pressed his stomach and ribs waiting for the pain which only occurred when he got to his kidneys, They seemed swollen and hurt when he tried to move faster but he could bear it. He then looked at the door. Then thought. He had no idea what or who was beyond the corridor but knew it would probably be just one shot. He looked around the room for something to cover him then saw a bundle on the floor next to his roommate's bed. A long, light-grey mac lay next to a trilby hat. He searched for a shirt or jacket but the coat and hat was all there was. He pulled on the coat and put the hat on his head. He picked up the steel bowl again and looked at the view. It was still definitely him but the wrecked face might draw attention. He turned and looked at everything in the room but there was nothing more. Until he looked at his roommate again. The eyepatch would help.

He crept along the corridor until it turned a corner. He peered around it and saw another longer corridor with a door at the end. *Doors lead to other doors*, he thought. Halfway along there was a wooden bench against the wall, quite incongruously, it appeared, until he reached it and opposite it hanging on the wall was a large framed picture of Lenin, bald-headed, bearded and in clenched-fist mode in mid rant. Some perverted means of re-indoctrination to those who would disapprove of Karl Marx's first revolutionary leader, he assumed. And then he heard footsteps and a human noise from beyond the door at the end which was definitely sailing his way. He didn't know what to do. Panic overcame him but he quickly sat down on the bench and stared at Lenin. A woman in a headscarf and coat, wet with rain, opened the door and came along the corridor muttering and crying, wiping tears and snot from her face. She cared little for the barefooted man in the grey mac, trilby and an eye-patch contemplating the vision of Lenin opposite him, and hurried away leaving Kelly there on the bench. He waited until it was quiet again. The door never creaked when the crying woman came through, he thought. Wooden doors with small windows accosted his view. They were twenty-feet from him and he could see streetlight coming through them. Locked.

They wouldn't move and he wasn't moving so well either, barefoot. There was a set of stairs opposite the doors going down into a basement level. The whole place reminded him of his old school, tiles, stone floors and bad paint job. He went down two flights and tried another door which opened into a yard which held two large steel vats each about seven feet high. It was dark but the smell in the summer heat was sick-making. He retched which gave away that it was refuse, rubbish and the like, but above them was a small wrought iron fence on the street level. A set of wooden steps, stained with every kind of detritus leaned against a brick wall next to the vats. He grabbed them and put them against the exterior wall and climbed up. He had trouble climbing the ladder as it was dark and his renal pains stopped him moving, freely. He struggled but slowly got over the fence and looked up and down the alleyway then walked towards the streetlights of a main road. He had no idea where he was. There was nobody out on the street, no cars but for the odd one passing occasionally as he walked trying to look as though he knew where he was going but the pains in his back altered his gait and he travelled as would an incoherent drunk.

He scanned the buildings and lamp posts looking for a sign directing him towards the city centre for half an hour until he saw one and gingerly walked on the cobbles whenever they were available, which were smoother than the pavements. It was obviously the early hours of the morning and although the odd car passed, it was getting busier, which meant he was nearing the city centre. He wanted to rest but his absence would soon be discovered and if he was to avoid a stint in chokey either here or in Scotland, had to get back to his rented room fast to get some money and disappear. He had little idea of how eccentric, homeless and lost he looked. Trilby, coat, bare legs and feet and an eyepatch but it was hardly a consideration as he made his way along a straight road of closed shops and flats above. As he pushed forward he saw a pair of feet sticking out of a shop doorway, which were unmoving but he still cautiously approached. A vagrant, or what he thought was a Czech version of a wino lay there asleep with an empty bottle close to him. Kelly quietly went past him but then stopped, thought and turned. He went back and looked up and down the road. It was quiet. Careworn and uncaring, he started to remove the man's shoes. They were of broken brown leather and exceedingly worn but they were better than nothing. He pulled them on to his feet and stood. They were slightly tight but he felt better for the protection and started off again.

A huge swathe of greenery to his left opened up on the road he was on and then he saw a sign *Kinsekho Zahrada*. No idea. The name of the park, presumably? He must have travelled for two miles or more since he acquired his new footwear, which were now hurting beyond the pain of being barefoot so he opted for the soft grass. He took off the shoes and threw them away into the darkness of the park. *Holeckova* was the name of the road he was on and made decent progress without the shoes but suffering the pain of small stones under his feet, however he hobbled on for another mile or so until he came to a fork in the road. To the left the park continued.

To the right was a street called *Petrinska*. On a sign pointing down *Petrinska* was the words *řeka Vlatava* and a few wavy lines. The river. He knew the river was central and The Charles Bridge, which went over it, was close. When he reached the river he saw a bridge to his left about half a mile away and quickly made towards it like a drunk desperate to reach home and his enthusiasm to get there left him breathless again as he walked across the bridge. A few cars passed and their drivers took in the picture and he knew they were looking at him. He stopped on the middle of the bridge and looked down at the water and across the city. The fact that Prague was beautiful passed him by. He knew it was beautiful but he felt that a joy freely expressed of the beauty around them was lost to the people in the nullifying system they lived with. Something grey and rank killed it every day, something fearful of joy and human expression, and likewise he knew something, too, was now dead within him. He looked up the water at the reflections of the lights and buildings, then he reflected on.... *everything,* then, from somewhere, he wasn't sure where, thought that the world would be a better place without him and of the pain he felt in his body and heart and at this moment he knew that in every sense of the word, he was utterly *lost.* Then he considered leaning forward and letting the Vlatava take him. He thought it could be his one mighty gesture to the world, his life's greatest selfless act, to remove this human callus, rid this postulating lesion of disease from humanity with one last, but fruitful exertion..... then he heard a car slowing behind him and the creak of Eastern Bloc brakes. He didn't want to turn. He was scared but he didn't want to be. If it was them, Grey Suit, Alexej and the torture team...one last leap would fix everything. *Fuck them. I'm in control, I'm the sole arbiter of who decides the fate of this carcass, not them!*

A voice said, *"Ahoj"*

He remained where he was and didn't turn.

"Ahoj! Co děláš?"

He remained statuesque. The voice sounded a little louder and more aggressive.

"Hej, co se to kurva děje!"

Something started to rumble and growl from deep within him. An out of body experience observed what was happening quite objectively as if he was a psychological lab-rat and then heavy sobs arrived with the tears as his torso heaved trying to retain its oxygen amid the manifestation of human despair. He turned slowly. Before him was a police car with two uniformed officers inside. They both drew a frown as the picture became clear. His coat was open. Beneath it was a hospital smock barely covering his genitals. A trilby hat sat above a cut eye, a bruised face with a black eyepatch. Bare legs and bare feet completed the cartoon figure, perfectly, but it was the streams of tears pouring from his eyes and unashamedly dripping from his cheeks that prompted a quick discussion.

The policeman in the driver seat said something quickly to his mate along the lines of,

This will be the third suicide in a fucking fortnight! I'm not writing up any more fucking reports. If we stop him now we have to find the asylum, or wherever the fuck he's escaped from and that could take ages. Whatever happens, look at him! He's going to do it either now, tomorrow or next fucking week, whatever we do! We can't stop him and our Jan is getting married tomorrow and I need to get some sleep and for our shift to end when it supposed to, that is exactly thirty-seven minutes from now. Drive! We never saw him! We were never here!

A tad reluctantly, the other policeman drove on looking back and left Kelly alone on the bridge. Relief that it wasn't them and that a police patrol weren't interested in this sorry madman drew him from his dejected state, somewhat. He looked down at the water again and looked across the river into the town. He could hear voices and the faint sound of music. His legs involuntarily dragged him across the bridge into *Narodni*, a wide and busier street. The music became more discernible and he passed a doorway and large window with *Státní Jazyková Skola* written across it. He continued down the street desperately looking for signs to Wenceslas Square. Nothing. A door opened further down. Music, jazz music, got louder and three young women walked out onto the street one hundred yards in front of him. There was a neon sign above the door which read, *Reduta Jazz Club*. They were laughing animatedly. He heard the babble of Czech spoken quickly, more laughter, and then a Czech accent asked,

"How you say....erm, job...future...I want.... big coronas....?"

The spoken English grabbed his attention. He halted suudenly and listened. Then a Scottish accent replied,

"I think you mean...ermm.. I would really like to have a successful career in the future and earn a lot of money!"

He leaned forward and started to breathe heavily with his good eye straight on these women.

More laughter. They walked towards him. He stood there, barefoot with the coat open, before them square on the pavement. He had pulled the trilby tight onto his head to ensure it stayed on and now sat misshapen on his head and shadowing the eyepatch. The image was correctly described by the policeman. He did look as though he was an asylum escapee who'd had an argument with a speeding truck.

The first Czech accent spoke again,

"Yes, yes...successful career...lots of money..."

The other Czech woman said, "Lots of men!"

More raucous laughter.

They were now no more than fifty yards from him. He looked at them again. Then he stared. Then he craned his neck. Twenty yards from him. They looked up together and the laughter subsided and the smiles dropped becoming aware of the obvious danger of the madman in front of them, his face and wounds advertising the obvious danger he posed. The Czech girls both took the arm of the woman in the middle and went to guide her around Kelly. They passed widely and quietly around this barefooted, bruised and bloodied pirate and he stared like the lunatic they assumed him to be. He turned his head and body to stare even more at them. His eyes widened and his jaw dropped. They were now a little unnerved and picked up their pace, then returned to the centre of the pavement with their backs going away from him. Then, in his attempt to speak, a noise slowly rasped out of Kelly, a sort of throaty *arrghh* sound and the three of them turned their heads to see just in case he was about to attack. Then he tried to say something but his mouth was still swollen and there was phlegm, dried blood and snot lodged in his throat.

"Mmmenn..."

They were now convinced he was dangerous. He followed them for a few steps as he became seemingly desperate to keep their company and they kept looking over their shoulders ready to hurry away. He tried again as his knees began to bend,

"Megnnn.... Megnnn..."

The woman in the middle stopped. She turned. Kelly dropped to his knees. He tried again except this time it was happiness, relief and tears of pure joy that stopped him saying her name. However he sputtered out,

" Megn... Megan.....Megan!!"

Beneath his obvious difficulty to speak, Megan heard the semblance of a familiar voice

"Megan...it's me!" he managed to utter and at that moment Kelly either forgot or couldn't say his name. Megan rescued him.

"Kells?"

She couldn't believe it. This vision of beaten, comic, half-naked, despair on it's knees before her in this far-off place couldn't be him?

"Megan.... it's me... *Kells*... Kelly..." Tears flowed from him as water from a tap. ".....my name is *Leonard Kelly.... Leonard Kelly...*"

Megan put her hands to her head in disbelief as her two companions shared a bemused look between them. Megan moved slowly at first and then rushed towards the bubbling idiot before her.

"Oh my God! Kells! What ...? *Kells?*"

She bent down and lifted the hat slowly from his head, revealing more weals of his torture and couldn't hide her shock and she put her hand to her mouth. He attempted to stand all the while saying *it's me, it's me,* started to take off the coat, and tore off the eyepatch. Then he pulled the smock quickly over his head before she could stop him and he stood naked before her with his arms out there on *Narodni Street,* in Prague. She was about to try to cover him up with the coat but saw the red weals on his back and legs and the burn on his nipple and the red exposed flesh at the end of his fingers. A moment passed as she forgot his nakedness and cried for him.

Her two friends now started to question if this wasn't selflessness and altruism Britishly extended to a ridiculous length? Prague had these eccentric homeless characters who fought each other and the law, securing a few nasty wounds along way. What was she doing?

"Look at you, Kells....what happened....?" she said touching his renal area. He cried out. She cried more. "Why are you.... how have you...?"

Megan stopped talking abruptly realising practical measures were now required and turned to the other two and bid them leave with a wave of her hand. They acceded quickly and left them there chattering covertly between them and occasionally snatching a disbelieving look back. She picked up the coat and wrapped it around him and pulled the hat back onto his head, then picked up the smock and eyepatch and threw them into a bin at the side of the road. She then guided him gently into a doorway told him to wait as she went to the roadside. She stood under a streetlight and within a minute she'd hailed a taxi.

Megan gave the driver the name of the street she was living in but Kelly said no and told him to go straight to his place *Toulovska* but it took him a while to check his map and even then he wasn't entirely happy taking these westerners in his cab. Especially the one in the coat that looked fucked. He would only bring trouble.

Kelly babbled out everything to Megan on their way to his room. She was shocked and really couldn't quite believe it all but he assured her that it was the truth and that he *was sorry.... I'm sorry*..he said over and over. Megan consoled him like a child and held him in the back seat. Gradually he quietened as the streets became familiar to him then he shouted *There! There!,* to the driver.

Megan looked down at him on her shoulder and ventured a stab at the inevitable.

"Kells...where will you go! What are you going to do?"

A semblance of his wits returned with the question. Quietly he said,

"I don't know. I can't stay and I can't go back. I have money, though, if they didn't find it. Lots of it. Enough to disappear."

"To where. This is crazy!"

"I'd be crazy to go home. I'd go to prison. I can't do that. I'd die."

"You might die all alone here in Czechoslovakia and nobody

would know. Go home and explain!"

"Something has happened to me Megan....."

"I can see that, Kells."

"No, no... In here...." he tapped his head. "I'm ready to take what life throws at me and be straight with it. Honest. I'm going to do something, something good, and I don't know what, yet, but I will and if it's here, well...."

"I have no idea what you're talking about Kells."

"I do. I have to hurry, grab my things and go.", then from nowhere he said, "I loved you, Megan."

Megan's face tightened as she held back her emotion.

"Did you? I knew you liked me. I never thought I'd ever be loved. Why? I'm not all that."

"Who is? You are someone, though, but you made the same mistake as me with all your moneyed university friends. You tried to be someone you're not. Don't do that!"

"I know. I won't. I'll be okay, Kells it's you I'm worried about."

"Don't be. What day is this?"

"Friday."

"That doesn't help. I don't know how long they've kept me asleep. I have to hurry."

The taxi pulled into *Toulovska*. Megan paid the fare and they went up the stairs. He realised he didn't have his key but tried the door anyway. Quietly they entered and closed the door behind them. The room had been trashed. The StB had left no stone unturned. The bedstead was on its side, the mattress was torn and the stuffing was strewn around the room. His clothes were lying about everywhere, the rug was in a pile by the window, the curtains had been torn down and a wooden panel by the window smashed. Floorboards had been torn up and all the drawers of the cupboard were hanging open. Megan stared with her mouth agape.

"Look at the state of the place!" Megan said. Then a voice from behind them said,

"You have a terrible habit of leaving flats in a shit state, Kells...." They both turned in unison. "....there's not a body in the bath, here as well, is there?"

McQuarrie sat on a chair and looked at them both. "I couldn't imagine you being part of this, Megan?"

Another face from home she'd tried to leave behind her. This was all becoming far too much for Megan. "Mr McQuarrie! *Mr McQuarrie.....*I'm not. I got a job...here...You're here, Kells is....."

".....here, too. I was brought here by some of your StB secret police chums and got the key from your landlady, Kells, I hope you don't mind but it became necessary to get into your room just to check....*things*. I believe they have gone to bring you to me now but you seem to have the advantage of them. Oh dear, you look shocked....and, well, let's not beat about the bush, really not good, Kells. *Fucked,* some would say. But that would be our friends the StB, would it not?"

Kelly, slowly removed the hat and stared for a moment. "You worked it out?"

"We got a call. The Greyfriars thing. Quoted your name courtesy of Her Majesty's Government they said. Searched your flat and found...*her*. Not in great nick, she wasn't."

"It was an accident. Honestly." Kelly said.

"Now I know you're lying." McQuarrie quickly threw back.

"It's the truth. She gave me something. A disease. Lived upstairs and was on the game. That's why I became so horrible at the party, Megan. I didn't want you to like...*love* me. I found out that night. I'm sorry."

Megan had started to quietly shed tears. " It's okay...it's okay..."

"So how did you work out I was here?"

"*The Good Soldier Sveyk?* If you're anything, Kells, you're a romantic. However, we got a call four days ago from Mi6, believe it or not, who'd been made aware by the Czech Stb, the secret police here...."

"I know who they are! Bastards!"

"......yes you do... saying they, errrmm.. *had you*, you were being a pest, as usual, pretending to be Joe, I believe, and....erm *Spiderman...* a ridiculous extension of your acting abilities if you'll forgive me for saying, Kells,...and that you should be returned to us forthwith. So....here I am, and DC Jones, with the assent of the Czech government and on behalf of Her Majesty's Government."

"Where is she?"

"Jones? Well, as we thought we had a bit of time to kill in your new place here, she insisted, despite the early hour, that she go out and find coffee for us both. Old habits die hard, eh.... and you didn't seem to have the equipment here.... so she'll be back presently....unless she's picked up by the secret police, eh!"

McQuarrie chuckled fraudulently. Kelly didn't, then said,

"What happens now?"

"Well normally, I'd read you your rights cuff you and take you to a waiting police car, however, no police car because you've arrived early and *without* the secret police. Well done. So it's fair to say that these are not the most usual of circumstances, you'd agree?"

"Yes."

McQuarrie looked at Megan who was still crying.

"Why don't you sit down? Megan?"

McQuarrie carefully tipped the bedstead back on to its feet. Megan sat down with McQuarrie next to him and he gave Kelly the chair.

"Joe sends his best wishes."

"I don't think so." Kelly replied.

"No he's not very happy, really, however it is a crime and the banks are insured against fraud so Joe's actually okay, you'll be pleased to hear. And I believe he's recently had something of a windfall. Some sideline I'd rather not know about but he and May....are *doing okay.*"

"May?" Megan looked puzzled.

"Hasn't Kells told you? I suppose he has had other things on his mind. They're together. Have been for years. And May is actually....*a man.*"

Megan didn't need another headfuck but there it was. McQuarrie continued,

"Anyway you didn't steal from Joe, you stole from the bank."

"I took his name. That's worse."

McQuarrie pursed his lips and thought for a second.

"Quite unusual to hear you being so contrite, Kells. I told the StB about your financial misdemeanours and they've gone to town looking for it in here, but apparently couldn't find any *evidence,* and as they were close to killing you, gave up, didn't want an international incident, as it were, made a big deal about saying you were *nobody* and just wanted you out of their hair. However, that leaves us with a massive quandary, doesn't it?"

Kelly waited as McQuarrie held the tension, then said.

"You'd like some *evidence* to take back with you?"

"How *much* evidence is there?"

"A lot. Thousands. Pounds, dollars and crowns."

McQuarrie changed to a colder tone.

"Where have you just come from?"

"Some sort of hospital. Just me and another man in a room. Nurse kept firing something into him to keep him out. I pretended I was still under and made a run for it. They'll be coming here to try and find me when they realise I'm gone, I expect. Soon, I would think. Then you can cuff me read me my rights and take me to the airport.....*or...?*"

Megan just stood listening. Then McQuarrie considered her for a moment and said,

"Megan, I'm delighted to hear that you've got yourself a job... *teaching....?*"

"....English... Státní Jazyková škola."

"...which is great. Erm, would you mind if I had a private chat with Kells, Megan?"

"Yes...of course....I mean no.... I'll be just outside..." she flustered and exited quietly.

McQuarrie and Kelly faced each other.

"Time seems to be of the essence, Kells, so I'll get to the point. Give me *the evidence* that the StB didn't find and I never saw you. You weren't here. Then go. Wherever. You're a big boy. You'll get by. My dad needs it more than you."

"How is he Mr McQuarrie?"

"Ermm..totally shite wouldn't be an understatement. Well?"

Kelly looked at McQuarrie and said nothing. Then,

"You never liked me, Mr McQuarrie."

"Really, however did you get that impression? No. I didn't. You respected nobody. You had a superiority complex, you thought you were much cleverer than everyone, else. You were selfish, thoughtless of others and condescending whenever the opportunity arose and liked to merely give the impression you were well-read. Those are usually the actions of a narcissistic and compulsive liar. What was there to like?"

"Nothing. You're right."

For the first time he could remember, a sigh and a sympathetic tone for Kelly came from McQuarrie as he gently shook his head.

"Look at the state of you *Leonard Kelly*. Look at the pain you've suffered and the lengths you've gone to. For what? To avoid that which the rest of the world have get on with. To opt out. Be no-one. What a waste. Anyway, the clock's ticking, Kells... what's it to be, my offer or ten years in Saughton?"

Kelly took only a moment's thought, indicated McQuarrie should wait and went out into the common stairwell, down into the dark recess. He passed Megan drinking coffee with DC Jones who had an arm around her shoulder. Jones took an eyeful of the mess he was in and watched him descend the stairs. She didn't know what was happening. Was he leaving? Why wasn't McQuarrie with him? Then he returned with the shoulder bag. Jones was relieved and returned to comforting Megan. Kelly went back into the room. He held out the bag to McQuarrie who went to take it then Kelly pulled it back quickly.

"Leave me something."

McQuarrie became agitated. "Take the Crowns! Then go! We haven't got time for this!"

Kelly took the crowns quickly from the bag and started to lay them down on the floor. McQuarrie cleared his throat and said,

"By the way.... your mother died."

Kelly stopped what he was doing and just stared at the floor. "I know." He quietly said, then finished his task. Kelly handed him the bag. McQuarrie looked into the bag at the mess of Sterling and Dollars and closed it up.

Both looked at each other and silently acknowledged they'd seen each other for the last time. Some sort of regret and respect passed between them. McQuarrie made to leave,

"One last question, Mr McQuarrie?"

"Quickly Kells or this might not end well for either of us."

"How did Trotsky die?"

McQuarrie looked frustratedly at him.

"What? *How did Trotsky die?*"

"Yes."

"He had an ice-pick thrust into his head, as I recall."

Kelly digested this then said, "Thanks."

McQuarrie nodded then quickly left.

Megan came in. "Why has he gone?"

Kelly said, "He has to get home to look after his dad."

Then he pulled on what clothes were closest to hand, a T-shirt, jeans and the jacket he travelled in, while Megan's eyes widened at the sight of the money on the floor. Kelly then asked Megan if she had keys, which didn't do anything more to enlighten the scene for her but she gave him her keys, anyway, and he quickly used it to tear a hole in the lining of the jacket, then lifted the money and dropped it inside and closed it up.

"What now?" Megan asked putting the keys back in her pocket.

"Bohemia. Vagabonding."

*

Kelly and Megan stood on the platform looking like a young couple dreading the long goodbye. Megan had bought him a ticket on the night train to Ceske Budjovice in the south. He had no idea where he was going to get off but a quiet contentment radiated through him. Something was about to happen. Something he had no control over. He had no passport, no right to be there but was about to disappear deep into Europe, just as Jaroslav Hasek, that other wandering wastrel, had done years before him but there was no trepidation at the prospect for him. Only the fear of being apprehended by the authorities. His train crawled up to the platform and creaked to a standstill.

"Get something to eat. You look terrible." Megan said avoiding the inevitable conversation.

"I will."

Megan was about to throw another pithy phrase at him but he

interrupted her.

"We never kissed each other." He quietly said looking directly into her eyes.

"No." She softly said.

A hesitant pause, but they kissed each other gently and held each other close for a few precious moments. They broke and Megan smiled at him and touched his cut eyebrow and said,

"I'm using *The Good Soldier Sveyk* in my teaching, you know. They were delighted I knew it. So happy that someone knew their literature, knew who they were. They like me."

"Why wouldn't they, Megan? You're a beautiful person."

"Look after yourself."

"I don't care that much about me anymore, Megan."

He walked to the carriage door.

"Try to." she said and weakly smiled.

He smiled back and boarded the train. It was quiet. Megan remained where she was on the platform and cried when the train pulled out of the station, and she knew she was crying for something lost, something painful, something learned but also for something about to begin without her. An old woman saw her and said something to her while smiling and put her arms around her shoulders and gave her a hug, said something again that Megan did not understand and smiled and touched her on the chin. Words weren't necessary. Megan understood the kindness she was being offered, thanked her and then wandered slowly out of the station and occasionally catching a loose tear.

Kelly stayed on the train for four hours. He'd fallen asleep in an empty carriage and when he woke up he saw that his ticket had been punched. He smiled and looked out of the window. The sun was coming up and the light started to wash across the landscape. Everything looked bigger to him. The forests were spread over the land for miles and when pasture arrived the greenery was vibrant, the countryside dense with woodland and fields. They crossed rivers which were wider than most he'd crossed in Scotland and the villages they passed were so remote, it seemed, that he questioned whether anyone knew they existed. Something inside him decided it was time to get off the train, that this was the right place, that this was where his life began again. It pulled into a small town called *Horusice* and he got off and walked out into the early morning dawn. He walked up a rough dirt road leading away from the station and then had a left or right turn. Right was a road away from the cluster of buildings, left looked best. He walked through the small town. It was still very early. Nobody was yet about, which made him look very conspicuous, so he went on and out the other side towards the countryside where he came to a massive lake and he followed the shoreline for a few miles. Then appeared a clutch of houses close to the waterside and he stopped to see if there was anyone around. He pulled out a small note from the lining and put it in his jeans. In his inability to fight off sleep and haste to be unseen he'd forgotten to eat. He walked up to the first house, ramshackle as it was, and knocked on the door. The door opened and an older woman opened the door. She had a shawl around her shoulders and a headscarf tied under her chin and a black skirt. She looked at him knowing he wasn't one of theirs. Kelly brought out the note and put his fingers to his mouth. She understood but then said something,

"Co se ti stalo s obličejem?" and pointed at his face.

Kelly understood and made a fist and softly punched his own face, shrugging at the same time and forcing a slight smile.

"Pojď sem." She said and beckoned him to come in.

She sat Kelly down at a rough table next to a fire that had just been set and poured a coffee into a cup and put it in front of Kelly. He drank it quickly and she poured him another then cut a doorstep of bread and put it onto a wooden cutting board with some hard looking cheese and beckoned him to eat. Then she went to a shelf of jars on a wall of exposed plaster and took one down and untied the cloth cap around the neck..

"Cikáni? Romů?" she asked. "Romanie?"

He got Romanie. "Ano." he said but felt bad as he'd given the gypsies a bad press without just cause. Then she took the bread from his hand, just as he was about to take another mouthful, with a practical but gentle authority and laid it on the wooden board. She then pushed his head back to the light and dabbed a sweet-smelling oily liquid onto his face with a cloth and beckoned him to give her his hand. She gently laid some of the ointment onto his finger. He smarted a little as it touched the exposed end where his nail should be but she made some noises that were obviously meant to console him. She held his hand looking at the mess of his finger and sighed. Then she laid on some more of the oily balm. She nodded satisfied when she'd finished and told him to eat. Then she went to tend the fire and muttered something about *Romů* aggressively poking the wood into place. Kelly smiled. A small girl of about ten years entered the room carrying another child of about two years and spoke to her grandmother? Kelly was unsure what the relationship was but surmised she had to be the grandmother. In the hour that he spent in that house no other adult arrived or was seen to be there.

"Jste maďarsky?" she asked him as she dressed the two year old boy and the other girl drank milk.

Kelly shrugged.

"Hungari? Magyar?"

"Ano" he replied. He didn't want to tell any more lies, so he stood up and nodded to her but had to duck as there were baskets of all shapes hung above his head hanging on hooks.

"Děkuju." he said to her.

He pointed to the baskets. Ineptly and quite out of keeping with the older generation he gave her a thumbs up. It was all he had.

"Děkuju" she thanked him back and smiled.

He held up his finger as if remembering something and went into his pocket and drew out the thousand crown note but before he could offer it to her, she had started to say,

"Ne, ne, ne, ne...." and waved both her hands making her way to the door. Kelly tried to push it into her hand but he had a notion that there might be a tradition of travellers being helped, fed, or something similar that hung onto Bohemian culture for centuries, which made him feel better about it but really wanted her to take the money. He stayed there for an hour drinking the coffee, eating and staring into the fire as a comfortable silence wrapped around him and these strangers. Eventually he was drawn out of his reverie by the discussion the woman was having with the children and he pointed at the baskets and rubbed his fingers onto his thumb signifying money and she smiled ruefully and made a picture of the swaying scales with her hands. Kelly tried again and dug out the word for *please,*

"Prosím!" he said,

but she had become insistent and opened the door for him but smiling at the same time. Kelly crossed the threshold and lifted his hand in goodbye. The old lady put the jar of ointment into his hand and mimed putting it on his face and rolled her hand in the air to indicate every day. She still smiled.

"Dekuju, dekuju." he repeated and she waved and smiled then closed the door.

Kelly walked for a while close to a wooded track near the lakeside. He sat under a tree and enjoyed the heat of the sun for the first time that day and thought it glorious. He dozed for an hour or so until he heard scraping and footsteps coming along the track. The ten-year old girl from the house was coming up from the woods near the lakeside and she was carrying dozens of cut saplings intended for basket-work, tied with an old linen rag, probably an old bed sheet to spread the weight and the rest of it went around her shoulder. It all looked too big for the kid, he thought. Then he thought again. Now he knew the something he was going to do.

He stood to meet her and he said "Dobrý den." to her.

She was a little shy but said "Dobrý den." politely back to him and shifted her load to a better position. Kelly gestured to her that he would carry it for her but she said, *ne, ne...* but Kelly gently insisted and took it anyway.

"Dekuju." she politely said.

They walked together in silence back toward the house. Kelly pointed to some birds up in the trees and smiled. She smiled back. Then she started to talk pointing up at the birds,

...that one is an omen of bad luck if it sits alone on your roof but the small ones that flock together that are yellow are the sunshine in the morning, my Granma says. That is a pigeon. They are many and are good to eat if you can trap them or hit them with the sling. I can't but my father could when he was taken away....

Kelly looked up with her but dropped his hand into the lining of his jacket and grabbed every note he could as she was talking and jammed it all behind the linen rag holding the saplings. They reached a short distance from the house and he gave the load back to her. She smiled and thanked him and watched her walk back down to the house. He imagined the scene of joy he would never see. He envisioned the smiles and laughter he would never hear or feel the relief the house would have but he was glad to do it, he needed to do something for someone else for the mere pleasure of making them happy and enriching their lives. Then he turned and left.

Miles further on, now utterly penniless, a traditional painted gypsy's wooden wagon came up behind him pulled by a single horse and he stood aside to let it past. It was brightly decorated in greens and blues with pictures of flowers everywhere. Sprigs and bunches of drying plants were tied and hung on the arch and doorway along with a few assorted tools which clinked gently as the wagon slowly shifted along.

"Ahoj! Jeďte s námi, cestovateli!"

A tawny-faced man holding the reins leaned out and gestured for him to leap up and sit with him. Kelly climbed up and the man offered his hand and said,

"Vaclav...." Kelly could smell the hanging plants and herbs. He shook his hand. Vaclav then pointed behind him with his thumb and said, "Maria, Dominic."

Mother and child smiled at him and nodded. Vaclav then pointed upwards and said,

"Wenceslas!"

Kelly stood up and looked on the wooden roof at a large white cat sitting above their world, magisterially. He sat back down, smiled, nodded his thanks put his hand to his chest and said,

"Kel.... Leonard....ermm... *Lenny*......"

Vaclav said,

"Lenny? Dobrý den, Lenny."

"Dobrý den, Vaclav." he replied. "Dobrý den Maria, Dominic." They smiled and nodded back at him.

Vaclav started to sing quietly at first but then got a little louder as he shared a smile with Kelly. It was something quite uplifting with a *hey* repeated often as the chorus arrived. Kelly smiled and Dominic inside the wagon quietly joined in with his father. Vaclav pointed at the trees and flowers all around him and saying the name with a wave of an arm as his verses rolled forward with the movement of the wagon, along the rough track, under verdant trees and summer sun, to where and to do what? Perhaps to riches coin could never buy? Nobody knows, but it travelled with *Lenny,* deep into the heart of Europe.

The End.

Acknowledgements

Thanks to *Hana Deringerova* a complete stranger I contacted online, who was very helpful. Twice. She gave the information of a Prague language school.

Thanks to my son, Alex, for being here. Him being here motivated me. He'll realise that one day.

Thanks to Arthur, the mechanic who fixes my car, who said it was great that I was writing a novel. I like him.

Thanks to everyone who rolled their eyes and sighed when I told them I was writing a novel. They motivated me.

Thanks to June Deuchars who, enthusiastically, declared she wanted to read it before it was finished then, honestly told me it wasn't for her. I knew it wouldn't be. That's ok.

All the rest was me.

Matt Mason was born in Weymouth, Dorset, left when he was three months old and has never been back. He spent his next six years in a small mining village in County Durham called Esh Winning then moved with his parents to Edinburgh. I suppose they had to come, too. He left school with a B in Arithmetic and became a Painter and Decorator, which always kept the wolf from the door. He moved to Liverpool in 1982 and went on to Further Ed., then studied Drama at Liverpool Polytechnic back in the good old days when grants were awarded and then became hugely successful at being a quite unsuccessful actor. He went on to study at Edinburgh University and became a teacher of Drama. He now lives in Livingston, Scotland....but he's going to move soon.

2019.©

mattie100@hotmail.co.uk

Printed in Great Britain
by Amazon